ALSO BY ELIN HILDERBRAND

BAREFOOT

a novel

Elin Hilderbrand

LITTLE, BROWN AND COMPANY

NEW YORK BOSTON LONDON

The characters and events in this book are fictitious. Any similarity to real persons, living or dead, is coincidental and not intended by the author.

Copyright © 2007 by Elin Hilderbrand
Excerpt from *The Castaways* copyright © 2009 by Elin Hilderbrand
All rights reserved. Except as permitted under the U.S. Copyright Act of 1976, no part of this publication may be reproduced, distributed, or transmitted in any form or by any means, or stored in a database or retrieval system, without the prior written permission of the publisher.

Little, Brown and Company
Hachette Book Group
237 Park Avenue
New York, NY 10017
Visit our Web site at www.HachetteBookGroup.com.

Printed in the United States of America

Originally published in hardcover by Little, Brown and Company, July 2007
First Back Bay paperback edition, June 2008
First mass market edition, August 2009

10 9 8 7 6 5 4 3 2 1

For Heather Osteen Thorpe: In honor of the dollhouse, the roller-skating shows, the Peanut Butter and Jelly Theater, the Wawa parties, and now, six kids between us. You are the best sister-friend a woman could ask for.

PART ONE

——

JUNE

Three women step off of a plane. It sounded like the start of a joke.

Joshua Flynn, age twenty-two, native of Nantucket Island, senior at Middlebury College, summer employee of the Nantucket Memorial Airport, where his father was an air traffic controller, noticed the women immediately. They arrived on a US Airways flight from LaGuardia. Three women, two small children, nothing unusual about that, so what caught Josh's eye? Josh Flynn was a creative-writing student at Middlebury, and his mentor, the writer-in-residence, Chas Gorda, liked to say that a writer smells a good story in the air like it's an approaching storm. *The hair on your arms will stand up,* Chas Gorda promised. Josh checked his forearms—nothing— and tugged at his fluorescent orange vest. He approached the plane to help Carlo unload the luggage. Josh's father,

Tom Flynn, would be at a computer terminal five stories above Josh's head, occasionally spying out the window to make sure Josh was doing what he called "a decent job." Being under surveillance like this provided as unsettling a work situation as Josh could imagine, and so in the two weeks he'd been at it, he'd learned to sniff for stories without giving himself away.

Two of the women stood on the tarmac. Josh could tell they were sisters. Sister One was very thin with long light-brown hair that blew all over the place in the breeze; she had a pointy nose, blue eyes, and she was visibly unhappy. Her forehead was as scrunched and wrinkled as one of those funny Chinese dogs. Sister Two had the same blue eyes, the same sharp nose, but instead of scowling, Sister Two's face conveyed baffled sadness. She blinked a lot, like she was about to cry. She was heavier than her sister, and her hair, cut bluntly to her shoulders, was a Scandinavian blond. She carried a floral-print bag bursting with diapers and a colorful set of plastic keys; she was taking deep, exaggerated breaths, as though the flight had just scared her to death.

The third woman teetered at the top of the steps with a baby in her arms and a little boy of about four peeking around her legs. She had a pretty, round face and corkscrew curls that peeked out from underneath a straw hat. She was wearing jeans with muddy knees and a pair of rubber clogs.

The sisters waited at the bottom of the stairs for this third woman to descend. Heavy-breathing Sister reached out for the baby, shaking the keys. "Come to Mama," she said. "Here, Melanie, I'll take him." In addition to the baby, Straw Hat held a package of Cheez-Its, a green plastic cup, and an air-sickness bag. She was two steps from the ground when the little boy behind her shouted, "Auntie Brenda, here I come!"

And jumped.

He was aiming for Scowling Sister, but in his excitement, he hurtled his forty-some-pound body into the back of Straw Hat, who went sprawling onto the tarmac with the baby. Josh bolted forward—though he knew he wouldn't be quick enough to save anyone. Straw Hat covered the baby's head with her hands and took the brunt of the fall on her knees and her left arm. Ouch.

"Melanie!" Heavy-breathing Sister cried. She dropped the diaper bag and raced toward Straw Hat. The baby wasn't making any noise. Neck broken. Dead. Josh felt his spirit trickle onto the tarmac as though he'd wet his pants. But then—a cry! The baby had merely been sucking in air, released now in heroic tones. The baby was alive! Heavy-breathing Sister took the baby and studied him for obvious injury, then shushed him against her shoulder. Scowling Sister approached with the perpetrator of the crime, older brother, clinging to her legs.

"Is the baby okay?" Scowling Sister asked. Her expression shifted from impatient to impatient and concerned.

"He's fine," Heavy-breathing Sister said. "Just scared." She reached out to Straw Hat. "Are you okay, Melanie? Are you okay? Do you feel okay?"

Melanie dusted the tarmac grit off her face; there was a scrape on her elbow, some blood. The Cheez-Its blew off down the runway; the plastic cup rolled to Josh's feet. He picked it up, and the air-sickness bag as well.

"Would you like me to get a first-aid kit?" he asked Melanie.

She put a hand to her cheek, and the other hand massaged her stomach. "Oh, no. Thank you, though. I'm fine."

"Are you sure?" Heavy-breathing Sister said. "What about . . . ?"

"I'm *fine*," Melanie said.

"Blaine will apologize," Heavy-breathing Sister said. "Apologize, Blaine."

"Sorry," the boy mumbled.

"You could have hurt your brother. You could have hurt Melanie. You just can't *do* things like that, sweetheart. You have to be *careful*."

"He said he was sorry, Vick," Scowling Sister said.

This was not joke material. The three women, collectively, were the most miserable-looking people Josh had ever seen.

"Welcome to Nantucket," Josh said, hoping his words might cheer them, though Carlo was always reminding him that he was not an ambassador. He should just tend to the bags; his father would be watching.

Scowling Sister rolled her eyes. "Thanks a lot," she said.

They should have driven to the island, Brenda thought as they climbed into a cab outside the terminal. She had been coming to Nantucket her entire life and they always drove, and then put the car on the ferry. This year, because of the kids and Vicki's cancer and a desire to get to Nantucket as expediently as possible no matter what the cost, they had flown. They shouldn't have broken with tradition in Brenda's opinion, because look what happened—they were off to a horrible start already. Melanie had vomited the whole flight; then she fell, giving Vicki something else to worry about. The whole point of the summer was to help Vicki relax, to soothe her, to ease the sickness from her body. *That's the point, Melanie!* Now, Melanie was sitting behind Brenda in the cab with her eyes closed. Vicki had invited Melanie to Nantucket for the summer because Melanie had "problems." She was dealing with a "complicated situation" back in Connecticut. But it was also the case that Brenda's company alone had never been enough for Vicki. All their lives, all through growing up—whether it was camping trips, nights at the summer carnival, or church on Sunday—Vicki had brought a friend.

This summer it was Melanie Patchen. The news that Melanie would be joining them was sprung on Brenda at the last minute, giving her no opportunity to protest. During the limousine ride from Darien to LaGuardia, Brenda had heard about the "complicated situation": Melanie and her husband, Peter Patchen, had been trying "forever" to get pregnant; they had, in the past calendar year, endured seven failed rounds of in vitro fertilization. Then, a few weeks ago, Peter admitted he was having an affair with a young woman from his office named Frances Digitt. Melanie was devastated. She was so upset she made herself sick—she couldn't keep food down, she took to her bed. Then she missed her period. She was *pregnant*—and the "complicated" part of her "situation" was that she had left Connecticut without telling her husband that she was leaving, and without telling him she was pregnant. She was stealing away with Vicki and

Brenda and the kids because she "needed time to think. Time away."

Brenda had taken in this information silently but skeptically. The last thing she and Vicki needed this summer was a stowaway from a complicated situation. Vicki had lung cancer, and Brenda had problems of her own. Earlier that spring, she had been fired from her teaching job at Champion University for sleeping with her only male student—and, as if that weren't catastrophic enough, there were "unrelated" criminal charges pending, concerning a valuable piece of university-owned art. *Sex scandal! Criminal charges!* Brenda had gone from being hot property—a celebrated young professor, the It girl of Champion University—to being the subject of rumor and gossip. Everyone on Champion's campus had been talking about her: Dr. Brenda Lyndon, who earned top teaching marks in the English Department her *very first semester,* had conducted an illicit affair with one of her students. And then, for a reason nobody could discern, she had "vandalized" an original Jackson Pollock—a bequest from a gung-ho alumnus—that hung on the wall of the English Department's Barrington Room. In addition to the mortifying shame of her relationship with John Walsh, Brenda had been forced to hire a lawyer she couldn't afford to deal with the vandalism charges. Best-case scenario, Brian Delaney, Esquire, said, would be the university's art restoration team deciding they could tinker with the painting, fill in the "divot," make the painting as good as new. Worst-case scenario would be irrevocable damage. The university was still looking into the matter.

Brenda had ostensibly come to Nantucket because

Vicki had cancer and needed help. But Brenda w̶
unemployed, unemployable, and in serious need of mo̶
Melanie wasn't the only one who needed "time away"
or "time to think"—Brenda needed it, too. Desperately.
She had devoted her entire career to one narrow subject: Fleming Trainor's novel, *The Innocent Impostor*.
This little-known volume, published in 1790, had been
the topic of Brenda's dissertation and of the surprisingly
popular seminar she taught at Champion. Since Brenda
would be forever ostracized from the world of academia,
the only way *The Innocent Impostor* could make her any
money now—at least the kind of money she needed to
pay a lawyer and / or a "hefty fine"—was if she used it
in some unconventional, and un-academic, way. It was
Brian Delaney, Esquire, who suggested Brenda write a
screenplay. At first Brenda scoffed, but as Brian Delaney,
Esquire, eloquently pointed out: *Hollywood loves that
old-time shit. Look at* Vanity Fair, *look at Jane Austen.*
The Innocent Impostor was so obscure it wasn't even
available on Amazon.com, but Brenda was desperate, not
only for money, but for a project, something to work on.
She batted the idea around for a while, and the more she
thought about it, the less outlandish it seemed. This summer, if anyone asked her what she did for a living, she
would tell them she was writing a screenplay.

The other reason that Brenda had come to Nantucket
was that John Walsh was in Manhattan, and even in a
city of eight million people, Brenda felt his presence as
acutely as if he lived on the other side of her exposed-
brick wall. She had to sever ties with John Walsh no matter how strongly she felt about him, she had to flee the
city of her disgrace, she had to help her sister. A summer

on Nantucket was the answer all the way around, and the cottage that had belonged to Brenda and Vicki's great-aunt Liv was, after three years, out of probate. The two sisters owned it now, officially.

The question wasn't, why was she here? The question was, why wasn't she happier she was here?

Brenda held the baby tightly on her lap and put an arm around her four-year-old nephew, Blaine, who was buckled in next to her. The cabbie said, "Where to?" And Brenda said, "Shell Street, 'Sconset."

Shell Street, 'Sconset: These were Brenda's three favorite words in the English language. It had not slipped Brenda's mind that one way to access a large sum of money was to sell out her half of Aunt Liv's house to Vicki and Ted. But Brenda couldn't bear to relinquish the piece of this island she now owned: half of a very small house. Brenda gazed out the window at the scrubby evergreens that bordered Milestone Road, at the acres of moors held in conservation. She inhaled the air, so rich and clean that it worked like an anesthetic; Blaine's eyelids started to droop. Brenda couldn't help thinking that Walsh would love it here. He was a man of the outdoors, being typically Australian; he liked beaches and waves, open space, clear sky. He was at a loss in Manhattan, all that manufactured civilization baffled him, the subway suffocated him, he preferred to walk, *thank you, mate.* How many times had he traversed Central Park in a snowstorm to get to Brenda's apartment? How many times had they met secretly in Riverside Park after class? Too many, apparently, and not secretly enough. One person had harbored suspicions, the wrong person, and Brenda's career in academia was over a semester and a half after it began.

She had been branded with the scarlet letter despite the fact that Walsh was thirty-one years old and Brenda herself only thirty. The situation at Champion had been such a hideous mess, the cause of such powerful shame, that Brenda had no choice but to end everything with Walsh. He wanted to come visit her here. It would be different, he said, out of the city. Maybe, Brenda thought. But not different enough.

Brenda was relieved that Aunt Liv wasn't alive to witness her fall from grace. Aunt Liv, a celebrated professor of Russian literature at Bryn Mawr College, had cultivated Brenda for a life in academia. She had served as a mentor and a role model. How many hours had they talked about Fleming Trainor—and Isaak Babel, Tolstoy, Solzhenitzyn, Dumas, Hugo, Whitman? How many times had they agreed there was no nobler pursuit than the study of literature, no better way to spend an evening than alone with Turgenev?

I was doing so well, Brenda thought. *Until Walsh.*

When Brenda thought of Aunt Liv now, the term "rolling over in her grave" came to mind. So in some way this summer on Nantucket was about seeking atonement. Brenda wanted others to forgive and, more saliently, forget; she wanted to find some peace for her roiling conscience. *Time to think. Time away.* Maybe it wouldn't be so bad, having Melanie around. Misery did love company.

Brenda checked behind her again. Now Vicki's eyes were closed. She and Melanie were both asleep, and weirder still, they were holding hands, like they were lovers. Brenda tightened her grip on the warm, doughy baby in her lap. She felt like a six-year-old, jealous and left out.

~~~~~

Victoria Lyndon Stowe had been making lists all her life. She attributed this to the fact that she was the first-born, a classic type-A personality, something her parents did nothing but reinforce. *Vicki is so organized, she never forgets a thing.* As early as the fifth grade, Vicki wrote down what she wore to school each day so that she didn't repeat an outfit. She made lists of her favorite movies and books. She made a list of what each friend gave her for her birthday, and she always wrote the thank-you notes in order so that she could check them off, boom, boom, boom, just like that. At Duke, there had been myriad lists—she was president of the Tri-Delts, the head of the Drama Society, and a campus tour guide, so there were lists for each of those things, and a separate list for her studies. Then, out in the real world, the lists multiplied. There were "single girl living and working in the city" lists, lists for her wedding to Ted Stowe, and finally the endless lists of a mother of young children. *Schedule doctor's appointment; return library books; save milk cartons for planting radishes; money for babysitter; playdate with Carson, Wheeler, Sam; call balloon man for birthday party; buy summer pajamas; oil the tricycle; have carpets cleaned in the playroom.*

When Vicki was diagnosed with lung cancer, the lists came to a halt. This was her doctor's suggestion, though Vicki initially protested. Lists kept her world in order; they were a safety net that prevented important things from falling through. But Dr. Garcia, and then her husband, Ted, insisted. No more lists. Let them go. If she forgot to pick up the dry cleaning, so what? She would undergo two months of intensive chemotherapy, and if the chemo worked as it was supposed to—shrinking her tumor to a resectable size—it would be followed by thoracic surgery in which they would remove her left lung and her hilar lymph nodes. Chemotherapy, surgery, *survival*—these things were too big for any list. And so, the lists had all been thrown away, except for the one Vicki kept in her head: the List of Things That No Longer Matter.

A brother and sister running across the street, late for their dentist appointments. A pretty skirt worn with the wrong shoes. Peterson's Shorebirds. (There was a group of retired women in Darien who wandered the beach with this exact volume in hand. Vicki hated these women. She hated them for being so lucky—they didn't have cancer, thus they had the luxury of spending precious minutes of their lives tracking an oystercatcher or a blue heron.)

Unfortunately for Brenda and Melanie, there were things about this summer on Nantucket that had initially been placed on Vicki's List of Things That No Longer Matter—such as whether Brenda and Melanie would get along, or whether all five of them would be comfortable in Aunt Liv's summer cottage—but now it seemed like they might matter after all. *Vicki's so organized, she never forgets a thing.* But the fact was, Vicki had forgotten the physical details of Aunt Liv's cottage. When Vicki made the radical decision to come to Nantucket for the summer, her only thought had been of the comfort that Aunt Liv's cottage, and Nantucket, would give her.

Every summer growing up she had stayed in the cottage with her parents and Brenda and Aunt Liv. It was her favorite place, it defined summertime, and Vicki's mother, Ellen Lyndon, had always sworn that any ailment in the world—physical or emotional—could be cured by a little Nantucket sand between your toes. Everyone else thought Vicki was crazy to go away for the summer, endangering herself even, but another thing that Vicki put on her List of Things That No Longer Matter was what everyone else thought.

Inviting Brenda to come along had been the obvious choice. Vicki needed help with the kids and getting back and forth to chemo, and Brenda, fired from Champion in a blaze of scandal with attendant legal trouble, was desperate to escape the city. It was summer, salvaged for both of them. In the harrowing days following Vicki's diagnosis, they talked about reliving their memories from childhood: long beach days, catching fireflies, bike rides to Sesachacha Pond, corn on the cob, games of Monopoly and badminton, picking blackberries, twilight walks up to Sankaty Head Lighthouse, which spun its beacon like a cowboy with a wild lasso, picnics of bologna-and-potato-chip sandwiches, spending every day barefoot. It would be just the two of them, creating memories for Vicki's own kids. It was a chance for Vicki to heal, for Brenda to regroup. They would follow their mother's advice: Nantucket sand between the toes. It might cure anything: cancer, ruined careers, badly ended love affairs. *Just the two of us,* they said as they sat under the harsh hospital lights awaiting a second opinion. It would be a sister summer.

But how, really, could Vicki leave her best friend behind in Darien—especially with the monstrous news of

Peter's affair followed by an even bigger stunner (whispered, frantically, at three in the morning over the telephone). Melanie was—after all this time, after so many costly and invasive procedures—pregnant!

Come to Nantucket, Vicki had said immediately, and without thinking (and without consulting Ted or Brenda).

Okay, Melanie had said just as quickly. *I will.*

As the taxi pulled up in front of Aunt Liv's cottage, Vicki feared she'd made a mistake. The house was smaller than Vicki remembered, a lot smaller. It was a shoe box; Blaine had friends with playhouses bigger than this. Had it shrunk? Vicki wondered. Because she remembered whole summers with her parents and Brenda and Aunt Liv, and the house had seemed, if not palatial, then at least comfortable.

"It's darling," Melanie said as she stepped out of the cab. "Oh, Vicki, it's all that I imagined."

Vicki unhinged the front gate. The landscapers had come, thank God. Melanie loved flowers. Pale pink New Dawn roses cascaded down a trellis, and the front beds had been planted with cosmos and blue delphiniums and fat, happy-faced zinnias. There were butterflies. The postage-stamp lawn had been recently mowed.

"Where's the sandbox?" Blaine said. "Where's the curly slide?"

Vicki produced a key from her purse and opened the front door, which was made from three rough-hewn planks and sported a brass scallop-shell knocker. The doorway was low. As Vicki stepped through, she thought of her husband, Ted, a hale and hearty six foot five. He had told her from the beginning that he was *vehemently against* her going to Nantucket. Did she really want to spend all summer with her sister, with whom her relationship was spotty at best? And Melanie Patchen, who would be as needy as Vicki, if not more so? And did she really want her chemotherapy—the chemo that she was asking to save her life—to be administered at the Nantucket Cottage Hospital? Wasn't that the equivalent of being treated in the Third World? *What the hell are you thinking?* he asked. He sounded confused and defeated. Ted was a hedge fund manager in Manhattan; he liked problems he could fell like trees, problems he could solve with brute strength and canny intelligence. The horrifying diagnosis, the wing-and-a-prayer treatment plan, and then Vicki's wacko decision to flee for the summer left him confounded. But Vicki couldn't believe she was being asked to explain herself.

It was, quite possibly, the last summer of her life, and she didn't want to spend it in stifling hot Darien under the sympathetic scrutiny of her friends and peers. Already, Vicki's circumstances were being repeated like the Song of the Day: *Did you hear? Vicki Stowe has lung cancer. They're going to try chemo first and then they'll decide if it's worth operating. They don't know if she'll make it.* A steady stream of food and flowers arrived along with the offer of playdates. *Let us take Blaine. Let us take the baby. So you can rest.* Vicki was the new Darien charity. She couldn't stand the casseroles or the calla lilies; she couldn't stand her children being farmed out like they were orphans. The women circled like buzzards—some close friends, some friends of friends, some women she barely knew. Ted didn't get it; he saw it as outreach by a caring community. *That's why we moved here,* he said.

These are our neighbors, our friends. But Vicki's desire to get away grew every time the phone rang, every time a Volvo station wagon pulled into the driveway.

Vicki's mother was the one who had suggested Nantucket; she would have joined Vicki herself but for an ill-timed knee replacement. Vicki latched on to the idea, despite the fact that her mother wouldn't be coming to help. Aunt Liv's estate had been settled in March; the house belonged to her and Brenda now. It felt like a sign. Brenda was all for it. Even Vicki's oncologist, Dr. Garcia, gave his okay; he assured her that chemo was chemo. The treatment would be the same on Nantucket as it would be in Connecticut, or in the city. The people in Vicki's cancer support group, all of whom embraced holistic as well as conventional medical treatment, understood. *Enjoy yourself,* they said. *Relax. Play with your kids. Be outside. Talk with your sister, your friend. Look at the stars. Eat organic vegetables. Try to forget about fine-needle aspirations, CT scans, metastases. Fight the good fight, on your own terms, in your own space. Have a lovely summer.*

Vicki had held Ted hostage with her eyes. Since her diagnosis, she'd watched him constantly—tying his necktie, removing change from his suit pocket, stirring sugar into his coffee—hoping to memorize him, to take him with her wherever she went.

I'll miss you, she said. *But I'm going.*

The cottage had been built in 1803—back, Vicki thought, when life was both busier and simpler, back when people were shorter and held lower expectations. The cottage had originally been one room with a fireplace built into the north wall, but over the years, three "warts" had been added for bedrooms. All of the rooms were small with low ceilings; it was like living in a dollhouse. That was what Aunt Liv had loved about the cottage—it was life pared down, scaled way back. There was no TV, no answering machine, no computer or microwave or stereo. It was a true summerhouse, Aunt Liv used to say, because it encouraged you to spend most of your time outside— on the back deck overlooking the yard and garden, or down the street at 'Sconset's public beach. Back in 1803 when the woman of the house had cancer, there were no oncologists or treatment plans. A woman worked right through it—stoking the fire, preparing meals, stirring the laundry in a cauldron of boiling water—until one day she died in bed. These were Vicki's thoughts as she stepped inside.

The cottage had been cleaned and the furniture aired. Vicki had arranged for all of this by telephone; apparently, houses that sat dormant for three years were common stuff on Nantucket. The house smelled okay, maybe a bit too optimistically like air freshener. The living room floors were made from wide, buttery pine boards that showed every scratch from a dragged chair, every divot from a pair of high heels. The plaster-and-wood-beamed ceiling was low, and the furniture was old-ladyish, like something out of a Victorian bed-and-breakfast: Aunt Liv's delft blue high-back sofa, the dainty coffee table with a silver-plated tea service resting on a piece of Belgian lace. There were the bookshelves bowing under the weight of Aunt Liv's summer library, there was the fireplace with mismatched andirons. Vicki moved into the small kitchen, appliances circa 1962, silver-threaded Formica, Aunt Liv's china, which was painted with little

Dutch girls in wooden shoes. The caretaker's bill was secured to the refrigerator with a magnet advertising a restaurant called the Elegant Dump, which had been defunct for years.

The west bedroom was sunny. That would be Melanie's room. Twin beds were made up with the pink-and-orange-striped sheets that Vicki remembered from her childhood. (What she remembered most vividly was staining the sheets during her first period. Aunt Liv had sensibly pulled out the hydrogen peroxide while Ellen Lyndon had chirped with over-the-top sentimentality about how "Vicki is a woman now" and Brenda glowered and chewed her cuticles.) Vicki would take the largest bedroom, with the king bed, where she would sleep with the kids, and Brenda would sleep in the old nursery, a room just slightly bigger than Vicki's walk-in closet at home. This was the room Aunt Liv had always occupied—it was called the old nursery because both Aunt Liv and Vicki and Brenda's grandmother Joy had slept in cribs in that room alongside the family's baby nurse, Miss George, more than eighty years earlier. Once Aunt Liv had arthritis and every other old-person ailment, Vicki's parents suggested she take the big bedroom—but that didn't suit Liv. She stopped coming to Nantucket altogether, and then she died.

There was a flurry of activity as everyone piled into the house, dragging luggage and boxes. The cabbie stood by the car, waiting to be paid. That was Vicki's department. She was going to pay for everything all summer. She was summer's sponsor. She handed the kid twenty bucks. *Enough?*

He grinned. *Too much.* "Thanks, ma'am. Enjoy your stay."

As the cab pulled away, Blaine started to cry. Vicki worried that all the change would traumatize him; there had been a scene at breakfast when he'd said good-bye to Ted, and then he'd knocked Melanie off the airplane's steps. He was acting out. It was three o'clock, and although he was outgrowing his nap, Vicki knew he needed some quiet time. She herself was bone weary. Just picking up her bag and walking five feet to the bedroom made her feel like she'd climbed Mount Kilimanjaro. Her lungs were on fire. She hated them.

Suddenly, Brenda made a noise even worse than Blaine's whiny cry. She was moaning in that *Oh no, oh no, no,* the-world-is-ending kind of way. What was it? A dead animal in the old nursery? A family of dead animals? Vicki lowered her bottom onto her bed's squishy mattress. She didn't have the energy to move, so she called out, "What's wrong, Bren?"

Brenda appeared in the absurdly low doorway of Vicki's bedroom. "I can't find my book."

Vicki didn't have to ask which book. This was Brenda, her sister. There was only one book: Brenda's two-hundred-year-old first edition of Fleming Trainor's *The Innocent Impostor.* This book, a little-known novel of a mediocre Early American writer, was the foundation of Brenda's career. Brenda had spent six years getting her master's degree and doctorate from the University of Iowa, she had written a dissertation and had part of it published in an obscure literary journal, and she'd landed the job at Champion University—all because of this book. The first edition was an antique, worth thousands of dollars, Brenda claimed. She had owned it since she was fourteen years old, when she bought it for fifty cents at a flea market. The book was, for all intents and purposes, Brenda's pet. She wouldn't *consider* leaving it in Manhattan, where the subletter could get at it. It had traveled with them in a special briefcase—temperature and humidity controlled, the whole nine yards. Now it was missing.

"Are you sure?" Vicki said. "Did you check everywhere?" Despite the fact that Brenda's missing book fell squarely onto Vicki's List of Things That No Longer Matter, she tried to summon sympathy in the interest of getting things off to a good start. And crises of this nature were Vicki's specialty. With the kids, her day was spent hunting for things: the other shoe, the ball that rolled under the sofa, the pacifier!

"Everywhere," Brenda said. It was amazing how quickly her demeanor had changed. She had been a bitch all day, but now that her book was missing, she was turning into the cake that someone left out in the rain. Her cheeks were blotching, her hands were twitching, and Vicki sensed tears weren't far off.

"What if I *lost* the book?" Brenda said. "What if I left it at"—the next word was so awful, it stuck like a chunk of carrot in the back of her throat—"LaGuardia?"

Vicki shut her eyes. She was so tired she could sleep like this, sitting up. "You carried it off the plane with you, remember? You had your little purse, and . . ."

"The briefcase," Brenda said. She blinked rapidly, trying to fend off the tears. Vicki felt a surge of anger. If Brenda had been the one to get cancer, she wouldn't have been able to deal. God never gives you more than you can handle—this saying was repeated with conviction at Vicki's cancer support group—and that is why God did not give Brenda cancer.

Somewhere in the house, the baby was crying. A second later, Melanie appeared. "I think he's hungry," she said. She caught a whiff of Brenda's desperate mien—the hands were still twitching—and she said, "Honey, what's wrong? What's *wrong?*"

"Brenda lost her book," Vicki said, trying to sound grave. "Her old book. The antique."

"That book is my life," Brenda said. "I've had it forever, it's priceless . . . okay, I feel sick. That book is my talisman, my good-luck charm."

Good-luck charm? Vicki thought. If the book really had supernatural powers, wouldn't it somehow have kept Brenda from sleeping with John Walsh and ruining her career?

"Call the airport," Vicki said. She took Porter from Melanie and latched him onto her breast. As soon as the chemo started on Tuesday, he would have to be weaned. Bottles, formula. Even Porter, at nine months old, had a more legitimate crisis than Brenda. "I'm sure they have it."

"Okay," Brenda said. "What's the number?"

"Call information," Vicki said.

"I hate to ask this," Melanie said. "But is there just the one bathroom?"

"Quiet!" Brenda snapped.

Melanie's eyes grew wide and Vicki thought for an instant that *she* might start to cry. Melanie was sweet and self-effacing to a fault, and she hated confrontation. When the whole ugly thing with Peter happened, Melanie didn't yell at him. She didn't break his squash racquet or burn the wedding photos as Vicki herself would have. Instead, she'd let his infidelity quietly infect her. She became sick and fatigued. Then she discovered she was pregnant. The news that should have caused her the greatest joy was suddenly a source of conflict and confusion. Nobody deserved this less than Melanie. Vicki had given Brenda a direct order—*Be nice to her!*—but now Vicki saw she should have been more emphatic. *Really nice! Kid gloves!*

"Sorry, Mel," Vicki whispered.

"I hear you," Brenda said. Then, in a businesslike voice, she said, "Nantucket Memorial Airport, please. Nantucket, Massa-chusetts."

"Anyway, yes," Vicki said. "Just the one bathroom. Sorry. I hope that's okay." Vicki hadn't poked her head into the bathroom yet, though she was pretty sure it hadn't changed. Small hexagonal tiles on the floor, transparent shower curtain patterned with red and purple poppies, toilet with the tank high above and an old-fashioned pull chain. One bathroom for a woman about to be served up a biweekly dose of poisonous drugs, a woman in the throes of morning sickness, a four-year-old boy unreliably potty trained, and Brenda. And Ted, of course, on the weekends. Vicki took a breath. Fire. She switched Porter to her other breast. He had milk all over his chin and a deliriously happy look on his face. She should have started him on a bottle weeks ago. Months ago.

"I'm going to unpack," Melanie announced. She was still wearing her straw hat. When Vicki and Brenda had arrived in the limo to pick her up that morning, she'd been in her garden, weeding. As she climbed into the

Lincoln Town Car, clogs caked with mud, she said, "I should have left Peter a reminder to water. I just know he'll forget, or ignore it."

"Your husband is still living with you?" Brenda had said. "You mean to say you didn't throw him out?"

Melanie had glanced at Vicki. "She knows about Peter?"

At that minute, Vicki's lungs had felt like they were filling with swamp water. It went without saying that Melanie's situation was confidential, but Brenda was Vicki's *sister,* and the three of them were going to be living together *all summer,* so . . .

"I told her," Vicki said. "I'm sorry."

"It's okay," Melanie said softly. "So I guess you know I'm pregnant, too?"

"Yeah," Brenda said.

"I'm sorry, Mel," Vicki said.

"I'm a dead end," Brenda said. "Really, I am. But if you want my opinion . . ."

"She doesn't want your opinion, Bren," Vicki said.

"You should tell the man to fuck off," Brenda said. "Twenty-seven-year-old adventure girl, my sweet ass!"

"Brenda, enough!" Vicki said.

"Just please don't tell anyone I'm pregnant," Melanie said.

"Oh, I won't say a word," Brenda said. "I promise."

A few minutes later, after enough time had passed for everyone in the limo to reflect on this exchange, Melanie had started vomiting. She claimed it was because she was sitting backward.

Vicki propped Porter up over one shoulder, and he gave a healthy belch; then he squirmed and let out a wet, vibrating gush from his rear. The tiny bedroom smelled funky and breadlike.

Brenda poked her head back in. "They have the book at the airport," she said. "Some kid found it. I told him I wouldn't have a car until Friday, and he said he'd drop it by on his way home from work." She grinned. "See? I told you the book was lucky."

⁓

Josh Flynn didn't have a mystical bone in his body, but he wasn't insensitive, either. He knew when something was meant to be, and for some reason as yet unclear to him, he was supposed to be involved with the three women and two small children he had singled out earlier that afternoon. They had left behind a very important piece of luggage, and because Carlo had to leave early for a dental appointment, Josh was the one who fielded the phone call and Josh was the person who was going to deliver the goods. A briefcase with a fancy dial next to the locks. If Josh had been writing a certain kind of novel, the briefcase would contain a bomb, or drugs, or money, but the other students in Chas Gorda's creative-writing workshop found thrillers "amateurish" and "derivative," and some nitpicker would point out that the briefcase never would have made it through security in New York. What was in the briefcase? The woman—and Josh could tell just from her voice that it was Scowling Sister—had sounded unnerved on the phone. Anxio[us] and worried—and then relieved when he said that [ ] he had the briefcase. Josh shifted it in his hands. N[ ] moved; it was as though the briefcase were stuffed with wadded-up newspapers.

It was four-thirty. Josh was alone in the small, messy airport office. He could see the evening shift getting to work out the open back door, other college kids who had arrived on the island earlier than he did. They were waving the fluorescent wands like they'd seen it done on TV, bringing the nine-seater Cessnas on top of their marks, staying clear of the propellers, the way they'd all been taught in training. The evening shift was the best—it was shorter than the day shift, and busier. Maybe next month, if he did a decent job.

Josh fiddled with the briefcase locks just to see if anything would happen. At the mere touch of his fingertips, the locks sprang open with a noise like a gun's report. Josh jumped out of his chair. Whoa! He had not expected that! He checked the office. No one was around. His father worked upstairs through the evening shift. He always got home at eight o'clock, and he liked to eat dinner with Josh by eight-thirty. Just the two of them with something basic that Josh put together: burgers, barbecued chicken, always an iceberg salad, always a beer for his father— and now that Josh was old enough, a beer for Josh. Just one, though. His father was a creature of habit and had been since Josh had bothered to take note of it, which he supposed was at the age of twelve, after his mother committed suicide. His father was so predictable that Josh ⬚ there was no way he would ever come down to ⬚ his father was the only person he feared,

the briefcase open. There, swaddled in ⬚ wrap, was a heavy-duty freezer bag, the kind of bag fishermen down on the wharves filled with fresh tuna steaks. Only this bag contained . . . Josh peered closer . . . a book. A book? A book with a brown leather cover and a title in gold on the front: *The Innocent Impostor. A novel by Fleming Trainor.* After three years of literature courses at Middlebury, Josh's knowledge of important writers was growing. He had read Melville, Henry James, Hawthorne, Emily Dickinson, Mark Twain, F. Scott Fitzgerald, Jack Kerouac. He had never read— nor heard of—Fleming Trainor.

Josh stared at the book and tried to put it together in his mind with Scowling Sister's panicked voice. Nope, didn't make any sense. But Josh liked that. He closed the briefcase, locked it tight.

The briefcase sat on the passenger seat of his Jeep for the ride out to 'Sconset. Josh had lived on Nantucket his entire life. Because there was a small year-round community, everyone had an identity, and Josh's was this: good kid, smart kid, steady kid. His mother had killed herself while he was still in elementary school, but Josh hadn't derailed or self-destructed. In high school he studied hard enough to stay at the top of his class, he lettered in three sports, he was the senior class treasurer and did such a fine job running fund-raisers that he culled a budget surplus large enough to send the entire senior class to Boston the week before they graduated. Everyone thought he would become a doctor or a lawyer or a Wall Street banker, but Josh wanted to do something creative, something that would endure and have meaning. But nobody got it. Even Josh's best friend, Zach Browning, had cocked his head and said, *Do something creative? Like what, man? Paint someone's portrait? Compose a fucking symphony?*

Josh had kept a journal for years, in a series of spiral-bound notebooks that he stashed under his bed like *Playboy* magazines. They contained the usual stuff—his thoughts, snippets of dreams, song lyrics, dialogue from movies, passages from novels, the scores from every football, basketball, and baseball game of his high school career, riffs on friends, girlfriends, teachers, and his father, memories of his mother, pages of descriptions of Nantucket and the places farther afield that he had traveled, ideas for stories he wanted to write someday. Now, thanks to three years under the tutelage (or "hypnosis," as some would say) of Middlebury's writer-in-residence, Chas Gorda, Josh knew that journal keeping was not only okay for a writer, but compulsory. In high school, it had seemed a little weird. Weren't diaries for girls? His father had caught Josh a couple of times, opening Josh's bedroom door without knocking the way he'd been wont to do in those days and asking, "What are you doing?"

"Writing."

"Something for English?"

"No. Just writing. For me." It had sounded odd, and Josh had felt embarrassed. He started locking his bedroom door.

Chas Gorda warned his students against being too "self-referential." He was constantly reminding his class that no one wanted to read a short story about a college kid studying to be a writer. Josh understood this, but as he rolled into the town of 'Sconset with the mysterious briefcase next to him, anticipating interaction with people he barely knew who didn't know him, he couldn't help feeling that this was a moment he could someday mine. Maybe. Or maybe it would turn out to be a big nothing. The point, Chas Gorda had effectively hammered home, was that you had to be *ready*.

Nantucket was the dullest place in America to grow up. There was no city, no shopping mall, no McDonald's, no arcades, no diners, no clubs, no place to hang out unless you were into two-hundred-year-old Quaker meetinghouses. And yet, Josh had always had a soft spot for 'Sconset. It was a true village, with a Main Street canopied by tall, deciduous trees. The "town" of 'Sconset consisted of a post office, a package store that sold beer, wine, and used paperback books, two quaint cafes, and a market where Josh's mother used to take him for an ice-cream cone once a summer. There was an old casino that now served as a tennis club. 'Sconset was a place from another age, Josh had always thought. People said it was "old money," but that just meant that a long, long time ago someone had the five hundred dollars and the good sense it took to buy a piece of land and a small house. The people who lived in 'Sconset had always lived in 'Sconset; they drove twenty-five-year-old Jeep Wagoneers, kids rode Radio Flyer tricycles down streets paved with white shells, and on a summer afternoon, the only three sounds you could hear were the waves of the town beach, the snap of the flag at the rotary, and the thwack of tennis balls from the club. It was like something precious from a postcard, but it was real.

The address Scowling Sister had given Josh over the phone was Eleven Shell Street. The Jeep's tires crackled over crushed clamshells as he pulled up in front

of the house. It was small, cute, typical of 'Sconset;
it looked like the house where the Three Bears lived.
Josh picked up the briefcase. He was officially nervous. The house had a gate with a funny latch, and
while he was fumbling with it, the front door swung
open and out came a woman wearing a pair of denim
shorts and a green bikini top that shimmered like fish
scales. It was . . . well, Josh had to admit it took him
a minute to get his eyes to focus on the woman's face,
and when he did, he was confused. It was Scowling
Sister, but she was smiling. She was getting closer to
him, and closer, and before Josh knew it, she was wrapping her arms around his neck, and he felt the press of
her breasts against his grubby airport-issued polo shirt,
and he smelled her perfume and then he felt something
unsettling happening—he was losing his grip on the
briefcase. Or no, wait. She was prying it from his hand.
She had it now.

"Thank you," she said. "Thank you, thank you."

"Uh," Josh said. He took a few steps back. His vision
was splotchy and green—green from the plot of grass
in the side yard, green from the shiny material cupping
Scowling Sister's breasts. Okay, now, for sure, the hair
on his arms was standing up. "You're welcome."

"I'm Dr. Lyndon," Scowling Sister said, offering her
hand. "Brenda."

"Josh Flynn."

"You're such a doll to bring this by," Brenda said. She
hugged the briefcase to her chest. "I thought it was gone
forever."

"No problem," Josh said, though it was more of a
problem than he imagined. He was thrown into a frenzy

by the sight of Scowling Sister. Her hair, which had been loose at the airport, was now held in a bun by a pencil, and little pieces fell down around her neck. She was very pretty. And pretty old, he guessed. Maybe thirty. She was barefoot and her toes were dark pink; they looked like berries. *Enough!* he thought, and he may have actually spoken the word because Brenda tilted her head and looked at him strangely, as if to say, *Enough what?*

"Do you want to come in?" she asked.

Chas Gorda would have encouraged Josh to say yes. One way to avoid being self-referential was to open your world up, meet new people. Listen, observe, absorb. Josh had never seen the inside of one of these little cottages. He checked his watch. Five o'clock. Normally, after work, he went for a swim at Nobadeer Beach, and sometimes he stopped by his old girlfriend Didi's apartment. He and Didi had dated all through high school, but then she had stayed on the island and Josh had left, and now, three years later, you could really tell the difference. Didi worked at the admitting desk at the hospital and all she talked about was her weight and *Survivor.* If she had found an old book nestled in bubble wrap, she would have snorted and chucked it in the Dumpster.

"Oh-kay," he said. "Sure."

"I'll make us some tea," Brenda said. But she was distracted by a noise, a computerized version of "Für Elise." Brenda pulled a cell phone out of her back pocket and checked the display.

"Oh, God," she said. "I am *not* going to answer that." She smiled lamely at Josh, and he watched the enthusiasm drain from her face. They were two steps from the door when Brenda stopped. "Actually, everyone in the house is asleep."

"Oh."

"The kids. My sister. Her friend. And I'm not sure we even have any tea, so . . ."

"That's all right," Josh said, backing away. He was disappointed, but also relieved.

"Another time," Brenda said. "You promise you'll come back another time? Now you know where we live!"

Melanie would never complain out loud, not with her best friend so gravely ill, but she felt like mold on the wall at a fleabag motel. Here, then, was a classic case of Be Careful What You Wish For. Her breasts felt like lead balloons. They hurt so much she couldn't sleep on her stomach, and yet that was her favorite position for sleep, facedown, without so much as a pillow. Now she had to contend with new sleeping quarters, a sagging twin bed in this strange, sunny room that smelled like artificial pine trees.

All she had wanted was to get away—as far away as possible. When she was in Connecticut, facing the utter wasteland her life had become, moving to Pluto had seemed too close. But now she was at loose ends; from a distance, things somehow looked worse than they did when she was standing in the middle of them. And the bizarre, unfathomable fact was, she missed Peter.

Peter, Melanie's husband of six years, was very tall for an Asian man. Tall, broad in the shoulders, startlingly handsome—people on the streets of Manhattan occasionally mistook him for the chef Jean-Georges Vongerichten. Melanie had met Peter at a bar on the East Side. Peter, at that time, had worked on Wall Street, but shortly after he and Melanie married he became a market analyst at Rutter, Higgens, where he met Ted Stowe, Vicki's husband. Vicki and Ted were expecting their first child; they were moving to Darien. Melanie and Vicki became good, fast friends, and soon Melanie was pestering Peter about moving to Connecticut, too. ("Pestering" was how Peter described it now. At the time, to Melanie, it had seemed like a mutual decision to move.) Melanie wanted children. She and Peter started trying—nothing happened. But Melanie had fallen in love with a house, not to mention the green-grass-and-garden vision of her life in Connecticut. They moved and became the only young couple in Darien without children. At times, Melanie blamed her fertility problems on the suburb. Babies were everywhere. Melanie was forced to watch the stroller brigade on its way to the school bus stop each morning. She was confronted by children wherever she turned—at the Stop & Shop, at the packed day care of her gym, at the annual Christmas pageant of St. Clement's Episcopal Church.

You're so lucky, the mothers would say to Melanie. *You're free to do whatever you want. You can sit through dinner and a bottle of wine at Chuck's without sixteen hundred interruptions, without all the silverware and half the dinner rolls ending up on the floor, without the waitstaff glaring at you like you're something stuck to the bottom of a mortician's shoe.* The mothers were kind; they pretended to envy Melanie. But she knew that they pitied her, that she had become a woman defined by her faulty biology. Never mind that Melanie had graduated from Sarah Lawrence, that she had taught English to the hill tribes of northern Thailand after college; never mind that Melanie was an avid gardener and a dedicated power walker. When the other women saw her, they thought: *That's the woman who's trying to conceive. The one who's having difficulty. Barren, maybe. Something's wrong, poor thing.*

Peter didn't acknowledge any of this, and Melanie knew now, in the post-breakup where deep, dark secrets oozed out like sludge from the sewer, that he'd never cared whether they conceived or not. (No wonder she'd had such trouble! Everyone knew the game was 90 percent attitude, positive thinking, visualization.) Peter had tried to make her happy, and the best way he knew to do this, being a man, was to spend money on her in flabbergasting ways. Weekend trips to Cabo, the Connaught in London, the Delano in South Beach. An Yves Saint Laurent velvet blazer that had a two-month waiting list. A twelve-ounce black truffle flown in from Italy in a wooden box packed with straw. Orchids every Friday.

As the months of infertility dragged on, Melanie immersed herself in starting seeds, digging beds, planting shrubs and perennials, mulching, weeding, spending nearly a thousand dollars on annuals and herbs and heirloom tomato plants. She let the two beautiful little girls who lived next door cut her tulips and hyacinths for their May baskets. She fed her hydrangea bushes clam necks from the fish market. A Saint Bernard would have been easier to take care of than the damn garden, Peter complained.

Peter had told Melanie about his affair with Frances

Digitt on the way home from the Memorial Day picnic that Rutter, Higgens threw every year in Central Park. There were softball, hamburgers and hot dogs, watermelon, egg-in-a-spoon races and water balloons for the kids. It was a nice event, but Melanie had suffered through it. She and Peter had tried in vitro seven times with no results, and they had decided not to pursue any more treatment. It just wasn't working. But still people asked, "Any news?" and Melanie was forced to say, "We've let it go, for the time being." Ted and Vicki had not attended the picnic at all because Vicki had just gotten her diagnosis confirmed with a second opinion from Mount Sinai and she didn't feel up to seeing anybody. So Melanie fielded inquiries not only about her infertility but about Vicki's cancer as well. With the number of people pursuing Melanie and pinning her down in conversation, it would have been easier to hold a press conference.

On the way home, Melanie mentioned to Peter that the afternoon had worn her down, she hadn't had much fun, probably because Ted and Vicki weren't there.

"Life is too short," Melanie said. She said this every time she thought of Vicki now. Peter nodded distractedly; Melanie intoned this sentiment so often, its meaning was diluted. But Melanie meant the words urgently: Life was too short to fritter away in a constant state of yearning, aching, wanting. Waiting for something to happen.

At Exit 1 on I-95, they hit traffic and Peter cursed and they slowed to a crawl.

Now's the time, Melanie thought. And she said, "I think we should try again. Once more."

She steeled herself for his reaction. He hadn't wanted to pursue in vitro at all. There was something about it that felt forced to Peter, unnatural. Melanie had pushed the issue not once, not twice, but *seven* times, promising that each round would be the last. And then, a few weeks ago, she had really, really promised; she and Peter had made a pact of sorts, sealing it with their first spontaneous love-making in nearly a year. Afterward, Peter talked about a trip to the Great Barrier Reef, just the two of them. They would stay at a resort that didn't allow children.

Melanie was ready for Peter to be annoyed that she was revisiting the topic *yet again*; she was ready for anger. But Peter just shook his head, and with his eyes on the bumper of the car in front of them, he said, "I'm involved with someone else."

It took Melanie a moment to understand what he meant by "involved," but even after the obvious occurred to her, she still wasn't sure. "Involved?" she said.

"Yes. With Frances."

"Frances?" Melanie said. She looked at Peter. He had drunk several beers at the picnic. Was he impaired? Should he even be driving? Because what he was saying didn't make any sense. "You're involved with Frances? Frances Digitt?" Melanie could only picture Frances as she had just seen her—in a pair of red nylon running shorts and a white T-shirt that said *Mad River Glen, Ski It If You Can*. Frances Digitt was twenty-seven years old, she had a butch haircut, she was into all these *extreme* sports, like rock climbing and backcountry skiing. She had hit a home run during the softball game and she ran the bases pumping her fist in the air like a sixteen-year-old boy. "You're having an affair with Frances?"

"Yes," Peter said.

Yes: They were having the sleaziest kind of office

sex—in coat closets, in the deserted restrooms after hours, on top of his desk with the door closed and locked, in his swivel chair, Frances's skirt hiked up, straddling him.

When they got home that night, Peter moved into the guest room while Melanie took a bath and cried. Peter did not move out—he claimed he didn't want to, and Melanie couldn't bring herself to demand it. They slept under one roof, in separate rooms. He was not willing to end his "involvement" with Frances Digitt, not yet, he said, but maybe someday. Melanie was tortured by this. She loved the man, and he was using her heart for target practice. Most nights he came home, but some nights he called to say he would be "staying in the city" (which meant, she could only assume, staying with Frances Digitt). He rendered Melanie powerless; he knew she didn't have the courage to divorce him and take all his money, which was what everyone encouraged her to do.

When Melanie started feeling sick, she wasn't surprised. Extreme emotional stress, she thought. Depression. She couldn't keep food down. She would think about Frances Digitt and gag. She was overcome with exhaustion; she took three- and four-hour naps in the afternoons. Her cycle had been manipulated for so long with hormones that she didn't notice when she missed her period. But then her breasts started to tingle and ache, and smells she normally loved—coffee, fresh sage from the garden—turned her stomach. She went to a drugstore three towns away, where nobody knew her, and bought a test.

Pregnant.

Of course, she thought. Of course, of course. She was

pregnant now, when it no longer mattered, when it was a painful and complicated discovery instead of a joyous one. Melanie was aching to tell Peter. Every time she looked at him, she felt like she was going to burst with the news. She thought he would be astute enough to figure it out on his own—because she rushed to the bathroom to vomit, because she slept all the time. Peter either didn't notice these obvious symptoms or he chalked them up to Frances Digitt–inspired melodrama. Melanie decided she would not tell Peter—she was resolved in this—until something changed. She wanted Peter to leave Frances Digitt because he loved her, Melanie, and not because there was now going to be a baby. A baby. Their baby. After all that trying, after all the needles, drugs, treatments, counting days, scheduling sex, it had happened on its own. Even Peter would be amazed, even he would shout with joy. But she couldn't divulge the news yet. The pregnancy was her only currency; it was all she had left, and she didn't want to share it.

So . . . get out of town. Go with Vicki—and her sister, Brenda—to an island thirty miles out to sea.

Melanie hadn't told Peter she was leaving; he wouldn't realize it until seven o'clock that evening when he found her note in an envelope taped to the door of the mudroom. He would be stunned by her departure. He would realize he'd made a horrible mistake. The phone would ring. Maybe. He would ask her to come home. Maybe.

But maybe he'd be happy she left. Relieved. Maybe he would count Melanie's departure as his good fortune and invite Frances Digitt to move into their house and tend Melanie's garden.

One bad thought was all it took. Melanie rushed to

the communal bathroom and vomited bitter green bile into the toilet, which was spotted with urine because Blaine could not yet clear the rim. She pooled water in her hand and rinsed her mouth, glanced at her reflection in the brown-spotted mirror. Even the mirror looked sick. She stepped onto the rickety bathroom scale; if the thing was right, then she had lost three pounds since discovering she was pregnant. She couldn't keep anything down, not ginger ale, not dry toast, but she kept at it, eating and vomiting, because she was hungry, ravenous, and she couldn't stand to think of her baby starving and dehydrated, shriveling up like a piece of beef jerky.

The house was quiet. Vicki and the kids were sleeping, and Brenda was outside talking to . . . that handsome kid from the airport, the one who had offered Melanie first aid. It figured. Melanie hadn't gotten the whole story about Brenda and her student, but it didn't take a wizard to figure out that Brenda was a loose cannon. Promiscuous. Easy. Look at the way she was touching the kid's shoulder, then shaking her boobs at him. And he was just a kid, in his twenties, though quite adorable. He had smiled at Melanie when he offered the first aid, like he'd wanted to help but wasn't sure how. Melanie sighed. When was the last time Peter had smiled at her? She pulled the shades against the sun. The only good thing about pregnant sleep was that she was too exhausted to dream.

Brenda was the only adult awake when the phone rang. She had cleared Aunt Liv's tea set and all the ceramic knickknacks and enamel boxes from the coffee table so that she and Blaine could play Chutes and Ladders. The baby, meanwhile, would sit in Brenda's lap for thirty or forty seconds, then climb over her folded knees like Hannibal over the mountains and he was off, crawling across the satiny floorboards, pulling at lamps, fingering electrical cords, plugs, outlets. Somehow, while Brenda was teaching Blaine to count out spaces on the board, Porter put a dime in his mouth. Brenda heard him gagging, and she picked him up and smacked him on the back; the dime went flying across the room. Blaine moved himself forward an illegal fourteen spaces, and Brenda, although desperate for the game to be over, made him move back on principle. He started to cry. Brenda gathered him into her lap, and Porter crawled into the kitchen. At least he was too short to reach the knives. But then, as Brenda explained to Blaine that if he cheated at games no one would ever want to play with him, she heard a muffled thud that sickened her heart.

"Porter?" she said.

He gurgled happily in response.

Brenda slid Blaine off her lap. Aunt Liv's banjo clock chimed; it was six-thirty. Vicki and Melanie had been in their respective rooms with the doors closed since three. Brenda would have welcomed three and a half quiet hours for herself—but she was not pregnant and she did not have cancer. *Cancer,* she thought. Did the word ever get less scary and horrible? If you repeated it often enough and understood it better, did it lose that Grim Reaper chill?

In the kitchen, Brenda found her two-hundred-year-old first edition of *The Innocent Impostor* splayed on the floor like a dead bird. Porter sat next to the book, chewing on something. The cap to Brenda's pen.

Brenda cried out. Gently, she picked up the book, amazed that as old as it was, it hadn't crumbled into dust from the impact. She never should have taken it out of the briefcase—the book, like an elderly person, needed to be coddled. She smoothed the pages and swaddled it in its plastic cover, nestled it in the bubble wrap and locked it up, safe from grubby little hands. She plucked the pen cap out of Porter's drooly little mouth and threw it, with some force, into the kitchen trash.

Her problems were small beans, she reminded herself. In comparison, that was. She did not have cancer, she was not carrying her cheating husband's baby. Out of three bad situations, hers was the least dire. Was that a blessing or a curse? *I am grateful for my health. I will not feel sorry for myself. I am here to help Vicki, my sister, who has cancer.* Two hours after the news of Brenda's dismissal hit Champion's campus, Brenda had received an e-mail from a colleague of hers at the University of Iowa. *Rumor has it you've been axed,* Neil Gilinski wrote. *Rumor has it you committed the only sin that can't be forgiven other than out-and-out plagiarism.* Brenda's heart had tumbled. The news of her disgrace had traveled halfway across the country in two hours. It might as well have appeared on Page Six. But she would not feel sorry for herself. She would be grateful for her health.

"Auntie Brenda!" Blaine called out. "Come on! It's your turn!"

"Okay," Brenda said. "I'll be right there."

At that moment, the phone rang. The phone hung on the kitchen wall; it was white, with a rotary dial. Its ring was cranky and mechanical: a hammer hitting a bell. The sound made Brenda's breath catch. Fear seeped into her chest. Brian Delaney, Esquire, had already left two urgent-sounding messages on her cell phone. *Call me, please. Dammit, Brenda, call me.* But Brenda didn't want—indeed, couldn't afford—to call him back. Every phone call cost her a hundred dollars. If Brian had good news, such as the art restoration professional at Champion had found no permanent damage to the painting in question and the English Department had decided to drop all charges, then he could leave a message saying as much. And if Brian had bad news, she didn't want to hear it. Every time her cell phone rang, she prayed it would be Walsh. That it should be her lawyer added insult to injury. But the cottage's ringing phone took Brenda by surprise. She had known the phone number at Number Eleven Shell Street since she was a little girl, but she hadn't given the number to Walsh or to Brian Delaney, Esquire. Which meant it was probably her mother.

"Hello?" Brenda said.

"Is my wife there?" a man asked. He sounded even angrier than Brenda.

How did people live without caller ID? "Ted?" Brenda said.

"I said, is my *wife* there? This is the number she left on the note. A note! 'Gone for the summer.' What the hell?"

"You mean Melanie?" Brenda said. She was impressed that Melanie had bolted with only a note.

"Yes, Melanie!"

"She's here," Brenda said. "But she's not available."

"What does that mean?"

"I can't explain it any more clearly," Brenda said. "She . . . is . . . not . . . available."

"Put her on the phone," the husband said.

"No," Brenda said. She gazed at her briefcase and felt fresh relief that it hadn't vanished into the purgatory reserved for lost luggage, and then she checked on Porter, who had found the other half of Brenda's pen. His mouth was bleeding blue ink. "Oh, geez," Brenda said. When she lunged for the pen, Porter crawled away and Brenda nearly yanked the phone off the wall. In seconds, Porter and the pen were inches from Vicki's bedroom door. "I'm sorry," Brenda said. She hung up on Melanie's husband.

As she buckled Blaine and Porter into the double jog stroller, she wondered, *Why isn't there an Olympic crawling event for babies?* Porter would win. Then she thought, Melanie's husband sounded pretty damn entitled for someone who was having an affair.

"I'm hungry," Blaine said. "When are we having dinner?"

"Good question," Brenda said. She hadn't eaten since Au Bon Pain in LaGuardia. There was no food in the house, and it was possible that Vicki might sleep until morning. Brenda ran inside and helped herself to forty dollars from Vicki's wallet—she'd earned it.

As Brenda pushed the stroller over the crushed shells toward the market, she thought, *I am helping my sister, who is very sick. Sick* sounded better than *cancer*. People got sick all the time, and then they got better. *Vicki is sick, but she will get better, and in the meantime, I will take care of everything.* But Brenda feared she wouldn't be able to handle it. She had visited with the kids often since the previous September, when she moved back east from Iowa City to take the job at Champion—but she'd never had both of them alone for three whole hours. How did Vicki do it—one crawling all over creation, into everything, while the other one asked a hundred questions a minute, like, *What's your favorite number, Auntie Brenda? Mine is nine. No, actually, mine is three hundred and six. Is that more than fifty?* How did Vicki keep her mind from turning into a bowl of porridge? Why had Brenda thought that spending the summer taking care of the children would be something she would excel at? What led her to believe that she'd have a single quiet hour to try her hand at screenwriting? Melanie had said she would pitch in, but look what happened—she'd nearly killed Porter coming off the airplane and then she dozed off like Sleeping Beauty. That left Brenda holding the bag. Brenda to cover the kids, Brenda to drive Vicki to chemo, Brenda to shop for the food—and cook? This was what Brenda had offered, earnest in her desire to redeem herself, to prove to her sister and parents that she was neither soft nor rotten, she was neither self-centered nor self-destructive. She was not a person who typically broke rules or committed sins. She was a nice person, a good person. But really, *really,* Brenda thought, it wasn't as easy as that. She *was* soft; she *was* self-centered. And Vicki was asking too much of Brenda this summer; she wanted Brenda to be her *wife,* and what if Brenda couldn't do it? What she craved the most right now was quiet, even the quiet solitude of her apartment back in Manhattan. But to free herself of the rent, Brenda had sublet the apartment to her best friend in the world, Erik vanCott, and his fiancée. Erik and Noel would be making love in the bed that had most recently been occupied by Brenda and Walsh. Brenda had an exquisite longing in her stomach that was unique to being separated from one's true love. She could call Walsh, she thought, palming her cell phone. But no. She wouldn't pitch all of her resolutions into the trash can just yet. It was only the first day!

At the market, Brenda bought milk, bread, a log of goat cheese, some purple figs, a pound of gourmet butter (this was the only kind they had), a bunch of bananas, a pint of strawberries, a bag of Chips Ahoy!, and a pint of Ben & Jerry's Phish Food. Thirty-five dollars. Even Brenda, who was used to Manhattan prices, gulped. She gave the bag of cookies to Blaine, snatching one for herself first and one for Porter to gnaw on. As she was leaving the market, she noticed a bulletin board by the door. Yoga on the beach at sunrise, missing cat, room to share.

Yes, she thought.

She went back to the counter and borrowed an old flyer from the deli and a nearly used-up black marker. In streaky gray letters, she wrote: *Babysitter wanted. Flexible hours, daily, in 'Sconset. Two boys, 4 years and 9 months. Experience required. References. Please call 257-6101.*

She pinned it to the bulletin board in a prominent place, and then she strolled the kids home with one hand and held the bag of very expensive groceries in the other. If Brenda had just a little assistance with the kids, she would be better able to help Vicki and she would be able to start her screenplay, which might possibly earn her money and keep her from being a financial burden to

Ted and Vicki and her parents. A voice in Brenda's head whispered, *Soft. Self-centered.*

Oh, shut up, Brenda thought.

⌒

That night at dinner—steak tips, a baked potato, iceberg salad—Josh told his father he was thinking of quitting the airport.

Tom Flynn didn't respond right away. He was a quiet man; Josh had always thought of him as stingy with words. It was as though he withheld them on purpose to frustrate and annoy people, especially Josh. What Josh realized was that in not speaking, Tom Flynn prompted other people—and especially Josh—to say too much.

"It's boring," Josh said. He did not share the story about the three women, the woman falling, the baby, the briefcase, or the delivery of the briefcase to 'Sconset, though Josh understood it was this incident that was causing him to think about quitting. "It's pointless. I'd rather be doing something else."

"Really?" Tom Flynn said. He cut into his wedge of iceberg lettuce. Always with dinner they had iceberg salad. It was one of the many sad things about Josh's father, though again, Josh couldn't say exactly why. It was his refusal to deviate, his insistence on routine, the same salad winter, spring, summer, fall. It was tied to the death of Josh's mother eleven years earlier. She had hanged herself from a beam in the attic while Tom was at work and Josh was at school. She hadn't left a note—no hint or clue as to why she did what she did. She had seemed, if not overly happy, at least steady. She had grown up on the island, she had gone away to Plymouth State College, she had worked as an office manager for a construction company. She had few close friends but everybody knew her—Janey Flynn, nee Cumberland. *Pretty lady, runs the show at Dimmity Brothers, married to Tom who works out at the airport, one son, good-looking kid, smart as a whip.* That was his mother's biography—nothing flashy but nothing sinister either, no quiet desperation that Tom or Josh knew of. And yet.

So at the age of twelve Josh was left with just his father, who battled against his anger and confusion and grief with predictability, safety, evenness. Tom Flynn had never yelled at Josh; he never lost his temper; he showed his love the best way he knew how: by working, by putting food on the table, by saving his money to send Josh to Middlebury. But sometimes, when Josh looked at his father, he saw a man suspended in his sorrow, floating in it the way a fetal pig in the biology lab at school floated in formaldehyde.

"Yeah," Josh said. "Well, I don't know. I don't know what I want." Josh wished he had taken a job off-island for the summer, at a camp in Vermont or something. He liked kids.

The phone rang. Josh finished off his bottle of Sam Adams and went to answer it, since, invariably, it was for him.

"Josh?" It was Didi. It sounded like she was a couple of drinks ahead of him. "Wanna come over?"

"Come over" meant sex. Didi rented a basement apartment in a house on Fairgrounds Road, less than a mile away. The apartment was all hers and Josh liked the privacy of it, though it was always damp, and it smelled like her cat.

"Nah," he said.

"Come on," she said. "Please?"

Josh thought of Scowling Sister in the green shimmery bikini top.

"Sorry," he said. "Not tonight."

<hr>

The duck-breast sandwich with fig chutney wrapped in white butcher paper from Café L'Auberge on Eleventh Street. Spinach in her teeth. The smell of a new car. Blaine's preschool field trip to the dairy farm. Colleen Redd's baby shower. The baseball standings.

At the end of every winter, Vicki became restless, and this past April the restlessness had been worse than ever before. The skies in Darien were a permanent pewter gray; it rained all the time; it was unseasonably cold. Vicki was trapped in the house; the baby still nursed six times a day and wouldn't take a bottle, which limited how much Vicki could get out alone. Some days she stayed in her yoga pants until Ted got home from work. She tried to enjoy the quiet rhythm of her days—her kids would only be little once—but increasingly she dreamed of a change in her life. Returning to work, maybe? She had graduated Phi Beta Kappa from Duke, after all, and at one point had entertained thoughts of going to law school. She craved something private, something entirely her own. An affair, maybe? She'd heard her friends whisper about similar longings—their biology was to blame, a woman hit her sexual peak in her thirties, it was their situation: a husband, small children. Wouldn't it be nice if there was someone tending *their* every need for a change? Suddenly, men everywhere looked good to Vicki—the mechanic who worked on the Yukon, the boys at the gym, the new associates, just out of business school, at Ted's office. Vicki needed something else in her life, otherwise she would turn into one of these women with too little to do who slowly lost her mind. She felt combustible, like she might burst into flames at any moment. Her anger and her desire scared her. She began to feel a tightness in her chest, and then the tightness, if she wasn't imagining things, became a pain. She was short of breath. One morning, she woke up huffing like she did when she was in the basement doing laundry and she heard Porter on the baby monitor and she raced up two flights of stairs. Something was wrong with her.

Vicki's disdain of doctors and hospitals was legendary. In college, she contracted a bladder infection that she left untreated, and it moved to her kidneys. She was so sick, and yet so averse to going to the doctor, that her roommates took her to the infirmary while she was asleep. Years later, when she had Blaine, she arrived at the hospital forty minutes before he was delivered and left twenty-four hours later. And yet that morning, she drove right to the ER at Fairfield Hospital. *What is wrong with me? Why can't I breathe?*

At first, the doctors thought she had walking pneumonia, but the X-ray looked suspicious. An MRI revealed a mass in Vicki's left lung the size of an apple. Subsequent tests—a PET/CT scan and a fine-needle aspiration—confirmed that this mass was malignant, and it showed suspicious cells in her hilar lymph nodes. She had robust stage-two lung cancer. She heard the oncologist, Dr. Garcia, say the words "lung cancer," she saw his melancholy brown eyes swimming behind the lenses of his thick glasses—and yet Vicki assumed it was some kind of joke, or a mistake.

"Mistake?" she'd said, shaking her head, unable to come up with enough oxygen to say anything more.

"I'm afraid not," Dr. Garcia said. "You have a four-centimeter tumor in your left lung that is hugging the chest wall, which makes it difficult to remove. It looks like the cancer may have also spread to your hilar lymph nodes, but the MRI didn't detect any additional metastases. A lot of times when the cancer is this far along it will turn up elsewhere—in the brain or the liver, for example. But your cancer is contained in your lungs and this is *good news*." Here, he pounded his desk.

Good news? Was the man stupid, or just insensitive?

"You're wrong," Vicki said. It sounded like she meant that he was wrong about the "good news," but what she meant was that he was wrong about the cancer. There was no way she had cancer. When you had cancer, when you had an *apple-sized tumor* in your lung, you knew it. All Vicki had was a little shortness of breath, an infection of some sort. She needed antibiotics. Ted was sitting in the leather armchair next to Vicki, and Vicki turned to him with a little laugh. Ted was a powerful man, big and handsome, with a crushing handshake. *Tell the doctor he's wrong, Ted!* Vicki thought. But Ted looked like he had taken a kick to the genitals. He was hunched over, and his mouth formed a small O. *Tell the doctor he's wrong, Ted!* Vicki did not have cancer, technically or otherwise. Who was this man, anyway? She didn't know him and he didn't know her. Strangers should not be allowed to tell you you have cancer, and yet that was what had just happened.

"I have children," Vicki said. Her voice was flat and scary. "I have two boys, a four-year-old and a baby, seven months. You would have a hard time convincing them or anybody else that their mother having lung cancer is good news."

"Let me tell you something, Victoria," Dr. Garcia said. "I'm a pulmonary oncologist. Lung cancer is my field, it's what I do. And if you take all the patients I've seen in the past fourteen years—let's say, for the sake of argument, a thousand patients—I would put you smack in the middle. It's a challenging case, yes. To give you the best shot at long-term remission, we'll try to shrink the tumor with chemo first and then we'll go in surgically and hope we can get it all out. But full remission is a viable outcome, and that, Vicki, is good news."

"I don't want to be a case," Vicki said. "I don't want you to treat me like your nine hundred and ninety-nine other patients. I want you to treat me like the mother of two little boys." She started to cry.

"Many of my other patients had children," Dr. Garcia said.

"But they're not me. My life is valuable. It's really fucking valuable. My children are young. They're babies." Vicki looked to Ted for confirmation of this, but he was still incapacitated. Vicki wiped at her eyes. "Am I going to die?" she asked.

"We're all going to die," Dr. Garcia said.

Just as Vicki was about to tell him to stuff his existential bullshit, he smiled. "The best thing you can do for yourself," he said, "is to keep a positive attitude."

Positive attitude? But that, in the end, was how he had won Vicki over. Dr. Garcia was the kind of oncologist who used phrases like *good news* and *positive attitude.*

She went for a second opinion at Mount Sinai right after the initial diagnosis, at Ted's insistence. That appointment was with a female oncologist named Dr. Doone, whom Vicki had immediately renamed Dr. Doom because she wasn't nearly as upbeat about Vicki's chances of recovery as Dr. Garcia. Dr. Doone basically told Vicki that IF chemo shrank the tumor in her left lung such that it receded from the chest wall (which, tone of voice conveyed, was doubtful), then POSSIBLY a pneumonectomy would solve the problem IF THERE WERE NO ADDITIONAL METASTASES. *It's not the tumor in your lungs that's the problem,* Dr. Doone had said. *It's where that tumor came from. It's where that tumor is going.* She made a comment about Vicki being FOOLISH to pursue treatment in the BOONDOCKS. Dr. Doone felt Vicki should be treated at Mount Sinai—but since Dr. Doone herself had enough cancer patients to fill ten city buses, Vicki should accept as a HUGE FAVOR a referral to Dr. Martine, an oncologist at Sloan-Kettering who also happened to have been Dr. Doone's roommate at Columbia Physicians and Surgeons.

No, thank you, Vicki had said. *I'm sticking with Dr. Garcia.*

And Vicki understood at that point that Dr. Doom wrote her off. As good as dead.

*   *   *

Vicki had two days until her chemo started. Two days until the doctors cut into her chest to install a port through which they would pump her full of poison twice a week for the next two months. It was, Dr. Garcia assured her, nothing to get frantic about. The problem was, the chemo wouldn't cure her cancer. It would merely discipline it. Vicki could feel the mean-ass, dumb-shit little cells throwing a beer bash, doing the bump and grind and drunkenly copulating and reproducing as she lay in bed trying to breathe, with Porter hiccuping at her side. *I have a malignant tumor in my lungs. Lung cancer.* She could say it in her mind and out loud, but it didn't seem true. It wasn't even a kind of cancer that made any sense. Breast cancer made sense, and Vicki irrationally wished she had breast cancer. She was a thirty-one-year-old nonsmoking mother of two. *Give me breast cancer!* Lung cancer was for old men, two packs a day for twenty years; it was for John Wayne. Vicki laughed joylessly. Listen to yourself.

The traffic on I-95, a sale on beef tenderloin at Stew Leonard's, the United States' involvement in Iraq. Powder-post beetles in the attic. Swim lesson sign-ups. Collecting pinecones for Christmas wreaths. Chapped lips. Uncut toenails. Pollution in the Hudson. Duke, once again, in the men's NCAA basketball finals.

The chemo regimen consisted of two drugs: gemcitabine and carboplatin. Vicki could barely pronounce the names, but she was well versed in the possible side effects: weight loss, diarrhea, constipation, nausea and vomiting, fatigue, confusion—and she would, most likely, lose her hair. She had to stop nursing and she might become sterile. It was enough to bring her to tears—she had cried many silent hours when Ted and the kids were asleep, when the dark house seemed as terrifying as death itself—but the chemo was nothing compared to the pneumonectomy. The surgery blocked Vicki's path; she couldn't see over, around, or beyond it. If the chemo worked as it was supposed to, they would operate at Fairfield Hospital in early September. Dr. Emery, thoracic surgeon, Dr. Garcia attending. Two resident surgeons, five OR nurses, six hours, the removal of her left lung and the hilar lymph nodes. Who survived a surgery like that?

Oh, lots of people, Dr. Garcia said. *Every day. And it has to be done, obviously. If you want to live.*

But it was as though he were asking Vicki to pass through a tunnel of solid granite, or travel into outer space and back. Impossible to come to grips with. Terrifying.

Vicki could have lain in bed all day, obsessing about her cancer, dissecting it until it was in ten or twelve comprehendible pieces, but the curse and the blessing of her present situation was that there was no time. She was in Nantucket with two children to look after, a household to run—and a sister and a best friend who were, after being together for less than twenty-four hours, arguing.

Vicki heard them in the kitchen—strained pleasantries that quickly turned bitter. By the time Vicki wrapped herself in her seersucker robe, collected Porter, and made it out to the kitchen, she had pieced together the gist of the argument: Peter had called the night before, but Brenda had neglected to give Melanie the message.

"You were asleep," Brenda said. "You'd been asleep for hours."

"You could have left a note," Melanie said. "Slipped

it under my door. Because now he won't answer his cell phone. He's furious with me."

"He's furious with *you*?" Brenda said. "That's rich. You'll pardon me for saying so, but I don't understand why you care. The man is cheating on you."

"You know nothing about it," Melanie said.

Brenda sliced a fig in half and tried to feed it to Blaine, who "yucked" and clamped a hand over his mouth.

"I know nothing about it," Brenda agreed. "I didn't write a note because I was busy with the kids. We were on our way out to buy groceries. You were asleep. Vicki was asleep. I was left to captain the ship by myself and I . . . just forgot. Honestly, it flew out of my mind."

"I hope you didn't tell him I was pregnant," Melanie said.

"Oh my God, of course not."

"Or even hint at it. I don't want him to know. And I mean that."

"I didn't hint at anything. I was very vague. I didn't even tell him you were asleep. All I said was that you were unavailable. You should be *thanking* me. I did a great job."

"Except you didn't tell me he called."

"I had my hands full!"

"Bren," Vicki said.

Brenda whipped her head around. When she did that, her hair was a weapon. "Are you taking sides?"

There can't be any sides this summer, Vicki thought. *I am too sick for sides.* But she knew it would be fruitless. There was Brenda, her sister. There was Melanie, her friend. They didn't have a single thing in common except for Vicki. Already Vicki felt herself splitting down the middle, a crack right between her diseased lungs.

"No," she said.

Vicki had come to Nantucket with the hope of re-creating the idyllic summers of her youth. Had those long-ago summers really been idyllic? Vicki remembered a summer with one hundred mosquito bites, and another summer, or maybe the same summer, when she had a gnat trapped in her ear overnight, and one year Vicki fought with her father about long-distance phone calls to her boyfriend Simon. But for the most part, yes, they had been idyllic. Vicki and Brenda left school and friends behind in Pennsylvania, so the summers had starred only them and, in a hazy, parallel adult world, their parents, Buzz and Ellen, and Aunt Liv. The sand castles with moats, the smell of a real charcoal barbecue—it had all been real. And so, even as Melanie pouted on the living room sofa and Brenda huffed around the kitchen—they were like boxers back in their corners—Vicki peeled a banana, eyed the sunlight pouring through the cottage windows like honey, and thought: *It's a beach day.*

This sounded like a simple idea, but it took forever to get ready to leave. The children had to be changed into bathing suits and slathered with lotion. (Skin cancer!) Brenda found plastic sand toys, bleached white by the sun, in a net bag in the shed. The toys were covered with years of dust and cobwebs and had to be rinsed with the hose. Then, lunch. Vicki suggested, for the sake of ease, picking up sandwiches at Claudette's, but Brenda insisted on a picnic hodgepodged together from the bizarre ingredients she had brought home from the market:

bread and goat cheese, figs and strawberries. At the mention of these provisions, Melanie gagged and ran for the bathroom. Vicki and Brenda listened to her throwing up as they folded the beach towels.

"Try not to upset her," Vicki said.

"She's pretty sensitive," Brenda said.

"She's going through a lot," Vicki said.

"*You're* going through a lot," Brenda said. She stuffed the towels into a mildewed canvas tote that had belonged to Aunt Liv. "What are we going to do on Tuesday, when I take you for your port installation? The doctors said it would take all morning. There is no way she can handle both kids by herself all morning."

"Sure she can."

"She cannot. I could barely do it myself. And, I hate to bring this up, I mean, I'm happy to help with the kids and all, that is why I'm here, but I was hoping to get some work done this summer. On my screenplay."

Vicki took a breath. Brenda was so predictable, but maybe only to Vicki. Vicki heard Ted's words: *Your sister says she wants to help, but she won't help. She'll be too busy reading to help.* That was how it always went. When Vicki and Brenda were children, Brenda had been excused from all kinds of chores—setting the table, folding laundry, cleaning her room—because she was *too busy reading.* Even if it was only the newspaper, when Brenda was reading, it had been considered sacrilegious to ask her to stop. Buzz and Ellen Lyndon had done a thorough (if unintentional) job of labeling their girls: Vicki was the go-getter, organized and hardworking, whereas Brenda had been blessed with the kind of rarefied genius that had to be coddled. Although Brenda was only sixteen months younger than Vicki, nothing was expected of her. She and her "great mind" were tiptoed around like a sleeping baby.

Melanie came out of the bathroom, wiping at her lips. "Sorry," she said. "Can I just have a piece of bread, please? With nothing on it?"

"Sure," Brenda said. "My pleasure."

"Thank you."

"You're welcome."

Okay, Vicki thought. *Okay?*

The morning sparkled. Vicki, Brenda, and Melanie rambled down the streets of 'Sconset toward the town beach. Vicki was carrying Porter, who kept sticking his hand into her bikini top and pinching her nipple. She had tried to give him a bottle that morning, but he threw it defiantly to the floor. Then he lunged for Vicki, fell out of the high chair, and bumped his head on the table. Tears. The subsequent fussing over Porter made Blaine irate—he proceeded to march out the front door and urinate on the flagstone walk. Lovely.

Vicki removed Porter's hand from her breast. "Sorry, buddy." Brenda was up ahead schlepping the beach bag with towels and lotion, the net bag of plastic sand toys, the cooler with lunch and drinks, two beach chairs, and the umbrella. Melanie was wearing her wide-brimmed straw hat and carrying a leather purse. Brenda had caught Vicki's eye when Melanie emerged with the purse as if to say, *Who the hell takes a* purse *to the beach?* As if to say, *I'm loaded down like a camel traveling across the Sahara and she's got a little something from Coach?* Vicki almost suggested Melanie leave the purse behind—

there was nothing to buy—but she was afraid she'd scare Melanie away. Melanie hadn't even wanted to come to the beach; she'd wanted to stay in the cottage in case Peter called.

Melanie was also attempting to hold Blaine's hand. She grasped it for five seconds, but then he raced ahead, into the road, around the corner, out of sight. Vicki called after him and removed Porter's hand from her breast. So much of parenting was just this mind-numbing repetition.

They all followed Brenda on a shortcut: between two houses, along a path, over the dunes. They popped out a hundred yards down from the parking lot, away from the clusters of other people and the lifeguard stand. Brenda dropped all her stuff with a great big martyrish sigh.

"I hope this is okay," she said.

"Fine," Vicki said. "Melanie?"

"Fine," Melanie said.

Brenda set up the umbrellas and the chairs, she stuck Porter in the shade next to the cooler, she spread out the blanket and towels and handed Blaine a shovel, a bucket, and a dump truck. He dashed for the water. Melanie pulled one of the chairs into the shade and took off her hat. Porter crawled over to the hat and put it in his mouth. Melanie made a sour face. Vicki snatched the hat from Porter and he started to cry. Vicki dug through the beach bag and handed Porter a spare pair of sunglasses. Immediately, he snapped off one of the arms.

"Great," Brenda said. "Those were mine."

"Oh, sorry," Vicki said. "I thought they were an extra pair."

"They were my extra pair," Brenda said.

"I'm sorry," Vicki said again. "He was eating Melanie's hat. He's like a goat."

"Well, we can't have him eating *Melanie's hat,*" Brenda said. "It's such a beautiful hat! Better he should break my sunglasses. Look at them, they're useless."

"Were they expensive?" Vicki asked. "I'll replace them."

"No, no," Brenda said. "I don't want you to worry about it. They're just sunglasses."

Vicki took a deep breath and turned to Melanie.

"What do you think about the beach?" Vicki said. She wanted Melanie to be happy; she wanted Melanie to love Nantucket. She did not want Melanie to think, even for a second, that she had made a mistake in coming along.

"Do you think Peter's trying to call?" Melanie said. She checked her watch, a Cartier tank watch that Peter had given her after the first failed round of in vitro. "Should I call him at work? He goes in sometimes on Sundays."

He doesn't go to the office on Sundays, Vicki thought. *He's just been telling you he goes to the office when really he spends Sundays with Frances Digitt making love, eating bagels, reading the* Times, *and making love again.* That was what a man who was having an affair did on Sundays; that was where Peter was this very second. But Vicki said nothing. She shrugged.

Brenda cleared her throat. "Vick, are you taking the other chair?"

Vicki looked at the chair. Brenda had hauled it; she should sit on it.

"No. You take it."

"Well, do you want it?"

"That's okay."

Brenda huffed. "Please take it. I'll lie on my stomach."

"Are you sure?" Vicki said.

"Sure."

"Should I call Peter at work?" Melanie said.

More breathy-type noises from Brenda. She pulled out her cell phone. "Here. Be my guest."

Melanie took the cell phone, set it in her lap, and stared at it.

Vicki heard a shout. She looked down the beach. Someone was waving at her. No, not at her, thank God. She settled in the chair.

"Will someone keep an eye on Blaine?" Vicki asked. "I'm just going to close my eyes for a minute."

"I'd like to try and write," Brenda said.

"I'll watch him," Melanie said.

"You're not going to call Peter?"

"No," Melanie said. "Yes. I don't know. Not right now."

Vicki closed her eyes and raised her face to the sun. It felt wonderful—sun on her face, her feet buried in the Nantucket sand. It was just as her mother had promised. The sound of the waves lulled Vicki into a sense of drowsy well-being. Was this what it was like when you died? Or was it completely black, a big nothing, oblivion, the way it was before you were born? She wanted to know.

"How long have you noticed this shortness of breath?" Dr. Garcia asked. They were in his office, which was bland and doctorish: medical books, diplomas, pictures of his family. Two children, Vicki noted. She liked Dr.

Garcia more for the picture of his daughter dressed up as a dragonfly for Halloween.

"I've had tightness in my chest, a little pain for a week or two, since Easter, but I didn't think anything of it. But now, I can't get air in."

"Do you smoke?"

"God, no," Vicki said. "Well, I tried a cigarette when I was thirteen, outside the ice-skating rink. One puff. I smoked marijuana in college, three, maybe four hits altogether. And for two years I had a Cuban cigar once a week."

Dr. Garcia laughed. "Cuban cigar?"

"It was a poker game," Vicki said.

"The MRI shows a mass in your lung."

"A mass?"

"It looks suspicious to me, but we're going to have to take a cell sample to figure out what it is. It could simply be a water-filled cyst. Or it could be something more serious."

Vicki felt her stomach rise up in revolt. She spotted a trash can next to Dr. Garcia's desk. *Something more serious? Do not,* she implored herself, *think about the children.*

"We'll do it now," Dr. Garcia said. "When I saw your scan, I blocked off time."

It sounded like he expected Vicki to thank him, but it was all she could do not to spew her breakfast all over his desk.

"It could just be a water-filled cyst?" she said. She held out hope for a juicy bubble of stagnant liquid that would just pop!—and dissolve.

"Sure enough," Dr. Garcia said. "Follow me."

* * *

"Vicki! Vicki Stowe!"

Vicki looked up. A woman *was* waving at her. It was . . . oh dear God, Caroline Knox, an acquaintance from Darien. Caroline's sister, Eve, had been in Vicki's Lamaze class when Vicki was pregnant with Blaine. Eve had brought Caroline as her partner a few times, and somehow Nantucket had come up—that Vicki stayed with Aunt Liv, that Caroline owned a house and came for the summer with her husband and kids. A few weeks ago, Vicki bumped into Caroline Knox in the parking lot of Goodwives, and Caroline asked Vicki if Vicki was going to Nantucket, and Vicki, not wanting to discuss the only topic on her mind that day, which was her cancer, had, without thinking, said, *Yes, we'll be there on June tenth.* To which Caroline had replied, *Oh, us, too! We must get together!* Vicki had agreed, though really, if she and Caroline Knox didn't get together in Darien, why would they get together on Nantucket?

Vicki pushed herself up out of the chair. Porter had crawled off the blanket and was sitting in the sand chewing on the handle of a plastic shovel.

"Hi!" she said, trying to muster enthusiasm at the sight of Caroline Knox, who, Vicki noted, looked very matronly in her black one-piece suit. And she'd cut her hair short. Not even forty and she looked like Barbara Bush. "Hi, Caroline!"

"Hiiiiiiiiiiiiiiiii," Caroline squealed. "Vicki, how are you? When did you get here?"

"Yesterday."

"We've been here a week already. It's heaven on earth, don't you think?"

Vicki smiled.

"When is Ted coming?" Caroline asked.

"Friday. He's driving up with the car."

"Well, we should have dinner while it's just us girls. Are you free on Wednesday?"

"I'm free . . . ," Vicki said.

"Oh, good!"

"But I start chemo on Tuesday, so . . ."

Caroline's face stopped its smiling. *"What?"*

"I have lung cancer," Vicki said. She felt mean dropping it on Caroline this way, in front of Brenda, who had just scrawled two lines on her yellow legal pad, and Melanie, who was still staring at the phone in her lap. But Vicki enjoyed it, too, making Caroline Knox uncomfortable, watching her grope around for something to say.

"I had no idea," Caroline said. "Eve didn't tell me." She dug her toe in the sand and the flesh of her thigh wobbled. "You know that Kit Campbell's father had lung cancer last year, and . . ."

"Yes," Vicki said, though she had no idea who Kit Campbell was. "I heard all about it."

"So you're getting chemo *here*? On the island?"

"At the hospital," Vicki said, in a voice that ended the topic. "Caroline, I'd like you to meet my sister, Brenda Lyndon, and my friend Melanie Patchen."

Caroline shook hands with Melanie. "Patchen, you say? Are you related to Peter?"

"He's my husband," Melanie said. She squinted. "Why? Do you know him?"

"He plays squash with my husband, Edgar, at the Y," Caroline said. "I didn't realize Peter was married. For some reason, I thought he was single."

It's official, Vicki thought. *I hate Caroline Knox.*

Brenda shifted on her towel, though she made no move to acknowledge Caroline's presence. Despite their mother's best efforts, Brenda had the manners of Attila the Hun. When Brenda spoke, she said, "Vick, where's Blaine?"

Vicki looked at the water. Blaine had been digging a hole just beyond where the waves broke so that the hole filled with water. That was what he'd been doing when she shut her eyes. But when she looked now, she saw the shovel, the pail, the truck, and the hole—but no Blaine.

Okay, wait. Vicki checked the perimeter of where they were sitting. He was behind them—no. He was . . . where was he?

"Mel?" Vicki asked. But Melanie looked even paler and more panicked than Vicki. *You were watching him, right?* Vicki thought. *You said you'd keep an eye on him.* Melanie stood up. Her left foot crushed her straw hat, and Brenda's cell phone fell into the sand.

"Oh, God," Vicki said. She jogged to the shoreline. Her insides twisted up in preliminary panic, and she felt her lungs tighten. "Blaine!" she called out. She looked to the left, to the right, and then all the way back to the dunes. Was he hiding in the dunes? Brenda grabbed her arm.

"It's okay. Do not panic. Don't panic, Vick. He couldn't have gone far."

"Did he go in?" Vicki said. The surface of the water was calm; small waves broke at her feet. She waded in up to her knees, scanning the dappled surface of the water. The only thing she had to worry about was Blaine under water. "Blaine?" she called out, looking for air bubbles.

"Blaine?" Blaine could swim a little bit. If he was drowning, he would have splashed and made a fuss; Melanie certainly would have noticed. If there was an undertow here, and sometimes there was, he would have called for Vicki. She would have heard him calling out.

"Blaine!" Brenda shouted. She turned back toward the beach. "Blaine Stowe! Where are you? Are there footprints? He was right here a second ago, wasn't he?"

Was he? Now Vicki couldn't remember if she'd seen him digging at all. But his toys were here. She'd had her eyes closed, she'd checked on the baby, she'd been thinking about Dr. Garcia, she'd assumed Melanie was watching Blaine. But then Caroline came.

"He's here somewhere," Vicki said. "He has to be here."

"Of course," Brenda said. "Obviously. We'll find him."

"I'll go to the left," Vicki said, though there was no evidence of humanity to the left—no people, no footprints, nothing but five or six plovers pecking at the sand. "I'll go to the right, I mean. You check the dunes. He probably had to go to the bathroom. Mel can stay with the baby."

"Is everything all right?" Caroline called out.

"I lost my son!" Vicki said in a lighthearted way. She didn't want to sound too frantic in front of Caroline. She didn't want Caroline to think that she'd *actually* lost Blaine—because what kind of mother took her eyes off her child when that child was playing at the water's edge? "He must have wandered away!" She waved at Caroline as if to say, *You know how kids are, always putting the fear of God into you,* as she speed walked down the beach. She couldn't go as fast as she wanted; she was wheezing already, and her heart was galloping at an un-safe speed. *Do not panic,* she thought. *He's here some-where.* She would find him any second, she would flood with relief. He's okay, he's right here . . . he just . . . but no, she didn't see him anywhere. Not yet. She was ap-proaching the main section of 'Sconset Beach, just thirty or forty yards away from the parking lot entrance. There were people here—families, couples, college girls lined up on a blanket. Vicki hurried to the lifeguard stand. As long as Blaine wasn't in the water, he was safe. Why, oh why, hadn't they sat between the two red flags? They were so far down that the lifeguard would never have no-ticed Blaine drowning.

"Excuse me," Vicki said.

The lifeguard didn't remove her eyes from the water. She was a chunky girl in a red tank suit; she had a sun-burn on her cheeks that had peeled, revealing raw pink skin underneath. *Skin cancer!* Vicki thought.

"My son is missing," Vicki said. "He's four years old. We're sitting down there." She pointed, but the lifeguard did not move her eyes. "He was wearing a green bathing suit with green frogs on it. He has blond hair. Have you seem him? Did he wander by, maybe?"

"I haven't seen him," the lifeguard said.

"No?" Vicki said. "Is there anything you can do to help me find him?"

"You're sitting beyond the flags?" the lifeguard asked.

"Yes."

"I have to keep my eyes on the people who are in the water between the flags," the lifeguard said. "Lots of times kids just walk away and get lost. Maybe you can ask some of the folks sitting nearby if they've seen him. I can't leave my post to help. I'm sorry."

Vicki studied the other families, the other children, many of them Blaine's age. The families reminded Vicki of herself and Brenda and her parents and Aunt Liv, sitting on the beach every single day, happy as larks, swimming, sunning, eating, sleeping in the sun. She had never gotten lost; Brenda had never gotten swept away by the undertow. They had been like the kids in front of Vicki now: whole, happy, in one piece. Blaine was someplace else, an unknown place. What if they couldn't find him? Vicki would have to call Ted—though there was no way she could tell him Blaine was gone; that was just not acceptable. *Three grown women on the beach, one of them his own mother,* Ted would say. How did he slip away? Why wasn't anyone watching? *I thought Melanie was watching! I asked her to watch! I closed my eyes for . . . three minutes. Maybe four.* Vicki felt like collapsing in a pile on the sand. *Okay, fine,* she told God, or the Devil, or whoever listened to pleas from desperate mothers. *Take me. Let me die. Just please, please let Blaine be okay.*

"Please," she whispered. "Please."

"Vick!"

The voice was far away, but Vicki heard it over the roar of anxiety in her ears. She turned and saw a woman in a green bikini waving her arms. Brenda. Vicki allowed her hopes to rise a little bit. She saw a figure under the umbrella—maybe a little boy wrapped in a towel? Vicki got closer, running, walking, stopping to control her breathing. Vicki saw Brenda on her cell phone. The "figure" under the umbrella was just a towel hanging from the cooler. Vicki burst into tears. How many hundreds of hours in the past month had she spent wondering: *What could be worse than lung cancer? What could be worse than chemotherapy? What could be worse than having my chest sliced open, my ribs spread, and my lung removed?* Well, here was the answer. This was worse. Blaine was missing. Where was he? Every molecule in Vicki's body screamed in chorus, *Find him, find him!* Porter was crying. Melanie was rocking him, but he pitched forward toward Vicki.

Brenda said, "I checked the dunes. He's not there. Your friend left. She really wanted to help us look, but she had a tennis lesson at the casino. She suggested I call the police, so that's what I'm doing."

"I am so sorry," Melanie said. She was weepy, though not actually crying. If it had been Brenda, Vicki would have lost her temper, but this was Melanie, her dear, sweet, heartbroken friend. *Kid gloves!* Vicki thought. Melanie had a lot on her mind; Melanie could not be held accountable.

"It's okay," Vicki said.

"It's not okay," Melanie said. "You asked me to watch him, and I was thinking about something else. I didn't even see him leave."

"Did you see him go into the water?" Vicki asked. "Did you see him swimming?"

"No," Melanie said. "I don't think so. I don't know. I was thinking about Peter, and . . ."

Brenda held up a finger and gave the 911 operator the information: four-year-old boy, blond, green bathing suit, 'Sconset Beach north. Missing for . . . twelve minutes. Only twelve minutes? Vicki could easily dissolve, but no, she was going to be strong. *Think!* she urged herself. *Think like Blaine.* Porter was screaming. Vicki took him from Melanie. She recalled the day before, Melanie falling from the steps of the plane. Melanie had been anxious, tired, sick, distressed, and wearing those ridiculous gardening clogs. She'd had her hands full, and Blaine had knocked her over. Yesterday was not Melanie's fault. Porter reached inside Vicki's bikini top and pinched her nipple. Her milk came in. She hugged Porter and whispered, "We have to find your brother."

Brenda hung up with the police. "They're sending a squad car," she said. "And a guy on a Jet Ski."

"Do they think he's in the water?" Vicki said.

"I told the police the last place we saw him was at the water's edge." Brenda glared at Melanie. *"Right?"*

Melanie made a retching noise. She bent in half and vomited into the sand. She staggered toward the dunes. Vicki followed her and gently touched her shoulder. "I'll be right back, okay?" Brenda had checked the dunes, but maybe not closely enough. Blaine might have found a nest of some kind, or maybe he had to go to the bathroom. She hobbled through the dunes, looking for a little boy crouched in the eelgrass. Porter held on tight, one hand locked on Vicki's breast, which was leaking milk. Her bikini top was wet, and milk trickled down her bare stomach. The path through the dunes funneled her between two private homes and then back onto the street, where a squad car waited, lights flashing. Vicki pried Porter's hand from her breast, and he started with fresh tears. Milk was leaking everywhere; Vicki needed a towel. She needed to wean the baby. She needed to find her child! Her exuberant, out-to-conquer-the-world firstborn. Would he have come this far by himself? Of course. Blaine was afraid of nothing; he was impossible to intimidate. Ted loved this about him, he *encouraged* Blaine's fearlessness, his independence—he fostered it! This was Ted's fault. It was Melanie's fault. She said she would keep an eye on him! Ultimately, however, Vicki blamed herself.

The policeman was a woman. Short, with a dark ponytail and eyebrows that met over her nose. When Vicki approached, she said, "You're the one who called?"

"I'm the mother," Vicki said. She tried to wipe the milk from her stomach, pull her bikini top so that it lined up evenly, and comfort her screaming baby. All this disarray, a missing child . . . *and I have cancer!*

"Where did you last see your son?" the policewoman asked.

"He was on the beach," Vicki said. "But now I'm wondering if he didn't try to walk home by himself. Or to the market. He knows there's ice cream there. Could we get in your car and drive around to look for him?"

"The fire department sent a Jet Ski," the policewoman said. "To check the waters."

"I don't think he's in the water," Vicki said. What she meant was: *He can't be in the water. If he's in the water, he's dead.* "Could we just go in your car?"

The policewoman murmured something into her crackling walkie-talkie and indicated with a tilt of her head that Vicki and Porter should climb into the back. As soon as Vicki was sitting down, she latched Porter onto her leaking breast. The policewoman caught a glimpse of this and her eyebrows wiggled like a caterpillar.

"Do you have children?" Vicki asked hopefully.

"No."

No, Vicki thought. The policewoman—Sergeant Lorie, her ID said—had no children, thus she had no earthly clue how Vicki teetered on the brink of insanity. Twelve minutes, thirteen minutes . . . surely by now Blaine had been missing for *fifteen minutes.* Sergeant Lorie cruised the streets of 'Sconset, which were only wide enough for one car. They were bordered on both sides by cottages, privet hedge, pocket gardens. *Where would he have gone?* Vicki thought of a fireman on a Jet Ski discovering Blaine's body floating a hundred yards offshore—and then pushed the image away. *Take me,* she thought. *Do not take my child.*

Sergeant Lorie pulled up in front of the 'Sconset Market.

"Do you want to run in?" she asked Vicki.

"Yes." Vicki unlatched Porter from her breast and threw him over her shoulder. He let out a belch. Sergeant Lorie murmured something else into her walkie-talkie. Vicki hurried into the market. She checked aisle by aisle—cereal, crackers, biscotti, chips, jasmine rice, toilet paper—she checked around the small deli case and the soda coolers, behind the spinning book racks, and then, finally, the only place Blaine would logically be— the ice-cream counter. No Blaine.

A young girl wearing a green canvas apron poised her ice-cream scoop in the air. "Can I help you?" she said.

"Have you seen a four-year-old boy in here by himself? Blond hair? Green bathing suit?"

"No," the girl said. "Sorry. I haven't."

"No," Vicki said. "Of course not." She zipped back

outside to the police car. "He wasn't there," she told Sergeant Lorie. "Let's try Shell Street."

They drove to Shell Street slowly—Vicki checking in every yard, in every climbable tree—but when they got to Aunt Liv's cottage, the gate was shut tight and so was the front door to the house. Vicki knew Blaine wasn't inside. Okay, that was it. She was free to flip out—to pull her hair and scream and pound the reinforced windows of the police car until they shattered. He was in the water.

"What would you like to do, ma'am?" Sergeant Lorie asked.

"Let's go back to the beach," Vicki said. Brenda and Melanie had probably found him.

They drove back to the spot where the squad car had waited initially and Vicki hopped out. Her lungs ached. She pictured her tumor glowing hot and red like an ember. Did things like this really happen? Did a woman get lung cancer and then lose her child? Did this much bad luck visit one person? It shouldn't be allowed. It wasn't allowed.

On the beach, a crowd had gathered—Caroline Knox had reappeared, and the lifeguard was there, as well as the college girls who had been snoozing on the blanket, and some members of the previously happy families that had been frolicking on the beach. Everyone was gathered in a loose knot, though some people stood at the water's edge or waded in, kicking up the sandy bottom. A teenage boy veered around with a mask and snorkel; the Jet Ski zipped back and forth, making small, predictable waves. Vicki was astonished at the gathering—part of her was embarrassed. She hated to draw attention to herself; she felt like telling everyone to go back to their business, Blaine was just hiding in the dunes, pushing things too far, he didn't know any better, he was only four years old. There were other mothers in the group—Vicki picked them out—women with the worst kind of sympathy stamped on their faces. *I can't imagine . . . thank God it's not my . . . why on earth wasn't she keeping an eye on . . .*

Brenda was in the center of things; it looked like she was organizing search parties. One for the beach to the left, one for the dunes. Melanie stood at the edge of the crowd, rubbing Brenda's cell phone like it was a rabbit's foot. Caroline Knox saw Vicki and rushed over.

"I feel awful," Caroline said. "This is my fault. If you hadn't been talking to me . . ."

"Did you see him playing?" Vicki asked. "Do you remember seeing him playing by the water? Blond hair, green bathing suit?"

"That's the thing," Caroline said. "I don't remember."

Vicki heard a motor approaching—three policemen on ATV's came sledding over the sand. These were summer cops, teenagers, basically, in fluorescent yellow shirts, with Ray-Bans and walkie-talkies.

"We're here to help," one of them said. He was the alpha dog, with linebacker shoulders and dark movie-star hair.

"I'm his mother," Vicki said, stepping forward. She pried Porter's hand from her breast once again, and he started to cry. "His name is Blaine. Blaine Stowe, he's four years old."

"Blond hair, green bathing suit," the policeman said.

"Yes," Vicki said.

"We'll find him," the policeman said. He was all of

twenty years old, but the sunglasses and the walkie-talkie gave him a cocky self-assurance.

"Please," Vicki whispered.

Brenda said, "We'll go this way, then," and she headed off to the left. A second group went to the right. Some people, seeing the police, wandered back to their camps. When the cops gunned their motors and left to search, the area cleared out, leaving Vicki, Melanie, and Caroline Knox. Vicki felt deserted; she couldn't stand being stuck behind to wait, and certainly not in present company. Blaine had been missing for thirty minutes at least. She would check the dunes herself. She took the cell phone from Melanie. "You stay here and hold down the fort," Vicki said. "I'm going to look."

"I'll come with you," Caroline said.

"No, no," Vicki said. "I'll go myself."

"I'll carry the baby," Caroline said.

"We'll be fine," Vicki said.

"This is all my fault," Melanie said. "Oh, Vicki, I am so, so sorry."

"It's okay, Mel," Vicki said.

"No, it's not okay! I should have been . . ."

But Vicki didn't have time! She turned and hurried for the dunes.

It was hot in the dunes, and Porter's head drooped. He made a sucking noise against Vicki's shoulder.

"Blaine!" Vicki shouted. "Blaine Theodore Stowe!"

It went on like this for fifteen minutes, thirty minutes, an hour. Vicki searched every inch of the dunes; they all looked the same, white bowls of sand crowned with eel-grass. Vicki got lost herself a couple of times; she had to climb into the eelgrass (which was just crawling with ticks, she knew) to get her bearings. She called Blaine's name until she was hoarse. She wandered back out to the street, all the way down to the market, all the way over to Shell Street. No Blaine. Vicki returned to the beach. She was parched, pain seared her lungs; she collapsed on a beach towel under their umbrella. Porter had fallen asleep. She laid him down and hunted through the cooler for water. Even if Blaine was alive, he would be thirsty by now, and hungry. Wherever he was he would be afraid, crying, alone.

Caroline Knox was gone—to her tennis lesson, Vicki thought angrily, though she was relieved. Melanie lay facedown on a towel, her face buried.

"I have to call Ted," Vicki said. "I don't know what else to do."

"This is all my fault," Melanie said. "I am going to be a terrible mother."

"No, Melanie," Vicki said. "Do not say that. Do not think that."

Vicki dialed home. Ted had promised to clean the attic and get someone to check for powder-post beetles. He would see Brenda's cell phone number on the caller ID, but he would have no idea what Vicki was about to tell him.

Four rings, then the answering machine picked up. Vicki's own voice—happy, unconcerned—a voice from another time, before today, before her diagnosis. "You have reached the Stowe residence . . ." The message played in one ear, and in the other ear, Vicki heard the growl of the ocean, like some kind of animal ready to attack. The growl grew louder—something about the sound made Vicki turn. Just as Ted snapped the receiver up, saying in a breathless voice, "Sorry, I didn't hear the phone. Hello?" Vicki saw the ATV, the smug *Top Gun* smile of the summer policeman, and two little hands clasped around the policeman's waist. She heard Melanie shriek. And then—a wave from the back of the ATV, like Blaine was the mayor in a parade.

"Mom!" he cried out. "Look at me!"

When Vicki woke up from her nap, Porter's hand was on her breast and Blaine was curled under her left arm. They had fallen asleep immediately upon returning home from the beach; Vicki hadn't even bothered to rinse off their feet, and now the sheets were sandy. The room was dark, though Vicki could see golden sunlight in the living room. She eased out of bed, then stood over her children and watched them sleep. In ninety harrowing minutes, her world had shattered and then, like magic, been made whole again. Blaine was alive and well; he'd wandered all the way down the beach throwing rocks into the water. He'd walked well over a mile, the policeman said, but he didn't seem upset or worried in the slightest.

"I've never seen such a brave kid," the policeman had said. "And he's got quite an arm. The Red Sox should sign him now."

The tops of Blaine's shoulders were sunburned. When he climbed off the ATV he suffered through Vicki's whimpers and sobs of relief and the tightest hug of his life; then he showed her a handful of shells and asked for his milk. Now, even with robust stage-two lung cancer and thirty-six hours until chemotherapy, Vicki felt like the luckiest woman on earth.

She tiptoed out and shut the door so the boys could

sleep awhile longer. Melanie's door was closed. She had slinked off once they reached home, apologizing again and again, until it was like a joke she'd told too many times. Vicki had done the best she could to assuage Melanie's guilt, but she knew Melanie would flagellate herself just the same. *It's my fault. I should have been . . .* Vicki considered tapping on Melanie's door. *Don't worry about it. You have enough on your mind as it is. Everything turned out okay.* Vicki put her ear to the door and heard nothing. Melanie was probably asleep.

A note on the kitchen table said, *Gone writing!* From Brenda. Predictable. Brenda swore up and down that this summer would be about helping Vicki, but Vicki knew better. She flipped Brenda's note over and started to make a grocery list. She wanted to walk to the market to get food for a proper dinner. They couldn't continue to eat like French college students.

The phone rang, loud and grating. Vicki leapt to answer it before it woke the kids or Melanie.

"Hello?"

A young female voice said, "I'm calling about the ad."

"Ad?" Vicki said. "I'm afraid you've got the wrong number."

"Oh," the girl said. "Sorry." She hung up. Vicki hung up.

A few seconds later, the phone rang again.

"Hello?" Vicki said.

"Hi," the girl said. "I dialed really carefully. 257-6101? The help wanted? For the babysitter?"

"Babysitter?" Vicki said.

"For the two boys in 'Sconset?" the girl said. "I live

in 'Sconset and my parents want me to get a job this summer."

"We don't need a babysitter," Vicki said. "But thanks for calling."

"Too bad," the girl said. "It sounded perfect for me. Not too hard or anything."

"Thanks for calling," Vicki said. She hung up. The house was silent. Vicki's brain started to fizz and pop. Babysitter, two boys in 'Sconset, this number? Brenda had placed an ad for a babysitter and hadn't checked with Vicki? And hadn't breathed a word about it? Vicki flung open the fridge, hoping to find a cold bottle of wine. No such luck. She wasn't supposed to drink anyway. What did Dr. Garcia say? Water, broccoli, kale, watermelon, blueberries, beets. But wine wasn't cigarettes. Vicki opened the cabinets, marveling at her sister's gall. She was farming out her own nephews!

The front screen door slammed. Vicki looked up. There was Brenda, looking like a supermodel in her bikini top and jean shorts. Holding a yellow legal pad. It was her "screenplay"—a screenplay based on a book that only six other people in the world had ever read, a screenplay that had no prayer of ever being produced. And yet this endeavor was more important to Brenda than caring for Vicki's children.

"What's the face for?" Brenda said.

"You know what it's for," Vicki said.

~

Melanie could hear Brenda and Vicki fighting in the living room even as she lay across her supremely uncomfortable mattress with a down pillow over her head. Her leg was throbbing; somehow in the midst of all the commotion over losing Blaine, she had acquired an angry sunburn. Her stomach was sour—she had kept nothing down all day, not even plain bread. And her heart was broken. Melanie pictured it as an apple: sliced down the middle, then into quarters, cored, skinned. She deserved it all, and worse. Yesterday she had fallen while holding the baby, and today she had failed at the simplest child-related task. *Will someone keep an eye on Blaine?* Make sure he doesn't die, or vanish. But even that had proved too much. Before Peter announced his infidelity, before Melanie learned of the living being inside of her, she had held great visions of herself as a mother. She would buy only wooden toys and only organic produce, she would spend hours reading colorful children's books with strong messages bought only from independently owned bookstores. She would never yell, never condescend, never pick a pacifier up off the floor, lick it and put it back into her child's mouth. She was going to do it right. She certainly never imagined getting so caught up in the disintegrating state of her marriage that she lost track of a child completely, that she couldn't say for certain whether or not that child had wandered away or drowned. It was, Melanie decided, all Peter's fault, but the result of this thinking only intensified her urge to speak to him. It was almost a physical need, more pressing than being hungry or thirsty. She needed to talk to Peter the way she needed oxygen.

Since she returned home from the beach, she had called him six times at the office, and all six times she had gotten his voice mail. His voice sounded cruelly jovial. "Hi!

You've reached the voice mail of Peter Patchen, senior analyst for Rutter, Higgens. I'm either on the phone or away from my desk, so please leave a message and I'll call you back. Thank you!"

The first message that Melanie had left was at 1:28 PM: *Peter, it's me. I'm on Nantucket with Vicki. I'm staying for the summer, unless you give me a reason to come home. What I mean is, I'm not coming home until you end things with Frances. Okay. Call me. You can call me at the number I left earlier, which is 508-257-6101—or you can call me on this cell phone, which belongs to Vicki's sister. The number is 917-555-0628. I'd like you to call me, please.*

She had lain facedown on the bed and waited until the banjo clock chiming in the living room announced two o'clock. Melanie had left her own cell phone in Connecticut specifically so Peter couldn't reach her and so she would be less tempted to call him. Ha. She called back. *Peter, please call me. My numbers, once again, are . . .*

She had called four other times at half-hour intervals, and on the quarter hour, she called him at their house, where her own voice greeted her. "You have reached the Patchen residence. We are unable to take your call. Please leave a message and your phone number and we will call you back." Melanie left no message. She called Peter's cell phone and was shuttled immediately to voice mail.

Peter, it's me. And then, in case he didn't recognize her voice, she said, *Melanie. Please call me at 508-257-6101. Or you can call me on this phone at . . .* She called the cell phone three more times and hung up each time.

Surprise! The phone rang. Melanie's heart leapt. She studied the number on the display. It was an unfamiliar Manhattan number. The display said *Walsh, J.*

"Hello?" Melanie said.

"Brindah?"

Deflation. Disappointment. Not Peter.

"No, I'm sorry. This isn't Brenda."

"Vicki?"

"No," Melanie said. "This is Melanie. I'm a friend of Vicki's."

"Oar right." The voice was heavily Australian. "Is Brindah available?"

Melanie listened. Out in the living room, the fight continued. *Never met such a selfish . . . the world doesn't revolve around . . .* "She's not available this very second."

"No worries. Would you tell her Walsh called?"

"I will," Melanie said. She paused. Was this the student? He sounded rather old to be the student, but then again, Melanie knew nothing about the student except that he was, in fact, Brenda's student. "Do you want to leave your number?"

"She has the number. Leaving it again would be pointless."

Pointless, Melanie thought. She had left her number again and again, as though it were the lack of a number that was Peter's problem.

"I'll have her call you," Melanie said in an authoritative voice, as though she had the power to make Brenda do a single thing. "I promise she will call you. You can count on me."

Walsh laughed. "Well, I thank you, Melanie."

"You're welcome," Melanie said.

Walsh hung up. Melanie hung up. The call had only lasted a minute and three seconds, but Melanie felt better. She felt less isolated somehow, knowing that this person Walsh was in New York City trying to reach Brenda. But she also felt pointlessly jealous. Men loved Brenda. Even the young stud policeman had been unable to take his eyes off of her. Melanie sucked in the stale air of her room. She should open the window. But instead she dialed Frances Digitt's apartment. She didn't even need to check her book for the number; she had it memorized. Frances Digitt answered on the second ring.

"Hello?"

Melanie wasn't worried about caller ID since she was using Brenda's phone. She hung on for a minute, listening for Peter. Was he there? What she heard was a dog barking (Frances Digitt had a chocolate Lab) and what sounded like the baseball game on TV. Dog, baseball. Of course. The irony of the situation was that Frances Digitt was not a woman who had ever threatened Melanie, or any of the other wives at Rutter, Higgens; she was the opposite of a bombshell. She was the girl who beat the boys in races in gym class, the one the boys forgot come seventh grade when all the other girls developed breasts. Frances was small and boyish. She was, Melanie reflected, the only kind of woman who could survive the locker-room miasma of Peter's office: She was the little sister, but smart as a whip, she knew the market, she did her research, she organized the office football pool and the brackets for March Madness. Everyone assumed she was a lesbian, but Melanie had seen it all along—she was too cute to be a lesbian! She had a certain recklessness that might translate to her being a dynamo in bed.

It made Melanie sick just to think about it. She hung up, then pressed Brenda's phone to her pounding heart. She dialed Frances Digitt's number again.

"Hello?" Now Frances Digitt sounded irked, and Melanie thought, *You have no right to sound irked. If anyone should sound irked here, it's me.*

Thus prodded, she said, "Is Peter there?" It was more a question than a request for his presence on the phone, and Frances, predictably, paused. No need to ask who was calling, no need to play games, or so Frances ultimately decided, because she said, "Yes. He is." She set the phone down a bit too firmly on what Melanie pictured as her cheap, shoddily assembled plastic-laminate-over-plywood side table from IKEA. People in their twenties had no taste.

"Hello?" Peter said, sounding wary.

"It's me," Melanie said. And then, in case he still didn't get it, she said, "Melanie."

"Hi," Peter said—and this was the syllable that squashed Melanie's heart once and for all. He sounded uninspired, uninterested; he sounded caught. Melanie felt like his truant officer, his Sunday school teacher, his dentist.

"I'm on Nantucket," she said.

"I know."

"For the whole summer."

"So the note said."

"Do you want me to come home?" she asked.

"What kind of question is that?" Peter said.

It was the only question that mattered. She had left because she wanted time to think, but as it turned out, all she could think about was Peter. She had wanted to get away, but now that she was away she wanted, more than anything, to be home. *I'm pregnant,* she thought. *You have a child in this world and you don't even know it.* Keeping this from Peter was cruel, but was it any worse than what Peter was doing?

No! He was at Frances's apartment. They were fucking! Melanie felt sick. She was going to . . .

"I have to hang up," she said.

"Okay," he said.

Melanie stared at the dead phone. She retched into the plastic-lined trash can at the side of her bed. Nothing came up. She was vomiting bad air, her own sadness, Peter's rejection. Out in the living room, Brenda and Vicki were still fighting. Something about a babysitter. Something about Brenda's screenplay, *a total sham,* then something about their parents, *that's the way things always are with you!* Then Melanie heard her name, or rather, what she heard was the absence of her name: a repeated "she," a repeated "her." It was Brenda in a stage whisper: *You want* her *to take care of the kids and look what happened! I understand* she *has shit to deal with, but we all do. You're sick! I refuse to spend the summer accommodating* her*! I just don't get it!* She's *one more person to take care of! Did you think of that before you invited her along? Did you?*

Melanie staggered to her feet and began tossing her belongings into her suitcase. She was going home. It had been an impulsive decision to come, and now she realized that it was a mistake.

She tiptoed to the bathroom for her toothbrush. They were still at it. It would be better for Brenda and Vicki to spend the summer alone, working through their issues.

Melanie didn't have a sister; she knew nothing about it, but it seemed like hard work.

Everything fit into her suitcase except for her straw hat. It was mangled from when she'd stepped on it at the beach, and she was tempted to leave it behind. It was a present from Peter last spring on her birthday; it was wide-brimmed and old-fashioned, but she loved it. It was her gardening hat. She put it on, tying the satin ribbon under her chin, then zipped her suitcase and looked around the room. This room was witness to her startling decision. She would go home and confront Peter in person. She would tell him she wanted an abortion.

She slipped into the living room. Brenda and Vicki were gone. Melanie heard them somewhere. Out back. One of them was in the outdoor shower. They were still arguing. Before Melanie walked out the front door, she scribbled a note and left it on the kitchen table: *Call John Walsh!* Strangely, John Walsh was the only person Melanie felt responsible to. She would call Vicki later, once she was safely home and there was no chance of Vicki talking her into staying.

Melanie extended the handle of her suitcase and tried to roll it down the shell-lined street. Shells caught in the wheels, and the suitcase jerked to a stop. She decided it would be easier to carry the suitcase, though it was heavy and she bent to one side in a way that couldn't have been good for the baby. *Abortion,* she thought. After all she'd been through. Seven times her hopes had been dashed at the sight of her own blood. Seven times she had failed; success had come unbidden, when she no longer wanted it.

She made it to the rotary, where she found a cab

waiting. Thank God! She climbed in and said, "Airport, please."

It was Sunday at five o'clock, and every plane back to New York was booked and overbooked. When it was Melanie's turn in line, she pushed her ticket across the counter, her spirits temporarily buoyed by the business of getting home—until the woman working the US Airways desk pushed the ticket right back.

"We have nothing tonight," she said. "And nothing tomorrow until three o'clock. I'm sorry."

"I'm happy to pay the change fee," Melanie said. "Or go standby, in case someone doesn't show."

The woman held up a piece of paper crowded with names. "This is the waiting list. You'd be number one sixty-seven."

Melanie stuffed her ticket into her purse and dragged her suitcase to a bench. The predictable thing would be for her to cry. She was about to start down that hackneyed road when she noticed someone walking toward her. A kid in a fluorescent orange vest. The one who had offered her first aid when she fell down the stairs. She smiled at him. He came right over.

"Hi," he said. He grinned. "Did you have a nice trip?"

"Very nice," Melanie said.

"That was a joke," he said. "'Trip,' you know? Because you fell down."

Melanie felt her cheeks burning. "Right," she said. "Well, as it turned out, that wasn't the stupidest thing I did this weekend."

The kid tugged at his vest and scuffed at the floor with

his sneaker. "I didn't mean you were stupid," he said. "I was just trying to . . ."

"It's okay," Melanie said. She touched her elbow. It was still tender, and yet with all that had happened, she had forgotten about it. "I'm Melanie, by the way."

"Josh Flynn," he said. He looked at her suitcase. "Are you leaving tonight? You just got here."

"I was supposed to stay longer," Melanie said. "But I have to get home."

"That's too bad," Josh said. "Where do you live?"

"Connecticut," she said. "But, as it turns out, I can't get a plane tonight. They're all sold out. I was just gathering my wits before I grabbed a taxi back to the place I'm staying."

"You're in 'Sconset, right?" Josh said. "I can take you home. I just finished my shift."

"Don't worry about me," Melanie said. "I'll take a cab."

"It's no problem for me to give you a ride," Josh said. "I even know which house. I was there yesterday to drop off a briefcase."

"Right," Melanie said. She eyed her luggage. She was so devoid of energy, she wasn't sure if she could even get herself to the curb. "I hate to impose."

"It's on my way home," Josh said. He picked up her suitcase. "Please. I insist."

Melanie followed him out to the parking lot, where he threw her luggage in the back of his Jeep. The Jeep had an inch of sand on the floor, and the passenger side was strewn with CDs. Melanie slid into the seat, stacking the CDs in her lap. Dispatch, Offspring, Afroman. She had never even heard of these bands. She felt old enough to be his mother.

"Sorry the car is such a mess," Josh said. "I didn't know I'd have female companionship."

Melanie blushed and straightened the edges of the CDs so that they made a perfect cube. *Female companionship?* She felt like a hooker. Then she caught sight of herself in the mirror. Her straw hat made her look like the Farmer in the Dell; it made her look like Minnie Pearl or some other character from *Hee Haw*. She took off the hat and set it in her lap as Josh buckled himself in, swiped at the dust on the dashboard, and turned down the radio. He stretched his arm over to Melanie's seat as he craned his neck to check behind him before backing out. His hand was resting an inch or so above her head. She could smell him. He was very handsome—*hot,* someone younger would have said— but he was just a child. How old? she wondered.

"Do you live here?" she asked.

"Born and raised," he said. "But I go to college. Middlebury, in Vermont."

"Good school," Melanie said.

"I'll be a senior," he said.

So that made him around twenty-one, Melanie thought. Maybe twenty-two. Which was how old she'd been when she'd met Peter.

They pulled onto the major road. Josh's window was unzipped and air rushed in as they sped toward 'Sconset. Melanie rested her head against the seat and closed her eyes. There was something therapeutic about this ride. *I feel okay,* Melanie thought. *Right this second I feel okay. How can that be?*

She turned to face the wind. Josh's brown hair ruffled up like a rooster's comb. In her lap, the brim of her hat flapped.

"How do you like your job?" she asked.

"I hate it," he said.

"That's too bad."

"Truly," he said. "My father's an air traffic controller. He sort of got me in there."

"Oh," Melanie said.

"I'm going to quit anyway," Josh said. "Life's too short."

"I agree. That is, basically, my mantra. But will your father be mad?"

"He'll be mad," Josh said. "But he can't stop me."

"All right, then," Melanie said. The road stretched out before them; to the left, across the moors, was a lighthouse, and beyond that, the ocean. "It's beautiful here."

Josh didn't answer, and Melanie chastised herself for saying something so obvious. He probably heard it from tourists all the time: how lovely, how quaint, how pristine, how beautiful. She tried to think of something witty to say, something bright, something that would make him think she was . . . cool. She had never been cool in her entire life, and she certainly wasn't cool tonight. But she wanted Josh to believe she was worthy of the ride.

"I just found out I'm pregnant," she said.

He looked at her quizzically. "Really?"

"Yeah." She stared at her knees. She would never make it in the CIA. She had just shared the strictest secret with someone she barely knew. "I'd appreciate it if you didn't tell anybody."

He seemed puzzled by this, and Melanie would have

laughed if she didn't feel like such a horse's ass. Who would he possibly tell?

Still, he humored her. "My lips are sealed, I promise," he said. "You know yesterday, when you fell? I thought your friend sounded pretty concerned. Overly concerned—about you, not her baby."

"She worries about me," Melanie said.

"Right," he said. "But I wondered if there was something else going on. Something no one else knew about."

"Oh," Melanie said. "Well . . . yes." She looked at him. "You have a good memory."

"The three of you were hard to forget," he said.

When the Jeep pulled up in front of the cottage on Shell Street, Melanie's spirits flagged. She didn't want the ride to end; she didn't want to have to face Vicki and Brenda like a child who had run away from home. Josh yanked the brake and hopped out of the Jeep to retrieve Melanie's luggage.

"Thanks for the ride," Melanie said.

"My pleasure."

Melanie reached for the suitcase, and their hands touched on the handle. *We're touching,* she thought. One second, two, three. Did he notice? He didn't move his hand. Slowly, Melanie raised her eyes and thought, *If he's staring at me, I won't be able to bear it.*

He was looking at the cottage. Melanie let her breath go. She felt like a thirteen-year-old.

"Well," she said. "Thanks again."

"Right," Josh said. "So, I'll see you, I guess. Good luck with everything." He smiled at her.

"Thanks," she said. "You, too." She smiled back. She smiled until he climbed into his Jeep and drove off. Then she took a deep breath. The air smelled like steak on a charcoal grill, and miraculously, she felt hungry.

As she rolled her suitcase down the flagstone walk, she met Blaine. His hair had been wetted and combed and he wore a fresh blue polo shirt.

"Where were you?" he demanded. *The inquisition starts,* Melanie thought. But then Blaine's face broke open into genuine curiosity and, if Melanie wasn't mistaken, a little bit of conspiracy. "Were you lost?" he whispered.

"Yes," she said. "I was lost."

That night, after dinner (cheeseburgers, Ore-Ida onion rings, iceberg salad), Josh drove to Didi's apartment. She had called during dinner and asked him to come over. He said no. When he sat back down to his father's silence, Josh felt he had to explain. "That was Didi. She wants me to come over. I said no."

Tom Flynn cleared his throat. "Dennis told me he saw you giving a girl a ride home tonight."

"Huh?" Josh said, then he remembered Melanie. "Oh, right." How to explain the "girl" Dennis was referring to was an airline passenger who was much older than Josh, and pregnant to boot? How to explain that he had driven her home in an attempt to catch another glimpse of Scowling Sister, who was another woman out of his league in every respect? "That was nothing."

Tom Flynn cut his iceberg salad, took a bite, wiped

ranch dressing from his chin. Drank his beer. The phone rang again. Again, Josh rose to answer it. Melanie had told him she was pregnant, but she hadn't seemed happy about it. In fact, she had seemed gloomy. But she was too old to have gotten knocked up. Josh hadn't thought to check if she was wearing a wedding ring. He wasn't doing a very good job observing or absorbing.

"Hello?"

"Josh?"

"What?" Josh said in an aggravated whisper.

"I really want you to come over. Really. It's important."

"You've been drinking," he said.

"Just wine," Didi said. "Please? Come over. I have something to tell you."

She had something to tell him. This was how it always went, since the end of sophomore year in high school when they'd started dating. Didi took everyday truths and twisted them like a kid with taffy until they were soap-opera dramas. Her doctor told her she was anemic, her brother threatened her with a carving knife because she borrowed his favorite sweater and got makeup on it, her father's friend Ed Grubb pinched her ass—all these became reasons why Didi needed consoling, protecting, and extra heaps of attention from Josh.

"What is it, Didi?" he said.

"Just come," she said, and she hung up.

Josh sat back down at the table. He stared at his onion rings, which had grown cold, limp, and soggy. "Sounds like I'd better go," he said.

* * *

At nine o'clock, when Josh pulled into Didi's driveway, the sun was just setting. *Summer,* he thought. *Drag-ass summer.*

He could hear the music from fifty yards away: Led Zeppelin. This was not a promising sign. He approached the stairs down to Didi's basement apartment in what might be considered a stealthy way and peered into the living room window, which was at ankle level. Didi was dancing on her coffee table wearing only a red negligee, waving around a glass of white wine so that it sloshed everywhere. During their senior year in high school, Josh's friend Zach had referred to Didi as Most Likely to Become a Pole Dancer, and although at the time Josh had been obligated to punch Zach in the gut, watching her now, he had to agree. Didi had been a better-quality person when Josh was dating her, or so it had seemed. She was a cheerleader, she was on student council, she'd had lots of girlfriends with whom she was constantly conferring—by passed notes, in the bathroom, at sleepovers on the weekends. She had been fun—not as smart as Josh, maybe, not "academically oriented," not exactly the kind of girl Josh's mother would have wanted for him in the long run, but perfect for high school.

They had broken up the first time a few weeks before Josh left for college. Tom Flynn had been away, in Woburn, renewing his controller's certification, and Didi had spent the night at Josh's house. It started out as a very pleasant playing-house fantasy—they ordered pizza, drank Tom Flynn's beer, and rented a movie. Then they brushed their teeth and climbed into bed together. In the middle of the night, Josh awoke to find Didi sitting on the floor by the side of the bed, reading through Josh's journal with a flashlight. They broke up that night—not because Josh was pissed at her for invading his privacy (though he was) but because Didi had either hunted for or stumbled across the pages in the journals that were dedicated to her. In these pages, Josh wrote about how needy Didi was and how he wished she would "locate her center" and "operate from a place of security." Didi took enormous offense at these statements. She threw the journal in Josh's face and stormed out of his bedroom, slamming the door, only to return a few seconds later, claim her overnight bag, and then slam the door again.

A little while later, Josh found her downstairs at the kitchen table, crying, with another of Tom Flynn's beers open in front of her. He went to her and held her, marveling at how his writing about how needy she was had made her even needier. She was terrified to let him go away to college. *You'll forget all about me,* she said, and he did not refute this, because Didi represented the things about high school that he wanted to leave behind.

That their relationship had endured three years hence—at least in its sexual aspect—was beginning to discourage him. Dealing with Didi was like Josh's job at the airport, it was like his living on the island at all—too safe, too predictable, too familiar. And yet he had never been able to shake her. She made herself available, and Josh could never quite turn her down.

Josh knocked on the door. The music switched to Blue Öyster Cult. Didi had a drinking problem, Josh decided, in addition to a self-esteem problem. He knocked again. No response. He was about to escape when the door swung open. Didi grabbed Josh by the shirt collar and dragged him inside.

They started kissing on the couch. Didi's mouth was hot and sloppy, she tasted like cheap wine, and Josh tried to ignore the feeling of yuck that crept over him. Lola, Didi's vicious cat, was lurking around somewhere—Josh could smell her, and the sofa was covered with her orange fur. Josh closed his eyes and tried to lose himself. *Sex,* he thought. *This is only about sex.* He reached up inside Didi's negligee. She had put on weight since high school, and whereas once her stomach had been smooth and taut, it was now fleshy, and her thighs were heavy and dimpled. Josh could not get excited; in fact, the longer they kissed, the more depressed he became. He tried to think of Scowling Sister, but the face that came to his mind was Melanie's. Okay, weird. She had a pretty smile and a perfect ass, but really, was he demented? She had told him she was pregnant! Josh pulled away from Didi.

"I'm not into this," he said.

At this announcement, she bit his neck and sucked. She was trying to mark him as her own. There had been so many hickeys in high school, his teachers had looked at him sideways. He pushed at her.

"Didi, stop."

She persisted, in what she wanted him to believe was a playful way, her forehead boring into his jaw, her mouth like a Hoover on his neck. Josh took hold of her shoulders and pried her off. He got to his feet.

"Stop it, I said."

"What?" Didi lay splayed across the disgusting sofa looking very much like a half-opened Christmas present in her red satin. Her makeup was smeared around her eyes, and one of the slinky shoulder straps had slid off her shoulders and threatened to expose her breast.

There was a bloodcurdling shriek. Josh jumped. Lola stood, back arched, on the top of the recliner.

"Okay, I'm out of here," Josh said.

"Wait!" Didi said. She gathered Lola in her arms.

"Sorry," Josh said. "This isn't working out for me."

Didi slugged back the rest of her wine and trailed Josh to the door. Didi draped Lola over her shoulders like a fur wrap. "We're still friends, right?"

Josh paused. He didn't want to say yes, but if he said no there would be a barrage of sad-sack nonsense and he would never escape. "Sure," he said.

"So you'll lend me the money?" she said.

This was another classic Didi trick: to refer to something completely out of the blue as if it were an already decided-upon fact.

"What money?"

"I need two hundred dollars for my car," she said. "Or they're going to repossess it."

"What?"

"I'm a little behind on my bills," Didi said. "I bought some summer clothes, my rent went up, my credit cards are maxed . . ."

"Ask your parents for the money," Josh said.

"I did. They said no."

"I don't have two hundred dollars," Josh said. "Not to spare, anyway. I have to save. College is *ex-pen-sive*."

"I'll pay you back at the end of the month," Didi said. "I promise. Please? I'm in really big trouble. Would you drop it off at the hospital tomorrow? I'm there eight to four."

"I work tomorrow."

"What about Tuesday, then?" Didi said. "Tuesday's your day off, right?"

Josh let his head fall forward on his neck. How did things like this happen? He should just say no and leave.

"If you lend me the money, I'll leave you alone forever," Didi said. "I swear it."

This was as blatant a lie as was ever spoken, but it was too tempting to ignore.

"You'll stop calling?" he said.

"Yes."

"And you'll pay me back? By the first of July?"

"With interest," Didi said. "Ten dollars interest."

Josh managed to get himself on the opposite side of the door. Lola scratched at the screen.

"Fine," he said. He was absolutely certain he would never see the money again, but if he could get Didi out of his life once and for all, it was a small price to pay. "I'll see you Tuesday."

According to Aunt Liv, there were only three kinds of women in the world: older sisters, younger sisters, and women without sisters. Aunt Liv was a younger sister like Brenda; Aunt Liv's older sister, Joy, had been Brenda's grandmother. Joy was prettier, Liv always thought, and luckier. They both got jobs working at a fabric store during the Second World War, but for whatever reason, Joy was paid a nickel more per day. *The owner was sweet on her,* Liv said, *even though I was the one who made him laugh.* Joy then married a boy from Narberth named Albert Lyndon, and they had four children, the oldest of whom was Brenda's father, Buzz. Liv, meanwhile, inherited her parents' stone house in Gladwyne, she attended Bryn Mawr College, she taught literature there for years. She read, she lavished her nieces and nephews with attention and love and money, she kept meticulous documentation of the family history. Aunt Liv was the only person Brenda had ever confided in about Vicki because she was the only person Brenda knew who would understand.

I spent my whole growing-up thinking Joy was born a princess and I was born a scullery maid, Liv said. *But then I realized that was my own delusion.*

Brenda had cherished those words at the time of their delivery (Brenda was ten, Vicki eleven), but there were no delusions about what was happening in Aunt Liv's cottage this summer. Brenda was not only serving as Vicki's scullery maid, but also as her nanny and her chauffeur. *Because Vicki had cancer!* If Brenda wanted to throw a pity party for herself, she would be the only one attending. More than once already, Brenda had sat on her bed in the old nursery, hoping to absorb some of Aunt Liv's strength, patience, and kindness.

On Tuesday, Brenda drove Vicki to chemotherapy in the neighbors' ancient Peugeot with the kids strapped into the backseat. Taking the kids had not been in the original plan; however, over the weekend, one thing had become clear: If the children were left in Melanie's care, they would die in a kitchen fire or drown drinking from the garden hose. Melanie was going to stay home and "rest," she said—and if she attempted another escape and was successful, so much the better in Brenda's opinion.

Brenda tried not to appear martyrish in her role as servant, because she knew this was exactly what Vicki expected. They had argued about Melanie on Sunday afternoon. Brenda expressed her discontent while Vicki made what Brenda could only think of as the "she's becoming our mother" face. Brenda couldn't stand that facial expression, and yet she sensed she would see a lot of it this summer. In the end, however, Vicki had—surprise!—agreed with Brenda, and apologized. *Melanie probably shouldn't have come. It seemed like a good idea at the time, but maybe we were hasty. I'm sorry. Yes, we'll look for a babysitter, and no, you won't get much of your screenplay written until we do.* Brenda had been impressed by Vicki's admission of her own poor judgment. It was, in thirty years of sisterhood, unprecedented. Vicki was always right; this was a fact of her birth. She had been born right—as well as pretty, talented, intelligent, and athletic; she was a model daughter, a natural-born leader, the gold-medal/blue-ribbon winner in whatever she did, a magnet for girlfriends and boyfriends alike. She was the sister people preferred. Again and again and again while growing up, Brenda had screamed at her parents: *How could you do this to me?* They had never once asked her to define the "this"; it was understood. *How could you make me follow Vicki?* Only sixteen months apart, they were constantly compared, and Brenda constantly found herself coming up short.

People are different. Ellen Lyndon had been telling Brenda this for thirty years. Even sisters were different. But, as Aunt Liv was quick to point out, Ellen Lyndon was a woman without sisters. Ellen Lyndon had grown up with three older brothers, and the fact that she had given birth to sisters in rather rapid succession left her perplexed, as though she had brought home not children, but rather a rare breed of chinchilla. Brenda thought her mother the loveliest of women. She was stylish, cultivated, and impeccably mannered. She was educated about art, poetry, and classical music. On the one hand, it seemed Ellen had been born into the world to be the mother of girls: to orchestrate the tea parties, buckle up the patent leather shoes, read *A Little Princess* aloud, and procure tickets to the *Nutcracker.* But on the other hand—and here was the one thing Brenda and Vicki had always agreed upon—she had no idea what it was like to have a sister. Ellen understood nothing of hand-me-downs; she didn't know what it felt like to walk into a classroom and watch the expression of delight on a new teacher's face when she learned that she was blessed with *another Lyndon girl this year!* Ellen, Brenda was sure, knew nothing of insidious jealousy. She would be appalled to learn that the deepest and darkest secrets in Brenda's life all somehow related to her envy of Vicki.

Vicki teased Brenda all the time about her devotion to *The Innocent Impostor,* but that book, discovered at the tender age of fourteen when Brenda was in danger of being crushed under the toe of Vicki's Tretorn sneaker, had served as Brenda's life raft. It gave her a focus, an identity. Because of that book, Brenda became a reader, a critical thinker, a writer, an American literature major in college, a graduate student, a doctoral candidate, a doctor, a professor, possibly the foremost authority on Fleming Trainor in the world. And now that Brenda would never be able to teach the book again, and would never be able to write about it with any hope of being published someplace even remotely legitimate and scholarly, she was forced to commit a transgression (seen by some academics as even more egregious than the ones she'd already committed) and commercialize the novel. Take it public, as it were. She would write a screenplay for *The Innocent Impostor*. Brenda vacillated between thinking this was a brilliant idea and thinking it was completely inane. She wondered: Do all brilliant ideas seem brilliant from the very beginning, or do they seem far-fetched until they come into clearer focus? Brenda had first considered writing the screenplay for the novel (or "treating it," as they say) back in grad school, when she was dirt poor, subsisting on green tea, saltines, and ramen noodles, but she had dismissed the idea as crass and ridiculous. She was, like every other academic worth her salt, a purist.

Now, however, Brenda tried to convince herself that the novel was perfect for Hollywood. Set in eighteenth-century Philadelphia, the book told the story of a man named Calvin Dare, whose horse kills another man, Thomas Beech, by accident. (The horse kicks Beech in the head while the two men are tying up in front of a tavern during a lightning storm.) Calvin Dare, through a series of carefully disguised coincidences, proceeds to *become* the deceased Beech. He applies for and is given Beech's old job; he falls in love with Beech's bereaved fiancée, Emily. He becomes a Quaker and joins Beech's meetinghouse. The book was unsatisfying to some critics because of its blissful ending: Dare marries Emily, produces healthy and loving children, and is happy in his work. Dare suffers no qualms about how he moved into Beech's life as though it were an abandoned house, fixed it up, and made it his own. Brenda had spent the greater part of six years parsing the book's definition of identity and holding the implied messages of the book up against colonial, and modern, morality. If you didn't like your life, was it okay to become someone else? What if that person was dead? Brenda had often felt like a lone traveler on the icy plateau of this topic. There was nobody else who cared. But that might change if *The Innocent Impostor* were produced. She, Dr. Brenda Lyndon, formerly Professor Brenda Lyndon, would be acknowledged for unearthing a lost classic; and more important, she would be forgiven.

And yet, even with redemption almost within her grasp, doubt plagued her. Why waste her time on an idiotic project that was destined to lead nowhere? The answer was, she had no other options. She wished again and again that her academic career had not been so gruesomely derailed. Even with millions of potential dollars in her future, Brenda dwelled on the "if onlys." If only she hadn't answered her cell phone the night John Walsh first called, if only she'd warned Walsh not to show his midterm paper to anyone, if only she hadn't lost her temper with Mrs. Pencaldron and thrown a book at the painting, if only she'd exercised a modicum of common sense . . . she would still be a professor. Professor Brenda Lyndon. Herself.

Her first semester at Champion had gone beautifully. Brenda was awarded the highest teaching rating of any professor in her department, and these ratings were published in the campus newspaper for all to see. Some said it was because Brenda was new blood, a professor half the age of anyone else in the department, and with such unusual subject matter (Champion was the only university in the country teaching Fleming Trainor). Brenda was attractive to boot—slender, with long hair, blue eyes,

Prada loafers. Some said the English Department offered no competition. The rest of the faculty were dinosaurs, wax dummies. Whatever the reason, Brenda blew away the other professors in her department, not only in the numerical ratings, but with the anecdotals. *Engaging, absorbing . . . we hung on every word . . . we carried the discussion into the quad . . . we were still talking about the reading at dinner. Dr. Lyndon is available and fair. . . . She is everything a Champion professor should be.* The *Pen & Feather* ran a front-page feature on Brenda the following week. She was a celebrity. She was part Britney Spears, part Condoleezza Rice. Each of Brenda's much-older colleagues—including the department chair, Dr. Suzanne Atela—called to congratulate her. They were envious, though not surprised. *That's why we hired you,* Dr. Atela said. *You're young. You have a passion for your subject matter that we outgrew long ago. Congratulations, Dr. Lyndon.*

Brenda had bragged to her family at Christmastime; she had bought a bottle of expensive champagne to celebrate, drank most of it herself, and then blew her own horn. *My students like me,* she said as they all sat around the harvest table in Vicki and Ted's dining room eating the impeccable meal that Vicki had prepared entirely from scratch. *They love me.*

These words took on a mortifying nuance second semester, when Brenda's class consisted of eleven females and one male, a fox in the henhouse, a thirty-one-year-old sophomore from Fremantle, Australia, named John Walsh.

I love you, Walsh said. *Brindah, I love you.*

*   *   *

In the passenger seat, Vicki coughed. Brenda peeked at her. She was pale, her hands were like restless birds in her lap. *I am driving my sister to chemotherapy,* Brenda thought. *Vicki has cancer and might die from it.*

Today, Vicki was having a port installed in her chest that would allow the oncology nurses to thread a tube into her vein and administer the poison. Installing the port was outpatient surgery, though the hospital told her to expect a three-hour visit. Brenda was supposed to take the kids to the playground, buy them an ice cream at Congdon's Pharmacy on Main Street for lunch, and be back at the hospital in time to pick up Vicki and get Porter home for his afternoon nap. Vicki had made it sound all nice and neat, the perfect plan, but Brenda could tell that Vicki was nervous. When other people got nervous, they tightened up, they became high-pitched and strained. Vicki was like this normally. When she got addled, she became floppy and indecisive. She was all over the place.

Brenda pulled into the hospital parking lot. As soon as she shut off the engine, Porter started to cry. Blaine said, "Actually, I want to go home."

"We're dropping Mom off, then we're going to the playground," Brenda said. She got out of the car and unbuckled Porter, but he screamed and thrust himself at Vicki.

"Give him his pacifier," Vicki said flatly. She was eyeing the gray-shingled hospital.

"Where is it?" Brenda said.

Vicki rummaged through her bag. "I can't find it right this second, but I know it's here," she said. "I remember packing it. But . . . maybe we should run home and get another one."

"Run home?" Brenda said. "Here, I'll just take him." But Porter kicked and screamed some more. He nearly wriggled out of her arms. "Whoa!"

"Give him to me," Vicki said. "I may be able to nurse him one last time before I go in."

"But you did bring a bottle?" Brenda said.

"I did," Vicki said. "This is going to be known as extreme weaning."

Brenda moved to the other side of the car and set Blaine free from his five-point harness. A person had to have an advanced degree just to operate the car seats. "Come on, Champ."

"Actually, I want to go home. To my house. In Connecticut."

"Actually, you have no choice in the matter," Vicki said in a stern voice. "Mommy has an appointment. Now hop out."

"Here," Brenda said. "I'll carry you."

"He can walk," Vicki said.

"No," Blaine said, and he kicked the seat in front of him. "I'm not getting out."

"After we drop Mom off, we're going to the playground at Children's Beach," Brenda said.

"I don't want to go to the beach! I want to go to my house in Connecticut. Where my dad lives."

"We should have left him at the cottage," Vicki said. "But I couldn't do that to Melanie."

Brenda kept quiet. She was not going to be predictable.

"I'm taking you to get ice cream for lunch," Brenda told Blaine. "At the pharmacy." This was the ace up her sleeve, and she was dismayed to have to throw it so early, but . . .

"I don't *want* ice cream for lunch," Blaine said. He started to cry. "I want to stay with Mommy."

"Oh, for God's sake," Vicki said. "Can we just get inside, please? Blaine? Will you help Mommy out here and come with me inside?"

Blaine shook his head. Strains of "Für Elise" floated up from Brenda's purse. Her cell phone.

"That's probably Ted," Vicki said.

Brenda checked the display, thinking, *Yes, it's probably Ted,* but hoping it was Walsh. The display said, *Delaney, Brian.* Brenda groaned. "Shit," she said. "My lawyer." She shoved the phone back into her purse and, fueled by her anger at the call, barked at Blaine, "Let's go. Right now."

Reluctantly, Blaine climbed into Brenda's arms. She gasped; he weighed a ton.

"I want to stay with Mommy," he said.

If only the university officials could see me now, Brenda thought as they walked through the sliding doors into the bright chill of the hospital. *They would have mercy on me. Anyone would.*

They slogged toward the admitting desk, where a busty young woman waited for them. She had blond hair held in a very sloppy bun with what looked like crazy straws, streaky blusher on her cheekbones, and breasts that were shoved up and out so far it looked like she was offering them up on a platter. *Didi,* her name tag said.

"Victoria Stowe," Vicki said. "I'm here for a port installation."

"Righty-o," Didi said. She had long painted fingernails with rhinestones embedded in them. Brenda wanted to whisk the girl home and give her a makeover. Pretty girl, bad decisions. Didi slid some forms across the desk to Vicki. "Fill these out, insurance information here, signature here, initials here and here. Sign this waiver, very important." She smiled. She had a lovely smile. "It's so you can't sue us if you die."

Brenda took a long, deep drink of the girl's cleavage. Could she buy the girl some tact?

"I'm not going to die," Vicki said.

"Oh, God, no," Didi said. "I was only kidding."

In the waiting area, they found a row of chairs in front of a TV. *Sesame Street* was on, and Porter became entranced.

"Go," Brenda said. "Get it over with. Go now while we're calm." Blaine emptied a tub of Lincoln Logs onto the polished floor.

"I can't," Vicki said, sitting down. "I have all these forms to fill out." As she said this, the forms slid off her lap and fanned out all over the floor.

Suddenly, a nurse appeared. "Victoria Stowe?"

Vicki bent over, scrambling to pick up the forms. "I'm not ready. Were these in any special order?"

"Bring them along," the nurse said. "You can fill them out upstairs."

"Yes, yes, yes," Didi called out. "Go now, or you'll back everything up."

Vicki remained in her seat. She looked at Brenda. "Listen, there's something I want to ask you."

"What?" Brenda said. Vicki's tone of voice made her nervous. Brenda traveled back twenty-five years: Brenda was five years old, Vicki was six and a half, the two of them were playing on the beach on a cloudy day in matching strawberry-print bikinis and yellow hooded sweatshirts. There was a bolt of lightning, then the loudest crack of thunder Brenda had heard either before or since. Vicki grabbed her hand as the rain started to fall. *Come on. We have to run.*

Until the obvious differences between them emerged, they had been raised as twins. Now, Brenda felt a fear as strong as Vicki's own. *My sister!* Fifteen years ago, when Brenda had spent her study halls as a library aide and Vicki was student council president, who would have guessed that Vicki would be the one to get cancer? It didn't make any sense. *It should be me,* Brenda thought.

"Mom?" Blaine said. He knocked over his log cabin running to her.

"If you can be strong and go with that nurse, I will take care of things here," Brenda said. "The kids will be safe. They'll be fine."

"I can't go," Vicki said. Her eyes filled with tears. "I'm sorry. I just can't."

"Victoria Stowe?" the nurse said.

"They need you in pre-op," Didi said. "Otherwise, I swear, things will get backed up and I will get blamed."

"Go," Brenda said. "We'll be fine."

"I want to stay with Mom," Blaine said.

Vicki sniffled and kissed him. "You stay here. Be good for Auntie Brenda." She stood up and crossed the room stiffly, like a robot.

"Vick?" Brenda said. "What did you want to ask me?"

"Later," Vicki said, and she disappeared down the hall.

*   *   *

An hour passed with Brenda feeling like a broken record. How many times had she suggested they leave—to go to Children's Beach, to get ice cream at the pharmacy?

"With sprinkles," she said. "Please, Blaine? We'll come back and get Mom in a little while."

"No," Blaine said. "I want to stay here until she comes back."

Porter was crying—he'd been crying for twenty minutes, and nothing Brenda did made him stop. She tried the bottle, but he wouldn't take it; he spitefully clamped his mouth shut, and formula ran all over his chin and the front of his shirt. His face was red and scrunched, tears squeezed out of the corners of his eyes; he threw back his head and wailed. Brenda plopped him down on the floor, put an orange plastic gorilla in front of him, and hunted through Vicki's bag for the goddamned pacifier. Porter shrieked and threw the gorilla in anger.

Brenda pulled out a box of Q-tips, two diapers, a package of wipes, a plastic bag of Cheerios crushed into dust, a set of plastic keys, two Chap Sticks, a box of crayons, a sippy cup of what smelled like sour juice, and a paperback called *When Life Becomes Precious*. Vicki could go on *Let's Make a Deal* with what she had in her bag, and yet there was no pacifier. Brenda checked the side pocket—the bottle was in there, and aha! Under the bottle, squashed at the very bottom of the pocket and covered with lint and sand, was the pacifier.

"I found it!" she said. She brandished the pacifier for the girl behind the desk, Didi, as if to say, *Here is the answer to all my problems!* Brenda stuck the pacifier in Porter's mouth and he quieted. Ahhhhh. Brenda sighed.

The room was peaceful once again. But not a minute later, Porter threw the pacifier across the room and started with fresh tears.

"Blaine?" Brenda said. "Can we please go? Your brother . . ."

"There's a soda machine at the end of the hall," Didi said.

Brenda stared at her. Soda machine? She had two tiny children here. Did the girl think her problems could be solved with a can of Coke?

"We're not allowed to have soda," Blaine said.

Didi stared. "Maybe you could use a walk."

The girl wanted to get rid of them. And could Brenda blame her, really?

"We *could* use a walk," Brenda said. "Let's go."

She carried Porter, who was whimpering, down the polished corridor. *Cottage Hospital,* she thought. The kind of place where they fixed up Jack and Jill after they fell down the hill. Nothing bad happened here. Vicki was somewhere in the cottage hospital having her port installed. For chemotherapy. For cancer.

It should be me, Brenda thought. *I don't have kids. I don't have anybody.*

Before she got the teaching job, Brenda had never seen Champion University, except in photos on the Internet. She had taken a virtual tour like a prospective student and checked out the neoclassical buildings, the geometric lawns, the plaza where students sunbathed and played Frisbee. It looked, while not bucolic, at least sufficiently oasis-like, a real college campus in the melee of Manhattan. But at the start of second semester, in

January, the blocks of Champion University were gray and businesslike. This only served to make the English Department, with its Persian rugs and grandfather clocks, its first-edition Henry James in a glass museum case, seem more inviting. Mrs. Pencaldron, the department's supremely capable and officious administrative assistant, had rushed to make Brenda a cappuccino, something she did for professors currently in her favor. *Welcome back, Dr. Lyndon. How was your break? Here is your class list and the syllabus. I had them copied for you.*

Brenda reviewed the syllabus. They would start by reading Fleming Trainor, and then they would compare and contrast *The Innocent Impostor* with the works of contemporary authors: Lorrie Moore, Richard Russo, Anne Lamott, Rick Moody, Adam Haslett, Antonya Nelson, Andre Dubus. The reading list was so delicious, Brenda wanted to eat it with a knife and fork. *There's a wait list for your class,* Mrs. Pencaldron said. *Thirty-three people long. In the fall, Dr. Atela wants to add another section. Does she?* Brenda had said. The department chair, Suzanne Atela, was only five feet tall, but she was exotic and formidable. She was a native of the Bahamas and had cocoa-butter skin without a single line of age, although Brenda knew her to be sixty-two years old, the mother of four, the grandmother of fourteen. She had published copiously on the literature of the Beat generation, and there were rumors she had slept with one of the minor players, a cousin of Ginsburg's, which seemed fantastical to Brenda, but who knew what the woman was like when she took off her harlequin glasses and unpinned her hair? Her husband was a handsome Indian man; Brenda had never met him, though she'd seen a photograph of him wearing a tuxedo, on Suzanne Atela's desk. Suzanne Atela was formidable only because she held Brenda's future, and that of every other untenured professor in the department, in her tiny, delicate hands.

Brenda surveyed her class list. Upon initial inspection, it looked as though she had struck gold. It looked like she had gotten a class of *only women*. This was too good to be true! Brenda started amending the reading list in her mind—with a class of only women, they could attack Fleming Trainor and the problem of identity with a gender slant. Just as Brenda started scribbling down the titles of some really incendiary feminist texts, her eyes hit on the last name on the list: *Walsh, John. Sophomore.*

Mrs. Pencaldron had tapped on Brenda's office door. "There's been a change, Dr. Lyndon," she said. "You'll be teaching your seminar in the Barrington Room."

Brenda grinned stupidly even as she crumpled her list of incendiary feminist texts and threw it away. First the cappuccino, then a mention of teaching two sections next year, and now the Barrington Room, which was the crown jewel of the department. It was used for special occasions—department meetings, faculty luncheons—and Suzanne Atela taught her graduate students in that room. It had a long, polished Queen Anne table and an original Jackson Pollock hanging on the wall.

"The Barrington Room?" Brenda had said.

"Yes," Mrs. Pencaldron said. "Follow me."

They made their way down the hushed hallway to the end, where the door, dark and paneled, loomed with importance.

"Now," Mrs. Pencaldron said, "I'm required to go over the rules. No drinks on the table—no cans, no bottles, no coffee cups. The room must be opened and locked by you and you must never leave the students in the room alone with the painting. *Capiche?*"

"*Capiche,*" Brenda said.

Mrs. Pencaldron gave Brenda a long, unwavering look. "I mean it. That painting was bequeathed to the department by Whitmore Barrington and it is worth *a lot* of money. So, for that matter, is the table."

"Gotcha," Brenda said. "No drinks."

"None whatsoever," Mrs. Pencaldron said. "Now, let me give you the security code."

After Brenda had practiced locking and unlocking the door and setting and disarming the alarm with a long, complicated security code, Mrs. Pencaldron left Brenda to her own devices.

"I hope you realize, Dr. Lyndon, what a privilege it is to teach in that room," she said as she walked away.

Brenda pitched her cappuccino cup into the trash, then organized her papers at the head of the Queen Anne table and took a second to consider the painting. Ellen Lyndon was a great appreciator of art, and she had passed this appreciation on to her daughters with museum trips that started as soon as Vicki and Brenda were out of diapers. But really, Brenda thought. Really, *really*—wasn't the Pollock just a mess of splattered paint? Who was the person who designated Pollock as a great artist? Did some people see beyond the splatter to a universal truth, or was it all just nonsense, as Brenda suspected? Literature, at least, had real meaning; it made sense. A painting should make sense, too, Brenda thought, and if it didn't make sense, then it should be pretty. The Pollock failed on both fronts, but there it hung, and Brenda, despite herself, felt impressed.

It was at that moment, of Brenda feeling impressed but not knowing why, that a man walked into the room. A very handsome man with olive skin and dark eyes, close-cropped black hair. He was Brenda's age and as tall and strapping as a ranch hand, though he was dressed like John Keats, in a soft Burgundy sweater with a gray wool scarf wrapped around his neck. There was a pencil tucked behind his ear. Brenda thought he must be a graduate student, one of Suzanne Atela's doctoral candidates, perhaps, who had wandered in accidentally.

"Hi?" she said.

He nodded. "How you going?" He had some sort of broad antipodean accent.

"This is the seminar on Fleming Trainor," she said. "Are you . . . ?"

"John Walsh," he said.

John Walsh. This was John Walsh. Brenda felt her good sense unraveling in her brain like a ball of yarn. She had not prepared herself for this—a man in her class, not a boy. He was beautiful, more beautiful than the girl-women who came streaming into the Barrington Room after him like rats following the Pied Piper.

Brenda wiggled her feet in her Prada loafers and stared down at her scrumptious syllabus. Day one, minute one: She was attracted to her sole male student.

Once everyone was settled, she cleared her throat and checked for cups and cans, bottles of water. Nothing. Mrs. Pencaldron must have screened everyone at the door. "I'm Dr. Brenda Lyndon," she said. "Please call me whatever makes you most comfortable, Dr. Lyndon or Brenda. We are here to study Fleming Trainor's novel, *The Innocent Impostor,* and to compare and contrast Trainor's concept of identity with those of contemporary authors. Was everyone able to get the books?"

Nods.

"Good," Brenda said. She stared at her hands: They were scaly with dry skin, and trembling. She needed a spa treatment. She made a mental note to call Vicki as soon as she got home. "Your assignment for Thursday is the first ten chapters of the book, and I'd like you to have the second half done by next Tuesday." She waited for the inevitable protests, but she only met with more nods. There was a woman in a wheelchair, a black woman with a short Afro, an Indian woman with fingernails the color of red currants. The other girl-women were varying shades of winter pale with light hair, dark hair, purple hair. And then there was John Walsh, whom Brenda did not look at. "Here is your syllabus." She closed her eyes for a moment, savoring the whisper of the papers being passed around. "You'll be graded on two papers, one at midterm and one at the end of the semester. You'll also be graded on your contributions to the discussion, so please notify me if you're going to miss class. My office hours will be Thursday from nine to eleven."

Brenda gave the class her cell phone number. She glanced at John Walsh and was both elated and mortified to find he was programming her number right into his phone.

She asked the students to go around the room and say their names, where they were from, and one thing about themselves. She started at the opposite side of the room from John Walsh on purpose—she started with the girl named Amrita from Bangalore, India, who told everyone she took the class because she'd seen that Dr. Lyndon had been given the top teaching marks last semester in the *Pen & Feather*.

"I've been here three years," Amrita said. "I've encountered many brilliant minds, but I've yet to find one decent teacher."

Amrita was blatantly brownnosing, but Brenda was too preoccupied by John Walsh's unsettling presence to take the bait.

"Thank you," Brenda said. "Next?"

The girls continued, and Brenda, half listening, made notes by each name. Jeannie in the wheelchair was a Democrat from Arkansas; Mallory and Kelly were fraternal twins: Mallory wore cat's-eye glasses, and Kelly, with the purple hair, played a minor role on the soap opera *Love Another Day*. There were three girls named Rebecca; a girl from Guadeloupe named Sandrine, who played guitar in a band called French Toast; the black woman, Michele Nathans, had just returned from a semester in Marrakech; short, squat Amy Feldman was a Japanese major and a sushi aficionado who also admitted, after prompting from one of the Rebeccas, that her father was the president of Marquee Films; and the last girl, named Ivy, announced that she was from the Upper Peninsula of Michigan, and a lesbian.

Was everyone extra quiet after this announcement, or was it just Brenda's imagination? Maybe they were, like Brenda, waiting to hear what John Walsh would say.

Slowly, Brenda turned to look at John Walsh, praying she would keep her composure. At the top of her class list, she wrote: *Call Vicki!*

John Walsh had removed the pencil from behind his ear, and was turning it slowly in his hands. He raised his eyes to the girl-women and Brenda.

"I'm John Walsh," he said. "Most people just call me Walsh. I'm from Western Australia, a town called Fremantle." He tapped his desk with his pencil. "So . . . you probably notice I'm a bit older than your average college sophomore."

"Yes!" In alarm, Brenda looked at the Jackson Pollock painting, as though it were the painting that had spoken and not her. She waited for the girl-women to giggle, or whisper, but there was silence. Maybe they could teach her how to keep her act together.

"I did my freshman year at the University of W.A."— this he pronounced *dubya-aye*—"and then I got caught up with a bit of the wanderlust. I dropped out of school. I traveled around the world."

Brenda knew she should keep her mouth shut, but that was proving impossible. "Around the world?" she said.

"To Thailand and Nepal and India, up through Afghanistan and China into Russia. I've been to the Middle East, Jordan, Dubai, Lebanon. And then there was one year in Britain, where I worked at a pub. I spent some time on the continent in Germany, Belgium, Italy, France, Spain, Malta, the Canary Islands, Iceland . . . until I got to New York, when I ran out of money." He stopped. "I'm talking too much, right?"

Right, thought Brenda. All of the incendiary feminist texts she had ever read would say: Just because you're the only man in the room does not mean that your life has been more interesting, more authentic, or more worthy than the rest of our (female) lives. But Brenda didn't want him to stop. For starters, she loved the sound of his voice. It was so . . . masculine. Part Crocodile Dundee, part Crocodile Hunter. Did the other women want him to stop? Brenda quickly surveyed the room. The women had the same expression of placid interest they'd had since they arrived. Well, except for Amrita, the brown-noser. She was agog over Walsh, leaning toward him, nodding. Brenda took this as a sign.

"Go on," Brenda said.

"From there it gets complicated. I needed a job; I met a bloke at Eddie's down in the Village whose uncle had a construction company and I started working for him, but that got old right on so I thought, the only way I'm going to get anywhere is to go back to school. So here I am, a thirty-one-year-old sophomore."

"Well," said Brenda. Thinking: *He's older than I am! But he's a sophomore in college. He's my* student*!* "Thank you all for sharing. Does anyone have questions about the course or the syllabus? The assignments?" She paused. Nothing but polite stares. "Okay, then, I think we can call it a day. Please read to chapter ten by Thursday."

She watched as the girl-women collected themselves and left the room—some alone, some chatting. Jeannie buzzed out in the wheelchair. A cell phone rang—one of the Rebeccas. She said, "Hello? Yeah, I'm out." As though she'd been in prison. Was it that bad? Had Brenda seemed anything like the person who'd taught last semester? Brenda was so preoccupied with her thoughts that she didn't realize John Walsh was still sitting. When she saw him, she jumped.

"Geez," she said, and she laughed. "You shouldn't sneak up on people like that."

"I was wondering," he said. He was turning his pencil again. "Would you like to grab some lunch?"

"What?" Brenda said. She checked the room. Who else had heard? Just her and the Jackson Pollock. Was John Walsh asking her on a date? Her, the professor? The first day of class? "I'm sorry, *what*?"

He didn't look embarrassed, not even a little bit. "I don't have another class until two," he said. "And I don't know anybody here. This is my first semester. I was kind of hoping there might be some people here my age. I went to the orientation for 'nontraditional' students, but . . . you know, there were a couple of fourteen-year-old whiz kids and a housewife in her forties and a guy even older than that who was some kind of tribal chief in Zaire. I'm looking to make some friends."

"But I'm your professor," Brenda said.

"So you can't go get a slice of pizza?"

"Sorry," Brenda said.

He sighed in an exaggerated way, and then he smiled. He was so attractive that Brenda didn't even feel comfortable sitting in a room alone with him. She had to get out!

"There are all these silly rules," she said. She had stumbled across the lines in her *Handbook of Employee Rules and Regulations* when she'd paged through it on the crosstown bus after her orientation. *Romantic or sexual relationships are forbidden between a faculty member and a student. Romantic or sexual comments, gestures, or innuendo are forbidden between a faculty member and a student and will result in disciplinary action. There are no exceptions made for tenured professors.*

"I'm over eighteen," he said. "It's just pizza."

"It doesn't matter," Brenda said. "I'm sorry."

Walsh slid his pencil behind his ear. "So I guess I'm eating alone again today. Ah, no worries. See you Thursday?"

"Yes."

Brenda let him out ahead of her because she had to lock the door and reset the security code to ensure the safety of the painting. But Walsh lingered in the hallway, and they walked toward Mrs. Pencaldron's desk together. Mrs. Pencaldron had her eyes trained on them all the way down the hall; Brenda felt herself emitting guilt. But why? He had asked her to lunch, she said no.

John Walsh pushed through the door that separated the English Department from the rest of the drab university.

"Ta!" he said—to Brenda or Mrs. Pencaldron, Brenda wasn't sure, nor was she sure what *ta* meant. She waved instinctively, relieved to see him go.

She handed the key to Mrs. Pencaldron. "He's Australian," she said.

"So I gathered."

"We had a good class," Brenda said. "Short. First day, you know. They hadn't read anything. I went over my expectations for the class and the kids introduced themselves. That's how I knew he was Australian." *Stop talking!* Brenda told herself.

Mrs. Pencaldron tilted her head. "You reset the security code?"

"Uh . . . yes."

"He didn't see you do it, did he?"

"Who?"

Mrs. Pencaldron smiled impatiently. "The Australian."

"Uh . . . no," Brenda said.

"You're sure?"

"I'm sure. He waited down the hall a bit. I shielded the keypad with my body."

"Okay," Mrs. Pencaldron said, though her voice sounded specifically not-okay. She sounded like she suspected an international art theft ring. "Giving the security code to a student is against the rules. Do you understand?"

"I understand," Brenda said. "And nobody brought cans or cups into the room, either. Or bottles. None whatsoever."

"Oh, I know," Mrs. Pencaldron said. "I saw to that myself."

So many silly rules, Brenda thought as they approached the hospital's soda machine.

She had sandwiched the note that said *Call John Walsh!* into her copy of *The Innocent Impostor* and then locked the book in its briefcase. Brenda wasn't sure why she was keeping the note. She couldn't think about John Walsh and Fleming Trainor at the same time; that much had already been proven.

"Are we getting a Coke?" Blaine asked. "Really, are we?"

"Really we are." If this was what it took, this was what it took, Brenda thought. It wasn't like she was offering the kids cigarettes, or shots of Jägermeister. She filched five quarters out of Vicki's bag and let Blaine carefully slip them into the slot, but she couldn't find any more change, and the smallest bill in Vicki's wallet was a twenty. Porter babbled. "Ba ba ba, da da da." The nonsense a person said before the real nonsense began.

"Wouldn't you know," Brenda said. "We need more money."

Blaine, panic-stricken, looked at Brenda as they walked back to the admitting desk. "What about the Coke?" he said.

"We need more money," Brenda said, and Blaine started to cry. Hearing Blaine cry made Porter start up again in louder tones. "Boys," Brenda said. "Please. Just wait a second." Was it any surprise that Nantucket had the world's most expensive soda machine? She would have to break a twenty for one lousy quarter, but that made perfect sense. That was how her day was going.

And of course Didi, at the admitting desk, was now deep in conversation with someone else, a guy her age. Brenda tried to wave the twenty over the guy's shoulder. Didi would hear the kids crying, she would sense urgency. But no—Didi was oblivious, she was completely focused on this other person, who was wearing a hunter green polo shirt and khaki shorts and grass-stained Adidas sneakers. He had a fresh haircut; there were short hair trimmings all over the back of his shirt. He was holding on to one end of a white envelope, and Didi held on to the other end, looking like she might cry.

"This is it," Haircut Guy said. "And I want it back!"

"I know," Didi said.

"By the first of July. Not the second. Not the fourth. The first."

"Righty-o."

"With interest."

"What about Friday?" Didi said.

"What *about* Friday?"

"Zach's party."

"Are you going?" Haircut Guy said.

"Yeah."

"Then I'm staying home."

"Excuse me," Brenda said, waving the twenty in the air. It was rude to interrupt, but Brenda couldn't stand around with two screaming kids while Didi and her friend discussed some kegger. "I need change. For the soda machine."

Didi wiped a finger under one eye. Her chest heaved. "I don't have any change," she snapped. "If you want change you'll have to go upstairs to the cafeteria."

Oh, no, Brenda thought. *No way.* "I only need one quarter," she said. "Please? Do you have a quarter you might just lend me?"

Didi snatched the envelope from her friend's grasp. "No," she said. "I don't."

Haircut Guy turned around. In his outstretched hand was a quarter. "Here," he said. Then he looked at Brenda. "Hey," he said. "It's you."

Brenda stared at his face for a second. She knew this person, but how? Who was it? One thing was for certain: She had never been so happy to see twenty-five cents in all her life.

Josh walked with Brenda and the kids to the Coke machine even though he heard Didi making noises back at the admitting desk. Blaine held the quarter and Josh lifted him up so that he could feed the machine, then push the button—and they were all silent as the Coke tumbled down the shoot. Even the baby was quiet. Josh took the Coke from the machine. "Shall I do the honors?"

"You're the guy from the airport," Brenda said. "The one who brought me my book. I'm sorry I didn't recognize you. You got a haircut."

She looked so astonished that Josh felt embarrassed. He cracked open the can. "Yep," he said. "I'm Josh."

"I'm Brenda Lyndon."

"I know," he said. "I remember. Dr. Lyndon."

"I'm not a *doctor* doctor," Brenda said. "I'm a doctor of American literature. The most useless kind of doctor there is. We're here because my sister, Vicki, is having a port installed for chemo."

"Chemo?" Josh said.

"She has lung cancer," Brenda whispered.

"You're kidding," Josh said. But what did he remember about the other sister? Her heavy breathing. "Oh, man."

Brenda shook her head, then made a motion over the kids' heads. Blaine said, "Coke! Coke!"

Josh knelt down and helped Blaine with the Coke. Lung cancer? Pregnant? *I'm not a* doctor *doctor.* The most miserable-looking people he had ever seen. That's what Josh had thought, right from the beginning. And no wonder.

"Are you here all summer?" he said. "Because I saw your friend Melanie at the airport a couple of days ago . . ."

"My sister and I are here all summer with the kids," Brenda said. "The jury's still out on Melanie."

"She seemed really nice," Josh said.

"Nice, yes, that she is. Very nice," Brenda said. "Hey,

you don't know anybody who needs a babysitting job this summer, do you?"

"What kind of babysitting job?"

"Watch the kids twenty-five hours a week. Go to the beach, the playground, throw the ball, build sand castles, take them for ice cream. Twenty dollars an hour, cash. We need somebody responsible. And I mean rock-solid. You would not *believe* the weekend we had . . ."

One thing about lending Didi the two hundred dollars was that it meant Josh couldn't quit his job at the airport. He had given her more than half his savings, and no matter what she promised him, he knew he would never see it again. But twenty dollars an hour cash was a lot more than he was making now. He had taken the job at the airport because of his father, though it was truly dull. The most memorable thing that had happened all summer was when Melanie fell off the steps of the plane.

"I'll do it," Josh said.

Brenda looked at him askance. "You already have a job," she said. "And you're a . . . guy."

"I'm quitting the airport," Josh said. "And I like kids."

Brenda stuck the nipple of the pacifier in the can of Coke, then popped it into the baby's mouth.

"Porter's only nine months old," she said. "He's very attached to his mother."

"I like babies," Josh said. This was only true in the hypothetical; Josh didn't know any babies. Out of the corner of his eye, he saw Didi rise from her desk and start over toward them.

"Can you change a diaper?" Brenda said.

"Of course."

As Didi closed in, Blaine chugged the Coke like a man who had been stranded in the desert. Josh gently pulled it away.

"Whoa there, pal. Easy, or you're going to get sick."

"You're available mornings?" Brenda said. "Weekdays, say, eight to one? Porter naps at one."

"I'm available."

"You have a car, right? The Jeep? Do you think the baby seats will fit in the Jeep?"

"Baby seats?" Didi said. She was upon them, sniffing around in an accusatory way, as though what they were talking about were her business if only because it was taking place in Admitting, which she considered her domain. She brandished a handful of quarters, as if to spite Brenda, and got herself a diet Dr Pepper.

"They should," Josh said. He had no idea if the baby seats would fit in his Jeep; he didn't know what baby seats *were* exactly, but the longer he stood here with this woman, the more desperate he was for a connection with her. "I can do it," he said. "I really want to do it."

"Do what?" Didi said.

"Do you have a criminal record?" Brenda asked. She wondered how pissed Vicki would be if she hired this guy herself, without consulting Vicki. A guy. Was that weird? With Ted gone, it might be good for the kids. It *would* be good for the kids, Brenda decided. It would be good for all of them to have a man around on a regular basis; it would even be good for Melanie.

"Criminal record?" Didi said, scoffing. "This guy is as straitlaced as they come."

"Okay," Brenda said. "You're hired."

◯⟋

Sand on the kitchen floor, a collar around the toilet bowl, dandelions, running out of hot water in the shower, a bug bite scratched until it bleeds, losing the plot strands of Desperate Housewives, *the* New York Times *Best Seller List, damp beach towels, mildew, Ted calling from the road to say he was stuck in a five-mile backup outside of New Haven, Ted calling to say the Yukon broke down and he was at a service station in Madison, Connecticut, Ted calling to say he was going to miss the ferry and not to expect him until tomorrow.*

"I'm sorry, sweetie," Ted said. "This is beyond my control."

Beyond your control? Vicki thought. *I thought I was talking to my husband, Ted Stowe, the man who rants and raves and throws money at problems until they're solved.* Vicki hated the defeated tone of Ted's voice. Her cancer was making him helpless. He couldn't even deal with traffic, or with an overheated engine. He was going to lie down and die.

"I need you here tonight," Vicki said. "The kids are expecting you. Blaine has talked about nothing else all week. You can't just *not show*. Take a taxi to the nearest airport and fly in."

"And do what with the car, Vick? It's full of stuff."

Ah, yes, the stuff: a case of Chardonnay from their favorite vineyard in the Russian River Valley that Vicki was craving, the items she'd bought in bulk at·BJ's— paper towels, cleaning supplies, juice boxes, diapers. Then there was Blaine's bicycle, a carton of the kids' favorite children's books, the paints and the Play-Doh, Vicki's vitamins (she'd forgotten them on purpose because they made her vomit). Her extra suitcases, one of which contained a blond wig.

Gingerly, Vicki touched her port. A surgeon had installed it, and Vicki's new oncologist, Dr. Alcott, decided to administer the first dose of chemo right away. *Why not?* Dr. Alcott said (cavalierly, Vicki thought, as though he were deciding to have a piece of Key lime pie for dessert). She had to admit that physically she felt no better or worse than she had all along. She kept waiting for a change—was the chemo working? Was it gobbling up the cancer cells like a Pac-Man with those stupid dots?—but the only thing the doctors could guarantee was that her breast milk would be poisoned. Her breasts grew warm and buzzed with pain every three hours like an alarm, but Vicki couldn't feed the baby. Porter had screamed through the first night. He refused to take a bottle, though Brenda had gotten him to drink a little bit of water from the bathroom cup. Still, Vicki told herself, things could have been a whole lot worse. She wasn't nauseous and her hair wasn't falling out in clumps the way she had feared. Brenda had hired the ramp attendant from the airport to babysit starting next week, and the sun was shining. As soon as Ted arrived, they could go to the beach as a family, proceed with the summer as though everything were all right. What Vicki realized during the phone call, however, was that she had pinned all her hopes on today, Friday, the day of Ted's arrival; he might as well have been riding in on a white horse. Now he wasn't coming. He couldn't leave the car full of stuff. Vicki waited for devastation to set in, but instead, all she experienced was a scary nothing. She didn't care. Ted's arriving one day late was just one more item on her List of Things That No Longer Matter.

She hung up the phone. Blaine and Brenda were sitting out on the front step, tossing pebbles into a paper cup. Porter sat on the tiny lawn in just his diaper, eating dandelions. Melanie was taking her third outdoor shower of the day. For some reason, the outdoor shower made Melanie feel better. She claimed it took her mind off Peter.

I'm sorry about all the hot water, she said.

Shower away, Vicki said.

Now, Vicki watched her children. They were happy, blissful, unaware. She wanted to be happy. What was going to make her happy? Anything? What would make her happier than she was now? She heard the voices of the people in her cancer support group chanting in her mind like a Greek chorus. *You have to make yourself fight. You cannot, under any circumstances, give up.*

Vicki tapped Brenda on the shoulder just as she sank the first pebble of the game.

"Yes!" Brenda said with a raised fist. "Two points for Auntie Brenda."

"Bren?" Vicki said.

Brenda looked up. "What?"

Vicki motioned for Brenda to step inside, though first she checked that the gate was latched—it would be just like her kids to take off on their own down Shell Street.

"Don't move a muscle," Vicki said to Blaine.

"And don't cheat," Brenda said. "I'll know if you cheated."

Blaine threw a pebble in anger and knocked the cup over.

"What is it?" Brenda said.

"Ted's not coming until tomorrow."

"Oh, shit."

"He got stuck in traffic, and I guess the Yukon overheated or something. He'll come in the morning."

"You're okay with that?"

"I want you to call the sitter."

"The sitter?"

"The boy. The guy. Josh. See if you can get him over here."

"Right now?"

"In an hour. I want to go out."

"You want to go *out*?" Brenda said. "Are you sure you feel . . ."

"I want to go out," Vicki said. "You, me, and Mel. I want to go into town and have a glass of wine. I want dinner. I want to go to the Club Car."

"You want to go to the *Club Car*?"

"Call the sitter. Call the taxi. Call the restaurant." Vicki took a breath. She was spewing out orders, but her desires were singular. *Go out with the girls. Feel like a person again.*

Josh pulled up in front of the house at seven o'clock. The gate was latched, the door was shut, there was a paper cup full of rocks sitting in the middle of the flagstone walk. Josh got out of the Jeep. He had showered and put on aftershave, but then, because he felt like he was going to too much trouble for a simple babysitting job, he put on jeans and a Red Sox jersey.

He'd had to call his father at work. "I'll leave dinner in the fridge," he'd said.

"You're going to Zach's party?" his father said.

"No," Josh said. "I'm babysitting."

Predictably, there was silence. Just as there had been silence on Tuesday night when, over fried chicken and deli potato salad, Josh announced that he had quit his job at the airport.

That night, after a longer-than-usual swill of Sam Adams, Tom Flynn had asked, "What will you do for money?"

"Babysit," Josh had said. He watched his father for a show of surprise or disbelief, but this was a man who had found his wife of fifteen years dangling from the attic rafters. His face registered nothing. "For these two boys out in 'Sconset," Josh continued. "It pays more than the airport. I'll get to spend time outside. There are these three women . . ." He shook his head; it was too complicated to explain. "The mother has cancer."

Tom Flynn cut through a wedge of iceberg. "You'll finish out the week?" he said.

Josh had finished out the week and that made today, Friday, his last day. Carlo treated him to a beer at the airport restaurant, then another, and then another, at which point Josh entertained thoughts of going to Zach's party despite Didi's inevitable and annoying presence. Then his cell phone rang with a New York number. It was Brenda. She sounded as desperate as she had when she called about her missing book. Could he be at their house to babysit in an hour?

Josh, not wanting to get off on the wrong foot with his

new employer, felt compelled to tell the truth. "It's my last day of work. I just drank three beers."

This was met with silence. Then Brenda said, "Have a cup of coffee. And come at seven. We'll get the kids all ready for bed. This will be the easiest money you've ever made."

When Josh knocked on the door, it swung open, taking him by surprise. He had never set foot inside one of these little 'Sconset cottages, and he thought it might smell like a library book or a museum—ancient, dusty, preserved. But instead the air was redolent of clean hair and perfumed shoulders, toenail polish and swinging skirts. This was the house of the three . . . the three what? The Three Bears? The three beers? *Three women step off of a plane.* Wasn't there some ancient tale about three sirens who led sailors astray? Josh knew what Chas Gorda would say: *Listen. Observe. Absorb.* Because Josh had finally found his story. The story of his summer.

Vicki, the mother, was the happiest-looking of the Three. She was wearing a sleeveless black sundress and a scarf in her hair. He tried to think *cancer, chemotherapy,* but the words didn't stick. She padded around in bare feet, a pair of black high heels in one hand and a glass of wine in the other.

"Normally I leave a list for the babysitter," she said. "But not this summer. There will be no lists this summer. Brenda assures me you're competent, you have lots of experience with kids, you can change a diaper."

Josh had had two cups of coffee, a Coke, and a bracing shower, but still his mind was hangover-fuzzy, either from the beers or from the oddness of this situation. He felt something grab the back of his ankle—it was the baby, who had crawled up behind him. Josh felt like a total charlatan as he bent down to pick up the baby. If any one of the hundred people at Zach's party could see him now . . .

"Yes," he said.

"Great. Stories are on the nightstand. Eight-o'clock bed. Porter's bottle is warming up on the counter. Give it to him before you lay him down." She paused. "Did that sound like a list?"

"No," he said. *Yes?*

"Good," she said. "My sister's cell phone number is on the table. We'll be at the Club Car."

"Okay," Josh said. The baby was chewing on his shirt, and a tiny moist hand grabbed his ear.

"Make sure Blaine pees twice before bed and brushes his teeth. Don't let him *eat* the toothpaste, which is what he likes to do. And put Porter in a clean diaper. It's too hot for pajamas tonight. The mattress on the floor is theirs, but normally I let them fall asleep in the big bed and then move them later. Feel free to do the same." She smiled at Josh. She was pretty, he thought. A really pretty mom. "I can't believe it," she said. "I just made a list. A verbal list with no less than ten items. I'm sorry. I'm getting out of here." She walked out the front door, then turned around. "You look darling holding the baby like that, by the way."

"Oh," Josh said. *Thanks?*

"Darling," a voice said in his ear. He turned to see Brenda, who had changed into a green strapless dress.

Green again. She was a mermaid. She went swishing out the door after her sister. The taxi pulled up.

"Hi, Josh." Melanie stood before him in white pants and a blue flowered halter top that left an inch of her midsection bare. Her hair was curly around her face, and she peered at him both shyly and hopefully.

"Still no word from my husband," she said.

"Huh?" he said. He wondered if they'd had a conversation that he'd forgotten about.

"He's such a jerk," she said. Her eyes shone. What was going *on* here? "Blaine's in the bedroom watching *Scooby-Doo,* by the way."

"Oh-kay," Josh said. Melanie walked out the door, and Josh watched her climb into the taxi. He tried to make the baby wave good-bye, but the baby started to whimper and Josh thought it best to close the door.

Time to get to work, he thought.

Josh poked his head into the bedroom. Blaine was splayed across the bed watching *Scooby-Doo* on a portable DVD player with a four-inch screen.

"Hey," Josh said.

Blaine glanced up, startled. "What are you doing here?"

"Babysitting."

"No!" Blaine said, and he started to cry. The baby, who had been content to slobber all over Josh's Varitek jersey, began to fuss.

"Hey, man, calm down. Your mom just went to dinner. She'll be back."

"What about my dad?" Blaine said. He kicked the DVD player off the bed. The machine landed upside down and a piece broke off and skidded across the floor, but Josh could still hear Velma's tinny voice talking about tracking down a phantom. Josh considered tending to the injured machine, then thought better of it. He remembered Blaine hurtling himself off the plane's steps and knocking over Melanie. The kid was a loose cannon.

"Do you want to finish watching? Or we could . . . play a game? I saw a cup of rocks outside. Want to throw rocks?"

"What about my dad?" Blaine screamed.

Porter was officially wailing now. A baby crying was, Josh decided, the world's worst noise.

"I don't know anything about your dad," Josh said.

"He's supposed to come tonight!" Blaine said. Blaine's face turned red right to the edge of his scalp, then the color crept through the part of his white-blond hair.

"Okay, well," Josh said. He'd wondered why the Three had left so quickly, why they tiptoed down the walk like cat burglars. Vicki had left something off the list, something crucial. Blaine was expecting his father to show up. "Do you want to eat some toothpaste?"

"No!" Blaine screamed. He ran to the front door, which was closed. He ran to the back door and bulldozed through the screen.

"Whoa!" Josh said. Ouch. Blaine bounced back onto his rear end, but not before leaving a Blaine-shaped-and-sized bulge in the screen. Blaine howled and put his hand to his face, then showed Josh blood. The Three had been gone less than ten minutes and already there was damaged property and blood. The kids cried in stereo. Josh shut the back door. If the neighbors heard, they would call the police. He set the crying baby down on the floor and went to the bathroom for a wet washcloth. Easiest money ever made? Hardly.

~~~~~~

This was more like it, Vicki thought. The cab was approaching town, bouncing over the cobblestone streets, which were crowded with loaded-down SUVs, many of which, Vicki guessed, had just come off the ferry that Ted was supposed to be on. The sidewalks were teeming with activity—couples headed for dinner or the art galleries on Old South Wharf, college kids aiming for drinks at the Gazebo, crew members coming off yachts, looking to stock up on provisions at the Grand Union—it was Nantucket on a summer night and Vicki loved it. She had been stranded on Planet Cancer for too long.

Muffled strains of Beethoven wafted up from Brenda's purse.

"That's probably Ted," Vicki said. "Calling to apologize."

Brenda pulled the phone out and checked the display. "Nope." She shut the phone and tucked it back into her purse. Vicki and Melanie waited a beat.

"Was it John Walsh?" Melanie asked.

"It was not."

"Was it your lawyer again?" Vicki asked.

"Please shut up," Brenda said, casting a sideways look at Melanie.

"I promised John Walsh you'd call him back," Melanie said. "You did call him back, I hope. He called, geez, last Sunday."

"I did not call him back," Brenda said. "And you had no right to promise him any such thing."

"Come on, now," Vicki said. "We're trying to have fun." The cab unloaded them at the restaurant. Melanie paid the driver. "Thank you, Mel," Vicki said.

"Yes, thank you," Brenda said, somewhat snidely.

"I'll buy dinner," Vicki said, as if there had been any doubt.

"This *was* your idea," Brenda said.

It *was* her idea, Vicki thought, and once they were seated in the dining room among the white linen and wineglasses and plates of pecan-crusted swordfish and phyllo-wrapped salmon revealed from under silver domes, it seemed like a grand one. She had ordered a bottle of riotously expensive Château Margaux, because if Vicki was going to drink wine she wanted it to be *good* wine. Even Melanie accepted a glass; Vicki encouraged her along like a bad teenager who had taken lessons in peer pressure. *One glass won't hurt.* But the wine went to Melanie's head, perhaps because she was out of practice, and she just started talking.

"I called Frances Digitt's apartment. Peter was there."

"Oh, Mel," Vicki said. "You didn't."

"I had to."

"You had to?" Brenda said.

"I asked him if he wanted me to come home."

"And what did he say?" Vicki asked.

"He didn't answer."

Brenda took a breath like she was about to speak, but then she clamped her mouth shut.

"What?" Melanie said.

"Nothing," Brenda said. "There are just a bunch of things I don't understand."

"There are a bunch of things *I* don't understand," Melanie said. "Like first of all, why you need a lawyer, and second of all, why you won't take his calls."

"Mel . . . ," Vicki said. She had told Melanie about Brenda's predicament at Champion—fired for her involvement with John Walsh—but she had only alluded to Brenda's legal trouble, primarily because all Vicki knew about it was what she had been told by their mother: Brenda was under investigation for vandalizing a piece of university-owned art. Brenda herself had said nothing about it to Vicki, probably because she figured Vicki had gotten the story from Ellen Lyndon. For years, information had been passed between the two girls via their mother, who had no understanding of confidentiality, at least not when it involved family.

"What?" Melanie said, her cheeks flaring red now. "She knows *my* dirty laundry. What's fair is fair."

"The only reason I know your dirty laundry is because you can't stop talking about it," Brenda said.

"Enough!" Vicki said. "Let's change the subject."

"Yes," Melanie said.

"Fine," Brenda said. "What do you think of Josh?"

"He's gorgeous," Melanie said. Her cheeks grew even rosier.

"Well!" Brenda said.

"That's why you hired him," Melanie said. "Don't pretend it isn't. I've heard you have a penchant for younger men."

Vicki touched Melanie's arm like a gentle referee. "How was your food?" Vicki asked. "Did you like it?"

Melanie poked at her steak, which she had barely touched. "It was fine. But rich. I don't want to make myself sick."

"You still feel bad?"

"Horrible," Melanie said. She pushed her wine away. "I don't want this."

"I'll drink it," Vicki said.

Brenda glared at Melanie. "Just so you know, John Walsh, my former student, was not a *younger man*. He's a year older than I am."

"Really?" Melanie said. "I thought Vicki said . . ."

"You know, Ted is bringing a box of that ginger tea I told you about," Vicki said. "It will help settle your stomach."

"So please, no more references to younger men," Brenda said. "It's not only insulting, it's inaccurate."

"Okay," Melanie said. "Sorry."

"You don't have to apologize," Vicki said.

"Sure she does," Brenda said.

Vicki set her fork down. All around them, people were having lovely dinners, pleasant conversation—was it too much to ask to be one of them, if only for tonight? "I want champagne with dessert," she said.

"Oh, Vick, are you sure?" Brenda said.

As Vicki flagged their waiter, Brenda's phone rang.

"You should turn that off," Vicki said.

Brenda checked the display.

"Ted?" Vicki said.

"John Walsh?" Melanie said. And then in a heartbreakingly earnest voice, "Peter?"

"Nope," Brenda said. "It's Mom."

"Oh, God," Vicki said. "Turn it off."

⁓

Somehow, Josh got Blaine's face cleaned up (the scratch was microscopic; Vicki might not even have noticed it had Blaine not insisted on the largest Band-Aid in the box). Blaine, patched up and abashed by his own antics, calmed down. Porter was still wailing, however, and Josh was at a loss as to how to make him stop.

"Give him a bottle," Blaine said. "He won't take it, but Mom says we have to keep trying."

Josh lifted the bottle out of the pan of hot water, tested the milk against the inside of his wrist like he'd seen it done in that movie where three grown men who don't know anything about babies are left in charge of one, and then tried, with Porter nestled in the crook of his arm, to feed it to him. No such luck. The baby was too heavy to hold that way and he didn't want the bottle. He threw it to the ground and shrieked with his lips curled back so that Josh could see all the way down his throat. Blaine looked on with mild interest.

"Does he always do this?" Josh asked.

"Yes," Blaine said. "But Mom says we have to keep trying."

"Okay," Josh said. He sensed Blaine warming up to him, although he dared not become too optimistic. He held Porter in one arm and the bottle in the opposite hand, just out of Porter's reach, hoping to entice him. Blaine, meanwhile, trudged back to the bedroom, where he unplugged the DVD player, pulled out the cord, wound it around his hand, shut the cover, retrieved the broken piece from under the bed, and set the whole thing on his mother's dresser. He was like a little adult, Josh thought. Then Blaine grabbed a pillow and a blanket and three storybooks and left the room without so much as a glance at Josh, though Josh understood he was supposed to follow.

They moved into the bathroom, where Blaine brushed his teeth, took a leak (he was too short to reach the pull chain to flush, so Josh helped him out), and climbed, like it was second nature, with his pillow, blanket, and the three books, into the bathtub. He made himself comfortable.

"You're kidding, right?"

"Sit," Blaine said. He held up *Horton Hatches the Egg*. "Read to me, please."

Josh sat and the baby sat. The baby was just as baffled as Josh, perhaps, because he quieted. Josh set the bottle on the closed toilet seat. He opened the book, cleared his throat, and started to read.

A few minutes later, Josh thought, *Yes, that's right. I am Horton the Elephant, sitting on an egg for lazy Mayzie bird who flew off to Palm Beach. If anyone at Zach's party could see me now, they would taunt and tease and torture me as surely as the other animals in the jungle taunted Horton. I am that unlikely. That well-meaning but misplaced. I am not competent. This is not easy money. I was led here by lust for the mermaid and a crazy sense that the Three and I were somehow connected. I am a fool, an idiot. I quit the airport. How dumb I am. Horton.*

And yet, before Josh had finished the book, peace settled over the bathroom. Blaine, in the tub, had fallen asleep. Porter, lying on his side on the cool tiles, was sucking down his bottle. It was too good to be true. He drained the bottle, then crawled over to Josh. Josh picked him up and he burped.

"Good boy," Josh said. "Good baby."

Josh changed Porter's diaper in the bedroom. The diaper was crooked, but it was on the right way and Porter seemed comfortable enough. Somewhere in the folds of the covers, Porter discovered his pacifier. He popped it in his mouth and kicked contentedly.

"Do you want to go to sleep?" Josh asked. He could have sworn he saw the baby nod. It was barely dark out, but Josh was exhausted. Those beers. He took off his shoes and climbed onto the bed next to Porter. Porter grabbed his ear. Whose bed was this? Josh wondered, though he knew it was Vicki's bed. The cancer bed. Josh thought about Brenda's bed and Melanie's bed. Then his cell phone rang.

He checked on Porter—asleep. Josh felt jubilant as he flipped open his phone. So jubilant that he answered even though he could see on the display that it was Didi calling.

"Hello?" he whispered.

There was loud, thumping music in the background. Then Didi's voice, as pleasant and soothing as smashing glass. "Josh? Are you there? Are you coming to Zach's? Josh?"

Josh hung up the phone and closed his eyes.

The story had been told so many times with such precise sameness that it no longer seemed true, and yet, it *was* true: Victoria Lyndon met Theodore Adler Stowe at a late-night high-stakes poker game.

Vicki had been living in Manhattan for a little more than a year when she discovered the poker game. She'd harbored a vision of herself as a party girl—nothing was too late or too wild for her, she never ran out of gas—though the fact of the matter was, her weeks were consumed by work as a paralegal at an all-female law firm and her weekends fell into a postcollegiate pattern of dinner at cheap ethnic restaurants followed by drinks at a string of bars on the Upper East Side populated by extremely recent graduates of Duke, Princeton, Stanford, Williams. Vicki was ready for something different, something edgier, more authentically *New York,* and so when a friend of a friend, a guy named Castor—who had long black hair and wore silver jewelry—invited her to a midnight poker game on the Bowery, she panted into the phone: *Yes, yes, yes!*

The address Castor gave her had once been a brownstone, but the windows were blown out and boarded over, the door was pocked with bullet wounds, and the place exuded an aura of shithole. Okay, Vicki thought, he must be kidding. Or he's trying to scare me. Or he's trying to kill me. Because how well, really, did she *know* Castor? Or maybe she had the wrong address. Except he'd been very clear, and this was the place. Half a block down, music pumped out of CBGB, but despite that, Vicki clenched her rape whistle. She had thirty dollars in the pocket of her leather pants, a lipstick, and her keys.

Castor pushed open the door of the building from the inside. "Come on in," he said.

The building had smelled like burning hair. The stairs were sticky with—blood? urine?—and Vicki heard the scuttling of rats.

"Where are we going?" she said.

"Upstairs," he said. "All the way up."

She followed Castor up the stairs, down a pitch-black hallway, up some more stairs, toward a door outlined with green light.

"The color of money," Castor said.

They pushed into a cavernous room, decorated like a 1920s speakeasy. It was someone's apartment—a little bald man named Doolie, who was, in fact, a squatter. He had transformed this room into the hottest poker game in the city. A three-piece jazz combo played in the corner. Juilliard students, Castor said. A bar was set up and a Rita Hayworth look-alike in a red flapper dress passed around fat corned-beef sandwiches. The center of the action was a round table that sat twelve, though half the seats were empty. It was a poker game, six men grimacing at one another.

"It's a hundred-dollar ante," Castor said. He handed Vicki a bill. "I'll spot you your first game."

"I can't," Vicki said. "I'll lose your money."

"You don't know how to play?"

"I know how to play." There had been some beer poker at Duke and, years before that, funny games with her parents and Brenda at the kitchen table. About as different from this kind of poker as Vicki could imagine.

"So play." Castor nudged Vicki forward and she stumbled into one of the empty chairs. Only one of the men bothered to look up. A young guy with brown hair and dark green eyes. Preppy-looking. A kid who, much to Vicki's dismay, looked like the hundreds of guys she met at the bars uptown. He was wearing a Dartmouth Lacrosse sweatshirt. Her first thought was, *If someone as standard-issue as you found this place, it can't be that hot.* But the other men were older, with the definite air that they knew what they were doing.

"You in the next hand?" Dartmouth Sweatshirt said.

She set the hundred out on the table. "I guess."

The other men licked their chops. They wanted her money.

She won the hand with three queens. The men pushed the pile of cash her way, chuckling. "Betty won."

"My name is Vicki," she said.

She played again and won with a full house. Castor brought her a martini. Vicki took an exultant sip, then thought, *This is where I get off.* Two more women joined the game and Vicki stood up.

"Oh, no," one of the older men said. He was the hardest-looking and the loudest-laughing, the leader. "You sit your pretty bucket back down and let us win our money back." She obeyed and won the third hand with a flush.

Then it was her turn to deal. Her hands shook as she shuffled. She thought of Crazy Eights with Brenda and shuffled with a waterfall. The men chuckled some more. *Betty.* She folded the next two hands, then won a hand. She ate half a corned-beef sandwich and had another martini. It was three o'clock in the morning and she had never felt more awake. In four hours, she would have to go to work, but she didn't care. Dartmouth Sweatshirt was smoking a Cohiba. *Do you want one?* he asked.

Sure, why not? She lost another hand then got up to join Castor at the bar. The band was still playing. Who were these people? Music and writing students, Castor said. Young Wall Street, young production designers, young Madison Avenue, young Seventh Avenue.

"It's who will be running New York ten years from now."

Vicki didn't belong there. She would never run New York; she couldn't even make a decision about law school. And yet she walked out of the building at five o'clock in the morning with twelve hundred dollars. Dartmouth Sweatshirt offered to walk her home; Castor was headed uptown to 120th Street, so Vicki had no choice but to agree. The streets were deserted and intimidating, and she had so much cash.

"You played well tonight," Dartmouth Sweatshirt said.

"Beginner's luck."

"Coming next week?"

"Maybe. Do you go every week?"

"Every week. I like it. It's different."

"Yes." Vicki looked at the guy. Out of the speakeasy, he seemed taller and more confident. He was very cute. Vicki sighed. The last thing she needed in her life was another guy. But she was grateful for the walk home. So many men were like Castor. *Sorry, going uptown.*

"What's your name?" Vicki asked.

"Ted Stowe."

Vicki went to the poker game the following Tuesday and the Tuesday after that. She didn't tell anyone else about it. She had two thousand dollars in cash in her sock drawer and Wednesdays at work she spent her lunch hour napping in the ladies' room. But Vicki craved the poker game. Castor gave it up at the end of October. He was on to other things, but not Vicki. She learned to tip Doolie from her winnings before she left, and she learned never to use the bathroom because there were always people in there—people who couldn't have cared less about poker and the pure high of gambling—doing drugs.

All Vicki had wanted in the world was her martini, her half a sandwich, her Cohiba, her hand of cards, the John Coltrane, and the green, glowing color of money. This, she thought, is what it must feel like to be a man.

Ted was there every week, despite the fact that he was an awful card player. Some nights he didn't win a single hand.

"You suck, Stowe," the leader said. Vicki had learned that the hard-looking man with the Bridge and Tunnel accent was Ted's boss on the trading floor at Smith Barney. Ken Roxby, his name was.

Ted was always good-natured, always even-tempered, even after losing five hundred dollars in half an hour, even at four o'clock in the morning, even drunk.

"I'll get you guys back at golf," he said.

One week, to her utter dismay, Vicki had a stomach virus and missed the poker game. Wednesday morning, her phone rang. Ted Stowe. "I won three hands last night."

"You did not."

"I made money," he said. "For the first time ever."

"And I missed it," Vicki said.

"And I missed you," he said.

Neither of them said anything for a second. Ted cleared his throat. "Hey, I was wondering if . . ."

"I don't think so."

"You haven't even let me ask."

"I don't want to date anyone in the poker game," she said. "I really, really like it and I want it to stay just the way it is."

"Okay," Ted said. "I quit."

Vicki thought he meant he was quitting her, but no. He meant he was quitting the game.

"You'd quit for me?" Vicki said.

"Well, you know what they say about hitting yourself over the head with a hammer," he said. "It feels good when you stop."

Now, here it was, more than ten years later: Vicki was lying in bed, nursing a hangover. She wanted to blame the malaise she felt on the chemotherapy, but the symptoms were all too familiar—the floury mouth, the fuzzy, buzzing headache, the sour stomach. She begged Brenda to take the kids for an hour, and bring her a chocolate milk, and Brenda did so huffily.

"I'm not actually your slave," Brenda said as she handed Vicki the milk.

Vicki nearly used the word "freeloader," which would have been like setting a match to hairspray, but at that moment the front screen door clapped shut. There was a shuffle, some heavy footsteps, and then Ted's voice. "Where are my little monsters?"

Vicki took a sip of her chocolate milk, then fell back into her covers. It was a little past nine; he must have gotten up at an ungodly hour to make the first boat. She listened to him horsing around with the kids. Ted Stowe, her husband. At another time, if she'd been separated from him for a week, she would have felt giddily excited about his arrival, nervous even. But now she felt the scary nothing.

He didn't come in to see her right away. He was busy with the kids first and then with all the stuff. Vicki had her eyes closed, but she tracked his presence, his footsteps on the flagstone path, the creak of the gate, the clicks and thumps of the car doors opening and closing. She heard him teasing Melanie, and indignation bloomed in Vicki's chest: *Your wife has cancer! You might take a few seconds to check on her and say hello!* By now, Vicki felt good enough to get out of bed, but she would wait (childishly?) for him to come to her.

When he did come, finally, it was all wrong. She knew it from the way he tapped on the door, from the tentative way he said her name. "Vicki? Vicki?" He never called her Vicki, only Vick. He was afraid of her now; she was a stranger to him.

And yet, they went through the motions. Ted knelt by the bed and kissed her forehead like she was a sick child. She pressed her face into his shirt and smelled him. He had a strange smell that she hoped was just hotel soap.

"How was the rest of the trip?" she said.

He eyed the glass of chocolate milk. "Well, I'm here."

He was there, yes, but in the weeks since Vicki's diagnosis, Ted had changed. He had become Mister Rogers. His voice used to boom and resonate, but now he sounded timid and supplicant, and if Vicki wasn't dreaming, he was getting fat. He had stopped going to the gym after work.

She knew that with her and the kids gone, he worked late and either grabbed fast food from Grand Central or foraged through the freezer for one of the leftover casseroles. In the evenings he did onerous chores, things Vicki had been after him to do for years, like cleaning the attic. He did them now because he thought she was going to die. The day before Vicki left for Nantucket he threw away thousands of dollars' worth of Cuban cigars by ceremoniously breaking them in half over the kitchen trash. *Really, Ted,* Vicki had said. *Is that necessary?*

Their sex life had come to a halt. Ted had taken to kissing her on the forehead and cheek; he hugged her like she was his sister. That afternoon, while Porter was napping, Brenda took Blaine to the beach with a wink and a nod so that Vicki and Ted could have some privacy. Ted closed the bedroom door and kissed Vicki in a way that let her know he was trying. They fell back on the bed, Vicki reached down his shorts, and . . . nothing. His body didn't respond to her touch. For the first time in ten years, he could not get an erection.

He pulled away, sank his face into the squishy mattress. "I'm tired," he said. "I barely slept last night."

Vicki's heart broke at this excuse. "It's me," she said.

"No," he said. He touched her lips. She was trying, too. She had risen from bed to put on lipstick, to put on perfume and a thong—all to try to disguise the fact that she was sick. The port alone was enough to turn any man off. She felt as sexy as a remote control, as desirable as a garage door opener. There was no pretending it didn't matter. Her husband had shown up, yes, but something vital, it seemed, had been left behind.

They fell asleep in the warm, stuffy bedroom and

woke an hour later to Porter crying and the sounds of Brenda and Blaine playing Chutes and Ladders in the living room. They might have been tender with each other, apologetic—but instead, they started fighting. Ted took issue with the fact that Vicki had gone out the night before. "To the Club Car, no less."

"What's wrong with the Club Car?" Vicki said.

"All those rich, divorced men on the prowl."

"No one was prowling after us, Ted. I promise you."

"And you got drunk," he said.

He had her there. She drank three or four glasses of wine at dinner, two flutes of Veuve Clicquot with dessert, and a glass of port at the bar. She had become utterly intoxicated, savoring the pure defiance of it. Her spirits lifted; she felt herself leaving her body behind. Dr. Garcia and Dr. Alcott had both told her *no alcohol,* but she felt so fantastic, she didn't understand why. She had even wanted to go dancing at the Chicken Box, chug a few beers and lose herself further, but Melanie had groaned and yawned and Brenda sided with Melanie.

It's late, Brenda said. *I think you've probably had enough.*

"I got drunk," Vicki admitted. The chocolate milk, now soured and separated, was still on her nightstand.

"It was irresponsible," he said.

"You're Blaine and Porter's father," Vicki said, rising from bed. She felt light-headed and nauseous. "You are not, however, my father."

"You're sick, Vicki."

Vicki thought of the circle of human beings that comprised her cancer support group. They had warned her this would happen: *You'll become your cancer. It will own you, define you.* That was true even within the group itself. Vicki knew the other members of the group only by first name, type of cancer, and stage. Maxine, breast, stage two; Jeremy, prostate, stage one; Alan, pancreatic (there was no stage with pancreatic, it was always terminal); Francesca, brain, stage two; and the leader, Dolores, Hodgkin's, five years in remission.

"So what?" Vicki, lung, stage two, said to her husband. "I'm an adult. I can do what I want. I wanted to have fun with my sister and Mel. Fun is allowed, you know. Even for people with cancer."

"You need to take care of yourself," Ted said. "Have you been eating kale, or broccoli? I noticed you left your vitamins at home. Dr. Garcia said . . ."

"You don't know what this is like for me," Vicki hissed. She marched into the other room, past Brenda and Blaine, to the kitchen counter, where she snatched up Porter's bottle. It was amazing how as some things fell apart, others came together. Porter had taken a bottle the night before for Josh, and another one this morning for Vicki, just like that, without a peep. Vicki stormed back into the bedroom and closed the door. Ted was bouncing Porter around, trying to get him to stop crying.

"Here's his bottle."

"Will he take it?"

"He took one last night from Josh and another one this morning from me."

"Who's Josh?"

"The babysitter."

"A guy?"

"A guy."

"What kind of guy?"

"He's going to be a senior at Middlebury. We met him at the airport the day we got here and now he's our babysitter."

Ted sat down on the bed and started feeding Porter the bottle. "I don't know how I feel about a male babysitter."

"You've got to be kidding me."

"What kind of guy wants to babysit? Is he a pedophile?"

"Do you honestly think I would hire someone like that? Josh is extremely normal. Athletic, handsome, trustworthy. He's a doll, actually."

"So you're trying to replace me?"

"Stop it, Ted."

"Was this Brenda's idea?"

"Well, sort of. But please don't . . ."

"Ha!" he said. "I knew it. Your sister's a pedophile."

"Ted, stop it!"

"She's going to have sex with the kids' babysitter."

"Ted!" Strangely, Vicki felt jealous. Josh didn't belong to Brenda! Last night when they got home, the three of them stood over Josh as he slept with Porter on the bed and they did everything shy of coo and cluck. Then Josh opened his eyes and startled—he was like Snow White waking up to the curious gazes of the dwarfs. Vicki had started to laugh, then Brenda laughed, then Melanie asked Josh if he wanted her to walk him out to his car and that made Vicki and Brenda laugh so hard they nearly peed themselves. Josh had seemed mildly offended, or perhaps just embarrassed that they had found him asleep, but he woke up enough to give Vicki a full report and she was so happy about Porter taking a bottle that she gave

Josh a hundred dollars and good feelings were restored all around. She did not want to be attacked for hiring a male babysitter, and she did not like anyone's insinuation that Josh was somehow around because of Brenda.

"Just please be quiet," Vicki said. She stopped herself from asking, *Why did you even come?*

Later, when it cooled down a bit, they went for a walk. *Get out of the house,* Vicki thought. The house was so small, the ceilings so low, that words and feelings got trapped, they ricocheted against the walls and floors instead of floating away.

Vicki and Ted put the kids in the double jogger and headed up Baxter Road, past the grandest of the island's summer homes, homes they had long fantasized about owning and now could probably afford, toward Sankaty Head Lighthouse. Ted was pushing the kids, Vicki was trying not to let on how much the simple walk winded her.

"Do you remember the poker game?" she said.

"Of course."

"It was like a lifetime ago," she said.

"I'll never forget you in those leather pants," Ted said. "Taking everyone's money."

"I've been thinking about all those cigars I smoked," she said. "One cigar a week for two years. You don't think . . ."

"No," he said. "I don't."

She was quiet. A white-haired man wearing madras Bermuda shorts strolled by, walking a golden retriever. Vicki smiled at him.

"Beautiful family," he said.

That was how they appeared to others, she knew. Blaine was asleep in the stroller, Porter was sucking on his pacifier. A man walking a dog on a mild summer afternoon would never know that Vicki was sick, and he would never know that Ted couldn't handle it.

But here they were on Nantucket, walking along the bluff with Sankaty Head Lighthouse like a giant peppermint stick in front of them, its flashing beacon steady and predictable. Being here made Vicki feel better. *Beautiful family,* the man walking his dog said, and whereas he was wrong, he was also right. They would grill fish for dinner, boil early corn, walk to the market for ice cream cones. After the kids were asleep, Vicki and Ted would try again in bed.

No sooner had these thoughts soothed Vicki, no sooner was the man with the dog past them and out of earshot, than Ted cleared his throat in a way that made Vicki nervous.

"I want you to come home," he said.

One of the things Vicki loved about her parents, Buzz and Ellen, was that they were still married; they had been married for thirty-five years. Vicki appreciated this more than Brenda did because she herself was part of a marriage, she was tied to Ted Stowe in a thousand ways—the children, the house, the friends, the community, their church, the ten years of breakfast, lunch, and dinner, bills paid, birthdays, anniversaries, vacations, dinners out, movies, parties, plays, concerts, the countless conversations. It seemed when they were first together that their conversations had been about other things—worldly matters, politics, books, ideas—and now the conversations were only about themselves. Did that happen to every couple? These endless discussions of schedules and logistics, squash games and Junior League lunches, of Blaine's fine-motor skills, his bowel movements, the amount of TV he watched, of Porter sleeping or not sleeping, of should they have a third child, go for the girl, of Ted's career, of their investments, their taxes, the warranty on the Yukon, of Vicki's involvement with the neighborhood association, of which day for what kind of recycling. Was everyone so inward-looking? Or was it just their family, the Stowes, and especially now, with Vicki's cancer?

A few years earlier, Ellen Lyndon had said something curious to Vicki. *Your father and I have been having the same argument for fourteen years,* she said. *Different manifestations, but the same argument.*

Vicki was both grateful and disturbed to discover that she didn't know what this argument between her parents might be about. She hadn't lived at home since the summer after her sophomore year in college, true, but it unsettled her to think that she didn't know her parents well enough to be privy to the subject of their one and only argument. And yet she understood, because she was married, that her parents' marriage was its own thing, an entity separate even from the children it produced; it was mysterious, sacred, unknowable.

Vicki's marriage to Ted had its own nooks and crannies, false starts and dead ends, with its own arguments, repeated and repeated again. *I want you to come home.* Ted didn't have to say another word—Vicki had the rest of his speech memorized. *I love you, I miss you, I miss the kids, I hate coming home to an empty house, I'm sick of Chinese takeout and frozen waffles. The house is too quiet. Porter's just a baby; he'll forget who I am—he already cries when he sees me. I want you to come home so you can have chemo in the city, let's not mess around, let's get serious, let's kill these cells, smug fuckers, get the best doctors, so what if the drugs are exactly the same, administered the same way? I want you at Sloan-Kettering so I can sleep at night, knowing you have the best money can buy, no second-guessing.*

But what Ted was also saying was, *I want you to come home because I'm afraid I'm going to lose you. Afraid like a little kid, Vick. Scared shitless. I'm going to lose you in September on the operating table, or at some point after that if the surgery doesn't work, if the tumors aren't resectable, if the cancer metastasizes to your brain or your liver, if they can't get it all out.*

I want you to come home, Ted said, because he had no faith. And that was what really stood between husband and wife, that was what had turned him into milquetoast, that was what caused Vicki's anger and Ted's impotence: He thought she was going to die. And, too, he didn't understand Nantucket the way Vicki did, he hadn't grown up in the house on Shell Street, he didn't feel the same way about the ocean, the sand, the reliable beacon of Sankaty Head Lighthouse. There were so many things that no longer mattered, but these things—this ocean, this air, this ground under her feet—did matter.

"I *am* home," Vicki said.

⁓

Vicki made it crystal clear: The most important thing when caring for children was to establish a routine.

Especially when those children's mother was sick. "The kids sense a change," Vicki said. "They sense uncertainty, they know something is wrong. Your job is to keep them calm and secure. Be consistent. Promote sameness."

"No problem," Josh said. "I'm all over it." He nearly went on to describe life with his father: dinner at eight-thirty, the beer, the iceberg salad. Josh knew all about routine, he knew all about sameness.

And so, the summer started: Monday through Friday, Josh's alarm went off at seven-thirty. It took him thirteen minutes to brush his teeth, shave, comb his hair, apply sunscreen, get dressed, and towel the dew off the seats of his Jeep—and anywhere from eleven to fourteen minutes to get from his house in Miacomet out to 'Sconset, depending on traffic by the high school. He pulled up to the cottage on Shell Street right before eight and invariably found Brenda and Blaine on the front step throwing pebbles into a paper cup. Brenda was always in a short nightgown—she had two, he'd learned, one pink and a white one with flowers. Josh was convinced she stayed in her nightgown to torment him. When Josh arrived, she stood up and said, *My work here is done,* and disappeared into the house, into her room, where she changed into a bikini. Josh was on board with establishing a routine, but he couldn't help appreciating variation—such as which nightgown Brenda was wearing, which bikini Brenda chose to put on, and the substance and duration of their conversations about her work. Because what Josh had learned early on, the first or second day on the job, was that Brenda was writing a screenplay. There had been one kid in Chas Gorda's writing workshop who aspired to write a screenplay, a sophomore named Drake Edgar.

Drake Edgar had the distinction of being the most earnest student in the class; he handed in scene after dreadful scene and wrote down everyone's criticism, verbatim. Chas Gorda himself—though his first and best-known novel had been made into a film that could now most generously be described as "cult"—suggested early on to Drake Edgar that the writing workshop was a place for pursuing serious fiction rather than scripts for horror films or thrillers. The other students, including Josh, dismissed Drake Edgar, considered him eccentric, borderline maniacal—though every conversation about Drake Edgar ended with the disclaimer that he would "probably laugh himself all the way to the bank."

Why not take screenwriters seriously? Josh thought. Everyone loved the movies. And movies had to be written.

"A screenplay?" Josh said to Brenda. "That's fascinating. I'm a writer, too. Well, I'm studying writing at Middlebury with Chas Gorda. You know of him?"

"No," Brenda said.

"He's great," Josh said. "He wrote this novel called *Talk* when he was only twenty-six."

Brenda smiled knowingly. "Oh, he's one of *those*. You know, prodigies who peak early and then never write another thing worth reading. God, I could teach an entire class on those people alone."

Josh felt uncomfortable hearing Chas Gorda insulted, and he considered defending his professor, but he didn't want to argue with Brenda. Instead, he said, "What are you working on?"

"Me?" Brenda said. "Oh, I'm trying to adapt this thing . . ." Here she stroked the gold-leaf lettering of her old book, *The Innocent Impostor*. "But I don't know. It's not going that well. It's like this book doesn't fit the screenplay formula, you know? There is no car chase."

Josh laughed—too loudly, probably, and with the unsettling eagerness of Drake Edgar. Still, what were the chances? He was a writer, sort of, and so was Brenda. Sort of.

"I can help you if you want," Josh said. "I can offer my opinion." (*That's our currency here,* Chas Gorda was always reminding the class. *Opinions.*) "I can give it a read."

"It's nice of you to offer," Brenda said. "But who knows if I'll ever finish. Are you writing a screenplay, too?"

"No, no, no," he said. "I'm more interested in writing short stories, you know, and novels." The way Brenda stared at him made him feel ridiculous, as though he'd just told her he was dressing up as Norman Mailer for Halloween. "But I could read your screenplay if you want feedback."

"Maybe," Brenda said. She tucked *The Innocent Impostor* back into its nest of bubble wrap and closed and locked the briefcase. "Maybe when I'm further along."

"Okay," Josh said. She was humoring him. He was a child to her, and yet he couldn't stop himself, each and every morning, as they helped Blaine pick the pebbles up off the flagstone walk, from asking how the screenplay was going. Some days she said, *Oh, fine,* and other days she shook her head and said nothing at all.

Another variation of Josh's day-to-day was what Vicki made for breakfast. Every morning it was something elaborate and delicious: blueberry pancakes, applewood-smoked bacon, cheddar omelets, peach muffins, eggs Benedict, crispy hash browns, cinnamon French toast, melon and berry salad. Josh and Vicki were the only ones who touched the breakfasts. Melanie was too queasy, she said, especially first thing in the morning. All she could handle was ginger tea and dry toast. Brenda didn't eat in the mornings, though she was a prodigious drinker of coffee and filled a thermos of it, doctored with a cup of half-and-half and six tablespoons of sugar, to take to the beach. The kids didn't eat the breakfasts because they were respectively too small and too picky. Vicki fed Porter pureed carrots or squash while Blaine ate Cheerios at the kitchen table. So the morning feasts were left to Josh and Vicki.

At first, Josh protested. "You don't have to go to all this trouble for me," he said. "I can grab something at home. Cereal, you know, or a bagel."

"You're doing me a favor," Vicki said. "I need to keep my strength up, and I would never make any of this for just myself." For Vicki, every forkful was an effort. She had no appetite, she felt specifically un-hungry. She gazed at the tiny portions on her plate and sighed. She picked a blueberry out of a pancake, she considered half a piece of bacon or a single cube of fried potato. "Here goes," she said. "Down the hatch."

Josh couldn't say how long it had been since someone had made a meal just for him; it was, he realized, one more part of having a mother that he missed. Vicki and Melanie watched him eat with appreciation, or maybe envy. They loaded his plate with seconds. Melanie nibbled her dry toast in the seat across from Josh; Vicki ate as much as she could, then she did the dishes, lifted Porter from his baby seat, washed his face and hands, changed his diaper, slathered him with lotion, and put him in his bathing suit. Blaine liked to dress himself—always in the same green bathing suit and then, as the days passed, in a shirt the same color as the shirt Josh was wearing. Yellow shirt for Josh, yellow shirt for Blaine. Green, red, white. Blaine cried the day Josh wore his Red Sox jersey.

"I'll have to buy him one," Vicki said.

"Sorry," Josh said.

"It must be tough being his hero," Vicki said.

Josh ruffled Blaine's blond hair, uncertain of what to say. There was no point denying it. Blaine hadn't given Josh a single bit of trouble since the first night of babysitting; he was resolutely well behaved, as though he were afraid that if he did something wrong, Josh would leave and never come back. Most days, Josh took the kids to the town beach right there in 'Sconset and sat in the shadow of the lifeguard stand (at Vicki's insistence). Josh and Blaine would dig in the sand, building castles, looking for crabs, collecting shells and rocks in a bucket. Porter spent time in his pack 'n' play under the umbrella chewing on the handle of a plastic shovel or chugging down a bottle or taking his morning nap. Blaine clearly liked it best when Porter was asleep; he wanted Josh all to himself. Other kids sidled up to Josh and Blaine with varying degrees of confidence, peering in the bucket, sizing up the sand castle. Could they play? Blaine shrugged and looked to Josh, who always said, *Sure.* And then, in the interest of fostering good socialization skills, he said, *This is Blaine. What's your name?* Josh had learned to be careful, though, not to show anyone more attention than

Blaine—otherwise Blaine would skulk off and sit under the umbrella, surreptitiously slipping rocks and shells of chokable sizes into his brother's playpen. Being with Blaine, Josh decided, was like being with a jealous and possessive girlfriend.

Babysitting was harder work than he thought it would be. It wasn't the hundreds of times Josh had to throw the Wiffle ball; it wasn't the half hour side by side eating the sandwiches that Vicki had packed talking about *Scooby-Doo;* it wasn't the fifty-seven items on Vicki's nonlist list, none of which could be forgotten (such as: never leave the house without a pacifier, make sure the milk stays cold, Blaine must finish his raisins before he has a pudding, *sunscreen, sunscreen, sunscreen!,* medicine for Porter's poison ivy to be applied every ninety minutes, shake the towels out, rinse off the Boogie board, stop by the market on the way home and pick up some Fig Newtons and some Bounce sheets, here's the money . . .). Rather, what drained Josh's energy was the emotional load of caring for two little people. From eight until one, five days a week, Blaine and Porter depended on Josh Flynn to keep them safe. Without him, they would dehydrate, drown, die. When viewed in this way, the job was *really important*. Despite the sort of flukiness of his taking this job, the oddness of it, and the suspicious nature of its beginning (his lust, plain and simple, for Brenda), Josh felt himself becoming attached to the kids. Hero worship? He loved it. At some point during the second or third week, Blaine took Josh's hand and said, *You're my best friend.* And Josh felt his heart grow three sizes, just like the Grinch in Dr. Seuss. A little kid affecting him this way? No one at the airport would have believed it.

Tom Flynn occasionally asked over dinner, *How's the new job going?*

Josh answered, *Good. Fine.* And left it at that. There was no use explaining to his father that he was making progress—he could now tell the difference between Porter's cries (hungry, tired, pick-me-up-please) and he was teaching Blaine to keep his eye on the ball. He would never admit that he had memorized entire pages from *Horton Hatches the Egg* and *Burt Dow, Deep-Water Man,* which Blaine liked to read upon their return to the cottage in the minutes before Josh left for the day. He couldn't articulate the tenderness he felt for these kids who were in danger of losing their mother. If Vicki died, they would be just like him—and although Josh would say he was well adjusted by anyone's standards, this made him sad. Every time Josh saw Vicki, he thought, *Don't die. Please.*

So with his father, he tried to stay noncommittal. *The job is good. I like it. The kids are a hoot.*

At this, Tom Flynn would nod, smile. He never asked what the kids' names were or anything else about them, and Josh, for the first time in his life, didn't feel compelled to explain. His job, the routine, his relationship with the kids and the Three—these were things that belonged to him.

Josh was so immersed in his new life that seeing Didi in the parking lot of Nobadeer Beach came as a very rude surprise. Josh had taken to swimming nearly every day at six o'clock, after most of the crowds had packed up and gone home, after the heat had dissipated but the sun was still mellow and warm. It was a fine hour of his day, and Josh usually toweled off and sat on the beach a few extra minutes watching the waves or tossing a piece of driftwood to someone else's dog, feeling fortunate, and smart, for taking control of his summer. So on the day that he climbed the narrow, rickety stairs from the beach and spied Didi sitting on the bumper of his Jeep, he filled with an old, familiar dread. There was no use pretending this was a happy coincidence; she was waiting for him. Staking him out. Josh thought back to the previous summer and the summer before that—Didi had surprised him every once in a while in this same way, and back then he had counted himself lucky. But now he felt creeped out. If her eyes hadn't been trained on him, he would have tried to sneak away.

As it was, he barely concealed his disgust. "Hey," he said. He whipped his damp towel into the open back of his Jeep.

She made a noise. At first he hoped for a snicker, but no such luck. She was crying. "You don't love me anymore," she said. "You fucking hate me."

"Didi—"

She sniffed and swiped at her nose with the heel of her palm. She was wearing her old cutoff jean shorts from high school, the ones with white strings dangling down her thighs, and a pink T-shirt that said *Baby Girl* in black cursive letters. She was barefoot; her toes, painted electric blue, dug into the dirty sand of the parking lot. Josh did a quick scan; he didn't see Didi's Jetta.

"How did you get here?" he said.

"Someone dropped me."

"Someone?"

"Rob."

Rob, her brother, who cruised around in a huge Ford F-350 with a shiny tool chest on the back and a bumper sticker that said *I give rides for gas, grass, and ass.* Rob was a carpenter with Dimmity Brothers, where Josh's mother used to work. The island was way too small. So Rob had dropped Didi off, and barefoot, no less; now Josh was trapped. He would be forced to give her a ride somewhere. She knew he was too nice a guy to strand her.

"Where's *your* car?" he said.

"They took it."

"Who took it?"

"The repo man." New tears fell; her mascara streaked. "It's gone forever."

Josh took a breath. "What about the money I lent you?"

"It wasn't enough. I'm in trouble, Josh. Big trouble. I can't make my rent, either. I'm going to get evicted and my parents have made it perfectly clear that they do not want me back at home."

Right. After twenty years of overindulgence, Didi's parents had moved on to tough love. Too little, too late, but Josh couldn't blame them for not wanting their grown daughter back in their house. She would drain their liquor cabinet and run up their phone bill.

"You have a job," Josh said. "I don't get it."

"I get paid shit," Didi said. "It's not like I'm a nurse."

"Maybe you should go back to school."

Didi raised her face. She looked like a zombie from *Night of the Living Dead.* "Now you sound like them."

Josh kicked at the ground. He wanted to go home and

shower. He was hungry; he was making quesadillas tonight for dinner. "What do you want from me, Didi?"

"I want you to care!" She was screaming now. "You
never call me anymore. You didn't show up at Zach's
party—"

"I had to babysit," he said.

"You're probably in love with that woman with the
kids," Didi said. "You're probably *sleeping* with her!"
This accusation was flung out there with such wild abandon that Josh didn't feel the need to respond. He didn't
like having Brenda or Vicki or the kids brought into the
conversation, especially not by Didi. She knew nothing
about them or about his time with them. If Brenda and
Vicki, or even Melanie, could see him now, they would
shake their heads. Poor girl, they'd say. Poor Josh.

He grabbed the car door. "Get in," he said. "I'm taking
you home."

Didi did as she was told, making Josh believe that he
was in control of the situation. But once Josh started driving, Didi started up again, bombarding him with nonsense.
"You're sleeping with her, just say it. . . . You don't love
me—you used to love me but now you're a real hotshot, a
college-boy hot shit, think you're better than . . . They don't
pay me shit, and after taxes . . . They took the car with my
Audioslave CD still in it . . . My own mother won't have
me." Tears, sobs, hiccups.

For a second, Josh feared she was going to vomit. He
drove as fast as he possibly could, saying nothing because
anything he said would be twisted around and used against
him. He thought of Brenda in her nightgown with her
notepad, her thermos of coffee, her briefcase for her old
first-edition book. Brenda was a different quality of per-

son: older, more mature, way past all this self-generated drama. Who needed fabricated drama when they were living through the real thing? Vicki had cancer. And Melanie had some kind of husband problem. Didi didn't even know what trouble was.

He swung into her driveway. "Get out," he said.

"I need money," she said.

"Oh, no," he said. "No way."

"Josh . . ." She put her hand on his leg.

"I lent you money," he said. "And you promised you'd leave me alone." He picked up her hand and dropped it into her lap.

"I only need—"

"The answer is no," he said. "And don't forget, you still owe me. Just because you asked me again and I said no doesn't mean you don't owe me from before. You owe me two hundred dollars, Didi."

"I know that, but—"

Josh got out of the car, stormed around to the passenger side, and opened her door.

"Out," he said.

"You don't love me."

So needy. All the time. Nothing had changed with Didi since senior year in high school. Her T-shirt caught his eye again. *Baby Girl. That's right,* he thought. He reached across Didi and unbuckled her seat belt. Then he took her arm and pried her from the car. He was gentle but firm, just as he would have been with Blaine. He knew how to handle Baby Girl; he dealt with children every day.

"I only need five hundred dollars," she said.

"I'm sorry," he said. "I can't help you."

"You're NOT sorry!" she screamed. Her nose was running and she was crying again and hiccuping like a cartoon drunk. "You're not *one bit* sorry, you don't care what happens to me!" Her voice was shrill and hysterical. It was like she *wanted* her neighbors to peer out their windows, sense a domestic disturbance, and call the police.

"Hey," he said. He looked at the house where Didi rented her apartment; he checked the yard and the woods around him. Now he wished someone would come out, ask what was going on, and help him deal with her, but there was no one around. "You just can't scream like this, Didi. You have to get ahold of yourself."

"Oh, fuck you," she said.

"I'm leaving," he said.

"I need the money," she said. She put her fists by her ears and shuddered until her face turned red. Josh watched her with disbelief. She was so far out of bounds that Josh thought maybe she was acting. Because hers was the kind of behavior Josh had only seen on soap operas; it was the behavior of the poverty-stricken, downtrodden, and criminally inclined people on *COPS*.

"Didi," Josh said. "Go inside and get a glass of water. Take a shower. Calm down."

She looked at him in a way that was both cunning and desperate. "If you don't help me," she said, "I'm going to kill myself."

He reached out and grabbed her chin. "You forgot who you're talking to," he said. "That isn't funny." He was really angry now, because he could hear the calculated tone of her voice. She *did* know who she was talking to. She was trying to use his mother's death to her advantage.

That was the kind of serpent Didi was; that was how she operated. Now Josh was the one with clenched fists. But no—in getting this angry, he was letting her win. Didi may have sensed that she'd crossed a line because her voice changed to a plea.

"It's just five hundred dollars. I know you have it, Josh."

"No," he said. Thinking: *Consistent message.* "Goodbye, Didi."

Nobody was more surprised by the passage of time than Melanie—the days passed, then a week, then another week. And here she was, still on Nantucket. She couldn't decide if she remained on the island out of sheer inertia (was she just avoiding the enormous effort it would take to get home?) or if she was starting to like it. The first days had been awful, with Vicki and Brenda fighting and then Vicki and Ted fighting and Melanie alternately vomiting, sleeping, or showering in an attempt to ameliorate the acute pain of Peter's affair with Frances Digitt. It was pain like Melanie had broken her arm and the bone was sticking through, pain like habanero chili sauce on an open cold sore. But one morning Melanie woke up and her first thoughts weren't about Peter and Frances, but rather about the secret that her body contained. She thought of the bud inside of her, the human being the size of a lima bean, a life that had taken root and held on in her body. This baby, unlike all the others (seven tries, eleven embryos), had recognized Melanie as its mother. She was seven weeks pregnant now, and although her body looked the same, she liked to lie in bed with her hand on her belly and imagine she could feel the flutter of a tiny beating heart. At this same time every morning, a wren perched on the gate outside Melanie's window and serenaded her. But the imagined sound of a beating heart and the wren's song were only preludes to what Melanie was really listening for. What she had started anticipating was the crackle of the Jeep's tires over crushed shells. Josh.

Okay, Melanie thought. *There is something wrong with me. He is nearly ten years my junior. He is in* college. *I am an old woman to him, an old pregnant woman.* And yet—what was it Woody Allen said?—"the heart wants what it wants." (Were her desires as morally ambiguous as Woody Allen's? Maybe they were; who was she to judge?) Melanie couldn't help what she felt, and what she felt when she heard the Jeep's tires crunch over the shells, when she heard the car door, the lifting of the gate latch, Blaine's delighted cry, and Josh's voice—*Hey, buddy, how's it hanging?*—was happy.

Melanie's routine, then, included climbing out of bed and making it into the kitchen for tea and toast while Josh was eating breakfast. Ideally, she would have liked to be home from a five-mile power walk, showered and dressed; she would have liked to be eating with him, buttering a scone, reading him something funny she had seen in the *Globe*. Instead, it was all she could do to sip her tea, nibble her toast, and make the most basic conversation.

She was dismayed to discover that he was a writing student—not because Melanie held anything against writing students, but because this gave him something in common with Brenda. Melanie heard them joking about writer's block. *Happens to the best of us,* Josh would say. And Brenda would point at him and say, *Keep telling me that.* The writing linked them in a way that irked Melanie and made her dislike Brenda more than she already did. It seemed hardly worth mentioning that Melanie also appreciated literature. She read serious, literary novels as well as trashy, commercial ones. She was a fan of Donna Tartt and Margaret Atwood—*and* Nora Roberts. She read the fiction in the *New Yorker,* maybe not every week, but often enough. Melanie understood, however, that reading was different from writing; she had no desire to write a short story or a novel. She wouldn't even know where to start.

Melanie searched for details she could share about herself that would resonate with Josh. She had been a history major at Sarah Lawrence. She had spent a year in Thailand teaching English: she had touched the Reclining Buddha's golden foot; she had commuted from her apartment to the school by water taxi; she had bought a parakeet at the bird market and named him Roger. Roger stopped singing after six weeks and then he died. When Melanie relayed these tidbits of her personal history, Josh nodded and chewed his food and seemed interested, at least until Brenda walked into the kitchen to get her coffee. Brenda stole his attention every time. Josh *looked* at Brenda. It became part of Melanie's routine to count the number of times Josh looked at Brenda and then feel jealous about it. How could Melanie blame him? Brenda was beautiful and oblivious; she lived in the house with the rest of them, but it was clear her mind was someplace else. On the lover back in New York, maybe, or on the lawyer whose phone calls she avoided each day, or on her stupid screenplay. Brenda had been fired from Champion University in the midst of a *sex scandal*—was Josh aware of this? Did he know she was in trouble with the *law*? Somehow Brenda rose above the smoldering fire of her recent past and managed to maintain a grip on her life. Not only was she writing a screenplay, which Josh found fascinating, but she had acquired something of a halo, taking care of Vicki and the kids in the hours when Josh and Ted weren't there. Melanie found herself detesting Brenda and at the same time wanting to be more like her.

In the afternoons, while Porter was napping, Melanie enlisted Blaine's help tending the gardens around the cottage. They weeded the front beds—Blaine trailing Melanie with a plastic Tupperware bowl that she filled and he dumped, periodically, in the kitchen trash. When the bed was weeded and the daylilies deadheaded, they patted down dark, sweet-smelling mulch. Melanie cut back the trellised New Dawn roses on the front of the house as well as the rosebushes that lined the back fence while Blaine watched. (He was afraid of thorns, and the bumblebees.)

That's the funny thing about roses, Melanie told him. *If you cut them back, they'll be even lovelier next time.*

Blaine nodded solemnly and then ran into the kitchen for a jelly jar filled with water. His favorite part of gardening was when Melanie cut flowers for the jar, which he then took inside and presented to Vicki.

"Those are pretty flowers," Josh said once, about a bunch of cosmos on the kitchen table.

"Melanie and I grew them," Blaine said. "Right, Melanie?"

"Right," Melanie said. Josh no doubt thought that gardening was a pastime for old ladies, but Melanie couldn't deny her proclivity for flowers, for privet hedge, for closely cropped lawn. She had always loved the sight and smell of things growing.

As the days passed, Melanie became more engaged in life on Nantucket, which meant Josh, the kids, Brenda—and Vicki. Melanie had been so consumed with her own woes that she had all but disregarded the fact that Vicki had cancer. Vicki went twice a week to chemo. Vicki was too sick—too weak, too exhausted and confused—to walk to the beach with Melanie, no matter how hard or gently Melanie prodded.

"It will be good for you to get out of the house," Melanie said. "And good for me, too."

"You go," Vicki said. "I'll wait here until the kids get back."

"I'll wait with you," Melanie said. "We can sit on the deck and drink iced tea."

They did this a few times, though for Melanie it was as awkward as a blind date. Vicki didn't seem to want to talk about her cancer, and the one time Melanie asked how Ted was dealing with it, Vicki said, "Ugh. I can't get into it." So there was something there—angst, anger, sadness—but when Melanie pushed a little harder, Vicki changed the subject to Peter, which was, for Melanie, like scratching a mosquito bite or wiggling a loose tooth. Painful, but irresistible.

"Have you spoken to him?" Vicki asked.

"No, not since before."

"So you haven't told him about the baby?"

"No."

"But you will."

"Eventually, I'll have to," Melanie said. "Does Ted know?"

"No. He has no idea. He's in his own sphere."

"Yeah, I guess. I just don't want Peter to find out from anyone but me."

"Obviously."

"Josh knows."

"He does?"

"I told him accidentally. Did you know Josh gave me a ride home that first Sunday, when I tried to fly back to Connecticut?"

"He did?"

"Yeah. Isn't that weird? I told him then, on the ride."

Vicki stared at Melanie in an inscrutable way. Melanie felt like she had just confessed that she and Josh had a secret history. Did Vicki disapprove? It was just a ride from the airport, nothing more, but how to explain the bizarre, nascent feelings she now harbored for Josh? She should keep them to herself. It was probably just her hormones.

"I don't know what to do about the baby, Vick."

"You're going to keep it, though, right?"

"Keep it, yes. But then what?"

Vicki was silent, sipping her iced tea. "There will be people to help you. Ted and I will help you."

"The baby needs a father."

"Peter will come around."

"You sound pretty sure about that."

"He must miss you."

Melanie scoffed. "He hasn't called once. Not once."

"And you haven't called him. I'm proud of you."

"I'm proud of myself," Melanie said. She hadn't called Peter; she hadn't tipped her hand. She was being patient, waiting things out. Along the back fence, the roses bloomed and the bumblebees were fat and happy. Ted had cut the grass over the weekend and it smelled wonderful and fresh. The sun was warm on Melanie's legs. Josh would return with the kids at one o'clock; this thought alone was enough to make Melanie glad she was here and not back in Connecticut. "Thank you for letting me come," Melanie said.

"I'm happy you're here," Vicki said.

"Are you?" Melanie said. Before the tumultuous events of the spring, Vicki and Melanie had talked on the phone three or four times a day; there were no taboo subjects. They excavated everything, leaving no stone unturned. Now, here they were, living under the same small roof, but they were each alone with their misery. Melanie worried that Vicki was angry at her for the things that happened the first week. Was she mad that Melanie had allowed Blaine to wander down the beach unnoticed, or that Melanie had fallen off the airplane steps with Porter? Was she pissed that Melanie had tried to leave Nantucket without saying good-bye? Did she resent having to hire a babysitter to take care of the children when her best friend should have been perfectly capable of doing so? Did she begrudge Melanie her pregnancy? Compared to Vicki's, Melanie's body was a piece of ripe fruit. And Melanie had done nothing to help Vicki with her chemo. Brenda had her role: She was the driver, the facilitator, the sister. Melanie was, and had been from the beginning, extra baggage. "Are you sure I'm not the worst friend you ever had?"

Vicki put her hand—which shook a little, like an old person's hand—over Melanie's, and instantly, the negative feelings receded. That was Vicki's gift. Kiss it and make it better. She was everybody's mother.

"Not even close," she said.

⁂

Every Tuesday and Friday when she took Vicki to chemo, Brenda sat in the waiting room pretending to read magazines and she prayed for her sister. This was secret, and strange, because Brenda had never been particularly religious. Buzz and Ellen Lyndon had raised the girls as lazy Protestants. Over the years, they'd attended church sporadically, in fits and bursts, every week for three months around Easter and then not again until Christmas. They'd always said grace before dinner, and for a while Ellen Lyndon attended early morning Bible study and would try to tell the girls about it as she drove them to school. Both girls had been baptized at St. David's Episcopal, then confirmed; it was their church, they considered themselves Christians, their pastor performed Vicki and Ted's wedding, a full service where everyone took Communion. And yet, religion had not played a central role in family life, not really, not the way it did for the Catholics or the Baptists or the Jewish people Brenda knew. There were no crucifixes in the Lyndon house, no open Bibles, no yarmulkes or prayer shawls. They were so privileged, so *lucky,* that they had never needed religion, maybe that was it. Buzz Lyndon was an attorney in

Philadelphia, he made plenty of money but not enough to cause trouble; Ellen Lyndon was a gifted housewife and mother. The Lyndon kitchen was, quite possibly, the happiest room in southeastern Pennsylvania—there was always classical music, fresh flowers, a bowl of ripe fruit, and something delicious about to come out of the oven. There was a blackboard in the kitchen where Ellen Lyndon wrote a quote each day, or a scrap of poem. *Food for thought,* she called it. Everything had been so lovely in the Lyndon household, so cultivated, so right, that God had been easy to overlook, to take for granted.

But now, this summer, in the pearl-gray waiting room of the Oncology Unit of Nantucket Cottage Hospital, Brenda Lyndon prayed her sister would live. The irony of this did not escape her. When Brenda had prayed at all growing up in the Lyndon household—if she had prayed secretly, fervently—then it was, without exception, that Vicki would die.

For years, Brenda and Vicki fought. There was screaming, scratching, spitting, and slamming doors. The girls fought about clothes, eyeliner, a Rick Springfield tape of Brenda's that Vicki lent to her friend Amy, who mangled it. They fought over who sat where in the car, who got to watch which TV program, who used the telephone for how many calls, for how many minutes. They fought over who collected the most beach glass from their walks around the Jetties, who had more bacon on her BLT, who looked better in her hockey skirt. They fought because Brenda borrowed Vicki's pink Fair Isle sweater without asking, and in retribution, Vicki ripped Brenda's paper about *The Adventures of Huckleberry Finn*—painstakingly typed on their father's Smith Corona—in half. Brenda smacked Vicki, Vicki pulled out a hank of Brenda's hair. They were separated by their father, Vicki called Brenda the *c* word from behind her bedroom door. Ellen Lyndon threatened boarding school. *Honestly,* she said, *I don't know where you girls learned such language.*

They fought over grades, teachers, test scores, and boys—or, Brenda corrected herself, *boy*—because the only boy who had mattered to Brenda for the first thirty years of her life (until she met Walsh, really) was Erik vanCott. Erik vanCott had been not only Brenda's best friend, but her secret, unrequited love. However, he had always nurtured a thing for Vicki. The pain of this alone was enough to fuel Brenda's fantasies of Vicki, dead. Car accident, botulism, heart attack, choking, stabbed in the heart on South Street by a man with a purple Mohawk.

All through high school the girls openly claimed they hated each other, though Brenda suspected it was she who had said the words more often, because what reason would Vicki have had to hate Brenda? Brenda was, in Vicki's opinion, pathetic. *Lowly Worm,* she called her to be mean, a name cruelly borrowed from their favorite Richard Scarry book growing up. *Lowly Worm, bookworm, nose always in a book, gobbling it up like a rotten apple.*

Can I invite a friend? Vicki always asked their parents, no matter where they were going. *I don't want to be stuck with Lowly Worm.*

I hate you, Brenda had thought. Then she wrote the words in her journal. Then she whispered them, then shouted them at the top of her lungs, *I hate you! I wish you were dead!*

Brenda shivered with guilt to think of it now. *Cancer.*

Their relationship hadn't been all bad. Ellen Lyndon, distraught by the girls' open hostility, was constantly reminding them of how close they'd been when they were little. *You two used to be such good friends. You used to fall asleep holding hands. Brenda cried the day Vicki left for kindergarten, and Vicki made Brenda a paper plate covered with foil stars.* There had even been a moment or two of solidarity in high school, primarily against their parents, and, in one instance, against Erik vanCott.

When Brenda and Erik vanCott were juniors in high school, and Vicki was a senior, Erik asked Vicki to the junior prom. Vicki was entangled in an on-again / off-again relationship with her boyfriend Simon, who was a freshman at the University of Delaware. Vicki asked Simon for "permission" to go to the junior prom with Erik "as a friend," and Simon's response was, *Whatever floats your boat.* Fine. Vicki and Erik were going to the junior prom together.

To say that Brenda was destroyed by this news would be an understatement. She had been asked to the junior prom by two boys, one decent-looking and moronic and the other just moronic. Brenda had said no to both, hoping that Erik would ask her out of pity, or a sense of duty, or for fun. But now Brenda would be staying home while Vicki went to Brenda's prom with Erik. Into this drama stepped Ellen, with her belief that all aches and pains—even romantic, sister-related ones—could be cured by a little Nantucket sand between the toes. When she got wind of the predicament and confirmed it with the sight of Brenda's long face, she took the bottle of Nantucket sand that she kept on the windowsill and poured some into Brenda's Bean Blucher moccasins.

"Put these on," Ellen ordered. "You'll feel better."

Brenda did as she was told, but this time, she swore to herself, she would not pretend that the sand treatment worked. She would not pretend that it was August and she was seven years old again, climbing the dunes of Great Point. Back then, the most important thing in her life had been her sea glass collection and her Frances Hodgson Burnett books—*A Little Princess, The Secret Garden.*

"See?" Ellen said. "You feel better already. I can tell."

"I do not."

"Well, you will soon. Is the sand between your toes?"

As the night of the prom drew nearer, Ellen plotted a distraction. She wanted Brenda to go with her and Buzz to the country club's annual Rites of Spring Dance, held the same night as the prom. Going to a different dance with her parents as her escorts was supposed to make Brenda feel better? Apparently so. Ellen asked if Brenda would prefer the salmon croquettes or the veal Oscar. When Brenda refused to answer, Ellen made a joke about Oscar the Grouch. The woman was a one-act in the theater of the absurd.

Brenda didn't watch Vicki get ready and she did not get ready herself. She hid under the comforter of her bed wearing sweatpants, reading *Vanity Fair* (the novel). She was boycotting the country club dance, salmon croquettes, Maypole and all. She was going to stay home and read.

An hour before Erik was to arrive, Vicki knocked on

Brenda's bedroom door. Brenda, naturally, did not answer. Vicki, who had no sense of boundaries, tried the knob. The door was locked. Vicki scratched on the door with her fingernails, a noise that Brenda could not tolerate. She flung open the door.

"What the fuck?"

"I'm not going," Vicki said. She was wearing her dress—a strapless black sheath—and her blond hair was in a bun. She was wearing Ellen's wedding pearl on a gold chain. She was as glamorous as a soap opera star to Brenda, but this fact only served to piss Brenda off. Vicki pushed into Brenda's room and threw herself facedown on the bed, as though she were the one with a broken heart. "He wants to meet up with all these people I don't know at the Main Lion. Lame. And afterwards, he wants to go to a breakfast party that some kid in the marching band is having. Lame." She lifted her head. "I just don't feel like making the effort."

"You don't feel like making the effort," Brenda said. Now here was a classic Vicki Lyndon moment. She had a great dress and an even better date to a dance Brenda would have murdered to go to—and she was threatening to stay home . . . why? Because it wasn't cool enough for her.

"You should go with him," Vicki said. "He's your friend."

Yes, Erik was Brenda's friend. However, in the universe of proms and prom dates, this mattered little. "He didn't ask me," Brenda said.

"Well, he's out of luck," Vicki said. "Because I'm not going."

"Mom will make you go," Brenda said. "She'll say it's rude to stand him up. *And in very poor taste.*"

"She can't make me go," Vicki said. She eyed Brenda in her sweatpants. "She's not making you go to Rites of Spring."

"She hasn't started trying yet," Brenda said.

Vicki unzipped her dress and wriggled out of it, like a snake shedding its skin. "We'll stay home together. Rent a movie. Drink Dad's beer."

Brenda stared at her sister. Was she being serious? Vicki didn't like staying home, and especially not with Brenda. But maybe . . . well, if nothing else, Erik would see Vicki's true colors. He would realize he should have asked Brenda instead.

"Okay," Brenda said.

Vicki called Erik at home to spare him the indignity of showing up at the Lyndon house in his tux with a gardenia in a plastic box.

"Sorr-eee," she said. "I don't feeeeel well. I have really bad men-strooool cramps. I'd better stay home." She paused. "Sure, she's right here."

Vicki passed the phone to Brenda.

"I just got dumped," Erik said. "What are you up to tonight?"

"I'm supposed to go out," Brenda said, though she did not tell him where or with whom. "But . . . since Vicki's not feeling well, I might stay home and keep her company."

"Can I come over?" Erik asked.

"Come over?" Brenda said.

"Yeah. To hang out with you guys."

Vicki sliced her hand across her throat.

"Sorry," Brenda said. "Not tonight."

In the end, Erik went to the prom by himself, and when word spread that he'd been stood up by Vicki Lyndon, his popularity swelled. The band let him sing a Bryan Adams song. It was the best night of his life. The next day, he called Vicki to say thank you. Brenda and Vicki had stayed home and made popcorn and drunk warm Michelobs and watched their favorite movie, *This Time Forever,* which made them both cry. They fell asleep on either end of the sofa, with their legs entwined in the middle.

Brenda sat in the oncology waiting room pretending to read *People* magazine, but in truth she was praying fast and furiously, her lips moving while she crossed herself with her right hand. *In the name of the Father, and of the Son, and of the Holy Spirit, Amen. Dear Lord, please let Vicki live. Please, Lord, please, I beg You, please: Let. Her. Live.*

It became usual that, at some point during Brenda's waiting-room vigil, her phone would ring. Brenda always checked the display with a mixture of hope (for Walsh) and dread (of Brian Delaney, Esquire)—even though it was almost always her mother. After a while the nurses who wandered in and out from behind the administrative desk knew to expect Ellen Lyndon's call. They thought it was cute—the call from Mama. Brenda vacillated between gratitude for the calls and annoyance. Ellen had had her left knee replaced just after Easter—*all that skiing caught up with me*—and she was still recovering. Otherwise, she would have been right there—either living in Melanie's room instead of Melanie, or renting Number Twelve Shell Street, where she could monitor all developments herself. Ellen Lyndon was more frantic about Vicki's condition than Vicki was, and thus it was left up to Brenda to placate her mother, to assure her that yes, everything was going along as expected, Vicki's blood count was holding steady, and the kids were fine. This gave Brenda a sense of empowerment and calm control. But Brenda became increasingly irritated by her mother's anxiety. Twice a week it became Brenda's responsibility to talk her mother off the ledge. Brenda found herself saying the same phrases over and over until her mother became hypnotized and repeated the phrases back to Brenda. Never once during these phone calls did Ellen Lyndon ask about Brenda. Brenda tried to ignore the fact that her mother had ceased acknowledging Brenda at all, except as a messenger. Now, Brenda took the call, saying, "Hello, Mom."

"How is she?"

Brenda couldn't help being maddening in return. "How are *you*? Still with the cane? Is there Nantucket sand in your knee brace?"

"Very funny, sweetheart. How's your sister?"

"She's fine, Mom."

"Her blood count?"

"Red cells steady. White cells down, but not by much."

"Has she lost . . ."

"Half a pound."

"Since Tuesday?"

"Yes."

"Has she been vomiting? What does her hair look like?"

"No vomiting. Hair looks the same."

"Your father and I should be there."

"How's your leg, really?" Brenda asked.

"When all was said and done, it would have been easier to amputate. But I'm finally off my painkillers."

"Good," Brenda said.

"How are the kids?" Ellen said. "And Melanie, poor thing. How is she doing?"

Brenda was in no mood to comment on poor Melanie. "Why not ask how I'm doing? You have two daughters, you know."

"Oh, darling, I know. You're such an angel to be there for your sister. If you weren't there . . ."

"But I am here. And everything's fine. Vicki is fine."

"You'll have her call me as soon as . . ."

"I'll have her call you," Brenda said. "I always have her call you."

"I worry so. You don't know how I worry. And your father, although he doesn't say it as much, worries just as much as I do."

"Everything's fine, Mom. I'll have Vicki call you."

"Everything's fine," Ellen Lyndon said. "You'll have Vicki call me."

"There you go. You got it."

"Oh, Brenda," Ellen Lyndon said. "You have no idea what this is like, sitting here a million miles away, unable to help. God forbid you ever have to go through something like this."

"I am going through it, Mom," Brenda said. "She's my

sister." *Repentance,* Brenda thought. *Atonement.* "Good-bye."

"Have Vicki call me!"

"Good-bye, Mom."

⌒

Needlepoint Christmas stockings, flossing, the score of the Red Sox game, corn silks clogging the kitchen sink, corn silk hair, clumps of it, clogging the bathtub drain, poison ivy, the weather, the outlandish price of gasoline, Homeland Security, money, erections, sex.

At first, the chemo was no more painful or inconvenient than a trip to the dentist. The Oncology Unit at the Nantucket Cottage Hospital was small, with a close-knit staff—or, as they liked to call themselves, "the team." (They all played summer league softball and had been champions three years running. *When you see what we see, day in and day out,* the head nurse, Mamie, said, *you need an outlet for your aggression.*)

The team consisted of Mamie, a woman about ten years older than Vicki who was single-handedly raising four boys, and two other nurses: a young black man named Ben and a heavyset girl with a pierced lower lip who was just out of nursing school named Amelia—and the oncologist, Dr. Alcott. Dr. Alcott, by happy coincidence, was an acquaintance of Dr. Garcia's back at Fairfield Hospital through years of tireless conference-attending.

We have a few drinks together now and then, Joe and I, Dr. Alcott said when Vicki first met him. *I promised him I'd take good care of you.*

Dr. Alcott was probably fifty but he looked about

thirty. He was blond and tan, with very white teeth and expensively tailored clothes underneath his white jacket. He told Vicki he liked to fish, loved to fish, actually, and that was what had brought him to Nantucket from Mass General in Boston—the potential for late-night and absurdly early morning trips to Great Point in his yellow Jeep Wrangler. Three or four times a summer he chartered a boat with Bobby D. to hunt down shark or bluefin tuna, but at heart he was a solitary catch-and-release man—a bluefish was good; a striped bass, false albacore, or bonito even better. Dr. Alcott was the softball team's secret weapon, an ace pitcher whom no one in the league could hit. Vicki was half in love with Dr. Alcott, but she supposed everybody was.

When Vicki got to the hospital, either Ben or Amelia weighed her, took her blood pressure, and drew a blood sample to check her white count. Then Vicki waited for Dr. Alcott to appear.

Just checking in, he said. *How are you? How do you feel? You're okay? You're hanging in there? You're a trouper. Joe told me you were going to be a star patient, a real fighter. The blood counts look okay, they look fine. You're okay. I'm proud of you, Vicki. You're doing a great job.*

These words of encouragement were ridiculously important to Vicki. She was used to excelling at things, though never once had she considered chemo something that a person might be good or bad at. It was random, the luck of the draw, how a body reacted to the chemicals. But she appreciated the cheerleading from Dr. Alcott nonetheless. He was going to save her.

The chemo room was small and pleasant, with three

recliners and two partial walls for privacy. Vicki chose
what she hoped was a lucky chair—it looked like the
chair her father had relaxed in all his life—and waited
as Mamie hooked her up to the poison. There was one
TV, always tuned in to ESPN's *SportsCenter* because the
oncology team took the Red Sox scores very seriously.

For the first week, then two, Vicki thought, *This is
okay. I can do this.* It wasn't great—of all the places on
Nantucket that Vicki wanted to be, this was a notch above
the island's one jail cell and the Lewis Funeral Home—
however, it was better than the horror stories she had
heard from people in her support group about the units
at bigger hospitals where chemo was unscheduled and a
person might sit around for three or four hours waiting
for a chair to open up. Vicki looked forward to her time
with Dr. Alcott, she listened to Mamie tell Ben about
her sons' escapades and mishaps (her fourteen-year-old
got caught at three o'clock in the morning driving a car
he had "borrowed" from the Grand Union parking lot),
she listened to Ben tell Amelia about the crazy, drunk
girls that he encountered in his second job as a bouncer
at the Chicken Box. There was a lot of animated chatter on mornings after their softball games. In short, the
Oncology Unit was its own universe where Vicki was a
visitor. She could contribute as much or as little as she
liked; nobody asked her about her cancer. Why would
they? It was a matter of fact, a given, her cells were like
rotten teeth the team had to extract. No judgments were
made; it was just business.

Vicki was almost embarrassed when the side effects
kicked in. It happened gradually; there was a noticeable
decline during the second week, and each day things got

a little worse. Vicki's appetite died; she had to make herself eat the way other people made themselves exercise. Her skin dried out and started to flake, she became confused (she repeated herself, she thought she was talking to Brenda but it was Melanie, she lost her train of thought in the middle of a sentence). She dropped ten pounds despite the fact that she was eating diligently, she became too weak to walk to the beach or even the market, she spent whole afternoons and then whole days—beautiful, sunny, perfect days—in bed. Brenda brought home sand from the beach and sprinkled it in every pair of Vicki's shoes. Melanie bought Vicki all the books on the paperback bestseller list, but Vicki couldn't concentrate for more than a few pages. The only good times of the day were the mornings, when she had enough energy to make breakfast, and at one o'clock, when Porter snuggled in next to her for his nap. She inhaled the scent of his hair, she stroked his satiny cheek, she watched his mouth work the pacifier. When Porter woke up, Blaine often came in with a jar of freshly cut flowers and a pile of picture books for Vicki to read to him. Vicki usually made it through one or two before her attention gave out.

That's enough for now, Vicki would say. *Auntie Brenda will finish. Mommy's tired.*

Vicki tried to store up her energy for the weekends, when Ted was around. When he appeared on Friday afternoons, she was always sitting up in bed, pretending to read, pretending everything was fine, she was okay—but the expression on his face told her that he knew otherwise. He would sit on the edge of the bed, his face an inch away from raw fear. *What are they doing to you?* he whispered.

I don't know, Vicki thought. Dr. Garcia had said the chemo would be brutal, but Vicki hadn't understood what that meant at the time. Now, of course, she did. She was weak, her finger bones as crushable as pieces of chalk, her lungs as brittle as honeycomb. Her breasts, because of the chemo and the normal shrinkage after nursing, didn't even fill a training bra. Her nipples were like two old raisins. Gone were her curves, her smooth skin, her silky blond hair. Now her body was twigs and leaves. Her hair was frayed thread. She was ugly, hideous, a carcass. Her sex drive had vanished, and yet in her mind, she didn't want to let that part of her life go. She was terrified Ted would seek out sex elsewhere—there were millions of women in the city, there were prostitutes, escort services, expensive ones that men on Wall Street knew about and utilized for clients. There were women in Ted's office, in his building; there might be a woman wearing a certain perfume on the elevator. It happened all the time, cheating. It had happened to Vicki's best friend! And so, Vicki pursued sex with Ted like she hadn't in all the years they'd been married, and he, clearly, thought she was nuts.

"I want this," she said, pulling him into bed. It was Sunday afternoon, and Brenda had agreed to keep the kids at the beach for an extra hour. "Let's take a shower together."

"Outside?"

"I want to be close to you."

"Vicki, Vicki, Vicki. You don't have to do this for me."

"For us," she said. "It will make me feel better."

"Okay," Ted said, and he kissed her hair. "Okay."

Vicki got up and pulled the shades; she wanted it dark. She went to her husband and slid his bathing trunks off his body. She took him in her mouth. Nothing. Ted lay back, pale, sweating, flaccid, his eyes squeezed shut, a pained look on his face. He was trying to block her out, probably. He was trying to remember the woman she'd been before, or he was thinking of some other woman.

"I'm sorry," he said.

"You're not attracted to me," Vicki said. She slumped on the floor. "You think I'm ugly."

"You're not ugly, Vick. You could never be ugly."

"What is it, then?"

"I don't know. It's a mind game. The cancer. I'm afraid I'm going to hurt you."

"I'll tell you what hurts," she said. "And that is not being able to excite my husband. Do you get an erection at home? When you wake up in the morning? Does it work then?"

"Vicki, please don't."

"Do you jerk off when I'm not there?"

"Stop it, Vick."

"I want to know."

"No."

"You don't? I don't believe you."

"Yeah? Well, why don't you come home and find out for yourself."

"Ohhhh," she said. "Okay, I see." There was going to be a fight, which was the last thing she wanted, but she was powerless to stop herself. "You're punishing me for leaving Connecticut? You won't have sex with me until I agree to come home?"

"That's not it, Vick. That has nothing to do with it."

"Well, what's wrong with you, then?" she said. She wanted to stand up, but she was too tired, so she remained on the floor, staring at Ted's knees. Their sex life had always been healthy; before Vicki got sick, Ted had asked for her every night. That was how it worked—Ted asked, Vicki gave in. Never once had Ted failed to show up like this. It was so unusual, they didn't even have the words to talk about it.

"I don't know what's wrong with me," he said.

"You've slept with someone else," Vicki said. "I know it."

Ted sat up. He pointed a finger at her. "Don't you ever say that again. Don't say it and don't think it. It's insulting to me and to our marriage and to our family." He pulled on his swim trunks and started pacing the room. "Do you honestly think I would do that to you?" he said. "After ten years of being my wife, do you honestly give me *so little credit*?"

Vicki started to cry. "I'm afraid," she said. "I'm afraid of what's happening to my body. I'm ugly. I left you by yourself at home and I know you're angry about that and I just have these awful thoughts about you screwing somebody else, of you falling in love with somebody else and the two of you waiting for me to die so that you can be together and raise the boys. . . ."

Ted knelt down. He held her face and she fell into him. She was overreacting, she knew it, but she was glad she had spoken because those *were* her fears. Sexually, she felt like a failure. Having cancer felt like a failure, and what Vicki realized was that she wasn't used to failing at anything. Things had always come easily to her; that was part of who she was.

Ted was due to leave at five o'clock, giving Vicki another five days to fret about trying again.

"Will you hold me?" Vicki asked.

Ted squeezed her tighter. "What do you think about trading in the Yukon?" he said.

"Excuse me?" she said.

"We could buy a Volvo. It's safer."

Vicki shook her head. It was such a non sequitur she wasn't even sure she'd heard him correctly. Could Ted really be concerned about the car? She forced herself to acknowledge the monstrous anger eating away at her. She couldn't *believe* the things that mattered to other people! A safer car? Mixed in with her anger was envy. Vicki envied everybody everything: Melanie's pregnancy, Brenda's screenplay, Josh's strong arms—he could carry the pack 'n' play, the umbrella, the towels, the cooler, and the baby and make it all the way to the beach without stopping or dropping anything. She envied Mamie her sons, all of them safely into teenagerhood; she envied Dr. Alcott the thirty-eight-inch striped bass that he decided to take home and grill for his family for dinner; she envied the tattoo on Amelia's lower back (her *tramp stamp,* Ben called it); she envied chatter about a missed fly ball. She envied Porter his pacifier—she wanted a pacifier! She envied Ted's career, its demands and rewards; he would fly back to New York and consume himself with making money. That was his job! Vicki wanted her job back— housewife, mother. She wanted a normal life, a life filled with things other than chemo treatments and a darkened bedroom and a wistful, impotent husband. She wanted a life busy with things other than cancer.

Brian Delaney, Esquire, had called nine times since Brenda had been on Nantucket, and Brenda had yet to return a single phone call. She had hoped that dealing with the charges the university was slapping her with in regard to the Jackson Pollock painting could be done via voice messages and e-mail, but Brian Delaney, Esquire, seemed intent on having a person-to-person chat on the phone at the cost of two hundred and fifty dollars an hour. The reason, plain and simple, why Brenda didn't want to talk to the man was that she didn't want to pay. He must have sensed this. On the tenth call, he said, *Call me back or I'm dropping your case.*

And so, once Brenda was safely away from the house, ensconced on a stretch of deserted beach that she'd discovered north of 'Sconset Bluff, she called him back.

Brian Delaney, Esquire's secretary, Trudi, put Brenda right through. Seconds later, Brian Delaney, Esquire's voice boomed over the line, with as much unleashed testosterone as a linebacker from Ohio State, which was, in fact, what Brian Delaney had been in his previous life.

"Brenda Lyndon! I thought for sure you'd fled the country!"

She should have a snappy comeback for that, she knew. When she'd first met Brian Delaney, Esquire, she'd been full of snappy comebacks, and that was one of the reasons he'd agreed to take her case. He liked her. It wasn't just his Big Ten jock inferiority in the face of a near–Ivy League professor; he also liked the fact that she was young, attractive, and sassy. *I can't believe you're a professor,* he kept saying. Despite the damage done to her reputation by her relationship with Walsh, Brenda had worn a snug pencil skirt and very high heels to her initial meeting with Brian Delaney, Esquire, in the hope that he might cut her a break on his fee. No such luck—though Brenda seemed to be rewarded by his confidence. This case was fun for him, it was a no-brainer. He was used to dealing with criminals, he said. Thieves, rapists, drug lords. Next to these people, Brenda looked like Queen Elizabeth.

"Nantucket *is* another country," she said. "It feels like it, anyway. Sorry I haven't called you back. I told you about my sister, right? She's going through chemotherapy? And I'm responsible for watching her kids? I'm very busy."

"Right," Brian said tentatively. Brenda had also thought that mentioning Vicki's cancer might inspire him to lower his fees, but it was clear he didn't remember what she was talking about. "Well, I've been in contact with the university's counsel, and she's been talking to both the head of the Art Restoration Program and the chair of the English Department—because, as you know, it's the English Department that technically *owns* the painting—and they are coming at this from two different places. The art restoration guy, Len, his name is, says that only a small amount of damage has been done to the painting. It just needs what he calls 'a little work.'"

"Thank God," Brenda said.

"Well, hold your horses there, sister. 'A little work' is going to cost you ten thousand dollars."

"What?" Brenda said. There wasn't another soul on

the beach for as far as she could see in either direction and so she felt free to shout. "What the hell?"

"There's a divot in the lower left quadrant of the painting where the spine of the book hit it. The divot is three-quarters of an inch long."

"A divot?"

"Would you rather I call it a gouge? Fine, it's a gouge. It needs to be stitched up, filled in, whatever it takes to restore the glory of Pollock's fine work. But that's not the bad news," Brian Delaney, Esquire, said. "The bad news is the other woman, the chair of your former department."

"Atela?"

"She's pursuing a grand larceny charge."

"Grand larceny?"

"It's art," Brian Delaney, Esquire, said. "The value is all perceived. It doesn't have to be taken from the room to be stolen. Atela is convinced you were trying to sabotage the painting."

"We went over this in the deposition. I threw the book in anger. It was the heat of the moment, which makes it second degree. Possibly even third degree because it *was* an accident."

"Listen to you with the legal jargon."

"I wasn't aiming for the painting."

"She's claiming that you went into that room with the intent to destroy."

"You've got to be kidding me, Brian. Doesn't that seem a bit extreme to you?"

"A jury might believe it."

"So what does *that* mean?" Brenda said. "Is there going to be a trial?"

"They'll threaten with a trial. But what they really want is a settlement. Which means more money."

"I am not giving the English Department a single dime," Brenda said.

"You may not have a choice," Brian said. "They're asking for three hundred thousand dollars."

Brenda laughed. *Ha!* Though the number was funny like a slap across the face. "No chance," she said.

"The painting's been appraised at three million," Brian Delaney, Esquire, said. "They want a tenth of the value."

"Do you think I compromised one-tenth of the painting's value?" Brenda said. "The art guy said there was just a little divot."

"What I know about art I could write on my thumbnail and still have room for one of Andy Warhol's soup cans," Brian Delaney, Esquire, said. "The point is, *they* feel you've compromised one-tenth of the painting's value. But I can get them down to a hundred and fifty."

"This is why I don't take your calls," Brenda said. "I can't stand to hear this."

"In some people's eyes you did a bad thing," Brian said. "You made a series of very bad judgment calls. It's time to own that."

She owned it, all right. Her fall from grace was spectacular. She felt not like Queen Elizabeth at all but rather like Monica Lewinsky, Martha Stewart, OJ Simpson. Her good name had been slandered across Champion's campus and campuses across the country. She would never work again, not like she was meant to. And if that weren't punishment enough, she had separated herself from Walsh. But, as with everything, there was the issue of money, of which Brenda had very little. Brenda couldn't own her mistake to the tune of a hundred and sixty thousand dollars plus however many millions Brian Delaney, Esquire, was going to charge her.

"I don't have that kind of money," Brenda said. "I just flat out do not have it."

"How's the screenplay coming along?" Brian asked. "Sell that baby for a million dollars and all the rest of this will look like milk money."

"The screenplay is going just fine," Brenda said. This was an out-and-out lie. In truth, she'd written one page. "I really have to go, so . . ."

"Time to flip over, huh?" Brian Delaney, Esquire, said. "Too much sun on your face?"

Was she really paying him two hundred and fifty dollars an hour for this?

"Good-bye," Brenda said.

A hundred and sixty thousand dollars. Each time Brenda thought it, it was like a medicine ball to the stomach. In other circumstances, she might have called her parents and asked for a loan. Despite the inevitable comments that she was thirty years old, and a reminder that they had subsidized her income through eight years of graduate school, the money would appear from somewhere. But Brenda had to downplay her misfortunes with her family. They knew the basics: fired from Champion, a "misunderstanding" about an important painting that was making it necessary for her to retain a lawyer, but she had kept it at that. The Lyndons had always been open-minded and tolerant, but this stemmed from a sense of their own superiority. Their behavior was impeccable; they lived up to very high expectations but they understood, in their infinite wisdom, that not everybody was like them. Vicki thought this way, too—and so, for a long time, had Brenda. She couldn't stand being numbered among the sinning masses, the morally bankrupt, which is right where her parents would place her if they found out what she'd done. They might lend or flat-out give her the startling sum of money, but they would think less of her, and Brenda couldn't abide that. And, too, she couldn't bear to burden her parents with the details of her own idiotic scandal when Vicki was so sick. As it was, Brenda was going to have to start lying to her mother about Vicki's condition. Because despite Brenda's prayers, Vicki was getting worse. The chemo was taking its toll. All the things the doctors warned might happen, happened. Vicki had lost more than ten pounds, she was chronically tired, she had no appetite—not even for grilled steak or corn on the cob. Her hair, which had always been like corn silk, began falling out in ghastly clumps; in places, Brenda could see right through to her scalp. Vicki had a wig in one of the suitcases she'd brought from home, though Brenda couldn't bring herself to suggest Vicki wear it.

One morning, a Tuesday, a chemo morning, Brenda found Vicki in her room, rocking back and forth on the bed with both of the kids in her lap, crying.

"I don't want to go," she said. "Please don't make me go. They're trying to kill me."

"They're trying to help you, Vick," Brenda said.

"Mom's not going to the hospital today," Blaine said.

"Come on," Brenda said. "You're scaring the kids."

"I'm not going," Vicki said.

"Josh will be here any second," Brenda said. "You haven't made him anything for breakfast."

"I can't cook anymore," Vicki said. "Just looking at food makes me sick. If Josh is hungry, Melanie will make him something." This had happened two or three times now: With Vicki too sick to cook, Melanie had attempted to step in and cook for Josh. There had been a platter of scrambled eggs, somehow both watery and burned, and some limp, greasy bacon—after which Josh said he would be happy with just a bowl of Cheerios.

"You can't skip chemo, Vick. It's like any medicine. It's like antibiotics. If you stop taking it, even for one day, you'll go back to being sick."

"I'm not going," Vicki said.

"She's not going!" Blaine shouted. "She's staying home!"

Vicki made no move to shush Blaine or reprimand him for yelling at his aunt who was, it should be pointed out, *just trying to do the right thing!* The family was going to hell in a handbasket.

"I'll give you a few minutes," Brenda said. "But we are leaving at eight-thirty."

Brenda left the room, dreading her mother's inevitable phone call. *How is she?* Ellen Lyndon would ask. And what could Brenda possibly say? *She's scared. She's angry. She hurts.* It wasn't possible to give their mother a dose of that kind of unadulterated truth. *She's fine,* Brenda would say. *The kids are fine.*

As Brenda was feeling guilty for lies she hadn't even told yet, she heard the predictable crunch of tires on shells. Josh. Somehow, Brenda thought, Josh would keep them afloat. Now that Brenda was a regular communicator with God, she believed Josh had been sent to them for a reason. Brenda tiptoed down the flagstone path and met Josh by the gate. She was still in her nightgown and it was a misty, chilly morning. She crossed her arms over her chest.

He furrowed his brow. "You're not throwing rocks today?" he said. "Is something wrong?"

"Kind of," Brenda said. "I need your help."

"Okay," Josh said. Brenda saw his eyes brighten. In this, he was like Walsh. Being typically Australian, Walsh loved to help. "Anything."

"I need you to talk to Vicki."

Another person might have said, *Anything but that,* but Josh had no problem with Vicki. He liked her; he wasn't afraid of her cancer. He called her "Boss," and each day he teased her about her "non-list list."

"Okay," Josh said. "Sure. What about?"

"Just talk to her," Brenda said. "She needs a friend. She's sick of me."

"No problem," Josh said. "I'm here for you."

Brenda was about to lead him into the house, into Vicki's bedroom, but those words, *I'm here for you,* even though they were said in a casual, lighthearted way, nearly made Brenda weep with gratitude. She suspected that Josh wasn't a college student at all, but rather, an angel. Brenda placed her hands on his shoulders, stood on her tiptoes, and kissed him. He tasted young, like a piece of unripe fruit; his lips were soft. She felt him move toward her, he took hold of her waist.

Immediately, Brenda realized she'd made a mistake. What was *wrong* with her? Gently, she pushed Josh away. "I'm sorry," she said. "That was unfair of me."

"You are so beautiful," Josh said. "You know I think so."

Yes, Brenda knew it. She had seen how he looked at her in her nightgown and her bikini, but she had done nothing to encourage him. When they spoke, she was friendly but never more than friendly. If anything, she had worked to keep Josh at arm's length. The last thing she wanted was for anyone to think . . . But, as ever, her good judgment fled her for one instant. She had kissed him—and it was a real kiss—so now, suddenly, on top of everything else, she was a tease. She had so much on her mind, so many heavy, difficult things, that the idea that there was someone willing to help, even a little bit, overwhelmed her good sense. She had made a mess of nearly everything in her life, but she didn't want to make a mess with Josh.

"It was unfair of me because I'm in love with someone else," Brenda said. "Someone back in New York." She thought of the damn napkin tucked into her book; the ink was smeared now. *Call John Walsh!*

"Oh," Josh said. He looked pissed off. He had every reason to be; he had every reason to leave Number Eleven Shell Street and never come back, but Brenda hoped he wouldn't. She hoped he was here for reasons a lot more powerful than any crush he might have on her.

"You'll still talk to Vicki, won't you?" Brenda asked. "Please?"

He shrugged. His eyes were filled with hurt and boyish disappointment. "Sure," he said.

The bedroom was dim, with the muted morning light peeking in around the edges of the pulled shades. Vicki rocked on the bed, holding both kids, but Brenda lifted Porter out of Vicki's arms and said to Blaine, "Come on out now. We have pebbles to throw."

"I want to stay with Mommy," Blaine said.

"Outside," Brenda said. "Now."

"I need to talk to your mom anyway," Josh said. "I'll be out in a couple of minutes."

This was so unusual that neither Blaine nor Vicki protested. Blaine left quietly, shutting the door behind him, and Vicki fell back on the bed. She was wearing gray athletic shorts and a navy Duke T-shirt that hiked up her midsection. She was a lot thinner than she'd been when Josh first saw her at the airport. She was wearing a bandanna over her head like a rap star; her hair was nearly gone.

"Brenda told you I don't want to take my medicine?"

"Actually, she told me nothing," Josh said. "Except that she's in love with someone else, not me."

At this, Vicki made a noise somewhere between a laugh and a hiccup. Josh was astounded at his own candor. But there was something about Vicki that put him at ease. She was too young to be his mother, though there had been times in the past few weeks when he'd felt like she *was* his mother, and he had relished it. She was sort of like an older sister might have been, or a very cool older girl best friend, the kind he'd never been lucky enough to have. He called her "Boss" as a joke, though why this was a joke he wasn't sure; she was his boss. And yet she didn't come across as his boss, despite the fact that she was always telling him what she wanted him to do and she was always asking for a full report of his and the kids' activities—their every word and deed and fart—when he got home at one o'clock. Still, she gave the impression that *he* was the boss, that he was ultimately in charge—and that was, he supposed, why Brenda had asked him to come in and talk. Vicki would listen to him.

"She's in love with someone named John Walsh," Vicki said. She sat up, plucked a tissue off the nightstand, and blew her nose. "One of her students, back in New York. I can't believe she told you."

"I can't believe I told you she told me," Josh said. "I thought I was sent in here to talk about something else."

"You were," Vicki said. She sighed. "I'm not going to chemo."

"Why not?"

"I've had enough," Vicki said. "It's not helping. I can feel it not helping. It's hurting. It's killing me. You know what chemotherapy is, right? It's controlled poisoning. They try to poison the cancer cells, but most of the time they poison healthy cells, too. So the way I feel is that I used to have healthy cells and now all I have are poisoned cells. I am a vessel filled with vile green poison."

"You look the same to me," Josh said, though this was a lie.

"I can't eat," Vicki said. "I've lost twelve pounds, and I'm bald. I can't cook, I can't stay awake through a *Scooby-Doo,* I can't concentrate long enough to play Chutes and Ladders, I can't land a single pebble in the damn paper cup. I can't do anything. What was the point in coming to Nantucket if I only go outside to get to the hospital? I want to go to the beach, I want to swim, I want to drink my Chardonnay on the back deck, I want to feel better. I'm done with chemo. There was never a guarantee it was going to shrink my tumor anyway. It's just a gamble the doctors take, a gamble with *my body*. But I'm putting an end to it today. I'm all done."

"I'll point out the obvious," Josh said. "If you don't go to chemo, your cancer might get worse."

"It might," Vicki said. "Or it might stay the same."

"But if they think the chemo will help, you should take it. You have the kids to think about."

"You sound like my husband," Vicki said. "Which is too bad. One thing I really appreciate about you is that you're nothing like my husband."

Josh felt himself redden. He had yet to meet Vicki's husband, Ted Stowe, though he had heard about him in detail from the kids. Ted Stowe came every weekend, he was some kind of financial wizard in New York, and Blaine had let it slip that Ted didn't like Josh.

But I don't even know your dad, Josh said. *We've never met.*

Trust me, Blaine said. *He doesn't like you.*

If Ted Stowe didn't like Josh, then Josh was determined not to like Ted Stowe. Josh understood, however, that whereas he filled a certain role, there were other men—Ted Stowe, Melanie's husband, Peter, and now this guy Brenda was in love with—who filled another role, a more important, more substantial role, in their real lives, away from Nantucket.

Josh sat down on the bed next to Vicki. He felt himself about to become self-referential and he recalled another one of Chas Gorda's much-repeated phrases: *Be wary of your own story.* Josh tried to stop himself, but it was pointless. *Just this once,* he told himself.

"My mother died when I was twelve," he said. "She killed herself."

Vicki did him the favor of being matter-of-fact. So many women—the girls he met at Middlebury, Didi—met this statement with a gush of sympathy, as useless to Josh as a lace handkerchief.

"Did she?" Vicki said.

"She hanged herself while I was at school."

Vicki nodded, like she was waiting for the rest of it.

There was nothing else to say. Josh had bounded off the school bus and headed home just like any other day. Except that day, his father was in the living room sitting on the sofa, waiting for him. There were no police, no sirens or lights, no other people. It was the lack of other people that Tom Flynn chose to address first.

I told them to wait, Tom Flynn said. *They'll all pour in around suppertime.*

Who? Josh said.

Josh didn't remember any other exact words. His father got the story across somehow—he'd come home for lunch as always (this was back when he worked the six-to-three shift) and found that the stairs to the attic had been pulled down. It was December; Tom Flynn thought his wife was up searching for Christmas decorations. He called to her but got no answer. He climbed the attic stairs and found her dangling. Tom Flynn cut her down and drove her to the hospital, even though it was clear she was already dead. He'd never described to his son how his wife had looked or what she'd used to hang herself or how he'd felt as he cut her down. Was he shaking? Was he crying? These were things that Josh would never know; they were things he'd been protected from. Not knowing if his mother's face was discolored, or if her head had hung at a funny angle because her neck had snapped, kept Josh from having to relay these details to others.

"She didn't leave a note," Josh said. "So I'll never know why she did it."

"Do you hate her?" Vicki asked.

"No," Josh said. "But if you stop going to chemo today and your cancer gets worse and you die and leave Blaine and Porter motherless, I'll hate you."

Again, the noise, the laugh or the hiccup.

"No, you won't," Vicki said. But still, she stood up.

Melanie threw open the lower-left kitchen cabinet, yanked out the only decent frying pan in the house, and slammed it against the largest burner of the electric stove. She was furious!

For the first time in nearly two months she had woken up early, feeling not only okay but good. She had energy!—and she rifled through her dresser for her exercise clothes. She power walked through the misty, deserted streets of early morning 'Sconset—all the way to the town beach and back—swinging her arms, breathing in through her nose and out through her mouth, feeling like she had finally, finally turned a corner. All the pregnancy books described how healthy and vibrant and capable a woman felt while carrying a child, and now, today, Melanie understood. Gone were the sickness and the fatigue—she had blossomed.

But then she turned a literal corner—from New Street

onto Shell Street. She was on her way home, her heart pumping, her blood surging in a way she had missed; she was actually *hungry,* craving protein, a couple of eggs over easy on buttery toast. She was so busy thinking of breaking the bright yellow yolks of the eggs and of the health of the fetus inside of her, grateful for exercise and nourishment, that what she saw taking place down the street inside the white picket fence of Number Eleven didn't, at first, register. What Melanie witnessed was two people kissing, then embracing. Melanie recognized the people, of course, at least she recognized them separately, but together, as a couple, they made no sense. It was Josh and Brenda.

Melanie stopped in her tracks. She ducked down behind the neighbor's Peugeot, which was parked in the street. She could hear Brenda's voice, though not her actual words. Whatever Brenda said was beside the point; Melanie had seen Brenda and Josh kissing, she had watched Josh grab Brenda's hips. It was an awful scene, worse somehow than the vision of Peter lying with Frances Digitt in Frances's early-nineties-model Japanese futon on sheets covered with brown dog hair. At that moment, Peter and Frances seemed very far away, whereas this betrayal by Josh and Brenda was immediate; it was a betrayal in Melanie's new life, her safe summer life.

Forget the sense of well-being. Melanie was going to be sick. She retched by the Peugeot's front tire. Jealousy and anger bubbled up from the pit of her stomach. It was gross, disgusting, Brenda and Josh together. It wasn't fair, Melanie thought. She spat at the ground, her knees wobbled. She raised her head, ready to catch them in the act, but the front yard was empty. They were gone.

Melanie took a shorter walk to the 'Sconset Market for a Gatorade, all the time talking to herself in her mind, and occasionally muttering a word or two out loud like a crazy person. Utterly revolting. Unacceptable. Josh was twenty-two. He was the babysitter. And yet there they'd been, in the front yard, like a couple of horny teenagers, Brenda still in her stripper's excuse for a nightgown. Melanie gulped the Gatorade and walked slowly back to the house, nurturing her hatred of Brenda. Brenda was a . . . slut, she was easy, she was after every man she met, she targeted them for sport, like a shameless game hunter poaching elephants for ivory or tigers for rugs. She had no scruples, she'd slept with her student, the Australian who had phoned. Next thing they all knew, she'd be after Ted Stowe—that was only logical with Vicki so sick—Brenda would sleep with her own brother-in-law.

"Arrumph," Melanie said. She walked down a side street in search of her favorite pocket garden. Brenda was as treacherous as Frances Digitt, as deficient in honor and integrity. What did she care if she slept with somebody else's husband? Melanie gazed at the neat patch of iris and bachelor's button. She closed her eyes and saw Brenda and Josh kissing.

Josh.

By the time Melanie got back to the house, the Yukon was gone, which meant Brenda had taken Vicki to chemo. Melanie stormed into the house, flinging open the screen door. Her body was still craving the eggs, and thus Melanie went rip-roaring through the kitchen slamming doors and surfaces, thinking, *Bitch, slut, bitch.* It felt like her hair was standing on end, like her skin was going to blister and pop.

"Are you okay?"

Melanie whipped around. Josh had emerged from Vicki's bedroom holding the baby. Blaine stood next to Josh, a mini-Josh, as he now emulated Josh's every word and gesture; his face held the same look of baffled interest. Melanie swilled the last of her Gatorade and pitched the empty bottle, with no small amount of force, into the kitchen trash.

"I'm *fine*," she said, making sure the word sounded as far from its actual meaning as possible. She turned her back on them. On the stove, the empty frying pan started to smoke. She dropped a pat of butter into the pan then pulled eggs out of the fridge, flinging the door open and shut so violently that the poor old fridge shuddered. Really, it was impossible to hate Josh, he was infuriatingly adorable, standing there with the kids. The boys loved him, he loved the boys, it made him irresistible. Damn it! This was awful. Melanie was jealous, as jealous as she'd ever been in her life. She wanted Josh to like *her,* she wanted Josh to kiss *her* in the front yard. She wanted Josh to look at her the way he looked at Brenda. Never mind that he was so young. He was an adult, sort of, a young man, kindhearted and well raised, as quality a person as a woman could ask for, and with the way Melanie was feeling, she might have been only fourteen herself. *I have a crush on him,* she thought. So embarrassing to admit, but true. I like him. I love him. This is ridiculous! Melanie cracked the eggs into the pan, where they sizzled. There was no noise behind her and she was afraid to turn around. Let him wonder what was wrong. Let him guess. Melanie salted her eggs and tried to flip them but failed. She was making a mess. She dropped two pieces of bread into the toaster. The room was silent and Melanie figured the boys had slipped out or retreated to the safety of the bedroom, but when she turned around to check, the three of them were sitting at the kitchen table, watching her.

"What?" she said. "Aren't you going to the beach?"

"In a little while," Josh said.

"These eggs are for me," Melanie said. "If you want to make your own breakfast when I'm finished, be my guest."

"I'm all set," Josh said. "If you're eating, you must be feeling better."

"I do feel better," Melanie said. She buttered the toast and slid the jumbled egg mess on top, then sat down.

"You seem really angry," Josh said. "Is it your husband?"

"No," Melanie said. "For once, it's not my husband."

"Is it anything you want to talk about?" Josh asked.

She glanced up from her plate. He was looking at her very intently. He was looking at her the way she wanted him to look at her, or maybe she was just imagining this. Those green eyes. Porter was working his pacifier, his head resting against Josh's chest. Melanie had hoped that because Josh was young, he would be different. He wouldn't have taken for granted, yet, his power over women. But clearly he understood it. He knew all of Peter Patchen's tricks and then some. It came with the territory of being handsome and strong and accomplished and, no doubt, spoiled by his mother. Any which way, he was showing what could only be described as undivided interest in Melanie for the first time ever, when less than an hour before, he'd been kissing Brenda. Was this some kind of parlor game—seduce all the women at Number Eleven Shell Street? Would Vicki be next?

"I have to pee," Blaine announced. He looked to Josh, as if for permission, and Josh nodded, his eyes still trained on Melanie. Blaine left the table.

Melanie cut into her eggs; the yolks weren't as runny as she'd hoped. "I saw you kissing Brenda," she said.

Josh hissed like a balloon losing air and leaned back in his chair. "Yeah," he said. "She kissed me, actually."

"It didn't look terribly one-sided," Melanie said.

"I thought maybe she meant something by it," he said. "But she didn't. She was just feeling desperate, you know, about Vicki, and she wanted my help." He shifted Porter in his arms and brushed his lips against the top of Porter's head. Melanie ate her eggs and toast. She couldn't bear to hear any more, and yet she had to know.

"Help how?"

"Talk to Vicki. Get her to go to chemo. Which I did, I guess. I mean, I don't know if *I* did anything, but she went."

Melanie nodded. The bereft, third-wheel, left-out feeling returned. There were dramas taking place all over this house that she didn't even know about. "So, what about Brenda?"

"Well, she's in love with someone else," Josh said. "Some student of hers back in New York."

"John Walsh," Melanie said. She took another, more

lustful bite of her eggs. Her anger and confusion were starting to clear. Melanie heard the toilet flush and Blaine called out for Josh. He smiled and stood up.

"So . . . whatever. It's no big deal. She digs somebody else. I mean . . . well, you know how it is."

"Yes," Melanie said. "I do."

PART TWO

❧

JULY

Brenda had been on Nantucket for more than three full weeks, and she had gotten nowhere on the damned screenplay. Day after day she left the house by nine o'clock for the beach, and she settled on her deserted stretch of sand with a thermos of coffee and her yellow legal pad. She knew the story of *The Innocent Impostor* so intimately it was as if she had written it herself. The book would make a great movie if she could get it right. It was an undiscovered classic with lots of drama and an ambiguous moral message. Brenda could keep it period, cast John Malkovich as Calvin Dare and dress him in frilly lace-collared shirts and a wig. Or maybe she should modernize it: turn Calvin Dare into a Jersey City construction worker who accidentally kills Thomas Beech with his Datsun 300ZX while backing out of a parking space at Shea Stadium after a Bruce Springsteen concert—and who then, through some carefully constructed coincidences, takes over for Beech on the trading floor of Goldman Sachs and starts dating Beech's fiancée, Emily, who manages the Kate Spade store in Soho. Brenda could visualize the movie as a huge critical and commercial success either way. She even had a tenuous connection in the "business"—her former student Amy Feldman's father, who was the president of Marquee Films.

But she couldn't write.

All her life, Brenda had been easily distracted. To work, she needed solitude and absolute quiet. Her parents had arranged for this in high school—Ellen Lyndon turned off the classical music she played on a Bose radio in the kitchen, she turned off the ringer on the phone, she allowed Brenda to skip dinner in order to study in the strictly silent reserve room of the Bryn Mawr College library. And then, in college and graduate school, Brenda sought out places where no one would ever discover her so she could have long, uninterrupted hours of reading and writing. She dead-bolted her apartment door and pulled her shades. One year for Christmas Vicki gave her a sign to hang from her door: *Do Not Disturb: Genius at work.* This was all very tongue in cheek; Vicki was the last person who understood single-mindedness. She had been born a multitasker before such a talent even had a name. But Brenda couldn't think about two things at once, much less four or five things, and therein lay her problem. How was she supposed to write a screenplay when her mind was crowded with the details of her disgrace, her legal and monetary worries, her absorbing concern for Vicki and the kids—and most of all, her lingering obsession with John Walsh?

Brenda couldn't stop thinking about Walsh. It was absurd! Brenda was now thinking that *she* should go to the doctor—she needed medication or, better still, surgery. *Remove the obsession with John Walsh. It's eating me up like cancer; it's growing in me like a baby.*

In three weeks, John Walsh had called only once, right at the beginning, on the day that Blaine was lost and then found, when Melanie answered Brenda's cell phone and scribbled the message that Brenda had since kept tucked inside her copy of *The Innocent Impostor*. She hadn't heard Walsh's voice since she left New York; she hadn't seen his face. He had pledged his love so ardently, so convincingly, that she thought the phone calls would be as incessant as those from her mother and Brian Delaney, Esquire; she thought Walsh would pursue her until she gave in. But no: There had been the one phone call and that was it. How typically Australian he was! *If you want me,* he was no doubt thinking, *you know where to find me.* Or maybe he just didn't love her anymore. Maybe he took her words to heart and decided that nothing good could come of their relationship. Maybe now that Brenda's career was in tatters and her good name sullied, he had lost interest. Maybe he had met someone else. It was fruitless to speculate, but she couldn't help wondering how he was spending his summer days in the city. Was he back working for the construction company? Was he sitting on scaffolding, hard-hatted and shirtless, eating a sandwich out of a metal lunch box? What did he do at night? Was he working the slow summer-evening shift at the law library as Brenda hoped—or was he out at the clubs, dancing and sleeping around? All of the girl-women in Brenda's second-semester class had been in love with him—even Kelly Moore, the purple-haired soap opera actress, even Ivy, the lesbian, and especially Amrita, the brownnoser. That had been the problem.

Brenda felt like she was trying to scramble out of a gravel pit but couldn't unbury her feet. She found it impossible to concentrate. Every five or six minutes she would stare at her yellow legal pad and see the faint blue lines and the empty space between them and she would admonish herself. "Focus!" But the movie playing in her mind wasn't *The Innocent Impostor*. The two reels endlessly spinning were Brenda and Walsh Together (*The Joy Ride*) and Brenda and Walsh Torn Apart (*The Crash*).

Brenda set her notebook aside and lay back on her towel, raised her face to the sun. She preferred to indulge in the first reel. *The Joy Ride*. The night Brenda and Walsh first got together had started out innocently enough. Brenda met her best friend and forever-secret-true-love, Erik vanCott, and his girlfriend, Noel, at Café des Bruxelles for *moules et frites*. Brenda hated Noel—she had always hated Erik's girlfriends—but she especially hated Noel because, according to Erik, Noel was "marriage material." Erik had actually spoken these words out loud, forcing Brenda to face a tough reality: Erik would, most likely, spend his life with someone else, someone who was not Brenda, despite her years of devotion and despite Brenda and Erik's rich, shared history. Brenda understood that she needed to break away from Erik; loving him was like staying on the *Titanic* and drowning in her stateroom. However, she couldn't give him up cold turkey, and to see Erik these days meant also seeing Noel.

Noel's eyes were a warm yellow-brown and her hair was as long and luxurious as a fur coat. She was wearing a white cashmere sweater and little pearl earrings. The three of them were seated at a table meant for two, with Brenda stuck off the side like a tumor. Before the famed *frites* even hit the table, a startling thing happened: Erik and Noel started fighting. Noel wasn't eating, and Erik had chosen this night of all nights to accuse her of being anorexic.

"You're not having any bread?"

"It's my business what I eat. Why do you care?"

"Why do I care? Are you asking me why I *care*?"

Brenda, meanwhile, busied herself with the crusty bread; she slathered it with butter as Eric looked on approvingly. "That's my girl," Erik said. "Brenda really knows how to eat."

"Yeah, well," Brenda said. "You know me. Indiscriminate."

A while later, the mussels arrived, with the fries: Noel made a face.

"You really don't want any?" Erik said to her. "Not a single *frite*?"

"No," she said.

"That's okay," Erik said. "That's just fine. Brenda will have some, won't you, Brenda?"

Brenda looked between Erik and Noel. She was being lobbed like a grenade at Noel's fortress. That was what happened when you were a single person out with a couple; you were either ignored or used as ammunition. Thus, Brenda did the only reasonable thing: She pretended to excuse herself for the ladies' room and she snuck out of the restaurant.

She stood on Greenwich Avenue at nine o'clock on a Friday night, with people streaming around her like a river around a rock, unsure of what to do next. Her confidence bobbled around like it was attached to a spring. She couldn't decide if walking out of the restaurant had been a brilliant move or an unforgivably rude one. What would her mother think? At that moment, Brenda's cell phone rang. *John Walsh,* the display said. She knew she should let the call go to her voice mail—because what were the chances John Walsh was calling to ask about the syllabus? However, Brenda was reeling from Erik and Noel–caused anxiety. Her good sense splattered all over the sidewalk, like she had dropped a melon. She answered the phone.

Brenda met John Walsh at the Cupping Room on Broome Street. She arrived first and ordered a fat glass of Cabernet to calm her nerves, and lo and behold, the bartender informed her that a man at the end of the bar had offered to pay for it. What man? A portly man in a suit with a gray handlebar mustache. A man slightly younger than Brenda's father. Brenda felt flattered, then creeped out. She was swimming in unfamiliar waters: She was alone in a bar waiting for her student to show up, and a stranger wanted to buy her drink. What was the etiquette here?

"Thank you," Brenda said to the bartender. "That's very nice. But I'm meeting someone."

"Fair enough," the bartender said. Meaning what, exactly?

No time to think because in the door strolled Walsh, looking so handsome that everyone at the bar stared at him, not least of all the man with the handlebar mustache. Walsh was wearing a black shirt and a black leather jacket, and with his close-cropped hair, his skin, his eyes, well, he was a lethal dose of something. College sophomore. Ha! Brenda took a mouthful of wine, hoping it didn't turn her teeth blue, and stood up.

He kissed her.

One of her heels slipped on something wet under the bar and she fell back. He caught her arm.

"Hi," she said.

"Hello." He grinned. "I can't believe you agreed to meet me."

That made two of them.

"This is very bad," Brenda said. "You're my student. If anyone sees us . . ."

"We're in Soho," Walsh said. "It's like another country."

For the next three hours, Brenda decided to pretend this was true. She drank her wine and Walsh drank Tanqueray. At first, Walsh talked, which allowed Brenda to obsess. *College sophomore, my student, what the fuck am I doing?* He told Brenda about the town he came from in Western Australia. Fremantle. South Beach, the Cappuccino Strip, the seafood restaurants on the harbor, the weekend markets, the taste of a passion fruit while sitting under a Norfolk pine with the Fremantle Doctor sweeping in off the Indian Ocean. The waves at Cottesloe, a day of sailing on the Swan, the wine and cheese from Margaret River. His family lived in a hundred-year-old limestone-and-brick bungalow in South Fremantle: his mum and dad, his sister, a niece and nephew he had only seen in pictures. His sister's partner, Eddie, lived there, too, though Eddie and the sister weren't married and to

make matters a bit more dickey—that was his word and
Brenda couldn't help grinning—Eddie was on the dole.

"Not to give you all the grim details up front," Walsh
said. "My mum has a rose garden and my dad finally
joined the twenty-first and bought a digital camera, so
he sends me pictures of the roses and the tots doddering
among the roses."

"Sounds lovely," Brenda said. And it did.

"It's paradise," Walsh said. "But there was no way for
me to know that until I left, only now that I'm here, it's
hard to get back."

"Will you go back?" Brenda asked.

"Either that or break my mum's heart."

The bartender appeared and Walsh ordered a burger.
Did Dr. Lyndon want anything?

"Please don't," she said.

"Don't what?"

"Call me Dr. Lyndon. Do it again and I'll leave."

He grinned. "Okay, then, Brenda." He pronounced it
"Brindah." "Want a burger?"

"I'll have a bite of yours, if that's okay."

"No worries. My burger is your burger."

"I ate a little something earlier," she said, and with
that, she ordered another glass of wine.

"You were out?"

"I was out." She told Walsh the short story of her
aborted dinner with Erik and Noel, then the long story of
Erik. "I've loved him since I was sixteen," Brenda said.
"Normally people grow up and move on. But not me."

"I reckon love at sixteen is the best kind of love," Walsh
said. "For its purity. I loved a girl named Copper Shay,
Abo girl, poorest girl I ever knew, and I loved her all the

more for it. When I think about Copper I think of choices I could have made that would have put me back in Freo with Copper and four or five kids, and I bet I would have been happy. But that wasn't how things worked out."

"No," Brenda said, and she was glad.

Another glass of wine and they were kissing. Their bar stools were practically on top of each other, and Walsh had his knees on either side of her legs. When he kissed her, his knees pressed her legs together, and Brenda couldn't help thinking about sex. At the end of the bar there was laughter, some sneaky applause, and Brenda thought, *Everyone is watching us,* but when she looked up, no one was doing anything but drinking and minding their own business, except the man with the handlebar mustache, who winked and raised a glass in their direction.

"You're not thinking of Erik now, are you?" Walsh asked.

"No," she said. "I'm not."

At quarter to one, Walsh switched to water. He had a rugby game in the morning at Van Cortlandt Park, he said. Did she want to come watch?

"I can't," she said. She was swimming in four glasses of wine, plus the drinks she'd imbibed earlier in the evening to blur the image of marriage-material non-eating Noel, and now, in this dark bar with the sexy jazz playing, she was a hostage to some very new feelings. She liked this guy, *really* liked him. The one man in Manhattan who was off-limits . . . and here they were.

"Okay," she said, pulling away, disentangling, trying

to orient herself with her bag, her cell phone, her keys, some money for the bill, her coat. "I have to go."

"Yes," said Walsh, yawning. He gave the waiter the high sign and a credit card slip arrived. Walsh, somehow, had already paid.

"Thank you," she said. "You salvaged my night."

"No worries." He kissed her.

She touched his ears, she ruffled his very short hair. She was melting away with desire. She wanted to hear his accent vibrate against her chest—but enough! He had rugby and she had . . .

"Cab?" Walsh said.

"I'll get my own," Brenda said. "East Side, you know."

"You sure? We can still share."

"I'm sure."

"Okay, then." Kiss, another kiss. Another, longer kiss. "I'll see you Tuesday. Brindah."

"Tuesday?"

"In class."

Brenda stood up from her beach towel; she felt dizzy. She walked toward the ocean. She had made no progress on the screenplay again today, and tomorrow was Friday, which meant taking Vicki to chemo, which meant Ted instead of Josh, which meant Brenda would be called in as backup to watch the kids and keep the peace. She had agreed to these duties wholeheartedly. (*Repentance,* she thought. *Atonement.*) This weekend they had an excursion to Smith's Point planned, complete with bonfire and boxed-up lobster dinners, in an attempt to get Vicki out of the cottage, to get her eating, to get her engaged in the summer and family life—and yet what this *really* meant was that no work got pursued again until Monday.

Brenda waded out past the first set of gently breaking waves and dove under. She wondered what the water felt like in Australia. Back at her towel, she scrolled through the previous ten calls to her cell phone, just in case Walsh had called during her three-minute dip, just in case she had missed his number in the hundred other times she had checked her messages. No, nothing. Brenda had left her copy of *The Innocent Impostor* at home in the briefcase, where it would be safe from the sand and salt air, but if she closed her eyes, she could see the smeared note. *Call John Walsh!*

She would call him; she would invite him to come to Nantucket. The beach, the swimming, the fresh air—he would love it here. Did Walsh like lobster? Probably. Being typically Australian, he would eat anything (including, he used to tease Brenda, what he called "bush tucker"—grubs, tree bark, snail eggs). But no sooner had Brenda punched the first four digits into her phone—1-212 (*I could be calling anyone in Manhattan,* she thought)— than the second reel started spinning against her will. *The Crash.* Brenda tried to block out the dominant image, but it came to her anyway. The Jackson Pollock painting.

It had taken weeks for Brenda to discover the painting's allure, but then, in the days when she was falling in love with Walsh, she became entranced by it. She had a favorite blue line in the painting that ran like a vein from a massive black tangle. The blue was a strand of reason emerging from chaos. Or so she had thought.

You will never work in academia again, Suzanne Atela had said, the harshness in her voice belied by her lilting

Bahamian accent. *I will see to it personally. As for the vandalism charges . . .*

Vandalism charges: The phrase sounded so crass, so trashy. Vandalism was a teenage girl taking a Sharpie to the bathroom wall, it was hoodlums spray-painting the skateboard park or breaking the front window of a pizzeria. It had nothing to do with Brenda and Mrs. Pencaldron exchanging words in the Barrington Room. But Brenda had been so, so angry, so confused and frustrated; she had wanted to *throw something!* Even as Mrs. Pencaldron shrieked and ordered Augie Fisk to stand in the doorway, lest Brenda try to escape, even as campus security arrived, Brenda could not take her eyes off the painting. The nasty black snarl mesmerized her; it was like hair caught in a drain, like real feelings shredded by a series of bad decisions.

A hundred and sixty thousand dollars, plus legal fees. This was only the monetary price; this did not even begin to address the damage done to Brenda's reputation. She would never work in academia again.

Call John Walsh! the note shouted. But no, she couldn't do it. She shut off her phone.

~~~

The first of July came and went—and still there was no sign of the two hundred and ten dollars from Didi. Josh wasn't surprised; lending money to Didi was as good as flushing it down the toilet. He wrote a threatening letter to Didi in his journal (*You need to grow up! Take responsibility for your actions! You can't keep jumping in the deep end and then crying out because you're drowning!*).

Writing was cathartic, and Josh decided to count himself lucky for not enabling Didi a second time. When she'd asked for more money, he had said no, and he hadn't heard from her since. She did not appear in the parking lot of Nobadeer Beach and she had stopped leaving drunk, late-night messages on his cell phone. Josh would have been happy to let the loan fade from his memory, but the problem was that somebody—Josh would never know who—had mentioned the loan to Tom Flynn, and in the world of Tom Flynn, when you lent out money that you'd earned with your own two hands, you should damn well make a point to get it back. Much to Josh's dismay, the topic came up at dinner.

"You lent the Patalka girl money?"

Josh had started dating Didi sophomore year in high school—so, six years earlier—and Tom Flynn still (and had always) referred to her as "the Patalka girl."

"She was in a pinch, she said."

"She always says. Doesn't she have a job now?"

"At the hospital," Josh said, though his father knew this.

"Then why . . ."

"Because she was in a *pinch,* Dad," Josh said. He did not want to be tricked into saying anything more. "I'll get it back."

"See that you do," Tom Flynn said. "What's yours is yours. You aren't working to support her. She doesn't have college bills to pay."

"I know that, Dad," Josh said. "I'll get it back."

Tom Flynn said nothing else, which was unfortunate because the "I'll get it back" hung in the air as the final words on the topic, making them into a promise Josh knew he couldn't fulfill. He would never, in a million years, call Didi up to ask for the money, if for no other reason than she obviously didn't have it and any exchange with her on the topic would be depressing and pointless.

And so, when Vicki mentioned, a few days later, that she wanted Josh to join them on an evening picnic out to Smith's Point on Saturday night, he said yes right away, thinking it would mean another hundred dollars that he could tell his father was from Didi. But it quickly became clear that Saturday night wasn't an invitation to work; it was simply an invitation. The Three were getting lobster dinners from Sayle's, they were going to build a bonfire and make s'mores with the kids, they were going to light sparklers and locate constellations and, if the water was warm enough, go for a nighttime swim.

"My husband, Ted, will be there," Vicki said. "I really think it's time you two met and hung out a little."

At that point, Josh tried to backpedal. His role at Number Eleven Shell Street was becoming blurry enough without having him join in on family beach picnics. And the last thing Josh wanted to do was meet Ted Stowe. Normally, Josh left Number Eleven at one o'clock on Friday afternoon and Ted arrived around four; Ted left on Sunday night and Josh returned at eight o'clock on Monday morning. With this schedule in place, Josh had hopes of avoiding Ted Stowe altogether—at least until Ted took his vacation at the end of August. Josh feared two things from Ted Stowe—his dislike (already in place) and his judgment. Josh, in one fleeting but beautiful moment, had kissed Brenda, and now he was starting to pick up funny vibes from Melanie. Ted might perceive this; he might, as the only other man in the house, sense a connection between Josh and one or more of the women. Josh didn't want to get fired, or beat up, by Ted Stowe. And so, a day after he'd agreed to go on the beach picnic, he took the path of least resistance and approached Brenda.

He caught her on his way out to his Jeep at one o'clock. She was returning from the beach with her notebook, her thermos, and her cell phone.

"How goes the screenplay?" he said.

"Don't ask," she said.

"Okay," he said. "I won't. Hey, listen—I can't make the picnic thing on Saturday night. I just remembered, I have something else. You'll tell Vicki?"

Brenda gnawed her lower lip. "Ohhhh," she said. "Shit."

"What?"

"Vicki really wants you to come," Brenda said. "I mean, she's talked about how much she wants you there. To meet Ted. He's bringing fishing rods so you guys can surf cast."

"Us guys?" Josh said. "Surf cast?"

"With Blaine," Brenda said. She took a deep breath; her chest rose and fell. Josh tried not to look. She was in love with someone else. "I'm afraid if you cancel, Vicki will do something funny. Like bag the whole thing. With the way she is now, that's exactly what she'll do. Toss the whole night out the window. And it's really important that we get her out. We have to boost her spirits."

"Right," Josh said. "But it's a family picnic. I'm not a part of your family."

"Neither is Melanie," Brenda said. "And she's going."

Josh looked at the ground. Thinking about Melanie only confused him further.

"Is there any way you can reschedule the other thing?" Brenda said. "Any way at all?" She lowered her voice. "I'm happy to pay you."

"No, no, no," Josh said quickly. He felt like his true motivation had been discovered and it embarrassed him. "You don't have to pay me. I'll come."

Brenda looked so happy and so relieved that Josh thought she might kiss him again. But no such luck. She just smiled in a really nice way and touched his arm. "Thank you," she whispered. "Thank you."

The high-performance rating of two fishing rods bought from Urban Angler on Fifth Avenue, the Yukon's tire pressure, four wooden pallets "borrowed" from the Stop & Shop, five adult lobster dinners complete with boiled new potatoes, corn on the cob, Caesar salad, buttermilk biscuits, half a dozen cherrystone clams, and a two-pound cooked and cracked lobster with drawn butter, a cooler full of Chardonnay and Stella Artois, three perfectly whittled roasting sticks, a box of graham crackers, a bag of marshmallows, a twenty-four-ounce Hershey's bar, a package of sparklers purchased in Chinatown, the National Audubon Society's Guide to the Constellations.

Vicki didn't care about the beach picnic. Any other year she would have been the organizing force—did they have bug spray? Was the beach permit prominently displayed on the bumper? Did they have jumper cables, just in case, and a tow rope? Were there hot dogs for the kids, and ketchup, and juice boxes? Did they bring baby powder to get the sand off the kids' feet? Extra diapers? Porter's bottle of warm milk? Trash bags? A corkscrew and a bottle opener? The camera? Now, Vicki lay back in bed, listening to Ted and Brenda and Melanie trying to cover all this ground in her stead. She didn't care. She had gone from feeling like her body was a box of broken toys to feeling nothing at all. A week earlier, in response to her complaints, to her tears, to her tantrum, Dr. Alcott had prescribed a new medication—for depression, he said. For six days, the world had come in and out of focus as Vicki's consciousness nuzzled the ceiling like a lazy balloon. It was a hundred times worse than pain; this loopiness, this numbness, this sense of disconnect from the real world—the island, the cottage, the people in the cottage, the kids. On Thursday, Vicki flushed the pills, which, she understood, was only a precursor to what she would do the following day. What she did on Friday was skip chemo.

It had been a piece of cake because Brenda was Vicki's gatekeeper, and although Brenda was doing a good job, exemplary even, Vicki knew Brenda inside and out and playing to her sister's weaknesses was *a piece of cake*. Friday morning they slipped into the car—discreetly, as always, so as not to alert the kids—and Vicki noticed the yellow legal pad and *The Innocent Impostor* crammed into Brenda's handbag. This was unusual because although Brenda took the yellow legal pad with her everywhere else, she had never once brought it to chemo. Chemo, for whatever reason, was the time Brenda reserved for reading out-of-date *People* magazines.

"Are you planning on writing today?" Vicki asked.

"I'm really behind," Brenda said.

"You know, you don't have to stay at the hospital with me," Vicki said. "In fact, the more I think about it, the more I think it's a waste of your time. I know the ropes now, and the team takes good care of me. They've never needed you for any reason. Why don't you just drop me off at the door and—oh, I don't know—go get a cup of coffee and sit and write at the Even Keel? You'd probably get a lot of work done."

"You're probably right."

"You should do it."

"I should."

"I mean it, Bren. It's two free hours. Come back and get me at eleven."

Brenda bit her bottom lip and said nothing further on the topic, but Vicki knew her sister. There was no chance that Brenda, after so many years devoted to quiet work—graduate school, dissertation, lecture prep, research—would be able to turn down this offer. Vicki's heart galloped at the thought of sweet escape. It would be just this once, like a single day of school skipped. There would be no needles, no poison, no Ben or Amelia or Mamie, no ESPN, no antiseptic hospital smell, and—for one summer weekend—no side effects. By next Tuesday, Vicki's resolve would return; she would store up strength and courage and she would walk back into the Oncology Unit, cheerfully even—if only she could get away with today.

Brenda pulled into the parking lot. She was still gnawing her lower lip, debating maybe, if it would seem selfish to . . .

"Just drop me off," Vicki said.

Brenda sighed. "Oh, Vick, are you *sure*?"

"Sure I'm sure. Go write. I'll be fine."

"I don't know . . ."

"You're worried about missing your update on Britney Spears?"

Brenda laughed. "No."

"Come back at eleven," Vicki said.

Brenda pulled up to the hospital entrance and Vicki hopped out. She caught a glimpse of Brenda's face as she drove away; Brenda looked like she felt as happy and as free as Vicki now did.

Vicki had spent her two stolen hours lounging in the shade of the Old Mill. Although it was a short walk from the hospital—a good arm could hit it with a baseball—it was as far as Vicki could get, and by the time she made it to the top of the hill, she was close to hyperventilating. She lay in the grass, hidden from passing traffic, and stared up at the sky, at the arms of the windmill slicing the sky into pieces of pie. For two hours she did nothing—and how long had it been since she did *nothing*? Even the hours spent in bed in the cottage felt like work; she was busy recovering, willing her body to fight, and she always kept one eye on the activity in the house—Brenda and Melanie, Josh and the kids. She was always trying to summon the energy to read a page of her book or a section of the newspaper so that her day wasn't a complete waste. But here, on Prospect Hill, in the shadow of what was still a functioning windmill, Vicki was set free from the rigors of recovery. No one knew where she was, and hence, it was as if she had ceased to exist. This was hooky, plain and simple. She harbored the singular delight of getting away with something. Mamie might call the house, but no one would be home to answer the phone. On Tuesday, Vicki would say she forgot (forgot chemotherapy?) or the car broke down or one of the kids got sick. Or maybe she would admit that she just didn't want to come. She needed a break. A personal day. *You know what they say about hitting yourself over the head with a hammer,* she would tell Mamie. *It feels good when you stop.*

It was only when Brenda swung back by to pick her up—Brenda getting out of the car to hold Vicki's arm and help her into the passenger seat because this was what Vicki normally required—that the guilt set in.

"How was it?" Brenda asked. "How are you feeling?"

These were the standard questions, but Vicki was at a loss for how to respond. What to say? What did she normally say?

She shrugged.

"The team had a game last night, right?" Brenda asked. "Did they win or lose?"

Again, Vicki shrugged. Did a shrug count as a lie?

On the way back to 'Sconset, Vicki opened her window and hung her elbow out; she tried to absorb the sunshine and the summer air. The bike path was crowded with people walking and cycling, people with dogs and children in strollers. *I skipped chemo,* Vicki thought. Suddenly, she felt monstrous. She recalled Dr. Garcia's words about the value of neoadjuvant chemo, hitting the cells hard, in succession. Kill them, clean them out of there, make it that much harder for the cells to metastasize. The tumor was impinging on her chest wall; it had to recede in order for the surgeons to operate. Chemo was a cumulative process. The most important thing was consistency. So . . . what was going on here? Did she not want to get better? Could she not endure the pain, the hair loss, and the confusion for the sake of her *children*?

And what about Dr. Alcott? How had she managed to fly in the face of his reaction? He would be all ready with his usual pep talk—*How do you feel? Are you hanging in there? You're a trouper, a star patient.* . . . He would wonder where Vicki was, he would call the house himself, maybe, and what if Melanie was home, what if she rushed in from the garden to answer the phone? *She went to chemo,* Melanie would say. *I saw her leave.* There would be no reason for any further pep talks because Vicki was *not* a trouper. She was not a star patient at all.

By the time they reached Shell Street, Vicki's guilt was paralyzing. She could barely breathe—but maybe this was a result of the missed chemo, maybe the cancer cells were strengthening, multiplying. She was no better than Josh's mother, hanging herself while Josh was at school. Vicki was committing her own murder.

Now, there was a knock on the front door, and Vicki sat bolt upright. She fingered the wig on her nightstand. It rested on a Styrofoam head that Blaine had named Daphne after the character in *Scooby-Doo*. Blaine had gone so far as to draw Daphne a face with his markers— two blue circles for eyes, two black dots meant to be nostrils, and a crooked red mouth. The Styrofoam head made Ted uncomfortable—last weekend he'd said he couldn't make love while the head was on the nightstand because he felt like someone was watching them—and the wig, as badly as she needed it, made Vicki shiver. She had tried to put both the wig and the head on the top shelf of the bedroom closet, out of sight, but Blaine had cried over this. *Daphne!* So on the nightstand Daphne now sat, like some twisted excuse for a pet. The wig was made from real hair. Vicki had gotten it from a shop in the city that Dr. Garcia recommended, a place that made wigs solely for cancer patients. The wig was blond, approximately the same color as Vicki's own hair. It didn't look bad on, but it gave Vicki the willies—another person's hair on her head. She was reminded of her sixth-grade science teacher, Mr. Upjohn, and his toupee. And so when the knock came at the door—meaning Josh had arrived—Vicki called out for Brenda. Brenda came right away, holding Porter, who was dressed in a diaper and bathing trunks.

Don't forget sweatshirts for the kids! Vicki almost said—but no, there wasn't time for that, she could remind Brenda later.

"Scarf!" she barked.

"Right," Brenda said. "Sorry." She set Porter down and plucked a scarf out of Vicki's top dresser drawer. Red, gold, gauzy: a very chic Louis Vuitton scarf that Ellen Lyndon had given Vicki for Christmas two years earlier. Brenda wound it deftly around Vicki's half-bald head until it was tied tight with two tails flowing down Vicki's back.

"Thank you," Vicki said. She climbed out of bed and peeked into the living room. She didn't give a hoot about the picnic but she was anxious about the moment that Josh met Ted. She wanted Josh to like Ted, to admire him; she wanted Josh to think that she, Vicki, had chosen well.

Because Vicki and Brenda were in the bedroom dealing with the scarf, however, Melanie had been left to do the introduction. Melanie knew Vicki was nervous about it. *It will be fine,* Melanie assured her. *Who wouldn't like Josh?*

It's not Josh I'm worried about, Vicki said.

Oh, Melanie said. *Well, who wouldn't like Ted? Ted is a great guy.*

He can be, Vicki said.

Now Melanie sounded as perky and confident as a talk show host on amphetamines.

"Hi, Josh! How are you? Come in, come in! *Ted,* this is the kids' babysitter, Josh Flynn. Josh, this is *Vicki's husband,* Ted Stowe."

Blaine locked his arms around Josh's legs in a way that seemed more possessive than usual. Ted would notice this, Vicki thought, and not like it.

Josh extended an arm as far as he could and gave Ted one of his gorgeous smiles. "Hey, Mr. Stowe. It's nice to meet . . . heard a lot about . . . yeah."

Ted regarded Josh's outstretched hand and took a prolonged swill of his Stella. Vicki could almost hear Josh thinking, *Rude bastard, Wall Street asshole.* Vicki watched her husband's face. Josh was clearly not a pedophile, that would be a relief to Ted; Josh was not so different from the kid that Ted had been fifteen years ago, when he played lacrosse at Dartmouth. But Ted might also be thinking Josh was too much like Ted himself at that age—and what would Ted have done, working all week for three beautiful women who lived alone? He would have tried to . . . He would have done his best to . . .

Oh, come on! Vicki thought. The scarf tickled the back of her neck. It seemed like Josh's hand was just *hanging* there; Ted was torturing him. But then Ted set his beer down with a definitive *thunk* and he stepped forward and shook Josh's hand with such force that Josh rattled.

"Same here, buddy," Ted said. "Same here. This guy especially"—Ted pointed to Blaine—"has nothing but great things to say about you. And my wife! Well, I really appreciate the way you've stepped in for me in my absence."

Ted's voice straddled the line of sarcasm. Was he being sincere? Vicki was suddenly glad that she'd skipped chemo; she felt stronger now than she had in weeks. She marched into the living room.

"That's right," Vicki said. "We'd be lost without Josh."

"I got lost," Blaine said. "At the beach, remember?"

Vicki glanced at Melanie, who reddened and looked at the ground. "Right," Vicki said. She was alarmed to see that Ted was still scrutinizing Josh. "Did anyone remember sweatshirts for the kids?"

~~~~~~

Twenty minutes later, squished in the third row of seating between Porter and Blaine in their respective car seats and feeling distinctly like one of the children, Josh chastised himself for not asking to be paid. This was, most definitely, *work*—as in not something he would ever have chosen to do on his own, for fun. And it was weird, too, driving out to Madaket and then stopping by the ranger station at the entrance of Smith's Point in the Stowes' car. The kid working the ranger station had graduated from high school a year behind Josh—his name was Aaron Henry—and under other circumstances Josh would have said hello, asked how Aaron liked the job, and teased him about his uniform. But tonight Josh was grateful for the tinted windows in the back of the Yukon; he didn't want Aaron to see him, because how would he ever explain who these people were or what he was doing with them?

Ted and Vicki sat up front. Ted Stowe came across as the type of guy who could be charming as hell when he wanted to be, but that depended on whom he was talking to and whether or not he was getting his way. Josh far preferred the kind of man his father was—Tom Flynn wasn't easy by any means, but at least you always knew what to expect.

In the middle seat, Brenda stared out the window while Melanie sat sideways so that she could chitchat with Josh. Melanie's breasts had swelled, and she had taken to wearing halter tops that cupped her breasts and flowed loosely over her stomach, which was still flat as a pancake.

"Since you grew up here," Melanie was now saying, "you must do this kind of thing all the time. Eat lobster on the beach."

"Not really," Josh said. Tom Flynn wasn't much for beach picnics. Josh did, however, have memories of Sunday afternoons at the beach when he was younger. His parents and a whole group of their friends congregated each week out at Eel Point. There were twenty or thirty kids, Wiffle ball games, charcoal barbecues with hamburgers and hot dogs. His mother, in particular, had seemed to enjoy these Sundays—she sat in her chair with her face raised to the sun, she swam twenty lengths of the beach, she helped Josh and the other kids collect horseshoe crabs, and she even pitched a few innings of Wiffle ball. At five o'clock she pulled a bottle of white wine from the depths of their icy cooler and poured herself some in a plastic cup. Every week, she insisted they stay until sunset.

We have to enjoy it now, she'd say. *Before winter comes.*

"Do you know how to drive on the beach?" Melanie said. "I'd get stuck."

"I can drive on the beach," Josh said. He kept his tire pressure low and put his Jeep in four-wheel drive; most of the time, it was as easy as that. "Years of beach parties."

"Sounds like fun," Melanie said. She smiled at him in a way that seemed to mean something. Josh felt his face growing warm and he looked at the kids. Porter was asleep already and drooling, and Blaine was getting that zoned-out look that came right before sleep. They weren't going to make one minute of the beach picnic.

Josh was relieved when Melanie turned her head away. Ted gunned the motor and sailed up over the big, bumpy dune. The car lurched and rocked; everyone pitched forward, and at one point, Josh was bounced right out of his seat. Melanie grabbed on to the back of Vicki's seat with one hand and clenched her midsection with the other.

"Hold on!" Ted called out, and he whooped like a cowboy.

Josh shook his head. *Tourists,* he thought. *Summer people.* It would serve Ted right if he got stuck in the soft sand, if he had to call on Josh to save his ass. But then Josh remembered that the picnic was supposed to be for Vicki's sake, and when he checked, Vicki was smiling. Ted careened down the smooth backside of the dune onto the beach, where he wisely placed the Yukon in the existing tracks. Melanie turned around and grinned at Josh.

"Look at the water," she said. "I can't wait to swim. Will you come in with me?"

"Oh," Josh said. "Well, I didn't bring my suit."

"Who needs a suit?" Melanie said, and she laughed.

"Right," Josh said. He glanced at Brenda, but she was still mooning out the window. It began to feel suspiciously as if he'd been asked along this evening as Melanie's date. Was that what Ted thought? Did that explain the cold reception? Melanie was stuck to Josh like gum on his shoe; he was a sitting duck, wedged in the back between the kids.

Melanie must have sensed his discomfort because she said, "I'm sorry. I'm bugging you." Her face got the same sort of crumpled expression that she had when Josh first saw her coming off the airplane. The expression addled Josh. It reminded him that she'd been abandoned, somehow, by her husband, even though she was pregnant. It made him want to help her, cheer her up. She was a nice woman and very pretty, but he didn't want anyone to think . . .

"You're not bugging me," Josh said. "I'm just hungry."

"Oh, me, too," Melanie said. "The smell of the lobsters is driving me crazy."

"I want a marshmallow," Blaine said.

Vicki piped up from the front. "After your hot dog."

Blaine rested his head against Josh's shoulder.

"He's going to sleep," Melanie said. "Vicki, do you want Blaine to sleep?"

Vicki turned around. Her eyes softened, and if Josh wasn't mistaken, they were shining with tears.

"Look at my beautiful boys," she said.

Instinctively, Josh mouthed, *Don't cry.*

That was all it took: Tears dripped down Vicki's face. Josh checked on Porter, who was mercilessly working his pacifier. Josh felt the bristle of Blaine's hair under his chin and relished the warm, heavy weight of Blaine's head on his shoulder. *Look at my beautiful boys.* Then he realized Vicki meant the three of them. She was gazing at them mournfully, and Josh wondered if his mother had looked at him in such a way in the weeks before she killed herself. He wondered if she had ever looked at him and questioned her decision to leave him. Just thinking this bugged him. He wasn't used to thinking about his mother at all, but being around Vicki, he couldn't help it. She looked like a foreigner in her scarf; her face was so thin, her eyes bulged. *She's vanishing,* Josh had written in his journal the night before. *By the end of summer, she'll be gone.*

Melanie took Vicki's hand. Brenda stared out the window at the waves breaking, the plovers and oystercatchers pecking at the sand. She was either oblivious, Josh thought, or purposefully trying to distance herself from the melancholy nature of this beach picnic. Josh was relieved when Ted banked a hard right and backed the Yukon up to a perfect stretch of beach.

"Here we are!" Ted boomed.

An hour later, Josh felt better, not least of all because Ted, maybe in an attempt to foster male bonding, or maybe as part of an evil plan Josh had yet to figure out, had offered Josh three ice-cold bottles of Stella, all of which Josh accepted, and drank, happily. They were drinking and fishing. Ted was fascinated by the bells and whistles of the new fancy-schmancy fishing rods he'd brought from New York and he wanted to show them off to Josh. Blaine had revived enough to ask Ted, five hundred times in ten minutes, when he was going to catch a fish. "Catch a fish, Dad. I want to see you catch a fish."

"You bet, buddy," Ted said. He fiddled with the reel, attached a twenty-dollar lure, and cast out, the line making a satisfying whizzing noise and then a *plop* as it landed. Ted looked to Josh.

"Go for it, man."

"Catch a fish, Josh," Blaine said. "Are you going to catch a fish?"

Josh hesitated. The rod felt sleek and expensive in his hand; it was the Maserati of surf-casting rods. Ted probably thought Josh was nervous about handling such fine equipment. Josh *was* nervous—but only because anyone who lived here knew that you could catch a bluefish with a hickory stick and a piece of string. Josh was nervous because he didn't want to show Ted up by catching the first fish. And so, he stood there with the rod in his hands.

"Do you need help?" Ted asked.

"Yeah," Josh said. "This rod is like nothing I've ever seen."

Ted beamed and reeled his line in. Nothing.

"Here," he said. "Let me show you." He took Josh's rod. "Hey, would you like another beer?"

~

Brenda had promised Vicki she would tend to all the details of the picnic, but she was happy when Vicki's old desire to be 100 percent in charge resurfaced, like something that washed up on the beach. Vicki laid the blanket down (*No sandy feet on the blanket, please!*) and unfolded chairs. She set out the boxed dinners, plastic utensils, and a tall stack of napkins, which she weighted down with a rock. She poured a glass of wine for Brenda, a small one for herself, and she cracked open a ginger ale for Melanie. She sank into a chair looking almost relaxed, but then she stood again, rummaged through the back of the Yukon, and returned with two citronella tiki torches, which she stabbed into the sand and lit up. She sank into her chair again. Her chest was heaving; she was winded by just that much activity, but the chemo was clearly working, Brenda thought, because this was more than she'd done in weeks.

Brenda and Vicki and Melanie touched glasses, and as they did so, Brenda heard everything click into place. The chemo was shrinking Vicki's tumor; she was getting better. Melanie had shed her woe-is-me attitude, she'd stopped vomiting and moaning about her marital troubles; she acted, at least half the time, like a nice, normal human being. And Brenda had written the first scene of her screenplay the previous morning, while drinking a decadent Milky Way coffee at the Even Keel Cafe. It was the scene where Calvin Dare and Thomas Beech meet up in front of the tavern, with nothing more in common than two people parking next to each other outside of a Chili's restaurant—and lightning strikes and Calvin Dare's horse bucks and whinnies and kicks Thomas Beech between the eyes. Men pour out of the tavern to tend to Beech—one of them a doctor, who proclaims Beech dead. The scene was five pages long, which meant, according to the *Screenwriter's Bible*, it would last five minutes, and Brenda thought it was pretty good.

She tried to analyze the day's success. Maybe she should abandon the beach and do all of her work at the Even Keel Cafe with the aid of a Milky Way coffee. Maybe it was the community nature of the cafe that had helped—there were other people sitting in the dappled shade of the cafe's back deck who were reading the paper, sketching, breezing through paperback novels, typing on their laptops. Maybe Brenda—like Hemingway, like Dylan Thomas—would do her best work in public places. However, deep down, Brenda suspected that it was the stolen nature of those two hours that transformed them. She was supposed to be somewhere else. She was supposed to be in the waiting room of the hospital's Oncology Unit praying for her sister's recovery. She had set aside those two hours—three, if you counted the driving—to be of service to her sister. The fact that Vicki had unexpectedly granted her leave gave those two hours a rarefied quality. What Brenda had thought was, *I'd better not waste them*. And, like magic, the words had come. The pages had filled.

As happy as Brenda was about writing the first pages of her screenplay, she still felt a twinge of guilt about abandoning Vicki. True, there was no reason for Brenda to sit in the waiting room while Vicki received her treatment; however, not being there felt like she was shirking her duties. Yesterday was the one and only time. She would never leave Vicki again.

She was proud of herself, however, for pulling together this beach picnic. The sun hovered over the water, there was a warm breeze, the waves washed over the sand in a rhythmic, soothing way. Down the beach, Ted and Josh and Blaine, bathed in the last rays of golden sunlight, cast their lines out into the water. They were like characters from a storybook. If this only lasted an hour or two, Brenda thought, that was okay. Walsh loved to point out the way Americans rushed from one thing to another. For people like Brenda, he said, happiness was always just around the bend; he accused her of being incapable of sitting back and enjoying a moment. And he was right. Now, Brenda tried to push every thought out of her mind except: *Please let Vicki enjoy this*.

There was shouting from down the beach. Brenda leaned forward in her chair. Someone had caught a fish.

When Josh felt a tug on his line, his gut reaction was excitement. Then, he thought, *Oh, shit*. He had no choice but to reel the fish in, even though Ted and Blaine hadn't yet realized he had a bite. Oh, well, Josh thought.

It was just a fish. It wasn't as though God had tapped Josh on the shoulder and declared him the superior man. As Josh's line tightened, he heard Ted shout, "Whoa! Josh has something! Look, buddy, Josh has a bite!" Ted didn't sound angry or jealous at all; he sounded as excited as a little kid.

Blaine jumped up and down. "Pull it in, Josh! Pull it in!"

Josh cranked the reel; the expensive rod bent like a rainbow, and Josh thought, *Lord, please do not let the rod snap.* No sooner had he thought this than the fish rose from the water, twisting and wriggling. Bluefish. Big one.

Ted was on top of the fish as soon as it hit the sand. He stood on the flapping tail and pulled a tape measure from his shorts pocket. "Thirty-four inches," he said. Josh wondered if this was the start of some sort of competition. Would Ted now try to catch a bigger fish? Would they make this about size in some pseudo-Freudian way? But then Ted held the end of the tape measure and dropped the spool end like a yo-yo. "They threw this in for free at the tackle shop," he said. He yanked the lure from the fish's mouth with a pair of pliers. He was deft and confident in all of this, which was a good thing because bluefish have a mean mouthful of teeth and Josh had seen plenty of people, including his father, get bitten.

"Look at that, buddy," Ted said to Blaine. He sounded as proud as if he'd caught it himself.

Blaine watched the fish do a dance across the sand. Ted slapped Josh on the back, and Josh felt the offer of another, celebratory beer on its way.

"Are we going to keep it?" Blaine asked. "Are we going to *eat* it?"

"No," Ted said. He picked the fish up by its tail. "We're throwing her back. We're going to let her live."

Vicki drank her three sips of wine and poured herself three more sips. Ted, Blaine, and Josh sauntered toward them, their rods slung over their shoulders. Blaine trumpeted the news: "Josh caught a fish, a really big fish! Dad unhooked it and threw it back!" The way the facts were relayed, both Ted and Josh sounded like heroes, and Vicki was relieved.

"Let's eat," she said.

They all sat on the blanket or in chairs and dug into their boxes. Ted started telling Josh a story about a boat he'd sailed from Newport to Bermuda the summer after he graduated from college. Brenda tried to entice Blaine into eating lobster.

"Look, Josh is eating it."

Blaine considered this for a second, then turned his nose up. He plopped in Vicki's lap, and his weight nearly crushed her. She gasped; Ted stopped talking and looked over.

"I'm fine," she said.

Blaine ate Vicki's biscuit and her corn on the cob. Porter was still asleep in the back of the car, and Vicki was about to ask Melanie to check on him—but when she looked at Melanie, Melanie was transfixed by . . . Vicki followed Melanie's gaze and then, inwardly, groaned. Melanie was staring at Josh in a way that could only mean one thing. *Do not judge,* Vicki told herself. After all, she was a woman who had skipped chemo. Still, Vicki hoped she was imagining things, and if she wasn't imagining things, if Melanie did harbor some sort of fascination with Josh, then Vicki hoped it was short-lived, a phase, like with the kids. Once Vicki made up her mind to worry about it, it would be over.

"Brenda?" Vicki said. "Would you check on the baby?"

Brenda rose. Melanie continued to stare at Josh with a vague smile on her face. Possibly she was following Ted's story about running aground on the Outer Banks, but Vicki kind of doubted it.

"Josh?" Vicki said. "Would you mind digging a hole for the fire?"

"I'll help!" Blaine said.

"I'll help, too," Melanie said.

"Not you, Mel," Vicki said. "You relax."

"Is there firewood?" Josh asked.

"Yes," Melanie said. "Brenda stole four pallets from the Stop and Shop."

"I did not steal them," Brenda said. "I do not *steal* things. They were left out by the Dumpster."

"How's the baby?" Vicki said. "Is he still asleep?"

"Yes, he's fine," Brenda spat. "I know you all think I'm a thief. I am *not* a thief."

"You robbed the cradle," Ted said.

"Ted!" Vicki said.

Over Blaine's head, Brenda shot Ted the finger.

"Lovely," Ted said.

"Thanks a lot," Brenda said to Melanie, "for bringing it up."

Vicki took a breath. She'd suspected things would explode one way or another.

Melanie rolled her eyes and stood next to Josh as he shoveled sand. A wailing noise came from the car.

"Ted?" Vicki said. "Will you . . . ?"

Ted was already up. He returned with a very cranky Porter. "I can't find his bottle."

"But you did pack it, right?"

"Right," he said uncertainly.

"Oh, Ted," Vicki said. "Please don't tell me . . ."

"Vicki . . . ," Brenda said.

"What?"

"Don't do that armchair Napoleon thing."

"*What* armchair Napoleon thing?"

"You just sound a little bossy is all. A little dictatorial."

"Josh?" Vicki said. "Do I sound dictatorial to you?"

"You have him digging ditches," Brenda said.

"A hole," Vicki said. "For the fire. So we can roast marshmallows."

"I want a marshmallow," Blaine said. "Mom told me if I ate . . ."

"So we can have a nice time!" Vicki said. She could hear herself above Porter's cries; her voice was loud and frustrated. "So we can have a bonfire and enjoy the evening."

"Vicki?"

The sun was setting over the water; it was a melting, golden blob. Vicki stared at the backlit figures of Josh digging the hole and Melanie standing beside him and Brenda with her hands on her hips declaring she was not a thief and Ted rocking Porter and giving him a bottle (that he found who knows where). They were, all of them, familiar to her. This scene was so familiar to her that she felt she had witnessed it before—and she had, maybe, in her mind's eye, when she'd imagined what this picnic might be like. They were having this picnic for her—to *get her out*—but there was also a summer-of-final-wishes element to it, a desire on everyone's part for this to be a perfect beach picnic, memories of which Vicki could take to her grave. So although the bickering was unpleasant, Vicki was glad they were letting the fantasy go and being themselves.

But then something odd happened. Brenda and Josh and Ted froze, they became perfectly still. Why? Vicki realized there was someone else among them, a foreign presence, the owner of the voice that had just spoken her name. *Vicki?* The voice was curious and kind, but with deep, authoritative undertones. She knew that voice, but how?

"Vicki Stowe?" the voice repeated. "Is that you?"

In general, Vicki hated to be recognized in public. (She thought back to the god-awful scene on the beach with Caroline Knox.) She didn't like to be caught unawares, and whoever was standing before her now—it looked like a man, in waders, with a fishing rod—was interrupting her family picnic and had, on top of that, interrupted a family squabble. Who knows what this person overheard and what this person now thought of them?

Vicki squinted. The sun was behind the man's head, radiating like a halo. "Yes," Vicki said.

"It's Mark."

"Mark?"

"Dr. Alcott," he said.

"Oh!" Vicki said. She leapt out of her chair. "Hi!" Once she stood, she could see him clearly: It was Dr. Alcott, but in his waders and Atlantic Cafe T-shirt and Red Sox cap, he was unrecognizable, and although she knew his first name was Mark, she had never once called him that. Vicki wondered if she should shake his hand, and as she was wondering this, he leaned forward and kissed her cheek, and Vicki felt like she had just been kissed by a new boyfriend in front of her parents. Ted and Brenda and Melanie, and even Josh, were watching this exchange like it was something that was being shown on TV. None of them knew who Dr. Alcott was— not even Brenda had met him—and she was just about to make the introductions when she remembered about the previous morning. *She had skipped chemo*—and now here was Dr. Alcott, appearing out of the blue to blow the whistle on her. To inform her family that she was sabotaging her own care. To tell them that Vicki didn't give a shit if she got better or not. At the very least, Dr. Alcott would ask Vicki where she'd been, and she would have no good answer; she would be forced to confess the truth in front of everyone. *I skipped.* The prospective humiliation of the moment was enough to leave Vicki temporarily tongue-tied.

Dr. Alcott took a step toward Ted and said, "Hi there. I'm Mark Alcott, Vicki's doctor."

"Aha!" Ted said. "It's a pleasure to meet you. I'm Ted Stowe."

The men shook hands.

Vicki, realizing she had to take control of the conversation, jumped in. "And this is my sister, Brenda. My friend Melanie Patchen, and our . . . friend Josh Flynn. And my sons, Blaine and Porter."

"Quite a group," Dr. Alcott said.

"Yes," Vicki said. She fingered one of the tails of her scarf. *Small talk!* she thought. Small talk might save her. "You're fishing?"

"You bet."

"Josh caught a fish," Blaine said. "A big one. And Dad threw it back."

"Good," Dr. Alcott said. "Great. It's a beautiful night."

"Beautiful," Vicki said. "We had lobsters."

"Yum," Dr. Alcott said. He eyed Ted's fishing rods, poking out of the sand. "Those are some real beauties."

"Thanks," Ted said. He grinned. "We might try again in a little while."

There was a beat of silence, then another beat. Vicki panicked. She was not a trouper, she was not a star patient—she was a fraud! Dr. Alcott had tracked her down, all the way out here on the far edge of the island, to call her bluff. "Okay, well," she said. "Don't let us keep you from your fishing." She cast around for someone safe to look at and came up with Melanie. "Dr. Alcott loves to fish."

Melanie widened her eyes and nodded in a good approximation of interest.

"Okay," Dr. Alcott said. He took a breath and seemed about to add something else. *No!* Vicki thought. He smiled at her blandly, and Vicki realized then that he didn't *know* she'd skipped chemo. Didn't know or didn't remember . . . or didn't care? "Good to see you. Nice to meet all of you."

"Likewise." Ted shook Dr. Alcott's hand again.

"Bye," Vicki said. She sat back down and exhaled as Dr. Alcott strolled off down the beach. She knew she should feel relieved—she'd dodged a bullet—but instead, she felt hollow. Here she was still alive, still among them—and yet, already forgotten.

Josh had thought that once they got back to Shell Street, he would be free to go. But everything had to be taken out of the car: the cooler, the chairs, the trash bag, the sleeping kids—and Josh offered to help. It was easy work, especially since Ted Stowe insisted they do it with the aid of yet another beer, Josh's sixth or seventh of the night. The beach picnic had been a success, or almost: There had been the fishing, the sunset, the lobsters—and later the fire and s'mores for Blaine. Melanie had made a big deal about going swimming in the dark. She'd changed into her suit behind the car and, despite protests from Vicki and Ted and Brenda, all of whom were pretty sure she would drown, charged into the water. She was gone all of thirty seconds before she returned, curled into herself, shivering and dripping. Josh handed her a towel, and he found himself gazing at her body—her breasts, the still-smooth plane of her stomach, bare in the bikini, her curly hair hanging in dark corkscrews around her face. Looking at Melanie that way had been careless, the result of too many beers too fast. The problem, Josh realized later, was that Melanie saw him looking, and that was all the confirmation she needed to move forward.

The moving forward happened after the remains of the

picnic were tucked away, after the Stowes and Brenda had said good night, after Josh, too, had said *good night, thank you for inviting me, nice to meet you, Ted, see you Monday, Boss.* Josh tripped as he headed down the flagstone walk. After six or seven beers, he thought, he shouldn't be driving, especially since the police loved to sit on Milestone Road picking off young drunk kids just like him. So he sat in his Jeep for a minute, searching through the console for his tin of Altoids, wondering if it was only his imagination or if the surprise appearance of the doctor had changed the night. Because after Dr. Whatshisface wandered away, Vicki clammed up, she burrowed into her chair and gave everyone the silent treatment. Everything had been going really well up until then, but the doctor's visit seemed to cast a shadow over things, reminding Josh and everyone else that Vicki was sick. For whatever reason, Josh thought again about those Sundays on the beach with his parents. If Josh went to Eel Point tomorrow, there would be a different group of parents playing with their kids. His parents' circle of friends had disbanded right after Josh's mother died—not because of Janey Flynn's suicide, maybe, but more likely because the kids were all older by then and asking to go to the big-surf beaches. But there was definitely a sense of loss, of an era passing.

We have to enjoy it now, his mother said. *Before winter comes.*

Those Sundays were over and done with, and hence at that moment they seemed unspeakably precious to Josh, as precious as his mother's lost love. Josh felt this so fervently, and he'd had so much to drink, that he thought he might cry. But then there was a tap on the Jeep window, frightening Josh. He yelped and put his hand to his heart like a woman.

It was Melanie.

He rolled down the window. "Jesus," he said. "You scared the shit out of me."

She didn't apologize or ask what he was still doing there. "Want to go for a walk?" she said.

"A walk?" he said, like she'd suggested a trip to outer space. It wasn't particularly late, maybe ten o'clock, and he was, at this point, too intoxicated to drive to the end of the street, much less home. A walk wasn't a terrible idea.

Josh looked at the house. It was dark, the door was shut tight.

"They've all gone to bed," Melanie said.

He heard conspiracy in her voice and he knew right then that agreeing to a walk with Melanie meant agreeing to some whole huge other thing that he wasn't sure he was ready for. She was ten years older than he was, she was pregnant, she was *married,* but overriding these compromising circumstances was the fact that the hair on his arms was standing up. *Listen. Observe. Absorb.* This was, he sensed, part of the story of his summer. He was supposed to walk with Melanie. He opened the car door and stepped out—and because there was no use pretending that it would happen any other way, he took Melanie's hand and they headed down Shell Street.

She was his second choice. As Melanie and Josh meandered down the narrow streets of 'Sconset along the short picket fences, past the tiny, ancient, rose-covered cottages—many of them dark, but a few here or there with a light on and one place ablaze with the end of a party—Melanie forced herself to acknowledge this fact: Josh had wanted Brenda first. And it was only because of Brenda's inexplicable devotion to her former student John Walsh that Melanie was now holding hands with Josh. Holding hands with Josh! The children's babysitter! It was funny and ridiculous and impossible to comprehend now that it was actually happening—and yet this was what she had wanted. This was what she had secretly hoped for, never once allowing herself to believe that it would ever come to pass. But here they were. Josh seemed to know where they were going. He led her past the tennis club, then through an arched opening in a pruned hedge. Suddenly they were in front of . . . a church. The 'Sconset Chapel, a shingled Victorian with white trim and a bell tower.

"There's a garden in the back," Josh said. "With a bench. We can sit."

"Okay," Melanie said. It was the cutest church in the whole world—something out of a storybook—and yet, she hesitated. Churches meant weddings and weddings meant marriage and marriage led Melanie right back to thinking about Peter.

So it was that they sat on the bench in the church garden—with Josh holding Melanie from behind—while Melanie told Josh a little something about her marriage.

What she chose to tell him about was Peter's office Christmas party the previous December. It had been in the city, all the way down on Elizabeth Street, at a restaurant called Public. Public was both hot and cool at the same time; it was so cool, they hadn't even bothered to decorate for the holidays.

Strange place for a Christmas party, Melanie murmured to Peter as she handed her fur wrap to a six-foot hostess.

Don't start, Peter had said. *I'd like to try and enjoy myself.*

"Peter was good at making me feel like a shrew," Melanie told Josh. She knew now that if she'd been even half paying attention, she would have seen the demise of her marriage at that party instead of floundering through five subsequent months and accidentally getting pregnant. She had gotten her period the day before the party, heralding failure for IVF round number five. It was another F on her body's report card. Everyone in Peter's office knew Peter and Melanie were trying to have children, hence Melanie expected an evening of inquiring glances and indirect questions. She didn't want to be there and Peter knew it. Melanie went directly to the long slate bar for drinks; she ordered two glasses of champagne for herself and a Stoli and tonic for Peter. She drank one of the glasses of champagne straight down, then tried to locate Peter in the crowd. She got caught talking to Peter's boss's wife for a while, then she saw Vicki waving from a corner of the room. Vicki was wearing a slinky red top and gold, dangly earrings; her hair was up. She had been gorgeous before she got cancer—gorgeous and fun and kindhearted and the world's greatest mother. She was the only person at the party, in the world, that Melanie could stand to be with. Melanie remembered excusing herself from the conversation with Cynthia Brenner and heading over to the safety of the space next to Vicki

Melanie told Vicki about failed round number five. *I'm being betrayed by my own body,* she said, and then she'd started to cry.

Vicki whisked her into the ladies' room, where the two of them sat on a velvet divan and finished their drinks. When they emerged, they bumped into Peter. He was standing near the emergency exit—Melanie remembered his face bathed in the red light of the exit sign in an otherwise dark alcove—talking to Frances Digitt. Frances Digitt was dressed in the suit she'd worn to work, a dark suit with a short skirt—and over the suit she wore a fleece vest. She looked like an executive for *Field & Stream.*

Melanie thought nothing of the sight of Peter and Frances together. She was more concerned with having to answer Frances's questions about the latest round of IVF. Frances showed enormous interest in the Patchens' quest for a baby; her sister, Jojo, in California was going through the *exact same thing,* or so she claimed. And, too, Melanie felt embarrassed about being caught emerging from the ladies' room with Vicki. This was one of the antisocial behaviors Peter always accused her of after an office party: *You snuck off to the bathroom with Vicki like the two of you were in junior high.*

"Now, if I'd been paying attention," Melanie said to Josh. "If I had seen past the end of my own nose . . ."

"He was having an affair with her?" Josh asked.

"Oh, yes," Melanie said. "Yes, he was. He still is."

"Still is? Even with . . ."

"He doesn't know I'm pregnant."

"He *doesn't?*"

"Nope."

"How come you haven't told him?"

"Ugh. Because he doesn't deserve to know."

Josh squeezed Melanie. It was exactly what she needed—a person to console her, a young, handsome, male person. She twisted around so that she was facing him. He was looking very serious.

"What?" she said.

"This is weird," Josh said. "Can we please just acknowledge how weird this is?"

"Why is it weird?" Melanie said. She knew why it was weird but she wanted to hear him say it.

"You're married," he said. "You're pregnant. I know you're pregnant but your own husband doesn't even know."

"You don't have to worry about Peter," she said.

"I'm not worried about Peter," Josh said. "I'm worried about what everyone is going to think. Vicki. Ted."

"They're not going to think anything," Melanie said. "Because they're not going to know."

"They're not?"

"They're not."

"Oh," he said. "Okay." He exhaled and seemed to relax a little bit. He was drunk, or nearly so. Whatever happened tonight happened *tonight*—and that would be the end of it. *Okay?* Melanie asked herself. Okay. She kissed him, and this seemed to catch him off-guard, though what were they doing on a bench in the church garden if they weren't planning on kissing? It only took a second or two for Josh to get it, and then it was as if Melanie were a car he decided he wanted to drive after all. The kissing, which Melanie had intended to keep sweet and soft, turned into something faster and more urgent. Josh ran his hands up and down her back, then up and down her back inside her shirt, and Melanie, who hadn't kissed a man other than Peter in nearly ten years, couldn't keep herself from wondering if this utterly intoxicating foreignness was what Peter experienced when he was with Frances Digitt.

Josh's youth was apparent in many ways. He was strong, forceful, intense. (With Peter, at the end, physical contact had been like work, like a duty—he complained of this and she'd felt it, too.) Josh fondled her tender breasts, he chewed on her earlobe and whispered into her ear, "God, you are so amazing." *Amazing?* Melanie thought. *Me?*

But when Josh moved his hands down over her stomach, he pulled back, like he was afraid he might burn himself. Melanie took hold of his hands and tried to place them on her midsection, but he resisted.

"It's okay," she whispered.

"It is?" he said. He allowed her to press his hands to her belly, but still she sensed reluctance. What was she doing, forcing a drunk college student to acknowledge her budding pregnancy?

"Relax," she said. "It's okay." She should just let it go, she realized. Let him take what parts of her he wanted and choose to ignore the parts that lay outside his comfort zone—but if they were to go any further, Melanie wanted him to accept her as she was. Thirty-one years old. And pregnant.

It occurred to Melanie for a second that maybe Josh wasn't mature enough to handle this, maybe he didn't *want* to handle a woman like her, with baggage, emotional and physical. She was his second choice for a reason. How could she blame him for wanting Brenda, who was not only beautiful but also unencumbered? How could she blame him for wanting some easy girl his own age that he met at a bar or a bonfire instead?

It seemed like they stayed in that moment for a very long time—with Melanie holding Josh's hands to the life inside of her—enough time for Melanie to travel down the road of insecurity and doubt, enough time for her to reach the conclusion that she'd made a mistake. She let Josh's hands go—in fact, she pushed them away—feeling stupid and foolish. She had been wrong to pursue him; she had been wrong to put any stock in her own kooky, adolescent feelings.

Josh separated from her. She heard him inhale, as if in relief of being cut free. But what Josh did next was so unexpected, it took Melanie's breath away. He lifted up her shirt and lowered his head. He pressed his face to her belly, and he kissed her there, like it was the most natural thing in the world.

~

*S*leep.

Vicki left a note. *Gone for a walk,* it said. *To Sankaty Light.*

She couldn't sleep—or rather, after the beach picnic she fell asleep like a rock sinking to the bottom of a riverbed and then she awoke with a jolt. She lifted Ted's arm and looked at his watch: 1:00 AM. Vicki's head was buzzing; she was *wide awake.* The room was dark, the house quiet except for Ted's gentle snoring. Vicki flipped over and caught sight of the Styrofoam head, the wig, the ghoulish face, *Daphne,* and it freaked her out. She rose from bed, picked the head up, and set it in the back of the closet. In the morning, it was going to the dump.

The boys were sleeping on their mattress on the floor. They were on their backs, their heads together at the top of the mattress. Blaine had an arm flung protectively across Porter's chest. They were sleeping with just a sheet, which was now bunched down by Blaine's ankles. Vicki stood at the foot of the mattress, watching them. Because it was so warm, Blaine slept in only short pajama bottoms and Porter in just a diaper. Their torsos were perfectly formed—Blaine lean and muscular, Porter chubby with baby fat—and their skin was milky white; it glowed. Vicki could pick out a pattern of poison ivy on the back of Porter's leg, she could discern a juicy new mosquito bite on Blaine's forearm. Their dark eyelashes fanned out against their cheeks; Blaine's eyelids were alive with movement underneath. What was he dreaming about?

There was, she decided, no more beautiful sight than her children sleeping. She loved her sons so profoundly, their perfect bodies and all the complexities each contained, that she thought she might explode. *My children,* she thought. They were bodies that had come from her body, they were a part of her—and yet she would die and they would live.

Vicki had entered into motherhood wholly unprepared. She had woken up confused when the nurse brought Blaine in to feed on the night he was born. The reality had sunk in, gradually, over the past four and a half years. *This child is my responsibility. Mine. For the rest of my life.*

Being a mother was the best of all human experiences, and also the most excruciating. Getting the baby to nurse, getting the baby to eat solids, getting the baby to sleep, the teething, the crying, the crawling, into everything, can't take my eyes off him for a second, a whole roll of toilet paper stuffed into the toilet, the first steps, the falling, the trips to the emergency room (*Does he need stitches?*), the Cheerios that stuck together and nearly choked him, the weaning from the breast, the bottle, the pacifier, the grating squeal of Elmo's voice, the first playdate, the hitting, the grabbing, the first word, *Dada* (Dada?), the second word, *mine,* the earaches, the diaper rash, the croup. It was a constant drone, all day, every day, occupying Vicki's hands, her eyes, her mind. *Invasion of the Body Snatchers.* Who did she used to be? She couldn't remember.

Vicki used to think that Blaine was born for her mind and Porter was born for her heart. Blaine was so damn capable, so independent, so smart. Before Vicki was diagnosed, he had taught himself to read, he knew his states and state capitals (*Frankfort, Kentucky*), and he kept a list of animals that were nocturnal (*bat, opossum, raccoon*). A day with Blaine was one long conversation: *Watch me, watch me, watch me, Mommy, Mommy, Mommy. Will you play Old Maid? Will you do the puzzle? Can we paint? Do Play-Doh? Practice numbers and letters? What day is today? What day is tomorrow? When can Leo come over? What time is it? When is Daddy coming home? How many days until we go to Nantucket? How many days until Porter's birthday?*

How many days until my birthday? Blaine's favorite time of day was story time, and better than the stories Vicki held in her hands, he said, were the ones in her mind. He loved the story of the night he was born (Vicki's water breaking unexpectedly, ruining the suede Ralph Lauren sofa in their pre-kids Manhattan apartment), he liked the story of the night Porter was born (her water breaking in the Yukon on her way home from dinner in New Canaan; Ted drove like a banshee to Fairfield Hospital, and Vicki delivered in time for Ted to get their babysitter home before midnight). But Blaine's favorite story was about how Vicki had punched Auntie Brenda in the nose when Auntie Brenda was a newborn, freshly home from the hospital, and how Auntie Brenda bled, and Vicki, feeling scared of what her mother would say, locked herself in the bathroom, and a fireman had to come get her out. As Vicki watched Blaine sleep, she realized she hadn't told him any real stories in a long time—and what was worse, he'd stopped asking for them. Maybe someday she'd tell him the story of how she had lung cancer and they came to Nantucket for the summer and she got better.

What *was* he dreaming about? A bike without training wheels, a scooter, a skateboard, bubble gum, a water pistol, a pet? These were the things he wanted most, and he made Vicki set timelines. Can I have a hamster when I'm six? Can I have a skateboard when I'm ten? Blaine wanted to be big, he wanted to be old; this had been true even before Josh came into the picture, and now, of course, Blaine wanted to be exactly like Josh. He wanted to be twenty-two, he wanted a cell phone and a Jeep. Vicki always told Blaine that the day he became a teenager was the day her heart would break, but now she thought that if she lived to see Blaine turn thirteen, she would count herself the luckiest woman alive.

The other morning, Vicki had awoken to find Blaine standing by her bed, a silent sentry. She smiled at him and whispered, *Hey, you.* Blaine pointed to the corner of his eye, he pointed to the center of his chest, and then he pointed to Vicki, and Vicki did the best she could to keep from crying. *I love you, too,* she said.

And then there was Porter, her baby. She missed him so much. He'd stopped nursing, and suddenly it was like he'd grown up and gone off to college. He took bottles from Josh, from Brenda, from Ted—all Vicki got was two and sometimes three hours during the heat of the afternoon when Porter took his nap tucked into the crook of her arm. He made sweet cooing noises when he slept, he babbled when he was awake, he sucked his pacifier like it was his job. His body was a pudding; when he smiled there was a dimple in his cheek. He was almost totally bald now and he only had two teeth—in truth, he looked like an old man. But he was so sweet—that smile could make anyone love him. *Don't grow up!* Vicki thought. *Stay a baby, at least until I'm healthy enough to enjoy you!* But Porter was chasing after his brother, the trailblazer. He would not be left behind! He was determined to conquer his developmental milestones early and with ease. Already, he had started cruising around the living room while holding on to Aunt Liv's dainty furniture. Soon, he would be walking. Her baby would be gone.

Blaine stirred. He made a snorting noise like a startled horse, and his eyes opened. He looked at Vicki. She held her breath—the last thing she wanted was for him to wake up, or to wake up his brother. His eyes drifted closed. She exhaled. Even this hurt. *I love you,* she thought. *You were both born for my heart.*

She tiptoed into the living room. Quiet, dark. The banjo clock ticked. Brenda's door was shut, Melanie's door was ajar about an inch. Vicki stepped out onto the back deck. The night sky was achingly beautiful. Vicki couldn't believe that people slept through nights like this. Back in the kitchen, she wrote the note, and then she left.

Gone for a walk. To Sankaty Light. In her ersatz pajamas—a pair of gym shorts, her Duke T-shirt, and flip-flops, with a bandanna on her head. This was, she realized, another crazy escape, just like the previous morning's jaunt to the Old Mill. She felt like a burglar as she padded down Shell Street. Every other house was pitch-black. The air was sweet with flowers and the ocean, and busy with the sound of crickets. Vicki was leaving the house with just a note. She thought of Josh's mother hanging herself without any explanation, and shuddered.

She made it to Sankaty Head Lighthouse, but barely. She was coughing and wheezing; her legs hurt, her head was throbbing, she touched her forehead—it was dry and hot. And yet, she felt proud. She had walked nearly a mile, some of it uphill, and now here she was, in the middle of the night, standing at the foot of the giant peppermint stick. To one side lay the rolling greens of the golf club, and to the other side the bluff dropped dramatically to the pounding surf. Vicki moved as close as she dared to the edge of the bluff. The ocean was before her, and the magnificent sky. Stars, planets, galaxies, places so far away human beings would never reach them. The universe was infinite. It was terrifying, really, incomprehensible, and had seemed so ever since she was a little girl. Vicki used to imagine the universe as a box that God held in his hand. Time would go on forever, she thought. But she would die.

She wondered what it would be like if she had always been as alone as she was this second, with no one else in her life—no husband, no children, no sister, no parents, no best friend. What if she were a homeless person, a drifter, without connections, without relationships? What if she were an island? Would that make dying easier? Because, quite frankly, she could imagine nothing more lonesome than dying and leaving everyone else behind. Dying was something a person did on her own. Dying only proved that no matter what bonds human beings formed with other human beings, everyone was, essentially, alone.

A voice cut through the darkness. "Vicki!"

Vicki whirled around. Ted was marching up the hill toward her, huffing and puffing himself. He could have been her father, coming to scold her for sneaking out. But as he got closer, she saw the look of concern on his face. He was worried about her, and he should be. What, exactly, was she doing?

"Vick," he said. "Are you okay?"

"I'm going to die," she whispered.

He made a shushing noise, the same noise he used to make when Blaine was a baby. He wrapped his arms around her. She was burning hot, not just the embers in her lungs, but her whole body. It was ablaze with sickness, with renegade cells. It wasn't something that could be exorcised. She *was* sickness. Once in Ted's arms, however, she started to shiver. She was freezing up there on the bluff, with wind coming off the water. Her teeth chattered. Ted's arms were the strongest arms she had ever known. She breathed in his smell, she absorbed his warmth, she rubbed her cheek against his cotton T-shirt. This was her husband, she knew him, and yet he was so far away from her.

"I can feel it," she said. "I'm going."

"Vicki," he said. His arms tightened around her and that felt good, but then he started, almost imperceptibly, to shake.

"I got up to look at the boys," she said. "I just wanted to watch them sleep."

"*You* should be asleep," he said. "What are you doing up here?"

"I don't know." She felt reckless then, and irresponsible. "What about you? What if the boys . . . ?"

"I woke Brenda once I realized you were gone," he said. "She said she'd stay in our room until I brought you back."

Like a runaway, she thought. But she couldn't run away, she couldn't hide. How long would it take her to understand that?

Ted held her by the shoulders, forcing her to look at him. His face was shining with tears. He was strong and masculine and competent, her husband, but the tears fell steadily and his voice was supplicating. "You have to get better, Vick. I can't live without you. Do you hear me? I love you in a way that is so powerful it lifts me up, it propels me forward. You propel me forward. *You have to get better, Vick.*"

Vicki tried to recall the last time she'd seen Ted like this, stripped down to bare emotion. The day he proposed, maybe, or the day Blaine was born. Vicki wanted to tell him, *Yes, okay, I'll fight for you, for the kids.* It would be like in the movies, it would be the scene where everything turns around, with the two of them standing on the bluff next to the lighthouse under the great dark sky; it would be the epiphany. Things would change; she would get better. But Vicki didn't believe in the words, she knew them to be false, and she wouldn't say them. So she said nothing. She tilted her face up to the sky full of stars. The problem with having everything, she thought, was that she had everything to lose.

"I can't make it back," she confessed to Ted. "It's too far. I feel like hell."

"I know," Ted said. "That's why I came to get you."

They hadn't made love in nearly a month, and yet Ted had never touched her more intimately than at that moment. He picked her up, he carried her home.

Brenda's phone rang. She was on page thirty of the screenplay and screaming along; the words were coming faster than she could write them. She was too busy to even check her phone's display. It wasn't exactly a mystery: the call was from either Brian Delaney, Esquire, or her mother. The phone stopped ringing. Brenda heard the soft dinging of an elevator somewhere in another part of the hospital, and then the gung-ho voice of the ESPN *SportsCenter* anchorman.

Vicki was meeting with Dr. Alcott behind closed doors. Vicki's white blood cell count had dropped dramatically, and she was running a fever of nearly 104. Dr. Alcott wanted to defer chemo until her counts rose and the fever abated. If ever there was a day when Brenda should have been praying, it was today—but for whatever reason, Brenda found that the only place she could now get any writing done was the oncology waiting room. It was all such a head game! Brenda had a block of time to work in peace at the beach each morning. But when she was at the beach, she got stuck, she was a dry well, she thought only of Walsh. She had tried the Even Keel Cafe one more time, but that had been worse—she fixated on the other couples eating breakfast, holding hands, whispering to each other, sharing sections of the newspaper. The Milky Way coffee seemed too sweet. Brenda found she could write her screenplay only when she was supposed to be doing something else. Like praying. Like worrying.

Her phone rang again. Brenda was smack in the middle of the scene where Calvin Dare attends the funeral service for Thomas Beech—hiding in the back so as not to be recognized as the man who owned the murderous horse—and this is when he first sets eyes on Beech's beautiful, bereaved fiancée, Emily. Brenda could see the scene with cinematic clarity—the tilt of Dare's black hat, the meeting of gazes across a dozen crowded church pews, Dare's decision then and there to summon the courage to speak to Emily. He approaches her on the church steps after the service to offer his condolences.

Did you know my Thomas? Emily asks, perplexed. *Were you a friend?*

And Calvin Dare, taking a chance, answers, *Yes, a friend from boyhood. I had not seen him in some time. I have been away.*

Away? Emily asks.

Abroad.

Emily's eyebrows arch. She's young, she was only engaged to Beech for a short while, and (as Brenda argued in her thesis) she is something of an opportunist. She's saddened by the death of her intended but also intrigued by this stranger, this friend of Thomas's from boyhood who has just returned from abroad.

Really? Emily says, in a way that could mean almost anything.

The phone stopped, then rang again. "Für Elise," the ring tone, was truly awful—it sounded like an organ-grinder monkey inside a tin can. Brenda reached blindly into her purse and pulled the phone out.

Her mother.

Brenda sighed. Put down her pen. Ellen Lyndon had gone into conniptions upon hearing about Vicki's fever; she would want to know what the doctor said. Brenda had to go to the bathroom anyway. She took the call.

"Hi, Mom."

"How is she?"

"Still in with the doctor."

"Still?"

"Still."

"Well, what did he say about the fever?"

Brenda moved down the hall to the ladies' room. "I have no idea. She's still in with him."

"They didn't tell you anything?"

"They never tell me anything. They tell Vicki and Vicki tells me. So, we have to wait." Brenda pushed into the ladies' room, where her voice bounced back at her from off the tile walls.

"How long did they say . . . ?"

"They didn't say, Mom." Brenda chastised herself. She should never have answered the phone. This kind of conversation frustrated them both. "Listen, I'll call you when . . ."

"You promise?"

"I promise. In fact, I'll have Vicki call so you can hear it straight from the horse's . . ."

"Okay, darling. Thank you. I'm here waiting. I canceled my physical therapy appointment."

"Why?" Brenda said. "You want your knee to get better, don't you?"

"I wouldn't be able to concentrate," she said. "Kenneth always asks for a 'dedicated effort' with the exercises, and I wouldn't be able to give it to him. He always knows when I'm distracted."

I should be distracted, Brenda thought. *But the opposite is true. Because I'm wired the wrong way.*

"Okay, Mom," Brenda said. "Good-bye."

"Call me when . . ."

"You bet," Brenda said, then she hung up. There was a flushing noise and a bathroom stall opened. A girl stepped out. Brenda smiled sheepishly and said, "Mothers!"

The girl ignored Brenda, which was fine. But when Brenda stepped out of the stall herself a few minutes later, the girl was still there, eyeing Brenda in the mirror.

"Hey," the girl said. "I know you. Josh works for you."

Brenda looked at the girl more closely. Of course. A push-up bra peeked out from the scoop neck of the girl's white T-shirt, and then there was the streaky blusher. It was the little vixen from Admitting. Brenda eyed the name tag. *Didi.* Ah, yes.

"That's right," Brenda said. "I'm Brenda. I forgot that you knew Josh."

"Damn right I know him."

Brenda washed her hands and reached for a paper towel. Didi rummaged through her bag and pulled out a cigarette, which she proceeded to light up.

"We really like Josh," Brenda said. "He does a great job with the kids."

"You pay him a fuckload of money," Didi said. This sounded like an accusation.

"I don't know about that," Brenda said. "I'm not in charge of paying him."

"Have you slept with him?"

Brenda turned to Didi just as Didi blew a stream of smoke from her mouth. Brenda hoped her face conveyed her disgust, combined with the fact that she was too dignified to answer such an absurd question. But Brenda couldn't help remembering the kiss on the front lawn. Certainly Josh hadn't told anyone about *that*?

"You're not supposed to be smoking in here," Brenda said. "It's a *hospital*. Some people have *lung cancer*."

Didi curled her lip into a snarl, and Brenda was overcome with the feeling that she had somehow reverted back to high school—she was trapped in the girls' bathroom with a rebellious smoker who was threatening her.

"You're fucking Josh," Didi said. "Admit it. Or maybe it's your sister who's fucking him."

"That's it," Brenda said. She whipped her wadded-up paper towel into the trash can. "I'm out of here. Good-bye."

"He never would have turned me down if he wasn't giving it to one of you," Didi called out as Brenda flew out the door. "I know it's one of you!"

Okay, Brenda thought. *Weird.* And weirder still, Brenda was trembling. Well, maybe it wasn't so weird that she was rattled—after all, the worst moment of her life had shared certain elements with that little scene in the bathroom. A girl, young enough to be Brenda's student, accusing her of improper relations.

Rumor has it you committed the only sin that can't be forgiven other than out-and-out plagiarism.

Romantic or sexual relationships are forbidden between a faculty member and a student. Romantic or sexual comments, gestures, or innuendo are forbidden between a faculty member and a student and will result in disciplinary action. There are no exceptions made for tenured professors.

We understand, Dr. Lyndon, that you've been having improper relations with one of your students.

The "improper relations" were Brenda's fault. It would have been nice to blame Walsh for pursuing her, but ultimately Brenda was the professor and Walsh the student and Brenda had let it happen. There had been the drinks at the Cupping Room and the kissing—when Brenda woke up the following morning she felt deeply ashamed and terrifically energized. She thought perhaps John Walsh would call her cell phone but he didn't, and by Tuesday morning, she thought maybe she had imagined the whole thing. But in class Walsh sat in his usual seat, surrounded by lovely girl-women, all of whom now seemed to Brenda to be flaunting their bright intelligence like feather boas for his sake. Every time Amrita the brownnoser contributed to class discussion, she looked to Walsh right away, to see if he agreed with her point or not. And Kelly Moore, the soap opera actress, was even worse, with all of her theatrics aimed in his direction. The three Rebeccas had basically formed a John Walsh Fan Club. *He's so hot,* Brenda overheard one of the Rebeccas saying. *Everybody wants him.* Walsh, for his part, was disarmingly blasé. He had no idea that he was sitting in a classroom of adoring fans.

At the end of class, Brenda handed out the topic of the midterm paper: *Compare and contrast Calvin Dare's identity crisis with an identity crisis of a character from contemporary literature, either on or off the reading list. Fifteen pages.* The girls groaned and filed out. Walsh stayed put.

Brenda looked up. "No," she said. "Go. You have to go."

He stared at her in a way that made her sick with desire. He didn't say a word; as Brenda remembered it, he didn't say one thing. He just stood there, looking at her. Brenda was stupid with her longing for him—and, too, she was egotistical. The other girls—girls far younger and prettier than she—all wanted him, but she was the one who was going to get him. She scribbled her address down on a piece of paper and pressed it into his hand, then she ushered him toward the door.

"Go," she said. "I have to lock up." She tilted her head. "Because of the painting."

He didn't show up that night or the next night, and Brenda felt like an idiot. She thought maybe he was a double agent hired by the other professors in the English Department who, jealous about her top teaching marks and subsequent superstar status, were trying to frame her. She thought maybe this was an elaborate practical joke dreamed up by the girl-women in the class. On Thursday, she vowed not to look Walsh's way, though of course she did, several times. Sandrine, the singer from Guadeloupe, had managed to sneak a can of Fresca, which she was resting on her thigh, past Mrs. Pencaldron's drinks radar. Brenda asked her to please throw it away. Sandrine had risen, reluctantly, and murmured something in French that half of the girl-women laughed at. Brenda became furious, though she was cognizant of the fact that she was not furious with Sandrine, or even with Walsh, but rather, with herself. She was fretting about the piece of paper with her address on it. It was just a piece of paper, just her address—it didn't *mean* anything—and yet, it did. Brenda had given Walsh her permission, she had given him her heart. This may have sounded ridiculous, but that was how she felt. She had pressed her heart into his palm and what had he done with it? Nothing. Walsh didn't linger after class; he filed out the door behind miffed Sandrine and the rest of the girl-women, and Brenda was crushed.

That night, Brenda was to meet Erik vanCott for dinner downtown at Craft. They were going alone, the two of them, without Noel, which should have made Brenda happy. Craft was a real restaurant, a *New York*–magazine type of restaurant. It had leather walls and a bottleneck of people at the door. Everyone was dressed up, smelling good, using important voices, talking on cell phones (*I'm here. Where are you?*), waiting to get in, in, in. Brenda stood on her tiptoes and tried to see over shoulders and around heads, but she couldn't locate Erik. She stood in the general mass waiting to talk to the gorgeous woman at the podium (her name was Felicity; Brenda overheard someone else say it). Brenda worried that she had the wrong place or the wrong time or the wrong night, or that she'd dreamt the phone call altogether. When finally it was Brenda's turn to talk to Felicity, she said, "I'm meeting someone. Erik vanCott?"

Felicity's eyes flickered over her very important reservation sheet. "Here it is: vanCott," Felicity said in a minor-league, *how-about-that* voice, as if she'd just found a dollar on the sidewalk. "Mr. vanCott has not yet arrived and the table isn't quite ready. Would you like to have a drink at the bar?"

At the bar, Brenda downed two cosmos. Then Felicity announced that the table was ready, and Brenda decided to sit, despite the fact that she was alone. She ordered another cosmo from a waiter who also appeared to be a professional weight lifter.

"I'm meeting someone," Brenda told him, hoping this was true. She checked her cell phone for a message. Nothing. It was eight-thirty. She had officially been stood up by two men in one week. But then she looked up and saw Erik darting toward her from across the room, the tails of his Burberry raincoat flying. The boy who'd chased Brenda on the playground, who once ate a whole jar of pistachios in one sitting in Ellen Lyndon's kitchen and then threw up in Ellen Lyndon's powder room, the lovelorn boy who had sung a Bryan Adams song at his prom after being ditched by Vicki, was now a man who made money, who wore suits, who met Brenda in snazzy New York restaurants.

"Am I late?" he said.

"No," Brenda lied.

"Good," he said. He collapsed into the chair across from Brenda, shed his raincoat, loosened his tie, and ordered a bottle of wine in impeccable French.

Brenda was dying to tell him the story of Walsh. There was no one else she could tell; her life was devoid of close girlfriends, and she couldn't tell Vicki and she couldn't tell her mother. Plus, Erik would be able to give her a male perspective, plus Brenda wanted Erik to know that yes, she did have men in her life other than him. However, in the twenty million years of their friendship, rules had developed, and one of those rules was that Brenda always asked about Erik first.

"So," she said, dipping into her third cosmo. "How's everything?"

"You mean Noel?"

"We can talk about Noel if you want," Brenda said, though, really, she had hoped for a Noel-less evening.

"I have something to tell you," Erik said.

We broke up, Brenda thought. If that was the case, she would talk about Noel all night. Good-bye to Noel, closure with Noel, and, of course, the requisite Noel-bashing.

Erik pulled a blue velvet box out of his suit jacket, and Brenda thought, *He has a ring. For me?* But even three cosmos didn't alter reality that much.

"I'm going to ask Noel to marry me," Erik said.

Brenda blinked. Marry him? She gazed at the box. She was sure the ring was lovely, but she didn't ask to see it. She had no right to be surprised—Erik had warned her. He had called Noel "marriage material." But Noel had a flaw: She didn't eat. A person who didn't eat had a serious esteem problem, a self-image problem. Brenda had written Noel off at Café des Bruxelles, and she thought Erik had, too. Brenda was mute. If Erik knew how much Brenda loved him, he would have done her a favor and called her on the phone so she could just hang up.

"Bren?"

"What?" Brenda said, and she started to cry.

Erik reached across the table for her hand. He held it tight and stroked it with his other hand. The blue box sat on the table between them, unopened. Brenda heard whispers, and she realized that somehow she and Erik had attracted the attention of their neighboring diners—who thought, no doubt, that Erik was proposing to Brenda.

"Put the ring away," Brenda whispered. "Please."

Erik slid the box back into his pocket but he didn't let go of Brenda's hand. They had never actually touched this way, and Brenda found it both breathtaking and exquisitely painful.

"Are you happy for me?" Erik said.

"Happy for you," she said. "Unhappy for me."

"Brenda Lyndon."

She saw the weight lifter approaching their table, but she couldn't deal with another minute of this date. She pushed away from the table. "I'm going."

"You're walking out on me again?" Erik said. "Again, in the middle of dinner?" He started in with the awful David Soul song. *"Don't give up on us, baby. We're still worth one . . . more try . . ."*

"That's not going to work," Brenda said.

"Brenda," Erik said, and Brenda looked at him.

"What?"

"I love her."

Brenda stood up and left Erik at the table. She was crying for many reasons, not least of all because true love always seemed to happen to other women—women like Vicki, women like Noel. Brenda could practically see Noel, naked in Erik's bed, which he had always fondly referred to as his nest. Noel was in the nest, naked, nesting, not eating. Alabaster skin, hair like a mink, naked except for pearl earrings. Ribs showing through her skin like the keys of a marimba that Erik could play while he sang. Brenda left the restaurant.

"Eighty-second Street," Brenda told the cabdriver waiting outside of Craft, who was, of all things, American. Benny Taylor, the license said. "And do you have any tissues?"

A small package of Kleenex came through the Plexiglas shield. "Here you go, sweetheart."

Benny Taylor delivered Brenda to her apartment at ten minutes to ten.

"Are you going to be okay, sweetheart?" Benny Taylor said.

He was asking not because she was crying, but because there was a man lingering by the door of Brenda's building. The man was tall and dressed entirely in black. Brenda squinted; her heart knocked around. It was John Walsh.

"I'll be fine," Brenda said. She tried to straighten her clothes and smooth her hair. Her makeup would be a wash. She pulled money out of her purse for Benny Taylor and ransacked her brain for something to say when she got out of the cab. *Hi? What are you doing here?* Brenda's ankles were weak, and the three drinks had taken custody of her sense of balance. Benny Taylor drove away; Brenda walked as steadily as she could toward Walsh, who was smiling. He was as dashing as the hero in an old Western. Strong, masculine, Australian. Brenda tried to be cool, but she found it impossible to wipe the stupid grin off her face.

"Hi," she said. "What are you doing here?"

John Walsh became her lover. He was her lover for days, weeks, months. It was exhilarating, delicious, and a holy, guarded secret. They never spoke on university property except during class, and Walsh stopped hanging around afterward. He called her cell phone—two rings then a hang-up was his signal—and they met at her apartment. If they couldn't wait the forty-five minutes it would take to get across town, they met in Riverside Park, where they kissed behind a stand of trees. They hunkered down in Brenda's apartment through one blizzard, eating scrambled eggs, drinking red wine, making love, watching old Australian movies, like *Breaker Morant*. John Walsh told Brenda things—about a girl he got pregnant in London who had an abortion, about his grandfather who worked in the interior of Western Australia shearing sheep. He told her about his travels around the world. Brenda talked about her life growing up in Pennsylvania, her parents, Vicki, summers in Nantucket with Aunt Liv, college, graduate school, Fleming Trainor. It was dull in comparison, but Walsh made her life seem fascinating. He asked the right questions, he listened to the answers, he was emotionally available and mature. What Brenda loved most about Walsh was his gravity. He wasn't afraid of serious topics; he wasn't afraid to look inside himself. Maybe that was how Australians were raised, or maybe it was because of his travels, but Brenda didn't know another man like this. Even Erik, even Ted, even her father. Ask them to talk about their feelings and they looked at her like she was asking them to shop for tampons.

During the second blizzard that winter, Brenda and Walsh bundled up so completely that no one would ever recognize them and they went sledding in Central Park. As the days passed, they got braver. They went to the movies (Brenda wore a baseball hat and sunglasses. She did not let Walsh hold her hand until the theater went dark). They went to dinner. They had drinks out, they went dancing. They never once saw anyone they knew.

At some point along the way, Brenda stopped thinking of Walsh as her student. He was her lover. He was her friend. But then came the Monday night that changed everything. Brenda was home alone, grading the midterm papers. She had put this off for as long as possible, and the girl-women in the class had started to complain; Brenda had promised the class their papers back the following morning and she had one paper yet to read. To his credit, Walsh hadn't asked her about it. Possibly he'd forgotten it was her job to grade it. It was with great trepidation that she picked up the paper with their names typed together at the top—*John Walsh / Dr. Brenda Lyndon*—and read.

What was she afraid of? She was afraid the paper would be bad—poorly organized, poorly argued, with typos and misspellings and comma splices. She was scared he would write "different than" rather than "different from." She was scared he would regurgitate what she'd said in class rather than think for himself (as one of the Rebeccas did, earning a flat C); she was scared he would accidentally quote somebody without noting a source. The paper was a potential relationship-ender—not only because he might get angry at a lousy grade, but because Brenda would not be able to continue seeing him if she had any qualms about his intelligence.

Nearly everyone else in the class chose to compare Calvin Dare to one of the characters from the books on their reading list. Not Walsh. He picked a book that wasn't on the reading list, a book Brenda had never read, a novel called *The Riders* by a Western Australian named Tim Winton. Walsh's paper targeted what he called the "identity of loss"—or how losing something or someone in one's life caused a change in that person's identity. In *The Innocent Impostor,* when Calvin Dare's horse kills Thomas Beech, Dare loses his confidence in his life path. The event shakes him to the core and causes him to relinquish his own dreams and ambitions and take up those of Beech. In *The Riders,* the main character, Scully, has lost his wife—quite literally *lost* her. She flies to Ireland with their daughter, but mysteriously, only the daughter gets off the plane. *The Riders* was a search for Scully's wife but it was also a study of how one man's identity changes because of this loss. Brenda was riveted. Walsh presented his thesis statement clearly in the first three pages, he backed it up with ten pages of textual support from both novels, and he ended, brilliantly, by citing other instances of the identity of loss across a wide scope of literature. It could be found, Walsh said, everywhere from *Huckleberry Finn* to *Beloved.*

Brenda put the paper down, stunned. For a point of reference, she reread Amrita's paper (which she had given an A) and then she read Walsh's paper again. Walsh's paper was different, it was original, as fresh and sun-drenched as the country he came from, but with a depth that could only come with age and experience. She gave Walsh an A+. Then she worried. She was giving Walsh the highest grade in the class. Was that fair? His paper was the best. Could she prove it? It was a subjective judgment. Would anyone suspect? Was the A+ in any way related to the fact that John Walsh made love to his professor on this very couch, bringing her enough pleasure that she cried out?

Brenda wrote the grade at the top of the paper in very light pencil, in case she changed her mind. But in the end, she couldn't bring herself to change the grade: He had earned it, fair and square. Still, she worried. She worried she was falling in love.

* * *

By the time Brenda made it back to the oncology waiting room, her concentration was shot. Amrita's accusations (true) blended with Didi's accusations (untrue). *You're fucking Josh. Admit it.* Brenda packed up her screenplay and decided not to tell anyone about what had transpired in the ladies' room.

A few seconds later, Vicki came down the hall, escorted by Dr. Alcott. Brenda blinked. Was that her sister, really? It looked like Vicki had shrunk—she seemed to have lost height as well as weight. She was as frail as Aunt Liv had been in the month before she died (and Aunt Liv had been petite anyway, eighty-five pounds in her wool overcoat). Vicki was wearing the Louis Vuitton scarf on her head, a pair of white shorts that sat on her hips, a pink tank top that made it seem like she had no breasts at all, and a navy cashmere zip-up hooded sweater because with a fever of 104, she was freezing. Brenda's mind had been far away in both time and place, but in a flash she resumed her attitude of urgent, incessant prayer. *Dear Lord, please, please, please, please, please . . .*

Dr. Alcott handed Vicki over. The waiting room was empty, but still he lowered his voice. "We've given her a shot of Neupogen, and she'll have to be brought in tomorrow and the following day for shots. That should get her counts to rise. I'm also prescribing antibiotics, and Tylenol to get her fever down. She should be feeling better in a few days. We'll try again with a reduced dose of the chemo when her counts are up." He looked at Vicki. "Okay?"

She shivered. "Okay."

Brenda clenched Vicki's arm. "Is there anything else?"

"She should rest," Dr. Alcott said. "I don't know about any more beach picnics."

"Okay," Brenda said quickly. She was already so racked with guilt (about Walsh, about kissing Josh, about writing instead of praying) and regret (about the goddamned A+, about the Jackson Pollock painting, about not telling Didi to fuck right off)—what did it matter if Dr. Alcott placed blame for the beach picnic at her feet as well? *I was trying to make her feel better,* Brenda might have said. *I was taking a holistic approach.* But instead, she bleated, "I'm sorry."

Out in the car, Vicki pulled a fleece blanket around her legs and melted into the seat.

"I got what I deserved," Vicki said.

"What do you mean?" Brenda said.

"I wanted to be done with chemo," Vicki said. "And now chemo's done with me. Once a week, a low dosage. It wouldn't kill a one-winged fly."

"You don't think?"

"The cancer's going to rally," Vicki said. "It's going to spread."

"Stop it, Vick. You've got to keep a positive attitude."

"And I will have brought it on myself."

"I don't see how you can say that," Brenda said. "It's not your fault you're sick."

"It's my fault I'm not getting better," Vicki said. "I suck at getting better." She leaned her head against the window. "God, the guilt."

Brenda started the car. "Amen to that," she said.

The heart wants what it wants, Melanie thought. And so, on the morning after her first prenatal appointment, she called Peter at the office.

Melanie was lying in bed, listening to the wren that habitually sang from its perch on the fence outside her window, with her eyes closed. She was tired because she and Josh had been out again the night before—to Quidnet Pond—and she hadn't gotten home until after midnight. Earlier that day, Melanie had gone with Vicki to the hospital. While Vicki was getting a shot to bring her blood counts back up, Melanie had an appointment with a surly GP, a white-haired doctor perhaps a month or two shy of retirement. The man had zero bedside manner, but Melanie didn't care. She had heard her baby's heartbeat. *Whoosh, whoosh, whoosh.* What she hadn't anticipated was the enormous chasm between imagining the sound of the heartbeat and actually hearing it. The pregnancy was real. It was healthy and viable. She was ten weeks along; the baby was the size of a plum.

Now, she placed a hand on her abdomen. "Hello," she whispered. "Good morning."

She had been waiting for a sign. It had been easy to keep the news from Peter because, although Melanie had been sick and so, so tired, there had been no visible manifestation of the pregnancy. She didn't even look pregnant. But that heartbeat had been real, it had been undeniable, and that was her cue. It wasn't that she felt she had to tell Peter. She *wanted* to tell Peter.

And so, once Josh and the kids left the house and once Brenda headed out to write, and once Vicki's bedroom door was securely closed, Melanie scuffed down to the 'Sconset Market and called Peter from the pay phone outside.

Melanie took a deep drink of 'Sconset morning: the blue, blooming hydrangeas, the freshly mown grass of the rotary, the smell of the clay tennis courts across the street at the casino, the scent of coffee and rolls and fresh newsprint coming from the market itself. And then there was the smell of Josh on her skin. Even if Peter was mean to her, even if he refused to believe her, he would not be able to ruin her day.

"Good morning," the receptionist said. "Rutter, Higgens."

Even if he said he didn't care.

"Peter Patchen, please," Melanie said, trying to sound businesslike.

"One moment, please."

There was a pause, a click, then ringing. Melanie was overcome with fear, anxiety, the same old negative Peter-feelings that she thought she'd buried. *Shit!* she thought. *Hang up!* But before there was time to orchestrate a hang up, Melanie heard Peter's voice. "Hello? Peter Patchen."

His voice. Amazing, but she had forgotten it, or half forgotten it, so that now these three words shocked her.

"Peter?" she said. "It's me." Then she worried he would mistake her "me" for Frances Digitt's "me," and so she added, "Melanie."

"Melanie?" He sounded surprised, and if she wasn't deluding herself, *happily* surprised. But no, this wasn't possible. It was a trick of long distance, of the rusty old pay phone.

"Yes," she said, trying to keep her voice clipped and cool.

"How are you?" Peter said. "*Where* are you?"

"Nantucket," she said.

"Oh," he said. Did she sense *disappointment* in his voice? Not possible. "How is it?"

"Great," she said. "Beautiful. Warm, sunny, breezy, beachy. How's New York?"

"Hot," he said. "Sticky. A cauldron."

"How's work?" she said.

"Oh, you know. The same."

Melanie pressed her lips together. *The same,* meaning he was still screwing the girl down the hall? Melanie wouldn't ask; she didn't care. She did care about the state of her garden, however—her poor perennial beds!—but she wouldn't ask about that either.

"Okay, well, I'm just calling to let you know . . ." God, was she really going to say it? "I'm pregnant."

"What?"

"I'm pregnant." The words seemed smaller when she spoke them than they did in her mind. "Pregnant with a baby. Due in February."

There was silence on Peter's end. Of course. Melanie focused on a nine- or ten-year-old girl walking into the market with her father. *Bubble Gum Princess,* the girl's T-shirt said. She had long, thin legs like a stork.

"You're kidding me," Peter said. "This is a joke."

"It is not," Melanie said. Though wasn't it just like Peter to think so. "I would never joke about something like this."

"No, you wouldn't," he said. "You're right, you wouldn't. But how? When?"

"That time," she said. "You remember."

"During the thunderstorm?"

"Yes." She knew he remembered, of course he remembered. Even if he'd had sex with Frances Digitt a hundred times that very week, he would remember. Melanie had been out in the garden cutting lilies. She ran into the house because it had started to pour. In the mudroom, she peeled off her soaked clothes and announced to Peter that she was all done with IVF. The disappointment was killing her, she told him. She wanted to get on with life. Melanie's face had been wet with raindrops and tears, naturally. Peter cried a little, too—mostly out of relief, she suspected—and then they made love, right there in the mudroom, up against the porcelain front of her gardening sink. Outside, it rained harder and harder; there was a sharp thunderclap that sounded like a very large bone breaking. Peter and Melanie made love like they hadn't in years—she hungrily, he gratefully—while the stamens of the lilies bled a deep orange into the sink.

Afterward, Peter said, *We could never have done that if we had children.*

The stains from the lily stamens remained in the sink, a lingering reminder of their coupling, which made Melanie wistful before she learned about Frances Digitt and bitterly angry afterward. She had been able to forget those stains now that there was something even more permanent. A heartbeat. A baby.

"You're sure, Mel?"

"I went to the doctor," she said. "I'm ten weeks along. I heard the heartbeat."

"You did?"

"Yeah."

"Jesus," he whispered. And then he was silent again. What was he thinking? Melanie was pleased to discover that she didn't particularly care.

"So, anyway," Melanie said. "I just thought you should know."

"Know? Of course I should *know*. I am the father." His tone was approaching that of an accusation, but Melanie would not be bullied. He had given up the right to the secrets her body contained when he slept with Frances Digitt. Melanie could close her eyes and picture Frances rounding the bases of the softball field, pumping her fist in the air.

"I wanted to wait until I'd been to the doctor before I told you. I wanted to make sure everything was okay."

"How do you feel?" he said.

"I've been pretty sick," she said. "I'm tired a lot, but otherwise, I feel fine."

"You sound great," Peter said. "You sound really *great*." He paused, cleared his throat. Melanie listened for the sound of his fingers on the computer keyboard. It would be just like him to check the market or play Snood while he was on the phone with her. But what she heard was silence; he didn't even seem to be breathing. "God, I can't believe this. Can you? After all we went through?"

"I know," she said. "Pretty ironic."

"You do sound great, Mel."

"Thanks," she said. "Okay, well, I'm on a pay phone so I should probably hang up. I'll see you . . ."

"When?" Peter said. "I mean, when are you coming home?"

Melanie laughed. "Oh, geez," she said. "I have no idea." She felt wonderful saying this. She was 100 percent in control. When she got back to the house, she would kiss Vicki and thank her again for letting her come to Nantucket. Tonight, she would kiss Josh, and then some.

"I'll be in touch, Peter," Melanie said.

"Um, okay, I'll—"

Melanie hung up.

E very morning when Josh walked into Number Eleven Shell Street, he asked himself what he was doing. *What am I doing? What the fuck am I doing?* The answer was: He was sleeping with Melanie Patchen, a woman both married and pregnant, he was having an affair with her, and he was keeping it a secret not only from Brenda and Vicki and his father, but from Blaine and Porter. He felt the guiltiest, perhaps, when he looked at the two kids, because he wanted to set a good example for them. They were going to emulate him any which way, a fact that would be easier to accept had he not been screwing their mother's best friend. It was always first thing in the morning, when he saw their round, wide-eyed faces at the breakfast table, that his remorse was the keenest. By ten o'clock at night—which was when he met Melanie at the town beach—it had dissipated enough for him to carry on with his treachery.

How long would it be until they got caught? Josh

asked himself this a hundred times a day, though he never put the question to Melanie because she had enough to worry about as it was. And they were very, very careful. Melanie went so far as to climb out her window into the garden rather than leave the house by the front door; she went so far as to straddle the picket fence rather than use the gate. She built a body out of spare pillows in her bed, and she padded along the side of the road in the grass rather than crunch on the shells. She arrived at the parking lot of the town beach between ten and ten-thirty; she climbed into Josh's Jeep, and he whisked her away to one of a dozen secluded spots where they made love either in his car or, if they were feeling brave, on the beach. Twice, Josh had gotten the feeling that they were being followed. One time, he had turned down a dirt road that led them deep into the moors, and the other time he pulled into an empty driveway. Those incidents made Melanie squeal with nervous excitement, and Josh had to admit, his adrenaline surged in a way that was not unpleasant. They were living a movie script—the secret, forbidden relationship complete with dramatic escapes, and the explosive sex that followed.

The sex was, in fact, astonishing. It became abundantly clear to Josh that having sex with a girl was one thing and having sex with a woman was quite another. Josh had thought Melanie's pregnancy would make things weird, or uncomfortable, but it was just the opposite. Melanie was completely in tune with her body, her hormones were flowing, she was always ready for Josh, she craved him. She complimented him, she encouraged him to be creative. Yeah, the sex was a fantasy, Josh couldn't deny it, but if the relationship with

Melanie had been only about sex, Josh would have tired of it. The problem was that the relationship quickly became about more than just sex. Melanie talked to him, she told him things—real, adult things; she trusted him with details. It was different from the dreck Josh usually got from girls. When Josh thought about the stupid drivel he was used to hearing from girls his age (*My hair goes frizz-city in this humidity. . . . Ohmygod, look how many grams of fat! . . . Who's going to be there? That bitch? . . . I downloaded it for free on . . .*), he was amazed his brain hadn't turned to tapioca. At first, Josh wasn't sure that hearing about Melanie's shattered marriage or her quest for a child would be any better, but he was wrong. It was a story that sucked him right in.

A marriage, as you'll no doubt discover one day, is a pact you make with another person. It's a vow you take, it's sacred, or so you believe on the altar. It's a promise that you'll never be alone, you're part of a team, a unit, a couple, a married couple. That's the dream, anyway, and I believed it. The baby thing was another dream. For most couples, it's a given. They don't even think about it and—bam!—pregnant. I thought it would be that way with Peter and me. I always wanted lots of kids. And then we tried and it didn't happen and people said, Give it time, because what else can they say? And so we kept trying and kept trying, but the more I thought of it as "trying" the more stressful it became and I got sad and Peter got angry because there was nothing either of us could do. So then we went to see a doctor, and I was, of course, thinking there was something wrong with Peter, and Peter was thinking there was something wrong with me. But the frustrating thing was that there was nothing wrong with either of us. We were both perfectly healthy, we just weren't connecting. So I took fertility drugs, which had unpleasant side effects, and they didn't seem to be working anyway, so I stopped those, and we tried the holistic approach—powder from rhinoceros horn and making love upside down at midnight during a full moon—and then we just threw in the towel and admitted it wasn't working. So what were our options? In vitro. But in vitro is tricky—there's a timetable, they harvest eggs, they take Peter's sperm, they fertilize the eggs in a laboratory, then they implant the eggs and hope they take root. There's a lot of hospital time involved, lots of other people, health professionals helping you along, and meanwhile you're thinking how unromantic it all is, and you're wondering why you couldn't just have conceived after three martinis or a weekend in Palm Springs, like everybody else. You start to hate yourself. Seven times I went through in vitro cycles. It was over a year of my life spent holding my breath, basically, and praying— then crying when it didn't work, blaming myself, blaming Peter. I'm not going to say I was easy to live with—I wasn't. Peter got tired of hearing about my cycle, ovulation, fertilization, implantation, viable embryos, but that was all I could think about. The real difference between Peter and me was that I kept the faith in our marriage. I thought we were on the same team—in a tug-of-war, let's say, against whatever forces were working to keep us childless. But then it was like I looked behind me and Peter was gone, I was tugging alone. Or worse. It was like Peter had joined the other team. He and Frances Digitt. He was my dearest love, my best friend, my safe place, my hero, Josh—and then I discovered I was noth-

*ing to him. Less than nothing. It was—it is—the betrayal
of a lifetime. I thought affairs were only in soap operas. I
thought they were only in Cheever. I didn't know they really happened. I was so fucking naive. Peter is having an
affair with Frances Digitt, he is* involved with *Frances
Digitt. You can't imagine. You just can't imagine.*

She was wrong there. All he could do was imagine, and
when he did so, he found himself hating Peter Patchen.
Because what Josh quickly learned was that Melanie was
a sweet person, a genuine person, she thought of others,
she was kind and vulnerable and trusting. Of course she
believed in love that lasted forever, of course she wanted
a house full of children—and she deserved it. The more
time Josh spent with Melanie, the more he wanted to
help her, to save her. *He* wanted to be her hero. He realized he'd felt this way from the very beginning—when
Melanie fell off the airplane's steps and he offered her
first aid, and then again when she was stranded at the
airport and he gave her a ride home. Late at night, when
Josh lay sleepless in bed trying to figure out *what the fuck
he was doing with Melanie,* he wondered if there was
something in him that needed to be needed—but if that
were the case, he might as well have stayed with Didi.
She was the neediest person he knew. In the end, Josh
would have to say that he didn't know what he was doing
with Melanie, but he was powerless to stop.

The nights passed in what felt like a blaze of light, at
once slow-burning and quick as a flash. Neither of them
was willing to skip a night, take a break, although they
both pretended to think it was a good idea. (*We should
probably take a breather at some point,* Josh said. And
with a yawn, Melanie: *I don't know how long I'll be able*

to keep these late nights up.) Josh figured that at some point the novelty would wear off; his insanely absorbing anticipation of the moment when Melanie climbed into his Jeep would diminish. A lackluster night would come upon them, a night when he just wasn't that into it, a night when Melanie seemed less dynamic than usual, or too familiar. This was how things went with Josh and girls. Eventually he felt—as with Didi—that he was being pulled along against his wishes.

But with Melanie, it was different. With Melanie, it was like climbing a mountain to a breathtaking view, and each time it was as novel and captivating as the first time.

More and more, he wanted to be with Melanie in a real bed, but that wasn't possible. His bed, his child-hood bed, in his room with his model airplanes and soccer trophies, his journals now tucked into the drawer of his nightstand? No. And Josh would never have the guts to sneak into Number Eleven Shell Street knowing that Vicki and Brenda and Blaine and Porter (and Ted, on the weekends) were all *right there.* Josh found himself brainstorming for an alternative—a night in a bed-and-breakfast, maybe? It was an expensive option and risky to boot because Tom Flynn knew everyone on the island. Somehow, Josh was sure, word would get back to his father that Josh had paid three hundred and fifty dollars for a room, which he had shared with an "older woman."

Josh hadn't seen much of his high school friends all summer. He was busy with work, they were busy with work—and going to the parties or meeting up at bars meant risking a run-in with Didi, which Josh was happy to avoid. Josh felt bad calling up Zach for what was, basically, the first time all summer—but Zach could help him. Zach was spending his summer working for Madaket Marine, the business his parents owned, but as a sideline, he served as caretaker for a house in Shimmo, right on the harbor. The house was modest for Nantucket's waterfront—it had five bedrooms and three baths, with a deck that extended the length of the second floor. The house was only used two weeks of the year—the first two weeks of July—and the rest of the time, it sat empty. It was Zach's responsibility to let the cleaners in every two weeks and arrange for the landscaping—and in winter to shovel the snow and check for burst pipes or leaks. The owners lived in Hong Kong; they never showed up without warning, and in fact, Zach spent the weeks before their arrival ensuring that every detail was perfect and in place—Asiatic lilies on the dining room table, Veuve Clicquot in the fridge. People had been urging Zach for the years that he'd been taking care of the Shimmo house to *throw a party, man!* But Zach was even more intimidated by his father than Josh was by Tom Flynn, and the owner of the house was a longtime Madaket Marine client. So Zach's answer was always, *No way, man. Are you kidding me?* Zach threw his parties at the beach.

Zach had been known, however, to entertain women at the house in Shimmo, especially summer girls (he told them the house was his). So Zach's scruples were negotiable (this had always been the case), and Josh thought, *Well, it's worth a shot.* He called Zach one night on his way home from swimming at Nobadeer Beach.

"I want to use the Shimmo house," Josh said. "One night. Any night next week."

"What?" Zach said. "Who is this?"

"Shut up."

"I haven't heard from you in ages, man. You skipped my party. You never go out. And now you want to use the house?"

"Don't be so sensitive," Josh said. "You sound like a woman. Can I use the house?"

"You have a girl?" Zach said.

"Yeah."

"Who is it?"

"None of your business," Josh said.

"Oh, come on."

"What?"

"Tell me who it is."

"A girl I met in 'Sconset."

"Really?"

"Really. There are girls in 'Sconset who never show their faces in town."

"What's her name?"

"None of your business."

"Why so secretive? Just tell me her name."

"No."

"If you tell me her name, I'll let you use the house. Next Wednesday."

"Her name is Merrill," Josh said. He wanted to use a name he would remember—and Merrill was Melanie's maiden name.

"Merrill?"

"Yeah."

"Is she in school?"

"She just graduated," Josh said. "From Sarah Lawrence."

"Sarah Lawrence?"

"Yeah."

"She graduated? So she's older?"

"She's older. A little bit older. I'd like to impress her. Hence, the request for the house."

"And I take it this Merrill person is why I haven't seen your ass all summer."

"Pretty much."

"Well, okay," Zach said. "Next Wednesday. I'll get you the keys. But you must promise to strictly adhere to all the rules."

"I'll adhere," Josh said.

The following Wednesday, instead of driving to the beach, Josh turned down Shimmo Road and pulled into the last driveway on the left. He was all wound up with anxiety and sexual anticipation and an overwhelming desire to surprise Melanie. He dug the keys to the house from the console and jangled them in her face.

"What are we doing here?" she said.

"What we normally do," he said, grinning.

He got out of the car and hurried around to open Melanie's door for her.

"Whose house is this?" she said.

"It belongs to a friend of mine," Josh said. "He's not using it this week."

He watched for her reaction. She seemed nonplussed. It had occurred to him since the moment that Zach handed him the keys that Melanie would think borrowing someone else's house was cheesy and juvenile.

Peter Patchen made serious money. He was the kind of guy who booked a suite at a five-star resort in Cabo. He could have rented a place like this with ease.

Josh's hands shook as he unlocked the front door. He checked over his shoulder at the neighbor's house, where a single onion lamp burned. These neighbors, according to Zach, were real watchdogs, and so one of the rules Josh had to strictly adhere to was not to turn on any lights on the north side of the house.

Inside the house, Josh took off his shoes.

"Take off your shoes," he said.

Melanie laughed. "Ohhhh-kay."

"I know," he said. "Sorry." The floors were made of some rare wood, Zach said, and the rule was: No shoes, not even if you were the Queen of England.

Josh walked up a curving staircase to a great room with windows overlooking the harbor. He turned on some lights and immediately set them on dimmers, way down low. There was a fancy bar with mirrors and blue granite and a hundred wineglasses hanging upside down. On the counter, as promised, Zach had left a bottle of champagne in a bucket of ice and a plate of cheese, crackers, strawberries, and grapes.

"For us," Josh said, brandishing the champagne bottle.

"Oh," Melanie said. She walked to the sliding glass door and stepped out onto the deck. "This place has some view!" she called out.

Josh nearly asked her to lower her voice. The last thing he wanted was for the neighbor to hear them and come over to investigate—or worse, to call the police. Since he'd gotten the keys, a hundred ruinous scenarios had presented themselves in Josh's mind, making him wonder if all this was even worth it.

But later, after they had used the bed (not the master bed, of course, but the best guest-room bed, which was a king and very soft and luxurious, a five-star bed, in Josh's estimation) and after they had showered together in a bathroom tiled with tumbled marble and after they had consumed the entire bottle of champagne (this was mostly Josh, since Melanie was pregnant) and the plate of cheese and fruit (this was mostly Melanie because she was ravenous after sex)—he decided that yes, it was worth it. The champagne had gone to his head, but that only intensified his enjoyment of these moments stolen, borrowed. Josh turned on the flat-screen TV at the foot of the bed. He had never done anything normal with Melanie, like watch TV.

"What do you watch?" he said.

"Nothing," she said. "Well, *The Sopranos.* And *Desperate Housewives,* if I remember to Tivo it. And football."

"Football?" he said. "College or NFL?"

"NFL," she said.

He fed her Brie on crackers, and the cracker crumbs fell onto the sheets. Josh tickled her and she squirmed and Josh noted how squirming on 400-count sheets was far superior to squirming in grainy sand. He tickled her so relentlessly that she squealed, and Josh stopped immediately, cocking his head like a dog, listening. Had anyone heard them?

"What's wrong with you?" Melanie said.

"Nothing."

"We're not supposed to be here, are we?"

"Of course we're supposed to be here," Josh said. "*We* are supposed to be here."

He and Melanie wrapped themselves in white, waffled robes that were hanging in the closet and stepped out onto the deck. Josh found himself wondering where he might find six million dollars, so he could buy the house. So they could just stay there. So they would never have to leave.

He pulled Melanie back into bed. "Are you happy?" he asked. "Do you like it here?"

"Mmmhmmgwshw," she said. Her mouth was full of strawberry. "Yeah. It was very sweet of you to arrange this. You didn't have to, though, Josh. The beach is fine."

"You deserve better," he said.

"Oh," she said. Her eyes misted up. She touched his cheek. "You are better."

You are better: She said things like this and rendered Josh speechless. *You are better:* He replayed the words over and over again in his mind, even after he took Melanie back to Number Eleven Shell Street, even after he returned to Shimmo to wash the sheets and wipe down the bathroom, even as he fell into bed at three o'clock in the morning. *You are better.*

The following night, it was back to the beach.

"I almost got caught today," Melanie said.

They were lying next to each other on an old blanket. (It was, in fact, the blanket that Vicki had given Josh to take to the beach with the kids. Earlier, he'd had to shake it free of raisins and graham cracker crumbs.) They were on the very small beach in Monomoy, hidden on the far side of two stacked wooden dinghies. To their left was tall marsh grass, which thrummed with the sound of bullfrogs. The best thing about Monomoy was the view of town, which glittered in the distance like a real city. Monomoy was one of Josh's favorite spots on the island, though compared to the night before, it was camping. Riches to rags, he thought.

Josh propped himself up on his elbows. Melanie wasn't trying to scare him. It had become part of their ritual to detail the ways in which they had almost gotten caught. There were a hundred pitfalls. Josh himself had nearly blown their cover that morning by showing up at Number Eleven with Melanie's watch in his pocket. She had left it on the bedside table in Shimmo the night before and he had meant to slip it to her or leave it, casually, on the kitchen table, but the second he walked through the gate, Blaine grabbed him by the pocket and the watch fell onto the flagstone path. Brenda was sitting on the step at the end of the path, but she was so intent on landing a pebble in the paper cup that she didn't notice the watch. Blaine noticed, however—it was impossible to get anything past that kid—because later, when Josh asked the family beside them at the beach for the time, Blaine scrunched his brow.

I thought you had Melanie's watch, he said.

Right, Josh said, determined not to get flustered. *I found it in the yard. But I gave it back to her.*

Oh, Blaine said. He might have looked at Josh suspiciously for an extra beat, or that might have been Josh's paranoid imagination.

"What happened today?" Josh asked Melanie now. He leaned over and kissed her neck. She smelled like chocolate. Immediately after sex she had pulled a bag of M&M's from her pocket, and now she was letting them dissolve, one by one, on her tongue.

"I sat with Vicki after dinner," Melanie said. "I read to her. And when I left, I told her I'd check on her when I got in."

"And she said, 'Get in? From where? Are you going out?'" Josh said.

"Exactly," Melanie said. "So I told her I was planning on walking to the market to call Peter from the pay phone."

Josh stiffened. Peter? Call Peter?

"That was a stupid excuse," he said. "Because why wouldn't you just call Peter from the house?"

"There's no long-distance from the house," Melanie said. "So to call Peter I'd have to go to the market."

"It was still a stupid excuse," Josh said. "Why would you want to call Peter? He's such an asshole."

"Right," Melanie said. "That was just what I told Vicki."

"So you didn't call Peter?"

"God, no. Not tonight."

"Another night? Did you call him another night? Last night?"

"Last week," Melanie said. "In the morning, I called him. About a household thing."

They were quiet. Josh heard the clanging of a buoy somewhere offshore. Normally, he enjoyed Melanie's too-close-for-comfort stories. It was thrilling, the secret of the two of them, the forbidden aspect of it. Josh's senses were heightened, his desire doubled and tripled by the simple fact that they were flying under everyone's radar. And yet now, with the mention of Peter, with the confession that she had spoken to him earlier in the week, he felt confused and jealous. He felt like he had been deceived. If she had talked to Peter *earlier in the week,* she should have told him. He might not have gone to all the trouble that last night entailed had he known Melanie was back in touch with Peter the creep, the lowlife, the philanderer. He might have skipped it and saved the ninety dollars he'd had to pay Zach for the champagne.

Why the hell would Melanie be calling Peter? A household thing? Which meant what, the electric bill? Josh didn't get it. He wanted to ask Melanie to explain, he wanted her to clarify. But Josh was halted by the sensation that this relationship was becoming too important to him—and one of the deals he had made with himself was that this was fun, yes, and exciting, certainly, but it was also short-term. For the summer only. He and Melanie had real lives to live—Josh would return to Middlebury, Melanie would go back to Connecticut and have her baby. There wasn't really room for jealousy or hurt feelings, and yet Josh was dangerously close to suffering from both.

Melanie offered Josh the bag of M&M's, but he pushed her hand away.

"Uh-oh," she said. "Someone's upset."

"I'm not upset."

"It was nothing, Josh. One phone call. I probably won't call him again this summer."

"Go ahead and call him," Josh said. "He's your husband." He took a breath of pungent air. At that moment,

Monomoy seemed like less of a haven and more of a swamp. "Let's get out of here."

Melanie eyed him for a second, and he thought she might protest, but Melanie wasn't silly or desperate like the other girls he knew. She folded the top of the M&M's bag over neatly, stood up, and brushed herself off.

"Fine," she said. "Let's go."

They walked back to the Jeep in silence, with Josh thinking alternately that this whole thing was stupid, they should just end it now. Deep down, however, Josh knew he would never be able to end it, and why would he want to? Melanie wasn't going back to Peter any time this summer, and summer was all he cared about so he should stop whining and enjoy himself.

Fine. That conclusion reached, he felt much better. At the Jeep, he opened Melanie's door and kissed her as he helped her in.

Headlights swooped in on him so fast he didn't know what they were at first. He felt caught, like a cartoon convict pegged by searchlights. He shouted at Melanie to *get down,* but she didn't hear him or she heard him but didn't listen because when he checked she was staring into the front of the big, black truck like she thought it might run them over. The engine gunned and the truck swerved into the spot next to the Jeep for just long enough that Josh could see who was driving; then the truck reversed and pulled out, leaving behind the proverbial cloud of brown dust and a spray of sand that peppered Josh's legs like buckshot.

Shit, Josh thought, and he said it over and again as he climbed into the Jeep next to Melanie. *Shit, shit, shit.* It might have been a coincidence, Josh thought. It wasn't like parking in Monomoy was an original idea. But who was he kidding? Rob Patalka, Didi's brother, was following him, stalking him, or driving around the island at Didi's insistence trying to hunt him down. Didi certainly wasn't paying Rob, so what incentive did Rob have to do her bidding? Was it out of loyalty? Brotherly love? Josh didn't want to think about it. All he knew was that the thrill and rush of almost getting caught had turned, like sour milk, into the reality of getting caught.

Melanie, not knowing this, looked amused. "Friend of yours?" she said.

"Not exactly," he said.

A card came in the mail. It was from Dolores, the leader of Vicki's cancer support group back in Connecticut. Alan, the member of the group with pancreatic cancer, had passed away the previous Monday. Vicki stared at the words "passed away" in Dolores's spidery handwriting. Alan was fifty-seven years old, he'd been married for thirty-one of those years, he was the father of one son and two daughters; he had a grandchild, the son of his son, a baby named Brendan, who was the same age as Porter. Alan, either coincidentally or on purpose, always chose the seat next to Vicki in the support group circle; they held hands during the opening and closing prayer. This was all Vicki knew of the man, and yet as she read Dolores's note ("passed away") she felt cold and numb. Alan had kissed Vicki's cheek before she left for Nantucket. She'd said, *I'll see you when I get back.* And he'd said, *You bet.*

The support group had been Dr. Garcia's idea. Vicki had attended half a dozen times—twice a week for the three weeks before she left for the summer. What she had learned, perhaps the only thing she had learned, was that cancer was a journey, a series of ups and downs, of good days and bad days, of progress and setbacks. Vicki yearned to be back in the circle so she could tell the story of her own journey and hear murmurs from people who understood.

The fever, which lasted five days, was like nothing Vicki had ever experienced. She was alternately burning up and freezing cold; she shook so violently in the bathtub that the water splashed over the sides. She wore a sweater to bed, she slept fitfully and had horrible nightmares—armed robbers in ski masks with guns in her bedroom, demanding that she hand over one of her boys. *Choose one!* How could she choose? *Take me!* she'd said. *Take me!* Yes, they would take her. They carried her out of the room by her arms and legs.

Her vision, during the day, was splotchy, she suffered from insidious headaches; it hurt just to look out the window at the bright sunlight and the green leaves. Her brain felt like a piece of meat boiling in a pot. She was dehydrated, despite the fact that Brenda replenished a frosty pitcher of ice water with lemon slices floating on top every few hours. Brenda held the straw to Vicki's lips, as did Melanie, as did Ted. Ted laid a washcloth across her forehead—a washcloth that they started keeping in the freezer, that made her cry out with pain and relief. Once, Vicki opened her eyes and was certain she saw her mother standing in the doorway of the bedroom. It was Ellen Lyndon, come from Philadelphia, despite the fact that her leg was imprisoned in a complicated brace. Ellen's hand was cool on Vicki's forehead; Vicki inhaled her mother's perfume. Vicki closed her eyes and suddenly she was back at her parents' house, in her childhood bed, with a cup of broth and angel toast dusted with cinnamon, with strains of Mozart floating up the stairs from the kitchen. Vicki rose from her bed. There was something in her shoes. Sand.

She was taking antibiotics, strong ones, although no one in the hospital could tell her where the infection was. Her fever dropped to 101 then shot back up to over 104. They threatened to admit her while she was at the hospital getting an injection of Neupogen, the drug that was supposed to boost her white count. She was taking four painkillers every six hours, and every two hours she suffered through the goddamned thermometer under her tongue or in the crook of her arm. Vicki started moaning about her missed chemo. Now that she couldn't have it, she wanted it badly. Dr. Alcott told her not to worry. Blood count up first, then they would let her return for treatment. Vicki's body felt like a murky soup, her blood poisoned and diluted. All the colors of the rainbow mixed together, Blaine had once informed her, made brown. That was Vicki.

All across the globe, mothers were dying. Engulfed in fever, Vicki tried to count them—women she remembered from childhood (Mrs. Antonini next door died of Lou Gehrig's disease, leaving behind seven-year-old twins); people she didn't know (Josh's mother, hanging herself); people she had read about in the newspaper (a Palestinian woman, eight months pregnant, blew herself to pieces at an Israeli checkpoint. In Royersford, Pennsylvania, a disgruntled client walked into the headquarters of his insurance company with an AK-47. His first victim was the receptionist, Mary Gallagher, who was on her first day back from maternity leave. Seven mothers were killed in Los Angeles when a commuter bus flipped on the freeway and caught on fire). These women floated over Vicki's bed, she could see them, sort of, she could hear them crying. Or was that Vicki crying? Curse the God who took mothers out of this world! But no sooner was she cursing Him than she was praying. Praying! *Don't let it be me. Please.*

The only pleasure she had, if you could call it pleasure, were those sips of water. The water was so cold and Vicki was so, so thirsty. Half the time, she swore, she didn't even swallow it. It was absorbed instantly by the chalky insides of her mouth, the dry sponge of her tongue. She had to be careful to ration herself. If she drank too much at once, she would spend torturous moments hanging off the side of her bed, sweating, her stomach twisting and clenching, her back spasming, her shoulders and neck as tense as steel cable as she fought to bring up teaspoons of bitter yellow bile.

On the sixth day, she woke up and her sheets were soaked. She feared she'd wet the bed, but she could barely bring herself to care. On top of everything else, what was a little incontinence? But no—it was sweat. Her fever had broken. Vicki took her temperature herself, then had Brenda double-check: 98.6.

Blaine ran into the room to see her, and she barely recognized him. He was brown from the sun. His hair, so blond it was almost white, had been cut to reveal pale stripes behind his ears and around his neck. Porter had a haircut, too.

"Who took them to get haircuts?" Vicki said. "Ted?"

"Josh," Brenda said. "But that was last week."

Already it was the middle of July. Where had the time gone? Vicki's fever had subsided and she and everyone else were glad about that, but Vicki was left feeling like a hollow log, one that the cancer cells might carry away, like so many ants. She went back to the hospital, they drew more blood, Vicki's count rose. On Tuesday, they would resume treatment, though slowly at first. She had lost an additional five pounds.

Melanie came in to read to Vicki every evening after dinner. Melanie was reading from *Bridget Jones's Diary* because it was light and fun, and both Vicki and Melanie wanted to spend time in a place where the only things that mattered were boyfriends, calories, and designer shoes. Vicki was embarrassed, being read to like a child, but she enjoyed the time with Melanie. They had been living under the same roof but they had lost each other. Now Melanie was coming back into focus, and she seemed different. Certainly she looked different—her body was simultaneously swollen and tight, she was tan, her hair was growing lighter from the sun. She was beautiful.

"You're beautiful," Vicki said one night as Melanie took the seat beside her bed. "You look fabulous. You're glowing. You should be in a magazine."

Melanie blushed, smiled, and tried to busy herself with finding the correct page in the book. "Stop it."

"I'm serious," Vicki said. "You look happy. Are you *happy*?" She hoped her voice conveyed that although she herself was dying, she could still celebrate the good news of others.

Melanie seemed afraid to speak, but the answer was obvious. And to Vicki, this change in Melanie seemed like the biggest thing of all that she had missed. Melanie was happy! Here on Nantucket!

Vicki resumed chemo. She returned to her lucky chair, the pearl-gray walls, the sports news, Mamie, Ben, Amelia, Dr. Alcott. She was happy to hear they were still undefeated in softball. Vicki gasped when Mamie inserted the needle into her port—the skin there was as tender as it had been in the beginning—but she was determined to think of the chemo as medicine. Positive attitude!

"Your sister seems very busy over there," Mamie commented. "She's writing something?"

"A screenplay," Vicki said. For the first time, this didn't sound completely ridiculous. "She's almost half done."

Vicki had one good day followed by another. The lighter chemo regimen took less of a toll on her body. She was able to cook dinner—grilled salmon, barbecued chicken, corn and early tomatoes from the farm—and she was able to eat. After dinner, she devoured ice-cream cones from the market. She gained two pounds, then three, and she joked that the weight went right to her ass. The weekend came, which meant Ted, and she felt so much better and looked so much better that sex came easily and naturally between the two of them. Sex! She might have lain in bed afterward savoring the first postcoital glow she'd enjoyed in nearly two months, but she didn't want to lie in bed when she could be up, when she could be outside.

"Let's go!" she said. She felt wild and carefree; she felt like Bridget Jones.

She went to the beach with Ted and the kids, though it was still too far for Vicki to walk, so they drove the Yukon. Vicki was the palest person on the beach and grotesquely skinny, and because of the port, she wore a nylon surf shirt over her bathing suit—but these things went immediately onto her List of Things That No Longer Matter. A few yards down the beach Vicki spied a familiar figure in a matronly black one-piece bathing suit. It was Caroline Knox with her family. If Vicki wasn't mistaken, Caroline was looking her way but trying not to be caught looking. She turned to say something to a bald man in a webbed chair next to her. Probably: *There's Vicki Stowe, lung cancer, poor woman. Just look at her, a skeleton. She used to be so pretty. . . .*

Vicki didn't care. She waded into the water with Blaine, and then she swam out a few yards by herself. The water felt incredible. It cradled her. She floated on her back and closed her eyes against the sun; she flipped over and floated on her stomach and opened her eyes to the green, silent world below. The waves washed over her, she was suspended, weightless, buoyant. How long did she stay out there? One minute, five minutes, twenty? She lost time the way she used to as she lay in bed, only now it was liberating. She was alive, living, out in the world, floating in the ocean. When she raised her head and looked back toward shore, she saw Ted standing at the edge of the water with Porter in his arms and Blaine standing beside him. They were searching for her. Could they not see her? She waved to them. *Hi! I'm right here!* For a second, she panicked. This was what it would be like once she was gone. She would be able to see them but they wouldn't be able to see her. Vicki raised her arms a little higher; she called out. *Hey! Hello!* And then Ted saw her; he pointed. *There she is! Hi, Mom!* They waved back.

First Vicki felt good, then she felt great. She called her mother and, for the first time all summer, put the woman's mind at ease. *You sound wonderful, darling! You sound like your old self!* Vicki felt like her old self— even breathing came easier. She imagined the tumor in her lungs shrinking to the size of a marble, she imagined the cancer cells giving up and dropping dead. It was easy to keep a positive attitude when she felt this good.

On Monday, when Josh took the kids to the beach, Vicki persuaded Brenda and Melanie to go shopping with her in town. The day was dazzling, and Main Street was a hive of activity. Vicki stood for nearly twenty minutes at the Bartlett's Farm truck picking out a rainbow of gladiola, six perfect tomatoes for sandwiches and salad, ten ears of sugar-butter corn, the perfect head of red leaf lettuce, and cucumbers that she would marinate in fresh dill, tarragon, and vinegar. Vicki carried this bounty herself—though Brenda strongly suggested putting it in the car—because Vicki liked being healthy enough to carry two shopping bags of vegetables, and she liked the way the stems of the gladiola brushed against her face.

Brenda wanted to go to the bookstore, and so they lingered in Mitchell's for a while, where Vicki paged through cookbooks. Melanie bought the sequel to

Bridget Jones. Vicki dashed up to the bank for cash and she picked up lollipops for the kids. When she got back to the bookstore, Melanie was standing outside, waiting for her. Brenda had gone to the Even Keel Cafe for a coffee. They proceeded down Main Street to Erica Wilson. Melanie wanted some new clothes. She tried on a long embroidered skirt with an elastic waist, and a tunic that she could wear over her bathing suit. Each time she came out of the curtained dressing room to model for Brenda and Vicki, she twirled. Her face barely concealed her delight.

Vicki was about to mention Melanie's unprecedented ecstasy to Brenda, but Brenda beat her to it. "What is *up* with her?" Brenda said. "She's been Suzy Sunshine lately."

"I know," Vicki said. "She's happy."

"But why?" Brenda said.

"Does there have to be a reason?" Vicki said.

"Don't you think it's strange?" Brenda said.

"Maybe it's the pregnancy hormones," Vicki said. "Or maybe she just loves it here with us."

Brenda looked skeptical. "Oh, yeah, it's us." Her cell phone started its strangled jingling. "I'm certainly not going to answer that."

"What if it's Josh?" Vicki said.

Brenda checked the display. "It's not Josh."

"Not Mom?"

"No."

"Your lawyer?"

"Mind your own business, please."

Melanie came bouncing up, swinging the shopping bag in her hand. "Okay!" she said. "I'm ready!"

Brenda furrowed her brow. "If you're taking happy drugs, it's time to share."

"What?" Melanie said.

"Onward!" Vicki said.

They hit Vis-A-Vis and Eye of the Needle, Gypsy, and Hepburn. Brenda looked long and hard at a reversible Hadley Pollet belt at Hepburn but then declared loudly that she couldn't afford anything new. Vicki thought this sounded suspiciously like fishing, but she let it go. They moved on.

Vicki bought a straw hat at Peter Beaton. The salesgirl was careful not to stare at Vicki's head when the scarf came off; Vicki could feel her not-staring, but she didn't care. She caught up with Brenda and Melanie at the top of Main Street. Melanie was standing outside Ladybird Lingerie, gazing at the door as if waiting for it to magically open.

"Do you want to go in?" Vicki asked.

"No, no," Melanie said. "What use do I have for lingerie?"

At Congdon's Pharmacy, the three of them sat at the lunch counter and ordered chicken salad sandwiches and chocolate frappes. Brenda's cell phone rang again. She checked the display.

"Not Josh," she said.

"I feel guilty," Vicki said. "Having this much fun while someone else is watching my children."

"Get over it," Brenda said. "You deserve a morning like this. We all do."

Melanie lifted her frappe in a toast. "I love you guys," she said.

Brenda rolled her eyes and Vicki almost laughed. But

this was the old Melanie. Before Melanie became obsessed with having a baby and devastated by Peter's betrayal, she had been one of the finest girlfriends around. She was always up for a twirl outside the dressing room and for cozy lunches where she would propose lovey-dovey toasts.

"Cheers!" Vicki said. They clinked glasses. Brenda joined in reluctantly.

"Oh, stop being such a sourpuss," Melanie said. "I got you something."

"Me?" Brenda said.

Melanie pulled the Hadley Pollet belt out of a small shopping bag at her feet and handed it to Brenda. "For you," she said.

"No . . . way!" Brenda said. Her expression was one Vicki remembered from childhood: She was excited, then suspicious. "What for? Why?"

"You wanted it," Melanie said. "And I know I horned in on your summer with Vicki. The house is yours, too, and I'm grateful to you for letting me stay. And you're taking such good care of Vicki and the kids. . . ." Melanie's eyes were shining. "I wanted to do something nice for you."

Brenda cast her eyes down. She wound the belt around her waist. "Well, thank you."

"That was really thoughtful, Mel," Vicki said.

Brenda narrowed her eyes. "Are you sure there's not something else going on?"

"Something else?" Melanie said.

Something else.

Later that afternoon, the phone rang in the cottage. Vicki was in bed, napping with Porter, and the phone woke her up. She was the only one home; Melanie had taken the Yukon to her doctor's appointment, and Brenda had walked with Blaine to the swing set on Low Beach Road. The phone rang five, six, seven times, was silent for a minute, then started ringing again. *Ted,* Vicki thought. She climbed out of bed carefully, so as not to disturb Porter, and hurried through the living room for the phone.

"Hello?"

There was silence. Somebody breathing. Then a young, female voice. "I know you're sleeping with him."

"*Excuse* me?" Vicki said.

"You're sleeping with him!"

Carefully, quietly, Vicki replaced the receiver. For this she had gotten out of bed? She poured herself a glass of iced tea and repaired to the back deck, where she stretched out on a chaise longue. The sun was hot; she should go back inside and put on lotion, but she was so dopey from her nap that she indulged herself for a few minutes. She thought about the phone call and laughed.

A little while later, the phone rang again. Vicki opened her eyes. Took a deep breath. She had been working hard on visualizing her lungs as two pink, spongy pillows. She rose and went to the phone; she didn't want it to wake up Porter. Though God knows if it was another wrong number, or the same wrong number, she would take the phone off the hook.

"Hello?" She tried to convey impatience.

Silence. This was ridiculous! But then, a throat clearing. A man.

"Uh, Vicki?"

"Yes?"

"It's Peter. Peter Patchen."

"Peter Patchen." Vicki couldn't disguise her shock. "Will wonders never cease." *You jerk,* she thought. *You coward.*

"Uh, yeah. Listen, I realize you probably hate me . . ."

"To be honest, Peter, I haven't given it that much thought."

"Right. You're busy with your own stuff, I get it. How are you feeling?"

"I'm feeling fine, actually."

"Yeah, that's what Ted told me. That's great."

Vicki didn't want to discuss her well-being or otherwise with Peter Patchen. But being on the phone with him made wheels turn in her mind. Melanie had told Peter about the pregnancy; this Vicki knew, and while Vicki was glad it was now out in the open, she didn't necessarily think Melanie should take Peter back right away.

"What can I do for you, Peter?" Vicki said.

"Well, I was wondering if Melanie was around."

"No," Vicki said. "She's out."

"Out?"

"Out."

"Oh. Okay."

"Would you like me to tell her you called?" Vicki said.

"Yeah," Peter said. "Tell her I called. Tell her I miss her."

Vicki rolled her eyes. *Yeah, you miss her now. Jerk! Coward!* Still, this was what Vicki wanted to see: Peter coming back on his hands and knees, groveling.

"I'll tell her," Vicki said.

Later, when the Yukon pulled up in front of the house, Vicki stepped out onto the flagstone path.

"I know what's going on," she said as Melanie got out of the car.

Melanie stared at Vicki; she had one hand resting on her belly. All the color drained from her face. "You do?"

"I do," Vicki said. "Peter called."

Melanie looked at Vicki strangely. She undid the latch of the gate and stepped inside slowly and carefully, as though Vicki were holding a gun to her head. "He did?"

"He said he misses you."

"He *did*?" Now Melanie looked perplexed.

"He did. He called, I told him you were out, he said, 'Out?' I said, 'Out.' He said to tell you he called. He said, 'Tell her I miss her.'"

Melanie shook her head. "Wow."

"'Wow'?" Vicki said. "'Wow'? Yeah, wow. That's right, wow. This is exactly what I said was going to happen. Didn't I tell you he'd come around?"

"He only cares about the baby," Melanie said.

"Maybe," Vicki said. "But maybe not. Are you going to call him back?"

"No," Melanie said. "Not today." She rubbed her belly.

"My hormones are all over the place, Vick. I don't know what I want."

"Right," Vicki said. "I can understand that. I'll tell you what, it was weird having him call."

"Yeah, I'll bet."

"In fact, I got two weird phone calls this afternoon."

"Who else?"

"Some girl," Vicki said. "Some crazy girl. A wrong number."

The longer Vicki felt good, the more frequently she wondered when the other shoe was going to drop. Could the worst be over? Vicki had three weeks of chemo left, then she would have another CT scan, the results of which would be sent to Dr. Garcia in Connecticut. If her lungs looked okay, if the tumor had shrunk, if it had receded from the chest wall, then Dr. Garcia would schedule the surgery. Now, because Vicki was feeling good, she allowed herself an occasional glimpse at herself *after* surgery: She pictured herself waking up in the recovery room, attached to an IV and five other machines. She imagined pain in her chest, soreness around the incision, she pictured herself bracing her body when she coughed or laughed or talked. All this would be fine because she would have survived the surgery. She would be clean. Cancer-free.

Vicki felt so good for so many days that one night at dinner she mentioned she was thinking of letting Josh go.

"I can take care of the kids myself now," she said. "I feel fine."

Brenda made a face. "I promised Josh work for the whole summer. He quit his job at the airport for us."

"And he has to go back to college," Melanie said. "I'm sure he needs the money."

"It's not fair to fire him at the beginning of August just because you feel better," Brenda said.

"I can't really imagine the rest of the summer without Josh," Melanie said. She set down her ear of corn; her chin was shiny with butter. "And what about the kids? They're attached."

"They're attached," Brenda said.

"They're attached," Vicki conceded. "But would it devastate them if he stopped coming? Don't you think they'd be happy to have me take them to the beach every day?"

"I promised him a summer of work, Vick," Brenda said.

"I think the kids would be devastated," Melanie said. "They love him."

"They love him," Brenda said.

"Do they love him, or do you guys love him?" Vicki said.

Brenda glowered; Melanie stood up from the table.

"Oh, who are we kidding?" Vicki said. "We all love him."

The next day Vicki invited herself to the beach with Josh and the kids. Josh seemed happy to have her come along, though he might have been pretending for her sake.

"I can help out," Vicki said.

"That's fine," Josh said.

"I know you guys have your own routine," Vicki said. "I promise not to cramp your style."

"Boss," Josh said, "it's fine. We're happy to have you come with us. Right, Chiefy?"

Blaine locked his arms across his chest. "No girls allowed."

Vicki ruffled his hair. "I'm not a girl," she said. "I'm your mother."

"This is where we usually sit," Josh said, dropping the umbrella, the cooler, and the bag of toys in the sand. "As you can see we're spitting distance from the lifeguard stand and close enough to wet sand that we can build sand castles."

"And dig holes," Blaine said.

Josh put up the umbrella, laid out a blanket, and set Porter in the shade. Immediately, Porter grabbed the pole of the umbrella and pulled himself up.

"He normally stands like that for five or ten minutes," Josh said.

"Then he chews on the handle of the orange shovel," Blaine said.

"Then he gets his snack," Josh said.

"I see," Vicki said. She had brought a chair for herself, which she unfolded in the sun. "You guys have it all figured out."

"We're all about routine," Josh said, winking at Vicki. "We're big fans of *consistency* and *sameness*." He waved at a woman down the beach who had two little girls. "There's Mrs. Brooks with Abby and Mariel. Blaine *loves* Abby."

"I do not," Blaine said.

"Oh, you do so," Josh said. "Go ask her if she wants to dig with us."

"Hey, Josh," a man's voice said. Vicki turned around. A tall, dark-skinned man with a little boy Blaine's age and a baby girl in his arms waved as he moved down the beach.

"Omar, my man!" Josh said. Then to Vicki, he whispered, "That's Omar Sherman. He brings the kids to the beach every morning while his wife talks to her patients on the phone. I guess she's some hotshot psychiatrist in Chicago and deals with a bunch of complete basket cases."

"Geez," Vicki said. "You know everybody."

She sat back and watched as Abby Brooks and Mateo Sherman helped Blaine and Josh dig a hole and then a tunnel in the sand. Porter stood holding on to the umbrella pole, and then he tired out and plopped onto the blanket. He reached for his orange shovel and started chewing. Vicki watched all this with the distinct feeling that she was a visitor. Josh was 100 percent in control. At ten-thirty, he pulled snacks from the cooler: a bottle of juice and box of raisins for Blaine, a graham cracker for Porter. Blaine and Porter sat on the blanket and ate neatly and without complaint, like a model of two children having a snack. Josh produced two plums from the cooler and handed one to Vicki.

"Oh," she said. "Thank you." She took a bite of the cold, sweet plum, and juice dripped down her chin. Josh handed her a napkin. "I feel like one of the children," she said, wiping her face. Vicki liked this, but it made her feel guilty, too. Guilty and unnecessary. She was the children's mother and they didn't need her. *No girls allowed.* Josh was taking care of everything and everybody.

Josh sat on the blanket. Porter pulled himself up to standing, holding on to the umbrella pole in a way that reminded Vicki of an old man on the subway. Blaine had dutifully collected the trash from snack and walked it over to the barrel behind the lifeguard stand. "You're a model citizen," Josh said. Blaine saluted. He joined Abby a few yards down the beach, where they busily filled up buckets with sand and then water.

Vicki couldn't believe she'd been thinking of letting Josh go. "I'm so glad you're here," she said. "With us, I mean."

"I like being here," Josh said. "With you."

"I don't mean to embarrass you," Vicki said. "Or get all serious on you."

"You can be as serious as you want, Boss."

"Okay, then," Vicki said. "I don't know what we would have done this summer without you."

"You would have found someone else," he said.

"But it wouldn't have been the same."

"Things happen for a reason," Josh said. "I knew when I saw you coming off the plane . . ."

"When Melanie fell?"

"Yeah, I knew then that something like this would happen."

"Something like what? You knew you'd be our babysitter?"

"I knew our paths would cross."

"You did not."

"I did. First Brenda left the book behind, then I saw Melanie at the airport. . . ."

"She was trying to leave," Vicki said.

"But I brought her back," Josh said. "It's like it was all part of some greater plan."

"If you believe in a greater plan," Vicki said.

"You don't believe in a greater plan?" Josh said.

"Oh, I don't know," Vicki said. When she looked at the ocean, or at some smaller, more delicate perfection—like Porter's ear, for example—it was hard to deny there was a force at work. But a plan into which everyone fit, a plan where everything happened for a reason? It was a convenient fallback. How many people in Vicki's cancer support group had said they believed they got cancer for a reason? Almost everyone. But look at Alan—he was dead. What was the reason there? The woman in Royersford, Pennsylvania, shot in the face, leaving her three-month-old motherless. That didn't happen for a *reason*. That was a mistake, a tragedy. If there was a greater plan, it was full of holes and people dropped through all the time. Vicki thought back on her own life. It had progressed in a way that made sense . . . right up until the cells of her lungs mutated and became life-threatening. "I've never been good at these meaning-of-life conversations."

Just as Vicki said these words, an amazing thing happened. Porter let go of the umbrella pole and took two, three, four steps forward.

Vicki leapt from her chair. "Oh my God! Did you see that?"

Porter stopped, turned to his mother with a triumphant expression that quickly became bafflement. He fell back on his butt and started to cry.

"He took his first steps!" Vicki said. "Did you see him? Josh, did you *see* him?"

"I saw him. He was walking."

"He was walking!" Vicki swept Porter up and kissed his face. "Oh, honey, you can walk!" She held Porter so tightly his cries amplified. Forget trying to find the meaning of life in some greater plan—it was right there in front of them! Porter had taken his first steps! He would walk for the rest of his life, but Vicki had been there, watching, the very first time. And Josh had seen. If Vicki hadn't come to the beach today, she might have missed Porter's first steps—or maybe he only took them because Vicki was there. Or maybe, Vicki couldn't help thinking, maybe seeing Porter's first steps was a small gift for Vicki before she died. *No negative thoughts!* she told herself. But she couldn't help it; doubt followed her everywhere.

"Amazing," she said, trying to hold on to her initial enthusiasm. She called out to Blaine. "Honey, your brother can walk. He just took his first steps!" But Porter was crying so loudly Blaine couldn't hear her. "Oh, dear. I scared him, maybe."

Josh checked his watch. "Actually, it's time for his nap."

"Eleven o'clock?" Vicki said.

"On the nose. Here, I'll take him."

Vicki handed Porter over to Josh, who laid Porter on his stomach on a section of clean blanket. Josh patted Porter's back and gave Porter his pacifier. Porter quieted, and as Vicki sat and watched, his eyes drifted closed.

Josh stood up carefully. "Now is when I play Wiffle

ball with Blaine," he said. "He's really learning how to connect with the ball."

"You're going to be a great father," Vicki said.

"Thanks, Boss." Josh smiled, and something about the smile gave Vicki a glimmer of hope. Josh would get older, fall in love, marry, have children. One thing, at least, would be right with the world.

PART THREE

~

AUGUST

There was a lot to be learned from children's games, Brenda thought. Take Chutes and Ladders, which she and Blaine had played umpteen times this summer and which they were playing again now on the coffee table. The board, with its 100 spaces, was a person's life, and a random spinner dictated which space a person would land on. *This little girl did her chores so she earned money to go to the movies:* short ladder. *This boy stood on a wobbly chair to reach the cookie jar, but he fell and broke his arm:* steep chute. As Blaine assiduously practiced counting out spaces, he looked to Brenda for nods of affirmation, but she was musing about all the things that had happened to her in the past year. Brenda had sailed up a tall ladder with her doctorate and the job at Champion and the highest teaching rating in the department, but all this seemed to do was to elevate her to a place where there were more perilous chutes. A professor has an affair with her student. . . . A woman throws a book in anger. . . .

Blaine won the game. This always made him happy. "Want to play again?" he asked.

It was August, everybody's summer, though for Brenda the month heralded the beginning of the end. They would be leaving the island in three and a half weeks. It made Brenda physically sick to think of leaving Nantucket and returning to the city, to the apartment she could no longer afford and the pervasive back-to-school atmosphere that now meant nothing to her. For the first time in her memory, Brenda would not be going back to school. She had been banned from school. *You will never work in academia again.* It was almost too much to bear. And so, Brenda did her best to ignore the fact that it was August.

Brian Delaney, Esquire, however, would not let her forget. His calls came so frequently that Brenda's life felt like a video game in which Brian Delaney, Esquire, popped up in her path to thwart her.

She finally called him back from a bench in the small park next to the 'Sconset Market. Even 'Sconset, quaint village that it was, was bursting at the seams with people now that it was August. There was a line out the door of the market for coffee and the paper, and there were no fewer than five people on cell phones in the small park, but none of them, certainly, were conducting business more unpleasant than Brenda's.

Trudi, Brian Delaney, Esquire's secretary, sounded relieved to hear it was Brenda calling. "He wants to get this settled," Trudi confided to Brenda, "before he goes to the Hamptons!"

"So now we're working around your vacation?" Brenda said when Himself came on the line. She meant to sound snappy-funny-sarcastic, but for once, Brian Delaney, Esquire, wasn't biting.

"Listen," he said. "The university is willing to settle at a hundred and twenty-five. Are you jumping for joy? One twenty-five. And they'll waive the ten grand you owe them to work on the painting. I guess the guy Len, or whomever, is going to write a paper about the restoration. So that's a clean and clear one twenty-five. That is as good as it's going to get, Dr. Lyndon. I strongly advise you to take it."

"I don't have a hundred and twenty-five thousand dollars," Brenda said. "And I don't have a job. How can I settle when I don't have the money?"

"We have to settle," Brian Delaney, Esquire, said. "How's the screenplay coming?"

"Fine," Brenda said. Which was true—the screenplay, which had started out as a wing and a prayer, was now nearly done. But the problem with finishing the screenplay was the incipient worry about selling the damn thing.

"Good, good," Brian Delaney, Esquire, said. "There's your million dollars right there."

"Yeah," Brenda said. "In my dreams."

"And there's that pretty piece of real estate you're sitting on. You could sell out to your sister."

"No," Brenda said. The cottage was the only thing

Brenda owned. If things didn't work out in the city, she would have to live on Nantucket year-round. She would have to get a job as a landscaper, or as a salesperson at one of the shops in town. She would have to make friends with other year-rounders who had failed to make lives in the real world. "I've told you I don't know how many times, my sister is sick. She has cancer. I can't bother her or her husband with a real estate thing now, just because I need money."

"But you do need money," Brian Delaney, Esquire, said. "We can't leave this hanging. Everything doesn't *stop* just because it's summer and you're on Nantucket. The university will take us to trial, where, I assure you, we will lose—to the tune of three hundred grand, plus all the money you'll have to pay me to prepare. I don't know what you did to that woman Atela, but she is *pissed.* She wants *justice,* the university counsel tells me. *Justice!*" Brian Delaney, Esquire, huffed impatiently. "Do you want me to settle this thing or not?"

There was no justice, Brenda thought. There were only chutes and ladders.

"Settle," she said.

The beginning of the end with Walsh had arrived when Brenda handed back the midterm papers to her class. She knew students compared notes and shared grades, but she never expected that Walsh would do so. Then again, she never told him (as perhaps she should have): *Don't tell anyone what grade I gave you.* The fact of the matter was, Brenda and Walsh didn't discuss the paper, or his grade, at all. It wasn't relevant to their relationship; it might have been someone else who gave Walsh the grade.

On the first day of April, no one showed up for class. At five past eleven, not a single student. This struck Brenda as odd, but she relished the quiet. She was tired. She had spent the night before at her parents' house in Philadelphia; she and Vicki had gone to their father's law office and signed the papers that made them the official owners of Number Eleven Shell Street. Ellen Lyndon had persuaded Brenda to stay for a dinner that featured roast chicken and several bottles of celebratory wine. Brenda missed the last train back to New York and had spent the night in her childhood bed. She'd awoken at six that morning to get to Thirtieth Street Station. Her day had been a blur of Metroliner, subway, crosstown bus.

So as she waited for her class to arrive, she rested her head on the Queen Anne table. It smelled like lemon Pledge. She closed her eyes.

And jolted awake! A minute later, two minutes? No, it was eleven-fifteen and still no one had come. She checked her syllabus; spring break wasn't for two weeks. But then she thought, April first, April Fool's. The class was playing a trick on her. Ha, ha. But where *were* they?

Brenda walked down the hall to Mrs. Pencaldron's desk, and on the way, she was passed by the university caterers rolling a tray of linens and dishes toward the Barrington Room.

Mrs. Pencaldron was on the phone. She saw Brenda but looked right through her. She said something about shrimp in the pasta salad, Dr. Barrett was allergic, if he ate it, he'd die. She hung up, huffing.

"Impossible!" she said.

"Am I missing something?" Brenda said.

Mrs. Pencaldron laughed with a false brightness. It

had become clear to Brenda over the course of the year that Mrs. Pencaldron regarded all the professors in the department as pets she was trying hard to train, but to no avail.

"Your class," Mrs. Pencaldron said. "What are you *doing* here?"

"No one's in the Barrington Room," Brenda said. "Except now it looks like they're setting up some kind of lunch."

"The department's spring luncheon," Mrs. Pencaldron said. "The notice has been in your box for ten days."

"It has?" Brenda was guilty. She never checked her box.

"It has. Along with a memo informing you that because of the luncheon your class is being held in Parsons 204."

"It is?"

"It is," Mrs. Pencaldron said. She was all gussied up in a floral-print dress. Should Brenda have gotten gussied, too?

"Should I go to the luncheon?"

"Are you a member of this department?"

That sounded like a rhetorical question, but was it?

Mrs. Pencaldron sighed in a way that made Brenda feel like a hopeless case. "We'll see you at one."

Brenda booked it over to Parsons 204. It was a beautiful spring day—finally!—and the quad looked like one of the pictures on the university Web site. Champion University had grass after all! It had daffodils! It had students eating Big Macs on beach towels! Brenda hurried, but she was almost certain her effort would be in vain. After twenty professorless minutes, the class would have left, and on such a sublime day, how could she blame them? So there was one precious seminar wasted. Brenda prayed that, at the very least, Walsh waited around. The weather had put her in a flirtatious frame of mind. Maybe they could go out tonight, to the Peruvian chicken place. Maybe they could stroll in Carl Schurz Park and check out barges on the East River. She would tell him about the cottage on Nantucket, half of it now hers.

Just outside Parsons 204, Brenda heard voices. She opened the door and there was her class, thick in discussion of the week's reading, Lorrie Moore's short story "Real Estate." The kids were so into it, they didn't even notice her standing there, and Brenda nearly burst with pride.

Brenda's good mood got better: Walsh grinned when she told him, after everyone else had filed out of the room, that she wanted to go on a chicken-eating, park-strolling, barge-watching date, and then—because they were in a strange classroom in the Biology Department—they kissed.

"I have to run," Brenda said. "I'm expected."

The department's spring luncheon was in full swing by the time Brenda arrived. The Barrington Room looked very elegant with the layered tablecloths, flowers, tiered silver trays of tuna and egg salad sandwiches, radishes with sweet butter, the shrimpless pasta salad, a bona fide punch bowl. There was a cluster of female graduate students by the door, teaching assistants, who greeted Brenda like a group of teenagers might greet Hilary Duff. Brenda was the department's rising star, but to the teaching assistants, Brenda tried to come across as a nice, regular, down-to-earth person. She complimented Audrey on her skirt and told Mary Kate that she'd be happy to proofread the first chapter of her thesis. Brenda chatted with Dr. Barrett, the Russian literature authority who had been friends with Aunt Liv, and then Brenda found herself in conversation with Elizabeth Graves's secretary, Nan, about the gorgeous weather and the weekend forecast. Across the room, Brenda saw Mrs. Pencaldron, Suzanne Atela, and a graduate student named Augie Fisk, who was a Chaucer specialist and who had asked Brenda out to dinner no less than three times. It would have been a beneficent gesture to seek out Augie Fisk and talk with him, it would have been wise to schmooze with Suzanne Atela—but Brenda was tired, and hungry. She fixed herself a plate and took a seat in a chair along the far wall next to a stout gentleman in a gray suit.

"I'm Bill Franklin," he said.

Aha! Bill Franklin was the drama professor, a famous queen, known among the students as "Uncle Pervy." Brenda had never met him. He taught at night, in the university theater. He had an office in the department, but the door was always closed.

"Oh, hi! It's nice to finally put a face to the name. I'm Brenda Lyndon."

"Yes, I know."

She smiled, trying not to let his unfortunate nickname color her first impression. Bill Franklin was in his midfifties, he had a nondescript, semi-desperate travelingsalesman aura about him. Something about him was familiar. She had seen him before. Around campus, maybe. Brenda sneaked another look at him sideways as she nibbled on a radish.

"This is a very nice event," she said.

And at the same time, he said, "You seem to be quite popular with the kids."

"Oh," she said. "Well, who knows? I like teaching. I love it. Today I was late and the class just started up without me."

"You're very young."

"I'll be thirty this month," Brenda said.

"Much closer to their age. They must find you intriguing."

"Intriguing?" Brenda said. "Oh, I kind of doubt that."

Bill Franklin was drinking a Michelob. He brought the bottle to his lips. He had a gray handlebar mustache. A handlebar mustache. Something about the mustache rang a bell, but why? Brenda got a funny-sick feeling in her stomach. It was a really bad paranoid suspicion. Really bad. Through three bites of pasta salad, she watched Suzanne Atela conferring with the head caterer. Dr. Atela was pointing; Brenda heard the word "coffee." Brenda had to stand up. She wanted to look at Bill Franklin from across the room. She pretended to be headed for the punch bowl, though the punch was the color of Pepto-Bismol, and no one had touched it. She lingered, trying to get a good, long look without getting caught. Okay. He drank from his bottle, he saw her, he winked. Winked.

Brenda looked away, horrified. Horrified! *We're in Soho. It's like another country. The man at the end of the bar would like to pay for your drink.*

The man at the end of the bar at the Cupping Room the night Brenda met Walsh, the night she kissed Walsh and flaunted her hot longing for all to see . . . the man who offered to buy her a drink was Bill Franklin.

Brenda canceled Walsh without explanation, and nine o'clock found him leaning against Brenda's buzzer until she let him in.

On purpose, she was wearing sweatpants. Since they were no longer to be lovers, he could see her looking grubby. Ancient Philadelphia marathon T-shirt, ponytail, no makeup. Well, a little makeup. Brenda took a long time with the dead bolts. She didn't want to see him.

"What's going on?" he said. "You sounded bloody awful on the phone. What happened?"

Walsh stepped inside, and she locked the door back up. Her apartment, at least, was safe. She took her clothes off before Walsh could get a good look at them.

Later, as they lay in bed sweating and spent, Walsh kissed her temple. Some days he seemed much older than he really was. Maybe because he was from Australia.

"You're upset," he said. "Tell me what happened."

She inhaled. "One of the professors in the department . . . the drama guy, Bill Franklin . . ."

"Uncle Pervy?" Walsh said.

"Yes. He was at the Cupping Room the night we were there."

"He was? How do you know? Did he tell you?"

"I recognized him," Brenda said. "He tried to buy me a drink. I remember him. At the other end of the bar. He was wearing the same suit he wore to the luncheon. And his mustache, with the curlicue ends all waxed, you don't forget something like that. He winked at me. Oh, God. It's awful."

"You're sure it wasn't some other bloke with the same suit?"

"I wish it was," Brenda said. "But I'm sure. And I mean, *sure*. Same guy. And he knows. I'm sure he knows. He said all this stuff about my being young. He said the students must find me 'intriguing.'"

"Intriguing?"

"He knows. It was the way he said it. He knows, Walsh. Okay, that's it. I *will* be fired. You will be . . . well, hopefully nothing will happen to you."

"Come on," Walsh said.

"We have to stop," Brenda said. "If I get fired, my career is over. My whole professional life. Everything I've worked for, the things I'm building on. Because I would like to stay at Champion, and if Champion doesn't want to offer me anything permanent, then I would like to teach someplace else. I can't have a weird sexual thing on my record. No one will hire me."

"I can't stop," Walsh said. "I don't want to stop."

"I don't want to stop, either," Brenda said. "Obviously. But is this any way to conduct a relationship? Sneaking around, hoping nobody catches us?"

"It hasn't seemed to bother you before."

"Well, now everything's different."

"Just like that?"

"Just like that."

"I can't believe you care what Uncle Pervy thinks. I hear stories about that guy all the time."

"Yeah, but not with undergraduates. Not with his *own* students."

"No, but still. That guy has too many skeletons in his own closet to blow the whistle on us . . ."

Brenda slid out of bed and stumbled through the dark apartment to the front door, where she found her sweats in a pile on the floor. Brenda put them on. She thought about how much she loved her class. But Walsh was part of that class and part of why she loved it was because he was in it. She thought of Bill Franklin winking at her. Ugh! *They must find you intriguing. Because I saw you kissing one of your students at a bar.* But that night in the Cupping Room had been nearly two months earlier, and if Bill Franklin hadn't said anything about it to Suzanne Atela yet, he might be planning to keep it under his hat. After all, he had no reason to sting Brenda. He didn't even know her. There were only five weeks left in the semester, anyway. The other day Walsh had told Brenda he wanted to take her back to Fremantle and introduce her to his mother, and Brenda had gone so far as to check flights from New York to Perth on the Internet. Brenda thought about their names, side by side at the top of his paper. *John Walsh /Dr. Brenda Lyndon.* He was a college sophomore. He was her student. *Romantic or sexual relationships are forbidden between a faculty member and a student.*

"Brindah," he called out.

Her mind was a muddy puddle.

. . . and will result in disciplinary action.

"Brindah?"

She couldn't come up with an answer.

I can't stop. I don't want to stop.
  I can't stop.

Brenda didn't stop. Her relationship with Walsh had too much momentum. And so, they continued to see each other, but only at Brenda's apartment. Brenda was firm in this. The beautiful weather beckoned; Walsh wanted to be outside. He wanted to walk with Brenda, lie in the grass with Brenda. It was against his nature to be cooped up in her apartment, where the windows didn't even open. But no, sorry—Brenda said no. She wouldn't budge.

In class, Brenda was increasingly businesslike, serious, professional. She was young, but that didn't mean she was frivolous! That didn't mean she would fly in the face of the strictest university rule and sleep with one of her students!

Brenda was consumed with anxiety, but she had no one to talk about it with. She couldn't tell her parents or Vicki and she hadn't spoken to Erik vanCott since their dinner at Craft. The bad news of Erik marrying Noel seemed very minor when compared to the bad news of Brenda losing her job and watching her good name go up in flames. Besides, what would she possibly say? *I'm sleeping with one of my students.* When phrased like that, which was to say, bluntly, without nuance or detail, it sounded tawdry and lecherous. It was the kind of secret that Brenda would have been ashamed to tell her therapist, if she had a therapist. The only person Brenda could vent to was Walsh himself, and he was growing weary of it. Brenda yammered on about getting caught, getting fired, what if, God forbid . . . until the words clinked like worthless coins. *Relax,* he said. *You're acting like such an American. Obsessing like this.*

Brenda's class read Anne Lamott's *Crooked Little*

Heart, which was the book Amrita the brownnoser had chosen to write her midterm paper on, and yet Amrita's customary seat, to Brenda's right, was vacant first on Tuesday and then again on Thursday.

"Does anyone know where Amrita is?" Brenda asked.

There was throat-clearing, a noise that sounded like a sneeze but could just as easily have been a snicker from one of the Rebeccas, a bunch of downcast eyes. Brenda got a funny vibe, but she couldn't pinpoint it and no one in the class was going to talk. Brenda scribbled, *Call Amrita!* at the top of her notes.

Spring break arrived. Walsh had rugby games in Van Cortlandt Park, he wanted Brenda to come watch him, they could picnic afterward, but she refused. *I can't. Someone will see me. Someone will figure it out.* Erik vanCott called and left a message, asking Brenda to be the best man in his wedding. Brenda thought he was kidding, but then he left another message. *Best man?* she thought. Would she have to stand on the altar looking like Victor Victoria while "marriage material" Noel looked stunning in silk shantung and tulle? For her vacation, Brenda took the train up to Darien to see Vicki, Ted, and the kids. Vicki wasn't feeling well; she'd been to the hospital for tests. Walking pneumonia, they thought it was. Brenda said, *Ugh, are you contagious?* She washed her hands, she kept a safe distance. She asked Vicki about being Erik vanCott's best man. *Tuxedo?* she said. *Black dress,* Vicki said. *But nothing too sexy. You're not allowed to upstage the bride.* One night, when Ted was out with clients, Brenda nearly confessed to Vicki about Walsh, but she held her tongue. Instead, they talked about Nantucket. Would they go, together, separately, when would they go, how long would they stay? Vicki said, *I have a family, Bren. I have to plan.* Brenda said, *Just let me get through this semester.*

After spring break, Brenda started holding class outside, in the quad, under a spindly, urban tree. She was thinking of summer, of time on Nantucket, she was thinking: *Walsh wants to spend time with me outside, here it is.* She also wanted to keep a low profile in the department. If she wasn't there, she reasoned, nothing bad could happen.

She left three messages for Amrita—two on Amrita's cell phone and one at Amrita's apartment, where a roommate promised to pass the message along. Had Amrita dropped the class? That seemed so unlikely that Brenda figured she must have contracted mono, or had to fly back to India to bury a dead grandmother. Students like Amrita didn't drop a class they were acing.

And then, one day, two weeks before final papers were due, two weeks before Brenda and Walsh were in the clear, Brenda found a note taped to her office door. SEE ME! S.A.

Brenda removed the note and held it in her hand. Her hand was steady. She wasn't nervous. Suzanne Atela could want a hundred things. The semester was ending; there was next year to consider. There had been talk of Brenda picking up another section. It was either that or some other administrative thing. Brenda wasn't nervous or worried.

Suzanne Atela wasn't in her office. Brenda checked with Mrs. Pencaldron, who without a word uncapped her

Montblanc pen and elegantly scripted a phone number on a peach-colored index card.

"She wants me to call her?" Brenda said.

Terse nod. Mrs. Pencaldron picked up her own phone and handed the receiver to Brenda.

Suzanne Atela wanted to meet at Feed Your Head, in the student union. Brenda agreed, handed the phone back to Mrs. Pencaldron, stifled a groan. She wasn't nervous or worried; she was merely inconvenienced. She was supposed to meet Walsh at her apartment with take-out Indian food at one. In the stairwell, she called Walsh to cancel.

At quarter to twelve, Feed Your Head was packed. Packed! Brenda realized how removed she had been from the student body of Champion University. She knew twelve students out of six thousand. She'd been teaching for nearly an entire school year and she'd never once eaten on campus. And no wonder. She paid twelve-fifty for a soggy tuna sub, fruit salad, and a bottle of water. She wandered past a bunch of girl-women watching a soap opera as she searched for Suzanne Atela. It took a few minutes to find her because Brenda was, of course, looking for a woman alone. Dr. Atela was not alone, however. She was sitting at a table with Bill Franklin and Amrita.

Brenda nearly turned and ran—it would have been easy to get lost in the crowd—but Amrita saw her and frowned. She nudged Dr. Atela, and Dr. Atela turned and drew Brenda over to the table with a steady, disapproving gaze over the top of her glasses. Bill Franklin was wearing a blue seersucker suit and a bow tie. With his waxed mustache, he looked old-fashioned and ridiculous, like a carnival barker. His attention was glued to the soap opera, showing on a screen over Atela's head.

As Brenda approached the table, her bowels did a twisty thing that made her think she might need a bathroom. She eased down in a molded plastic chair next to Atela.

"Hi," she said. "Amrita. Dr. Franklin. I didn't realize this was a meet—"

Suzanne Atela sliced through the air with her arm and checked her slim, gold watch. "I have a lunch at Picholine in an hour," she said. Her voice was so taut there was no trace of her accent. "I'll get right to the point. There are some indelicate rumors circulating about you, Dr. Lyndon."

"Rumors?" Brenda said. "About me?"

Amrita clucked and made eyes. Brenda regarded the girl. Her long black hair was parted in the middle and combed slick against her head; it was gathered in a schoolmarm's bun at the nape of her neck. Her skin was grayish, and she wore red lipstick, the same crimson as her fingernails. She was wearing jeans and a yellow Juicy Couture hooded sweatshirt. She did not look so different from the rest of Champion's students, and yet she stood out, not because of her culture, but because of the intensity with which she pursued her education. She had missed five classes, which was enough for Brenda to fail her for the semester. *What did I do to you?* Brenda thought. *You wanted teaching and teaching you got. I engaged you, I took your points, I showered you with praise. What more did you want?*

Bill Franklin cleared his throat, and then, with difficulty it seemed, he ripped his attention away from the TV.

"We're talking about more than just rumors, Suzanne," he said. "Otherwise we wouldn't be wasting our time. Or Dr. Lyndon's time."

"Quite right, Dr. Franklin," Suzanne Atela said.

For some reason, the TV above Dr. Atela's head snagged Brenda's attention. On the screen was Brenda's student Kelly Moore, her purple hair spiked like a Muppet. So this was *Love Another Day.* Kelly Moore's character kissed a man twice her age, then there was a struggle, a slap. She escaped the man and ran out of the room, flinging the door closed.

Amrita reached into her ornately embroidered silk book bag and pulled out her midterm paper, which had copious notes and exclamations of praise from Brenda in blue pen, and an A at the top.

"We know what's going on with you and Walsh," Amrita said. "Everybody knows. It's disgusting."

Dr. Atela removed her harlequin glasses and placed them on the sticky Formica table with a sigh. Brenda took a yoga breath. She was prepared for this, wasn't she? She had lived through this scene in her mind a thousand times in the last three weeks. And yet, the word "disgusting" threw her. "Disgusting" was the teacher who became impregnated by her seventh-grade student. Walsh was a year older than Brenda; a relationship between them was natural. Except he was her student. So it was wrong. It was indelicate, as Atela had said, unwise, a bad decision. It was against university rules. But it was not disgusting. Brenda was so busy thinking this through that she didn't say a word, and after a number of seconds had passed, this seemed like a brilliant strategy. Don't even dignify the accusation with a response.

"Dr. Lyndon?" Suzanne Atela said.

"I'm sorry. I don't know what you're talking about," Brenda said.

"We understand, Dr. Lyndon, that you've been having improper relations with one of your students."

"I saw you with him downtown," Bill Franklin said. "At the beginning of the semester. One of the things I noticed—in addition to your obvious attraction to one another—was that he paid the bill. The reason why faculty are forbidden from dating students is because of the power differential. He buys you drinks, you give him grades . . ."

"What are you suggesting?" Brenda said. "I'm sorry, I don't . . ."

"I really respected you," Amrita said. She fingered the zipper of her sweatshirt, unzipped it an inch, zipped it back up. Up, down, up, down. She was nervous. Brenda should capitalize on that fact, but she didn't know how. "I loved your class. I thought, finally, a real teacher, someone young, someone I could *relate* to." Here, Amrita's voice wavered. "But then it turns out that *you're* the impostor—and not so innocent. You're having a . . . *thing* with Walsh. You gave him an A plus on his paper!"

Brenda stared at her inedible lunch. She wanted to dump the bottle of water over Amrita's head. *You little snot!* she thought. *Is that why you're doing this? Because I gave him the grade he deserved? Or because you yourself are in love with him?* She wanted to smash the tuna sub into Bill Franklin's face. He had shown his true colors that night at the Cupping Room. Sitting at the end of the bar, getting drunk, waiting to prey on any young woman—or man—who came in unescorted.

Uncle Pervy—*that* was disgusting. And then there was Dr. Atela. She was the worst of the three because Brenda could see that beneath the somber concern and measured disapproval, she enjoyed watching Brenda suffer. If they were in ancient Rome, Atela would have thrown Brenda to the lions and applauded at the sport of it. But why? Because Brenda was young? Because she was a good teacher? Was Suzanne Atela jealous of Brenda? Did she feel threatened? Another department head might have emitted disappointment, but Suzanne Atela's face conveyed resignation, as though she'd known all along this would happen, as though she had predicted it. Brenda was so appalled, she stood up.

"I have a lunch at one myself," she said. "So if you'll excuse me . . ."

Brenda picked up the bottle of water but left the rest of her tray for Suzanne Atela to deal with. In seconds, Brenda was swallowed up in the crowd of hungry undergraduates.

She reached into her bag for her cell phone. Call Walsh, instruct him to deny everything. They had no proof! Bill Franklin saw them together at the Cupping Room. And maybe someone saw them kissing in Parsons 204. Why had she been so stupid, so cavalier? It didn't matter if they had proof or not, it was true—Brenda could deny it, but she would be lying. She was having a romantic and a sexual relationship with one of her students. Disciplinary action would be taken. Her job was gone and with it her good name, her reputation. Brenda might have walked off Champion's campus, taken the crosstown bus home, and never looked back, but there were things in her office she could not leave behind—certain papers, her first-edition Fleming Trainor. She raced back to the English Department.

Mrs. Pencaldron's chair was empty, and a half-eaten Caesar salad sat on her desk blotter. When Brenda reached into her bag, her fingers came across a single key on a thin wire ring with a round paper tag that said (in Mrs. Pencaldron's penciled script) *Barrington Room*. Brenda looked down the hall at the heavy, paneled door. There wasn't time! She had to get out of there! Go to her office, get her things! The door seemed even more formidable now than it had been at the beginning of the semester, but in spite of that, or maybe because of that, Brenda was drawn down the hall. In the copy room, Augie Fisk stood at the Xerox machine, and his presence almost deterred her, but when Brenda breezed by, he didn't even look up.

In her deposition, Brenda had admitted to being only partly conscious of her actions that afternoon. What she said was, *I was upset. I was stunned, mortified, terribly confused. I wasn't thinking clearly. I didn't know what I was doing. I wasn't planning on stealing the painting. I just wanted . . .*

Wanted what, Dr. Lyndon?

To see the painting one more time, she'd said. *To say good-bye to it.*

Brenda punched in the security code and unlocked the door to the Barrington Room, fully prepared to find Mrs. Pencaldron sitting at the Queen Anne table, waiting for her. But the room was empty, hushed, just as it had been in the moments before Brenda's class all semester long. Brenda felt an enormous sense of loss, the beginnings of mourning. Her career was dead, but the body not yet cold.

And it was all her own stupid, stupid fault. Temptation had been placed in Brenda's path, and instead of swerving around it, she had met it at a bar.

Brenda set her purse and the bottle of water down on the Queen Anne table, and she stood before the painting. She was trying to absorb it, to internalize it, because, certainly, she would never see it again. She wanted to rest her face against its surface, feel its texture under her cheek; she wanted to climb into the painting and lie down.

Brenda heard a noise. She turned to see Mrs. Pencaldron clapping at her, like she was a wayward dog. Mrs. Pencaldron snatched up the bottle of water from the Queen Anne table (it would indeed leave a pale ring).

"What are you doing in here?" Mrs. Pencaldron said. "You don't belong in here! And this—" She shook the bottle of water and wiped at the table with the bottom of her blouse. "What were you thinking? You know the rules!"

"Sorry," Brenda said. "I'm so sorry."

"You know the rules, but you don't follow them," Mrs. Pencaldron said. "Sorry does not begin to address your transgressions."

Brenda held up her hands. "Okay, whatever. I came to get my things. I'm leaving."

"I will pack your things properly and send them to your home address," Mrs. Pencaldron said. "I suggest you leave this room and the department now, otherwise I will call campus security."

"Campus security?" Brenda said. "There's no need for that . . ." Brenda was dying to address Mrs. Pencaldron by her first name, but she didn't know what it was. "I'm leaving."

Augie Fisk appeared in the doorway. He looked at Brenda with a combination of pity and disgust. "We all heard," he said. "Everyone knows. Did Atela fire you?"

"She didn't have to," Brenda said. "I'm leaving."

"This isn't going to be something you can walk away from," Augie said. "This is going to *stick*. I mean, you can try to find another job, but you won't be able to work anywhere accredited. Hell, you won't even be able to teach *high school*. Maybe you should look into one of those online universities, where they don't care what crimes you've committed."

"It's disgraceful," Mrs. Pencaldron said. "I knew something wasn't right with the two of you. Couldn't put my finger on it, though, and certainly never expected that . . . but *something,* yes, I sensed something from the beginning."

"We all thought you were a flash in the pan," Augie said. "A woman as attractive as you, with your boutique subject matter, a specialty that no one else on earth knows about, that has no relevance to the rest of the canon. I knew you weren't for real. There was something fishy about you, something artificial. We all knew it."

"Stop it," Brenda said. Couldn't they see she was upset enough as it was?

"You stop it," Mrs. Pencaldron said. She pointed to the door. "Leave, or I call security."

Not in her right mind. Terribly confused. And angry. Brenda *hated* Mrs. Pencaldron. She had never liked her but now she really despised her. And Augie Fisk— yuck!—with his thick shock of red hair and his pale, pinched lips. *Flash in the pan?* He had asked her out again and again, and each time Brenda turned him down, she felt worse. Not in her right mind. *Fishy and artificial? An online university?* After eight years of graduate school, the thousands of hours of reading and research? All that *work*? The slavish devotion? Suddenly, Brenda was furious. She would not be ordered out of this room. She had done a good job; she was a good teacher.

We all knew it. Well, wasn't it easy to say so. Now.

Brenda reached into her bag and grabbed a book— one of the nearly impossible to find paperbacks of *The Innocent Impostor* that she had ordered for her class— and flung it. She threw it, she told the university counsel in her deposition, just to throw something. *Have you never thrown anything in anger? Have you never felt that impulse?* Brenda was not aiming the book at Augie Fisk or Mrs. Pencaldron or the painting. But hit the painting it did. (Lower left quadrant, three-quarter-inch "divot" or "gouge.") Brenda sucked in her breath, horrified, and Mrs. Pencaldron shrieked, and Augie Fisk said, "Oh, shit. You've really done it now."

Mrs. Pencaldron said, "I'm calling security. Block the door, Augie. We are not letting her leave. She has to answer to this."

Brenda gazed at the painting through her tears. She understood it perfectly now. The splatter, the mess, the tangle, the chaos. That painting was her life.

Settle, she thought. It was a word with multiple meanings. On the one hand, it was comforting. The matter would be settled, finally. Cleaned up, laid to rest. *Champion University v. Brenda Lyndon* would become another file in the law offices of Brian Delaney, Esquire, closed away in a drawer. But settle also meant doing without. She would have to settle for a life excluded from academia, and for a life without Walsh.

Her heart longed for him, her body ached for his arms around her. She wanted to hear his voice; it didn't matter, particularly, what he said. But Brenda couldn't make herself call him; her relationship with Walsh was intertwined with the loss of her career, her life's work. Brenda hurt now, but it would hurt more to talk with Walsh, to relive, day in and day out, the humiliation of that afternoon with Suzanne Atela, Bill Franklin, Amrita, Augie Fisk, Mrs. Pencaldron, and, finally, campus security.

Where was she going to find the money? Could she declare bankruptcy? Would she be forced to ask her parents? In Brenda's mind, a hundred and twenty-five thousand dollars was no different from a hundred and sixty—they were both unattainable. She would have to sell her half of the cottage, but she couldn't drop that on Vicki now—and what if Vicki and Ted, for whatever reason, didn't have the money to buy Brenda out? Would Brenda force a sale of the whole property? She could just hear the thoughts of Vicki and her parents: *Brenda is book smart, yes, but she has no common sense. She is unable to make her way in the world. We always have to bail her out.*

How to defend herself? What else could she do? One thing. There had always been only one place for Brenda to hide. *Lowly Worm, bookworm, nose always in a book.* She pulled her yellow legal pad out of her bag, poured a cup of coffee from her thermos, and started to write.

It was nothing he would ever be able to use on his résumé, but Josh was proud of his Wiffle ball pitching ability. Josh gave the ball perfect arc and speed—and in addition, Josh had taught Blaine stance and swing so that Blaine hit the ball nearly every time. Yes, the Wiffle ball was satisfying, it was one of the things Josh would miss most about babysitting, and he was glad that he'd been able to show off his pitching prowess for Vicki.

Vicki was feeling better, she looked healthier and stronger, and Josh found himself wanting to spend more time with her. She was his boss, yes, but she was also his friend and he found her easy to talk to and fun to be with. Josh's relationship with Brenda had basically been whittled down to pleasantries and an occasional short conversation about the progress of her screenplay—and Josh's relationship with Melanie had morphed into a whole, huge, complicated and secret thing. Josh's feelings for Melanie were running amok; they were growing like some crazy, twisting vine, strangling his heart. He wanted to talk to someone about Melanie—and strangely, the person who came to mind was Vicki. But this was out of the question.

Melanie was thirteen weeks pregnant. Her stomach held the slightest swell—rounded, smooth, tight. She was luminous—always smiling, radiating good, sweet, sexy Melanie-ness. He was crazy about her, he couldn't wait for the day to pass, for night to come, for his father to switch off the TV and retire to his bedroom, because this was when Josh left the house, driving out to 'Sconset with a sense of fervent anticipation. *Melanie.*

Since the beginning of August, his longing for her had

intensified. One night, she didn't come to meet him at all. Josh waited patiently in the beach parking lot until eleven o'clock, then he drove, as stealthily as possible, past the house on Shell Street. The house was dark and buckled up for the night. In the morning, Melanie told him in a quick whisper that she had simply fallen asleep.

Simply? he thought. What had developed between them was well beyond simple.

She admitted to him that she was talking to Peter. Not just the one time and not just to discuss "household matters." He knew about the baby; she had told him.

"I had to," she said. "He's the father. He deserves to know."

Josh disagreed. "Is he still having the affair?"

"I don't know."

"Have you asked him?"

"No."

"Well, what does he say when he calls?"

"He says he misses me. He asks when I'm coming home."

"That's just because of the baby," Josh said. "He cares about you now because you're pregnant."

Josh said these words without realizing how hurtful they were. Melanie's eyes widened in shock. Right away, he knew he should apologize, he did apologize, and Melanie said, "No, no, you're right. I can't trust him. I don't trust him. He's only calling me because I'm pregnant."

"He's stupid," Josh said. And when Melanie didn't respond, he said, "It might be better if you didn't tell me about the phone calls anymore."

"Okay," she said. "Sure thing. I just don't want to keep anything from you."

But this wasn't exactly true. What she kept from Josh was how the phone calls made her feel and what she intended to do about Peter once the summer ended and she returned to Connecticut. Peter was her husband, yes, but was she going to take him back? Melanie never said, and Josh was afraid to ask. He needed someone to talk to, but there was no one. He spent all day with a four-year-old, throwing perfect pitches, fielding perfect hits.

"Josh? Josh?"

Blaine was standing at "home plate" with his bat poised when Josh, who had been ready to pitch, froze. It was his custom, between pitches, to check on Porter, who was asleep on the blanket under the umbrella. Was he still asleep? This was increasingly important now that Porter could walk; the last thing Josh wanted was for Porter to toddle off down the beach unnoticed. But when Josh checked on Porter this time, he was taken by surprise. There was a person sitting under the umbrella next to Porter, a person who had appeared out of nowhere, like a ghost, like a bad dream. It was Didi.

"What—" Josh said, but he stopped himself. He didn't want to get noticeably angry or flustered in front of Blaine.

"Hi," Didi said.

"Josh!" Blaine said. "Pitch!"

Josh looked at Blaine waiting—and then back at Didi. Josh felt as threatened as he would have by a cobra under the umbrella with Porter, or a Siberian tiger. What if Didi snatched Porter up and disappeared with him?

Josh pitched the ball, Blaine smacked it over Josh's head. Didi made a big show of clapping and cheering, and at that point, Blaine realized there was someone under the umbrella with his brother. A stranger. But no, not a stranger.

"Hey, I know you," Blaine said. "From the hospital." As Josh retrieved the ball, Blaine approached the umbrella. *Not too close!* Josh thought. He jogged over.

"Blaine, do you want to play with Mateo now?"

"What about Wiffle ball?"

"I have to talk to Didi."

"Is she your girlfriend?"

At this, Didi laughed, a forceful, one-syllable blast. "Ha!"

"No," Josh said. "But I have to talk to her. Will you play with Mateo?"

"How many minutes until lunch?"

Josh checked his watch. "Eighteen minutes."

"Okay," Blaine said. He wandered a few yards down the beach to where Mateo Sherman was burying his father's feet in the sand. Omar Sherman looked over to Josh and said, "I've got him."

"Thanks!" Josh said. Omar would be wondering who Didi was, as would Mrs. Brooks two umbrellas down. Josh smiled at Didi, but this was purely for show. "What are you doing here, Didi?"

"I know about her."

"You know about who?" Josh said wearily.

"You're screwing the mother's friend," Didi said. "And she's pregnant. I know all about it. It's weird, okay, Josh? It's twis-ted."

"You don't know a damn thing," Josh said. "You are

so far off base, you're just making shit up. You sound like a crazy person."

"Rob saw you with a woman with curly hair. Older. And I did some further research. It's the mother's friend. She came to the hospital for a prenatal appointment. I know you're sleeping with her. I know you took her to the house in Shimmo. Zach told me."

Stop! Josh thought. *Stop and think!* But if he paused, even for a second, if he faltered or showed a crack, she would get a fingerhold and pull him apart.

"You owe me money," Josh said. "Two hundred dollars, plus interest. Are you here to pay me?"

"Don't try to change the subject," she said.

"You're the one who's trying to change the subject," Josh said. "Because the only thing between you and me is that money."

"I need five hundred dollars to get my car back," Didi said. "Give me five hundred dollars and I won't tell anyone."

"Won't tell anyone what?"

"That you're sleeping with a woman who is pregnant. I could see if you hit on the other one, the sister. She, at least, is attractive, though waaaaaaayyyyy too old for you."

"Stop it, Didi. You can't blackmail me."

"Sure I can."

"No, you can't," Josh said. "What you're saying is outrageous. No one will believe you."

"Rob saw you, Josh. Out in Monomoy. With the woman. At midnight. How do you explain that?"

"I don't have to explain it because it isn't true. Rob is untrustworthy. He's as crazy as you are." Josh looked over at Blaine, happily playing with Mateo Sherman. Omar gave Josh the thumbs-up. Porter's breathing was deep and even. *Everything is okay,* Josh told himself. *You can handle Didi.*

"Everyone will believe it," Didi said. "Because you're different this summer. You never come to parties, you don't go out. You don't do anything except hang around with those women and the kids. Everyone's noticed, Josh. I'm sure even your father's noticed. Although, maybe not. Your father is pretty oblivious."

"Stop it, Didi."

"I'll have to clue him in."

Josh tried not to let any emotion cross his face. He felt like he was onstage. Still, he couldn't let Didi get anywhere near his father. That would be a complete disaster.

"Whatever," Josh said. "My father already thinks you're wacko, Didi. Anything you try to tell him will fall on deaf ears."

"That's a chance I'll have to take," Didi said. She stood up and brushed off the seat of her shorts. "Give me five hundred bucks and I'll let this go. I won't tell your father. I won't tell anyone."

"Get out of here, Didi."

"You'll be sorry."

"Why are you doing this?" Josh asked.

"You really want to know?"

"Yes," he said. "I really want to know."

Didi sidled up to him and tucked herself right under his ear. "Because I love you," she whispered.

* * *

A few days later, the heat arrived. Real heat, and humidity—and as in the case of an unwelcome houseguest, no one knew how long it was staying. Josh was glad he wasn't working at the airport. How the kids could stand on that asphalt all day without feeling like they were sausages on a griddle, Josh had no idea. Even the beach wasn't much of a reprieve. The sand was too hot for Blaine to walk across, so Josh had to carry Blaine in addition to his usual load. The three of them abandoned their routine and spent all morning swimming in the shallows. The water was as warm as a bathtub, and strewn with tangles of seaweed. It cooled down a little at night, but there was no breeze. The humidity hung in the air in damp sheets, and the mosquitoes hatched. Josh's Jeep had no air-conditioning, so he and Melanie made love on the beach, where they got eaten alive. They were sticky and sweaty, and their skin became breaded with sand.

"Yuck," Melanie said. "This is when you want the Four Seasons."

Josh's house had no air-conditioning either, so Tom Flynn set up a big square fan at one end of the table that blew on them while they ate. Josh liked the fan; its noise took the place of conversation.

"Hot one," Tom Flynn would say when he sat down. Josh was making cold things for dinner: Italian subs, tuna fish, sliced watermelon; the iceberg salad had never tasted so good.

"Hot one," Josh agreed.

Maybe it was because of the noisy fan, but Tom Flynn did not bring up Didi's visit at the table. Instead, he caught Josh in the morning, as Josh was getting out of the shower. It was Saturday, not a day Josh worked, and so he was in no particular hurry. Josh came out of the bathroom with a towel around his waist to find Tom Flynn standing in the hallway. Waiting for him. His presence was so surprising, Josh sucked in his breath.

"Jesus, Dad. You scared me."

"Do you have a minute?" Tom Flynn said. This was very much the rhetorical question, and Josh tensed. He knew what was coming, sort of.

"Can I get dressed?"

"By all means," Tom Flynn said. "I'll be out on the deck."

"The deck" was off Josh's parents' bedroom. Because it was on the second floor, it caught the breeze. It was by far the most comfortable place in the house in this kind of weather, and yet Josh never used the deck, and as far as Josh knew, his father never used it, either. In fact, it had been a year, maybe two, since Josh had set foot in his father's bedroom at all. He wasn't exactly surprised to find that it was still the same—same dark-patterned bedspread that Josh and his father had bought at Sears in Hyannis shortly after Josh's mother died, same neat-as-a-pin dresser, same lineup of shoes in the closet. A picture of Josh's mother hung on the wall, a picture of her from high school, in which she was barely identifiable as the woman Josh had known. Still, Josh stopped and looked at the picture on his way out to the deck.

Do you hate her? Vicki had asked.

Tom Flynn was already outside, his arms crossed on the railing, his head focused in the direction of Miacomet Pond and the eleventh hole of the golf course in the distance. He was wearing a white undershirt and a pair of belted khakis. He was barefoot. Josh couldn't remember the last time he'd seen his father barefoot. If Tom Flynn could be described in any way, it would be as tightly laced, buttoned up. But half dressed and without shoes, Tom Flynn seemed vulnerable, human. For this reason, Josh relaxed a little.

"Hot one," Josh said, trying to be funny.

Tom Flynn nodded. "Your mother loved summer."

Again, Josh tensed. His neck was so stiff, it felt like a steel column. *Your mother loved summer:* It was a perfectly innocuous statement, but Josh could count on one hand the number of times his mother had been mentioned in the past ten years.

"I know," Josh said. "I remember."

"Someone once suggested she had that seasonal mood disorder," Tom Flynn said. "People suffer from it when they don't get enough sunlight." He paused. Josh thought, *Well, she did kill herself in December.* He pictured her on the beach with her glass of wine. *We have to enjoy it now. Before winter comes.* "It's probably a bunch of bullshit."

"Probably," Josh murmured.

Tom Flynn's hair was damp and held teeth marks from his comb. He smelled of aftershave and hair oil. The hair oil alone was enough to place Tom Flynn in a separate category of man from Josh. A different generation. Tom Flynn had been in the military in the eighties—he had been stationed near Afghanistan for two years—something about intelligence and aircraft. Josh wasn't sure what his father had done, but Josh attributed most of his father's behaviors—his silence, his promptness, his stiff upper lip, even his neat dresser and closet—to this time in the military. Although Tom Flynn was a supremely competent and dedicated air traffic controller, he made it clear to Josh that the job at Nantucket Memorial Airport, even on the most hectic summer days, was too easy; it was a walk in the park compared to what he'd done "before." The military, then, felt like Tom Flynn's "real job." Nantucket was a pale replacement, time put in until retirement.

Tom Flynn took a deep breath and stared down at his bare feet as though he were surprised to find them there, sticking out past the cuffs of his pants. Josh followed his father's gaze. His father's feet were pale and fishy-looking, the nails square-cut and yellowing. Josh looked up. As hard as it was for Josh to listen, it would be even harder for Tom Flynn to speak.

"What is it, Dad?"

"I don't know if I should even bring this up," Tom Flynn said. "You are an adult, after all."

"What is it?"

"The Patalka girl stopped me in the parking lot at work," Tom Flynn said. "Yesterday, on my way home. She told me you've been seeing one of the women you work for. There's one who's pregnant?"

Josh nodded.

"But it's not your baby?"

"No. God, no."

"I've noticed, obviously, that you've been leaving the house quite late and getting back in at God-knows-what hour. Every night, it seems like. So I figured there was a girl. But this . . . woman? Older than you? Pregnant with another man's child? Do you know what you're *doing*, Joshua?"

Josh stared at the thin blue ribbon on the horizon that was Miacomet Pond. Under other circumstances he might have been supremely embarrassed. He and his father never talked like this; there hadn't even been a sex talk when Josh was growing up. Now, however, he was relieved. He'd denied everything to Didi, but he wouldn't be able to lie to his father. It might feel good to talk about it.

"I thought I did at the beginning," Josh said. "But now I'm not so sure."

"This woman, she has a husband?"

"They're separated."

"But the baby . . ."

"Right. It's complicated."

"How old is she?"

"Thirty-one," Josh said. "Although how old she is doesn't matter."

"It's unusual," Tom Flynn said. "And the fact that she's pregnant . . ."

"Dad, I know, okay? It just happened, I'm not sure how, and now I'm in it. I love her." Even as Josh spoke the words, he was surprising himself. *Did* he love Melanie? Maybe he did. One thing was for sure: He had never felt as alive—happy, self-aware, conflicted, engaged—as he did this summer, with those three women. Maybe love wasn't the right word for it, but it was the only word he had.

Josh thought his father might laugh at this declaration, but Tom Flynn's expression held steady.

"I didn't argue when you said you wanted to quit the airport. I figured you knew what you were doing. Babysitting a couple of little kids . . . well, you're a people person and the money was good and I know the mother is sick and you felt invested, for some reason, in helping her out." Here, Tom Flynn stopped and took another breath. This was a marathon of talk for him. "Now I'm wondering if there's something else at work."

"What do you mean?"

"These women . . ."

"You mean sex?"

"I mean, why were you drawn to working for these women? Maybe it was about sex. But they're a lot older than you, Josh. And it crossed my mind—even before I was accosted by the Patalka girl—that you're out there in 'Sconset trying to find your mother."

"Jesus, Dad . . ."

"I'm the last person to deal in Freudian bullshit," Tom Flynn said. "But I'm not blind and I'm not stupid. You lost your mother at a young age. I dealt with it the best way I knew how, but maybe not the best way there was, you know what I'm saying?"

Josh nodded.

"Maybe we should have talked about your mother until we were blue in the face. Maybe we should have raked ourselves over hot coals about why she did it. Was it something I said or did, was it something you said or did, was it seasonal fucking mood disorder, what? What was it? Maybe we should have cried about it, screamed, yelled, hugged, maybe we should have punched holes in the plaster, smashed the toaster oven, ripped up the snapshots. Maybe those were better ways to deal with it, *healthier* ways. Instead of what we did, which was one foot in front of the other. Head up, eyes forward. There are lots of things we'll never know, never understand,

and why your mother took her own life is one of them."
Tom Flynn lifted a hand—it was trembling—and put it
on Josh's shoulder. "I can tell you one thing for sure.
Your mother loved you."

"I know."

"You don't have to go out and about looking for that
love elsewhere, Josh. Your mother loved you, and wherever she is now, she loves you still."

She loves you still. This was a huge statement, especially considering the source. It was a gift from his father. And yet, it was too much to process on a flat, hot
morning at the end of the most tumultuous summer of
his life. He would have to pocket the statement and think
about it later.

"Right," Josh said. "But I don't think what's happening this summer has anything to do with . . ."

"That may be," Tom Flynn said. "It was just a thought
I had."

"Okay," Josh said. "Thanks."

Tom Flynn stood up to his full height and squared his
shoulders. "As for being in love, I'm out of practice. I
don't have any fatherly advice other than: Be careful."

"Be careful," Josh repeated. "Okay. I will."

⁓

Heat and humidity were no friend to the pregnant woman.
Melanie couldn't stand to be in her own skin. She felt fat
and sweaty and lethargic. The cottage was unbearable,
it was a kiln, even with all of the windows open and the
three oscillating fans running on high. Melanie made two
or three trips to the market per day—primarily for cold

juice, Cokes, and Gatorade for herself and Vicki, but also because the market was air-conditioned. She went to the beach and swam, but it wasn't unusual for Melanie to feel faint walking home, confused, fatigued, forgetful. It was less than half a mile from the beach back to Number Eleven Shell Street, but Melanie arrived home feeling like she'd been lost in the desert.

And so, on the day that she saw Peter standing at the front door, she thought she was hallucinating.

She saw the cab first, an Atlantic Cab right in front of Number Eleven, and a cab, generally, meant Ted. But it was a Wednesday, not Friday, although Melanie had some vague sense that Ted was coming earlier than planned for his vacation so that he could be with Vicki for her post-treatment CT scan. But that was still another week away, wasn't it? This was the kind of thing Melanie kept forgetting. Still, when she saw the cab, she thought: Ted. Because who else could it possibly be? They never had visitors.

It took another few seconds for Melanie to notice the man standing in the shade of the overhang, a very tall man in a suit. From the back he looked like Peter. Melanie blinked. It was always like this at the end of her walk home; her vision splotched. She was thirsty and tired. She had been out with Josh the night before, back home so late it was early.

The man turned, or half turned, searching the street. Melanie stopped. It was Peter. Her stomach dropped in a quasi-thrilling way, like she was careening down a roller coaster. The voice in her head screamed: *Holy shit! It's Peter! Peter is here!* How was this possible? He took off from work? He *flew* here? He thought it would be okay to show up without *asking*? There had been phone calls, three to be exact, not counting the call that Melanie had placed from the market, not counting the call that Vicki had answered. So five calls in total—but not once did Peter hint that he was thinking of doing this. He asked Melanie when she was planning on coming home—and that was the correct question. That left Melanie in control. She would come home when she felt like it, and at that point they would deal with the detritus of their marriage. Melanie could not *believe* Peter was standing by the front door of the cottage. She imagined the baby inside of her doing backflips. *How dare he!* she thought. And simultaneously, she thought, *Thank God Josh is gone for the day.* Josh. A second later she realized that she was not only horrified by Peter's arrival, she was flattered by it. Before everything happened with Josh, this was exactly what she had wished for.

She couldn't make herself move forward; she wanted to remain in this moment of seeing Peter but being unseen herself. The front door of Number Eleven was always unlocked. Had he tried the knob? Had he knocked? Vicki would be asleep with the kids, Brenda was probably still out. Melanie stood in the shade of the neighbor's elm tree, watching him. He looked distinctly out of place in his suit, but the suit also brought to mind the fact that Peter was an adult, a man with a job in the city—and not a college student.

Melanie remained there a few seconds longer, but she was a hostage in her own body. She was dying of thirst—and, as ever, she had to pee. She moved forward, pretending not to have noticed him and trying not to worry about her appearance. She hadn't seen the man in nearly two months. She was bigger now, with a swell at her abdomen. She had been swimming at the beach, and her hair looked like . . . what? When she touched it, it was curly and stiff with salt. The skin of her face was tight from too much sun. And yet, Melanie felt beautiful. Because of Josh, she told herself. She felt beautiful because of Josh.

She opened the gate and strolled down the flagstone walk. Peter saw her, she could feel his eyes on her, but she would not look at him, she would not acknowledge him, she would not be the first to speak.

"Melanie?"

His voice was not filled with wonder, as she had hoped. Rather, his tone was the one he used when he wanted to call attention to something that was right in front of her face. *Earth to Melanie!* She responded to this not by acting surprised but by cutting her eyes at him, then quickly looking away. She reached past him for the doorknob and he touched her shoulder. His voice softened considerably.

"Hey, Mel. It's me."

"I can see that." She looked at him. It was both familiar and strange, the way her neck arched so she could look him in the eye. Peter was tall, six foot six, whereas Josh was just a few inches taller than Melanie. Peter's skin was a warm, golden color, despite his claims that he'd been trapped in the office all summer, and she'd missed his almond-shaped eyes, the intricate creases of his eyelids. This was her husband. The man she'd been with for nearly ten years.

Before she knew what was happening, he bent to kiss her. She closed her eyes. The kiss was distinct from the thousands of other kisses of their marriage, many of which had been dutiful, passionless, dry, quick. This kiss was searching, lingering, it was exploratory and apologetic. It took Melanie's breath away.

But come on! Melanie told herself. She was not such an easy mark. She pushed into the house. Peter had to duck to get through the doorway.

"Be quiet," Melanie said. "Vicki and the kids are sleeping."

"Okay," Peter whispered. He followed Melanie into the big room. She noticed he was toting an overnight bag. "This is a cute place. Not exactly what I imagined, but cute. Old-fashioned."

"I love it," Melanie said defensively, as if Peter had been insulting it. "It was built in eighteen oh-three. Vicki's family has owned it for over a hundred years."

"Wow," Peter said. Because of the low ceilings, he was hunched in the shoulders. Melanie watched him take in the details of the room—fireplace, bookshelves, coffee table, sofa, kitchen table, rotary phone, silver-threaded Formica, sixty-year-old appliances, braided rugs, ceiling beams, doors with glass knobs leading to various other rooms, presumably rooms as small and precious as this one. He stood there, nodding, waiting maybe, for Melanie to invite him into her room.

"Where are you staying?" she asked.

"Oh," he said as if she'd startled him. "Actually, I haven't booked a place."

"It's August," Melanie said. "It would have been smart to make a reservation."

"I thought I would stay here," he said. "With you. I thought . . ."

Melanie cut him off with some high-pitched laughing.

Laughing because she didn't know what to say or how to feel. She had to pee.

"You'll excuse me one second?" she said.

"Uh, sure."

She shut the door of the bathroom and locked it for good measure. *I thought I would stay here. With you.* Melanie pictured Frances Digitt with her cutesy-butch haircut and her lively blue eyes. Frances had always asked about Vicki's in vitro in a confidential sotto voce. *How's it going? My sister, Jojo, in California, the exact same thing. Must be so tough . . .* For months, Melanie had thought that Frances Digitt was genuinely sympathetic, but it was clear now that Frances Digitt hadn't wanted Melanie to conceive at all; most likely, her sister, Jojo, in California, was fictional. Frances Digitt skied the backcountry of the Canadian Rockies; she was dropped into remote mountain terrain by helicopter. She was a person who sought out danger—so, another woman's husband? Sure, why not? Frances Digitt's chocolate Lab was named Baby; she was one of these women whose dog was her child. The dog probably knew Peter by now, the dog probably licked his hands and rested his head in Peter's lap and whined to be stroked between the eyes.

I thought I would stay here. With you.

Melanie flushed the toilet. When she stood, her legs were jelly. She staggered to the brown-spotted mirror and smiled at herself. She looked okay; she looked better than okay. Her fury was empowering—and she was furious! She was about to pitch a fit like a little kid. *How dare you! You bastard! You asshole!* No doubt Peter expected Melanie to happily invite him back into her bed. He was, after all, her husband and the father of her child.

Melanie didn't care!

She washed her hands and face, patted them dry with a towel, and drank from the children's bathroom cup. Vicki could wake up at any moment, and Brenda would come home. Melanie had to figure this out, and soon.

Peter was standing right where she'd left him. A giant in the dollhouse. The cottage was hot, she realized. He must have been sweltering in his suit.

"Would you like a drink?" she said.

"I'd love one."

She poured two glasses of lemonade and added ice. She sucked hers down and poured herself more. She collapsed in a kitchen chair; she couldn't stand up another second. Peter remained standing until she nodded to the chair across from hers. He took off his suit jacket, loosened his tie, and sat.

"How do you feel?" he said. "You look great."

"What are you doing here, Peter?"

He rolled up his shirtsleeves. There were things about him that she'd forgotten—the muscle tone of his forearms, for example, and his brushed-chrome Tag Heuer watch, which he always kept facedown and jangled on his wrist when he was nervous. She'd forgotten how smooth his skin was, practically hairless; he only had to shave twice a week. And the glossy pink wetness of his lips and the faint scar on his nose, a half-inch white line with hash marks (he'd gotten the cut as a child in a bus accident). Melanie had touched that scar innumerable times, she had kissed it, licked it, batted it with her eyelashes. This was her *husband*. Before Frances Digitt, what had that meant? At first, they'd lived in Manhattan, they rode the subway, ate take-out food, went to movies and readings, worked out at the gym, volunteered at a soup kitchen and a shelter. They tried new restaurants and met in hotel bars for drinks with people from Peter's work, people like Ted and Vicki. They had shopped for things: a new sofa, window treatments, a birthday present for Peter's mother, who lived in Paris. They had plenty of money, and, more important, they had plenty of time. They spent hours reading the paper on Sundays and going for long walks in Central Park. Once they moved to Connecticut, they raked leaves and mowed the lawn, painted the powder room, and worked in the garden. But something was missing, a connection, a purpose to their union beyond the acquisition of things, the completion of tasks. Children! Melanie wanted children. That was when her marriage came into focus, or so it had seemed to Melanie. She and Peter embarked on a quest; they were united by their wanting. The gifts and the trips that arrived in place of a child—the orchids, the truffles, the oceanfront suite in Cabo—were meant to console Melanie, to make her happy. But they had only served to anger her. She was, in the final months, a woman who could not be made happy, except by one thing. The lovemaking became a job; Melanie did everything short of bringing her basal thermometer, calendar, and stopwatch to bed. Was it any wonder Peter had begun an affair with someone young, someone daring and fun, someone whose idea of a child weighed a hundred pounds and was covered with brown fur?

Yes, to Melanie it was a wonder. Peter was her husband. She'd assumed that meant they owned if not each other, then at least the relationship. The marriage was something they had agreed to value, like a Ming vase; it was something they were entrusted to carry, each holding equal weight. But Peter had dropped his end.

"I wanted to see you," Peter said. "You've been gone forever. I miss you."

"That's bullshit." Melanie touched her belly. "You're only here because I'm pregnant."

"That's not true."

"Oh, God, of course it is. Why pretend otherwise?"

"It's over with Frances," Peter said.

Melanie did not respond to this, though she was keenly interested by it. Did Peter end the relationship with Frances because he was overcome with love and longing for his wife? Or did Frances Digitt simply meet someone else at her share in the Hamptons?

"I said, it's over with . . ."

"I heard you."

"I thought you'd be . . ."

"What? Overjoyed? Relieved? I don't trust you, Peter. You cheated on me and you cheated on our marriage and although you didn't know it, you cheated on this baby."

"I knew you'd overreact."

Now, *there* was the Peter she recognized. It was as though he was torn between the mean person he really was and the kind, conciliatory person he was trying to be.

Melanie smirked. "Right. I'm sure you did. Get out of here, Peter."

"Sorry," he said. "Sorry, sorry." He leaned forward and gave her a look that could only be described as beseeching. "I love you, Mel."

"You do not."

"I do. I want you to come home."

"I don't want to come home. I'm happy here." She took a breath and counted to three, the way she did each afternoon before she plunged into the ocean. "There's someone else."

"There is?"

"There is." Melanie's stomach made some weird squelching noise, loud enough to offer some comic relief, but Peter's expression remained shocked, incredulous.

"Who is it?"

"It's none of your business," Melanie said. Already she was chastising herself—Josh was secret from everybody, and that meant secret from Peter, too. But Melanie couldn't help herself. She had wanted to tell Peter about Josh since the first night of her and Josh together, in the garden of the 'Sconset Chapel. She wanted Peter to know that she had settled the score. She had a lover, too!

"Well," Peter said. "Okay then."

"Okay then," Melanie said.

"He stays with you here?" Peter said.

"No," Melanie said. "But that doesn't mean that you can stay here."

Peter held up his palms. "Say no more. I get the picture. I'll book myself a room. Maybe at that place out by the airport."

Melanie tilted her head. She was torn, too, between the nice person she really was and the mean, spiteful person she wanted to be. "They might not have anything available."

"I'll check."

"Why don't you just go home, Peter?"

"Oh, no," he said. "I'm not giving up that easily."

"This isn't a game, Peter. I'm not a trophy you can win back."

"I know that," he said. "But I'm not leaving this island until you're certain with every cell of your body that I love you. I'm a genuine person, Mel."

"You are not."

"I am genuine in this," he said. He came around the table and folded himself in half to embrace her. The hug was awkward, but like the kiss, there was something distinct about it, something earnest.

"Let me take you out," Peter said. "Anywhere you want to go."

This was the old Peter talking. *Let me spend money on you.*

"No," Melanie said.

"So, what are you saying? I get to see you for five minutes and that's it? You won't even eat with me?"

"That is correct."

"Oh, come on, Mel. I took off from work. I flew all the way up here."

"No one asked you to. If you had called, I would have told you to stay home."

"You *have* to have dinner with me. Please?"

"You don't get it, Peter. You hurt me. You broke my heart. You destroyed my trust in you."

"I know, Mel, I know. I'm trying to tell you it's over and I'm sorry. That's why I'm here. Just let me stay and have dinner with you. That's all I'm asking for. Dinner with you. Please, Mel."

"Fine," Melanie said. "But we eat here."

"With Vicki? And . . ."

"Her sister, Brenda. Yes."

"Ahhhh," Peter said. He didn't want to have dinner with Vicki and Brenda, of course he didn't, but this was the first test. "Okay. Sure thing." He hoisted his overnight bag. "Would it be okay if I changed my clothes?"

"Peter!"

Melanie ground her molars together as Blaine launched himself into Peter's arms. Here was something Melanie hadn't considered. Vicki and Brenda might not mention Peter's presence to Josh (she would ask them not to, for what reason, Melanie had yet to conjure)—but Blaine would tell Josh immediately, first thing.

Peter laughed. "At least someone is happy to see me. How're you doing, buddy?"

"Good," Blaine said.

Peter set Blaine down. "You're getting tall. How old are you now? Seven?"

Blaine beamed. "I'm four and a half."

"See? You're so tall I thought you were seven."

"Did you come with my dad?" Blaine asked.

"No," Peter said. "I came by myself. I wanted to see Melanie."

Blaine looked puzzled. "What for?"

"Melanie's my wife. Remember?"

"She is?"

"Well . . . ," Melanie said.

"What?" Peter said. "You are my wife."

Vicki and Brenda were as quiet as thieves in the kitchen as they pulled dinner together. They had been shocked by Peter's presence, but Melanie couldn't tell if they were happy for her that her husband had come back, or if they were angry and disapproving. Brenda had been more visibly stunned, Vicki more openly cynical with Peter, but she had known him a long time.

"And the baby in here," Peter said, patting Melanie's belly, "is my baby and Melanie's baby."

"It is?" Blaine said.

"Amazing," Brenda said from the kitchen. Her voice was just loud enough for Melanie and Peter to hear.

Angry, Melanie thought. *Disapproving.*

"Peter brought some wine," Melanie said. "Brenda, would you like some? Vicki?"

"Yes," Brenda said.

"Yes," Vicki said.

Melanie poured three glasses. She was dying to take a sip herself, but no, she wouldn't.

Blaine said, "Want to go outside and throw rocks with me?"

"Sure," Peter said. "I love to throw rocks."

The front screen door slammed behind them.

"I'd like to throw some rocks at him," Vicki said.

"Vick . . . ," Melanie said.

"Sorry," Vicki said. "Couldn't help myself."

"I don't feel sorry," Brenda said. "You spent so many weeks feeling miserable because of that jerk, I think we have a right to be angry. I mean, what is the deal with the show-up-out-of-the-blue tactics?"

"He knew if he asked, I'd say no."

"You should have told him to go to hell," Brenda said.

"He's not staying here," Melanie said.

"He got a hotel?" Vicki said.

"I think he's planning on staying out by the airport," Melanie said, though she knew Peter had done nothing about booking a room. And not only that, but Peter's overnight bag was resting possessively on the other twin bed in Melanie's room.

"I see they gave you the nun's quarters," Peter had said when he walked into Melanie's room. "Do you and your lover share a twin bed?"

"I told you, he doesn't stay here."

"I can see why," Peter said. He'd proceeded to make himself comfortable, changing into shorts and a polo shirt right in front of Melanie. Watching him undress had seemed strange, and she'd nearly excused herself from the room. But he was her husband. How many times had she seen him undress before? Hundreds. Thousands.

"Who is it?" Peter said. "Some rich guy with a house on the beach?"

"I'm not telling you who it is," Melanie said. "It doesn't concern you."

"It does concern me. You're my wife. You're carrying my child."

Melanie poured herself a club soda. What would she do about Josh? Would she go to him tonight? Would she tell him? Was Melanie prepared to go back with Peter? She felt like the answer should be no, but he was her *husband*. Was she willing to raise this child alone, as a single parent, without a father?

"I don't know what I'm doing," Melanie said to Brenda and Vicki. "And I'm going to ask you to respect that. I'm playing this by ear. I'm going to hear what the man has to say for himself. I'll think about it. I'll make him go home tomorrow."

"Okay," Vicki said.

"And there's something else I want to ask you."

"What?" Brenda said.

"Please don't tell Josh that Peter came here."

"Why not?" Brenda said.

"Why not?" Vicki said.

They were both looking at her.

Melanie took a sip of club soda and fervently wished for some vodka.

"All the things I've said to Josh about Peter, he'd feel like you two do, but he's young, you know, and he's a guy. He won't get it."

"You have feelings for him," Vicki said. Her eyes were so dead-on certain she could have drilled holes through a two-by-four. "You have feelings for Josh."

Brenda's expression bloomed with what looked like childish delight. "You mean *feelings* feelings?"

Melanie could feel her face turning the color of the tomatoes in the Caprese salad. She forced a laugh. "For God's sake, Vick. Would you please give me a break?"

"Am I wrong?" Vicki said. Her tone was more curious than judgmental, but that would change if she knew how far things between Melanie and Josh had progressed.

"Just please don't mention it to Josh, okay?" Melanie said. "Please keep Peter's visit between us."

"*Feelings* feelings," Brenda said. "I can't believe it."

"Brenda," Vicki said.

"What? You're the one who said it."

The front screen door slammed. The women all turned. Peter said, "Oops, sorry. Am I interrupting something?"

There was conversation at dinner—Melanie may even have participated in it—but afterward, she didn't recall a thing that was said. Her mind was wholly occupied with the enormous mess she'd made of things. It was a ball of yarn, tangled in her lap. Slowly, she thought, she would have to unravel it.

After dinner, Peter did the dishes. Vicki excused herself to give the kids a bath, read them stories, and put them to bed. Brenda lingered in the kitchen for a while, finishing up the bottle of wine, watching Melanie a little too closely. Finally, she gave up, much to Melanie's relief. Melanie and Peter were polite to each other—washing the dishes, drying them and putting them away, wiping down the Formica, wrapping up the leftovers—they were too boring for Brenda.

"I'm going to read," she said. "Good night."

It was nearly nine o'clock. Dark outside, now that it was August.

"Want to go for a walk?" Peter said. "I've been here all day and I haven't seen the beach."

"Have you called for a hotel room?" Melanie said.

He walked toward her, wrapped his arms around her waist. "No."

"You're not staying here, Peter." Melanie tried to lean back, away from him, but he hugged her tight. She held her body rigid, resisting. In an hour, she would have to sneak out to see Josh.

"You have two beds. I'll just sleep in the other bed. All very innocent."

"No," Melanie said. "The answer is no."

"I love you, Mel."

"I don't believe you."

He bent down and kissed her hair. "I'm sorry about Frances."

"I can't even stand to hear her name, you know that?" Melanie said. "Thinking about her makes me want to vomit. It makes me break out in a rash."

Peter held Melanie apart so he could look at her. "What I did was wrong. I was confused and angry and frustrated with you, Melanie, and with the whole *process* you were putting us through. The only thing that seemed to matter to you, at all, was having a baby. There were times, lots of times, in bed and otherwise, when I was pretty sure you didn't even *see* me, I mattered to you so little. We lost each other, Mel, and I'm not blaming you for what happened because it was my fault. I did the wrong thing. I take full responsibility and I am now asking you to forgive me."

"Now, because I'm pregnant."

"That's *not* it."

"Well, why now, then? Why not my first week here? Why not when I called you sixteen times?"

"I was angry that you'd left."

Melanie laughed. "That is so rich."

"I was confused. Did you know you were pregnant when you left?"

"I did."

"See? I could be furious with you, too. But I'm not. I forgive you and I want you to forgive me."

"What if I can't forgive you?" she said.

"Ah, but I know you, Mel. And I know that you can."

"Except every time you call to say you're working late, or have to stay in the city . . ."

"Frances is leaving New York," Peter said. "When I ended things, she put in for a transfer. She's going to California to be closer to her sister."

"There will be someone else," Melanie said. "Even if Frances goes, there will be someone else."

"Yes," Peter said. "There will be you. There will be our child."

Melanie sighed. She heard the crunch of tires on shells out on the street and she cocked her head. Josh? She looked out the window. The car moved along down the street.

"You have to go," Melanie said. "To the hotel. I'm not willing to let you stay here."

Peter whipped out his cell phone. "Fine," he said. He sounded angry and officious. "I'll just call the cab and have him take me someplace."

"Good idea," Melanie said. "I'm going to bed. I'll pack your things and set them outside the door."

"Will I see you tomorrow?" Peter asked.

"Maybe just for a minute," Melanie said. "Call me in the morning and tell me where you're staying. I'll come to you. But you should go home tomorrow, Peter. Ted comes on Friday and this house is too small for . . ."

"Come home with me tomorrow," Peter said.

"No," Melanie said. "I'll be home in a few weeks."

"You're staying because of your . . ."

"I'm staying because I'm happy here."

"Happy with him?"

"Happy here."

"But you will come home?"

"Eventually, Peter . . ."

"I love you. What can I say to make you believe me?"

"Will you get out of here, Peter?" Melanie said. "Please?"

* * *

Peter stood on the flagstone walk until his cab pulled up, but by then it was nine-thirty. Melanie watched him from her bedroom window. Josh: She had to tell Josh. Melanie lay back on her bed. She was exhausted. Josh would not take the news well, even though they had both acknowledged that theirs was a summer romance. He was going back to Middlebury right after Labor Day; the story of Josh and Melanie ended there. To take it any further was comical. Melanie pictured herself and her newborn baby bunking with Josh in his dorm room. Absurd. Ridiculous. They had two and a half weeks left. Then it was over. Melanie closed her eyes. It would have been better if Peter had waited, she thought. Why he felt compelled to come now . . .

But, she thought, the heart wants what it wants.

When Melanie woke up, soft light was peeking in around the edges of the shades and the damn wren was chirping. She sat up in bed and checked the clock. Six-thirty. Her feet tingled, and it felt like she was suffering from an irregular heartbeat. She had missed Josh, again. And on the worst possible night. Melanie fell back against her pillows; she was still in her clothes, and hence, her body had that stiff, grungy, slept-in-her-clothes feeling. She would have to corner Josh this morning somehow. But she would have to be so, so careful because of Vicki and Brenda. Vicki knew, or thought she knew, but how? Did cancer give a person a sixth sense, or was Melanie simply transparent to her best friend? It didn't really matter. Melanie would deny it—and certainly Josh would deny it. But they would have to redouble their efforts to keep it a secret.

Melanie heard voices in the living room. Blaine was awake. Melanie rose from bed and undressed. It was still hot, still muggy; even with open windows, her room was a roasting pan. She put on a robe. Outdoor shower, she thought. Talk to Josh, go to Peter's hotel (meet him in the lobby, where it was safe), get Peter to the airport.

Melanie stepped out into the living room. Her bare feet hit the buttery floorboards at the same time that Peter cleared his throat and launched into *Make Way for Ducklings* in a soft but charming reading voice. *No,* Melanie thought. *Not possible.* But yes—Peter was sitting next to Blaine on the blue sofa, reading. Melanie stopped in her tracks. Peter's overnight bag sat open behind the sofa; he was wearing his light-green pajamas. Had he slept here? Not possible. Melanie had stood at the window until the cab whisked him away.

Melanie approached the sofa. Peter's voice was engaging and whimsical as he recited the names of the ducklings: *Jack, Kack, Lack, Mack, Nack, Ouack, Pack, and Quack.* . . . For someone who claimed he had never wanted children, he was doing a remarkable job.

"What are you doing here, Peter?" Melanie said.

He looked up, as though astonished to find her there. "Good morning!" he said. "We're reading."

"I told you . . . you said that . . . I thought . . ."

"No hotel rooms," Peter said. "Every room on the island, booked."

"I find that hard to believe."

"So did I. But it was true. Because of the heat wave on the East Coast, I guess. So I came back. The door was open. I didn't think you'd mind."

"I do mind," Melanie said.

Blaine's facial expression was pained; he looked like he was going to burst. "I want Peter to finish reading," he said. "Please?"

"By all means," Peter said. He smiled triumphantly at Melanie and continued regaling Blaine with the plight of the Mallard family.

Melanie stormed out to the shower.

When Melanie emerged, clean and dressed and ready to take Peter to the airport—because this was where they were going, most immediately, before Josh showed up— Blaine was at the kitchen table eating his Cheerios. It might have been any other morning, except for the presence of Peter's overnight bag, which was as unsettling as a dead animal in the room. Melanie smiled at Blaine; the poor child had been through enough this summer, he did not need to witness the decaying insides of Melanie's marriage.

"Where's Peter?"

"At the beach," Blaine said. "He wanted to see it. And he was wearing his bathing suit. He's going swimming. I wanted to go with him but he said I had to stay put."

Melanie sank into a kitchen chair. It was seven-fifteen. She could take the Yukon to the beach, pick up Peter, bring him back to shower and change and get him out of here. But could she do it in forty-five minutes? Would Peter sense urgency and wonder about it, and resist? Would Vicki or Brenda wonder why Melanie was so eager to get Peter out of the house by eight o'clock?

She took a breath. *This is all going to blow up in my face*.

"Blow up?" Blaine said.

"Did I say that aloud?" Melanie asked.

"What's going to blow up?" Blaine said.

"Nothing," Melanie said. "Nothing."

~~~

Be careful. That was the best advice his father had to offer, and the more Josh considered things, the more he realized these were the only words anybody could offer to someone in Josh's position. Josh wrote the words in his journal: *Be careful.*

Melanie had pulled a no-show again last night—so that was twice now. Josh had only waited around until ten-thirty, and he, pointedly, did not drive past Number Eleven on his way home. He had better things to do with his evening hours than track Melanie down. Maybe tonight he would be the one to stay home. Or better still, maybe he'd call up Zach and some of his other buddies from high school and go to the Chicken Box. Drink beer, check out the summer girls, dance. But as ever, Josh gave Melanie the benefit of the doubt. She was pregnant after all and, hence, legitimately tired. Or maybe there had been some kind of medical emergency—maybe she had pains, maybe something happened with Vicki. Melanie wouldn't stand him up on purpose; she wasn't like that.

Josh pulled up in front of Number Eleven. He smelled bacon and his stomach rumbled. The paper cup of pebbles was in the middle of the flagstone walk. Josh picked it up on his way in.

"Hello?" Josh said. He set the cup of pebbles in its customary place high up on the windowsill, out of Porter's reach.

"Hi, Josh," Vicki said. Her back was to him, she was at the stove, but her voice sounded different. It sounded strained, stressed, stretched. Josh looked over and saw a man at the kitchen table eating a stack of blueberry pancakes.

"Hi," Josh said. Porter was in his high chair with his bowl of mush, and Blaine was in the seat next to the unfamiliar man, rolling a Matchbox car along the edge of the table.

The man seemed eager to stand. He bumped the table, and his napkin slid off his lap to the floor as he reached over Blaine and Porter to shake Josh's hand. The man had extremely long arms.

"Hey," he said. "How're you doing? I'm Peter Patchen."

"Josh Flynn," Josh said.

He was grateful that his name came automatically, because shortly thereafter, Josh's mind switched over to white noise. *Peter Patchen. Peter Patchen.*

"Hungry?" Vicki said.

"Ummmm," Josh said. "Ahhhh. Actually, not really."

"No?" Vicki turned around.

Josh shook his head, or he meant to shake his head, but he was too busy staring at Peter Patchen, who was very tall, who was eating blueberry pancakes that in other circumstances would have been meant for Josh. Peter Patchen's hair was wet, his hair was very black, it was Chinese-black. The man was Asian. So this couldn't be Peter Patchen because Melanie had never mentioned that Peter Patchen was Asian. Though why would she? Peter Patchen was wearing a white T-shirt with writing on it, some kind of event T-shirt, Corporate Challenge or some such. And shorts. Regular khaki shorts. He was in bare feet. So he was staying here, he had stayed here, he had showered here. Josh cast his eyes around the room—he was a detective, looking for clues, and too, he was looking for Melanie. Where was Melanie? He wanted to see her. She couldn't keep a secret and she didn't know how to lie, so her face would tell him what was going on. But come on! Josh told himself. It was apparent what was going on—Peter Patchen, the cheating husband, was here on Nantucket, here in this house, eating pancakes meant for Josh and buddying up to Blaine—asking him about his Matchbox car, which, it just so happened, was a miniature Shelby Cobra that Josh had bought for Blaine when Vicki was so sick with her fever. Peter was holding the car now, turning it in the light, whistling with admiration.

It was very, very hot in the kitchen.

"Hey, Josh." Brenda passed by him, lightly touching his back, on her way to her coffee. "You met Peter? Melanie's husband?"

"Yep," Josh said. *Be careful* was flashing in neon lights behind his eyelids, and this flashing was accompanied by a high-pitched ringing, like an alarm. But still, he couldn't help himself. He said, "Where is Melanie, anyway?"

Both Vicki and Brenda turned to look at him. He could feel them looking, but his eyes were trained on Peter Patchen, Melanie's husband.

If he answers, Josh thought, *I will beat the shit out of him.*

But everyone was quiet—extra quiet?—and all Josh

could hear was bacon sizzling in the pan, hissing and spitting like it was angry.

Blaine looked up. "She went for a walk," he said.

What to do? Josh had taken care of the boys for seven weeks, and yet he stood in the kitchen with Vicki making breakfast and Brenda filling her thermos with coffee, and Porter and Blaine, and Peter Patchen, who was devouring pancakes like some kind of hungry animal—and Josh couldn't imagine what his next word or deed should be. Continue on as normal? It was impossible.

Vicki brought a plate of bacon, draining on paper towels, to the table. "Josh, are you okay?"

"You look sick," Brenda said. "Do you feel all right?"

"Fine," Josh said.

"Do you want to get stuff ready for the beach?" Vicki said.

"Beach!" Blaine shouted. He looked at Vicki, then at Josh. "Is it all right if Peter comes?"

If Peter comes? Josh thought. He should tell everyone he was sick. He should go home.

"I just went to the beach," Peter said. "And I have to leave today."

"Leave today?" Blaine said. "You just got here."

"This was a quick visit," Peter said.

"To see Melanie?" Blaine said.

"To see Melanie," Peter said.

One more word, Josh thought, *and I'm going to kill him.*

Vicki took Josh's elbow. "Why don't you get stuff

ready for the beach," she said. Her voice was kind and indulgent.

She knows, he thought.

"Okay," he said. "Right."

Towels, cooler with lunch, snacks and juice, lotion, umbrella, blanket, orange shovel, pacifier, buckets, change of clothes, extra diapers. Josh knew the routine by heart, he could do it in his sleep, and yet it took him forever to pull it all together. Blaine was champing at the bit, Porter was in a smiling mood; it should have been full-steam ahead. But Josh dragged his feet. He was waiting for Melanie to get home. Where was she? He tried to surreptitiously peer into the black overnight bag behind the couch. This was Peter's bag? Josh felt grateful that it was behind the couch and not in Melanie's bedroom. Josh wanted to say something to Peter before he left—but what? Peter was still at the kitchen table yapping to Vicki about this person and that person, friends and enemies back in Connecticut and "the city."

Josh stood at the front door. He tried to hoist an arm. "Okay, we're going."

Vicki looked over. "Okay."

Peter did not acknowledge Josh's impending departure. *You'd better not be here when I get back,* Josh thought. *Or I will kill you.*

"Do you need anything from the market?" Josh asked. "On the way home?"

Vicki smiled mildly. "No. I don't think so."

"Okay," Josh said. Where was Melanie? "See you."

Still no flicker of interest from Peter. Peter thought of Josh as the help. A servant, a slave. Whereas Peter was the husband, the neighbor, the peer, the equal, the chieftain in Melanie's real life. But Peter Patchen was also a genuine crumb who cheated and lied—*that* was Melanie's real life.

Josh trudged down the street, Porter in one arm, his pack-mule load in the other, beach umbrella slung across his back. The white shells of the street reflected the sunlight in a way that hurt Josh's eyes. The glare made Josh squint and gave him a headache; he'd had nothing to eat and his stomach was sour, and he was transporting a hundred pounds at least. He felt weak and shaky in the knees. He was stupid, an idiot; he should have declared himself sick when he had the chance. He encouraged Blaine to walk in the shade.

Josh found Melanie waiting for him at the rotary. She was leaning against the railing outside Claudette's, where he couldn't miss her. He saw her and flooded with relief and love, but this was replaced with a rush of fury and suspicion. *Be careful* blinkered in his mind.

"There's Melanie," Blaine said.

"I see her."

She was all decked out for power walking—the stretchy shorts, the white sneakers. Her hair was in a ponytail, but she'd been sweating and curls fell around her face. Her cheeks were hot and pink. She took up stride alongside of them and reached for the handle of the cooler.

"Let me help."

"I've got it." Josh's voice sounded angry, so he said, "You're carrying your own load."

"Josh?"

He stopped in his tracks and turned to her. "What?"

Blaine stopped, too, and looked up. "What?"

They both looked at Blaine and continued walking.

"I didn't know," she murmured. "I had no idea. It came as a total shock. You have to believe me."

"What about last night?" he said. "Where were you?"

"I fell asleep."

"Don't lie to me."

"I'm not lying."

"Where did he stay? With you?"

"He said he was getting a hotel, but he couldn't find a room, so he came back—this was after I fell asleep—and crashed on the sofa. When I woke up this morning, he was there. No one was more surprised than me . . ."

"Are you guys talking about Peter?" Blaine asked.

"No," Josh and Melanie said together. The parking lot of the public beach was up ahead. "The beach is crowded today," Josh said to Blaine. "Do you want to run ahead and save our spot before someone else takes it?"

"Takes our spot?" Blaine said, clearly worried. "Okay." He dashed off.

"Be careful!" Josh called out.

Be careful. To Melanie, Josh said, "I think we should end things."

"No," she said.

"Yeah," he said. His voice was thick; his throat felt like it was coated with a film or mucus. "It's going to be over in a couple of weeks anyway."

"But that's a couple of weeks . . ."

"Melanie," he said. "You're going back to Peter. He came to take you back."

"He came to take me back," she said. "But I said no. I'm staying here until . . ."

"But you will go back to him eventually. When you leave."

She was quiet.

"Right?"

"I don't know what I'm going to do."

"You're going back to him. Just say it."

"I don't want to say it."

Girls, women, Josh thought. They were the same. Lure you in, trample your heart, but instead of letting you break away clean, there was all this muddling confusion, all this *talking*.

"I have feelings for you, Josh."

"I have feelings for you, too," he said. "Obviously." He had called it love to his father and he might have used the word with Melanie if it hadn't been for this morning.

"It's only two more weeks," Melanie said. "What's the point of ending it now?"

What *was* the point in ending it now? Well, for one thing, Josh felt in control right now. Sort of. Peter's visit was a blessing in disguise, maybe; it gave Josh the impetus to get out while his head was still above water—because the possibility of drowning in Melanie, in his feelings, his love for her, was very real.

Suddenly, Melanie screamed.

Up ahead, Blaine was running through the parking lot toward the sandy entrance of the beach. A car, a behemoth green Suburban with a Thule car carrier and tinted windows, was backing up. There was no way the driver could see Blaine.

Josh yelled, "Blaine!" He dropped his load and handed Porter to Melanie.

Blaine stopped, turned around. The Suburban was still

backing up. Josh ran, yelling, "Stop! Get out of the way! Stop! Stop!"

The Suburban bucked to a stop a few feet shy of mowing Blaine over. Josh raced to Blaine, scooped him up. The window of the Suburban went down, and a woman who looked sort of like Vicki poked her head out, her hand to her chest.

"I didn't see him," she said. "Thank God you yelled. I just didn't see him at all."

Josh was too keyed up to speak. He clung to Blaine for a second, while the vision of Blaine struck in the head by the Suburban's bumper and Blaine crumpling to the ground before being flattened under the Suburban's crushing weight played its course, then evaporated with a shudder. *Thank God,* he thought. *Thank God.* There was bad like he was going through with Melanie, and then there was *really bad.*

"You have to be careful, buddy," Josh said. Relief flowed through him so fast, it made him dizzy. "Jesus God, Lord Almighty, thank you. Holy shit. Oh, man, you have to *watch.* You could have been killed. Geez."

Melanie hurried over to them; Porter's legs were straddling her. "Thank God you're okay," she said. "Thank God you didn't get hit."

Blaine looked like he was about to dissolve into tears. He grabbed Josh around the waist. "I was trying to save a spot at the beach, like you told me to."

"Right," Josh said. "I know. It's not your fault. But you have to *watch.*"

"I'm sorry," Blaine said.

"I shouldn't have told you to run ahead." Josh took Porter out of Melanie's arms. He'd been lucky, this time.

He felt like that was some kind of sign. "Okay." He corralled Blaine into the space beside him. "Stay with me."

Melanie touched Josh's arm. "We'll talk about things . . . later?" she said.

"No," Josh said. "I don't think so."

"What?"

"Good-bye, Melanie." And without turning back, he headed up over the sand dune with the kids, to the beach.

⌒

Vicki's last dose of chemo should have been cause for celebration. She had seen other patients show up on the day of their final treatment with roses for Mamie or banana bread for Dr. Alcott. But Vicki was too anxious to feel relief about the end of her regimen, and hence, she did nothing to mark it. She was used to doing things correctly, completely, and in a timely fashion—however, in regard to her chemo, she had failed. There was the day she'd skipped, followed by the five days of fever, and the subsequent lower dosage. The most important protocol of her thirty-two years, short of giving birth, and she'd gone at it half-assed. If she went for her CT scan and they found cancer all through her lungs, she shouldn't be surprised. She would deserve it.

The CT scan was scheduled for Tuesday, and Ted would be there. He had arrived on Friday, as usual, but this time with greater fanfare because he was staying. He was staying for the rest of the summer, until it was time to pack up the Yukon and drive it back home to Connecticut. He seemed different—happier, giddy even, at times. He was in vacation mode. Vicki could only guess how good it felt to leave the pressure of the market and Wall Street behind, along with the concrete blocks of Manhattan baking in the sun, the drudgery of the commute on the train, the confines of summer-weight suits, and, in Ted's case, the big, empty house. He reveled in being cut loose from all of that; he would finally be able to enjoy summer without the pall of Sunday evening hanging over his head. He walked around the cottage in his bathing trunks and a polo shirt and his flip-flops. He sang in the outdoor shower, he roughhoused with the boys, he suggested they go for ice cream every night after dinner. Vicki enjoyed his good mood, but she was worried by it, too. Because it was evident that part of Ted's gleeful demeanor was due to his unflagging belief that Vicki was getting better.

You look great, he kept saying. *God, you look wonderful. You've beat it, Vick. You've beat it.*

Ever since Vicki was diagnosed, she'd been hearing about the power of visualization and positive thinking. But Vicki's mind had never worked that way. She was *afraid* to imagine herself clean of cancer—because what if she tempted fate? Jinxed herself? What if the CT scan showed her lungs riddled with diseased cells, worse than ever? Or what if the tumor was exactly as it had been back in the spring—stubborn, immovable, straddling the line of surgical feasibility?

Ted's good mood would not be deterred. He kissed Vicki's scalp where her hair was slowly but surely growing back in—though the color was darker than Vicki's original blond, and it was tinged with gray. Ted's sexual appetite had returned with a vengeance; he basically bribed Brenda with cash to take the kids on Saturday and

Sunday mornings so he could lounge in bed with Vicki. *You look great,* he said. *You look beautiful. You're yourself again. You've beat it.*

"I haven't beat it," Vicki said angrily to Ted on Monday. In fact, when she woke up that morning, her breathing was labored, her chest was tight; she had to suck air in and squeeze it out. The mere fact that she had to *think* about her breathing was a very bad indicator. "Even if the tumor has shrunk, they still have to operate."

Ted looked at her like she'd insulted him. "I know," he said. "Baby, I know."

As the hour of her appointment on Tuesday approached, Vicki grew more and more tense. Her hands shook as she flipped pancakes and turned bacon for Ted's breakfast. Josh came and took the kids. Josh had been quieter than usual over the past week. He seemed withdrawn, though Vicki didn't have the time or wherewithal to ask him if everything was all right. Still, Josh made a point of giving Vicki a hug and a kiss before he left with the kids for the beach.

"Good luck today," he whispered.

"Thanks," she whispered back.

Later, she spent a long minute locked in an embrace with Melanie, who looked dangerously close to weeping. There should be a handbook, Vicki thought, for the friends and relatives of people with cancer, and in this handbook it should be mandated that the friend/relative be neither too upbeat (Ted) nor too gloomy (Melanie) about one's chance of survival. The friend/relative, Vicki thought as Melanie clung to her, should act like Josh.

Josh had wished her luck. Luck was useful. Luck, perhaps more than anything else, was what she would need.

"I'm going to be okay," Vicki said. "I'm going to be fine." *This is just great,* Vicki thought. *I'm the one whose head is on the chopping block and I'm comforting Melanie.*

"Oh, I know," Melanie said quickly, wiping at her eyes. "It's just all this stuff. The summer. Peter, the pregnancy. You. It's a lot, you know?"

"I know," Vicki said.

Brenda insisted on coming along with Ted and Vicki. "I've been with you all summer," she said. "And I am not missing today. Today is the big day."

Yes, the big day. There had been any number of big days in Vicki's life: her first day of kindergarten; the opening night of the school play with Vicki in the lead; the night of her first school dance, where she received her first kiss. There were Christmases, graduations, first days on the job, there was the day Duke won the NCAA Tournament, there was her wedding day, the nine perfect days of her honeymoon in Hawaii, there was the day she found out she was pregnant, the day she gave birth, the day she and Ted closed on the house in Darien, there were nights of charity benefits, three of which she had co-chaired, there were nights in New York City at restaurants and Broadway shows. There were days cluttered with commitments (the Yukon serviced, root canal, a field trip with Blaine's preschool, free box tickets for the Yankees–Red Sox game). All of these were big days, but none as big as today. Today would be the day Vicki looked at her cancer a second time and heard Dr. Alcott, or Dr. Garcia on a conference call from Fairfield Hospital, say, *Better? Worse? Live? Die?*

Nothing prepared a person for this, Vicki thought as she fastened her seat belt. Ted was driving; Brenda was in the backseat. When Vicki checked on Brenda in the rearview mirror, she saw Brenda's lips moving.

Nothing.

As they pulled into the hospital parking lot, Brenda's cell phone rang.

"That would be our mother," Brenda said.

"I can't talk to her," Vicki said. "I'm nervous enough as it is. Can you talk to her?"

"She doesn't want me," Brenda said. "She wants you."

"Give her to Ted," Vicki said.

Ted swung into a parking spot and took the phone from Brenda. That was for the best. Ellen Lyndon would be reassured by Ted's optimism.

Brenda took Vicki's hand as they headed for the door. She patted her bag. "I brought the book."

Vicki raised a questioning eyebrow.

"*The Innocent Impostor.* My good-luck charm. My talisman."

"Oh," Vicki said. "Thanks."

"And I've been praying for you," Brenda said. "Really praying."

"Praying?" Vicki said. And that reminded her. "You know, there's something I've been meaning to ask you."

"Yeah?" Brenda said. "What is it?"

Ted strode up alongside them. "Your mother wants us to call her as soon as we know anything."

"Okay," Vicki said.

"I don't get it," Brenda said. "Does she think we'll forget about her?"

"She's a mother," Ted said.

"What did you want to ask me, Vick?" Brenda said.

Vicki shook her head. "Later," she said. Though she was running out of time.

"Later for what?" Ted said.

"Nothing," Vicki said.

Brenda narrowed her eyes at the front of the hospital, the gray shingles, the white trim, the blue-and-white quarterboard that said NANTUCKET COTTAGE HOSPITAL. "Do you realize this is the last time we're coming here?" she said. "Strange, but I think I'm going to miss this place."

For all the anticipation and all the worry, for every strained breath and the eight fitful hours of sleep the night before, Vicki found that the actual CT scan itself wasn't that bad. The hospital was short-staffed, it seemed, because the person who administered the CT scan was . . . Amelia, from oncology.

"Yeah," Amelia said in a bored response to Vicki's excitement about seeing a familiar face. "I cover in radiology when they need me. What can I say? I'm multitalented. Now, everything above the waist comes off, including your . . . necklace."

The necklace was a piece of blue yarn strung with dried rigatoni that had been colored with Magic Marker, a present from Blaine on Mother's Day that he'd made in preschool. Vicki didn't have a goodluck charm like Brenda did; the necklace would have to suffice. Vicki removed her clothes, put on the paper robe that Amelia handed her, and clenched the necklace.

Amelia spoke formally, like an operator from a catalog, the ones whose calls were being monitored for customer service purposes. "Would you please lie on the examining table?" she said, indicating the narrow table with a Vanna White–like flourish of her hands.

Vicki complied, adjusting her paper robe. Amelia manipulated the machine into place. "I suggest you take four to five deep breaths in preparation."

"In preparation for what?" Vicki said.

"I'm going to ask you to hold your breath for twenty seconds," Amelia said. "Some patients find they like to exercise their lungs before commencing this process."

"Okay," Vicki said. She sucked air in and squeezed it out; her lungs felt like faulty bellows.

"In those twenty seconds, this machine will take nearly five hundred pictures of your lungs." Now, Amelia's voice was smug; she was obviously proud of the machine.

Could Vicki hold her breath for twenty seconds? She took one look at the ebony and silver stud protruding from Amelia's lower lip, and closed her eyes. Last night, in bed, Vicki had promised herself that she wouldn't think about Blaine and Porter, but as she silently counted out twenty Mississippis, they came to her anyway, only they weren't little boys; they had transmogrified into insects with gossamer wings. They flew, they dove, they hovered over Vicki as she lay on the table. They were dragonflies.

Nothing prepared a person for this. The five hundred pictures from the CT scan were loaded onto Dr. Alcott's computer, but he said he wouldn't have a conclusive answer for Vicki until later in the day. He wanted to look the results over; he wanted to think about them. Dr. Garcia would be examining the scan simultaneously in Connecticut, and the two of them would confer by telephone. Discuss the next step.

"How long do you think that will take?" Vicki asked. She had expected the answer to be clear-cut; she had expected an immediate verdict. She wasn't sure she could wait any longer than a few minutes.

"I really can't say. Depending on what we see, a few hours to a day or so."

"Another day?" Vicki said. "So we just can't . . . go out into the waiting room?"

"I'll call you at home," Dr. Alcott said. His voice was serious, businesslike. He was not his usual chummy, fisherman self. Vicki's spirit cracked and oozed like an egg.

"Thank you, Doctor," Ted said. They shook hands.

Vicki couldn't bring herself to say anything, not even good-bye. The delay disheartened her. *It's over,* she thought. *Palliative care.*

They filed out into the hallway, and Dr. Alcott closed his door. Brenda groaned.

"Here comes that girl," she said.

Vicki was so racked with anxiety that she didn't ask which girl Brenda was talking about. But then she saw a girl walking toward them, scowling. She was blond and disheveled-looking. Vicki remembered her now, though only vaguely, from their first visit here. The port installation.

"She stopped me in the ladies' room one day," Brenda

whispered. "And accused me of all kinds of nonsense. I guess she knows Josh."

Vicki nodded. She could not have cared less. She sucked air in and squeezed air out. Breathing was so difficult, she thought she might flatline right there. And her hand hurt. She gazed down. Ted was squeezing her hand so hard her fingers were turning white. He sensed bad news, too. Palliative care. Hospice. Outside, an ambulance whined, there was a flurry of activity as they walked past emergency. In one of the waiting rooms, the TV news was on: The president was cracking down along the Mexican border.

Vicki closed her eyes. Everything around her, absolutely everything, fell on her List of Things That No Longer Matter. Everything except her life, everything except her children. Blaine and Porter would be at the beach with Josh, digging in the sand, enjoying their snack, playing with their summer friends. But when Vicki tried to picture them ensconced in this idyllic scene, nothing came. Her mind was black. She thought about the boys as dragonflies. (To see them as dragonflies had been comforting, but why?) Again, nothing. She opened her eyes and turned to Ted. "Do you have a picture of the boys?"

Ted's eyes were trained on the girl from Admitting; she was approaching them with purpose. She wore a red cotton sundress that was too short and a pair of battered gold ballet slippers with ribbons that laced up her ankles. Vicki blinked—the girl's bra straps were showing, she wore hastily applied makeup, her blond hair was uncombed. What did she want? Ted absentmindedly handed Vicki a snapshot of the kids from his wallet. Brenda narrowed her eyes at the girl and shook her head. "Whatever you have to say, we don't want to hear it."

"I think you do want to hear it," Didi said.

"No, we don't," Brenda said.

"What is it?" Ted asked.

"Josh is sleeping with your friend," Didi said. "The one who's pregnant."

"Whoa-ho!" Ted said. "That's a pretty big accusation." He looked at Vicki first, then Brenda. His brow creased. "You're talking about Melanie, right? Melanie? How do you know this? Did Josh *tell* you this?"

"Go away," Brenda said. "Please."

"My brother saw them together," Didi said. "Out in Monomoy. In the middle of the night."

"Your brother?" Ted said.

"She's full of shit, Ted," Brenda said. "I don't know what your problem is with our family, but we really need you to leave us alone. We're under a lot of stress here."

Stress, Vicki thought. *There should be another word.*

"Fine," Didi said. She crossed her arms over her chest in a way that seemed diffident. "But I'm not full of shit. They are sleeping together." She spun on her heels and marched away.

Yes, Vicki thought. The girl was probably right. Josh and Melanie. Strange, nearly unbelievable, and yet Vicki had picked up on a bunch of clues that made her believe the girl was correct. Josh and Melanie together: It should have been the biggest revelation of the summer, but Vicki threw it into the basket with everything else. It didn't matter.

* * *

At home, the routine went to pot. Josh returned with the kids.

"How did it go?" he asked.

"We don't know," Ted said. "The doctor is going to call later."

"Oh," Josh said. He looked at Vicki quizzically. "You okay, Boss?"

Melanie and Josh, she thought. Possible? She couldn't waste time wondering. *Palliative care.* A year, maybe two. Blaine would be six, Porter three. Blaine would remember her, Porter probably not. There would be long hospital visits and drugs that put her mind on Pluto. Vicki felt like she was going to faint. She collapsed in a chair.

"Ted, can you take the kids out, please? I can't deal."

"Take them out where? What about Porter's nap?"

"Drive him around until he falls asleep. I can't lie down. What if the phone rings?"

Josh cleared his throat. "Okay, I'm going to go, then."

Blaine protested. "What about a story, Josh? What about *Kiss the Cow*?"

"You're going with Daddy," Vicki said.

Josh slipped out with a wave; he seemed eager to leave.

"I don't know about this, Vick," Ted said. "You're going to sit here by yourself and obsess."

"I'll take the kids," Brenda said. "That way you can both sit here and obsess."

Vicki felt like screaming, *We are talking about my health, my body, my life!*

"Go," she said. She hid in her hot bedroom with the door closed. She opened the window; she turned on the fan. She sat on the edge of the bed. All over the world mothers were dying. Palliative care: steps that could be taken to prolong her life. There was a question she needed to ask Brenda, but they never seemed to get a minute alone so Vicki could ask her. Because Melanie was always there? Melanie, twirling outside the dressing room. *Are you sure there's not something else going on?* Melanie and Josh. But when? Where? And why wouldn't Melanie have told her? But maybe the answer to that was obvious. She thought Vicki would be mad. Would Vicki be mad? She sat on the edge of the bed with her feet on the floor. Her feet, her toes, her body. Ted tapped on the door.

"Come in," she said.

He handed her the phone. "It's Dr. Alcott."

So soon? But when she checked the clock, she saw it was quarter to four. "Hello?" she said.

"Vicki? Hi, it's Mark."

"Hi," she said.

"First of all, let me tell you that Dr. Garcia has scheduled your surgery for September first."

"My surgery?" Vicki said. "So it worked? The chemo?"

Ted clapped his hands like he might have at a sporting event.

"It worked exactly the way it was supposed to," Dr. Alcott said. "The tumor has shrunk significantly, and it has receded from the chest wall. The thoracic surgeon should be able to go in and get it all out. And . . . assuming the cancer hasn't metastasized, your chances of remission are good."

"You're kidding me," Vicki said. She thought she

might laugh, or cry, but all she felt was breathless wonder. "You are *kidding* me."

"Well, there's the surgery," Dr. Alcott said. "Which is never risk-free. And then there's the chance that the surgeon will miss something or that we've missed something. There's a chance the cancer will turn up somewhere else—but this is just my ultracautious side talking. Overall, if the surgery works out like it should, then yes, remission."

"Remission," Vicki repeated.

Ted crushed Vicki in a bear hug. Vicki was afraid to feel anything resembling joy or relief, because what if it was a mistake, what if he was lying . . . ?

"This is good news? I should feel happy?"

"It could have been a whole lot worse," he said. "This is just one step, but it's an important step. So, yes, be happy. Absolutely."

Vicki hung up the phone. Ted said, "I'm going to call your mother. I promised her." He left the room, and Vicki sank back down on the bed. On the nightstand lay the snapshot of the boys, the one Ted had handed her at the hospital. It was of Blaine and Porter in a red vinyl booth at Friendly's. They had been eating clown sundaes, and Porter's face was smeared with chocolate. Vicki had taken them for lunch one day last winter because it was cold and snowy and she had wanted to get out of the house. It had been just a random day, just one of hundreds she had all but forgotten. Just one of thousands that she had taken for granted.

Looking back, Brenda couldn't believe she had ever been worried. Of course Vicki's news was good, of course the tumor had shrunk, of course surgery would be successful and Vicki would beat lung cancer. The woman was the luckiest person on the planet. Her life was Teflon—mess happened, but it didn't stick.

And why, Brenda wondered, should Vicki be the only one with luck? Why shouldn't Brenda be able to emerge from her own morass of problems in a similarly exultant way? Why shouldn't Brenda and Vicki be like sister superheroes, overcoming adversity in a single summer, together?

Ted had brought his laptop with him, but he only used it to send e-mail and check the market in the morning. Sure, Brenda could use it. Of course! Because of the good news of the CT scan, the whole house was in a generous frame of mind. Brenda took advantage of this— she set herself up on the back deck with the laptop and a thermos of coffee and her stack of yellow legal pads and she got to work typing in *The Innocent Impostor,* the screenplay. She was able to revise as she went along, she used an online thesaurus, she referenced a copy of *The Screenwriter's Bible* that she had checked out of the Nantucket Atheneum. The movie script had started out as a lark, but it had become something real. Was this how Pollock had felt? He'd dripped paint over a canvas in an approximation of child's play—and somehow it became art? Brenda tried not to think about Walsh or Jackson Pollock or one hundred and twenty-five thousand dollars as she worked. She tried not to think: *What am I going to do if I don't sell it?* Her mind flickered to the phone number she had programmed into her cell phone for Amy Feldman, her student whose father was the president of Marquee Films. To Brenda's recollection, Amy Feldman had liked *The Innocent Impostor* as much as anyone else; she had turned in a solid midterm paper comparing Calvin Dare to a character from Rick Moody's novel *The Ice Storm*. Had Amy Feldman heard about what happened to Dr. Lyndon right before the end of the semester? Of course she had. The students were officially told that Dr. Lyndon resigned for personal reasons; the last two classes were canceled, and Dr. Atela took responsibility for grading the final papers. But the scandalous stories—sex, grade inflation, vandalism—would have been blown up and distorted, told and told again until they reached cinematic proportions. What did Amy Feldman think of Brenda now? Would she pass the screenplay on to her father, or would she throw it into a Dumpster? Or burn it, in effigy, on Champion's campus?

Brenda typed until her back was stiff, her butt sore from sitting.

Occasionally, the other people in the cottage checked on her. People passing to and from the outdoor shower, for example.

TED

How's it going?

BRENDA

Fine.

BRENDA stops, looks up. She is eager to get some of her eggs out of Amy Feldman's basket.

Hey, do you have any clients who are in the movie business?

TED

Movie business?

BRENDA

Yeah. Or made-for-TV movies?

One hundred and twenty-five thousand dollars, BRENDA thinks. She can't be picky about medium.

Or just regular TV?

TED

Mmmmmmmmm. I don't think so.

*   *   *

VICKI

(touching BRENDA's back)

How's it going?

BRENDA

Fine.

VICKI

Can I bring you anything?

BRENDA

Yeah, how about a pile of money?

BRENDA clamps her mouth closed. She hadn't said anything to anybody about the money and she won't until she is desperate. She isn't desperate now; she is working.

VICKI

(laughing, as though what BRENDA said was funny)

How about a sandwich? I can make tuna.

BRENDA

No thanks.

VICKI

You have to eat.

BRENDA

You're right, Mom. How about a bag of Oreos?

*   *   *

MELANIE

How's it going?

BRENDA

BRENDA stops typing and looks up.
Fine. How's it going with you?
There was the outlandish assertion by DIDI-from-admitting on the day of VICKI's CT scan—BRENDA, unbeknownst to anyone, had called the hospital administration to complain—and ever since then, BRENDA had been watching MELANIE closely, especially when JOSH was around. But she saw no interaction between them. They barely spoke. When MELANIE walked into a room, JOSH walked out.

MELANIE

(taken aback by BRENDA's sudden interest)
I'm okay.
MELANIE's voice is melancholy. It harkens back to their first days in the house, when MELANIE moped all

the time. There had been some recent phone calls from Peter, but MELANIE spoke in a clipped tone and ended the calls quickly.

I'm bummed about the end of summer.

BRENDA
Well, that makes two of us.

MELANIE
What are you doing after we leave?

BRENDA
(focusing on the computer screen, ruing her decision to engage MELANIE in this much conversation)
That remains to be seen. How about you?

MELANIE
Ditto.

There is a long pause, during which BRENDA fears MELANIE is trying to read the computer screen. MELANIE burps.

MELANIE
Sorry, I have heartburn.

BRENDA
You're on your own there.

* * *

JOSH
How's it going?

BRENDA
Fine.

JOSH

Do you think you'll sell it?

BRENDA

I have no idea. I hope so.

BRENDA thinks, *Hell, it can't hurt.*

You don't know anyone in the business, do
you?

JOSH

Well, there's Chas Gorda, my creative-writing
professor at Middlebury. The writer-in-residence, actually. He had his novel, *Talk,* made
into a film back in 1989. He might know somebody. I could ask him when I go back.

BRENDA

Would you? That would be great.

JOSH

Sure.

BRENDA

When do you go back?

JOSH

Two weeks.

BRENDA

Are you looking forward to it?

JOSH

(staring into the cottage, where—by chance?—MELA-
NIE sits at the kitchen table reading the *Boston Globe*)
I guess so. I don't know.

BRENDA
(thinking, *Horrible Didi was right. Something is going on between them. Something the rest of us were too self-absorbed to notice.*)
BRENDA smiles kindly at JOSH, remembering back to when he lent her the quarter at the hospital, remembering back to when they kissed in the front yard.

> Maybe someday I'll be adapting one of your novels.

JOSH
(looking at BRENDA but diverted by something—someone?—inside the cottage)

> You never know.

*　　*　　*

BLAINE
(eating a red Popsicle)
Popsicle juice drips down BLAINE's chin in a good approximation of blood.

> What are you doing?

BRENDA
Working.

BLAINE
On Dad's computer?

BRENDA
Yep.

BLAINE
Are you working on your movie?

BRENDA

Mmmhmm.

BLAINE

Is it like *Scooby Doo*?

BRENDA

No, it's nothing like *Scooby Doo*. Remember I
said it's a movie for grown-ups?

BLAINE reaches out to touch the computer.

Ah, ah, don't touch. Do not touch Dad's computer with those sticky hands. Go wash.

BLAINE

Will you play Chutes and Ladders with me?

BRENDA

I can't now, Blaine. I'm working.

BLAINE

When you take a break, will you play?

BRENDA

When I take a break, yes.

BLAINE

When's that—

BRENDA

I don't know. Now, please . . .

BRENDA checks the cottage. She wonders, *Where's
Josh? Where's Vicki? Where's Ted?*
Auntie Brenda has to work.

BLAINE

How come?

BRENDA
Because. (in a whisper) I have to make money.

Brenda finished typing in the screenplay for *The Innocent Impostor* on the third day, in the middle of the night. She was sitting on the sofa with Ted's computer resting on Aunt Liv's dainty coffee table. There was a breeze coming in through the back screen door. 'Sconset was quiet except for the crickets and an occasional dog bark. Brenda typed in the last page, the scene where Calvin Dare, as an older gentleman with his career behind him, enjoys an afternoon of quiet reflection with his wife, Emily. Dare and Emily look on as their grandchildren frolic in the yard. The scene was taken directly from the last page of the book; it was the scene that gave critics pause. Was it right for Dare to enjoy such bliss when he had all but coopted the life of the man that he had all but killed? Brenda meant to include some kind of questioning imagery in her cinematography notes—but for now, dialogue and direction were . . . DONE! She stared at the computer screen. Fade out. Roll credits. DONE!

Brenda pushed Save and backed up the screenplay on a disc. It was twenty minutes after one, and she was wide awake. She poured herself a glass of wine and drank it sitting at the kitchen table. Her body ached from so much sitting; her eyes were tired. She cracked her knuckles. DONE! Euphoria like she thought she would never feel again. This was the way she'd felt when she finished her dissertation; this was the way she'd felt when she finished grading final papers her first semester at Champion. Job completed, job well done. Tomorrow she would worry about what to do with the damn thing; for tonight, she would just savor the euphoria.

She finished the glass of wine and poured herself another. The house was filled with the sounds of people breathing, or so Brenda imagined. She thought about Walsh—then blocked him out. She found her cell phone on the side table and carried it and her wine out to the back deck. She scrolled through her numbers.

What was she doing? It was quarter to two; any normal person would be asleep. But Brenda couldn't afford to let that matter. She was excited about her screenplay now; in the morning, when it was printed out, she might find flaws, she might question its big-screen potential.

She dialed Amy Feldman's number and tried, in the split second of silence before their lines connected, to remember everything she could about Amy Feldman. Brenda had now spent enough time with Blaine to know that Amy Feldman looked like Velma from *Scooby-Doo*. She was short and squat with a grandmotherly bosom, she had short hair, she wore square glasses with dark frames, and she kept the glasses on a chain so that, when the glasses were óff, they rested on her bosom. Amy Feldman was like an intellectual beatnik from forty years ago, and this, somehow, translated into her being cool, or if not cool, then at least accepted. The other girl-women in the class had seemed to like her; they'd listened respectfully when she spoke, though this may have been because of her father, Ron Feldman. Brenda's class had been, she saw now, a class of aspiring actresses, playing themselves up not only for Walsh but for Amy Feldman. Amy Feldman was majoring in Japanese. What was she doing this summer? Was she traveling in Japan? Had she stayed in New York? If only Brenda had known that she would be fired, and sued, and then in the hole to the tune of a hundred and twenty-five thousand dollars and hence dependent on the proceeds of a screenplay she had to sell, she would have paid more attention to Amy Feldman. As it was, what stuck in her mind were the glasses on a chain and the Japanese.

Like a thunderbolt Brenda recalled overhearing Amy Feldman talking to Walsh about sushi, a place called Uni in the Village that *absolutely no one knows about,* that was *undiscovered* and *completely authentic. Just like the sushi they have on Asakusa Road in Tokyo.*

You've been to Tokyo? Walsh, fellow world traveler, had asked.

I was with my father, Amy said, in a voice that was meant to impress. *On location.*

Amy Feldman, quite possibly, had been in love with Walsh, too.

Three rings, four rings, five rings. Brenda wondered if she was calling Amy Feldman's apartment or her cell phone. If she got voice mail, would she leave a message? A message was too hard to ignore, Brenda decided; Brenda wanted to connect with Amy Feldman in person.

"Yes?"

Someone answered! The voice was male, older, and overly pleasant, as if to say, in the nicest possible way, *Why am I answering the phone at two o'clock in the morning?*

"Hi," Brenda said, in what she hoped was a sprightly voice, to let this person know that she was neither drunk nor an obscene caller. "Is Amy there?"

"Amy?" the man said. Then, in a curious voice to someone else, he asked, "*Is* Amy here?" The other voice, female, murmured a response. The man said, "Yes. She's here, but she's sleeping."

"Right," Brenda said. *Hold it together,* Brenda thought. This was not Amy Feldman's cell phone, nor was it her apartment (insofar as Brenda meant "apartment": some college dive with roommates, laundry in the basement, and a hot plate). This was Amy Feldman's home number, her family home, probably some extremely fine pad overlooking Central Park. *Amy Feldman lives at home,* Brenda thought. *And I am now talking to her father, Ron Feldman.*

Ron Feldman said, "Would you like me to leave Amy a message?" Again, his voice was so pleasant that there was no possibility he was sincere.

"This is Brenda Lyndon calling," Brenda said. She was speaking very quietly because she didn't want to wake up anybody in the cottage. "*Doctor* Lyndon? I was Amy's professor last semester at Champion."

"Ohhhh-kay," Ron Feldman said. "Do I have to write this down or can you call back in the morning?" It was clear he would prefer the latter, but Brenda was as shameless as a telemarketer. She had to keep him on the phone!

"Would you mind terribly writing it down?" she asked.

"All right," he said. "Let me find a pen." To his wife, he said, "Hon, a pen. It's a professor of Amy's from Champion . . . I have no goddamned idea why." To Brenda he said, "What's your name again?"

"Brenda Lyndon. Lyndon with a *y.*"

"Brenda Lyndon," Ron Feldman repeated. The voice in the background raised an octave. Ron Feldman said, "What? Okay, wait. Honey, wait." To Brenda, he said, "I'm going to put you on hold for one second. Is that all right?"

"All right," Brenda said.

The line went silent, and Brenda kicked herself. She was a complete idiot. She had decided, only seconds before making this phone call, that she wasn't going to leave a message, and here she was leaving a message. And this was the one and only time she would be able to call; she couldn't stalk the Feldman household.

The line clicked. Ron Feldman said, "Are you there? Dr. Lyndon?"

"Yes."

"You're the one who got in all the trouble?" he said. "With the student from Australia? You're the one who nicked up the original Jackson Pollock?"

At that second, a light went on in one of the cottages that backed up to Number Eleven Shell Street. In the newly brightened window, Brenda saw the face of a woman her mother's age who appeared to be throwing back some pills and drinking water. Aspirin? Brenda thought. Antidepressants? Pills for arthritis? High blood pressure? Osteoporosis? When you peered into the windows of someone else's life, you could only guess what was going on.

"Well," Brenda said. "Yes, I guess I am."

"We heard all about you," Ron Feldman said. "Or my wife did, anyway. Amy told us you were a good teacher, though. She liked your class. She liked that book you taught."

"*The Innocent Impostor?*" Brenda said.

"*The Innocent Impostor,* hon?" Ron Feldman said. "Um, we can't remember the name, neither of us had ever heard of it. Anyway, Dr. Lyndon, it's late, but we will pass on to Amy . . ."

"Because that's why I'm calling."

"What is?"

"*The Innocent Impostor,* the book Amy liked, the book you've never heard of. I turned it into a screenplay. I have it right here in front of me, as an adapted screenplay."

"Waaaaaaaait a minute," Ron Feldman said. "Are you . . . ?" He laughed, but he no longer sounded overly pleasant or polite; he sounded suspicious, verging on angry. "Did you call here to *pitch* me?"

"Ummmmm . . . ," Brenda said.

"You call here in the middle of the night pretending to look for Amy when really you want to pitch me your screenplay?"

"No, no, I . . ."

"I've had people do it a hundred different ways. They leave the script with the maître d' at Gotham, because that's where I eat, or they bribe my doorman or my driver—or hell, they get *jobs* as my doorman or my driver just so they can get a script in my hands. I am not surprised to find that you, a recently fired Champion professor, have a screenplay, because everyone on God's green earth has a screenplay, including my periodontist's nephew, including my secretary's brother who's currently doing time in Sing Sing. But this is totally fucked-up. This is like nothing else. You . . . caught me with my guard down. Me! How did you get this number?"

"Your daughter gave it to me," Brenda said.

"Dandy," he said. "Dan-dee."

"You said she liked the book, right?" Brenda said.

He paused. "What's the name of the goddamned book?"

"*The Innocent Impostor.*"

"There's your first problem right there. You have to change the title. No one wants to see a movie about an innocent anything."

"Change the *title*?" Brenda said.

There was more yammering in the background. "Okay, right, yes. I stand corrected. My wife makes a point about *The Age of Innocence*. Edith Wharton, Martin Scorsese, nominated for an Oscar. Fine, okay, fine. Go ahead."

"Go ahead, what?"

"Pitch it. I'll give you thirty seconds. Go!"

"Uh, well," Brenda said, thinking, *Speak!* She knew the book inside and out; it was her passion, her baby. "It's a period piece, seventeen hundreds, this man, Calvin Dare, our protagonist, is tying up his horse in front of a tavern and there's lightning and his horse startles and kicks this other man, Thomas Beech, in the head and kills him."

"I'm practically asleep."

"So then the first man, Calvin Dare, goes through this process where he *becomes* Thomas Beech. He takes Beech's job, he marries Beech's fiancée, he lives Beech's life for him, basically, and sheds his own identity so that he can become Beech. Because Beech's life was better than his, maybe. Or . . . because he feels guilty about killing Beech."

"That's it?" Ron Feldman said.

"Well, no, but you'd have to read . . ."

"Thank you for calling, Dr. Lyndon."

"Can I send you . . ."

"Here's an idea: Write a screenplay about a professor who has sex with one of her students and then destroys millions of dollars of university-owned art. We're talking about small release for sure, but that, at least, has half a story line. The other thing, no."

"No?"

"Good night, Dr. Lyndon."

"Oh," Brenda said. In the other cottage, the light went off. The woman disappeared from view. "Good night."

~~~

Josh was going to quit.

There was only a week and a half of babysitting left anyway, and now that Ted was around, Vicki had cut back Josh's hours nearly every day. *Bring the kids home early. We're going to take them out to lunch. Drop them off at the casino. Ted is playing tennis.* Josh heard talk about another evening picnic out at Smith's Point but he had yet to be invited, and if they did invite him, he would say no. And yet, the fact that they didn't invite him bothered him. Was Josh no longer "part of the family"? Were they through with him? Was he expendable? Well, yeah, he'd have to be an idiot not to sense things coming to a close. After all, Vicki's chemo was over, it had been successful, she was gearing up for her surgery, which would be in Connecticut. Brenda had finished her screenplay and was now consumed with printing it, nestling it into cardboard boxes, and sending it out, cold, to studios. And Ted was here for his vacation. So there was no reason to include Josh on the family outing; they probably thought it wise to cut Josh loose from the kids now, otherwise the separation would be too hard on them. That was all fine and well, and yet Josh was hurt. He had been more a part of this family than anyone knew, because of Melanie. And yet, it was because of Melanie that Josh, ultimately, wanted to quit. He couldn't stand to be around Melanie, just to see her was excruciating. She had cornered him once since the day of Peter's visit. She'd begged him to meet her at the beach parking lot, she'd be waiting there as usual, ten o'clock. They needed closure, she said. *Closure,* Josh was pretty sure, meant a long, painful conversation as well as, probably, some good-bye sex, and that would be akin to ripping the Band-Aid off the fresh wound in his heart and would set it bleeding all over again.

Josh told Melanie no.

He was going to quit. The story of his summer was over.

When Josh walked into Number Eleven Shell Street with his resignation speech written in his mind, the house was silent. Ted, Melanie, and Brenda sat at the kitchen table, staring at one another. Through the screen door, Josh could see the kids in the backyard, rolling a ball in the grass. This was highly unusual. Vicki didn't like the boys hanging out in the backyard because she had found poisonous mushrooms along the fence line and the rosebushes attracted wasps. The front yard was much safer, according to Vicki, as long as they were always with an adult, which they always were. So out back, unsupervised—something was wrong.

"What's wrong?" Josh said.

The three of them looked up—Josh looked at Ted's

face and Brenda's face, both of which communicated dire happenings. Josh could not look at Melanie. And where was Vicki? The door to her bedroom was closed.

"It's nothing," Brenda said. "Vicki just has a headache."

"Oh," Josh said. A headache? That was the cause of the dolorous communion around the table like the three of them were government officials of a country that was collapsing? A headache? For this the kids had been either punished or bribed with unsupervised time in the fraught-with-peril backyard?

"She's in a lot of pain," Ted said. "She can't tolerate the sunlight. She can't stand the kids' voices."

"Oh," Josh said. "Did this just come about out of the blue?"

"Out of the blue," Ted said. "We called Dr. Alcott for some pain pills. He wants to see her."

"See her?" Josh said.

"He wants to do an MRI," Brenda said. "But Vicki, of course, refuses to go."

Melanie was silent. She was as marginal to this drama as Josh was. That was part of their connection, that was how they'd found each other in the first place—involved but not connected. Connected but not related. Melanie's eyes were locked on him in a way that was almost impossible to ignore.

"So . . . I should take the kids?" Josh said.

"Please," Ted said.

"I'll go with you," Melanie said. "To help."

"No, that's all right," Josh said. "We'll be okay."

"No, really," Melanie said. "I don't mind."

"Well, I . . . ," Josh nearly said "*do* mind," but he already had Ted and Brenda peering at him curiously. "Okay, fine," he said. "Whatever."

As they ambled down Shell Street, Josh felt supremely self-conscious. He had walked this way dozens of times with Blaine and Porter—and yet with Melanie at his side, he felt like this was his family: Blaine and Porter his sons, Melanie his pregnant wife. The people they passed in front of the 'Sconset Market easily could have believed this was the case—and what was worse, Josh realized, was that a part of him *wanted* this to be the case. Part of him wanted to marry Melanie and have children with her. And yet, he was angry with her, he'd been hurt by her, and he resented the way she'd just insinuated herself into his routine with the boys, giving him no chance to protest or assert his control. Hence, he said very little. But that didn't stop Melanie from blundering ahead.

"I miss you," she said.

He met this with silence. He was happy to hear her say it, but it wasn't enough.

"Do you miss me?" she asked.

"Melanie," he said.

"What?"

"It doesn't matter."

"It does matter."

"I'm not going to do this all morning. This 'I miss you, do you miss me' thing. Why did you even come with us?"

"I wanted to get out of the house. It was tense."

Josh eyed Blaine. Blaine was in one of his rare mellow, reflective moods—Josh could tell he wasn't listening with his usual acuity.

"Is it serious?" Josh said. "The headache?"

"It could be, I guess."

"Oh," he said.

They walked in silence all the way to the beach parking lot.

"Do *not* run ahead," Josh said to Blaine. "We'll all go together."

"I know," Blaine said.

Melanie sniffed. "I want you to meet me here tonight."

"No."

"It's only for another week."

"I know, so what does it matter?"

"It matters," she said. "I want to be with you."

Josh looked at Blaine. His head seemed to be cocked at the perfect angle for listening; maybe this was Josh's imagination, but Josh didn't care. He shook his head at Melanie. Porter babbled in Josh's ear.

Later, when Blaine was playing two umbrellas down with Abby Brooks and Porter was halfway through his bottle on his way to la-la land, Melanie hoisted herself up out of the chair and plopped down next to Josh on his towel. He readied himself for another onslaught, but Melanie was quiet and as still as a statue, and yet she was most definitely *there*; Josh could smell her hair and her skin. They sat side by side, staring at the ocean and the people in it, and it should have been tense, but surprisingly, it was okay. Coexisting, without touching or talking. Josh found himself afraid to move, afraid to break whatever spell had been temporarily cast over them. Maybe this was what Melanie meant by closure. It wasn't the rapture he'd experienced all summer—the night at the Shimmo house came to mind, rolling around with Melanie on those sheets, holding her close as they stood on the deck taking in the view—but it wasn't bad or painful, either. He felt like he was suspended directly between the best minutes with Melanie and the worst, and there was something comforting in the neither-good-nor-bad of it. Ten days from today Josh would be beside his father in their Ford Explorer, driving back to Middlebury. He would see his friends, girls, people he hadn't thought of in three months, and they would ask him, *How was your summer?* And all he knew for certain as he sat, sharing his towel with Melanie, was that there was no way he would ever be able to explain.

First, there was the dream. Vicki couldn't remember it completely. It was a surgery dream, the doctors were going to perform Vicki's surgery right then and there and not on September first as they had planned. There was urgency, secrecy—somehow Vicki was told, or perhaps she discerned, that what they were removing from her lungs wasn't tumors at all, but rather, precious jewels. Huge rubies, emeralds, amethysts, sapphires—the biggest in the world, right there inside Vicki's chest, embedded in the healthy tissue of Vicki's lungs. The doctors weren't doctors, they were thieves of some international acclaim; they were planning on doing the surgery, she learned, without any anesthetic. Vicki would die from the pain; they were planning on killing her.

She woke up. Not with a start, like in the movies, not

sitting straight up in bed gasping for breath, but quietly. She opened her eyes and felt tears on her cheeks. Ted was beside her, breathing like a man on vacation. With a crook of her neck, Vicki saw both her children asleep on the mattress on the floor. It hurt to breathe. Vicki wondered what the inside of her chest would look like after the surgery. Would there be a big hole where her lung used to be?

The surgery, now that it was a reality, was newly terrifying. *It has to be done, obviously*, Dr. Garcia had said months ago. *If you want to live.* Funny how the surgery was what Vicki had wished for, it was the *goal* of the chemotherapy, and yet it frightened her beyond all comprehension. It made her insides twist, her pelvis tighten, it made her shoulders and wrists stiff with anxiety. The anesthesia alone was nearly impossible to come to grips with. She would be out, way out, for more than six hours. It was different from sleep, she understood that. It was forced unconsciousness, a place between sleep and death. Vicki would be kept there, in that purgatory of nothingness, while they cut through her chest muscles, spread open her rib cage, collapsed her lung, and then removed it. It was worse than a horror movie. A hundred things could go wrong during the surgery and a hundred things could go wrong with the anesthesia. What if the surgery was a success but they pushed her too far under with the anesthetic and she drowned in it? What if she crossed to the other side?

She lay in bed, ticking like an overheated engine. Was it any wonder she couldn't sleep? Was it any wonder she had nightmares?

Next came the headache.

When Vicki woke up in the morning she felt like she was wearing a lead helmet. There was not only pain, there was pressure. Blaine launched himself onto the bed as he did every morning when Ted was there—no need to worry about Mommy not feeling well when Dad was around—and Porter whined to be lifted up. He was still too little to climb. Vicki opened one eye. This wasn't intentional; it seemed, for whatever reason, that she could only get one eye open. And even that took a Herculean effort. And it hurt—sunlight coming in around the edges of the shades hurt, and Porter's whining hurt. She tried to extend a hand to the baby, thinking she might haul him up onto the mattress with one arm despite the fact that he weighed nearly twenty pounds, but she couldn't sit up to get leverage. She couldn't lift her head.

"Ted?" she said. Her voice was dry and papery. She was just dehydrated, maybe. She needed water. She reached for the glass she kept on the nightstand, but her arms trembled and she could not lift her head to take a sip. Ted was busy with the kids, tickling and teasing, rough-housing and kicking—and he didn't hear her. The glass slipped, or she dropped it, it got away from her somehow, and fell to the floor, spilling everywhere, though it didn't break.

"Jesus, Vick," Ted said.

"My head," she said.

"What?"

"My head," she said, "is killing me." This sounded colloquial—it was, after all, a popular turn of phrase—and hence there was no way Ted would know Vicki meant it literally. Her head was killing her. Her head was trying to kill her.

"The light," she said. "The kids." She pulled the sheet over her head but it was as effective at blocking out noise and sunlight as a Kleenex.

"Do you want aspirin?" Ted said. "Some chocolate milk?"

As if she had a hangover. There had been some wine the night before—wine every night since her CT scan—but this was not a hangover. Still, Vicki wasn't hearty enough to turn down the offer of medicine.

"I might have painkillers left," she said. Just eking out this sentence hurt.

Ted sloughed the boys off the bed and scooted Blaine out the door of the bedroom. "Go out. Mom doesn't feel well."

"Again?" Blaine said.

Ah, the guilt. Blaine would probably end up in therapy due to Vicki's cancer, but she couldn't worry about that now. *Get better*, she thought. *Then worry about it.*

Ted held Porter in one arm and checked the prescription bottles on Vicki's dresser.

"Percocet," he said. "Empty."

"Shit," she said. She was pretty sure there'd been three or four left. Brenda? "Would you call Dr. Alcott?"

"And tell him what?" Ted was like Vicki used to be: supremely uncomfortable around doctors. But since Vicki had begun regularly relying on doctors to save her life, her attitude had changed.

"Call in more," Vicki said. And then she became confused. Why was she asking Blaine to call the doctor? Would he, at the age of four and a half, be able to do it?

He wasn't even good at talking on the phone with his grandmother. "Magic words," Vicki reminded him.

Who knew how many painful moments passed? It felt like forever. Vicki moaned into her pillow. She could hear noises from the rest of the house, domestic noises—the frying pan hitting the stove, eggs cracking, the whisk chiming against the side of the stoneware bowl, the butter melting, the refrigerator door opening and closing, ice in a glass, Porter crying, the rubber squeal of the high chair sliding across the linoleum, Blaine's constant stream of chatter, Ted's voice—yes, on the phone, thank God. So much noise—and all of it as loud and unpleasant to her ears as a jackhammer in the room. Vicki grabbed Ted's goose-down pillow and covered her head.

The pain was a hand squeezing water from the sponge of her brain. Let go!

There was a tap on the door. Brenda. "Vick, are you okay?"

Vicki wanted to scream at her sister for stealing her Percocet, but screaming was beyond her.

"Headache," Vicki mumbled. "Unbearable pain."

"Ted just called Dr. Alcott. He wants you to come in."

Come in where? Vicki thought. Come into the hospital? Impossible. The whole idea of getting out of bed, getting into the car, driving through the eyeball-bursting sunny day to the hospital, completely preposterous.

Ted's voice was alongside Brenda's now. "Dr. Alcott wants to see you, Vick."

"Because I have a headache?" Vicki said. "What about the Percocet?"

"He's calling them in," Ted said.

Vicki felt something like relief, though it was difficult to identify under the blanket of pain.

"But he wants you to come in," Ted said. "He wants to take a look at you. He said it might not be a bad idea to have an MRI."

"Why?" Vicki said.

"I don't know."

That was a big, fat lie. Metastasis to the brain, she thought. Dr. Alcott's suspicions were correct; she could feel it. The cancer was a hand, fingers spreading through her brain, pressing down. The cancer was a spider, nesting in her gray matter. The pain, the pressure, the increased sensitivity to sound, to light. This was what a brain tumor felt like; she had heard someone in her cancer support group describe it, but she couldn't remember who. Alan? No, Alan was dead. It wasn't Alan. Vicki said, "I had too much wine last night."

"One glass?" Ted said.

"Water," Vicki said. "Magic words. Please. Thank you."

The pillow was lifted. Vicki smelled Brenda—what was it? Noxema. Piña colada suntan lotion.

"You're not making sense, Vick. Open your eyes."

"I can't."

"Try."

Vicki tried. The one eye opened. There was a very blurry Brenda. Behind her, a form Vicki knew to be Ted, but could just as easily have been an international thief, come to cut her open and take the jewels.

"You stole my Percocets," Vicki said to Brenda.

"Yes," Brenda said. "I'm sorry."

"I need them," Vicki said. "Now."

"I'm going, I'm going," Ted said. "I'll take the kids."

"I'll get you water," Brenda said to Vicki. "Ice water with paper-thin slices of lemon, just how you like it."

"No hospital," Vicki said. "I'm never going back."

Brenda and Ted left the room. The click of the door shutting was like a gunshot. Brenda said to Ted, "Her pupil was really dilated. What do you suppose that means?"

There's a spider on my brain, Vicki thought. Brenda was whispering, but her voice reverberated in Vicki's head like she was back at CBGB at a B-52's concert standing next to the chin-high speaker, which was blaring at a bazillion decibels. *Quiet!*

"I have no idea," Ted said.

The drugs helped, at least enough so that Vicki could limp along through the next few days. Dr. Alcott had prescribed only twenty Percocets, and Vicki found that by taking two pills three times a day the pain was ratcheted down from unbearable to merely excruciating. Her left eye finally did open, though the lid was droopy, as though Vicki were a stroke victim, and both of her pupils were as big as manhole covers. Vicki wore her sunglasses whenever she could get away with it. She didn't want Brenda or Ted to know that it felt like she was wearing a Mack truck tire around her neck, she didn't want them to know it felt like someone was trying to pull her brain out through her eye socket, and she especially didn't want them to know about the hand squeezing water from the sponge of her brain or the spider nesting. She wasn't going back to the hospital for any reason, she would not agree to an MRI, because she absolutely would not be able to handle the news of a metastasis to the brain.

And so, she carried on. They had a week left. Ted was trying to cram everything in at the last minute; he wanted to spend every waking second outside. He played tennis at the casino while Josh had the kids, and he took Vicki, Brenda, and Melanie to lunch at the Wauwinet, where Vicki spent the whole time trying to keep her head off the table. Ted wanted to go into town every night after dinner, to walk the docks and ogle the yachts—and one evening, impulsively, he signed himself and Blaine up for a day of charter fishing, despite the fact that the captain eyed Blaine doubtfully and told Ted he would have to come prepared with a life jacket for the little guy. Ted bought a sixty-dollar life jacket for Blaine at the Ship's Chandlery, seconds later.

Whereas Vicki once would have staged a protest (*he's too little, it's not safe, a big waste of money, Ted*), now she stood mutely by. Ted didn't ask her how she felt because he didn't want to hear the answer. There were only seven days of summer left; surely Vicki could hang on, could act and pretend, until they got home.

Vicki called Dr. Alcott, Mark, herself, for more drugs.

"Still the headache?" he said.

"It's not as bad as before," she lied. "But we're so busy, there's so much going on, that . . ."

"Percocet is a narcotic," Dr. Alcott said. "For extreme pain."

"I'm in extreme pain," Vicki said. "I qualify as a person who needs a narcotic, I promise."

"I believe you," Dr. Alcott said. "And that's why I want you to come in."

"I'm not coming in," Vicki said.

"There's nothing to be afraid of," Dr. Alcott said.

Oh, but there was. Vicki said, "Is there anything else I can take?"

Dr. Alcott sighed. Vicki felt like Blaine. *Can I have a hamster when I'm six? A skateboard? Bubble gum?* "I'll call something in."

Later, out of desperation, Vicki called the pharmacy. "Yes," the pharmacist said, in a way that could only be compared to the Angel Gabriel announcing the impending birth of Christ to the Virgin Mary, "Dr. Alcott called in a prescription for Darvocet and six-hundred-milligram Motrin."

"Is Darvocet a narcotic?" Vicki asked.

"No, ma'am, it's not."

"But it is a painkiller?"

"Yes, indeed, it is, and it can be taken to greater effect with the Motrin."

Greater effect. Vicki was mollified.

Ted lobbied for another beach picnic. He wanted to use his fishing poles one more time, he wanted lobsters again. This time Vicki could organize, right?

Right, Vicki said weakly.

That afternoon, when Josh dropped off the boys, Ted thumped him on the back and said, "We're going back out to Smith's Point tomorrow night for dinner and some more fishing. Will you join us?"

"I can't," Josh said. "I'm busy."

"Busy?" Ted said.

Vicki looked at Josh's face. She was in the kitchen with her sunglasses on and everyone looked shadowy and dim, like actors in an old black-and-white movie.

"Really?" she said. "We'd love to have you. It's the last . . ."

"Really," he said. "I'm busy."

Later, after Josh left, Ted said, "We could invite Dr. Alcott to the picnic. *He* likes to fish."

"No," Vicki said. "No way."

Numbed by Darvocet and Motrin (ramped up with the addition of three Advil and two Tylenol), Vicki pulled the picnic together in a near-exact replica of the previous picnic. Except, no Josh.

"Who's coming?" Melanie asked.

Vicki said, "Just us."

As Ted drove west toward Madaket and Smith's Point, Vicki felt the summer ending. It was closing, like a door. The sun hung low in the sky, barely hovering over the tops of the scrub pines of Ram Pasture; its last rays dripped onto the rooftops of the huge summer homes in Dionis. Or so it seemed to Vicki, through her sunglasses. The world was slowing down, the light was syrupy. Melanie sat up front next to Ted, and Brenda and Vicki sat in the Yukon's middle section, where they could tend to the kids in the way-back. Blaine had his hand arched over his head because Ted had asked him to *take care of those rods* and Blaine thought that meant he had to hold them for the entire ride. Porter babbled, alternately sucking on his pacifier and popping it out, which made a hollow noise he liked. *Babble, suck, pop*. The car smelled like lobster. Vicki had accidentally ordered an extra dinner—for Josh, she realized, who wasn't coming. The car felt empty without him. Was she the only person who felt this way? The kids missed him. Melanie, probably, too, though Vicki hadn't felt well or brave enough to talk to Melanie about Josh. Maybe later, down the road, after surgery and the baby, maybe when they more closely resembled the people they'd been before this summer. (A memory came to Vicki out of the blue: a dinner party at Melanie and Peter's house, a catered party that featured black truffle in every course. Peter had bought the truffle from a "truffle broker" in Paris after another failed round of in vitro; it was his idea to hire the caterer and throw the party. Vicki had appeared at the party with an ounce of outrageously expensive perfume from Henri Bendel as a gift for Melanie. Melanie had seemed delighted by the perfume. Vicki guarded the conversation at that dinner party like the gestapo; every time one of the other guests mentioned anything having to do with children, Vicki changed the subject.)

They would never go back to those former selves. They had changed; they would change again. As if reading Vicki's thoughts, Brenda let out a big sigh. Vicki looked her way.

"What?"

"I have to talk to you," Brenda said. She slid down in her seat, and Vicki, instinctively, did the same. They were like kids again, talking below their parents' radar, where they wouldn't be heard.

"About what?" Vicki said.

"About money," Brenda said.

The car's radio was on. Journey, singing "Wheels in the Sky." Vicki thought, *Wheels in the sky?* What did that mean, exactly? Did that mean the plan that God was endlessly spinning for us? In the front seat, Ted was blathering on to Melanie about the fishing trip he and Blaine were going to take on Tuesday. Apparently, Harrison Ford would be on the boat, too, with his nephew. Did *wheels in the sky* refer to the wheels turning in Vicki's mind, the gears that were supposed to move at lightning speed, shuttling thoughts in and out, but that now kept getting stuck and going in reverse, as though they needed oil? *About money?* Why would anyone want to talk about *money?* Did *wheels in the sky* mean the actual sky? Outside, the sky was dark already. How was that possible, when just moments before, the sun . . . *babble, suck, pop.* Ted said, *They can pretty much guarantee you'll catch a bluefish, but everyone wants stripers.* The car smelled like lobsters. Seven mothers died when a bus on a Los Angeles freeway flipped and caught fire. Only seven? Josh was busy. *Really,* he said. *I'm busy.* Greta Jenkins had started telling a story about her daughter, Avery, four years old, taking dance lessons and what a hassle it had been to find the right kind of tights. *Tights without feet,* Greta said. A look of loss and despair had flickered across Melanie's face (but just for a second because she was, after all, the hostess of this dinner party, with its shavings of truffle over everything—like shavings from a lead pencil, Vicki thought). Vicki had changed the subject, saying, *Did anyone read the Susan Orlean article in the* New Yorker *about pigeon fanciers? Babble, suck, pop. About money?* Vicki missed Josh. He was busy. It was dark everywhere now.

"Ted!" The voice was Brenda's serious voice, even more serious than when she said, *I have to talk to you.* It was her urgent voice. Signaling: *Emergency!* "Ted, pull over right now. She passed out or fainted or something. I'm calling nine-one-one."

"Who?" Ted said, turning down the radio. "What?"

"Vicki," Brenda said. "Vicki!"

It wasn't the sirens that woke her or the incredible rush of pavement beneath the ambulance's tires, though Vicki could feel the speed, and the sirens were as upsetting as the screams of one of her children, hurt or terrified. What woke her was the smell. Something sharp, antiseptic. Something right under her nose. Smelling salts? Like she had fainted in a Victorian parlor? An unfamiliar young man, Josh's age but with hair pulled back in a ponytail (why such long hair on a guy? Vicki should have asked Castor, from the poker game, back when she had a chance), was gazing down at her, though he was blurry. Again, Vicki could only get one eye open.

"Vicki!" There, moving in to her limited field of vision, was her sister, and Vicki was relieved. Brenda. There was something important Vicki had wanted to ask Brenda all summer long, but she had been waiting for the right moment and, too, she had been afraid to ask, but she would ask now. Before it was too late.

Vicki opened her mouth to speak, and Brenda said, "I'm sorry I brought up money. God, I am so sorry. Like what you need is more upset. And . . . don't kill me, but I called Mom and Dad. They're on their way up. Right now, tonight."

Before it's too late! Vicki thought. But her eyelids

were being pulled down like the shades on the windows of her bedroom at Number Eleven Shell Street. She was tired, she realized. Tired of fighting, tired of denying it: She was very sick. She was going to die. It had been mentioned in Vicki's cancer support group that when you got close, fear vanished and peace settled in. Vicki was tired, she wanted to go back to where she'd been before she woke up, to the lost place and time, the nothingness. But resist! Stay with us a little longer! She had to ask Brenda something very important, the most important thing, but Vicki *could not* find her voice, her voice eluded her, it was gone, it had been stolen—and so Vicki just squeezed Brenda's hand and thought the words and hoped that Brenda, as brilliant as she was, could intuit them.

I want you to take care of Blaine and Porter. I want you to take my little boys and raise them into men. Ted will be there, too, of course. He will do the ball games and the skiing and the fishing, he will talk to them about girls and drugs and alcohol, he will handle the guy stuff. But boys need a mother, a mommy, and I want that person to be you. You know me, I'm a list person, I always have been, even when I was pretending not to be. So here is the list. Remember everything, forget nothing: Kiss the kids when they fall down, read them stories, praise them when they share, teach them to be kind, to knock on a door before they enter a room, to put their toys away, to put the toilet seat down when they finish. Play Chutes and Ladders, take them to museums and zoos and funny movies. Listen when they tell you something. Encourage them to sing, to build, to paint, to glue and tape, to call their grandmother. Teach them to cook one thing, make them eat grapes and carrots, and broccoli if you can, get them into swimming lessons, let them have sleepovers with friends where they watch Scooby-Doo and eat pizza and popcorn. Give them one gold dollar from the tooth fairy for each lost tooth. Make certain they don't choke, drown, or ride their bike without a helmet. Volunteer in the classroom, always be on time picking them up and dropping them off, go to extra lengths with the Halloween costumes, the Christmas stockings, the valentines. Take them sledding and then make hot chocolate with marshmallows. Let them have an extra turn on the slide, notice when their pants get too short or their shoes too tight, hang up their artwork, let them have ice cream with jimmies when they're good. Magic words, always, for everything. Do not buy a PlayStation. Spend your money, instead, on a trip to Egypt. They should see the Pyramids, the Sphinx. But most important, Brenda, tell them every single day how much I love them, even though I'm not there. I will be watching them, every soccer goal, every sand castle they build, every time they raise their hand in class with an answer right or wrong, I will be watching them. I will put my arms around them when they are sick, hurt, or sad. Make sure they can feel my arms around them! Someone once told me that having a child was like having your heart walk around outside of your body. They are my heart, Brenda, the heart I am leaving behind. Take care of my heart, Bren.

It's a lot to ask, I know. It is the biggest, most important thing, and I am asking you because you are my *sister. We are different, you and me, but if I can say one thing about you it's that you* know *me, inside and out, better than Mom and Dad, better, even, than Ted. You are my sister, and I know you love my children and will take care of them like they're your own. I wouldn't ask anyone else to do this. To do this, there is only you.*

Brenda was gazing down at her. Had she heard? Vicki released Brenda's hand.

"Okay?" Vicki whispered.

"Okay," Brenda said.

Brenda prayed, fast and furiously. *Please, please, please, please, please.* Ted was pacing the waiting room like a raving lunatic; they took Vicki upstairs for tests, but neither Ted nor Brenda had been allowed to accompany her. Melanie, in a moment of clarity that was previously unthinkable, volunteered to drive the kids back to 'Sconset, get them an ice cream at the market, pop in a *Scooby-Doo* video, and let them fall asleep in Ted and Vicki's bed.

"Thank you," Brenda said.

Brenda had called her parents in the frantic moments before the ambulance arrived, with Vicki unconscious in Ted's arms. What Brenda said to her mother was, "Vicki's unconscious."

Ellen Lyndon said, "We're on our way."

And Brenda, realizing that (a) it would be fruitless to dissuade her mother and (b) her mother and father were exactly what she needed right now, some backup, some help, some support, said, "Yes, okay."

They wouldn't be able to get to the island until the morning, though, and Brenda needed comfort now. There was a worm of guilt chewing a tunnel through Brenda's brain. Brenda had brought up money; she had meant to initiate a conversation about the hundred and twenty-five thousand dollars, and it was at that moment that Vicki lost consciousness. And it was now, ironically, that Brenda realized money didn't matter. Money was the last thing that mattered. (Why did human beings believe otherwise?) What mattered was family. What mattered was love.

Love.

Brenda pulled out her cell phone and walked to the end of the hospital corridor. She dialed the number from memory. All summer she had tried to forget that number, and yet, it came automatically.

One ring, two rings.

And then, Walsh. "Hello?"

His voice. It threw Brenda off balance. She took a stutter step backward. *Rumor has it you committed the only sin that can't be forgiven other than out-and-out plagiarism.*

"Hi," she said. "It's Brenda."

"Brindah." There was a pause. "Brindah, Brindah."

Oh, God. She was going to cry. But no.

"I'm on Nantucket still," she said. "At the hospital. Vicki is upstairs having tests. Because one minute she was fine, and the next minute she was unconscious. It could be nothing, or it could be something awful. I've done a good job all summer. Taking care of Vicki, I mean. Not a perfect job, but a good job. I've been praying, Walsh, but I kind of get the feeling no one is listening."

"Yeah, I know that feeling."

"Do you?"

"Well, I did," he said. "Until now."

"I'm sorry I haven't called," she said.

"Ahhh," he said. "Yeah."

"I just felt like . . . all that stuff back in New York, with the university . . . it was all *wrong*."

"They made you feel like it was wrong."

"There were things about it that *were* wrong," Brenda said. "The time and place. We should have waited."

"I couldn't have waited," Walsh said.

Could I have waited? Brenda thought. *To save my career? To salvage my reputation? Could I not just have* waited? Down the hall, Brenda watched Ted sink into a chair and drop his head in his hands. His ship was going down.

"I should go," Brenda said. "My sister . . ."

"Is there anything I can do?" Walsh said.

"No," Brenda said. "There's nothing anyone can do."

"Ahhh," he said again. "Yeah."

Love is all that matters, Brenda thought. *Tell him!* But she couldn't. She was too rattled by the sound of his voice, she was too mired in the nonlanguage of ex-lovers. There was too much to say, so she would say nothing at all.

"Well, okay," Brenda said. "Good-bye."

"Good-bye," Walsh said.

* * *

They were keeping Vicki overnight for tests, they said. One of which would be an MRI, in the morning, when Dr. Alcott could be present.

"Your sister has lung cancer," the doctor, a trim, handsome Indian man visiting from Mass General, said. "We're looking for metastases to the brain. Tumors in her brain."

"Right," Brenda said. "I understand that."

"You can see her before you leave," he said. "You can say good night."

"Okay," Brenda said. "I will."

Brenda and Ted took the elevator upstairs in silence to Vicki's room. It was a private room, quiet and white. Vicki had an IV and wore an oxygen mask. Brenda kissed her cheek, and Vicki opened one eye.

"I was really hoping I'd never come back here," Vicki said into her mask.

"I know," Brenda said. "I know."

Ted sat down on the bed and wrapped Vicki up in his arms. "I love you, baby," he said. "You have to hang in there. You have to get better." Ted was crying and Vicki was crying, and watching the two of them together made Brenda choke up. One of her secret goals was to someday have a man love her the way that Ted loved Vicki. He always referred to her as "my bride" or "the beautiful mother of my beautiful boys." If Vicki was in the room, she was Ted's sole focus. He did act like an alpha male a lot of the time—with his hedge-fund-manager big-shot spiel—but really, he was a man on his knees in front of his wife.

Brenda thought of Walsh. *I couldn't have waited.*

No, she thought. *Me either.*

Josh was at the Chicken Box drinking Bud drafts, shooting pool with Zach, trying not to think about the beach picnic that was taking place out at Smith's Point without him, although certain images flashed through his mind, unbidden: fishing poles sticking out of the sand, Blaine's face in firelight, Melanie dripping and shivering from her nighttime swim. In the name of getting the night off to a good start, Josh and Zach had done a couple of tequila shots at Zach's house before they went out, but what this had led to, in the car on the way to the bar, was Zach's unwieldy confession that he had had sex with Didi twice over the summer and had paid her a hundred dollars each time.

"And I don't think I was the only one, man," Zach said. "I think she's a prostitute or something."

Now they were stuck in an uncomfortable silence, which was only partially ameliorated by the pool cha (*nine ball, side pocket*) and by the Bruce Springsteen cover band wailing their hearts out on the far side of the bar. If this was what Josh had been missing all summer, then he was glad he'd missed it.

Josh was relieved when his phone rang. He checked the display: It was Number Eleven Shell Street calling. was nearly ten-thirty. They were probably just back from the beach, carrying the sandy, sleepy boys off to bed And they were calling him because . . . ? It was probabl Vicki, cutting his hours, or it might be Melanie. She ha missed him at the picnic, she had been remembering th first picnic, when they . . . and wouldn't he meet her now tonight, one last time? How could it hurt? Well, it would hurt, it was like any addiction—you couldn't keep going back for quick fixes, you had to cut it out all at once, cold turkey. Didn't she *see* that? Didn't she get it? She was the one who was *married*! Josh watched Zach, formerly his best friend, bent in half over the table, shutting one eye in concentration and jimmying his stick back and forth in front of the cue ball. Josh could totally blow Zach's mind with the story of Melanie. As far as shock value was concerned, it would be an even trade for the news of Didi (a *prostitute*?), but Zach wasn't worthy of the information. Josh let the call go to his voice mail.

Later, much later, after Josh had dropped Zach off at home (the two of them shaking hands, Zach saying in an upbeat, conciliatory way, reminding Josh why they'd been friends in the first place, *Hey, man, it was good to see you. It was good to hang out*), Josh listened to the voice message.

Josh, it's Ted Stowe. Listen, some things have come up here at the house. Vicki is in the hospital, she had an episode, she's in for testing, we don't know what the hell is going on, but her parents, my in-laws, are coming over in the morning and they'll take care of the kids. So you don't have to worry about coming to work on Monday. Vicki probably has your address somewhere; I'll write you a check for this week, plus a bonus..Vicki said you did a great job, and I really appreciate it, man. You don't know how critical it was to have rock-solid help, someone to fill in the gaps, I know it couldn't have been easy, and man, the kids . . . they love you and Vicki loves you and she's going to be okay. We just have to keep believing that. Anyway, thanks again for your help. And good luck at school. I can't believe I'm leaving such a long message. I hate talking to machines.

Click. Josh listened to the message a second time as he drove home. It was a good-bye, good-bye a week early, which was fine, in theory, and Josh was certain he would be paid handsomely, but the good-bye bugged him. It had come from Ted, who was the wrong person. Ted, who suggested the only form of closure Josh might need was a check. What about saying good-bye to the kids? What about finding out if Vicki was okay or not? Episode? What kind of episode? An episode serious enough that she had to spend the night in the hospital? Serious enough that her parents were coming in the morning? Josh, helped along by the tequila and the beers he'd consumed at the bar, was both enraged and confused. It was another murky question—was he part of Number Eleven Shell Street or not? Could he be dismissed with a phone message? Apparently so. Thanks again, good luck, good-bye. Josh was tempted to call back and inform *Ted Stowe* of Josh's importance to the women and children of that house. He had loved those kids and cared for them better than anyone else could have. He earned their trust; he knew them. He became their friend. He had pulled Melanie out of a quicksand of self-hatred and misery; he gave her confidence. He made her feel beautiful and sexy. He had confided in Vicki, he had treated her not like a sick person, but like a person person. He'd made her smile, even when she was at death's door. He had confided to her about his mother. And Josh was going to help Brenda with her career; he was going to ask Chas Gorda how to sell a screenplay. He had done all of that—

and Ted had written Josh off, cut him loose with a *phone message*. As if Josh were the plumber, the exterminator, someone who could be *canceled*. *I'll write you a check*.

Be careful. Not just because of Melanie, but because of the whole family. He had loved the family, and the family had broken his heart.

~~~

At a quarter to seven the next morning, Brenda heard what sounded like a suitcase on wheels bumping down the flagstone path, and then the creak of the ancient plank door opening. But no, she thought. It was impossibly early. Even people who went to church weren't awake yet.

Seconds later, there was a tap on her bedroom door. Brenda opened her eyes to see . . . Ellen Lyndon poking her head in. Her mother. Brenda sat up.

"Mom!" she said.

The room filled, immediately, with the aura of Ellen Lyndon: her frosted-blond hair cut into a lovely bob, sunglasses pushed on top of her head, her permanent scent of Coco Chanel and vanilla, her pale pink lipstick. Her left knee was sheathed in a blue neoprene brace, and she wore tennis shoes in lieu of her usual espadrilles. But still, her pink tank was crisp and fresh and there were matching pink embroidered turtles on her Bermuda shorts. Who looked this wonderful so early in the morning?

My mother, Brenda thought. *She goes to bed beautiful, she wakes up beautiful*.

Ellen limped over to the bed, held Brenda's face, and kissed her on the lips. Brenda tasted lipstick.

"Oh, honey!" Ellen said. "I've missed you!"

"I can't believe you're here," Brenda said. "Already."

"First plane. We drove until midnight and stopped in Providence. And you know your father. Up at five-thirty." Ellen Lyndon eased down on the bed, removed her tennis shoes, and said, "Scoot over. I'm climbing in."

Well, it wasn't exactly the person Brenda wanted to be welcoming into her bed that day, but it was a kind of salve—even at age thirty—to be held by her mother. To have her mother stroke her hair and say, "You have been such a pillar, honey. Such a support for your sister. What would she have done without you? She was so lucky to have you here."

"I didn't do all that much," Brenda said. "Drove her to chemo, mostly."

"And you watched the kids and you helped out around the house. And you gave her moral support."

"I guess."

"And you dealt with me, your wacky mother."

"That I did. How's your knee?"

"It's fine. I've had a few setbacks that weren't important enough to tell you about. My physical therapist, Kenneth, does not know I've crossed the state line, but when he finds out, he's going to be very cross."

"Because it's too much," Brenda said. "I wouldn't have called you, but . . ."

"Oh, God, darling, of course you were right to call me. Half the reason why I'm not healing as I should is because of the stress of your sister. I'm distracted." Ellen Lyndon lay on her back and stared up at the ceiling. "This used to be Aunt Liv's room."

"I know. I remember."

"Liv was a strong woman. Stronger than your grandmother, even. She was a great role model for you and your sister."

"Yes," Brenda said. *And if she's been watching me the past year, she's dumbfounded.*

"I know they think Vicki might have a brain tumor," Ellen said. "Nobody said that to me, but I know that's what the doctors think."

"I guess it's a possibility."

Ellen took a deep breath. "You know, as a mother, you're never ready to hear that your child is sick. It is . . . the *worst* news." She gazed at Brenda. "There's no way for you to understand. Not yet. Not until you have your own children. And even then, I hope you never experience it." Ellen Lyndon relaxed into the bed a little and closed her eyes. "But you know, it feels good just to be here. In this room, especially. This was the nursery for your grandmother and Aunt Liv. The cradle of strong women. I can feel their strength, can't you?"

"Sort of," Brenda lied. In truth, Brenda felt weak and tired. The conversation with Walsh hurt, like a scrape on her knee, every time she thought about it.

Ellen Lyndon shifted her knee a little, and in another moment, she was breathing steadily, asleep. Brenda slipped out of bed and pulled the sheet up over her mother's shoulders.

Buzz Lyndon was in the kitchen with Ted, Blaine, and Porter, but no move had been made on breakfast. They were waiting for a woman to do it, Brenda supposed. Ellen Lyndon and Vicki had created these monsters themselves, but since Ellen was asleep and Vicki was gone,

that left Brenda. Brenda hoped they liked cold cereal.
She pulled out the Cheerios and started pouring.

"Hello, Daddy," she said, kissing her father's unshaven
cheek. Unlike his wife, Buzz Lyndon looked like he had
gotten five hours of sleep in a roadside motel. He looked
like a long-haul trucker three years past retirement.

"Oh, honey," Buzz said. "How are you?"

"Fine," Brenda said. "Mom's asleep."

"Yes, she's tired," Buzz said. "When can we go see
your sister?"

"Her MRI is at nine," Ted said. "Which means I have
to get going. She'll be finished by eleven. They should
know more by then."

Brenda fixed four bowls of Cheerios, she poured coffee and made a second pot, and she even managed to
get Porter his mush. Melanie emerged and, after greeting
Buzz Lyndon, made a plate of toast. A little while later
Ellen Lyndon shambled out to the kitchen, where she
sat at the table, cutting up a fruit salad. The boys were
bouncing off the walls, thrilled by the unexpected presence of their grandparents. Here was a new audience!

"Will you come to the beach with us?" Blaine said.

"Grandpa will take you," Ellen Lyndon said. "After
we see your mommy."

Brenda escaped to the back deck with her coffee. The
kitchen was crowded and noisy, and although the arrival of her parents gave the day a festive air, it also felt
strangely like a funeral. Everyone there except Vicki.

Please, please, please, please, please, please, she
prayed. The backyard fluttered and chirped in response:
butterflies, bees, rosebushes, a picket fence, green grass,
blue sky, robins, wrens, sunshine. If God was anywhere

He was in this backyard, but there was no way to tell if He was listening!

Hands landed on Brenda's shoulders. Firm, male hands. Her father. Buzz Lyndon dealt only in tangibles: *Is there anything your mother can do? Does anybody need money?* Well, yes, Brenda needed money, but what she realized now was that she wasn't willing to ask anyone for it, not even her father. She would finance her debt, get a job, pay it off. She had spent enough nights in the cradle of strong women to know this was the right thing.

There was a voice in her ear. "Brindah." The voice was a whisper; it was too intimate for her father. The hands on Brenda's shoulders were not her father's hands. Their touch was different. And then there was the voice. *Brindah.* Brenda was confused; she whipped around.

Brenda set her coffee down, afraid she would spill it. Her hands were shaking. Walsh was here! Not here in her mind, but here in person: His dark hair was close-cropped, his olive skin bronzed from the sun, and he wore a white polo shirt that she had never seen before. He smiled at her, and her stomach dropped away. It was him. Him! The only "him" that mattered: Walsh, her student, her Australian lover. *I couldn't have waited.* Walsh had come! He must have left New York as soon as he hung up the phone. Brenda wanted to know everything: how he got here, why he'd decided to come, how long he would stay, but she made herself stop thinking. Stop! He was here. The one person here just for her.

She put her hand over her mouth. She started to cry. He took her in. Brenda dissolved against his chest. Touching him, holding him, hugging him felt illicit. It had always felt sneaky, like she was getting away with something.

Romantic or sexual relationships are forbidden between a faculty member and a student. But none of that mattered anymore.

We didn't choose love; it chose us, right or wrong—and realizing this, for Brenda, was a kind of answered prayer.

Love was all that mattered.

⌒

As Josh got out of the water at Nobadeer Beach, shaking his hair like a dog, he wondered how he would ever write about what had happened to him this summer. He had been wounded so badly he deserved a Purple Heart, but the upside was that he had learned some things (hadn't he?). He now understood the tragic hero.

You'll sense the story like an approaching storm, Chas Gorda had said. *The hair on your arms will stand up.*

These words rang out distinctly—maybe because it looked like there *was* a storm approaching—dark, billowy clouds were blowing in from offshore. It had been beautiful all day—clear, sunny, and windless—but this had only served to annoy Josh. He was hungover from his night out with Zach, and now that he was essentially unemployed, he felt aimless and without purpose. He'd spent all day trying to write his feelings down in his journal—but what this had turned into was a lot of sitting on his unmade bed, thinking of Number Eleven Shell Street and then admonishing himself for thinking of it. His cell phone had rung incessantly—but three times it was Zach (calling to apologize?) and Josh let the calls go to voice mail, and twice the display said *Robert Patalka*, and there was sure as hell no way Josh was going to take that call.

He was relieved when five o'clock rolled around. He was hot and discouraged—he hadn't managed to get any worthwhile thoughts on paper (*Avoid being self-referential. Be wary of your own story*). There was cleaning and packing and laundry to do before he left for school, but those tasks were too heinous to even consider undertaking in his fractious state of mind. The only thing he had to look forward to was his swim at Nobadeer; however, he made himself wait until he was sure most of the families and otherwise jolly beachgoers would be gone. He couldn't stand to see other children at the beach, or other parents; he didn't want to have to witness everyone else's happy end-of-summer. He decided, bravely, on the way to the beach that he wouldn't cook dinner for his father tonight. He would pick up a pizza on the way home, and if his father wanted an iceberg salad, he could make it himself.

Josh swam for the better part of an hour, and the swimming improved his mood. He was proud of himself for not calling Number Eleven Shell Street—if they didn't need or want him, then so be it, the feeling was mutual—and he was glad he'd fought his urge to stop by the hospital to see if Vicki was all right. He couldn't concern himself with their dramas anymore. He had to let go. He did feel pangs of regret when he thought about the boys, but he had their birthdays marked down on his calendar and he would send presents—big, loud monster trucks, he decided, the kind that had flashing lights and played rock music, the kind that would drive Vicki nuts. Just thinking of it, Josh smiled for the first time all day.

But then, as Josh climbed out of the waves, the sky grew cloudy and ominous, and Chas Gorda's words came to him. Fat, warm raindrops started to fall. Josh grabbed his towel and raced up the stairs to the parking lot, cursing. Naturally, the top to his Jeep was down.

You'll sense the story like an approaching storm.

The hair on your arms will stand up.

Josh held his towel over his head like a canopy when the real rain arrived. The hair on his arms was standing up. There was a flash of light and, a split second later, a crack of thunder.

"Shit!" he cried out. His Jeep was getting soaked.

"Josh! Joshua!"

His name.

"Joshua!"

He lifted his towel. There was his father's green Ford Explorer, lights on, wipers whipping back and forth—and standing out in the rain without an umbrella or hat, or anything, his father. They locked eyes for a moment, then Josh looked away; he looked at the ground, at his feet in flip-flops, at the dirt and sand and pebbles of the parking lot and the rushing rivulets of water and the puddles forming. *No,* Josh thought. *No fucking way.* He grew dizzy and he realized he was holding his breath. He was having an awful, horrible memory—not a picture memory so much as a feeling memory. What it had felt like when his father said—and Josh heard the exact words, though he would swear he hadn't thought of them in more than ten years— *Son, your mother is dead.* Like a single blow to the gut. The rest, Josh assumed, came later; it may have been explained to him that she took her own life, that she hanged herself in the attic, or he may have been left to piece together facts from what was implied or what he over-heard. Josh couldn't remember. But he remembered the look on his father's face. It was a look he never wanted to see again, and he hadn't, until this very moment. Tom Flynn was standing out in the rain like he didn't even notice it, he was here at Nobadeer Beach, instead of being in his rightful place behind his computer terminal five stories up in the airport control tower.

Vicki is in the hospital, Ted Stowe said. *She had an episode.*

Vicki.

Son, your mother is dead. Twelve-year-old Josh had vomited, right there on the spot, without thinking or even noticing. He had vomited all over his new sneakers and the living room rug. And now, thinking, *Vicki,* Josh leaned over and retched.

No, he thought. *No fucking way.*

"Joshua!"

Josh looked up. His father was motioning; he wanted Josh to get in the car. Josh would have given anything to turn away, but he was standing in the middle of a downpour—there was another crack of thunder—and Josh's Jeep didn't offer much in the way of refuge. Josh dashed to the Explorer and climbed inside.

His father got in next to him, and they both sat there as if stunned, staring at the rain pummeling the windshield. Tom Flynn wiped his face with a handkerchief. His dark hair was plastered to his head. He said, "I have some bad news."

No, Josh thought. He put his hand up to let his father know he couldn't stand to hear it. *She had an episode.*

Tom Flynn cleared his throat and said, "The Patalka girl . . ."

Josh jerked his head. "Didi?"

"She's dead."

Josh sucked in his breath. The truck was close and warm, but Josh's body convulsed with cold. Didi? Not Vicki, but Didi? Didi dead?

"What?" Josh said. *"What?"*

"She's dead. She died . . . early this morning."

"Why?" Josh said. "What happened?"

"Drugs, they think. Pills, with alcohol."

"But not—"

"They're pretty sure it was accidental."

Tears sprang to Josh's eyes. The mix of emotions that assaulted him was confusing; it was like too many keys played at once on a piano. Discord. Didi was dead. Didi was *dead*? She had, by anyone's estimation, made a royal mess of her life—car repossessed, behind on her rent, prostitution? But Josh had assumed she would get her act together eventually; he had thought her parents would bail her out, or she'd meet some poor soul who wanted to take her on. Didi dead seemed impossible. She was such a force, so much herself—with the jean shorts with the white strings, front and center on the cheerleading squad, with the notes she used to pass to Josh between classes, marked with *X*s and *O*s and the stamp of her lipsticked mouth. With her hickeys and her adoration of her ferocious cat and her exhaustive knowledge of classic rock, the Allman Brothers, Lynyrd Skynyrd, Led Zeppelin. There was a time, a long period of time actually, when Josh had used the word "love" with Didi. She had said the word more often and with greater conviction: *I love* *you, I love you so much, you're my true love, always and forever.* Josh, being male, had responded with: *Ditto. Roger that. Yep, me too.*

Now, however, he knew more about love, and looking back at what he experienced with Didi, he could see its immaturity, its imperfection. So there was guilt mixed in with his shock and disbelief. He hadn't loved her well enough or genuinely enough. He hadn't given her a strong foundation on which to build future relationships. He may, in fact, have crippled her—unintentionally—because she never moved on.

And, too, in the melee of what Josh was feeling was relief that the news wasn't about Vicki. That was a horrible thought, and he didn't quite know how to deal with it. He certainly wasn't *happy* Didi was dead and Vicki was alive. He was just happy Vicki was alive.

Still, there was loss. Still, there was a hole inside of him. The funeral for Deirdre Alison Patalka was held two days later, and Josh attended, wearing his gray interview suit. He may have been imagining it, but he thought he sensed a buzz go through the church when he walked in; he saw heads turn, and the whispering grew louder, though not loud enough for him to make out any actual words. He had no idea how much people knew—maybe they were whispering because they thought Josh and Didi were still together and hence he would be cast as the devastated lover. Or maybe everyone knew of Josh and Didi's falling-out, maybe they'd heard that Josh paid Didi off just so she would leave him alone, maybe they held him responsible for Didi's demise, for her turn to drugs and alcohol, maybe they blamed him for not saving her.

Josh had no way of knowing. He saw everyone he used to know—high school friends, teachers, his friends' parents, doctors and administrators from the hospital, guys from Rob Patalka's crew, and the actual Dimmity brothers themselves, Seth and Vegas, whom Josh hadn't set eyes on since his mother ran their office. Josh's dentist was there, the ladies who worked in the post office, the manager of the Stop & Shop, the chef and waitstaff of the Straight Wharf, where Didi used to waitress in the summer, the librarians from the Atheneum. The police had to close off Federal Street because there were so many people attending Didi's funeral that they spilled down the church steps onto the sidewalk and over the sidewalk onto the cobblestone street and the far sidewalk. Didi arrived in a hearse, in a closed casket that was a somber navy blue, not at all a Didi color, Josh thought, which made it harder for him to believe that she was actually inside. He was glad, however, that the casket was closed. He didn't want to see Didi dead, all made-up by the mortician, wearing whatever "suitable" outfit Mrs. Patalka had picked out. He didn't want to have to gaze at Didi's face and acknowledge its unspoken accusation: *You failed me.*

After the funeral, there was an official reception at the Anglers' Club, but Josh stayed only a few minutes, long enough to kiss Mrs. Patalka and receive, in a somber handshake, an envelope from Mr. Patalka containing two hundred dollars.

"There was a note on her desk," Mr. Patalka said. "Saying she owed you this."

Josh tried to refuse the envelope, but Mr. Patalka insisted. Josh used some of the money to buy beer at

Hatch's; he was taking the beer to the house in Shimmo, where Zach was throwing the unofficial reception for "Didi's real friends," "the people who knew her best."

Josh set the beer down on the passenger side of his Jeep, which he tried not to think of as Melanie's seat. He took off his suit jacket and threw it into the back; even at four o'clock, it was too hot for it. He hadn't called Melanie to tell her about Didi, not only because of his self-imposed ban on calling Melanie but because Melanie knew nothing about Didi, and how cumbersome would it be to explain that Josh had had this friend—not even a friend, really, but an ex-girlfriend, a person who defied easy categorization in his life—who had died? Melanie wouldn't get it, but because she was Melanie, so incredibly kind, she would pretend to get it, and how could Josh find that anything but patronizing? Didi and Melanie were from separate parts of Josh's life, they weren't connected, and trying to connect them would require stretching something that might break and end up in a mess. Still, on his way out to Shimmo, with his tie off now as well as his jacket and the windows open, allowing the last of summer's warm, fresh air to rush in, Josh fondled his phone. He scrolled through his calls received—there were the two calls from Rob Patalka, three calls from Zach, all to tell him the news, he now knew—until he found the call from Number Eleven Shell Street, from Ted, and he nearly hit the button that would dial the house, but then it was time for him to turn, which he did, abruptly, and the beer slid off Melanie's seat and clunked to the floor, and while Josh was half bent over trying to upright the beer, he saw Tish Alexander's car in front of him and the moment to call Melanie was lost.

It was another beautiful afternoon. If they hadn't been attending a funeral, people might have come to the Shimmo house in bathing suits. They might have gone swimming right there in the harbor in front of the house. The water was very blue and calm; Josh had never seen water look more inviting. He stood for a minute in the driveway, gazing out across Nantucket Sound. He had been born and raised on this island; there was a sense that this view belonged to him and the others who grew up here. And if it belonged to them, then it belonged to Didi, too, but that fact hadn't been enough to keep her on the straight and narrow, to keep her alive. Didi—and how many times had Josh uttered this sentence in his mind, hoping that it would start to make sense?—was dead.

Josh entered the house and took off his shoes. He tried to push away thoughts of his night here with Melanie. Strains of Bon Jovi floated down the stairs. Josh ascended, glad for the case of beer in his arms because it gave him something to hold. There were a few people in the living room, mostly girls, all of whom Josh had known forever, but whose names he could not, at that second, summon, crying on the sofa. Josh nodded at them. Everyone else was out on the deck. The guys, like Josh, had their jackets and ties off, their shirts unbuttoned; they were drinking beer, talking quietly, shaking their heads, gazing off into the distance. *Why?* Josh heard someone say. And someone else answered, *I don't know, man.*

Zach was in the kitchen, fussing like Martha Stewart. He was dumping bags of Doritos into fancy, hand-painted ceramic bowls, he was setting out cocktail napkins, he was sponging off the countertop. He saw Josh and said, "You got beer?"

"Yeah."

"This fridge is full," Zach said. "Can you put it in the fridge under the bar?"

"Sure."

"They're not smoking out there, are they?" Zach said. He craned his neck to spy on the activity on the deck. "There's no smoking allowed anywhere on the property. Not even outside."

"No one's smoking," Josh said. He carried the case of beer over to the bar, which brought him into close proximity with the girls who were crying. Their talk stopped when he approached. It became silence studded with sniffles.

"Hi, Josh."

He turned. Eleanor Shelby, Didi's best friend, sat between Annelise Carter and Penelope Ross; it was the queen of sorrow and her two handmaidens. Eleanor's voice, even in its greeting, was accusatory. Josh realized this should come as no surprise—Didi obviously shared every last thing with Eleanor, and with Annelise and Penelope as well, probably—but he was unprepared for the blitz. He opened the door to the fridge under the bar and noted the slab of blue granite, the mirrors, the one hundred wineglasses hanging upside down. He pushed the six-packs into the fridge, he shoved them with some aggression because against his will he was thinking of Melanie and their night here, in this house. They had made love in a bed in the next room, they had showered together, they had stood on the deck in robes, and Josh, anyway, had allowed himself the five-minute fantasy that all this was his, or could be.

Behind him, Eleanor cleared her throat. "We haven't

seen you around much this summer, Josh," she said. "Rumor had it you were babysitting out in 'Sconset."

He smiled at Eleanor in the mirror, not because he was happy or trying to be nice, but because he was freshly surprised by the difference between girls and women.

"Yes," he said. "That's right."

Penelope Ross, whom Josh had known literally all his life (they were born the same week at Nantucket Cottage Hospital, their mothers in adjoining rooms), said, "And there were other rumors."

He glared at Penelope with as much disdain as he could muster. "I'm sure there were."

"Like, you have a baby on the way."

He scoffed. There was no point getting drawn into a discussion like this one, but the day had worn on him and he felt his fists itching. Part of him wanted a fight.

"That's ridiculous," he said.

"But your girlfriend is pregnant, right?" Penelope said. "Didi told us your girlfriend is pregnant."

"And older," Eleanor said. "Like, our parents' age."

Josh shook his head. Didi, now that she was dead, had a new, irrefutable authority, and an air of celebrity that she would have relished had she been alive. Josh could have pulled out his ammunition against Didi—her money problems, her drinking problem, the prostitution—but what would that accomplish? Josh eyeballed the girls and said in a quiet, serious voice, "I don't have a girlfriend."

This silenced them long enough for Josh to escape down the stairs and out into the driveway. He couldn't stay. The party for "Didi's real friends," "for the people who knew her best," was not for him. He backed out of the driveway, trying to control his breathing. He was

ery, very nervous. He headed out Shimmo Road toward
olpis. He waited until he had turned onto Polpis Road
efore he picked up his phone. He told himself he could
lways change his mind.

But then, as he knew he would, he dialed the number.

An unfamiliar voice answered the phone. A singsongy,
ulie Andrews–type voice. "Hel-lo!"

Josh was caught unprepared. Had he dialed the wrong
umber?

"Uh . . . hi," he said. "Is Melanie available, please?"

"Melanie," the voice said. "Yes. Yes, indeed, Melanie
s available. May I tell her who's calling?"

"Josh."

"Josh," the voice repeated. There was a pause, then an
ntake of breath. "Oh! You must be the young man who
elped out this summer."

"Yes," Josh said. He heard Penelope Ross's reedy
oice. *Didi told us* . . . "Yes, I am. Who's this?"

"Oooh, I'm Ellen Lyndon. Vicki and Brenda's mom.
hey just raved about you. Raved! So, I thank you and
eir father thanks you. We would have been here our-
elves if we could, but I had some ambulatory issues, knee
peration and all that. And Buzz, my husband, has work.
Ve only came now because it was a real emergency . . ."

"Right," Josh said. "Is Vicki okay?"

Another sharp intake of breath. And then it sounded
ke the woman was trying to hold herself together.
She's okay. Which is to say, she still has cancer. But it's
ıst the regular old cancer and not any new cancer. We
vere all sure it was going to be new cancer, but no, the
1RI was clear. She lost consciousness the other night
ı the car, and we all thought the cancer had gone to her

brain. But the doctors said she had overmedicated, her blood was thinned, plus there was the heat and the stress. You know Vicki. She feels an enormous amount of pressure because of the surgery and whatnot." Ellen Lyndon paused, and Josh heard her pluck a Kleenex from a box. "My daughter wants to live more than anyone I have ever known."

She wants to live, Josh thought. Unlike Didi. Unlike my own mother.

"Because of the kids," Ellen Lyndon said. "Because of everything."

"Right," Josh said. "I know."

Ellen Lyndon's voice brightened. "So, anyway! If you hold on one moment, I'll get Melanie."

"Okay," Josh said. "Thanks."

You should never underestimate the power of your mind, Dr. Alcott said. *The cancer isn't making you sick. You're making yourself sick.*

These words were delivered to Vicki, bedside, in the hospital. Coming from anyone else they would have sounded like an admonishment, but from Dr. Alcott—Mark—it just sounded like the truth, gently spoken.

"I'm going to release you," he said. "But you have to promise me that, between now and the date of your surgery, you'll relax. You'll drink plenty of water and take the vitamins and eat right. You will not self-medicate. You'll talk to someone when you feel anxious or upset. If you internalize your fear, it can turn around and destroy you."

Vicki tried to speak, but found she couldn't. She nodded, then choked out, "I know."

"You say you know, but you don't act like you know," Dr. Alcott said. "You're making the road harder for yourself than it needs to be. You took so many pills you nearly put yourself into a coma."

She tried again to speak but got stuck. Something was wrong with her voice. "S——orry." Her tone was not what she intended; she sounded like an automaton on a recording.

"Don't apologize to me, apologize to yourself."

"I'm sorry, s——elf," Vicki said. She was only half joking.

Dr. Alcott smiled. "I want you to take it easy, do you hear me?"

She nodded.

"Okay," Dr. Alcott said. He leaned in and kissed Vicki on the cheek. "This is good-bye. I won't see you again this summer. But Dr. Garcia has promised to call me after your surgery. And"—here he squeezed Vicki's hand—"I want you to come back and visit me and the rest of the team next summer. Promise?"

She couldn't speak! Something was wrong with her voice, or maybe she'd damaged her brain. She nodded.

"Good. Those are the visits we like the best." He held her gaze. "Because next summer you're going to be healthy."

Vicki's eyes swam with tears. It wasn't as easy as Dr. Alcott was making it seem. She was petrified; anxiety held her by the shoulders. She couldn't just click her heels like Dorothy and make that go away. She could not *relax;* she was incapable of *taking it easy.* She was stand-

ing on a ledge, fifty stories off the ground; she couldn'
pretend that she was safe, or that everything was going
to be okay. She couldn't even speak properly; something
had been lost, or altered, while she was unconscious
Maybe she'd had a stroke. Maybe the drugs had ravaged
her central controls. Vicki let a few tears drop. What she
wanted more than anything was to be out of this hospital for good and back home with her family at Number
Eleven Shell Street.

"Thank you," she mumbled.

"You're welcome," he said.

At home, she still had trouble speaking. She had a stutter
The words and sentences were fluid in her mind, but in
delivering them, she hit the same frustrating stumbling
block again and again, even with Ted and the kids, ever
saying phrases she had said thousands of times. *Magic
words. Hold on. Be careful. I love you.* Vicki was concerned about this but she was incapable of articulating
her concern, and no one in the cottage seemed to notice
her speech impediment, or the fact that, in order to hide
the impediment (she would not be able to tolerate another trip to the hospital or any more drugs), she said
next to nothing. The announcement of no metastases had
put everyone's mind at ease; the implication that Vicki's
"incident" had come at her own hands (overdoing it with
the painkillers) or that it was all in her mind made her
feel like a malingerer. If she complained now of something else, no one would believe her. They would think
she was making it up. At times she thought perhaps she
was making it up. She whispered to herself in the shower

I'm making it up. She got stuck on the *m* and stopped trying.

Ted, in an attempt to wring every bit of fun out of what remained of the summer, cajoled Vicki into joining him and Blaine on the fishing trip. He arranged for Ellen to stay home and watch Porter. It would be good for Blaine to have Vicki there as well as Ted; it would be good for the three of them to spend the day together. It would be good for Vicki to be out on the water; in years past, Ted had chartered a sailboat, and Vicki had loved it. *Remember, Vick, how you loved it?* Vicki couldn't protest. She nodded. Ohhhhh——kay.

It was just the three of them—plus the captain and first mate—because Harrison Ford canceled. Ted was disappointed, but only for a minute, and Vicki found it nicer without any other people. It was like they had their own boat. Blaine was over the moon to be on a real fishing boat, with a fight chair and special holders for his pole and his very own can of Coke. He bounded from one side of the boat to the other, bundled in his brand-new orange life jacket. He had both his parents to himself for the first time in a long time, and Vicki could see that while he was feeling very adult to be on this excursion, he was also relishing his role as the only child of his two parents. He let Ted hold him up high as they motored out of the harbor, past the jetty and around the tip of Great Point.

It was a stunning day. With the drone of the engine making conversation unnecessary, Vicki was set free for long periods of time. She basked in the sun, she sat up to feel the spray of the waves and to see Nantucket as just a sliver of pale sand in the distance. She watched the

business of catching a fish as though it were a movie. Ted
was doing most of the fishing while Blaine sat in the fight
chair, a captive audience through one, two, three bluefish. With the fourth fish, Blaine said, "Another blue."
His voice was weary and disappointed beyond his years.
With a wink between Ted and Pete, the captain, it became
clear that the mission was to now catch a striped bass.
Pete motored all the way to the other side of the island; if
they set up right between Smith's Point and Tuckernuck,
he said, they would have better luck. The first mate, a
kid named Andre, sat next to Vicki. He reminded her of
Josh; he was on Nantucket for the summer, working. The
following week he would head back to the College of
Charleston.

At lunchtime, Vicki pulled out the lunch she had made:
chicken salad sandwiches, potato chips, cold plums, watermelon slices, and chocolate peanut butter cookies.
Pete and Andre devoured the sandwiches and cookies
Vicki had included for them, and Andre said it was the
best lunch he'd had all summer.

"Leave it to my wife," Ted said.

"Leave it to my mom," Blaine echoed proudly.

Vicki smiled at them and felt happiness, fleeting
though it was. After lunch, she went up to the bow of
the boat and closed her eyes as the boat sliced through
the water. *This will not be my last day on the water,* she
thought. But then she had a vision of herself on the operating table, the surgeon brandishing a scalpel. *Why not
just cut me open with a saber?* The night before, Vicki
had watched Brenda and Walsh holding hands. Walsh was
the kind of person Ellen Lyndon referred to as a "gem,"
or "a real treasure"; he was immediately recognizable as

good, kind, and sensitive, as well as extremely attractive (well, there had never been any doubt about that)—he was the kind of person that it might be reasonable to lose one's job over. Brenda and Walsh were so visibly happy together that Vicki thought, *They will get married. But I won't be alive for the wedding.* Where did these thoughts come from? How could she make them stop? Dr. Alcott was right about one thing: Fear was its own disease.

Vicki handed Ted his cell phone; she wanted him to check on Porter. It would stand to reason that since she was enjoying herself, something must be horribly amiss at home. Ted dialed the number and it rang once, then the connection cut out. *Call ended.* As Ted dialed again, Vicki pictured Porter's face in a purple squeal. It used to be when Porter got upset, he would throw up, and though he hadn't done this all summer, it was the vision that came to Vicki: Porter spewing pureed carrots all over Ellen Lyndon's white linen pants and choking on the vomit until he stopped breathing.

The second call didn't go through at all, and Ted shook the cell phone in frustration. "There's no reception out here, hon. Just relax. Everything is fine."

You always say everything is fine, Vicki thought angrily. *How am I supposed to relax when Porter is probably in the hospital on a respirator?*

She was distracted from these thoughts by a shout from her other son. "Dad! Daddy!" It had only occurred to Vicki a hundred times since the day began that Blaine would fall overboard and be sucked under the boat by the power of the engines. When Vicki looked up, however, what she saw was Blaine holding on to the fishing pole for dear life. The line was taut, and Blaine was pulling back in a professional way, bracing his bare feet against the side of the boat.

Ted said, "You've got a bite! Here, let me bring him in."

Vicki thought Blaine might protest, but he handed the rod over to Ted right away, with relief. Vicki, too, was relieved. She didn't want Blaine pulled into the drink by the resistance of some monstrous fish, nor did she want to see Blaine lose the rod altogether, which was the more likely outcome. Vicki thought there might be a long, drawn-out Ahab versus Moby Dick–like struggle, but Ted landed the fish in a matter of seconds. Even in the overwhelming sunlight, Vicki could see the glint of silver scales. The fish was sleek but long, much longer than any of the bluefish Ted had caught.

"Striped bass?" Ted said uncertainly.

The captain whistled. "Better. You caught a bonito. She's a beauty." He pulled out a tape measure and pressed the flopping fish to the deck with his shoe. "Thirty-seven inches. She's a keeper."

"What's it called?" Blaine asked.

"Bonito," Ted said. "Bone-ee-to."

"They're good eating," the captain said.

"Do you want to keep it?" Ted said. "Do you want to take it back to the docks so Grammie and Grandpa can see it?"

"We could gr——ill it for dinner," Vicki said.

Blaine sucked his lower lip as he studied the fish. In his sun visor with his hands on his hips and the look of deliberation on his face, he could have been fourteen. He could have been twenty-four.

"Nah," Blaine said. "I want to throw her back. I want to let her live."

They threw the bonito back, but to celebrate their day of fishing, Ted stopped at East Coast Seafood on the way home and bought salmon, swordfish, and tuna. It was their next-to-last night on the island, the evening of the last big dinner, and it would be really big with the addition of Buzz and Ellen Lyndon and John Walsh.

When Ted pulled the Yukon up in front of the house, Vicki blinked with disbelief. Josh's Jeep was parked out front.

"Josh," she said. His name came easily, all in one piece.

"Josh!" Blaine shouted.

"Good," Ted said, unbuckling his seat belt. "I can give him his check."

Vicki felt unaccountably happy when she walked inside. She expected a house full of people, but the only person waiting for them was Ellen Lyndon, who was relaxing on the sofa, gimpy leg up.

"Hello, all," Ellen said. "How was fishing?"

"We caught fish!" Blaine said. "Seven bluefish and one . . ." Here, Blaine looked to his father.

"Bonito," Ted said.

"Bonito!" Blaine said. "But we let them go."

"Josh?" Vicki said. Again, no stutter, no stumble.

"Josh?" Ellen Lyndon said.

"Is heeeee——here?" Vicki said.

"Yes," Ellen Lyndon said. "Josh and Melanie took Porter for a walk."

Josh and Melanie, Vicki thought.

"And Brenda and Walsh are at the beach," Ellen said. "And I sent your father to the farm for corn, tomatoes, and blueberry pie."

"We bought . . ." Vicki held up the fish to show her mother. She set the fillets on the counter and immediately started thinking: eight adults for dinner if Josh would stay; she had to marinate the fish, chill wine, soften butter, set the table, and get a shower. Plus, food for the kids. Shuck the corn when her father got home, slice and dress the tomatoes. Would there be enough food? Should she run to the market for a baguette?

The lists were back. Vicki scribbled some things down on a tablet. But as she unwrapped the beautiful fish fillets from the butcher paper, the terror returned. Terror! When Ted passed behind her, she turned and grabbed his wrist.

"What is it?" he said.

"We're leeee——aving."

"We have to go back sometime," Ted said. "We just can't stay here forever."

Of course not, Vicki thought. However, back in Connecticut, reality awaited.

From her outpost on the sofa, Ellen Lyndon sang out, "Nantucket will always be here, honey."

Yes, Vicki thought. *But will I?*

⁓

Josh might have been more comfortable in the house with the women—Vicki, Melanie, Brenda, and Mrs. Lyndon—but he found himself, instead, out on the deck with "the men." The men included Buzz Lyndon, Ted, and John Walsh, Brenda's student, Brenda's lover, who had (Josh learned from Melanie) shown up without warning a few days earlier. Initially, Josh felt threatened by John Walsh, but it quickly became apparent that John Walsh was different from the likes of Peter Patchen, or even Ted. To begin with, John Walsh was Australian, and his accent alone made him seem cheerful and approachable, open, friendly, and egalitarian. When Ted introduced Josh, John Walsh stood up right away from the deck chair and gave Josh a hearty handshake.

"Hey, mate. Name's Walsh. Nice to meet you."

"Likewise," Josh said.

"Beer?" Ted said.

"I'll get it," Buzz Lyndon said. He handed Josh a Stella.

"Thanks," Josh said. He took a long, cold swallow.

"Not your usual duds," Ted noted.

"No," Josh said. He was wearing the bare bones of his gray suit—the gray pants, the white dress shirt (unbuttoned at the neck, cuffs rolled up), and his dress shoes with black socks. He had walked with Melanie and Porter to the beach in this unlikely outfit, and whereas he felt overdressed, the suit made him feel older, like an actual grown-up. "I had a funeral."

"Who?" Ted said.

"Friend of mine from high school," Josh said. "A girl. My ex-girlfriend, actually. Didi, her name was. She worked at the hospital."

Ted stared at him. "Blond girl?"

"Yeah."

"I met her," Ted said. "Briefly. When we were there for Vicki last week. That's terrible. God, I'm sorry."

John Walsh raised his beer bottle. "Sorry for your loss, mate."

"Oh," Josh said. "Thanks. She had . . . a lot of problems."

"That's too bad," Buzz Lyndon said. "Young girl like that."

"Was she sick?" Ted asked. "She didn't look sick."

"No, not sick. She overdosed. It was a combination of pills and alcohol." Already he had said more about Didi than he wanted to. He had hoped to leave behind the sadness of the funeral and the discomfort he felt around his high school friends, but that was proving to be impossible. All summer, he'd tried to keep his job at Number Eleven Shell Street separate from his life at home, but he saw now it was pointless. The island was so small that everyone intersected. Thinking back, Josh realized he wouldn't even be working here if he hadn't shown up at the hospital that day to lend Didi the two hundred dollars. So in a way it was like Didi led him here. "It was an accident," Josh added. "Her death was accidental."

"When I think back on the stuff I tried as a kid . . . ," John Walsh said. "It's a bloody miracle I didn't accidentally off myself."

Ted swilled his beer, nodding in agreement. Buzz Lyndon cleared his throat and settled in a deck chair. Everyone was quiet. The silence was similar to the silence Tom Flynn liked to immerse himself in; it was this silence that Josh had always found intimidating. But now, he savored it. Four men could drink beer on a deck and not say a word and not find it awkward. Women would talk, say whatever came next to their minds. Men could keep what was on their minds to themselves. And what was on Josh's mind was . . . Melanie.

The anticipation of seeing her that afternoon had nearly strangled him; he felt like a half-crazed animal pulling on its chain. As soon as Josh set eyes on her (a little rounder in the midsection, a little tanner, a little more luminous), as soon as they were pushing Porter in the baby jogger down Shell Street, he filled with quiet elation. She asked about the suit, and he told her about Didi. Talking to Melanie was as therapeutic as crying. A sudden, unexpected death, the death of someone young, the death of someone Josh hadn't always treated nicely, a death that caused him to fill with guilt and regret—Melanie got it; she understood. Josh and Melanie became so engrossed in talking about Didi that they managed, for a while, to forget about themselves. But then, when talk of Didi was exhausted, Josh felt he had to address the issue of their relationship.

"I hadn't planned on coming back here," he said.

"I didn't expect to see you," Melanie said. "I thought you were gone."

"Well," Josh said.

"Well what?"

"I wanted to see you."

Melanie smiled at the ground. They had made it all the way to the beach and were on their way back to Number Eleven. In the stroller, Porter was fast asleep. They could have turned right, back onto Shell Street, but Josh suggested they continue straight.

"Past the 'Sconset Chapel?" Melanie said.

"Yes."

They walked for a while without speaking. Then Josh said, "You're going back to Peter?"

Melanie pressed her lips together and nodded. "He's my husband. That counts for something. The vows count for something."

"Even though he broke them?" Josh said.

"Even though he broke them," Melanie said. "I realize that must be hard for you to hear."

"It's hard for me to think of you getting hurt again," Josh said.

"He won't . . . well, he said he wouldn't . . ."

"If he does," Josh said, "I'll kill him."

Melanie leaned her head against Josh's shoulder. The church was in front of them; there were white ribbons fluttering on the handrails of the three stone steps that led to the front door. The vestiges of someone's wedding. "Finding you was the best thing that could have happened to me," she said.

It was another line that rendered Josh speechless. As he stood now on the back deck drinking his beer, he thought: *Yes*. It had been the best thing for both of them, as unlikely as that might seem to outside eyes.

Josh was startled when the back door opened and Vicki poked her head out to say, "Josh? D——inner? You'll . . ." She nodded at the picnic table.

"Sure," he said. "I'd love to."

At dinner, Josh sat between Melanie and Vicki. Melanie kept a hand on Josh's leg while Vicki loaded his plate with food. Talk was light: Josh heard all about the fishing trip, the bluefish, the bonito. Then Buzz Lyndon told some fishing stories from his youth, then John Walsh told fishing stories from Australia, which quickly turned into stories about sharks and saltwater crocodiles and deadly box jellyfish. Josh had consumed no small amount of wine—Ted, at the head of the table, kept leaning forward and filling Josh's glass—and the wine, along with the candlelight and the pure lawlessness of Melanie's hand on his leg, gave the evening a surreal glow. Over the course of the summer he had made a place for himself at this table—but how? He thought back to the first afternoon he set eyes on them: *Three women step off of a plane.*

Brenda sat in the crook of Walsh's arm with a contented smile on her face. Scowling Sister. Except now she seemed happy and at peace. Vicki—Heavy-breathing Sister—seemed melancholy and very quiet, though now Josh understood why. The summer had left Vicki physically transformed (her blond hair was gone, and she was leaner by at least twenty pounds), but she still retained what Josh thought of as her "mom-ness," that quality that brought everybody together and made sure every detail of the day was tended to. She was the glue that held everyone here together. If they lost her, they would break apart, splinter off. Fall to pieces. That was the cause of her melancholy, perhaps: She understood how important she was to other people and she couldn't stand to let them down.

Finally, next to him, touching him, was Straw Hat. Melanie. He liked to think he had saved Melanie, but it was probably the other way around. Melanie had taught Josh things he never even knew he wanted to learn. She would go back to Peter—that fact was as real and hard and smooth as a marble that rolled around in Josh's mind—and Josh would be heartbroken. He was on his way to heartbreak now, sitting here on this last night, but that heartbreak—along with everything else that had happened today—made him feel older and more seasoned. He had his story; nobody could take that away. Chas Gorda would be proud.

After dinner, there was pie, ice cream, the last of the wine, and smaller glasses of port passed around for the men. Buzz Lyndon produced cigars. Ted accepted one, though Josh declined and so did Walsh. Brenda said, "Daddy, cigars stink."

"Keeps the bugs away," Buzz Lyndon said.

Vicki stood up. "I have to . . ." She touched the top of Blaine's head. "Josh? Will you r——ead?"

Blaine, who was almost asleep on his grandmother's lap, revived enough to say, "Stories! Please, Josh?"

Melanie squeezed his knee. Josh stood up. "Ohhhh-kay," he said.

He lay down with Blaine on the mattress on the floor of Ted and Vicki's bedroom. Porter was already fast asleep, sucking away on his pacifier. Vicki sat on the bed. She handed Josh *Sylvester and the Magic Pebble*.

"It's sad," she said.

"Mom cries whenever she reads it," Blaine said.

"Does she, now?" Josh said. He winked at Vicki, then cleared his throat and started to read.

The story was about a donkey named Sylvester who finds a shiny red pebble that turns out to have magic powers. When Sylvester wishes for rain, it rains; when Sylvester wishes for the rain to stop, it stops. One day, when Sylvester is out, he sees a hungry lion approaching, and in a moment of panic, he wishes he were a rock

Sylvester turns into a rock and he is saved from the lion—but because Sylvester drops the magic pebble, he has no way to turn himself back into a donkey. He is stuck being a rock, no matter how hard he wishes otherwise. When Sylvester does not return home, his parents grow sick with worry. After weeks of searching, they come to the conclusion that Sylvester is dead. They are nearly destroyed by the loss of their only child.

In the springtime, however, Sylvester's parents venture out for a picnic and they come across the rock that is Sylvester, and they use him as a table. Then Sylvester's father spies the magic pebble in the grass—and, knowing it is an object his son would have loved, he picks it up and places it on the rock.

Sylvester can sense his parents' presence; he can hear them talking. No sooner does he think, *I wish I were myself again, I wish I were my real self again,* than this becomes true—he turns back into a donkey, right before his parents' eyes. And—oh!—what happiness!

In the end, Sylvester and his parents return home and put the marble in an iron safe.

"'Some day they might want to use it,'" Josh read, "'but really, for now, what more could they wish for? They had all that they wanted.'"

"They had all that they wanted," Blaine repeated. "Because they're together again."

Vicki nodded. Her mouth was a line.

Josh closed the book. He found it difficult to speak. It would be impossible to say good-bye to the boys right now, and so he kissed first Porter, and then Blaine, on the top of the head.

"Yes," he said.

When Josh and Vicki emerged from the bedroom, the dinner party was breaking up. Ellen Lyndon was finishing the dishes, Brenda and Walsh had left for a walk up to the lighthouse, Ted and Buzz Lyndon were standing on the back deck, blowing smoke into the night air. Josh had wondered all through dinner if he would have the guts to stay here with Melanie tonight, and now he saw the answer was no. There was an unspoken understanding about him and Melanie, but it had to remain unspoken; there was no point lifting the veil now, on the final day. Josh said his good-byes to the elder Lyndons and gave Ted his best interview handshake.

Ted said, "Oh, wait, I have something for you," and pulled a check out of his wallet.

"Thanks," Josh said. He was embarrassed by the money; he stuffed the check into the pocket of his suit pants, though he couldn't help noticing, in a quick glance, that the check had one more zero on it than usual.

By the time Ted and Josh made it inside, the elder Lyndons had left for the Wade Cottages, down the street where they were staying. So it was just Ted, Vicki, Josh and—pouring herself a glass of water at the kitchen sink—Melanie.

Ted said, "I'm going to bed. Good night, all."

Vicki said, "Me, too. Tired." She looked at Josh, and her eyes filled with tears. "I can't say good——bye to you."

There was a lump in his throat and it ached. "Oh, Boss," he said.

She hugged him tight. "Josh," she said. "Th——ank you."

"Stop it. You don't have to thank me."

"I'm grateful."

"I'm grateful, too," he said. He paused, thinking of his father's words: *It crossed my mind . . . that you're out there in 'Sconset trying to find your mother.* Well, it wasn't impossible.

Vicki wiped her eyes. They separated.

"Get better," Josh said.

"Okay," she said.

"I mean it, Boss."

"I know," she said. "I know you do."

Vicki disappeared into the bedroom, and Josh turned around. Melanie was standing there, sniffling.

"That was beautiful," she said. "But you know me these days, reading the phone book makes me cry."

Josh unrolled the sleeve of his white dress shirt and used it to wipe the tears from Melanie's face. It had been a very, very long day, perhaps the longest day of his life, but even so, he wasn't ready for it to end.

"Let's get out of here," he said. "You can drive."

~~~~~~

For weeks, Brenda had dreaded the day they were to leave Nantucket—but now, with Walsh at her side, it didn't seem so bad. They would return to Manhattan together, Brenda would assess the damage and make some decisions. As Brenda was packing up, Ellen Lyndon teetered into Brenda's room and handed her a jelly jar filled with sand.

"For your shoes," Ellen Lyndon said. "I just gave your sister some."

Brenda shook her head. "You're insane, Mother."

"You're welcome," Ellen Lyndon said.

Brenda considered the jar. She didn't really have room for it in either of her bags. She would just leave it on the dresser. But first, just in case Ellen Lyndon actually wa the owner of divine intuition, Brenda sprinkled some o the sand into her Prada loafers, shoes she had not wor since arriving on the island. And then, in the end, sh stuffed the jelly jar into her duffel bag. She needed all th help she could get.

Brenda's parents left first on the fast ferry; they woulc pick up their car in Hyannis and drive back to Philadelphia Melanie was the next to go. Josh appeared in his Jeep t deliver her to the airport so she could make her fligh to LaGuardia. Ted, Vicki, and the boys were taking th noon boat and driving back to Connecticut in the jam packed Yukon. So that left Brenda and Walsh to close up the house. Brenda was amazed that her parents and Vick had entrusted her with such a massive responsibility, anc she wanted to do a thorough job. The fridge was empty and shut off, the gas line disengaged from the grill, the beds stripped. Brenda returned Aunt Liv's enamel boxes silver tea set, and lace doilies to their rightful place or the coffee table; she tucked the key under a shingle fo the caretaker, who would come the next morning. Righ before Brenda closed the door to the cottage for good she noticed the paper cup of pebbles sitting on a high windowsill. Should she leave it there or throw it away?

She left it there. There was always next summer.

Brenda's cell phone rang in the cab on the way to the airport. For the first time in months, the Beethoven-in-a blender ring did not cause her any anxiety.

"Well, I know it's not you," she said to Walsh. "Not that it was ever you."

"I called once," he said.

Brenda checked the display: *Brian Delaney, Esquire.* Her instinct was to let it go to voice mail, but she couldn't run away forever.

"Hello, Counsel," she said.

"I just got the strangest phone call," said Himself.

"Did you?" Brenda said. Her mind started running like a taxi meter times ten. "Pertaining to me?"

"Someone called asking about the rights to your screenplay," he said.

"What?"

"This guy, Feldman? He called the university and they gave him my name, as your attorney."

"Feldman?" Brenda said. In the end, she hadn't sent her screenplay to Ron Feldman or anyone else at Marquee Films. Because after that horrible phone call, what was the point?

"Yeah. I guess he borrowed his daughter's copy of the book and he liked it and he wants to see your screenplay. He was very clear that he makes no promises. I guess Marquee is already doing something similar, a book by some guy named George Eliot, more of that old-time shit, but he did like the Fleming Trainor, he said, and he wants to see the script. You know, I sort of got the impression he thought I was your *agent*."

"So what did you tell him?"

"I told him the script was out with various studio execs, we had lots of interest, but that we would keep him in the loop before we made any decisions."

"You're *kidding* me," Brenda said. "God, I cannot believe this."

"He makes no promises, Brenda. In fact, he said even if he did option it, it might molder for years, unproduced. I asked him what his ballpark was for an option, and he made it clear it was five figures, not six, so don't go jumping over the moon."

When Brenda hung up, she threw her arms around Walsh's neck. "Feldman wants to see it. He makes no promises, but he does want to see it." This was good news, not great news, not the best news, but not bad news either. For the first time all summer, Brain Delaney, Esquire, had called without bad news.

Brenda rested her head against Walsh's sturdy Australian shoulder as the taxi barreled down Milestone Road toward the airport. She was already over the moon.

EPILOGUE

◡

WINTER

All over the world, mothers are dying, but at eleven o'clock on the morning of January 29, a mother is born. Melanie Patchen delivers a baby girl, Amber Victoria, weighing eight pounds even and measuring twenty inches long. Healthy.

When the nurses wheel Melanie out of recovery (after eighteen hours in labor, an epidural, a shot of Pitocin, and a distressed heartbeat, the doctors performed a C-section), Melanie is able to hold her daughter and nurse her for the first time, and she feels like the world is brand-new; she feels like she is seeing everything for the first time.

When she conveys this feeling to Peter, he says, "That's the morphine talking."

I have a baby, Melanie thinks. *This baby is mine. I'm her* mother.

Melanie becomes mesmerized by the impossible smallness of Amber's every feature—her small mouth, her tiny ears, her fingers and toes, her beating heart the size of an egg. The baby cries, she opens her eyes and turns her head toward sound, she roots against Melanie until she latches onto a nipple. Melanie feels an explosive, protective, overwhelming love. She wants to tell everyone about this new love, how it puts everything else into perspective. But what she quickly discovers is that the world falls into two categories: those who don't care and those who already know.

For three days straight, flowers arrive. There are orchids from Vicki and Ted, pink roses from Melanie's parents, a cyclamen from Peter's mother in Paris, an embarrassingly lavish and funereal arrangement from "the gang at Rutter, Higgens," red gerbera daisies from Melanie and Peter's neighbors, a potted chrysanthemum from Brenda Lyndon and John Walsh, forced paperwhites from Melanie's college roommate . . . the flowers keep coming until the nurses start to joke about Melanie being "quite the popular one." Melanie sends the next three arrangements over to the cancer ward.

On the afternoon of the fourth day, when Melanie is nursing Amber in bed, more flowers arrive. The arrangement is modest, sparse even. It's tea roses and carnations, a few sprays of baby's breath; it comes in a mug that says *Mommy* and has a pink, heart-shaped Mylar balloon attached.

"Another one," the nurse says. It's Stephanie, Melanie's

favorite nurse, the head of Labor and Delivery. She is blond and pretty, kind and capable; she was with Melanie through the last part of her labor and her C-section and she has done most of the teaching—how to feed and burp the baby, how to give her a sponge bath, how to clean around the umbilical cord.

Melanie smiles. "And here I thought everyone had forgotten about me."

"Apparently not," Stephanie says. She sets the mug down on Melanie's meal tray. "Would you like me to read you the card?"

Melanie studies the flowers. What she realizes is that she's been waiting for flowers just like this: inexpensive but earnest. Easily purchased online.

"No, thanks," Melanie says. "It'll give me something to look forward to when I'm done feeding her."

"You're doing a great job, by the way," Stephanie says. "The baby's already back up to her birth weight. That's what we like to see."

Melanie gazes down at Amber's soft head, covered with dark fuzz. Stephanie leaves the room.

Later, when the baby is asleep in her bassinet, Melanie removes the envelope from the prongs of the plastic fork sticking out of the arrangement. *Melanie Patchen,* the envelope says.

Peter is picking up his mother at JFK; Melanie expects them at dinnertime.

She takes out the card. It says: *I know she's beautiful.*

Melanie's eyes flood with tears, and in an instant, she is sobbing. Stephanie had told her to expect this—sudden tears, for no apparent reason. Her hormones are all over the place. Melanie looks first at her baby sleeping and then out the window—the late-afternoon sky is gray and there are snow flurries. In the hallway, Melanie can hear strains of Muzak. She has just given birth to a gorgeous, healthy baby, and yet all she can do is cry, cry until she is struggling to catch her breath. She is back together with Peter; they are a couple again. All she can do is hope; she likens her marriage to the New Dawn roses that hung on the front of Number Eleven Shell Street. *If you cut them back,* Melanie had told Blaine, *they'll be even lovelier next time.* Melanie is filled with love and joy and wonder, and yet, she is empty. She has everything she ever wanted, but she longs for . . .

For what?

For summertime. For an hour on a sunny deck, for a perfect slice of tomato, for the song of the wren that perched outside her window, for the way her body felt when it was cradled by the ocean's waves, for a perfect blue hydrangea hanging over a white picket fence, for butterflies and bumblebees, for ice-cream cones after dinner, for the passenger seat of the Jeep. How intoxicating it had felt to ride down Milestone Road with the windows open and the night air rushing in, how quickening to pull up to the beach and see the water before them and the night sky spread out like a blanket, how lucky she had felt simply to sit beside someone as extraordinary as Josh Flynn.

Melanie wipes her tears and reads the card again. (She will read it every day at first and then only on days when she needs a lift, when she needs a reminder of happiness.)

I know she's beautiful.

The card is unsigned.

Today, Vicki's list runs two pages long. It's a Thursday in early February, and it also happens to be Blaine's fifth birthday. Vicki is throwing a party that afternoon at four o'clock at Chuck E. Cheese. This is the venue Blaine ardently lobbied for, and Vicki acquiesced, as it conveniently placed the chaos outside the house. Still, there are balloons to pick up as well as the cake and presents. There is a Valentine's Day charity auction on Saturday night, and Vicki had hoped to get into the city to shop for something to wear (everything she has is too big; she still hasn't recouped from her weight loss), but the shopping will have to wait, as will the hundred other things on her list. The birthday party is important, yes, but there is something else in the early part of Vicki's day that's even more important.

Her cancer support group at ten-thirty.

Vicki manages to get there on time, or almost. She slips into a seat just before Dolores begins with opening prayer. Vicki hasn't been to the group since three days before her surgery, when she had been too tongue-tied and paralyzed with fear to even say her name. She feels guilty now, like the lapsed returning to church. She holds hands with Jeremy and another person—a woman younger than she is, dressed in a denim jumper—whom she's never seen before.

When the prayer ends, Dolores raises her head and beams at Vicki.

"Would you like some mulled cider?" Dolores asks her. "It's organic."

Vicki notices that the rest of the group have cups, but she demurs. "Maybe after."

"Very well," Dolores says. "Let's start by introducing ourselves. Dana? Will you go first, please?"

The woman in the denim jumper speaks. "My name is Dana. Breast cancer, stage three."

Vicki's throat constricts. She is relieved when they go the other way around the circle. Ed, prostate cancer, stage two, Josie, breast cancer, stage three; Francesca is still there, as is Jeremy. There's another woman Vicki doesn't recognize who does not have cancer at all; she's there because her seven-year-old daughter has been diagnosed with leukemia.

Vicki is so moved by this declaration that she finds herself lapsing back to her stutter.

"Vicki?" Dolores says.

"I'm V——icki," she says. "Lung cancer." She pauses, swallows, collects herself. "Survivor."

Survivor. The other people in the circle stare at her, and Vicki feels self-conscious. Dolores continues to beam. Dolores had called a few days ago and asked Vicki to come back to the support group. Implored her, really.

"It will be good for the others to see," Dolores said. "Especially at this bleak time of year. It will deliver a message of hope."

Except what Vicki sees now in the others' eyes is envy, resentment even. She recognizes it because she was in their shoes once, listening to Travis, who beat liver cancer, and Janice, who, against all odds, beat ovarian cancer. While Vicki was happy for them, she also hated them. And now here she is. She wants to tell this circle of people the whole story, every detail, but mostly she wants to convey that she is one of them. She is them, they are her, they are all in this together. She calls herself a survivor, but the term, as they all know, is conditional, because maybe the cancer is all gone, but maybe it only went into hiding, like an evil jack-in-the-box face that will, eventually and to her sudden surprise, resurface. Vicki lived for thirty-one years as a confident, capable person, but now she is shackled by fear and uncertainty. Nothing will ever come easily again.

"Tell us," Dolores says. "Tell us about your journey."

Vicki is cautious about what she says. She wants to be honest but not confessional, straightforward but not graphic. She was afraid of the surgery, she tells the group, so afraid that she developed a stutter. She was unable to speak clearly; her tongue was a lump in her mouth. Every sentence was garbled. When she returned to Darien from Nantucket, she was unable to keep food down, and she was hospitalized for dehydration. Dr. Garcia referred her to a psychotherapist. The therapy worked in reverse, her stutter worsened, and Ted was forced to acknowledge that something else was wrong with her. She wrote notes on paper, but even the notes were confusing and disjointed. She couldn't concentrate on anything except her own fear and anxiety—it was a minute-by-minute battle to keep it from escalating into full-blown panic. The anesthesia, they're going to kill me, I'm going to die. She dropped Blaine off at preschool, she picked him up, she shopped for diapers and Oreos and rib-eye steaks, she oiled her butcher-block countertops and did laundry, but the question was always with her: Why bother? Was this how she

wanted to spend her final days? Wasn't there something
else she should be doing to stop the train that was speed-
ing toward her? She couldn't sleep, and when she did
sleep, she had nightmares. Dr. Garcia prescribed Ativan.
Vicki and Ted met with their attorney and signed a new
will. Vicki named her sister as guardian. She donated her
organs, lungs excepted. She signed a Health Care Proxy,
a DNR order, and gave Ted power of attorney. She vomited in the bathroom of the lawyer's office. She wrote
the boys each a long letter, and she wrote a long letter
for Ted, and she wrote a shorter letter for everyone else
that she wanted Brenda to read at her funeral. The night
before her surgery, she went to church; she knelt in the
empty sanctuary and prayed, then felt like a hypocrite
because she didn't know what she believed. She went
home and sat on the side of the bed as Ted read to the
children. She kissed them good night and thought, *What
if this is the last time?*

"What I'm telling you," Vicki says, "is that I thought I
was going to die. I was sure of it."

Around the circle, there are nods.

Vicki was so terrified that pre-op was a blur. She had
vague recollections of listening to the anesthesiologist
and the head surgical nurse. She remembers changing
from her clothes into the gown and wondering if she
would ever wear clothes again; she remembers trembling and feeling cold. She remembers the IV stuck, after
three tries, into the back of her hand. She remembers Ted
wearing khaki shorts and a cheerful, red polo shirt; he
was there the whole time, whispering, it seemed like.
Whatever he was saying, Vicki couldn't hear him. Both
Ellen Lyndon and Brenda were at home with the kids.

Vicki had (irrationally) insisted that she wanted them to hold Blaine and Porter the entire time she was in surgery. She remembers being wheeled down a series of hallways, with as many tight turns as a Moroccan souk, Ted at her side, in turquoise scrubs now. He was going to stay with her until they put her to sleep. She remembers the incredible gravity of the surgical team, the meticulous professionalism, the nurses going through an inscrutable protocol—numbers, codes, her blood pressure, her temperature. It was as dramatic as the theater, and for good reason—they held Vicki's life in their hands! But, too, it was just another day at work for these people. Hers was the body today; tomorrow it would be someone else.

The OR was cold. Vicki's feet were bare, sticking out from under the sheet like a TV corpse. Everyone wore scrubs and masks. Vicki couldn't tell one person from another, man from woman; it was as if she had arrived on another planet. Ted was there at her side and then a second familiar face—those thick glasses—Dr. Garcia.

"You're going to be just fine," Dr. Garcia said.

There was a stirring, a soft commotion, then a parting of the seas. The surgeon had arrived. His name was Jason Emery, and he was a giant—taller and broader than Ted, and very young. A superstar, Dr. Garcia had called him, the best thoracic surgeon in Connecticut. (How many could there be? Vicki wondered.) The nurses worked as quickly as a NASCAR pit crew, pulling on Dr. Emery's gloves and getting him his equipment. When he took his spot at the helm, his mask stretched, and Vicki knew he was smiling.

"Hi, Vicki," he said. "It's Jason."

They had met the week before in his office, where he

explained every step of the surgery. Vicki had liked him
Like Dr. Garcia, Jason Emery was unshakably optimis
tic. But so young! How old? He would turn thirty-two on
October 9, and so would Vicki. They had the same birth
day, they were twins, it was a sign, he could save her.

"Hi, Jason," she said.

"Everything's going to be fine," he said.

He started barking orders, all of them unintelligible
It reminded Vicki of a quarterback calling out plays. A
rubber mask went over her face. The mask smelled like
vanilla. It was the same smell, she thought, as her moth
er's kitchen when cookies were baking.

This is it, she thought. Ted squeezed her hand. Vicki
thought: *Blaine! Porter!* She imagined them in her moth
er's arms, in Brenda's arms. Safe and sound.

She woke up in pain. Hideous pain, straight from the fir
pits of hell. She woke up screaming.

A nurse gave her a shot in the arm. "Morphine booster,"
she said. "You have Duramorph going into your spine a
well."

Still, Vicki screamed. She thought she might feel ela
tion or at least a deep relief at finding herself alive; she
had, somehow, made it through the granite tunnel. Bu
as miraculous as that seemed to her intellect, it was im
possible to process because of the pain. With the pain
there was only one thought. And therein lay the irony
The surgery that had saved her life made her wish tha
she were dead.

It lasted an eternity. There was a blur of activity
people, machines, procedures—but none of it translated
Vicki, who hated to call attention to herself, especiall

a public place, among strangers, screamed for hours. Vicki, who liked to be in control at all times, was not only screaming and howling like an animal, but begging, too. *Help me! Help me! Dear God, please help me!*

And then, quiet. Dark. A soft beeping. A dark face hovering above hers. A nurse. *I'm Juanita,* she said. *How are you feeling?*

Vicki was sore in some places, numb in others. Her throat was killing her. Her mouth was dry, her lips cracked. She was thirsty. Juanita put a straw to her mouth. The water was cold, as cold as the ice water with paper-thin slices of lemon that Brenda had put by her bedside all summer. Vicki started to cry. The water tasted so good. The summer had been so beautiful, despite everything. She was alive.

Vicki does not want to frighten anyone in the group, but she can't bring herself to candy-coat things, either. The recovery was long, it was hard (Vicki means to use the word *horrible,* but she stops herself at *hard*). She had seven million stitches through all the muscles she needed to get anything done. With every cough, every sneeze, every laugh or exclamation, she felt stabbing pain along the miles of her incision. She felt like she was going to break open, burst apart. If the cancer had hurt, and made breathing hard, it was nothing compared to how she hurt now, to how she labored for air. Vicki only had one lung remaining. Even feeding herself, even taking a shower, even reading a picture book wiped her out. She couldn't stand to be awake, and so she slept for great portions of the day. Morphine gave way to Percocet and Percocet to Advil. Vicki went through fifty Advil a week. And

still, the pain. For weeks, Ted carried her up and dow
the stairs. Friends and neighbors brought meals, the
sent cards, books, flowers; she heard them whispering
How is she? What else can we do? They took Blain
and Porter for playdates. Ellen Lyndon had to go bac
to Philadelphia at the end of the month. Brenda cam
two days a week, but the rest of the time she was busy
working as a manager at Barnes & Noble and trying t
sell her screenplay to a studio that would actually pro
duce it. Brenda's life, in essence, was busy and bac
on track, which was great news for her, but Vicki stil
needed help. *Don't leave!* Vicki's voice had returnec
like magic she could speak again and she was amaze
by this restoration, relieved at how the words she hel
in her mind flowed right out into the world—but every
thing she said was negative, unpleasant, confrontationa
When Ted suggested hiring a live-in nanny, Vicki said,
*don't want a stranger taking care of my children. I onl
want Josh.* To which Ted snapped, *Well, I doubt Josh i
available.*

After six weeks, Vicki went in for her postoperativ
scan. Dr. Garcia said the pictures looked "clean." Vick
appeared to be "cancer-free." Ted bought champagne
Vicki drank some from a Dixie cup, but that night Porte
howled from his crib and the next day he broke out i
red spots. Chicken pox, contracted on one of the play
dates. Ted took the week off from work. Vicki curse
herself for not being able to deal with it. She couldn't d
anything—she couldn't care for Porter, she couldn't g
to the grocery store, she couldn't trick-or-treat with th
kids, she couldn't plan a baby shower for Melanie. Sh
was still in such pain, her faculties were compromise

Her body had been invaded. She had been sliced open and stitched back together like a rag doll. Part of her incision became infected. There was an unusually severe soreness, a smell, redness, and an oozing pus. She ran a fever. Dr. Garcia prescribed antibiotics.

Vicki felt empty, and she imagined her chest cavity as literally empty. She imagined that, along with the cancer, Dr. Jason Emery had removed her capacity for getting things done, her good luck, and her happiness. She went to physical therapy; she went back to the psychotherapist.

She was better, yes. She was cancer-free, cured, a survivor. But she wasn't herself—and what was the point of getting better if her essential Vicki-ness had been lost? All her life, things had come easily. Now, the only thing that came easily was lying in bed and watching TV. She became addicted to the soap opera *Love Another Day* and hated herself for it.

"Recovery is a long, tough road," Vicki tells the group. "But in my case it was a road with an end."

Somehow, she pulled herself up. In spite of her deep despair, the lingering pain, the adjusted expectations, or perhaps because of them, she got better. It might have started with something little—a note came from Dr. Alcott, Ted made a joke and she laughed without splitting open, she had enough stamina to stand at the counter and make a sandwich. She followed her therapist's advice and built on these minor successes rather than dismissing them.

Now look at her: Five months later, she is here, in the circle, head bowed for closing prayer. She has changed. She is cancer-free, yes, but the change is something else, something more elusive, harder to pinpoint. She has been on a journey, and the place she finds herself now is the place she hopes everyone else in this circle will arrive. It is a place of wonder. It is a place of enormous gratitude.

You don't believe in a greater plan? Josh had asked her.

Vicki's answer—still—is *I don't know.* Some people in the circle will die, some will live. Who's to say which will happen, or why?

I want to throw her back. I want to let her live. Could it all be just that random?

Vicki recalls the night she stood on Sankaty Bluff, with the waves pounding the beach below her and the embarrassing riches of the night sky above.

Everything matters. Every little thing.

"Amen," Dolores says.

The closing prayer is over. Vicki has missed it. Or has she?

ACKNOWLEDGMENTS

This book marks a new beginning for me. I would like to thank my agent, Michael Carlisle, for his wise counsel; he has been with me every step of the way. Also, David Forrer, for his canny suggestions, which resulted in a better book all the way around. I thank Jennifer Weis and Sally Richardson for sticking with me through seven years and five books; they are both extraordinary women. At Little, Brown, I would like to thank Reagan Arthur and Michael Pietsch for taking me on with such enthusiasm, as well as Oliver Haslegrave for his gallant assistance. I feel like I have been born anew.

Thank you to Dr. William G. Porter, who is not only a friend and a discerning reader/critic, but an oncologist. We talked extensively about lung cancer and its various treatments. Any inaccuracies in the text, however, are mine alone. Thank you to Dr. Jason Lamb, thoracic surgeon, who briefed me on the pertinent details of a pneumonectomy. And thank you to my aunt, Ruthann Hall, who is a cancer survivor. Her details of chemotherapy and its mental / emotional/physical side effects were both inspiring and helpful.

One of the beating hearts of this novel is the parenting of small children. I am blessed to have a close-knit circle of friends on Nantucket who are rearing young families right alongside of me. My friend Debbie calls it "the vil-

lage." My friend Liz calls it "the squad." So thank you
to said village/squad for your support and your friend-
ship: Amanda and Richard Congdon, Elizabeth and Beau
Almodobar, Rebecca and John Bartlett, Debbie and
Jamey Bennett, Leslie and Tom Bresette, Betty and Rhett
Dupont, Renee and Joe Gamberoni, Anne and Whitney
Gifford, Sally and Brooks Hall, Wendy and Randy
Hudson, Wendy Rouillard and Illya Kagan, and Marty
and Holly McGowan.

I could not have written a word of this novel without the steadfast kindness and rock-solid care that our au
pair, Suphawan "Za" Intafa, provided to my three children. Thank you, Za. You will never know how much I
appreciate your help.

Thank you, Dan Bowling, for giving Nantucket a shot
in the summer of 2004. I exonerate you from all com-
parisons to Josh Flynn, except that you will always be a
favorite with my boys.

As for Chip, Max, Dawson, and Shelby Cunningham,
my family: When I wake up each morning, I marvel at
how lucky I am. Everything, always, is for you.

ABOUT THE AUTHOR

Elin Hilderbrand is the author of six previous novels, including, most recently, the celebrated bestseller *Barefoot*.

Hilderbrand lives on Nantucket with her husband and their three young children. She grew up in Collegeville, Pennsylvania, and traveled extensively before settling on Nantucket, which has been the setting for each of her novels. She holds degrees from Johns Hopkins University and the graduate fiction workshop at the University of Iowa.

For more information, visit ElinHilderbrand.net.

. . . AND HER MOST RECENT NOVEL

In July 2009 Little, Brown and Company published Elin Hilderbrand's *The Castaways*. Following is an excerpt from the novel's opening pages.

THE CHIEF

Because the accident occurred out on the water and not on the land that fell under his jurisdiction, it was unusual that the Chief was the first one to find out. But that was the benefit of an official position: He was a lightning rod for information, a conduit. Everything went through him first.

Dickson, his best sergeant, came into the office without his usual peppermint breeze of self-confidence. Was he sick? His skin was the color of frostbite, even though it was the first day of summer. In the seconds immediately before Dickson shuffled in, the Chief had been thinking of Greg with envy. The wind was strong; you couldn't ask for a better day to sail. Greg planned to go all the way to the Vineyard and if he caught the gusts, he would be there in five minutes. Tess would hate it; she would be clinging to the mast or down

below in the cramped head, her face as green as a bowl
of pea soup.

"What's up?" the Chief said. Dickson, who had the
broadest shoulders the Chief had ever seen on a human
being, was hunched over. He looked like he was going
to upchuck right there on the Chief's desk. He had
gotten a haircut that morning, too, his summer buzz,
which made his head seem square and strange, his scalp
vulnerable.

"The Coast Guard just called," Dickson said. "There's
been an accident on the water."

"Hmmm," Chief said. This was the stuff of his days:
accidents, crime, people fucking up in big ways and
small. Mostly small, he had come to realize after seventeen years on the force.

"Chief?" Dickson said. "The MacAvoys are dead."

The Chief would have called himself impossible
to faze. Even on an island as privileged and idyllic as
Nantucket, he had seen it all: an eight-year-old boy shot
in the face by his father's hunting rifle, a woman stabbed
fifty-one times by a jealous ex-boyfriend, heroin over-
doses, a Bulgarian prostitution ring, cocaine, ecstasy,
moonshine, high school kids stealing diamond rings
from beach cabanas, gangs, and a host of domestic dis-
putes, including a man who broke a chair over his wife's
head. As it turned out, the Chief was right, he was impossible to faze, because when Dickson said, *The MacAvoys
are dead*—the MacAvoys being Tess, Andrea's cousin,
and Greg, the closest thing to a brother or a best friend
the Chief had ever had, the Chief coughed dryly into his
hand. That was the extent of his initial reaction—one
raspy cough.

"What?" the Chief said. His voice was barely a whisper. *What? What are you telling me?* His hands were cold and numb, and he stared at his phone. It was not reasonable, at this point, to panic, because there might have been a mistake. So many times, there were mistakes, messages got crossed, people jumped to conclusions; so many times things weren't as bad as they seemed. He could not call Andrea until he spoke to the Coast Guard and found out exactly what had happened. It was four-thirty now. Andrea would be . . . where? At the beach, still, he supposed. The kids, finally, both had summer jobs and by Memorial Day weekend, Andrea had embarked on what she called "the Summer of Me." She had been good to her word, too—doing her power-walking every morning, and spending the afternoons on the south shore, swimming like the Olympic Trials qualifier that she was. She was getting fit, getting tan, and exercising her mind by reading all those thought-provoking novels. She tried to talk to the Chief about the novels when they climbed into bed at night, but the Chief's life was its own novel and he didn't have room in his mind for any more characters. Just yesterday, he had heard Andrea on the phone with Tess, talking about her book. He had overheard words like *ambivalence* and *disenchantment*, words he had no use for.

The Chief could not raise his eyes to Dickson's about-to-puke face. He could not call his wife and drop the bomb that would destroy the landscape of her life. Her first cousin, her closest friend—a person Andrea held dearer, possibly, than himself—Tess MacAvoy, was dead.

Maybe.

"I don't know what happened," Dickson said. Chief couldn't look at him or the haircut so short it looked painful. "They just called to say there was an accident. And the MacAvoys are dead."

ADDISON

Addison Wheeler was having cocktails at the Galley with clients. It was a celebration, and Addison had ordered a bottle of Cristal. A Purchase and Sale agreement had just been signed for a $9.2 million waterfront home on Polpis Harbor. But even as Addison was sipping champagne, even as he was mentally spending his whopping commission, his eyes scanned the white caps that frosted Nantucket Sound. The restaurant had plastic siding to protect diners from the wind, which was driving out of the north. There were boats out on the water, a lot of boats, despite the six- to eight-foot seas. Was one of them Greg and Tess? They would have made it to the Vineyard by one or two, and now would be returning home. Unless, of course, they had decided to spend the night. Addison would have said he was beyond this kind of jealousy, this kind of obsession, but he was feeling both things, jealousy and a panicky obsession. If Tess and Greg stayed on the Vineyard, in a room at the Charlotte Inn, would they make love? Addison sipped his champagne. Of course they would. Today was their twelfth anniversary.

He had tried to call her no less than five times before she left, but she didn't answer.

There were many indications that the day was special. They were taking champagne and a picnic that Andrea had prepared them as a gift. Greg was bringing his guitar. He had stopped by Addison's office that morning on his way to the dock.

"Your guitar?" Addison said.

"I'm a better singer than I am a sailor," Greg said. He shook his head to get his floppy bangs out of his face, a gesture that made Addison shudder. "I wrote her a song."

Wrote her a song. He would play the troubádour, try to win Tess back. After all that had happened last fall, Greg needed to make Tess trust him again.

"Good luck with that," Addison said

The final time Addison called Tess, he left a message. *Are you going to tell him? Are you going to tell him you love me?* The question was met with electronic silence.

The maître'd caught his eye. Addison tilted his head. His clients were talking between themselves now, awkwardly, about the quality of the champagne, and about the water, the impressive wind. It would sweep Greg and Tess to the Vineyard, but they would have to come back in the teeth of it. Would they risk it? If they spent the night at the Charlotte Inn, Addison would lose his mind. The place was too romantic, with its pencil post bed, white grand piano, towel warmer, silver buckets filled with blooming roses. Addison had stayed at the Charlotte Inn with his first wife twenty years earlier, and he remembered that the hotel had had the magical power to improve their relationship, for the nights they stayed there, certainly, and for several days afterward. Addison did not want Greg and Tess to stay there, because what if they experienced the same balm? He reached into his pocket to touch the heart Tess had given him on his birthday. She had cut the heart out of red felt, using child's scissors. Addison treated it like a talisman, though he was far too old and reasonable to believe in such things. He fingered the heart—now grotty and pilled and dangerously close to ripping—and wondered if Tess was thinking about him. Would she have the courage to tell Greg? Addison could hope all he wanted, but he knew the answer was no. Never in a million years.

The wife of the client couple asked Addison a question, but he didn't hear it. He was dropping the ball conversationally; he had to get back into the game, $9.2 million, and his office had the listing as well as the buyer. This was the biggest deal of the year so far. But something was going on at the front of the restaurant. Was the maître'd signaling him? He wanted Addison's attention?

"Excuse me," Addison said. He stood up, forced a smile. "I'll be right back."

Phoebe was in the parking lot. It *was* Phoebe, right? There was her car, the red Triumph Spitfire, and there was a woman Phoebe's shape and size with the shining blond hair—but her face was pink and crumpled like a dropped handkerchief, her cheeks were streaked with makeup, she was keening, hiccuping, *freaking out*. Losing her shit, here in public! This was not his wife. His wife, Phoebe Wheeler, rarely cracked a smile or shed a tear. Addison grabbed her by the shoulders. Was it really her? Yes, those eyes, blue fire. She was emotionally absent, a woman made of ice, steel, chalk, plastic, stone, rubber, clay, straw—but her eyes revealed a spark, and that was one reason Addison hung in there. He was convinced she would return to him, one day.

"Phoebe?" he said.

She pushed him away. She was making noises like an animal; her beautiful hair fell into her face. She was trying to speak, but she could not form any coherent words. Well, there was one word, over and over again, like a hiss: *Tess*.

"Tess?" Addison said. Did Phoebe know, then? She'd found out? This was impossible, because no one knew and there was not one scrap of evidence that would betray them. The cell phone bill, maybe, but only if Phoebe had gone through it with a fine-tooth comb and seen the calls that Addison made to Tess while he was golfing two weeks ago, in North Carolina. Yes, that must be it. Addison's heart cracked and sizzled like an egg on the hot griddle of the parking lot. He could explain away the phone calls; he and Tess were, after all, friends. He could come up with a plausible reason for the calls.

"Honey, you have to get ahold of yourself," Addison said. He could not believe his marriage was going to explode here, now, when he was completely unprepared—but a part of him was intrigued by Phoebe's unbridled reaction. She was hysterical. He couldn't believe it. He would have said that when Phoebe found out about Tess she would have done nothing more than roll over and sneeze.

Just like that, her meds kicked in. She reined in the horses that were running away with her. She stopped crying, she sniffed. Addison had only seen her crumble like this one other time—September 11. Her twin brother, Reed, worked on the 101st floor of the second tower. He had jumped.

"Tess," Phoebe said. "And Greg. Tess and Greg are dead."

VISIT US ONLINE

@ WWW.HACHETTEBOOKGROUP.COM.

AT THE HACHETTE BOOK GROUP WEB SITE YOU'LL FIND:

A drop of ~~w~~ ~~~~ ~~~~ ~~~~ ~~~~ ~~~~
on her lips.

Nobody was more surprised than he when he leaned in.

He barely brushed his lips across hers, but he felt the impact all the way to his toes.

For a moment so brief that he might have imagined it, she went with the flow. Then she was pushing against him. He pulled away, searching her stunned face, trying to gather his scattered thoughts.

And with the symbolic distance between them, whatever craziness had possessed him disappeared. He didn't know where it had come from, but he did know one thing for sure: under no circumstances would he ever touch this woman again. She was nothing but trouble.

"We shouldn't be doing this. You are—" She paused. "I am—" She made a soft noise of frustration. "We can't do this again."

His gaze strayed to those ruby lips that were pressed into a severe, angry line. Then, instead of agreeing, he flashed the woman his most wicked grin and said, "I think we're definitely going to do this again."

DANA MARTON

STRANDED WITH THE PRINCE

HARLEQUIN®

TORONTO • NEW YORK • LONDON
AMSTERDAM • PARIS • SYDNEY • HAMBURG
STOCKHOLM • ATHENS • TOKYO • MILAN • MADRID
PRAGUE • WARSAW • BUDAPEST • AUCKLAND

With many thanks to Allison Lyons

Recycling programs
for this product may
not exist in your area.

ISBN-13: 978-0-373-69473-0

STRANDED WITH THE PRINCE

Copyright © 2010 by Dana Marton

Printed in U.S.A.

ABOUT THE AUTHOR

Dana Marton is the author of more than a dozen fast-paced, action-adventure romantic suspense novels and a winner of the Daphne du Maurier Award of Excellence. She loves writing books of international intrigue, filled with dangerous plots that try her tough-as-nails heroes and the special women they fall in love with. Her books have been published in seven languages in eleven countries around the world. When not writing or reading, she loves to browse antiques shops and enjoys working in her sizable flower garden where she searches for "bad" bugs with the skills of a superspy and vanquishes them with the agility of a commando soldier. Every day in her garden is a thriller. To find more information on her books, please visit www.danamarton.com. She loves to hear from her readers and can be reached via e-mail at DanaMarton@DanaMarton.com.

Books by Dana Marton

CAST OF CHARACTERS

Lazlo Kerkay—The "rebel prince" is a successful entrepreneur and a ladies' man. But he hasn't seen trouble until he meets a determined matchmaker from the U.S. who is set on ending his freedom.

Milda Milas—The last in a long line of matchmakers, Milda is brought in from New York by the queen to help tame the wildest of the princes. Finding a match for Lazlo turns into the most difficult task she's ever attempted.

Roberto—The leader of a small group of criminals from Bogotá. He is in Europe to penetrate the European drug market and to gain revenge for his brother's death.

The Freedom Council—A secret group of prominent businessmen whose sole purpose is to destroy the royal family and break the country into small republics that they could each rule individually.

Arpad Kerkay—The crown prince is a colonel in the air force. Since the queen is ill, soon he will inherit the crown.

Miklos Kerkay—Second to the throne. He is an army major and a happily married man.

Janos Kerkay—Third in line to the throne. He is an economist and a superb yachtsman who also regularly wins golf championships.

Istvan Kerkay—The fourth prince in line to the throne is a cultural anthropologist who is obsessed with preserving the past of his country.

Benedek Kerkay—Lazlo's twin. The youngest prince has two passions: architecture and his wife, Rayne Williams, the opera singing sensation.

Chapter One

Sagro Prison island, Italy

Boots slapped on the concrete floor, keeping a regular rhythm. The night security lights were on, enough to see the guard who was texting on his phone as he strode out of sight, a sly grin on his pockmarked face. A minute went by, then another. The steel door opened then closed at the end of the cell block.

The 2:00 a.m. check was complete. Nobody would be by again until morning.

Roberto, fully dressed, slid out of bed, making no more noise than his shadow as it moved across the floor. He laid his pillow lengthwise on the bare mattress then draped the bed with his blanket, creating a bulky form.

His sheets had been ripped, twisted into rope and wrapped around his waist before he'd gone to bed. Now he bent and squatted one more time to make sure the cumbersome arrangement wouldn't limit his movement. He adjusted a tight strip under his left armpit before he stole to the door and pressed the top part of the lock hard.

Click. The sound was so soft even he barely heard it.

José had fixed the locks. The oldest of the team, José had been a locksmith before a drive-by took out his family in the godforsaken backstreets of Bogotá. With nothing to live for, he'd signed up for the rival gang. José understood revenge.

So did Roberto. It pushed him forward as he stole down the hallway, moving fast in a crouch. He listened to the snoring of the other inmates. A bed creaked now and then as someone turned over in his sleep. He listened for any indication that someone noticed him, not trusting—despite substantial bribes and dire threats—that they wouldn't betray him and sound the alarm.

José was waiting for him at the water block, along with Marco, the third member of the team.

"Any trouble?" Roberto kept his voice to a low whisper.

Marco shook his head. He was young and sullen, still not over the fact that they'd been imprisoned. That here, on the other side of the ocean, the boss couldn't protect them. He was ready to go, but didn't think it fair that they had to orchestrate the escape themselves. He'd griped and whined through the preparations. Which better stop right now, right here. Roberto flashed him a sharp look that warned him to be on his best behavior.

The young thugs coming out of the slums these days

were too hotheaded, only after the glory, and rarely willing to put enough effort into a job to get it done right. They wanted the fastest car and the biggest gun, wanted to build reputations overnight, which led to too much senseless killing.

"All's according to plan," José was saying.

Exactly what Roberto wanted to hear. His sticker, a spoon handle sharpened into a knife, waited stashed inside a showerhead. He retrieved the makeshift tool then went to work on removing a wall panel.

A hundred years ago, Sagro Prison had been the hunting castle of some Italian king. When they'd rebuilt it into a prison in the fifties, they changed just about everything. Security had been upgraded several times since, but the prison's waste and sewer system still connected to the old castle's cistern.

All Roberto and his men had had to do over the endless months that they'd been locked up here was dig through the wall. The cistern's ducts, carved from stone, were plenty wide to accommodate a man.

José squeezed in first, then Marco, Roberto going last, pulling the wall panel into place behind him. By morning they'd be free men. His to-do list was simple: get food, finish the boss's business in Trieste, then get the hell out of Italy.

But he wouldn't go back to Bogotá, not straightaway. He had personal business in the area which he meant to see handled. He was going to Valtria, the small kingdom to the north, to gain retribution for his brother's death.

An eye for an eye, a life for a life. He might have been too old-school to condone all the senseless killing the new gangs did these days, but revenge was part of a man's honor. And he did believe in that. He certainly did.

Island of Morka, Nature Preserve, Valtria

SHE WAS THE SCOURGE of his life, a relentless thorn under his royal skin. Prince Lazlo of Valtria watched Milda Milas bear down on him and knew what it felt like to be hunted.

A professional matchmaker from New York. He loved his mother as much as all his brothers did, but the Queen had gone too far this time. One of her ladies-in-waiting had a cousin in New York who'd been Milda's client. Apparently, a recommendation had been made. He didn't like the idea of his mother discussing his personal life with her ladies-in-waiting. Shouldn't they have been talking about the royal gardens or copying antique tapestries and the like when they retired to the Queen's private quarters?

Despite the calming, balmy breeze that streamed from the endless azure water, Lazlo's sense of peace was fast disappearing. He'd been looking forward to spending the day away from the palace, away from Milda's harping. He should have known she wouldn't let a perfectly good day go by without doing her best to ruin it. A dull throb started up in the knee he'd once injured in a crash. Maybe his subconscious was beginning to associate her with pain.

"And there I was, thinking I could hide from you here," he said when she reached him.

He liked the island of Morka, fifty miles off the Italian coast, an inhabited chunk of land in the Mediterranean Sea, owned by the Valtrian royal family and set up as a nature preserve. With its wild olive and orange groves, the place was a veritable paradise—but for Milda Milas's unfortunate presence.

"Your Highness." She stopped in front of him with that ra-ra-hurra look that hardly left her face whenever she dealt with him. She seemed to think that if she smiled wide enough and pretended that what she was doing to him was normal—wonderful, even—somehow he could be tricked into agreeing with her.

"I don't know how you got here. Never mind that." He reconsidered and cut to the point. "You should leave," he told her firmly. "I'm not playing your games today. I've made other plans."

Since the top of her head only came up to his shoulders, she usually rose to the tips of her toes when she wanted to browbeat him into yet another one of her crazy plans. She was stretching up so hard at the moment that she looked like a ballet dancer. The wind whipped her long, reddish-brown hair around her slim face. Her eyes, the exact dusky blue of his first race car, narrowed as she dropped the smile, recognizing smartly that it wasn't going to work today.

"You should face your responsibilities, Your

Highness. Don't you think all this endless evasion is childish?"

She had his gander up in thirty seconds flat. A new record. She knew she was annoying him, but she didn't care. She had the Queen's protection. She'd been given free reign, God help him.

"I'm childish?" He drew up an eyebrow slowly, regally, and regarded her with a chilly expression he'd learned early on in life from his mother. "You torture me for money. What does that make you?"

She dropped back on her heels and stuck her chin out, her eyes and lips narrowing. "To be honest, I'd torture you for free. If that makes you feel better."

He was taken aback for a moment. He was used to more respect as a prince. Although not from her, admittedly.

"You know what I think?" she asked with a smirk, losing the last of her polite veneer.

He allowed a subtle sneer. "A better question is, mademoiselle, do I care?"

"I think you're afraid that you couldn't hold an intelligent woman's attention over the long term. That's why you engage only in nightlong, scandalous affairs with those twits." Her tone turned to lecturing. "Your conduct is embarrassing the monarchy and the Queen. You were caught on tape in a compromising situation, for love's sake." She rolled her dusky blue eyes in a way that told him exactly what she thought of that.

Not that until now he'd been forced to guess. She

had expressed her opinion a number of times since the unfortunate incident.

He tried to put this latest scandal out of his mind. No chance of that with her around. *She* was going to lecture him on his duties as a prince? His blood pressure inched up. He drew a long, slow breath.

"You know what I think?" he asked, and kept going, without giving her a chance to pipe up. "I think American kamikaze nuptial consultants should stay in their own country."

He was pleased with himself for resisting the urge to raise his voice. He was not going to lose control because of her. He was a prince. He was certainly up to the challenge of ignoring a troublesome matchmaker. "Where are my brothers?"

He was supposed to be on the island with them, and *only* them, on a day hike. Miklos's idea. Since the failed rebel attacks of the past two years, the six royal brothers hardly got to spend time together anymore. If he didn't like Miklos's and Benedek's wives so much, he would have blamed it on them, but Princess Judi and Princess Rayne were too lovely to fault for anything. He couldn't truly blame his brothers for not wanting to leave home, even if he never understood what had possessed them to rush into marriage.

Single life suited him just fine. Being a prince, he already had more expectations and regulations, more rules governing his every move than he cared to think about. Marriage would have been just another prison.

Which Milda refused to understand.

"Your brothers aren't coming." Her slim fingers worried the colorful bead bracelet on her left wrist.

Why couldn't they just call, instead of sending a message with her, of all people, when— Lazlo froze, a terrible premonition holding him speechless for a moment before he could ask, "This is another one of your traps, isn't it?"

So help him God—

"You'll be going hiking with the Lady Lidia, the Lady Szilvia and the Lady Adel." Her "this will be fun, you'll see" smile returned.

He swore in a way that should have been beneath him as a prince. "My brothers helped you set me up?" A new low. Incomprehensible, really. The sense of betrayal was overwhelming.

And her guilty look confirmed everything.

His brothers probably thought it was a grand joke. "I'm going to murder them," he muttered.

History was full of princes who killed their own brothers to get closer to the throne. He didn't care about the throne. But he might be driven to murder by Milda Milas yet. Except, then centuries from now historians would speculate that maybe he'd been secretly in love with her, and the act had been motivated by jealousy or some such nonsense. That would be intolerable. She was already messing up his life; he wasn't going to let her sully his legacy.

"How dare you?" He stepped toward her, ready to take her to task, but caught sight of a sizable pile of duffel bags farther up the beach. He'd thought them a pile of rocks earlier, with the sun in his eyes, but now that a small cloud blocked some of the brilliant rays, he could see that he'd been mistaken. "What is that?"

They couldn't have needed all that equipment for one day. His own guards were in the process of unloading his speedboat, removing the two boxes that contained the food and drink he and his brothers would have needed until they returned to the palace this evening.

"A two-week hike?" she squeaked, cleared her throat, went back up on her tiptoes then said again, in a deeper tone of self-confidence she must have practiced in the mirror, "A two-week hike with the ladies." Her damned smile was in full bloom.

He glanced around but didn't see any desperate women ready to drag him to the altar. Excellent. He had plenty of time to run for the boat. "Have you lost your mind?"

She drew her slim shoulders up, looking like some sort of exotic bird taking up defensive position. Or getting ready to attack. He had the uncomfortable feeling that he was about to be pecked to death.

"The ladies went to see the Painted Rocks. They should be back shortly. You need to spend time with intelligent, self-sufficient women, and stay away from your empty-headed beauties for a few days," she stated.

So she admitted that the three ladies in question weren't beauties. Not that he could bring that up without proving himself to be shallow—of which she accused him endlessly.

The impatient growl that escaped him didn't seem to alarm her in the least. "Once you calm down, Your Highness, you'll see this was a good idea." She didn't back away. She never backed down from him, one of her many annoying qualities. "By tonight, I promise you'll feel a lot better about all this."

The only thing that would have made him feel better would have been tossing her into the sea. Sadly, being a prince, he'd been raised better than to threaten bodily harm to a woman. Not even a woman who was dead set on ruining his life.

She wasn't going to quit until she saw him married. She was the type to see that the job got done. No matter what. In anyone else, he could have appreciated the drive. He could appreciate little in her. They'd been doing battle for months now.

A wave of weariness hit him. "Why are you doing this to me?"

Her gaze never wavered. "For one, as you pointed out, I get paid for it."

"I could pay you more to go away."

"I would never break my contract. You should be grateful. I'm here to help you. The Queen gave you six months to announce that you've chosen a bride. She wants to see you settled down. You must end the scandals."

"I still have another month." In fact, he'd been counting on that last month of freedom rather desperately.

"Exactly."

"Two weeks on this blasted island would waste half.

Absolutely not. When that boat leaves in a few minutes, I'm leaving with it."

"And the ladies? Common courtesy—"

"If you want to stay with the ladies, be my guest. Have a pajama party." He ignored the intriguing picture that flashed into his mind and focused on her clenched jaw instead.

But the next moment she was forcing a smile again. He hated how cheerful she always was while she tortured him.

"Two weeks in this beautiful place is exactly what you need." She sounded like she actually believed it. "By the time we come back for you, you will have made your choice. The Queen and the country will be happy."

"Dare I ask, what about me?"

"Try to give these women a chance. Maybe you'll fall in love with one of them." Her eyes brightened at the mention of the L word.

"In two weeks?" Was she for real? Sadly, she was. She had an unshakable, deep-seated belief in romance that annoyed the hell out of him. He gave her his most discouraging expression, the one he normally reserved for ambushing paparazzi.

But her eyebrows stayed up, the corners of her lips tugged into that fake encouraging smile, her gaze steady on him. "Stranger things have happened."

A *lot* of strange things had happened to him lately, his mother hiring the pushiest woman in the world to force him to wed being one of them. But the chances of him falling in love were slim to none. For that to happen, he would have to believe in love to begin with.

There was no point in further bickering with her. They were too different. They'd never understand each other. He glanced at the boat, ready to go, and realized that the two guards had disappeared, leaving the boxes of food on the bluff above the tide line. "Where did Ben and Vince go?"

She worried her bead bracelet again for a brief, unguarded moment before she responded. "They'll guard the island's perimeter. They'll be in radio contact with each other, but not with you. I can't risk you bullying them with some fake emergency into coming to pick you up."

The woman boggled his mind. She was beyond all belief. "Good plan." He couldn't help a sneer. "And what would have happened if there'd *been* an emergency?"

"I'm not at liberty to say," she said, apparently still thinking that she could make him stay.

He glanced toward his jacket, draped over the side of the boat, his cell phone in the pocket. He needed to pay closer attention to her. She wasn't to be underestimated. With some luck, she *could* have stranded him. The thought was disturbing.

He needed to make her see reason and quit this sordid business. "You really expected me to spend two weeks in the bush with a bunch of wilting lilies? I'm a racer, not a camper. And I bet your ladies haven't seen more nature than what can be found at the palace gardens. What, exactly, did you think we would be doing out here?"

She put that pert nose of hers into the air and flashed him a smug look. "Lady Lidia is an herbalist, Lady Szilvia is a survival specialist and Lady Adel is a doctor at your favorite ski resort."

He sure didn't remember her. Which must have meant she wasn't a looker. Then again, he preferred to sustain his injuries at the racetrack, so maybe he hadn't been visited by the resort's doctor in the past.

"I'm to attend a race tomorrow evening." It was to be the first time one of his cars was running with a modified engine, a major invention he needed to see in action. He needed to make manufacturing decisions based on tomorrow's race. She was interfering with his business.

"Prince Lazlo—"

"Enough." He was out of patience with her and her meddling. She'd been relentlessly after him for the past five months, since the Queen and Chancellor Egon had sicced her on him. "So you decided to parade the country cows." He practically growled the words. "You need to understand, Milda, that I'm not some prize bull you can lead into the pasture for breeding."

"Prince Laz—"

"No." He raised a hand, palm out. "I don't care what these women want from me—title, money or their children in the line of succession. They need to find another way of getting it. So you collected a homely bunch of ambitious—" he swallowed the word that a prince wouldn't utter "—ladies. Read my lips. I don't want any of them." He pushed by her to stride toward the boat.

"Prince Lazlo!"

"Goodbye, Milda."

But something in her voice as she called his name again stopped him. He turned to give her a piece of his mind, in case she still harbored some doubts regarding how he felt about the evil job she'd been hired to do.

And he saw the three ladies.

They had come out of the wild olive grove. From the look on their faces, they'd been standing within hearing range when he'd made that country cow comment. *Blast it,* he thought.

By God, he was tired of this. He liked the chase between the sexes, another sport to him. But, call him old-fashioned, he liked to be the one to do the chasing. He inclined his head, his jaw so tight he could barely push out the single word. "Ladies."

They looked vaguely familiar—and were pretty, to be fair—but he couldn't place them. No big surprise there. He'd run into a lot of women over the years.

"Your Highness." They curtsied, but if looks could kill...

Which was surprising. The women he regularly saw at court were more of the simpering kind—lots of eyelash batting and that sort of thing. He hated simpering. But maybe these three were different. Maybe Milda had done her homework.

He still didn't care. He wasn't going to be forced into marriage.

What a crazy, absolutely insane idea this has been—him on a deserted island with three proper young ladies. Ridiculous, really. For two weeks!

He gave them an apologetic smile he had to force. They'd been inconvenienced as much as he had. "I'm sorry you've been misled. Why don't you wait in the boat? I'll take you back to the mainland in a minute."

The boat could only seat four. Which meant Milda and the two bodyguards would have to wait until someone returned for them. Now there was a happy thought. With some luck, the pickup would take a long time. For a moment, he even toyed with the thought of not sending his boat back. Two weeks of freedom without her hounding him... The idea held considerable merit.

"See what you've done?" he asked, once the ladies were out of earshot, as they marched toward the boat. Obedient they were, he couldn't help noticing. After dealing with Milda for the past five challenging months, he was beginning to appreciate obedience more and more in a woman. "You managed to further damage my reputation. You should quit and go home to New York. You're a PR liability."

No evidence of her infamous smile now. Her face was turning red. Her delicate nostrils flared. He wouldn't have been surprised to see smoke coming out of her dainty ears.

"I damaged your reputation?" She put her hands on her slim hips. The movement stretched her shirt over her breasts. They were one of her very best features, made the endless hours she spent lecturing him bearable. "*I* damaged your reputation?" She was sputtering.

"You can think of ways to make it up to me while you wait for someone to come for you." He smirked as he stepped away from her, ready to saunter across the beach.

"I'm fighting for my business," she warned him. "My livelihood and my heritage. I will *not* give up. I will not give in."

"And I'm fighting for my freedom. Something I most cherish," he told her…and heard the motor start.

He spun around in time to see the boat pull away, steered by Lady Adel.

"Wait!" Sand flew up around him as he broke into a sprint. His busted knee slowed him. And the boat was too far, pulling away rapidly.

They couldn't leave him, dammit. Not here, not with Milda. "Wait!" He dashed into the surf after them to no avail. But he refused to give up. He swam like he never swam before. Like his life depended on it.

One of the ladies gave him a smug little wave.

The distance between them was growing.

And growing.

His lungs burned from the effort he put into propelling his body through the water. Then he stopped completely, at last accepting the unacceptable. He swore an unprincely streak and let himself sink for a moment, let the waves wash over his head before he pushed up to the surface again. He treaded water for another few seconds, too stunned to think. Then, as outrage took over, he turned to swim for the shore.

He strode back onto dry land, fuming and dripping. "You!" He bore down on the woman of his nightmares. "Get on your cell phone and get another boat out here."

Her stricken look stopped him. They were practically nose to nose anyway, only inches separating them from each other. Her big blue eyes went impossibly wide. She smelled like spring, the perfume the Queen's own *parfumerie* had created for her, a scent that lately haunted him, even in his sleep.

"I want another boat. Pronto. As in yesterday." He barked the words at her.

She was very quiet all of a sudden.

He didn't have the patience for this. "Speak."

"My organizer fell into the water on the way here with the ladies." She winced. "I'm a bad swimmer. I always get nervous around water. I should have—"

"I don't care about your organizer." The damn thing was her ever-present companion. Her nefarious plans for his life were no doubt in it. He'd been so disconcerted by her sudden appearance on the island that he hadn't even noticed it was missing. "Good riddance."

"My cell phone was tucked in the front."

He walked away from her before he said something he regretted. But called back, after a moment, "Will the guards be checking on us?"

"No." Her voice was small. A first. "They're supposed to avoid contact at all costs. They're to stay out of sight at all times. They won't be following you or anything. We, um, wanted to give you and the ladies privacy. The guards are only here to prevent the paparazzi from getting on the island if they get wind of your trip. For all intents and purposes, we're alone on an uninhabited island. That's the feel I was going for to foster a certain sense of..."

He glared, daring her to say the word "romance." That and true love were her favorite things. He'd tried to tell her in vain that there came a time when a grown woman should stop believing in fairy tales.

She closed her mouth without finishing the sentence, but she didn't fool him. She was hopeless. He turned from her again, to survey the shore. There had to be a way off.... He thought of something suddenly. She was very methodical about ruining his life. She was definitely the type to plan for contingencies.

He turned back to her. "What was the emergency plan? If I broke an arm, how would I have called for help?" He was a royal person. There was always a backup plan for unforeseen contingencies.

She was studying her feet, her sandals half sunk into the soft sand. "The Lady Adel had an emergency radio in her medical bag," she muttered.

"The red bag on her shoulder?" He distinctly remembered the bag. It was the one the doctor walked to the boat with.

Milda nodded weakly. "They'll send someone back for us as soon as they land." She looked after them, biting her bottom lip. The women and his speedboat were a dot over endless blue waves. "We'll be back at the palace before nightfall, I'm sure."

He wouldn't bet on it. "So basically, we could be stranded here for two whole weeks."

She still avoided his gaze. "I wanted to give you sufficient time to get comfortable with each other. I wanted to give the ladies enough time for their true colors to start showing. I only meant the best for you. For everybody."

A minute or so passed in uncomfortable silence, as they both contemplated the absurdity of the situation.

Then she finally looked him in the eye. "Have you camped before?"

He shook his head. "You?"

Her face looked pinched. "I have a demanding business that I run all by myself. I don't usually leave the city."

ROBERTO PUT ONE HAND above the other as he climbed the guard tower soundlessly. Below him, Sagro Prison was clouded in darkness, the island quiet. He gripped his sole weapon, the sharpened handle of a spoon, between his teeth. When he reached the top, he vaulted over and cut the guard's throat before the man could raise the alarm.

Had to be done.

There was no way around it. He lowered the body to the wooden boards, wiped the warm blood off his fingers and took the rifle, waited.

No siren sounded. He hadn't been detected. The

small Italian prison island was well guarded, but it was no high-security facility.

He lowered himself to the ground where José and Marco crouched in the shadows. He was the boss of the small team, though they were all hired hands, working for a new Colombian drug lord who was trying to break into the European market via Italy, among other places. Except that they'd been caught on this trip.

But he wouldn't rot in a dank cell, he thought as they crawled their way to the fence where the hole they'd painstakingly prepared and covered awaited. He wouldn't end up like his brother, Miguel, trapped in a Valtrian prison, then knifed by some local hotshot, dead two weeks before his release.

The drug lord they both worked for was trying to wiggle his way into the European market at multiple points of entry. Roberto had a cousin with a small team in Romania. He wondered how the bastard was faring. Hopefully better than this.

He was the first to reach the unfinished tunnel and head into the darkness. What little they'd left for tonight could be done in an hour. He dug with the flat rock they'd used to get this far, sweated, swore, but never stopped working. When at long last he'd reached the opening, only just clearing the fence, he tossed the stone aside then brushed the dirt from his eyes.

"Hurry," he said, speaking for the first time. This far out, nobody should be able to hear them.

He came up into a crouch, suddenly dizzy from hunger. All three of them were starving. Over the past few weeks, they'd had to bribe too many inmates with food to get what they needed for the escape. They could have just as easily beaten the bastards into obedience, but fights drew the guards' attention, and their small team needed to fly below the radar. They had to remain invisible. Then and now.

"Keep low to the ground," he said as they crossed the narrow slice of flat plateau. Then they unraveled their makeshift ropes, tied them together and lowered themselves down the rock face.

Roberto reached the beach first. When they were all down, they gathered as much driftwood as they could find, then they used the ropes to tie a raft together. Marco was the fastest with the knots, the son of a fisherman, pulling his weight for the first time. They swam out beyond the breakers before climbing on, then paddled with their shoes as best they could—which wasn't easy at all, as the waves were getting angry.

Real paddles would have helped, but they'd had no place to steal them from and no time to make them. Using their shoes required too much effort for too little result. The three were weak and exhausted, but they would work until their last breath.

They'd all sworn not to go back behind bars. They would either escape today or die trying.

"Get your ass moving." Roberto snarled at Marco when he slowed. The other apparently thought that having worked on the raft, he was now entitled to a break.

José shook his head and spit into the waves.

Marco got back to the paddling sullenly.

More trouble than he was worth. But they weren't out of danger yet. Roberto still needed him.

They needed to take the current to the mainland, land in an out-of-the-way spot and disappear deep into the country by morning, when their breakout would be discovered and law enforcement would start their coastal search.

But a storm was coming in and the waves didn't cooperate. The current seemed to be changing, taking them in another direction entirely.

Chapter Two

In hindsight, they shouldn't have wasted so much of the daylight on fighting.

Milda wrestled with the tent she'd dragged into the olive grove. She could see Prince Lazlo's outline a few hundred yards from her. She hadn't gone too far—was kind of scared of the darkness of the grove, the trees throwing shadows in the moonlight. The island was a nature preserve. Which meant wild animals for sure. She didn't want to think about that.

"I don't think that's how it goes," the prince called across the distance that separated them. He hadn't bothered bringing the second tent up from the beach.

"I got it," she answered over her shoulder. *Don't come over. Please, don't come over.*

If he helped her set up her tent, he would probably expect to sleep in it. With her. She couldn't handle that.

She glanced toward him. He rested—probably thinking dark, murderous thoughts about her—sitting up, his back against a tree, his shoulders outlined in the dim light. His body was lithe and powerful. He wasn't her favorite person in the world, but even she had to admit that he was incredibly handsome, with that debonair, devil-may-care attitude.

And beyond his good looks, he was intelligent as well. And a prince. At first, she'd been foolish enough to think that marrying him off would be easy. He'd certainly taught her better since.

She couldn't pin the man down, not for a second. Like seawater through a fishnet, he ran through her fingers over and over again. He could have made it all work. He had incredible focus when he chose. He owned one of the best speed car factories in Europe, built it himself from nothing but a dream. When he wanted something, he applied himself to the task until he achieved his goal. He could have made her job easy. Instead, he was doing the opposite. He didn't want anything to do with the Queen's plans, so he resisted Milda at every step.

Like the damn tent was doing at the moment.

She was going to figure this out. She gathered her last reserves and fitted the poles together at last. And felt triumphant.

Until she tried to get the structure in through the tent's door. She struggled for at least five minutes before she figured out it wasn't going to work this way. The poles were probably supposed to be snapped into place *inside* the tent. She stifled a groan and took it all apart.

"Need help?"

"Almost done. I'll be ready in a minute." She looked up to make sure he wasn't coming over.

But he was still sitting by the tree, his aristocratic profile outlined by the last of the light—a strong chin, straight nose and lips that looked as if they were carved from granite. Aside from the occasional debauchery— or even *with* that—he could have been one of those heroes of ancient Rome. She could definitely see him at the chariot races. She'd seen him at a modern racetrack, behind the wheel.

He was mesmerizing, had charisma in spades. No wonder women fell at his feet left and right. He certainly spent more time with them than pondering the duties of royalty. To the point that the media had taken to calling him The Rebel Prince. She filled her lungs with the salty sea air and turned away from him, giving the impertinent tent her full attention once again.

"I can't believe the women didn't send the boat back," she said after another five minutes of struggle.

"You know, the blonde looked familiar. I think I might have dated her in the past."

"You dated all three of them. With time being so tight, I wanted to go for certainty. A shortcut, you know? If you were attracted to them once, you could be attracted to them again."

Silence was the only answer.

"Right?" she asked, then immediately hated that she was second-guessing herself because of him. He was terrible for her self-confidence.

"'Heaven has no rage like love to hatred turned, nor

hell a fury like a woman scorned.'" He quoted William Congreve. "Better settle in for the full two weeks."

"They couldn't have been that mad at you. They agreed to another try."

"Could be they planned to kill me in the wilderness," he remarked dryly.

"What on earth have you done to them? No, never mind." The fact that he didn't even remember that he'd dated them gave her a clue. Plus his tirade on the beach that the ladies had overheard. She'd never dated him, and even she was about ready to strangle him and leave him in the wilderness for the vultures or whatever.

So maybe the ladies were somewhat justified in their fury. But leaving *her* stranded here with the prince was completely uncalled for. What harm had *she* done to anyone? She was doing the best she could, with everyone's best interests at heart. She was beginning to feel decidedly underappreciated. The least of her problems, all considered, when her whole world was threatening to come right down around her ears.

She was the last link in a long line of matchmakers. And the business hadn't been doing well for the past couple of years. If she failed, the family tradition would end with her. Her grandmother was probably rolling in her grave.

Poles miraculously snapping into place and holding the tent up from the inside at last distracted her from any further thoughts on what a disappointment she was turning out to be, compared to her more talented ancestors. The tent was standing. So there. That was something. She pulled herself straight proudly, grinning into the darkness. But then she tripped over the blanket she'd already tossed into the tent, not wanting it to get dirty or bugs to crawl inside, and fell with her full weight against one of the poles and the whole thing came apart all over again.

She could have howled with frustration. She didn't. She'd be damned if she'd lose control within hearing distance of the prince.

"Everything okay in there?" His voice dripped with mockery.

She climbed out on her hands and knees, the definition of undignified, stood and brushed herself off. "I decided to take it down. The air is too stifling in there."

The breeze coming off the ocean was balmy. She simply adjusted the waterproof material on the ground so the collapsed poles wouldn't be sticking her in the ribs, then lay down at last. There. She was perfectly content. Who needed the tent?

She was blissfully comfortable for five full minutes. Except maybe her neck. She adjusted a wadded-up blanket under her head just as a fat raindrop fell on her face. Wind ruffled her hair. Another raindrop followed.

She squeezed her eyes closed for a moment. She was *not* going to be defeated. She got up and tried to unfold the tent, to get in the middle somehow, sandwiched between protective layers. But the rain picked up long before she finished. And by the time she was settled

horizontally again, she realized she was lying in mud.
She cursed the prince under her breath.

She was so not supposed to be here.

He was supposed to be snug in his tent, with three
intelligent, great women, each with the pedigree and
temperament to become a fantastic princess. Why
couldn't he have just gone with that plan? What did he
have to complain about?

"It's raining," he said from a few feet away, his rich
baritone startling her.

She hadn't noticed him coming closer. "Cry me a
river," she muttered through clenched teeth. Or not.
They seemed to have more than enough water already.
She pulled her head into her cocoon. She'd been about
to get out of the mud, but she would pretend that everything was well if it killed her.

"The water running down the hillside will be heading this way," he observed with perfect aristocratic
nonchalance.

Maybe it would wash him away. That could be another solution to the problem. He couldn't very well
embarrass the monarchy any more if he disappeared,
could he?

But the water would wash her away, too, if she stayed
like this. She crawled out and was soaked to the skin
the next second. "You know how to set this thing up?"
She gestured toward the tent. If they had it anchored to
the ground, maybe the water would run around them.
The canvas was waterproof.

"Forget it." He grabbed the muddy, dripping tent,

tossed it over his shoulder and headed inland. His slight limp did nothing to detract from his powerful appearance.

She reluctantly followed him, carrying her soggy blanket. With the cloud cover thick now, and the rain coming down hard, she could see little, even with the flashlight. Once she thought she caught a moving shadow up ahead, but by the time she looked closer, it disappeared. Maybe one of the guards. Their gear and supplies had been dropped off on the other side of the island earlier. They'd probably gotten their tents up around the perimeter in time for the rain. Lucky them.

"Hello!" she called out. "We need help. We're here."

She waited, but no response came. Maybe they couldn't hear her. Or she'd only seen a bush moving in the wind.

Should have looked for the men this afternoon, instead of waiting for a boat by the beach and fighting, she thought as she pushed ahead, mud squishing in the front of her sandals and leaking out the back.

An hour of miserable marching got them to a rocky cliff wall. The famous Painted Rocks, not that she could make out any of the images in the rain and the dark. Soon blind luck brought them to an overhang that shielded them from most of the rain—if they sat far back in the rock's crevice and very close to each other.

He positioned the rolled-up tent in front of them to

block as much rain from that side as was possible. "You might want to take a minute and ponder where meddling gets you." His tone was lecturing. "I hope you're happy."

She would have been happy if she'd never heard of Prince Lazlo of Valtria. "I'm wet."

Her side was plastered to his. He was a full head taller than her, long limbs, muscles in all the right places. According to her research, he was an avid sportsman. Highly competitive, highly seductive, highly annoying. And, unfortunately, he was her cross to bear.

He relaxed his shoulders against the rock. His masculine scent of leather and motor oil reached her even through the rain. He'd probably spent his morning at the racetrack as usual.

She needed to think about something other than him, or she'd never relax enough to fall asleep. She gave that a valiant try for as long as she could. With her clothes soaked, she was cold to the bone, but she resisted moving even closer to him.

"First thing in the morning," she said when she could stay silent no longer, "we'll set up the tent and find our breakfast in the bags. I had the royal cook pack plenty of food for you and the women. If the rain stops, we can make a fire and signal for help."

He didn't say anything.

She thought of her small walk-up in Brooklyn, New York, that was mortgaged to the hilt. She couldn't fail here. If she pulled this off, she'd have enough money to throw some serious advertising out there and save her business.

The matchmakers' second rule was: *Win each client's goodwill. Only then can you work productively together.*

And she badly needed to keep this client.

Having to apologize, when she'd done nothing wrong, just about killed her, but she was willing to make that sacrifice. She had a month left to claim the exorbitant fee the Queen had promised her if she succeeded. She needed to gain Lazlo's cooperation and goodwill.

"I'm sorry. This isn't how I planned this."

Once again, he didn't respond.

But she did hear a sound, so she turned and saw his head resting on his shoulder, at what looked like an uncomfortable angle. He softly snored into her face.

And then he began leaning and sliding against her. She tried to move away, but somehow ended up on the ground, practically pinned under him.

"Your Highness!" She shoved him toward the edge of their shelter.

"Mmmm," he said without opening his eyes as he rolled onto his side.

Wedged between him and the rock, she had no room to pull away. She was practically spooning him. She had to get out of there. Except, the spot *was* comfortable. And his body heat was slowly drying her. And it was dark and scary out in the open.

She decided to stay put. For comfort's sake. She did her best to ignore that they were touching. Still, sleep didn't come easily.

Every noise the rain didn't drown out startled her. At one point, she could have sworn something big moved through the woods nearby. She could hear branches cracking, but as she waited with her breath held, nobody materialized from the darkness.

When she did sleep, her dreams were strange. She was with the prince on the beach, entangled, naked, waves licking their feet. He was kissing the sensitive skin of her neck, sending spirals of need through her body. In her dream, he wasn't the least annoying. The hands that at times molded metal at his auto factory, now caressed her breasts. She arched to press them into his palms as her nipples pebbled and begged for more. She tried to shift closer to him, but hit her head on rock.

What rock? They were making love in the surf on the beach. The sand was soft...except it wasn't. She was lying on rock. She slowly came awake.

The wetness on her feet was rain, not playful waves. She'd stuck them out of their shelter while she slept. Prince Lazlo had turned in the night, one arm under her head, his other hand cupping one of her breasts gently.

Heat rushed to her face. "Your Highness!" She squeaked the words as she tried to wiggle away from him, but the rock provided no space.

Firmly, she pushed the hand away. "Prince Lazlo, this is not—" She glanced up into his face.

His eyes were closed, his aristocratic mouth lax. He was still fast asleep.

ROBERTO SPIT SAND as he crawled out of the water, too exhausted to stand. The waves had broken their raft, taken their weapons—the makeshift knife as well as the guard's rifle—and separated the small team from each other.

He scanned the beach where he landed. Nothing but darkness and rain. He couldn't even tell if he'd reached the mainland or only another island. He rolled to his side and puked up some of the saltwater he'd swallowed. Then he flopped onto his back, letting the rain beat his face, unable to move another inch.

Endless hours passed. Each time the waves came up to lick his feet, he crawled a little higher. Then the rain stopped, the clouds cleared out and he could see two dark forms on the beach—either his men, driftwood or clumps of seaweed. He stood from the wet sand and staggered toward them, squinting his eyes to see.

He came across Marco first, shook him, pounded his back. When the man coughed up water at last, Roberto moved on to José. Then the three of them dragged themselves into the low brush that edged the narrow, rocky shoreline.

And for a while, they rested.

"Where the hell are we?" José spoke first, sounding

hoarse. Their throats were raw from swallowing too much seawater and vomiting.

"Close to a house, I hope." Marco shook wet sand from his curly black hair, looking the most chipper among the three. "A house full of food and women."

But instead of a house, the first thing they spotted once they got going was a tent, about a hundred meters or so inland.

Roberto signaled to the others, then picked up the largest stone within reach. They spread out and circled their target, caught the man inside the tent unawares. The guy had a weapon, but no time to use it before they smashed his skull in.

They stood over the body, breathing hard, adrenaline pumping, the scent of blood in their nostrils. They waited, listening. When they were sure that the man had been alone and nobody was coming, Roberto lit a lamp. He grinned as he looked around. His friends didn't call him a lucky bastard for nothing. "We have food, shelter and a gun again." Not a bad start to the day.

Marco was stuffing his face already. Crumbs rolled down his cleft chin as he made an animal-like sound.

"Give me that." Roberto snatched the rucksack away from him. He went through the contents, then tossed José a neatly packed sandwich, laying claim to the rest. He was the boss; he would hand out the food when and where it pleased him.

He took the largest sandwich for himself and bit into it with only slightly more restraint than Marco. They were safe for the moment, out of the weather and soon their bellies would be full. Nobody knew they were here. Probably nobody knew the man they'd killed was here, either. Surveying his gear, he looked like a lone hiker out camping.

But before they could settle in comfortably, a radio he hadn't noticed before came on, startling José into jumping.

The small device was hanging on a peg in a dark corner of the tent. "Station two, come in."

MORNING COULDN'T COME soon enough. Every inch of Milda's body ached. The only comfort she'd had over the long night was the heat radiating off the prince. Since their sole blanket was wet and muddy, she hadn't been able to use that for anything.

She looked around, rubbing the sleep from her eyes.

Lazlo was gone.

Thank God.

She ran her fingers through her hair. She wasn't one of those women who woke with perfect style and grace. At least she would have a little time to get herself together before she had to face him. A drowned rat had to look better than she did.

She ran her fingertips under her eyes to take off any smudged mascara. Not that she wanted to look attractive for the prince, but looking put together gave her self-confidence, and she had a feeling she would need all the self-confidence she could get when dealing with this client on this particular morning.

She crawled out from under the overhang, smoothed down her soiled, ruined clothes. Then the pictures that covered the rock wall caught her attention, the paintings that had been nothing but darker smudges in the dark night when they'd arrived here.

She'd heard of them when she'd been asking around for information on the island, trying to figure out whether it would be right for this project, but she'd had no idea what they depicted. She'd expected horses and buffalos like other nonhomicidal cavemen left all over Europe. She blanched now as she looked at scenes of wholesale murder. Blood splashed everywhere, necks cut, bellies opened. Shocked, she snatched her gaze away.

Good thing she hadn't seen the paintings the night before. They would have given her nightmares.

She stumbled away from the images, heading for the beach. The gear she'd put together, with professional help, included a number of toothbrushes and plenty of toothpaste. And breakfast. Most importantly, coffee. She'd have her first cup here, then another cup when they were back in the palace. They made the most amazing cappuccinos there, the frothy milk dusted with cinnamon.

She was one hundred percent certain that the boat would come for them today. The ladies had been angry. They'd made their point. The rescue team had to be on their way, if not already here.

But when she came out of the grove, she found the beach empty. No boat. No prince. And more alarmingly, no gear.

She swirled around. Maybe the boat had come and gone already. Was Lazlo mad enough at her to leave her like this?

"Your Highness?"

No response came, save the slapping of the waves.

"Your Highness?" she shouted more loudly as a twinge of panic squeezed her chest.

He couldn't just leave her. *He wouldn't,* she thought, openmouthed with shock, still scanning the empty beach. He was a gentleman.

In most situations.

But he did seem to have developed some sort of unreasonable dislike for her. Crazy, really, when one considered that she was here to help him. She was instrumental for his future happiness. That he wouldn't see that was most frustrating.

She was close to making him see reason, though. She was pretty sure. The two weeks with those ladies on this island would have done it. Once she got back to the palace, she needed to come up with another plan, and quickly.

She looked toward the mainland. The sunrise over the endless blue of the ocean filled the sky with pink. The scene was beautiful enough to take her breath away, but after a few moments her instincts prickled. Something didn't feel right. There was something…sinister in the air.

She shook her head. She thought that just because the prince was missing. Or maybe because she'd seen those dreadful pictures.

She ignored her prickling senses, although she'd always been proud of her keen intuition, a must in her line of work, a strong family trait. Having excellent intuition was essential in matching up couples.

Except, she'd never felt that sense of rightness when she'd considered a candidate for the prince. Not even with the three women she'd invited to the island, if she were to be honest, and the present moment seemed like the perfect time to face certain truths. She didn't feel that certain zing. Didn't see that image of the young couple leaving the church and rice flying. Didn't hear the proverbial wedding bells ring. Maybe that had been the problem to begin with.

Every time she'd looked at a woman and thought of her with the prince, the image brought only one thought to her mind: *wrong.* And she didn't have all that much time to keep looking.

She picked up a chunk of driftwood by her feet, walked to get another. Even a couple of larger pieces had washed onto the shore overnight. She could use smoke to signal for help. Not that she had any matches. Those were in the gear, which was presumably with the prince. Still, there was that Boy Scout thing of making a bow with a string and rubbing things against each other. She'd seen that once on TV. But before she could bring up in her mind's eye exactly how that was done, she saw a man bobbing in the water a few hundred feet from shore. He hadn't been there a moment before.

Then he was close enough for her to recognize Prince Lazlo. Relief flooded her. He was swimming for shore, pulling something with him. A green bag, dripping with water, she realized, when he was close enough to stand up and start walking.

Naked!

Her dreams rushed back. Her eyes went wide. Her throat constricted. Her heart put on a drum festival in the middle of her chest, the beat growing faster and faster, not slowing until he was out of the water enough so she could see that he was still wearing his underwear. *Phew.* Royal-blue boxer briefs.

Thank God for small mercies.

Not that the rest of his nakedness wasn't distracting enough. His upper torso was all lean muscles, drops of seawater running down his tanned skin. The rising sun was behind him, outlining his perfect shape.

Then her gaze dropped to the scars on his left leg.

She bit her lip. The skin was pulled together and a shade darker than the rest, white stripes going through the angry red here and there. He'd gotten trapped in a wreck at a racetrack crash and had been burned a few years back, an accident he so downplayed that, before now, she hadn't even been aware of the extent of his injuries. From what she was seeing now, he must have suffered horribly. That he was even walking had to be a miracle.

His stunning scars didn't detract anything from his

absolute masculine beauty. If anything, they gave him an edge that she imagined drew women even more. His physique drew *her,* for love's sake, and he was the last man on earth she would have ever been seriously interested in.

The first rule of matchmaking was: *Do not get involved with a client under any circumstances.*

He pulled his left hand through his dark hair to get it out of his eyes, shaking the bag with his other hand to dislodge a long strand of seaweed. His breathing was labored, as if he'd been swimming for a long time.

"What are you doing?" Had he tried to swim off the island with some of their supplies? That made no sense whatsoever.

"Saving the remains of our gear."

Her feet rooted to the spot. For a second, she couldn't move, couldn't speak. She couldn't really understand. "But—"

"The storm last night whipped up the waves. They ran farther up the beach than usual." He came over and lowered the bag to the ground at his feet.

"It's all gone?" She stared at him, still barely comprehending.

He nodded.

Disaster. Absolute disaster was all she could think.

"Can you go back for the rest?" She wasn't the best of swimmers.

He dropped to the sand, panting, stretching his muscular legs in front of him. "I've been at it for the last two hours. Everything else must have been carried far out to sea."

Her legs wouldn't hold her up. She sank down across the bag from him.

He opened the bag and pulled out ten jars of caviar— five red, five black—a dozen scented candles and a half-dozen bottles of champagne carefully wrapped in bubble bags.

She waited for more, then could have cried as he tossed the empty bag aside. She pulled it to herself and went through it again. And in one of the front pockets she found waterproof matches, one box of the two dozen she'd ordered from a camping supply store.

"Breakfast?" He held out a jar of caviar, the top already twisted off.

"No thanks." Her stomach was in a knot. No way could she put anything into it.

He shrugged and scooped some tiny, shiny, pearl-like beluga roe into his mouth. When he finished off the jar, he washed the food down with champagne. Then he lay back on the sand, his face to the sky, suddenly grinning while she did her best not to hyperventilate.

"How can you be happy at a moment like this?" she snapped at him.

He came up on one elbow—biceps bulging all over the place—and pinned her with those wicked dark eyes of his. "I have two weeks without you being able to do anything to get me married."

He was insufferable.

"You're missing your race," she pointed out, just to needle him.

He shrugged. "A little freedom might just be worth it."

She didn't say anything for a while, then, "We should light a fire and send smoke signals."

He looked over the meager pile of driftwood she'd collected. "If the guards are on the other side of the island, they won't see it. Better we save the wood for tonight to keep warm. It has to dry before we can light it anyway."

She couldn't bear the thought of another night. Under those rocks. With the prince. "The boat will come."

"Maybe. But we need a plan B."

"We should find another shelter. And we should go and find fresh water before the day gets too hot." They were in the Mediterranean. There was plenty of heat; his shorts were half-dry already. And they needed to do *something*. Sprawled on the sand, he looked like he was on vacation. He gestured toward the champagne bottles.

"That won't prevent dehydration. In fact, alcohol speeds it." Lady Szilvia, the survival expert, had told her that when she'd given advice about what to bring. And Milda had made sure to pack plenty of water. Except, those plastic bottles were now bobbing somewhere in the sea. "We need fresh water."

"We have nothing to put it in until we drink the champagne."

She hated that he had a point. "We could pour the champagne out."

He seemed to consider that, but then he said, "On the off chance that we might be here awhile without much food, we could need those calories."

She grabbed the bottle from him.

The bubbles tickled down her throat deliciously. After the ninth or tenth sip, she felt some of the tension leaving her body. "There." She took another gulp, then tossed the empty bottle onto the sand in front of him.

He picked it up with an amused look, stood and held out his hand.

She ignored him.

He walked to the bushes and came back with his clothes, a bundle she hadn't seen there in her frenetic search for him. He dressed, then slipped the waterproof matches into his pocket, packed everything else back into the bag before slinging it over his shoulder. "Let's stash this under the overhang before we go for a stroll. Wouldn't want to lose it again."

She walked after him, trying not to look at him too much. The only man she'd ever known who managed to swagger with a limp. Who did he think he was, John Wayne?

They crossed the wild olive grove, the tangy scent of the trees heavy in the air. That odd feeling returned to her again, a premonition she couldn't put her finger on, a sense of unease. Probably because they were going back to those gruesome rocks.

"So, what are those paintings about? I didn't realize Valtria's past was that bloodthirsty."

"It's not. The island was used by Etruscan priests back in the day, for their human sacrifices. Valtrians came here much later."

A shiver ran down her spine as she thought how many men and women must have died on the island over the centuries. Which would explain the bad vibes she'd been getting. By being here, they were probably disturbing some ancient burial grounds.

She tried not to look at the rock paintings as they emptied the bag and secured their meager supplies. Then they were finally heading for higher ground. The hillside wasn't too steep, solid rock in places, brittle shale in others where she had to watch her step in order not to slip. Here and there, thick woods appeared, especially close to the top, but on the bottom, the wild groves were sparse with plenty of open areas between them.

"Is there fresh water here, do you know?" She did her best to keep up with him. He was pretty fast, even with the limp.

She was wearing sandals. Only two-inch heels, but still... She hadn't planned on staying on the island beyond explaining the camping trip to Lazlo and introducing him to the ladies. She'd planned on being back at the palace by dinner, at the latest. At least she'd had the good sense to wear summer slacks, and brought a sweater in case the wind was too much on the boat ride over.

"There's a stream."

"Do you know where?"

"No idea. I was only here once, when I was a kid."

The higher they went, the denser the vegetation became.

"Wild animals?" She remembered last night's worry.

"Rabbits and foxes."

At least that was reassuring.

They walked until noon but found nothing. "We should switch tactics and walk the perimeter of the island," Lazlo recommended. "Even if the guards keep out of our way, we should be able to find one of their tents. We'd be set for supplies at least."

Exactly. Why didn't she think of that earlier? Had to be the champagne.

Downhill was a lot easier than up. She did slip a couple of times, but he always caught her easily. She didn't like when they were touching. He was the type of man a woman couldn't help but be aware of physically.

Several hours passed as they walked, keeping as much as possible to the shade of the trees. Her stomach growled.

"Should have brought some food and champagne," Lazlo said. "Sorry."

"We didn't know it would take this long."

It had to be midafternoon by the time he spotted the tent under a clump of trees and pointed it out to her.

She was so tired she could barely walk, but she broke into a run.

"Hello, we need help." She pushed through the open flap, relieved that the nightmare was over.

Then reeled back, was caught against Lazlo's wide chest. He swore softly, put his arms around her, tried to pull her back. But she couldn't move, couldn't take her eyes off the sight in front of her.

Inside the tent was the dead body of one of the guards. Lying in a pool of blood, stripped naked. A sight that eerily echoed the rock paintings.

Chapter Three

Lazlo searched for a weapon, but Ben's gun was gone. So was his radio.

"For love's sake." The mumbled words came through as Milda cupped her hands in front of her mouth. Tears filled her eyes, which were round with shock.

He looked outside. The woods seemed empty, the birds trilling in the air, no sign that anyone might be lurking in the bushes. He waited anyway, watching for any movement, listening for any sound that didn't belong. When he was certain that they were alone, he pulled the tent flap closed behind them.

"We'll be fine. I think we're alone for now. As soon as I take care of Ben, we should grab whatever we can use, then get out of here."

The young guard had only been working at the palace for a little over a year. He was a fine polo player and an antique car enthusiast. They'd had some conversations. Yesterday wasn't the first time the man had been assigned to Lazlo's personal detail.

He wrapped the man in his sleeping bag, then carried

him outside, to a spot they'd passed on their way to the tent. A storm had uprooted an ancient olive tree, leaving a giant hole in the ground. He laid Ben in the hole, then went back for the short camping shovel he'd seen in the tent's corner.

Milda still stood in the same spot, looking at the pool of blood, her arms folded in front of her, her face ashen.

He handed her their bag, the one he'd salvaged from the sea and brought along in case they found anything suitable to eat. "You should start packing." She needed a distraction.

He waited until her eyes focused on him at last and she gave a dazed nod.

Burying Ben took a fraction of the time it would have if Lazlo had to dig a hole, but still much longer than he preferred. He said a prayer as best he could, and marked the grave. His people would be back for the body, but he had no idea how many days that would take. First he had to get off the island. In the meantime, he didn't want to leave the guard to the birds and the foxes.

He wished he'd at least found Ben's radio so he could figure out where Vince, the other guard, was. Probably camping on one of the island's high points. If Ben took the shore, the other would take the highest lookout point. That would make the most sense.

Back in the tent, Milda was still standing and staring. He put a blanket in the bag she held. And he realized there wasn't much more to take. He tossed aside a pair of boots that wouldn't fit either of them. Then grabbed three books, highbrow literary novels. If nothing else, they could use the paper to start a fire.

A couple of plastic bags littered the tent's floor. He took those. Might come in handy for something. He rechecked the small tent, hoping for more, but whoever had killed Ben had cleared the place out fairly well.

At least they had their own tent back at Painted Rock. The bottom panel of this one was soaked with blood. He took the duffel bag from Milda and slung it over his shoulder. "Ready?"

For the first time ever, he hated that she was quiet. She was clearly rattled, but he couldn't give her time to gather herself. They had to get moving.

He turned to look around the campsite one last time before heading out. The grass had been trampled on and flattened. Ben had probably done a fair share of that. So had Lazlo and Milda for that matter. He could see cracked twigs and the soil disturbed here and there, a faint path leading into the woods, but couldn't tell how long it had been since anyone had walked that way, or whether it had been Ben or his killer.

Maybe Miklos or Arpad could have done better. They were the best hunters among the royal brothers. They went after elk and even bear. The most Lazlo ever did was join in the occasional fox hunt, which he did for the sake of riding. Nobody noticed his limp on a horse. He played polo for the same reason. But real sport, for him, began and ended on the racetrack.

"Who would do this?" Milda's voice trembled,

her blue eyes searching his face as she waited for an answer.

"Maybe a fugitive. Or someone who got shipwrecked and went crazy."

The island was supposed to be uninhabited. Only the odd ornithologist visited now and then, usually during the spring or fall, when migrating birds stopped to rest here. And even the ornithologists needed a royal permit to conduct their observations.

She rubbed her hands up and down her slender, bare arms. She didn't have that stunning cover model look that normally tended to capture his imagination, but she did have an earthy sort of wholesome thing going on. What they called the "girl next door" look, he supposed, and he kind of knew what that meant, although there were no girls next door to where he lived. The royal palace stood alone on Palace Hill.

At the moment, she looked frightened and fragile, but he'd fought against that steel core of hers too many times these past few months to forget that it was there. She kept looking back toward the clearing, slowing her steps each time.

He took her by the hand and led her deeper into the woods. "We need to keep moving. Whoever did this might come back."

She didn't pull away. "What about the other guard?" She seemed completely subdued. Downright meek.

He warned himself not to get used to that. She was scared, *not* reformed. "We'll find him. Don't worry about it."

She shivered. He almost pulled her closer on reflex, but he caught himself in time. Of all the women he knew, she was the one who would need comfort from a man the least. She was no shrinking violet. He had likened her to a she-dragon several times in the past, in fact.

She'd never shown an ounce of respect for his title. Every chance she got, she stood up to him. She was incredibly pushy. And when he'd tried to seduce her upon arrival, to distract her from her matchmaking, she'd resisted. Not that he was so vain that it would have bothered him. But still.

Yet the pluck now seemed to have gone right out of her. He watched her suspiciously. *Could be some new trap.* She was endlessly inventive when it came to tricking him into all sorts of things that pushed him closer to the shackles of matrimony. But try as he might, he couldn't figure out how acting meek now would benefit her.

Maybe she'd never seen a dead body before. Plus, she was a city girl. The whole nature thing was probably wearing her down, too. That thought cheered him up, so he spent some time on it. *Milda Milas subdued and malleable. Paradise at last!*

He mercilessly squashed whatever protective instincts her unusual mood brought out in him.

"I'm hungry," she said after a while, her voice still shaky. "Could we go back for food?"

She'd had nothing for breakfast but champagne.

"I'm afraid our stash of caviar will have to wait. We

need to find Vince. We need weapons and a way to communicate with the outside world."

"We can't keep walking if we don't eat." She pulled her hand from his.

To his regret, her subdued state seemed to be coming to an end. He stopped and faced her. "A person can go for days without food. You can't go nearly as long with a knife between your shoulder blades."

She paled.

Regretting his words, he drew a slow breath. "We'll come across something."

And a little while later, they did. They stopped and lunched on wild oranges that were small but plentiful on this side of the hill. The sweet juice was just the right thing to quench their thirst, while the pulp was enough to make them feel like their bellies weren't empty.

They were spending time together almost companionably. It was the strangest thing.

She sat cross-legged, her slim back against a tree, peeled her fourth orange with dainty fingers and bit in. A drop rolled down her chin before she caught it. Her lips were moist and shiny, like rubies in the noon light.

A honeybee buzzed by, circled her head. With her hair all wild, she looked like some woodland fairy. In the right light, from the right angle, she was almost pretty, he realized with some surprise. Yes, *definitely* pretty. He might have noticed it before if he weren't always trying to evade her.

The bee circled again. She swatted it away, but within

a few seconds another came by. And another. Coming from the same direction.

He pushed to his feet and walked that way, if for no other reason than because his sudden awareness of the woman, who'd been nothing but a thorn under his skin thus far, unsettled him. At the edge of the grove he found a hollow tree.

"Where are you going?" she called after him.

"For honey. Stay where you are."

He broke off a young branch, stripped the leaves then the bark with his fingernails and crept up to the tree. Very slowly he reached up and dipped the branch inside; very slowly, he pulled it out. When wild honey dripped to the ground, he grinned.

He carefully walked the loot back to Milda, who looked ready to run if they were attacked by the bees, but all they did was buzz around him. Still, a few seconds passed before she focused on the honey. But once she did, he didn't have to offer it twice. He held the branch. She put a hand next to his to steady it. Then she tilted her mouth up, and her small, pink tongue darted out to lick the sweet goo.

His groin tightened. A most unexpected reaction that jolted him.

Not possible. Not now. Not with *this* woman.

But his resolve weakened as her eyelids fluttered closed for a second and she gave a soft moan. Then she looked up at him with those dusky blue eyes. "This is beyond good. Thank you. I needed this."

He cleared his throat to respond. But as she went

back to her snacking, he forgot what he was about to say. Lost track of time there for a second.

Until she looked up at him again, sheepishly. "I ate it all."

He blinked hard and tossed the branch to the ground. He needed to snap out of it. They needed to get going and find the guard, make contact with the mainland. Instead, he hesitated.

She winced as she shot him a guilty look. "I was so hungry I wasn't even thinking."

A drop of wild honey still glistened on her lips.

He liked full, pouty lips. Hers were on the thin side and crooked when she smiled. Not particularly seductive. Nobody was more surprised than he when he leaned in.

She was soft and sweet; her mouth fitted his to perfection. He felt his body harden in a split second, his reaction disproportionate to the minor amount of bodily contact between them. He barely brushed his lips across hers, but he felt the impact all the way to his toes.

For a moment so brief that he might have imagined it, she went with the flow. Then she was pushing against him. He pulled away, searching her stunned face, trying to gather his scattered thoughts.

Her lips moved but no sound came out. She was probably looking for the words with which to best berate him.

And he definitely deserved that. What in hell had he been thinking? Her life mission was to make him miserable. Normally, he couldn't stand the sight of her.

He pulled his spine straight and stepped back, standing stiff and still.

And with that symbolic distance between them, whatever craziness had possessed him disappeared. He didn't know where it had come from, but he did know one thing for sure: under no circumstances would he ever touch this woman again. She was nothing but trouble.

"I—" She swallowed. "We shouldn't be doing this. You are—" She paused. "I am—" She made a soft noise of frustration. "We can't do this again."

For the first time they were in agreement. That threw him even more thoroughly off balance.

It wasn't right.

He weighed the issue at hand, his gaze straying to those ruby lips that were pressed into a severe, angry line. Then the solution came to him and he flashed the woman his most wicked grin. "I think we're definitely going to do this again."

And watched her sputter with outrage. Her magnificent breasts heaved with barely suppressed indignation. Her eyes were throwing thunderbolts.

Which made him relax. Everything was back to normal between them again.

ROBERTO STOLE FORWARD, breathing hard from the effort, wiping the sweat that ran into his eyes as he looked up. The top of the hill seemed a lot closer now than the last time he'd stopped for a breather. He needed high ground to see if his hunch was right and they were on an island. He wanted to know how many houses there were.

José and Marco had gone off in different directions to get the lay of the land. The three of them were to meet back in a couple of hours at the rocky beach where they'd landed.

Then Roberto reached the top at last, and could finally look around. An island, definitely. With no houses. A fishing boat passed by slowly to the north. He could see the mainland in the distance, a strip of gray at the edge of the azure.

They'd reached an uninhabited island, with two hikers. One now—whoever had spoken on that radio. Roberto scratched the stubble on his chin. Still, one was enough to spot them, to report them to the police. If they took that guy out, the island would be theirs for a few days, until people came to look for the hikers. A couple of days would be enough to recover from their near drowning. They needed rest and food to regain their strength before they made their way to the mainland. The first hiker had a considerable stash of food. And his buddy probably had supplies of his own.

The hikers had to have a boat, too, he figured. Although, so far he hadn't been able to spot it. But, between the three of them, they should be able to find the damn thing sooner or later.

He swept the vista again and thought he saw the tip of a tent by the edge of the trees to the north. He glanced at the watch he'd gotten off the first hiker. Plenty of time. And he could definitely handle one man.

He made his way down the hill, keeping the dead hiker's knife close at hand. Looked like military issue, but the man hadn't been in uniform, although his black clothes did have some sort of coat of arms on them. Maybe the two men were government surveyors of some sort.

But then, where was their equipment?

Maybe they were gamekeepers, here to keep hunters and fishermen off the island.

Roberto didn't much care one way or the other. One of them was dead, and the other was about to join his buddy.

A good hour passed before he reached the tent. He considered the gun for a second, but then grabbed the knife. With the fishing boat that close to the island, he couldn't risk someone hearing a shot.

He snuck up to the tent, burst through the flap, found the inside empty. But just then, a noise came from behind him.

MILDA MOVED ACROSS the rocky ground as if the devil was after her. They had to find the other guard. There was a killer on the island. They had no food or water, and she was getting weaker by the minute. The sooner they got to a radio the better. But that wasn't the only reason for her to hurry.

The prince had kissed her. Kind of.

Tasted her. Barely.

She'd blown the whole thing way out of proportion. She'd acted as if she'd never been kissed before. Which she had. On a few occasions. But she'd never felt that lightning of heat and need, the weakening of the knees that Lazlo's barely-there kiss had caused.

What did he kiss her for?

She pushed harder, needing to stay ahead of him and keep some distance between them.

His lips had been firm and warm and felt as good as they had in her dreams, for love's sake.

Thank God, she'd found the strength to pull away before she could completely embarrass herself. And that ridiculous threat of him wanting to do it again! She'd been marching forward in silence, rounding the island in search of the other guard ever since.

She kept going, trying to forget the kiss, trying to forget the dead guard. She had a feeling she wouldn't be able to do either. But at the very least, she had to find a way to put both out of her mind, because she had to function to stay alive.

In her haste to get away from him, she'd gotten quite a bit ahead of the prince. The sound of rolling rocks somewhere ahead of her on the hillside reached her. She couldn't see through the trees.

Could be a wild animal.

Or could be the other guard.

Or could be the killer.

She slowed, but it was too late. Since her eyes were on the woods, she didn't notice the crevasse in front of her, half covered by lush, green vines. She stepped onto the leaves, and her feet touched air. She tumbled, down, down, down, the earth swallowing her startled cry....

which ended abruptly when hitting bottom pushed the air from her lungs.

Just as well. Alerting the killer to her whereabouts was the last thing she needed.

Every part of her was sore as she stood. There were leaves in her hair and dirt on her face. Her arm stung where she'd scraped off the skin. She flexed her limbs. At least nothing felt broken.

The hole was as narrow as it was deep, probably carved by water running down the hill.

Lazlo was peering down from the mouth of the hole. "Are you okay?"

"Just get me out of here." She didn't even want to think of the snakes and spiders that were probably down there with her. Luckily, there was hardly any light filtering down to the bottom, so she couldn't see anything that would have started her screaming.

She looked up. The prince seemed to be lying down. He lowered his arm, but his hand remained out of reach. He moved forward and leaned into the hole up to his waist but, even like this, several inches still separated them.

"Can you climb up the side?" he asked.

She felt around and made contact with square stones. Maybe the hole hadn't been created by water after all. Could be that she'd fallen into an old well. She tried to climb, but the stones were covered with slippery moss and she slid back immediately. She grabbed on to some roots to support her weight, but that didn't work for long either. She jumped.

The very tips of their fingers touched.

She thudded back to the ground, panic flashing through her as dry branches snapped under her feet.

What if he couldn't pull her out of here?

Her heart beat in her throat as he disappeared from the mouth of the hole. What if he left her?

He'd disliked her from the get-go. He considered her a nuisance. She'd tricked him onto the island in the first place. It seemed unlikely that he would have forgotten that.

"Please, don't leave—" She dodged the duffel bag coming down on top of her. "What—" She scampered aside as he jumped in, nearly knocking her off her feet. "What are you doing?" Panic switched to anger. Didn't he think at all? Now they would both be trapped down here.

Instead of answering, he put a hand over her mouth and whispered into her ear, "Somebody's coming."

After a startled moment, she nodded.

He let her mouth go, but didn't step away. No place to go without rubbing against the dirt wall, roots sticking out and spiderwebs and God knew what else. Scorpions, probably. There were plenty of those on most Mediterranean islands.

But it was hard to think of the local flora and fauna when the tips of her breasts were touching his chest. The hollow of his throat was inches from her mouth. If there were more light, she could probably see his pulse beating there. She could feel his breath fanning her hair.

Last night, even being cold, wet and miserable, she'd been aware of his body lying next to hers. And then today, he'd kissed her. Now she knew how his mouth felt on hers. Their close proximity took the awareness to a whole new level.

Every time she took a breath, her breasts moved and her nipples rubbed against his chest. Heat shot through her and pooled low in her belly, as tension built. She pressed closer to him to stop the rubbing, not sure she'd improved the situation. Now her breasts were flattened against him. He put an arm around her.

She was about ready to jump out of her skin when she heard footsteps above.

They stood motionless, barely daring to breathe. Her fingers curved around Lazlo's arm. The footsteps neared, stopped. A moment passed before whoever it was began to walk away.

Then they could no longer hear him.

And with some of that acute fear gone, her full focus was back on Lazlo, against whose hard body she was plastered.

His head dipped forward.

"Don't kiss me again," she protested, then grew mortified when she realized that hadn't been his intention.

He was simply positioning himself to reach something at his back. "I haven't really kissed you yet." His voice turned low and wicked. "I was just tasting the honey."

He flipped on the flashlight and panned the sides

of the hole. Since she didn't want to look into his eyes, she kept her gaze on the walls instead.

Roughly carved, square stones peeked from the dirt here and there, their prison definitely a manmade structure. One spider that was big enough to give her nightmares for the rest of her days moved into a large crack between two rocks. She scooted closer to Lazlo, which hardly seemed possible.

He directed the light at their feet.

They were standing on old bones, most covered with moss. She couldn't even see the ground. Human, she realized when she spotted a yellowish jawbone. And about climbed the prince. *Yuck. Yuck, yuck, yuck. Oh, gross.*

"I'm guessing those would be the Etruscan sacrifices." Lazlo wasn't the least rattled. He gently peeled her off him, then bent his knees. "Get on my shoulders."

She didn't argue, for once, eager to get out any way she could. The maneuver began awkwardly, but then she thought, *to hell with it,* and grabbed on to his shoulders, stepped on his bent knee then worked herself up until she was standing with her feet next to his ears. She was just about to pop her head out of the hole when she heard a surprised shout. A man, close by.

"That was Vincent," Lazlo said beneath her. "Hurry."

She took a quick peek. Nobody within sight. She crawled out, kicking some dirt and small rocks back at Lazlo as she went. She whispered a low "Sorry."

Then Lazlo was next to her before she even began worrying about how to pull him up. He had more upper body strength than she did, she supposed. Probably could hang on to the roots more easily. He even had the bag with him.

Her gaze swept the area again as she stood. And what she saw made her heart beat faster. "Look."

A white fishing boat sliced the waves in the distance.

She waved her arms madly over her head.

"They can't see us," Lazlo said, his lips tightening. "But if we had a gun, they might hear the shots."

"We have to find Vincent."

He nodded. "Quickly."

The boat was heading away from the island.

He immediately took off in the direction of the shout, keeping himself between her and possible danger.

They walked too slowly, constrained by both the need to stay silent and the mess of vines and bushes. An eternity seemed to pass and they still couldn't hear or see the man they were seeking.

Then he stopped and swore under his breath, motioned for her to get down, behind the cover of a tree. She immediately obeyed, foreboding making her chest heavy. He crept forward, inch by inch, toward a prone body on the ground.

The black fatigues belonged to the royal guard.

Her heart lurched into a faster rhythm.

Lazlo stopped and listened. Waited. "Vincent," he

whispered after a while, and motioned for her to stay where she was while he checked out the body.

Despite the heat, she shivered behind the tree. Another body. Deep down she knew that Vincent was dead. But this time, she got herself together faster.

THIS TIME, SHE HELPED LAZLO bury the man with a knife wound in the back, and mark the grave. Then they tried to backtrack to the guard's tent, in the hope that they would find either his weapon or his radio—neither of which were with him—or at least some food for later.

"The boat is gone." She looked out over the sea when they were back at the well again.

"If there was one, there'll be others," Lazlo said.

What he didn't mention, probably to keep her spirits up, was that even if a boat did come sufficiently close to the island, they had no way of gaining the crew's attention. Her small pile of driftwood by the beach was nothing. They definitely needed to work more on that later.

But it was dusk by the time they found Vincent's campsite. His supplies were missing. At least his tent was on sandy soil, which provided some clues.

Lazlo inspected the ground carefully. "The prints are from three different sets of shoes. Only one would be Vincent's."

The implication wasn't lost on her. A shiver ran down her spine. "The killer is not alone."

"And they have weapons. Two guns now, at least. Knives."

"We could hide."

"Don't count on it. I don't know why these people are on the island, but something tells me they want the place for themselves. If they saw us land yesterday, they know that we're here. Sooner or later, we'll meet up with them. And when we do, it's either them or us," he said, laying it on the line.

Her mouth was as dry as the sand under their feet. She felt a new wave of panic wash over her, but then she steeled herself. She was no shrinking violet. She was a New Yorker. "Them," she said, without hesitation. "We need to get them before they get us." Not that she had the faintest idea how to go about that.

Prince Lazlo looked surprised for a moment. But then, for the first time perhaps ever, he flashed her a pleased grin. "That's my spunky matchmaker."

"Marital consultant," she corrected him, out of habit.

He good-naturedly nodded. "We'll go back to the Painted Rocks to spend the night there. We'll gather some oranges on the way."

"I really hate that place. The paintings give me the creeps."

"We need that caviar, and the champagne wouldn't be bad, either. If we emptied another bottle, we'd have two for water when we finally find that stream."

"Maybe we'll come across it on the way back." Just

their luck that they would find a hidden well with an ancient stack of bones, but they couldn't find water.

"There's something eerie about this island. Do you feel it?"

One aristocratic eyebrow slid up his forehead. "You should have thought of that before you booked me on a two-week pleasure trip here with three husband-hungry women."

"I was running out of time. It made me desperate."

He gave her a narrow-eyed look.

"I do feel bad about it. In hindsight," she confessed.

"You should. You're messing with my life. But I'm willing to let it go for now. We'll worry about that when we get back to the palace."

"I make most of my clients very happy." She prided herself on that. "Usually, they even invite me to their wedding. One couple asked me to be godmother to their little boy. And another named their girl after me." She didn't want him to think that she was a total loser.

"I dare say that's not going to happen with me, Milda. Why don't you quit now? Cut your losses."

"I need this assignment too badly to quit."

He gave her a questioning look, but she wouldn't elaborate. "Maybe you've been less than thrilled with me until now, but when I find you that perfect partner, you'll be happy. You'll be grateful that I tried so hard."

"And off she goes, down the track." He shook his head and turned to go, muttering a few words under his breath. Then he said, "I'll go first. I want you to follow at a distance. That way, if we run into anyone and they catch me, you'll have a chance to escape."

She wouldn't have thought of that, but it made sense, although she wasn't sure why a prince would risk his life for a commoner, a commoner who wasn't even one of his subjects. Self-sacrifice from Prince Lazlo? Not the image the media had painted of him, for sure. But maybe there was more to him than being a speed-obsessed, spoiled, womanizing prince.

They reached the wild orange grove at twilight, filled the bag and their shirts with fruit that provided both nourishment and moisture. But in all their wandering, they hadn't found any signs of the stream. Whatever else they did, the next day they had to find fresh water.

They ate more honey, then moved on. Night fell, clouds soon drifting in to cover the moon. She followed him, listening for the soft noises he made, nearly indiscernible from the noises of the forest. He was far enough ahead so that the sound his feet made on the ground barely reached her.

The footsteps she heard suddenly from behind were much louder, much closer.

Chapter Four

There were more people on the island. Roberto swore. He'd wondered about that, and followed the second hiker for a while this afternoon, hoping the man might lead them to others, if there were any. But the guy had noticed him and Roberto had to take him out. Not an easy task. For someone taken by surprise, he had put up a surprisingly good defense. Still, he wasn't a match for Roberto's prison brawl skills, skills that had taken his decades-long street fighting experience to a whole new level.

By the time Roberto got back to the man's tent, Marco had been there, rifling through the supplies.

They'd gathered up what they needed, then went to meet up with José. Then the three of them decided to bring one of the dead men's tents over and set it up, leaving behind the cave José had discovered high up the hillside. They'd spent the previous night in that place, grateful to be out of the rain. It was more easily defensible than a tent, should anyone come to the island to look for them; but the swarm of bats that returned from their night hunt at dawn had scared them.

So they'd set up the tent, then ate and rested. When twilight fell, José went on guard duty and Marco went to sleep. But Roberto was restless. He'd decided on a walk in the woods instead. And heard a man say something. A woman answered. Then they fell silent as they separated and passed through the forest. More hikers? For an uninhabited island, the place sure seemed popular.

He gripped his knife, moved closer to the woman. Then a branch snapped under his feet, and he swore silently, spotting her at last. She stopped and looked back. He remained still, in the shadow of a leafy bush. She didn't see him, and she turned back to the path.

He moved closer, watching every step, until he was close enough to lunge. He knew where the knife had to go, to hold her mouth shut so she couldn't give warning.

But as he got ready to make his move, the man strode into sight.

"Don't stay too far back. I don't want to lose you."

"I heard something," she said.

The man peered into the woods behind her.

Roberto held his breath. They were two meters from each other, impossible to miss, but for the thick vegetation and the dark of the night. The tree canopy was low, but sufficient to block out most of the moon above.

The man peered into the deep shadows, then, after a moment, shrugged. "The night noises of the forest, I'm sure. We should keep going, we're almost there."

They walked off together and soon came to the end of the woods, entering a flat and open area, where Roberto could no longer follow them unseen.

But at least, now he knew that they were here. He and his team had more work ahead of them before the island would truly be theirs.

MILDA WAS BONE TIRED by the time they reached the Painted Rocks, but she hadn't complained. She simply pushed forward and did what needed to be done. Most women Lazlo knew would have been whining for a limousine by now, to take them back to their five-star hotel.

Somehow, she managed to look more attractive without makeup and with smudges on her face, her hair all mussed. Spending the day with her, just trying to survive, was starkly different from the way they normally spent time together—her harping on him to get married and he trying to get away. Their trek across the island hadn't been bad. She'd been scared out of her wits, but held herself together. She even helped pick oranges, had offered several times to carry their bag. Had assisted in burying Vincent.

He was beginning to appreciate her company. And as much as he told himself that kissing her again would be a considerable mistake, truth was, he wouldn't have minded tasting her lips one more time, honey or no honey.

He shook his head.

Absolutely not. Not this woman.

When he'd threatened her with more kisses, he'd only said that to keep her off-kilter. He hadn't meant any of that. Definitely *not*.

Except, he was beginning to rethink the issue, once they were snuggled together for warmth under the overhang again. They hadn't dared to erect their tent. The tents of both guards had been discovered by the killers. He figured it'd be better if their shelter wasn't visible from a distance.

"We need to find water tomorrow," she said as she lay stiffly next to him.

"We'll have to be careful. If the men who killed Ben and Vincent have been living on the island for a while, they probably know the creek and use it."

She stilled. "I just thought of something."

He waited.

"When I first got the idea for your hike with the ladies, I talked with the chief of palace security."

"And he didn't talk you out of it? I'm disappointed in the man." How many people had a hand in setting him up? The sense of betrayal returned.

"He didn't know the details, just that I might be planning an event here that might involve some of the princes."

At least the man wasn't laughing behind his back.

"The point is," Milda went on, "that he sent a team to make sure the island would be a safe location for my plans. They didn't find anyone here."

"When was that?"

"Three weeks ago. But your brother Miklos also sent a group of his men the morning before our arrival, to do another sweep. He gave me the all clear."

"He should have given me a warning instead." He had a lot to say to his brothers once he was back at the palace.

"So these men must have come here after us. Maybe during the storm that first night."

"Could be their boat capsized near the island. But they are no fishermen in distress. These are killers." Again, all he could think of was the Freedom Council. More likely than the capsized boat with a couple of murderers inside, was that the men were here with a purpose, and that purpose was to kill him.

Milda had fallen silent. He decided to drop the topic. He had no way of gaining any information, and there was little sense in speculating. Nor did he want to scare her.

They listened to the noises of the night for a while, and he gradually relaxed. The stars were incredible, the moon lording over them like a king over his subjects. Milda would call him "typical prince" if he shared that thought with her, he realized, and grinned, forgetting the dangers around them.

In this moment it seemed that they were the only two people on the island, in the whole world perhaps. Far from being uncomfortable, the thought brought him an odd sort of contentment.

"Good night." She turned from him.

"Good night." He put his arm around her waist as he held her from behind.

And after a few minutes, she finally relaxed against him.

The crevice provided them with little room. They'd decided not to risk lighting a fire, so they had to snuggle together for heat. They had one blanket under them, on top of the folded tent, not that the thin layer could make them forget that they were lying on a rock bed. The lone blanket that covered them was insufficient against the chill of the night. They needed each other to be even remotely comfortable.

Their physical proximity meant nothing. At least, that was what he told himself.

"Milda?" he asked a few minutes later, just to hear her voice, which wasn't altogether unpleasant when she wasn't harping.

"Yes?"

"What kind of name is that? Is it short for something? It's not a typical American name."

"My family is Lithuanian American. My great grandparents came over on a ship, through Ellis Island." She paused, as if considering whether to say more. Then she did. "Milda is the name of a mythical Lithuanian love goddess."

He heroically held back any smart comments, saying only, "Perfect name for a matchmaker."

She wiggled around to face him. Enough moonlight spilled into the crevice to illuminate her face. "Marital consultant."

"Is that a legitimate occupation in Lithuania?"

She stiffened. "It's a legitimate occupation everywhere. I'm a certified, card-carrying member of MCA, Marital Consultants of America."

"Of course you are."

Her chin came up. "The women of my family were always in the business, one way or another. My family name, Milas, is short for Milasiniks—'love potion maker.'"

Unease crept into his mind. "You haven't—"

"I don't believe in potions. True love has to come from the heart, not from a bottle."

He normally wasn't crazy about her ideas on true love, but he appreciated this one. The last thing he needed was for a desperate matchmaker to poison him. "No potions. Promise."

She rolled her eyes. "I could be offended by all this mistrust."

"We're trapped on this godforsaken island because you tricked me," he reminded her. "Trust is not going to come easily."

At least she looked contrite for a fleeting second. "Fine. No potions. I promise. Are you happy?"

Not exactly, but as he lay next to her, his gaze straying to her crooked lips, he realized that it wouldn't take much to make him at least a little happier than he was at the moment. She had surprised him today. Not many women had ever done that. He'd seen another side of her, and this other side was...not at all like what he'd seen of her at the palace. She had gumption. She had common sense. She sucked it up and toughed it out when things turned bad.

If he wasn't careful, he was going to develop some misplaced admiration for her…. All right, probably not. That would be going too far. But there was some draw between them, for sure.

As he thought of their kiss in the orange grove, he could still taste the wild honey, and his head dipped forward without conscious effort. Her eyes went wide as their lips met.

Soft.

Sweet.

Not two adjectives he would have ever used in connection with Milda before, but there it was. He caressed her upper lip with his, then the lower, pressing kisses to the corners of her mouth.

One minute, her hands were between them, pushing him away. The next her eyes drifted closed as she capitulated. And what had begun as a lazy exploration turned serious all of a sudden.

Hot need shot through him as he gathered her tighter into his arms. The chaste tasting of her lips seemed woefully inadequate. So he deepened the kiss, his body waking up all over as she let him in.

All the tension, fight and fire that had built between them in the past five months, that whole giant ball of energy transformed in that moment, and the intensity of the desire he felt left his hands shaking.

That sobered him up.

He didn't even like her, for heaven's sake. Her job

was to make his life miserable. And so far, she had succeeded splendidly. What would she do if he gave her any kind of power over him?

He pulled away, his body reluctant to follow his mind's direction.

"Okay," he said, then cleared his throat to get the hoarseness out of his voice. "I'm not certain what's going on here, but it's not going to keep happening. You were right. We shouldn't do this. Ever again." His body loudly protested, but he ignored his baser instincts with the aplomb of a prince.

She was pulling back, too. Not that she had far to go. The small crevice only allowed an inch or two between them. Her warm breath still fanned his cheek. "Absolutely." The first word came out a little dazed, but then she recovered herself. "It's wrong. You're my client." A note of desperation snuck into her voice. "There are rules. I never should have— Could we please pretend this never happened?"

"That would be best."

They both stayed quiet after he said that. Another rare occurrence of agreeing on something. He suspected that neither of them knew what to do with this unexpected harmony.

"Why is this happening now?" she asked after a while, sounding frustrated.

What was he supposed to say to that? He had no idea why his body suddenly noticed her and wanted her. But he wouldn't make another move if it killed him. "Desert

Island Syndrome," he said as nonchalantly as he was capable.

Her eyes narrowed. "That's not too flattering."

"Neither of us is thinking rationally."

She nodded in agreement. "The important thing is that we seem to have come to our senses."

"Exactly."

Another stretch of silence followed.

"Tomorrow we figure out where those bastards are. We need to get one of the radios back from them, at least." He was the first to speak this time, needing to get his mind on another track so his body would calm down.

"Where do you think they are?" Milda obliged him, seeming just as anxious to forget that kiss.

"There are caves and Etruscan ruins on the other side of the hill."

More silence. Then her hand came up as she touched his arm lightly. "I'm sorry I've put your life in danger. It's the last thing that I wanted." She sounded sincere.

"Don't worry about it. This is Valtrian land. Those criminals are not going to claim it. I'm going to take care of them." He paused for a second as he thought of something. "You do realize that my brothers will actually be jealous of the adventure when I get back to the palace and tell them?"

A ghost of a smile played on her lips as she retrieved her hand. "And yet they seemed so sane."

"My brothers? You must not have looked too closely."

But *he* was looking closely. At *her*.

And he had to stop doing that before he forgot his resolution of not touching her again. Because every cell in his body still wanted her.

He did the only thing he could think of, and turned his back to her. "Good night," he called over his shoulder.

"Good night," she responded on a sigh behind him.

Then something rattled in the woods and she was plastered against his back again. "What was that?"

He listened, but the sound didn't come again. "Probably just the wind." He closed his eyes. Not that he expected to get any sleep, with her breasts pressing against his back. He fancied he could even feel the nipples.

Chapter Five

Milda soaked up the heat Lazlo radiated and wished she could sleep. She wouldn't have moved away for anything. She needed the reassurance of his nearness.

Cloud cover made the night too dark to see beyond a few feet. Tree branches rubbed together in the woods, moved by the breeze coming off the ocean. Now and then bugs chirped nearby. Or the screech of an owl interrupted the silence. She kept listening for other kinds of noises, those that would tell her if someone was out there.

The night before, her biggest problem had been the rain and Lazlo's fury at being stranded on the island. Amazing how much could change in just twenty-four hours. Two people had been killed. And the killers were somewhere on the island.

Forget sleep. She was too scared to even close her eyes. The rocks under their bedding dug into her side. She shifted. Sighed. She'd come to Valtria to save her business and get her life back on track. She didn't want to die here, like some sacrifice to the Etruscans.

"Are you all right?" Lazlo asked, without turning.

"Can't sleep."

"Stop thinking."

"Sure." If only it were so easy. "Those men are probably sleeping for the night. Right?"

"Of course they are." He didn't sound convincing. "Think about something else."

His nearness and kisses came to mind, but she didn't want to think about that, either.

"So everyone in your family is a matchmaker?" he asked after a minute, to distract her.

"Marital consultants. All seven of my sisters. If I can't make this work, they'll be coming over to help me," she said matter-of-factly. "We've been e-mailing almost every day."

He gave a choked sound that made her smile into the darkness. But then she felt bad for putting him on. It had been partially her fault that they were here on this island, in danger, in the first place.

"Take it easy. I'm an only child. The only Milas left, actually. I *am* the family," she confessed.

"What happened to the rest?"

"My parents died in a train accident when I was four. They were visiting Lithuania. Kaunas, where my family is from." She barely remembered them, which bothered her a lot. She clung to the few hazy memories. A visit to the zoo and her fourth birthday party were pretty much all she had. "My grandmother raised me. She passed away a couple of years ago."

Her grandmother had been the one to tell her about

her parents' death, had shown her the city of Kaunas on the map. She hadn't understood how her mother and father could have died on that piece of paper, kept looking behind it to see if they were there. To this day, the sight and sound of an unfolding map filled her with anxiety.

"I'm sorry," Lazlo said.

He probably couldn't imagine what it was like to be truly alone. He had a large family; and a prince would never be alone, anyway. The palace staff numbered in the hundreds.

"What's it like to have five brothers?"

"I'm reevaluating my feelings about that, since mine saw fit to set me up."

"They were only trying to help."

A groan was his only response.

"Must have been great growing up."

"You cannot underestimate the trouble we got into."

She didn't have a hard time picturing that. Although the Kerkay princes always behaved impeccably in public, there was something about them that suggested they could raise considerable hell if they put their minds to it. Those lively dark eyes they'd inherited from their mother had plenty of mischief and sparkle in them. There was Lazlo, for example. The paparazzi didn't call him "the Rebel Prince" for nothing.

"Who was the worst?" she asked, although she had her own suspicions.

He thought for a second. "I was the loudest for sure.

And the quickest. Took everything for a joyride, from the golf carts when I was six, to the royal ceremonial limousine when I was eight." There was a smile in his voice. "I think Istvan did the most damage. He was always quiet, but rather destructive. He always fancied being an archaeologist. I don't know how many times he dug up the palace gardens. And if he ever got his hands on any tools left lying around, he would hide in some quiet corner and go to work on the wall. One time, he caused a collapse in the royal chapel. He always wanted to know what was under and behind everything. Even back then, in his own mind, he was this great explorer."

Istvan was so reserved and withdrawn, she laughed out loud at the picture of him as the budding Indiana Jones of Valtria.

"Don't laugh. He ended up becoming a cultural anthropologist, and goes on digs every chance he gets. He's made some incredible discoveries in Valtria and abroad. You probably heard of those thirteenth-century royal graves up north." Warmth and pride came through Lazlo's voice; he obviously loved his brother. "I'll take you when we get out of here, if you haven't seen them yet."

For a moment, she was stunned by what he was saying. That he would want to spend time with her without being forced to. Normally, he did his best to avoid her at the palace.

"Actually, you should work on matching Istvan, not

me," he said thoughtfully. "I don't have any trouble getting my own dates."

That last bit was the truth and then some, even if he only said it to get rid of her. "I hardly think Istvan would have trouble getting a date if he wanted one. He's just focused on his work." He was just as handsome as the rest of the brothers. "I'd have a hard time believing that the ladies of the court aren't standing in line to go to dinner with him."

"He prefers people who've been dead for a few centuries. His nanny is to blame. The woman read him nothing but books on history and the adventures of famous explorers. She was the biggest know-it-all. I used to feel sorry for him."

"Who was your nanny?" She could easily picture him as a child who was more than a handful.

"A former model. A very distant cousin who got the job as a favor. She shaped my tastes considerably."

I'll just bet, she mused.

"How about Arpad?" That one looked as remote and withdrawn as Istvan on the few occasions that she'd seen him.

"Arpad was the big brother who taught us everything. And Miklos was born for the military. Even as a little kid, he always played soldier," he reminisced.

She didn't envy his wealth or power, but just a little, she did envy his family. The princes were really something. She couldn't remember ever seeing this many strong, honorable, outrageously gorgeous men all in one pack. The women of Valtria must have walked around in a continuous daydream.

Lazlo shifted next to her, causing the blanket to slip off. She reached out to cover herself again, her hand briefly brushing against his chest.

And because she was so ridiculously aware of even that small contact, she forced herself to focus on something else. Like his childhood. Maybe thinking of him as just a little boy would help. "So, did you ever crash any of the vehicles you misappropriated?"

He made a noise in his throat. "Are you trying to insult me?"

ROBERTO WALKED into the tent and caught Marco hiding something under his shirt. He glanced around. Nothing obvious was missing. The pile of food at the head of his sleeping bag looked undisturbed.

The tent provided cramped quarters for the three of them, but they made do. Only two slept at a time, anyway. One was always on guard—José was due to come in, and Marco was supposed to take over.

Still, the tent could have been bigger. He could always kick Marco out. Especially if the little bastard kept stealing food. Marco could go back to the cave where they'd spent the first night. Unease skittered down Roberto's spine at the thought of the cave. He hated bats. As perfect as the damn cave would have been for a hiding place, he was unlikely to go back there. Cramped or not, he preferred the tent.

"Hey, boss. I'm ready to go play night guard," Marco

said, with a little too much enthusiasm, stepping toward the exit.

Roberto blocked his path, keeping his right hand near the gun tucked into his belt. "What have you got there?"

"What are you talking about, this?" Marco pointed to the blanket at his feet. He scooped it up. "José said the mosquitoes were killing him out there, so I came back to grab it up. You want it?"

"What's under your shirt?"

Marco paled. "Nothing."

Roberto waited. Held his left hand out after a few seconds.

Marco's lips tightened, hate narrowing his eyes as he handed over two black leather wallets.

Where the hell did these come from? He didn't have to ask the question. Marco must have lifted them off the dead men. Roberto flipped one wallet open, then the other, saw the money with some disappointment. Valtrian currency. He would have preferred euros, that they could have used once they reached the mainland.

Then his eyes fell on the ID. *Valtrian Royal Security.*

For a second or two, he couldn't figure out what this meant, what those men were doing here. Why would "royal security" guard an inhabited island? Then he felt a smile spread on his face. "Find José and get ready. There is another man and a woman on the island."

"Do we have to go now? How long is this gonna take?"

"We'll go now and keep looking till we find them," Roberto snapped, dropping his voice into a warning growl. "And if you ever take anything without telling me again, I'll cut you open." He was on the younger man instantly, his knife at his throat, up against his Adam's apple.

Marco's eyes went wide as he stumbled back.

Roberto grabbed him by the arm and shoved him toward the opening of the tent. "Be ready to go in two minutes."

SHE WOKE TO THE SUN caressing her face and remembered only remnants of the stories Lazlo had entertained her with during the night. She loved it when he talked about his family. The love was palpable in his voice. Made her wonder what it would have been like to grow up knowing her parents, have siblings....

Whether intentionally or not, he'd done a good job of distracting her from her fears and setting her mind at ease. The awareness between them never did lessen, but she'd fallen asleep anyway, once she became completely exhausted.

Now she was alone again, like the morning before. Then, as she crawled from their shelter, she spotted the prince sitting on a rock not far from the crevice, surveying the sea.

The very last of her dreams still lingered. Of him. Kissing her again. She stifled a groan, but had a hard time putting the images and sensations out of her mind, couldn't shake the way he'd made her body feel. She'd never been this aware of a man before. This must be what people called blind lust. All he had to do was look at her and a zing went through her body.

It was exciting, but she would have appreciated if the source of her body's awakening had been anyone but the prince.

"Good, you're awake," he said, without turning. "Come look at this."

She finger-combed her hair and rubbed the last of the sleep out of her eyes, adjusted her pants and top, which were hopelessly wrinkled at this point. Then she walked up behind him, doing her best to forget her dreams. "What are we looking at?"

"There." He pointed.

And she saw, at last, a small, square shadow under the surface of the sea, at the rocky edge of the beach. "Is that…"

"One of our supply bags got stuck among the rocks. I didn't want to leave you here alone. Get ready as fast as you can. Before a wave washes it out to sea."

Her heart immediately thrilled. She practically ran into the bushes to complete her morning toilet. She was finished in under two minutes.

"Have you seen the others, the men who…" She couldn't finish.

Lazlo was covering their sleeping nook with some leafy branches. "No movement so far. They're probably on the other side of the island."

She hoped they would stay there until she and the prince had a chance to recover their bag from the sea.

They needed some real food desperately. Plus they needed to find that creek. And one of the radios the criminals had taken. Sure looked like they were going to have a busy day.

Which was fine with her. The less time she had to think about the prince's kisses the better. Because, now that her mind was fully awake, she was remembering that not all contact between her and Lazlo had been in her dreams.

The prince *had* kissed her.

And even he couldn't claim, this time, that it hadn't been a real kiss.

Thank God he didn't seem inclined to bring up the issue this morning. She would have died of embarrassment.

She'd about melted in his arms, forgetting all her reasons to resist. She had lost all ability to think, could only feel a fiery need that she had never felt before with any man. And she'd been willing to forget all the rules she had lived by until now. She would have been willing to give up everything.

But not him.

He had coolly pulled back. "Desert Island Syndrome," he'd called it.

And she called herself a hundred kinds of fool for falling for that kiss.

It wasn't going to happen again, he'd promised.

Damn right it wouldn't. Not if she had anything to say about it.

Temporary setbacks or not, she had to see the prince married. Her business and the rest of her life depended on it. She hadn't lied when she'd said she had appreciative clients. But not enough. These days, most of the people who came calling were mothers and grandmothers, asking for her help with their offspring. But today's young people didn't want to be married. They wanted to "hook up." They wanted to keep their options open. And as the years went by, Milda had to admit that she was part of a dying breed.

Hardly anyone believed in true love anymore. Few people wanted "happily ever after." For the short-attention-span generation, a lifetime with just one person didn't seem all that appealing.

She needed to succeed with Prince Lazlo. She needed it badly.

She followed him down the hillside, looking behind every few minutes. When they walked by a wild orange tree, she broke off the tip of a branch, chewed it up a little and used it for a toothbrush on the go.

They could have gotten down to the beach faster, but they walked slowly, making sure not to make too much noise, and stopped every once in a while to listen to see if anyone might be following.

"Stay in the cover of the bushes," Lazlo told her when they finally reached the sand. "We shouldn't both be out in the open."

"I don't want to separate. You might need help in the water."

He considered her for a moment. "All right. Let's make a run for it."

They did, choosing the shortest path to the large

pile of rocks that edged the sandy beach. Some were as big as nine or ten feet tall, others were the size of an overgrown otter. They got behind them and down as fast as they could, easing into the water.

The bag that had been easy to see in the clear, shallow sea from above was now harder to find among the rocks. But Lazlo did spot it after a few minutes. It was in deeper water. Not too deep, but above their heads, which complicated things.

He went under first, tugged at the bag. Came up for air. "Wedged in tight."

Made sense. That was why the waves hadn't washed it out to sea.

She went under to help him.

Trouble was, the bag was zipper side down, so they couldn't even open it.

They came up for air again.

"Hope whatever is in there wasn't ruined by water and we're not doing this for nothing," Lazlo was saying.

"I had to arrange for food that'd last you and the ladies two weeks without refrigeration. A lot of it is canned. The rest was sealed in airtight containers."

He gave an approving nod before going for another try. He was a stronger swimmer than she was, so it took her a few seconds to catch up with him.

He pointed to the bag then to her. Then he pointed to one of the rocks and to himself. Okay. She got it. He was going to roll the rock and she was to pull the bag.

She put all her strength into it, her lungs bursting.

Then the rock did move, and Lazlo was there helping her. Between the two of them, they dragged the bag toward the surface without much trouble.

She grinned at Lazlo and he grinned back. For the first time since they were left behind on the island, she was feeling optimistic. The food in the bag might last them a full week. Surely, help would come by then. She couldn't believe no boat had come for them yet. The ladies were taking their revenge too far. Maybe she'd been wrong about their character.

Then her head broke the surface and the first thing she heard was people talking.

"Where the hell are they?" a deep voice asked.

Another man answered him in a language that sounded Spanish. Or maybe Portuguese.

Definitely not a search crew that had come to save her and the prince.

"They went this way. Look at the footprints in the sand."

Lazlo grabbed her and pulled her tight against the rocks. She grabbed his arm as the sound of the men came nearer. They were walking onto the rocks. Before long, she and Lazlo would be seen.

He let her go and went under. He only broke the surface long enough to take a deep breath when he came back. Then he grabbed her and took her with him under the surface of the water.

She had to trust him against her most basic instincts. Since she was a poor swimmer, she didn't feel all that comfortable in the water. Going under scared her. But she followed him.

They came out just as her lungs began to ache, in a small crevice created by the haphazardly piled rocks. Their bodies were submerged, but at least they were breathing.

"Maybe they went for a swim," the deeper voice said.

A short response came in whatever language the other guy was speaking.

Something large moved next to her head. She nearly screamed. A moment passed before her eyes better adjusted to the semidarkness, and she realized that a turtle was wedged between the rocks that were covered with sea moss and even some clam shells here and there. Wedged tightly. The poor thing looked half-dead.

She signaled with her head toward the turtle.

Lazlo nodded.

Shoes scraped above.

Didn't seem like the men were going anywhere. Probably decided to wait out her and Lazlo until they came back from their supposed swim.

They could stick around for a while.

The muscles in her chest squeezed together tightly. She looked around the hole, realizing, all of a sudden, that their small shelter might not hold out that long. They were trapped in the water with barely enough room to breathe. What on earth were they going to do when the tide began rising?

Chapter Six

The men stuck to the beach and the grove, looking for a boat that might have been stashed among the trees. One of them spent an hour by the rocks, gathering clams. Only the merciless noon sun chased them away. By the time Lazlo and Milda could come out of hiding, they were weak with hunger and thirst.

The breeze coming off the sea was negligible. Coming from the shade of the rocks, the open air felt ten degrees hotter. A bigger wave washed over their heads. Even that felt balmy.

"The tide?" Milda sputtered, her eyes going wide, her wet lashes sticking together.

Had she been worried about that? No wonder she'd looked half scared to death. "Not until late afternoon. Keep down," Lazlo whispered over the sound of waves slapping against the rock and the cries of the seagulls circling above. "I'll get that turtle out." He hated to see anything or anyone trapped.

The loggerhead expressed his reluctance by sinking its horny beak—thicker than most other turtles', made to crush clam and crab shells—into Lazlo's hand. If it had been a fully grown animal, weighing more than its rescuer, Lazlo could never have managed. But a juvenile at only half a meter long, he could handle. The way the loggerhead was wedged in, he could only grab it from the front, which meant he had to keep his hand in harm's way. He did what he had to, ignoring the repeated attacks.

He freed the ungrateful thing at last and it immediately disappeared underwater. Lazlo watched it swim out to sea, then he came up next to Milda.

For the first time since they'd met, she was looking at him with approval in her eyes. Her smile was genuine, pleased—not the supercharged, let's-be-positive, this-will-work smile that was one of the tools of her trade. Her hair hung wet around her face, not a trace of makeup had remained; but beyond that smile she needed no enhancement. Even her crooked lips looked tempting. But, too quickly, she moved toward the beach, assuming they were ready to head back.

He caught up to her. "They'll be watching for us there." The men could still be close by. The fact that no voices came from the direction of the beach meant nothing. They could be taking a nap in the shade.

"Where can we get out?"

"How are you doing?" His body was weakened by the water, his muscles stiff from standing still for hours. She had to feel the strain, too. Although her body, with her clothes floating around her—allowing him a glimpse at her lace bra—looked more than fine to him.

"I'll do what I have to."

He raised his gaze to hers with effort. "This way."

On their left, the flat, sandy beach stretched for several hundred meters. On their right, the water met a rocky shoreline that was higher than the surface of the sea. He moved in that direction. If they swam close enough to the rocks, they wouldn't be seen by anyone on the shore. Once they'd swam far enough, they could climb out.

"What happened to your hand?" Her forehead wrinkled with concern when he brought the hand above water to grab on to a rock they were rounding.

"Unappreciative turtle." Red dripped into the water. Unfortunate, but they would have to swim. No way to keep that hand out. And no sense in worrying about something he couldn't help. "Be careful that the waves don't bang you against the rocks," he told Milda instead. "Some of them look sharp."

But she seemed to be considering something else. "Sharks?"

"It's a possibility."

Although, the only marine life they'd seen so far were the small, colorful fish that swam under the rocks, checking them out while they'd waited. And, of course, the ungrateful turtle.

"Keep your eyes open." He led the way, steering her clear of the most dangerous areas. If there were any strong currents or an undertow, he'd encounter it first and would have time to warn her. Not that they could put much distance between each other. Since they needed at least one hand to swim, plus a way to carry the hefty bag, they each hung on to a handle with their other hand, connected.

The first hundred feet or so went fine. Then the rocks became taller, steeper, the waves crushing against them harder. He banged his left shoulder at one point, but didn't break it, didn't even cut the skin, which was a miracle. He helped Milda through the rough spot, trying to ignore her trim body when she clung to him for a moment before she pushed forward.

They put all their focus and energy into battling the rocks and waves, but their progress was painfully slow. At least an hour must have passed before he estimated that they would be far enough from the beach so that it was safe to come out of the water.

He climbed up onto the rocks first, looked around, noted the dry brush a hundred feet or so ahead. Not much, but enough for cover. He went back, tossed the bag up, then helped Milda out of the water.

And tried not to look.

The thin material of her clothes was plastered to her body. The soggy material of her pants outlined the *V* of her thighs suggestively. She might as well have been naked. Her breasts made him ache, his fingers itching for the gentle swell of her hips. She had better curves than a top-of-the-line race car.

She pulled her clothes away from her skin and shook her legs, one after the other, like a dog, then moved on, having no apparent idea how tempting she looked, how erotic.

He kept his gaze averted as they dashed to cover, keeping down, and made their way farther and farther away from the shoreline. He led the way to higher ground, to the edge of yet another wild olive grove. From that vantage point, they would at least see if someone was approaching from below.

"Here is good," he said, and they both collapsed to the ground next to the bag.

She went through the contents immediately, not wasting any time. "Canned food, and some salmon."

That explained why the bag was so heavy.

She pulled out peaches first. "How are we going to open it?"

He searched for a small, sharp rock, then for a heavier one to use as a hammer. He managed to punch a hole in the top on the first try. He handed the can back to her. "Drink."

And she did, hungrily, dribbling the juice in through her parted lips. Lips that went crooked when she smiled. Lips that he'd tasted.

Again, he looked away. That he was becoming obsessed with her mouth was absolutely ridiculous. She wasn't even remotely his type. It had to be the island— or the heat. There was something strange going on with him.

He could understand liking her personality better, now that he'd had a chance to get to know her and she wasn't hunting him. But the sudden physical attraction was baffling.

Desert Island Syndrome.

That was what he'd told her, and he was sticking with it.

She swallowed one more time then stopped, with some reluctance, to hand him the syrupy juice. He drank a few mouthfuls, leaving a little more for her. Then, when they were done with the juice, he picked his rocks back up and set to getting to the fruit. It was a good start, but they needed protein. So he opened the shrink-wrapped smoked salmon next, and watched her inhale it while he feasted on a container of rare clams in truffle sauce, at which she only wrinkled her nose.

When they finished eating, they started back up the hill, taking the empty cans with them. No sense in leaving a trail, and they might need the containers for something.

"Might as well look for that creek while those men are lurking by the beach," she said.

"I doubt they're still there." He picked his way carefully over the loose soil. "They would have realized by now that we can't still be out there swimming."

"What will they do next?"

"If I were them, I'd round the island. They know where we went into the water. But we didn't come out there. So they're probably looking for where we came out. Then they could track us."

"Can they?" Alarm widened her eyes.

"I made sure we kept to rocky ground. No footprints."

Even here, on the side of the hill, they would be fine. The area was covered with loose gravel and brittle shale, their shoes leaving no trail.

He considered how long it would take these men to find them on this small island. It depended on how well they knew the place. "You said security checked the island over before giving the go-ahead for this trip?"

"Prince Miklos's soldiers were here all morning, to make sure the place was safe for you and the ladies. He insisted that his team would be used for this task, and no other."

Which didn't surprise him. Miklos was an army colonel and dealt with security issues regularly. "So these killers definitely came here after the island was cleared."

"Lucky timing? Just when you were supposed to arrive?" She looked skeptical.

Not more so than he felt. "The Freedom Council."

She blanched. "I thought that was finished. The rebellion was put down."

"But the Freedom Council was never caught. Maybe they're regrouping." He moved forward, his mind turning furiously, more and more questions filling it. "How many people at the palace knew about your plans for the island?"

"A handful. Only those who absolutely had to know. I had to make sure nobody told you." She winced.

Never mind that now. "But at least two dozen people know about my planned hike with my brothers. There wasn't any reason to keep that all hushed up, beyond basic security. A lot of the palace staff knew about the trip."

"And one of them could have betrayed you."

"The Freedom Council thought that all six princes would be here on this deserted island, with nothing but a few guards for protection. So they sent their assassins in."

She swallowed at the mention of the word *assassin*. He immediately regretted saying it. There was no point in scaring her. Those bastards weren't going to get to her. He was going to make sure of it.

"Why is the Freedom Council so set against the royal family? I heard bits and pieces about the rebellion, but I haven't had time to find out more."

"Too busy torturing me?" He tried to set a lighter tone.

"Too busy trying to help you." She glared.

He shook his head. Their ideas of what would have been helpful for his life were diametrically opposite.

"The Freedom Council wants the country," he explained in the most simple terms. Since there was a good chance that her life was being threatened by them, at least she should know why she was hunted all over the island. "Three prominent businessmen came up with it. They think if they do away with the monarchy, they can split the country up along ethnic lines."

"The three major ethnic groups? Italian, Hungarian and Austrian?"

Surprise sent his eyebrows up his forehead. "Good to know you didn't just hastily throw yourself into making my life miserable, but actually did some homework beforehand."

"I came to *help*." She paused. "Why is it good for them to split up the country?"

"They would each have full control over a small republic. Write their own laws. Do as they please."

"And what would happen to the monarchy?"

"The monarchy would be dead." He stopped for a moment to look around, then pointed east. "That way."

"Why? And what do you mean dead?" Her voice thinned.

He nodded toward the beach where they'd last heard those men. "Dead, as in not as fast as the assassins. And we're going this way because the vegetation is lusher up ahead. Might mean we're getting closer to the water."

"But why do they have to kill the royal family? Couldn't you abdicate or something? Why can't you just give up the throne?"

Her question set his teeth on edge. The Freedom Council had done its best to portray the royal family as dinosaurs, outdated, having no use, desperately clinging to power.

"We would, if that was what was best for Valtria. Fragmenting the country, pitching ethnic group against ethnic group, fracturing what industry we have, is not the way to a prosperous and peaceful future for the people."

"But some of the people think so."

"The Freedom Council has plenty of money to

spend on propaganda. And there are always people who are discontented with their lives. It's easy to convince them that someone else is to blame for all their misfortunes."

"But the royal weddings of Miklos and your twin, Benedek, brought the people together. And yours would give even more reason to celebrate. For a while, it would distract the people."

He blinked at her.

"Chancellor Egon told me that."

"No kidding. The chancellor is hell-bent on marrying off all the princes. It's easier than having to come up with a more serious plan, that would actually work for the long term. I'm afraid the man doesn't live up to his predecessor."

"A temporary solution is better than no solution at all." Not surprisingly, she stuck to her guns. For a matchmaker, the best solution for all the world's problems was probably marriage. "You could cooperate."

He shook his head, not expecting her to understand, but feeling compelled to try to make her see reason. "My life is not a circus act. I'm not here to distract the people from the real problems the country is facing. The chancellor needs to come up with a better solution."

"The Queen also wishes to see you wed."

"She wishes to see all her sons wed. What mother doesn't? She wants to see a roomful of grandchildren before—" He couldn't finish the sentence.

A moment of silence passed between them.

"How sick is she?" Milda asked.

For a while, he didn't answer. The Queen's state of health was a private matter. But then he ended up saying, "Sicker than the public realizes."

Milda startled him by giving him a hug. Too brief. She quickly drew back with a nervous smile. "Would it be so bad to set her mind at ease by settling down?"

He responded on reflex. "You're asking me to give up what little freedom I have left. I won't be trapped." He'd been trapped before. In a burning car. His worst fear was that he'd end up in a bad relationship, an entrapment that would last forever.

"You're a prince." She gave an incredulous laugh. "You have all the freedom in the world. You can do anything."

If only that were true. At the moment, for example, he wanted to kiss her. Since the moment he'd tasted that wild honey on her lips back in the orange grove, all he'd wanted was to kiss her again.

"Ninety percent of my life is choreographed," he said, telling her the truth. "Protocol above everything."

She watched him for a minute, looking incredulous. "What is it that you think you can't do?"

A great many things, he thought; but he gave her one that had nothing to do with her. "I can never be a professional race car driver, for one." The only thing he'd ever wanted to be, since as far back as he could remember.

Protocol wouldn't allow it. The racing associations wouldn't allow it. They couldn't handle the liability. His schedule couldn't handle it. Being a top driver took 110 percent. So did being a prince.

They reached an area of thicker grass, then bushes, then trees at last. And then finally, he could hear water trickling somewhere up ahead. He quickened his steps. They reached the water within fifty meters, a crystal-clear creek that was smaller than he'd remembered—maybe two meters wide and about thirty centimeters deep in the middle. It'd been a dry summer.

"Oh, God, we so needed this." She splashed water on her face and neck, getting her top partially wet all over again.

The creek rushed along over the rock bed—mossy in the areas of deep shade—tufts of water grasses edging the bank. He rinsed the peach can and filled it with water, wishing they had their empty champagne bottles. No matter. They would bring those back later.

She leaned to the surface of the creek and quenched her thirst from her cupped palms.

He did the same.

They looked at each other when they leaned back, satisfied, mirroring the smiles on each other's faces.

Clear droplets of water hung from her eyelashes. The sun filtering through the trees above bathed her face in soft light. *This is what Milda, the Lithuanian goddess of love, must have looked like on her best days,* he thought as warmth spread through his body. *Nothing to do with her,* he told himself.

The midafternoon heat was nearly unbearable, even by the creek. Here the air was a few degrees cooler than on the open hillside, but the humidity was getting to them. And the saltwater that had dried on his clothes and skin made him itchy. He pulled his shirt over his head.

She looked away.

Was she as aware of him as he was of her? It didn't seem possible. She'd never been anything but vocal about what she thought of him and his ways with women. And that angered him all of a sudden. What right did she have to judge him? What did she know about his life? So what if he acted out now and then? Being a prince was anything but easy. She was lucky to have been born into an average family and allowed to lead a normal life.

Well, perhaps not exactly *average*.

"Did you always want to be a matchmaker?" he asked.

"Of course," she said without hesitation, but there was something in her voice and in the way she wouldn't look at him.

"Maybe not," he observed, and thought about it for the first time. Maybe she was as bound by family expectations and traditions as he was. "You never wanted to be anything else?"

"What kind of question is that?" she snapped, with more heat than was warranted.

"A reasonable one." He watched her more closely now. "Why did you become a matchmaker?"

"Marital consultant," she said, emphasizing each word. "My mother was one."

"You barely knew your mother."

"My grandmother was one."

"And you felt like you owed her carrying on the family tradition because she raised you."

"Oh, that's good. What are you, a shrink now?" She stood and hopped over the creek in two graceful steps, anger clear on her face. "Analyze this—have you ever thought about what you're running from when you're running from a serious relationship?"

"That's ridiculous. I never ran from anything in my life."

"Maybe you drive away, then. As fast as you can, around and around the racetrack. Except, you're not getting anywhere."

"I don't want to get anywhere. I want to be at the racetrack. Have you even thought of where you'd really like to be?"

"Butt out of my life. It's none of your business."

"Where did I hear that before? That's right, I think I've told you that a time or two." *Or a hundred.*

"It's not the same." She looked thoroughly exasperated, which made her even more beautiful.

"Don't like the tables turned?" He wasn't seriously arguing with her, but would have liked to make her see his point, just for once.

"You're impossible. I'm not talking about this." She marched into the bushes on the other side, with one last murderous glance.

He'd hit a sore spot, apparently. Maybe she didn't really want to be a matchmaker after all. Could have fooled him. She'd always seemed more than committed to her task.

"You know, you're a complicated woman," he called after her. Intriguing, too, but he wasn't about to tell her that. Would sound too much like a compliment.

"All women are complicated," she called back. "You just never took the time to get to know any of them."

She was, of course, wrong about that. He paid plenty of attention to women. According to her and his mother, that was what had gotten him into trouble in the first place.

"Don't go too far," he called. He would give her enough time, in case she was doing her private business, then go after her.

He wanted to get back to their night shelter and bring some bottles over to the creek. And he wanted to get to higher ground, using the tree cover to see if he could spot the men who were after them. He had to find them, and somehow get ahold of a radio.

The babble of the creek drowned out most sounds around him. He was focused on the bushes she'd disappeared into. Hopefully, she hadn't gotten so mad at him that she'd walked off. He didn't want her to go, even beyond the fact that it was obviously not safe.

He wanted to keep talking with her, getting to know her better. He wanted to know what made her tick, what made her laugh, what made her blue eyes darken with passion. He couldn't remember his mind ever having been this preoccupied with a woman.

Too preoccupied, perhaps.

Because, when the barrel of a gun came to rest against the back of his neck, it caught him unawares.

"Make any noise and I'll blow your head off," a man with an Hispanic accent said. "Get up."

Lazlo got to his feet slowly. He couldn't see his captor, but he could smell the man's stale sweat.

"Now we'll wait for your little friend," the bastard announced.

Not a chance. Lazlo filled his lungs. "Don't come back, Milda. Run!"

Then the man behind him smacked the pistol butt into the back of his head, and the pain shot down his spine, taking all the strength from his legs.

SHE RAN AS FAST as her legs would carry her, until her lungs threatened to collapse. Was someone still following her? She was breathing too hard, the blood rushing in her ears too loudly to hear anything. When she could go no farther, Milda hid under a thick bush, pulling her limbs in, curling up into a ball, hoping to avoid detection if anyone came this way.

Someone *had* come after Lazlo's warning. But it had been a while since she'd heard any branches snap behind her. She lay still, not caring about the bugs or the small lizard that checked her out, stared into her face before turning its shimmering green tail and skittering off.

She was shaking, gasping for air, sweat soaking her skin. *Quiet. Don't make a noise.* Lazlo had been right. She was willing to admit that now. She would have willingly admitted anything, only to be back at home, or at least on the mainland. The island had been a terrible idea. She was never going to do anything like this, ever again.

A bird sang in a tree not far from her. She tried to focus on that instead of all her fears.

After a few interminably long minutes, her racing heart finally slowed. Her breathing was under control. Nobody came. She'd gotten away.

She closed her eyes for a split second, with pure relief, before the next thought hit her. She was alone in the forest. And she had no idea where she was. She'd run forward blindly, changing direction randomly, trying to lose the killer on her trail.

Lazlo would know which way to go. He always did. He seemed to have an innate sense of direction that she'd come to rely on. She relied on him for a number of things, to be fair. Strange for a man whom, for the longest time, she'd believed to be completely unreliable.

He was in the hands of his enemies.

If those men—assassins—she could barely even think the word—hated the royal family as much as he believed they did...

Pain streaked through her chest anew, and it had nothing to do with the way her lungs thirsted for air.

One thought circled her mind, one thought shrunk her stomach into a lead ball, one thought made her eyes burn so much that she had to squeeze them together.

It was entirely possible that they'd already killed him.

Chapter Seven

They had him tied up in Vincent's tent. Lazlo knew this because Ben's had been bloodstained, and this was clean, save for the dirt the three men had tracked in. They were outside at the moment, speaking Spanish, mixing in a lot of English words. Lazlo spoke fluent English, French, German and Italian, but he was unfamiliar with the language they were speaking. Add to that that they were keeping their voices down, and he was lucky to catch every tenth word, not enough to make sense of their conversation.

He still didn't have any idea, beyond guesses, who they were or how they'd gotten to the island. But as fiercely as they protected the place, they planned on leaving at some point. On the way here, he caught sight of a raft in the process of being constructed.

The good news was, they hadn't caught Milda.

The bad news was, they knew she was out there somewhere. And there were three of them. Armed.

He needed to come up with a plan. But even as he tried to loosen his ropes, the one they called Roberto walked into the tent. He'd been able to glean their names as they talked to each other.

"Who are you?" he asked.

Lazlo kept his mouth shut. If these men were with the Freedom Council, they knew exactly who he was.

The man came closer and fingered his clothes, kicked his new hiking boots. His eyes were mean and calculating. "You're a rich man. Give me your money and maybe I'll let you leave the island."

"I have no money." He was speaking the truth. He'd left his wallet in his jacket, which was on the boat that had returned to the mainland.

"Where is your boat?"

"No boat." Maybe the bastards weren't with the Freedom Council, after all. That gave him hope. If the men were after money and not after his life, they might be willing to negotiate.

"How did you get here?" Roberto asked. "You came hunting? Hiking?"

"Hiking. We were dropped off."

"Are you someone important?"

"Hardly."

"You lie," Roberto yelled, and kicked him in the side, this time more viciously.

Pain sliced through Lazlo's ribs. He clenched his jaw tight.

"Your two friends were Valtrian royal security." The man spat, missing Lazlo's head.

"As I am."

Roberto took in his clothes again and the gold watch

on his wrist and gave an evil grin that would have done any silver-screen villain proud. "On closer look, I think you're one of their damn princes."

If he worked for the Freedom Council, he'd know for sure, Lazlo thought. And decided to gamble. "Then negotiate for my release. You have the radios. Make contact."

The man's eyes narrowed suspiciously. He must have been thinking the same thing, but now that Lazlo brought it up, the bastard looked like he was beginning to smell a trap.

Not as stupid as he looked, after all.

"I can't do anything with money if I'm dead. The island would be too easily surrounded." He swore in Spanish, his face twisting into a fierce scowl, as if he blamed Lazlo for everything.

"Let us go then. You have nothing to gain by hurting us. We mean you no harm." He was talking to gain time. After seeing how these men had killed his guards, he had no illusions. The only reason he was still alive was because his apparent wealth and possible status had come as a surprise to Roberto, and it threw the man off temporarily.

The scowl disappeared from the guy's face, replaced by another slow, chilling smile. "Does the name Miguel Santos mean anything to you?"

Lazlo raked his brain. "No. I don't believe so."

Roberto's gaze turned frosty. "It will, before this is all over." He turned and strode out of the tent.

But Lazlo called after him. "Wait. Who is Miguel?"

Roberto stopped and looked back, one hand on the tent flap. "My brother. He was killed in a Valtrian prison. He appealed to the royal family but was denied early release. One of your Valtrian bastards knifed him to death before he could have walked out of there."

The man's chest heaved with emotion, the muscles of his face tight, his gaze burning into Lazlo's. "Before the sun comes up, Miguel will hear your screams in heaven." He spat toward Lazlo, but missed again. "Before the sun comes up, *mi amigo,* you will pray for death."

MILDA SPENT THE REST OF THE DAY under the bush where she'd collapsed, not daring to make any noise by moving, not even after hours had passed, and she was reasonably sure the men had gone. She was scared of everything around her, nearly startled out of her skin when a small animal—a mouse?—skittered across her leg.

But as night fell, she couldn't stop thinking about Lazlo in those killers' clutches. She pushed aside her fears and stole back to the creek, one careful step at a time. Nobody was there, everything was quiet.

She quenched her thirst and ignored her hunger. She couldn't go back to their shelter for food. The Painted Rocks were down the hill, and she needed to go up, in the opposite direction. She felt guilty about the time she'd already wasted.

Going after a group of murderous outlaws seemed insane, but she had to find Lazlo, had to see if she could do anything to help him. She knew she wouldn't be able to fight those men off, but if she could steal a radio while they were busy with Lazlo, at least she could call for help. The chances for dismal failure were astronomical, but she couldn't leave Lazlo to his fate.

She started up the hillside in the cover of the trees, putting one foot in front of the other carefully, stopping frequently to listen. Her pulse went into overdrive every time a piece of fruit fell from a tree. A snake that slithered across her path nearly gave her a heart attack.

At least two hours passed before she reached the top of the hill, the point from where she could see most of the island…and the blinking embers of a small fire in the distance.

There they were, for love's sake. She took a deep breath, relieved that seeking higher ground had been the right decision. Seeing the fire made her feel better about the mess they were in. Lazlo was alive—she felt more sure of that now. He was alive and she would find a way to save him.

She took off immediately, afraid that those embers would cool and she would lose direction. The moon came out from behind the clouds, and the silver light made her trek easier. For the moment, she was grateful for it, even knowing that, once she reached her destination, that light would be nothing but a hindrance, making it easier for the men to spot her approaching.

Another hour passed before she reached them. The

tent was set up next to a car-size rock that shielded it from the sea. That was why they'd been brave enough to light a fire, she realized. No passing boat could see it, especially with the stand of trees behind the rock providing even more thorough covering.

She waited carefully, looking for the slightest movement, listening for the smallest sound. They didn't seem to have a guard waiting. Maybe they thought that, with Lazlo captured, they didn't need one. They probably thought she was holed up somewhere, hiding. Which could work to her advantage.

She approached with as much care as she was capable of. The tent flap stood semiopen. One man slept inside. She couldn't see a radio from her vantage point, and she didn't dare move closer. At least not until she knew where the other one was.

There were two of them, she was pretty sure. She'd heard two when she'd been trapped with Lazlo beneath the rocks at the beach. They must have split up when they captured the prince. One had stayed with him and one had come after her. Thank God, she'd been able to find a good hiding place.

But where was he? And what did they do with their prisoner?

A low moan from the woods brought the answer as she rounded the tent. Her heart raced. She had no plan beyond finding them, but she was too scared to stop and think. And even if she did stop and come up with a plan before going farther, the best plan in the world wouldn't save Lazlo if he was dead by the time she got there.

She crept in the direction of the sound, making sure she was always in cover—not an easy task, as the trees weren't nearly thick enough here to hide her. Then she did see a man at last. Had to be one of the killers. She was so scared she could barely breathe as she watched him. Not stopping to make a plan or find some sort of a weapon seemed insanely stupid all of a sudden. But what experience did she have at something like this? She wasn't a warrior, she was a marital consultant.

The man was alone. Had he been the one to moan? That made little sense. A minute passed before she realized that the odd-shaped tree that held the guy's attention was a tree *and* a man. Her heart practically stopped beating.

Lazlo was tied, with his back against the trunk. His head hung forward and blood dripped from his forehead.

"NOT BAD," Roberto admitted with grudging admiration. He had figured he would have the bastard broken long before now. Many he knew would have already begged for mercy.

He didn't enjoy torture like some of his buddies, but he did it when necessary. He wasn't doing this for his own sake. But if Miguel was watching from above, Roberto wanted his brother to know that he took his death seriously. Where he grew up, women showed their love for a lost one with grief and mourning. A man showed his love for a murdered family member or friend by exacting revenge.

And he was about to kill a prince for Miguel. Brotherly love didn't get greater than that.

He was alone with the prince, not that he knew which one he was—there were four or five of them, he thought. José had gotten tired of the torture and had gone off to sleep. Marco was still out somewhere, looking for the woman.

Roberto drew back the stick he was holding and cracked the man across the shin again, careful not to break the prince's leg. Not yet.

He didn't want the man to go into shock and pass out. He wanted him conscious as long as possible while he beat him to death.

Like his little brother had been beaten and cut in that rat hole of a Valtrian prison. He dropped the stick and pulled the knife he'd gotten off the first man he'd killed on the island. Under other circumstances, he would have figured out a way to make money off the prince. Get the money, then shoot him. But the prince's people would be all over the island if Roberto made contact. And Roberto already had the Italian police after him. The island was too small, with very few places to hide. Bad location, bad timing. At least for a ransom gig. But he would have his revenge, and that in itself was worth something to him.

He had stayed alive this long because he knew the rules. And one of the rules was not to push his luck. Fate had dropped this man into his lap, bringing the revenge he'd so badly wanted right to his doorstep. Hell, the prince might as well have been gift-wrapped.

He planned on taking his sweet time opening this package.

THE VICIOUS CRACK at Lazlo's leg nearly made Milda sick to her stomach. Then the man drew a knife and she felt all the blood leave her head. She blinked a few times and mentally shook herself. She had to act. Now. Or in the next minute, Lazlo would be dead.

She looked for a weapon of any kind, hoping for a heavy, fallen branch. A fist-size stone was the only thing she found. She didn't dare throw it, didn't trust her aim when she had only one chance and her arm was shaking. She inched forward in the cover of the bushes and, when she thought she was close enough, she lunged at the man.

And hit her aim. The stone connected solidly with the back of the bastard's skull. She rolled away immediately, not wanting to get caught if she hadn't succeeded in knocking him out. But she didn't roll fast enough. Rough fingers closed around her ankle and yanked her back.

At least the man had been stunned enough by the blow to drop his knife. Milda saw it on the ground. Out of reach for the both of them.

The man kept her down with a hand splayed in the middle of her chest. She squirmed, but was no match for someone like him. With a roar, he raised the same stone she'd used.

She was a split second from having her skull smashed to pieces. She froze. She always froze when she was scared. She was a lover, not a fighter. She saw the stone come down as if in slow motion.

"Milda," Lazlo called out weakly by the tree.

Hearing his voice gave her strength. She brought her knees up and kicked the man as hard as she could, right where it counted.

The bastard collapsed, then she kicked him in the temple and watched with satisfaction as he fell flat on his back. He stayed on the ground and his eyes rolled back in his head.

She went for his knife and cut Lazlo free. *He was alive*—she hadn't been too late. She wanted to cry with relief. She could have hugged him. She could have kissed him. She held herself back.

He wiped the blood from his face with his sleeve, admiration glinting in his eyes. "You came back." His voice was hoarse, his gaze stunned as he took her in.

"Let's go. The other one is sleeping in the tent." She couldn't be sure if that one hadn't woken up to all the commotion. He could be on them any minute. She didn't have enough strength to fight off another attack, and Lazlo didn't look like he could handle hand-to-hand combat at the moment, either.

He glanced at the motionless figure on the ground, then looked toward the tent. "You go back up the path. I'll take care of that one."

He reached for the knife, and she gave it to him,

relieved to be free of it. "Are you sure? You don't look…"

"He's asleep now. He'll wake up eventually and come after us. We're in no shape to evade him. There's a third one, too. Have you seen him?"

She shook her head. "I'll come with you."

"It'll go faster and easier if I don't have to worry about you stepping into harm's way."

She nodded. Her knees threatened to buckle as she ran up the path, but she kept going. Until she ran into a solid body just around the corner. A young man grabbed her roughly, his face dirty, his thick lips stretching into a mean leer.

"*Puta*. You gave me much work tonight. You better make up for that." He yanked her against him.

His fingers bit into her arms. His breath was bad enough to knock her back. His gaze was emotionless, his eyes endless dark pools, as if there was no soul behind them, nothing whatsoever.

"Lazlo!" she screamed as a shot sounded somewhere behind her.

Then another.

Then Lazlo was running up the path, still bleeding and now breathing hard. He looked like he'd just escaped from hell. She'd never been so happy to see him.

The man shoved her roughly to the ground, pulled his gun and aimed at the prince. But Lazlo got off the first shot and hit his target. The man shouted in pain before he shot back. Then he threw himself into the bushes and ran away.

She remained flat on the ground, her hands over her head, not daring to move, barely daring to breathe.

Lazlo took another shot at the man who was now nothing more than a distant rustling in the bushes, then rushed to her side. "All you all right?"

She nodded, her heart going as fast as if they'd kissed. A nonsensical thought at a time like this.

"You?"

He was beaten and bloodied, but undefeated. He looked larger than life as he extended a hand to her, the kind of hero memorialized in those Valtrian myths on the bookshelves in her room at the palace. "Let's get out of here."

She didn't have to be told twice. She was only too aware that the man who'd grabbed her was still armed, still out there somewhere in the darkness.

HOURS HAD PASSED since they'd arrived back at the Painted Rocks, but Lazlo was still frustrated on every possible level.

He hadn't been able to protect Milda. That bothered him the most. He'd been captured. She could have been killed.

He hadn't been able to take out all three of the bastards. He didn't know for sure if Milda had gotten Roberto for good. He'd taken out José and was on his way back to his torturer when Milda had screamed and he'd rushed to her instead. He wasn't sure if his second bullet found Marco, either. Or whether the first one had caused enough damage to kill him eventually.

And without knowing that, he didn't want to leave Milda alone to go back and finish Roberto. Nor did it seem safe to take her with him since Roberto might have recovered enough to arm himself in the meanwhile.

Milda sat quietly, staring into the night.

She had saved him.

She had put her life on the line to rescue him. He didn't see that coming. He would have expected that from his guards and from his brothers, but not from a matchmaker he'd been less than civil to on a number of occasions.

She truly was one of a kind, the most extraordinary woman he'd ever met. She played no games. She asked for no gifts, accepted no bribes. She was honest, sometimes painfully so. Levelheaded. Brave. And she was beautiful, too. He couldn't understand why he'd ever thought her crooked lips less than the most tempting sight he'd ever seen.

"So how come a marital consultant like you isn't married? Wouldn't that be the best advertisement?" he asked, even as he found himself oddly annoyed at the thought of her with another man.

They were back in the crevice at Painted Rocks. They'd eaten more of their food. She had more smoked salmon. He had canned soup. She'd taken care of his wounds, disinfected them with champagne—reasoning that alcohol was alcohol. They only had a few hours to go until dawn. They should be resting, but they were both too wired to sleep.

The moon bathed her face, including her raised eyebrows, in a silver glow. "Marital consultant?"

He'd forgotten to tease her with the matchmaker thing. "Forget the things I said before," he told her. "You have my full respect."

The eyebrows went down. The pleased expression that appeared on her face made her look even more breathtaking.

"I've dated...." She hesitated as she answered his question. "Most of the time when I meet a guy, the first thing I think of is whether he'd be right for any of my clients."

"The cobbler who has holes in his shoes?"

She nodded.

"I can't imagine men not pursuing you," he observed, again, the thought uncomfortable. He didn't want to think of another man within a mile of her. She was too earnest, too honest, too well meaning. Someone could take advantage of her. It wasn't that he was interested in her personally, he told himself, but he didn't want to see her hurt.

"If they do, it ends pretty fast." She turned away, looking out at the sea. "They tend not to be crazy about my occupation. They're afraid that I know all the tricks of the trade to trap them."

He couldn't say much to that. He'd entertained the same thoughts when they'd first met. He'd avoided her every chance he got. What a fool he'd been, he thought. Five whole months wasted.

But then, did that mean that he *was* interested in her personally?

Only one way to find out.

He drew her into her arms slowly, gently, giving her time.

She didn't pull away. "How are you feeling?" she asked, snuggling closer to him.

And he felt a sense of peace that he'd never felt with a woman before. "Sore everywhere." But not too sore to do something about it if she turned in his arms.

She didn't. "At least I got there before he was able to use the knife."

"And for that, you have my undying gratitude." He meant that. He would never forget the way she had appeared out of the night, scared stiff, to save him.

"Tomorrow we'll go back to the stream, wash your wounds with clean water and rebandage them."

"Good. I don't think I can handle another champagne treatment." The alcohol might have been good for disinfecting, but it stung like hell. While she'd bandaged him in strips of his pants leg, he ended up finishing the bottle.

He must have looked like a mummy in raggedy shorts. He presented a less dashing picture than he was used to. But Milda had just smiled at him. And he found that, as long as she found it entertaining, he didn't mind being disheveled.

Peace surrounded them. He was almost certain that

they would be safe for the night. Roberto and Marco, if they were alive, would need time to regroup. One or both were seriously wounded. They wouldn't mount a manhunt in the middle of the night.

Gradually, the pain in his body abated, other sensations taking its place. To go with them or not, that was the question. To hell with hesitation, he thought then. He knew what he wanted with sudden clarity, and he'd just escaped death's jaw. Not that he'd ever been afraid of taking chances.

He reached up to caress Milda's arm, gliding his fingertip softly along her smooth skin, his touch barely a whisper. He didn't want to give her a reason to protest. She lay with her back to him. He pressed his lips behind her ear. Then down her neck, paying special attention to the heart-shaped mole there.

She was so incredibly soft everywhere. He wanted to investigate every inch of her body. His blood heated as it pumped through his veins. His fingers found their way over to the firm swell of her breast. His body hardened, predictably, and he kissed her neck again. His thumb found her nipple, a hard little knob that right now seemed the most fascinating thing in the universe.

So she wasn't completely unaffected by him.

He hated the obstruction of clothes between them.

His hand slid down to the button on her pants. He could already see them both naked, pressed together. He could no longer feel any pain. All he could feel was her incredible body against his. All he could think of was sliding into her tight heat, taking her.

He tugged her shirt loose. Then he splayed his fingers across her flat stomach, touching smooth skin again. He wanted to press his lips there. Not yet. But soon. For now, he went as slowly as he possibly could. He wanted to show her how good this could be between them.

He wanted her to feel. His hand moved up, his fingers reaching her bra. Lacy. Normally, he appreciated frills like that. But right now he resented any impediment. Still, he bade himself to be patient, and outlined the lace edging with his fingers.

A soft shiver ran through her, even as she put her hand over his to still it. "Shouldn't you rest?" Her voice was heavy, but not with sleep.

The sound shot even more desire through his body.

Rest? Not with her pressed against him. "I can't."

"And I can't do this," she said, but her voice was full of uncertainty, which gave him hope. "You're a client."

"The Queen hired you, not me."

She turned at last, but only to look into his eyes, not to throw herself into his arms. "We agreed that this wasn't going to happen."

"Because it would break some unwritten rule for you?" He reached a new level of frustration all of a sudden.

"Among other things."

"You could always quit and find another line of work."

She pulled back. There was that wall again. "What else would I be?" she asked, exasperated.

"A teacher. An actress…a princess," he added, before he could stop himself.

He'd never said that to any woman. Never thought he would, had always studiously avoided making any false promises.

For a moment, time stood still.

Then she shook her head. "Don't do this. You're a born seducer. You can't help yourself." She pulled back, out of his arms. "Look, you're very attractive. It's…it's not fair."

He didn't want to be fair. "Why couldn't it work? What do you have against me?"

"Are you kidding?" She gave a sour laugh. "You chase after anything in a skirt. You have no idea how to care about a woman, how to be faithful, how to love."

That stung. She was being incredibly unfair.

"I love my mother, I love my brothers and I love my country." And he knew how to care, too. He cared about his people, his employees at the factory. *About her.* Earlier, when she'd come to his rescue, he had spotted her in the bushes. And willed her to go away. He would have rather faced more of Roberto's torture than have something happen to her. His heart had nearly stopped when she'd lunged forward to stop Roberto.

The relief of having her back here with him, safe, was indescribable. Every cell inside him insisted on celebrating life in the most basic way possible.

"I care about a lot of things," he assured her.

"That's not the same, and you know it. With all due

respect, you have no idea how to be in a meaningful relationship."

Did he want to be in a meaningful relationship? He hadn't before. But with her... He didn't think he could tire of Milda anytime soon. Maybe never.

"Teach me then." He reached for her. "You're the expert."

She wouldn't move closer. She was visibly pulling herself together. The passion was gone from her voice when she said, "I came here to do a job, not to have my heart broken."

"I see." She was deliberately misunderstanding him. Again. He let it go, not wanting to push her. But he wasn't giving up. He was a prince. He wasn't easily thwarted.

Chapter Eight

Milda woke to an uncomfortable feeling in her stomach.

Alone.

Again.

Last night... She sat up when she remembered that she'd nearly given in to the prince. For a moment there she believed him, believed that he could be seriously interested in someone like her for a change. For love's sake, she couldn't be that foolish. She wouldn't.

She knew him. She knew how he was. He could never take a woman seriously, beyond a quick affair. Sure, that would have been fun. He was wonderfully male, had the greatest body she'd ever had the good luck to snuggle against—eyes and voice made for seduction. When he touched her, when he kissed her...her body responded to him fully. He would be a wonderful lover.

But she craved more. And less, in some ways. She wanted someone ordinary and simple. She wanted forever. She wanted a family. A family to replace the one she had lost, not that they could ever be replaced completely.

The part she loved most about her job was that she was creating families. That gave her a sense of satisfaction that nothing else could. It helped her forget, even if only temporarily, that she didn't have a family of her own. Being invited to those weddings and christenings mattered so much because there she could pretend that she was part of some unit and not all alone in the world.

A brief fling with Lazlo wouldn't solve anything. She had more self-respect than to allow herself to become another notch on the prince's bedpost—even if she was more attracted to him than to any other man she'd ever met. That would pass. She could ignore whatever insanity drew her to him. She was a professional.

She ran her fingers through her hair, then went to relieve herself in the bushes. A slight cramp ran through her stomach as she straightened. She pressed her hand against the pain. Here was the result of drinking champagne instead of water, and eating erratically.

She spotted Lazlo on her way back. He sat where he could see most of the area above and below them. She went to sit next to him.

"So, leaving before the woman you slept with wakes up is an ingrained habit with you, is it?" she asked, to remind herself what a colossally bad idea it would be to fall for him. A reminder she needed.

He looked at her, the rising sun behind him. His gaze took in her face, not missing any detail.

And she regretted her sharp remark. Her attraction to him wasn't his fault. She should be annoyed with herself, not with him.

"Maybe I don't trust myself around you in the mornings," he said quietly.

She felt her face heat.

"We need to go back to the creek and get some water today," he said, changing the subject suddenly, turning back to his survey of the island.

"What if the men go for water?"

"It's a chance we have to take."

He was right. They weren't drinking nearly enough, not even with the champagne. And maybe some cold, clear water would settle her stomach.

"Maybe those men are dead," she said, knowing she was probably being too optimistic. But it could have happened. Lazlo said he'd taken out the one in the tent. She'd hit and kicked the one who had tortured him as hard as she'd been able. And Lazlo had shot the young guy who'd run into the woods once for sure.

"That would be nice. But we shouldn't count on it." He stood and offered her his hand.

She accepted the help, acknowledged the electric current that passed between them and prudently let him go the second she was standing.

"How about breakfast before we head out?" he asked.

"Not hungry right now. Maybe when we come back. But you should eat. Go ahead."

"I'd rather go for water first, too. Before it gets too hot out here."

They walked back to the crevice together.

She'd had some practice at averting her eyes from the painted images, and did that now, as soon as they came into view. "I still wouldn't mind moving someplace else."

"The crevice is protected on two sides, and you can't see it until you're nearly upon it. We haven't been found so far. We should stick to what works." He dumped out the remaining food from the duffel bag, then placed the two empty champagne bottles and two empty cans inside.

She stumbled after him as he started out. She needed caffeine badly. Maybe her stomach problem was a withdrawal symptom. At home, the first thing she did each morning was drink a cup of coffee. She couldn't get dressed without it.

She might have given a little moan, because he asked, "What's wrong?" in a whisper, looking alert, looking her over.

"Just thinking."

He relaxed. "About what?"

"Everyone who complains about their job in an air-conditioned office, with the coffeepot around the corner, should try being a castaway for a week."

"You have an office?" He resumed walking.

That this would surprise him annoyed her. "I *am* a professional."

"Didn't mean it as an offense. All I meant was that

you're one person. No employees. You could work out of your house. Isn't that what everyone wants? To go to work in their pajamas?"

"Is that what you want?" She resisted picturing him in pajamas. Especially since her gut feeling said he was the type who would definitely sleep in the buff.

"I want to work, play and sleep at the racetrack," he confessed, with a disarming smile that she was beginning to like too much.

So she focused on something else instead. "I don't want to receive clients in my apartment." Aside from the privacy issue, they might lose confidence in her if they realized how modestly she lived. Her apartment didn't exactly portray an image of success. Her income was way down in the last couple of years.

"I do what they call 'office sharing.'" To keep costs down.

"With a divorce attorney?" he teased. "Get them coming and going?"

"You're hilarious." She made a face at him. "Lawyers can afford their own offices. I share with a psychic."

He made no comment, but she could tell from the expression on his face that it strained him.

"So, what's the most difficult part of your job?" he asked after a while, moving forward quietly, keeping his voice down, only turning to look at her now and then.

You, she wanted to say. But since she wasn't feeling up to par this morning, she decided it would be better not to start an argument with him. "Clients who know exactly what they need."

He did glance back at that. "How is that wrong?"

"They'll ask for someone who is professional, financially established, a certain religion. Then I find someone just like that and the client goes along for a while before he or she realizes that their date doesn't make their heart sing."

He sounded thoughtful as he said, "A person to make your heart sing?"

She nodded, even though he couldn't see her. "Exactly. You'll meet her one day. Soon, I hope," she added. And then, because the thought twisted something deep inside her chest, she added a snide remark. "You certainly seem to meet enough women."

He stopped and turned around to face her. "You do know that I don't bed every woman I meet?"

"Could have fooled me. How about the ladies who left us here?"

"I said I dated them. There might have been a couple of dinner invitations."

"As far as you remember."

"Fine, as far as I remember. I'm a sociable person. I like to go out. I like beautiful women." He paused. "Did they say that we—"

Her cheeks burned. Which was so insane. *He* should have been embarrassed. "I didn't ask intimate questions."

They fell quiet for the last leg of their trek, mindful that the men might be headed for the water, too. When she finally heard the creek—and then saw it—she realized Lazlo had picked a different spot, a little farther down the hillside.

The water felt incredible. She couldn't stop drinking. He rinsed the bottles. She rinsed the cans. Then they filled them.

"I'll hand-carry the cans so they don't spill. You can bring the bottles in the bag," he told her in a whisper, keeping his eyes on the surrounding vegetation. He was ready to go.

"Could I take a quick dip, you think?" The creek wasn't nearly deep enough to swim in, but she could sit in the water, or even lay in it. She'd sweated through her shirt on the way here. Feeling clean would have been nice. And the cold water might make her feel a little better. The sun was already high enough in the sky so that her clothes would dry in minutes.

He hesitated, but then he said, "All right. Try not to make any noise. You have two minutes."

He kept lookout while she bathed. Since she kept her clothes on, there was no reason to feel shy in front of him, but she did.

"You could turn around."

"I want to monitor both sides of the creek."

He was only a few steps away, the situation oddly intimate. He kept his eyes on their surroundings for the most part. But from time to time, his dark gaze did stray to her.

She splashed water into her face. On her neck. Oh, the hell with it, she thought then and lay right down, letting the water trickle over her, keeping only her face out so she could breathe. "I can't imagine anything more refreshing," she said as the dust and sweat of their long walk washed away.

He said nothing.

"Your turn." She submerged completely before she stood, nearly slipping, then walked out, keeping her arms crossed in front of her breasts.

He set the cans down and avoided looking at her. "We can probably spare another minute."

THIS TIME SHE STOOD sentinel and kept scanning the bushes, aware that any of them could hide an attacker. She studiously avoided looking at Lazlo. Managed for two whole minutes.

He didn't leave his clothes on.

He squatted, wearing his black shorts, in the deepest part of the water, which was only eight or nine inches deep at that spot. He was throwing water on his head, wetting his hair. Water ran down his impressive back in rivulets, dappled sunlight making the scene seem like an artistic photograph.

But not the kind he collected—antique photos of the first automobiles. This picture could have been in a wall calendar made for women. Even his scars looked artistic from this angle.

A deep yearning rose inside her, an elemental need she hadn't known was there. Her throat went dry as she watched him. Every movement showed the strength of the man. He was alert, unhurried, keeping his gaze on the opposite bank.

Then he turned.

And caught her watching him.

The expression on his face changed, heat coming into his gaze. He stood slowly, his tanned skin glistening. He took a step toward her. Then another.

A wave of dizziness washed over her. The next second, a cramp in her stomach made her double over. Then he was there.

"What's wrong?"

"I think I'm getting dehydrated."

"What hurts?"

"My stomach."

He helped her sit.

"I'm fine. It already passed." She glanced up at him, aware of his lack of clothing, of his hands on her shoulders.

"Let's get back to the Painted Rocks." He dressed hurriedly, then picked up their bag and the cans. "Stay behind me."

"I'm fine. Could be the sun." They'd spent too much time outside in the past couple of days.

He looked grim, as if not buying her explanation. "Did it just start hurting?"

"I had a few twinges yesterday."

He scowled. "Why didn't you say something?"

"We've been living on champagne, caviar and wild fruit. I thought my body was just adjusting to the circumstances."

Another cramp came, this one stronger, stealing her breath away. She felt the blood run out of her face and her knees weaken. She leaned against a tree. She was dizzy again.

He handed her the cans and picked her up. Suddenly, she was too weak to protest. "My ears are ringing."

By the time he got them back to their shelter, half the water had sloshed from the cans, but she was feeling better again—and foolish for having made such a fuss over what was most likely nothing. "I'll be fine in a couple of hours. Don't worry about it."

"As soon as night falls, I'm going back to the men. We need that radio. You're sick. You need medical help." He paced. "I think they're building a raft. I saw something in a clearing near the shore when Roberto was marching me back to their tent. We could steal that and get off the island."

"No," she said immediately.

"If we can't get the radio, that might be our only chance."

"The mainland is too far away. Maybe they can risk their lives like that, but you can't. You're a prince."

He poured the remaining water from the smaller can to fill up the bigger one, then sat on a rock and began hammering the empty can with a fist-size stone he'd wrapped in a piece of his shirt to muffle the sound. His mouth pulled tight as he looked out over the side of the hill. "I'll take my chances."

"I won't. I'm a terrible swimmer."

He only hesitated a second before he said, "It has to be the radio then."

"I'll be better by tonight, and we'll go get it together in the morning."

"I won't allow that."

Oh, please, she thought, but before she could object to his imperial style, a wave of nausea rolled over her. She got up, started toward the bushes. Lazlo stood to go with her.

"I need a moment of privacy."

"What if you fall?"

"Please." She didn't want to throw up in front of the prince.

He seemed to understand, but didn't look like he liked it. "Call if you need me."

She kept plodding forward. Then went a little farther. She didn't want him to hear her give back her last meal.

Another roll of nausea came. She squeezed her eyes shut. She was rarely sick. Catching some bug out here where she couldn't get any help was so unfair. If she got sick, she was going to hold Lazlo back. And she would be no help whatsoever if the men found them.

She braced an arm on the trunk of an old olive tree. A soft noise came from the bushes behind her. She didn't turn. "I'll be fine. Please go back."

But the prince didn't respond. Instead, she was grabbed roughly by the neck. She smelled unwashed, sweaty male. Opened her mouth to scream. But a large, dirty palm cut off her air.

She fought against the man who was dragging her away from Painted Rocks, fought as hard as she could until the next stomach cramp came and she lost all her strength for a minute.

Then she heaved.

The man swore in another language and snatched his hand from her mouth, but didn't let her go. Which meant that she ended up throwing up all over him.

Oh, God, that felt so much better. But he wouldn't let her sink to the ground. He slapped her across the face, then dragged her along as if nothing had happened.

He dragged her by the arm now, bruising her. She kicked out, too dizzy to put up a real fight. A murderous madman had her, and she could do little about it. Lazlo wouldn't even notice that she was gone until it was too late. And to be honest, part of her was glad about that. That way, at least the prince couldn't come after her, wouldn't come to harm.

She felt responsible for how things had turned out. She was the one who had tricked him into coming to the island.

Her stomach hurt and her head swam as the man dragged her along. When she realized that no amount of scratching and kicking would free her, she began grabbing for the branches they passed. But when she got a firm grip on one, it barely slowed the man's progress. He yanked her violently, nearly ripping her arm from the socket, and she was forced to let go.

She expected him to take her back to the campsite where she'd found Lazlo, but the man was carrying her up the hillside in another direction. This was the slope where they'd found the second guard's body in the woods.

Think, think, think. Not an easy task when her stomach was heaving and her head spinning.

She'd been gone for at least fifteen minutes now. Lazlo would start looking. She desperately wanted him to find her, but she wanted him to stay safe just as badly.

She had to save herself.

She refused to die here.

She was weak, thanks to her stomach, but the man was tiring, too. She dragged her feet, putting up as much resistance as possible, to exhaust him sooner. By the time they reached the clearing, his grip was loosening.

The well she'd fallen into was somewhere up ahead. Which gave her an idea.

She gave a loud moan, then made as if collapsing, heaved. The man let her drop to the ground this time, taking a quick step back. She rolled away from him as soon as she hit the ground. Then she was on her feet and running.

"You stupid—" The rest came out in his native language.

He was right behind her.

Her first burst of energy ran out quicker than she had anticipated. The nausea and dizziness weren't helping. If she could make it to the well… She gave everything she had.

The tip of his fingers touched her back, but it was too late. She jumped.

He went down the hole, shouting.

She collapsed on the other side, her knees wobbly, her lungs burning. She did her best to catch her breath. Almost succeeded, before she threw up again. When she was done, she rolled onto her back and stared up at the sky. God, she hated feeling sick. But at least she was safe for the moment.

Only a moment, she realized, as a noise drew her attention to the well. Rocks scraped under the man's shoes as he fought his way up, and she remembered that Lazlo had been able to get out of there without much trouble.

No time to rest now. She pushed to her feet, her limbs dangerously weak. But she didn't get farther than a few yards before the man shouted behind her. His head and arms were above the rim of the well. He was holding his gun on her.

How could she forget about the weapon? It must have been under his shirt all along. But he hadn't thought it was necessary to use until now. He'd thought taking her would be easy. And he'd probably wanted her alive. Now, with his head bleeding, he looked mad enough not to care anymore.

She froze as he pulled his body up and climbed out. This was it. The end.

But then Lazlo stole out of the woods behind the man, carrying a long, straight branch. She kept her eyes on her attacker, praying that he wouldn't turn. Of course, he did. And immediately took aim at Lazlo.

But Lazlo had already launched his makeshift spear. The sharp end went through the man's throat, and he fell to the ground, dropping the gun, clutching at the spurting blood, writhing.

She staggered toward Lazlo as he ran to her. "Where did you get that?"

"Made a tip from that can we weren't using." He pushed her behind him and walked toward the man carefully, grabbed the gun, then searched the man's pockets. "No radio. He must have passed it on to José."

"Finish him." She wanted to make sure the bastard was dead, that he could never come after her and Lazlo again.

"He's finished," he said simply, taking her hand. "And I might need all the bullets we have to keep us safe. Or to signal for help," he added, then paused for a second, as with a mighty groan, the man pulled himself to his knees.

He gripped the spear's handle with both hands, his eyes bulging. He was trying to remove the spear, but ended up lurching back instead. Into the well. Then everything went quiet.

Lazlo went to the well, holding the gun in front of him. He looked down. "Broke his neck," he said as he turned to her.

She looked away. The man had come to a gruesome end, but she couldn't feel sorry for him. Not when she remembered the two royal guards who'd been killed in cold blood. The man in the bottom of the well had gotten what he deserved.

Lazlo drew her forward. They didn't stop until they were in the woods, in the cover of the trees. Then he looked her over. "Did he hurt you?"

"He didn't have a chance. I fought him all the way."

The tight lines of his face relaxed. "How are you feeling?"

"Okay."

He tucked his gun away and picked her up without warning, carried her back to their crevice.

The closer they got, the worse she felt. By the time he gently placed her on their blanket, her head was swimming again. "Face it, Gilligan, you're never getting off this island," she muttered miserably, regretting that she'd ever set foot here.

Lazlo stilled. "Who is Gilligan?"

Of course he wouldn't get the cultural reference. Valtrian TV stations ran Valtrian shows. Although she'd seen some syndicated prime-time dramas since she'd been in the country, they tended to be the latest U.S. and U.K. top hits. He'd probably never seen a single rerun of *Gilligan's Island*. And she didn't have the energy to explain.

"An ex-boyfriend?" He frowned.

"A fictional character."

"Forget him. I'll get you back to the mainland. I promise you that."

The thing was, she believed him. She just hoped it wouldn't be too late.

He watched her for a few seconds, then moved to their food stock and began sorting it into four piles, carefully checking the cans and all the packaging. His movements were deliberate, unhurried, his focus on his task. Only the tight set of his jaw betrayed that he was fighting some emotion.

"What are you doing?" She hoped he wasn't going to eat. She was afraid the smell and sight of food would push her over the edge again. She needed a break. She was sure that if she could just rest for a few minutes, she would feel much better.

"This is what neither of us ate from." He pointed at the first pile. "This is what we both ate from. This is what only I ate from. And this—" his mouth tightened as he indicated the last pile "—is what only you ate."

The last thing she wanted to talk about was food. But something in his face made her ask, "And?"

He watched her as if weighing whether or not to say more. But then he drew a slow breath and held her gaze. "I think you've been poisoned."

Chapter Nine

When someone was dehydrated enough to have symptoms this severe, other signs showed as well, but Milda's eyes weren't sunk in, her skin felt elastic and supple. He checked.

His thoughts kept coming back to the smoked salmon that she'd eaten. Since she liked it so much, he'd left it all for her.

He made her drink as much water as she could keep down, hoping it would flush her system. By the time night fell again, she seemed to be resting more comfortably. He wasn't. Dark rage coursed through him. If anything happened to her, there'd be hell to pay. He could and would find the bastard who was responsible for this.

"Are you still hurting?" Lazlo asked, as calmly as he was capable, not wanting to let on just how precarious her situation was.

"The stomach cramps have passed." She looked pale in the moonlight.

Cooler night air came from the sea. "Do you want

me to light a fire?" Only, Roberto could still be alive. If the bastard *was* alive, and the light of the fire led him here, Lazlo would deal with him.

"No fire. It's too hot already."

Except it wasn't. He moved closer and placed a hand on her forehead. Worry tightened the muscles of his jaw. "You're running a fever."

She gave a resigned groan. "Figures." She closed her eyes. "I can't believe the food spoiled. The bag had been in the ocean, in cold water. That's as good as a refrigerator, isn't it? And everything was canned or shrink-wrapped. How could I get food poisoning from that?"

"Not food poisoning. Someone did this. On purpose." And now she had a fever. He had to do something about that.

"But these men had no access to our food." She opened her eyes and gave him a look of confusion.

"Not these men. The Freedom Council."

She fell silent. Then, after a moment she said, "That can't be. The food was prepared in the royal kitchen. No outsiders have access to it, do they?"

"They don't." The royal kitchen had top-notch security. And yet, it had somehow been infiltrated. "The Freedom Council thought, like I did, that the six princes would be coming to the island. They found a way to get to the food. The temptation was too much, I suppose."

"You mean, like the cook, or someone on his team, betrayed you?"

"Or someone who had access to the food during transportation. Between the kitchen staff and those who have access to the kitchen and transport, at least two dozen people could have found a moment to tamper with the packages." He remembered a discussion he'd had with his brothers a while back. "Benedek was right," he said under his breath. Of course, his twin brother often was.

"About what?"

"When he was in the catacombs with Rayne after the attack on the opera house, he heard a group of rebels down there. And one of the voices was familiar to him. He couldn't place it, but he swore that he'd heard that man speak before. He insisted that the enemy had someone inside the castle." He paused to think over the implications. "I didn't believe him."

"And now?"

"We need to get off this island and warn my family. I'm going to catch this bastard."

"Just be careful," she said weakly.

He watched her for a moment. Then he picked up the gun that was sitting on the rock beside him and handed it to her. "Hang on to this. If Roberto comes by, shoot him the second you spot him."

Her eyes went wide. "And you?"

"I'm going back to the creek." He gathered up all their empty containers in the canvas bag. "I'll be back as fast as I can."

"Please don't leave," she pleaded, pulling up to a sitting position.

He hesitated only for a second. Her fever had to be dealt with. "If I hear a shot, I'll come flying." Then he strode into the woods before he could change his mind.

That the Freedom Council had found a way, yet again, to get to the royal family didn't even surprise him anymore. They had money, which meant power. They were bound to find a way. He was a royal prince. He knew the risks. But Milda coming to harm...

Anger clenched his muscles tighter as he strode forward in the night. The need to stay quiet tempered his need for speed. The woods were considerably darker than the sparse area around their crevice, the branches above blocking out moonlight for the most part.

It didn't take long before he lost his points of reference. He stopped to regain his bearings, and realized that the unfamiliar feeling that was tearing him apart was despair. Except that he didn't despair. He was the easygoing prince.

But at some point Milda had become important to him. He cared more than he wanted to admit, about this pesky matchmaker—marital consultant, he corrected himself—holed up in a small crevice somewhere behind him, possibly dying.

Because of him.

And it was as if part of him was dying just thinking about that. Over the past couple of insane days, Milda Milas had come to *mean* something to him. She'd gained his trust and admiration, she'd become a friend—a sort of reluctant partner in survival.

It was a new experience for him, a relationship that he found he was desperate to keep. Even if the very word "relationship" scared him more than being stuck on the island with a cold-blooded killer who wanted to see him dead. Self-preservation dictated that he keep his thoughts on his enemy and on figuring out a way to defeat the man. But his mind wanted to dwell on Milda. As if somehow, in the middle of all the craziness, she had become the most important—

The thought stilled him. And in that moment of silence, he heard the distant call of the creek.

Ten minutes passed before he reached it. Then another forty minutes by the time he got back to Milda, careful again not to make too much noise, in case Roberto was out there hunting for them; careful, also, not to spill any water.

She was sitting with her back against the rock, the gun aimed at him as he stepped out of the bushes.

"It's me."

She lowered the weapon.

He noticed the small tremble in her arm. She looked weak, but she was still able to sit upright. That was something. "Feeling any better?" He searched her face.

She lay down on the folded-up tent, as if only nerves had kept her together while he'd been gone. "About the same." Her slim fingers worried the colorful bracelet on her left wrist.

"What's that made of, anyway?" he asked, to distract himself from how concerned he was about her.

"Love beads," she said sheepishly.

He resisted rolling his eyes. The woman took the whole love thing too far. He simply said, "Interesting," then lined up the water-filled champagne bottles and cans on the rock beside her. When he was done, he stepped back and used a sharp piece of metal that he'd scrapped when he'd put together his makeshift spear, and used it to slice off his other pant leg. His once elegant pants were now frayed shorts.

"If *Time* magazine could see me now," he muttered, with irony in his voice. They'd done a piece on him the year before, entitled: "Gentleman, Businessman, Prince." His normally impeccable style merited five whole paragraphs. As opposed to the single sentence about his charities toward the end of the article, the reason why he'd agreed to the interview in the first place.

They'd simply used him to sell more copies. Out of a hundred people he met, ninety-nine wondered how he could be of use to them. Yet another way his title trapped him.

Milda was giving him a weak smile. "You're beginning to look like a real castaway." She watched as he dipped the cloth into the largest water can, the one that at one time had held some incredibly delicious Valtrian peaches. "What are you doing?"

"I'm going to wash you off in some cool water. We need to bring down your fever."

He washed her face first, carefully, feeling the heat radiating off her. She closed her eyes, but it took little imagination to conjure up her familiar, knowing, lively gaze. Nothing was lively about her now. He hated the listlessness that took possession of her.

"You'll be fine. We'll get off this island. I promise."

She didn't say anything in response.

He dunked the cloth into the can, then squeezed out the excess water. He washed her face again, then her neck, as far as her shirt allowed. Not too far. She wasn't into plunging necklines.

He found now, to his surprise, that he liked that about her. She had an amazing body—he'd seen that every time her clothes got wet—but she didn't feel the need to put her assets on display every minute of every day. That spoke of self-assurance and the kind of sense of security that the models and actresses he'd dated rarely possessed.

She was different from most women he knew; he'd known that from the beginning, when he had come on to her. Her response had definitely not been the usual, what he'd come to expect.

They'd been in his office. She was working through an endless list of questions about him—his personality, what attracted him, and so on. He was nothing but a client to her. She was completely unaware of him as a man. And she was dead set on putting an end to his freedom. Which had seriously annoyed him.

So he strode up to her to take a look at the notes she was writing in her little personal organizer thing, thinking that he hadn't seen a paper one of those in years. She clearly hadn't yet moved into the twenty-first century. She'd worn a prim suit, her hair pulled away from her face. He'd leaned forward to see what she was writing.

And caught the scent of vanilla.

Nobody wore vanilla perfume. Absolutely nobody. Maybe young schoolgirls. He'd tried to discern what that told him about her, trying to pin down the enemy. But while he was thinking hard about his next move, that plain, faint vanilla scent had somehow gotten to him.

As did the soft strands of her hair, curled against her slim neck, hair that had clearly never seen artificial coloring. Her cheeks were not covered by foundation. And he'd marveled at her luminous skin.

The crook of her neck, the only bare spot exposed on her body, was inches from his lips. He wanted to kiss the heart-shaped mole there, even if he was certain that it was fake. She took the whole matchmaker/ambassador of love thing too far.

Not his type, some sane part of his mind had said.

But the rest of him hadn't cared.

She's going to be trouble. One last, reasonable thought surfaced.

But all he could think of was, *Well, if she's going to be trouble anyway...*

And then he'd leaned forward and kissed her soft skin. The heart-shaped mole was real.

She'd jumped out of her chair and was on the

other side of the table before he could blink. "Your Highness!"

"We could skip all the hard work and see if we might find a more pleasant way to pass the afternoon," he'd suggested.

She had succeeded in thoroughly distracting him. He'd thought maybe he could turn the tables on her and distract her from marrying him off to some woman of her choosing.

Women frequently developed passionate and mostly unrequited attachments to him. If she did, maybe she wouldn't push for some nightmare of a marriage with an "appropriate" lady. The idea had seemed brilliant. A lover who drew him for reasons he couldn't explain, and a way to gain safety.

But she had expressed, in the most polite—not to mention firm—terms, that she could never, under any circumstances—

"That feels nice." Her words cut off his memories.

Just as well. They were on the embarrassing side. He hadn't experienced much rejection as a prince. After that incident, they were firmly on opposing sides. She'd made it clear that she would do anything to see him married. He was equally determined to avoid that fate. He couldn't imagine coming home to the same person every night. *Having* to come home every night. Probably at the same time, or the wife would be upset that dinner had gotten cold, or that he left their guests waiting or whatever. Royal protocol already took up an inordinate amount of his time, time he would have rather spent on his cars and business.

Except, he'd barely thought about his cars and business since he'd been on the island with Milda. She had a way of filling out his time most interestingly, a way of invading his thoughts. And for some strange reason, he didn't even mind it.

Desert Island Syndrome, he reminded himself, then moistened and squeezed the cloth again, and after folding it, placed it on her forehead, leaving it there this time.

They sat quietly for the next few minutes. Then he reached for the cloth to change it again. Her forehead hadn't cooled enough. If anything, it was even hotter than before he'd started. His cure wasn't working.

He glanced at the bottles and cans of water, then at her. "I'm going to have to remove your clothes." He paused when her eyes went wide. "I'm sorry. It's a medical necessity."

"I bet you say that to all the women." She smiled weakly, but sat and pulled off her shirt and pants herself.

Moonlight gilded a body that would have thoroughly seduced him under different circumstances.

He busied himself by pouring out all the water they had, save one bottle, and soaking their only blanket. "Here." He lifted her up and wrapped her in the wet, soggy fabric.

In a minute, her teeth were chattering. "I'm freezing."

"You can put your dry clothes back on as soon as

your temperature comes down a little." He hated that he could do nothing for her beyond this. Or maybe one more thing. He lifted the bottle to her lips. "Drink."

"You're very bossy," she said before she did as he'd asked.

He shrugged. "Comes with the territory."

"Along with an endless supply of beautiful women?" she asked when she was done drinking. "You must be going through withdrawal by now."

He should be. He never lacked female company. But being on the island with Milda wasn't altogether bad. He had a feeling that, under different circumstances, they might have enjoyed their two secluded weeks. There were a couple of Etruscan ruins he remembered from his childhood that he wouldn't have minded showing her.

She tended to be amazed by anything older than a couple of hundred years—older than the U.S., her home country. She was forever admiring the palace and its artifacts. In fact, that had been one of the few things he'd been able to use now and then to successfully distract her from her matchmaking. Not nearly enough, but it had been something. He was grateful for even the smallest reprieve.

"You can catch up when we get back to the palace."

A moment passed by the time he realized she was still talking about women.

"I've cut back lately, actually."

She managed a weak snort.

But he was speaking the truth. He'd gone out less, and he kept his socializing to clubs and restaurants, going home afterwards. For the last couple of months, at least.

Maybe he was getting old.

Or maybe, with Milda trying to hook him up left and right with the most suitable women, he needed a break.

"Maybe I'm in a slump." He'd heard others talk about that before, but back then he hadn't fully understood what that meant.

Milda rolled her eyes. "I'm sure you'll recover."

He wasn't worried. They would get off this island; her assignment would be up. She would stop pestering him with her matchmaking. His strange new attraction to her would no doubt clear up as well, once he was back at court among all those ladies. Their friendship, or whatever it was that had grown between them, would fizzle out. She'd go back home to her life and he'd go back to his. Things would return to normal.

He couldn't wait.

Or could he?

SHE WOKE TO SUNSHINE and birdsong. Her fever was gone. She was freezing.

Milda kicked off the damp blanket, then grabbed her clothes. Lazlo slept sitting up, his back against the rock. He must have stayed up most of the night to watch over her.

She couldn't forget how he had gently washed her

face and neck over and over again, then carefully wrapped her in the blanket. It was a side of him she hadn't seen before. She had a feeling he hadn't seen it too often in the past, either. She had wanted him so badly to hold her. Had to be the fever, she'd told herself at the time.

His eyes popped open. His dark gaze immediately focused on her. "How are you?"

He looked all mussed and so incredibly handsome that it made her heart ache. *Don't fall for him,* she warned herself, and had a feeling that this would become her new mantra for as long as they were trapped on this island together. "Cold."

He pushed the damp blanket farther away and came to lie next to her, folding her into his arms. As always, he radiated heat. And she found herself molding her body against his. Her muscles relaxed, degree by degree, as she grew more comfortable.

Don't fall for him.

"Stomach pains?"

"None so far. Do you think the worst is over?" Please, please, for love's sake.

"Let's hope. Make sure you keep hydrated." He grabbed a water-filled champagne bottle.

She took it but didn't drink at first. "What will we eat?"

Not that she could think of food at the moment, not yet, but she had to have nourishment eventually. God forbid, Roberto found them and she was washed out and weak. She didn't want to become a liability. She needed to get back up to speed so they could work like a team.

"The food from that pile." He pointed. "I had some of it before, but you passed out."

Caviar galore. She wrinkled her nose. "What about the food we both tasted?"

"I thought about that. But it's possible that there was something that you ate more of than I did. Could be that my level of tolerance for whatever poison was used is higher. We should go with the safest option available. And have more oranges and honey," he added.

Mentioning the honey reminded her of his kiss. She couldn't take her eyes off his face all of a sudden. They were snuggled together in the breathtaking Mediterranean morning, the sea murmuring in the distance, birds singing in the air. She was pressed against him intimately, as if they'd just woken up after a night of lovemaking.

He must have been thinking the same thing, because his eyes darkened with heat. No man had ever looked at her like that before. That look made her feel like the most beautiful woman in the world. He lowered his lips.

To her forehead.

Disappointment sang through her.

But it was for the best. Definitely. One of them had to keep a cool head, and on this morning it seemed that person would be him.

She was grateful.

Under no circumstances would she acknowledge that she was also a little disappointed.

He FOUND THEM.

Roberto lay among the rocks halfway up the hillside, looking down. He saw some scattered cans and a blanket a hundred meters or so below him. This had to be their hideout.

A difficult spot to approach unseen. They were protected by the boulders. And since Marco hadn't come back last night, he had to assume that they had gotten to him and now had his weapon. He wasn't too upset over Marco. The man had been way too hotheaded. He might have gotten rid of the idiot himself before he left the island. He couldn't afford Marco messing up once they reached the mainland. His big mouth had been the reason they'd been caught and ended up in jail in the first place. And he never did listen.

Roberto had told the dumb bastard not to go out into the night alone. But Marco had wanted the woman badly. Like most young thugs his age, he had little discipline. In any case, looked like he was out of the picture permanently.

Roberto watched his enemies' lair with patience. He couldn't directly approach the crevice. He had to wait for them to leave it, had to be patient until he had a better opportunity. With any luck, they'd go foraging in the woods where he could easily sneak up on them. If they went to the beach—open land—he would just have to wait. Now that he knew where they were hiding, the rest should be easy.

He didn't for a moment consider hiding from them, keeping out of their way.

They'd killed Marco and José.

He had unfinished business with the prince, anyway. And they had seen his face. He was in no rush. He was so close now, the death of those two was a done deal. Everyone back home knew that he never let go of revenge. And he never left witnesses.

Chapter Ten

Lazlo had gone off to find Roberto and get the radio. *To kill Roberto and take the radio,* Milda thought. She couldn't picture the man handing over the damn thing any other way. Which meant a fight to the death.

She had refused to keep the gun for that very reason. After some heated words, Lazlo had agreed to take it, but insisted that she should at least have the knife she'd taken when she'd charged in to rescue him.

He was too stubborn to accept that she was too weak to fight off anyone, no matter what weapon he left with her. Her arms trembled too much to hold the heavy handgun steady. Even the knife...

If it came to hand-to-hand combat, she was dead. End of story.

Not that she thought the prince would let things come to that. He would defeat Roberto and then he would come for her. He would get them off the island somehow. She trusted him.

That was new.

So was the bad case of hero worship she was

developing for him. He made sure she was fed, kept her warm and saved her from Marco. And he was a dashing prince. Nobody could blame her if she had a few stars in her eyes when she looked at him.

A considerable change from before they'd gotten stranded on the island.

Desert Island Syndrome?

She didn't think so. She had the opportunity to see the prince under duress, stepping up to the plate, so to speak. And she liked what she'd seen.

Liked it too much, perhaps.

Especially his kisses.

Stop right there. There was no way she was going down *that* road. He was a client. A high-profile client. As high-profile as she was ever going to have for as long as she lived.

Thank God she wasn't developing a crush on him or, God forbid, any feelings. She was definitely smarter than that. The fact that she cared for him was completely normal. She cared for all her clients. A marital consultant was no good without an empathetic personality. And really, there was no such thing as too much caring when it came to another human being.

Soon she would find a match for him and he'd be married to a lucky woman. Very lucky. And the fact that she was feeling morose all of a sudden had nothing to do with jealousy. Which would have been ridiculous... completely.

A small noise came from her right, drawing her attention from the twisted path of her thoughts. She clutched the knife tighter, stiff with fear as Roberto stepped out of the bushes.

Oh, God.

She hadn't killed him then, with that rock. But he would know that she'd tried. She could expect little mercy.

The man pointed a gun at her, identical to the one Lazlo had taken. Standard-issue royal guard weapons. "Toss the knife to me."

He had quick eyes and likely just as quick hands. He probably figured he could handle her with one arm tied behind his back.

He was right.

But she didn't obey. Not the least because her muscles refused all movement.

"The knife." Roberto raised his voice, scowling with impatience. There was something savage in his face, in the way he took a deliberate step forward. His clothing—a Valtrian royal guard uniform he'd gotten from one of the men he'd killed—was dirty and torn. "The knife," he repeated, with venom in his voice.

And she had to admit that she didn't really have a choice. That she could defend herself against a seasoned killer had never been more than a fantasy. She couldn't defeat this man, not on her best day, and today was far from that.

If she put up some desperate fight now, she'd be shot for sure. But if she went along with him, maybe that would give Lazlo enough time to return and save her. She tossed her sole weapon toward the man, worrying that this could be her biggest mistake yet. But the knife was no good against the gun anyway, even if she had the strength to wield it.

He picked it up and stuck it in his belt. "Get up. You're coming with me."

A moment of relief came. Maybe he would take her back to his campsite. And Lazlo would be there, waiting. Then her sad reality hit. "I can't." She didn't have the strength to follow his orders. No way could she march halfway across the island.

"Walk or die." The look in his eyes said it wasn't an idle warning.

I'm walking to Lazlo. The thought gave her enough strength to push to her feet shakily. She took a few steps, steadied herself, took a few steps more and realized she might be able to pull it off after all.

She headed up the hill, but Roberto shoved her in another direction. He wasn't taking her to his camp. They were walking away from Lazlo, not toward him.

She dragged her feet, desperate for an idea that might set her free, trying to come up with something that would help her get away from the man. A quick scan of her surroundings didn't help any. There were plenty of loose rocks, but she was too weak to throw with any force, her arms too unsteady to hit her aim.

"That way." He motioned with the gun. "Keep moving forward."

She did as he asked, hanging her head in defeat, her gaze falling on the colorful beads that circled her wrist. She brought her hands in front of her and slid the bracelet off. He said nothing. She took that to mean he hadn't noticed. So she snapped the band and, every twenty feet or so, she surreptitiously dropped a love bead. The dots of color seemed pitifully small on the ground. Even she could barely see them, and she knew what she was looking for. But she could think of no better way to leave a trail for Lazlo.

Roberto marched her up the hillside, keeping in the cover of the bushes. He kept looking back. Was he afraid of Lazlo? He should be. But thinking of him distracted Milda and she tripped, scraping her palms on the ground. Which was the least of her problems. Roberto swore and kicked her. Pain shot down her thigh. Getting back to her feet took all her strength, but she did it, not wanting to give him any further reason to abuse her.

He took her around the side of the hill, into a long valley she hadn't yet seen. Old ruins littered the hillside here. The view would have been breathtaking under other circumstances.

"That way," he directed her, panting.

She was out of love beads. Desperation made her glance around for another idea, but nothing came to mind. She was too sick and too tired to think. She simply put one foot in front of the other, telling herself that he wasn't going to kill her as soon as they reached their destination. If he wanted to shoot her, he could have done that at Painted Rocks, where he'd found her. He had a plan for her. And if she went along with it, she could gain time, maybe enough time for Lazlo to find them. That was her only hope.

She put one foot in front of the other and plodded forward until he signaled that she could stop at last. She was beyond tired and thirsty.

The large stone boxes and boulders seemed solemn, the figures etched into them barely visible, worn down by rain during the past centuries. Some were broken, some surprisingly whole. One still had its lid on, although shoved to the side.

Roberto picked that one. "Get in there."

She stepped up to it and peeked in, seeing nothing but dirt and leaves the wind had blown inside. Still, the stone box gave her the creeps. "Please don't do this."

His face was as hard as the stone carvings around them. He didn't seem to be in the mood to bargain. He shoved her roughly, banging her hip against the box.

"Okay. Wait." She moved at last. If she didn't climb in there on her own, he certainly had the strength to make her, and possibly injure her in the process.

"Get your head in," he ordered, and swung his arm her way.

She ducked quickly.

"And stay down." He heaved against the lid.

Panic squeezed her chest.

The lid didn't budge. Thank God for small mercies.

"Don't move," he ordered as he walked off.

This was her chance. She had to do something. But she was too weak to take advantage of the opportunity.

If she could climb out and run for the trees... He was coming back all too quickly, with a branch that he wedged against the lid to use for leverage.

And to her horror, the lid began to slide over, inch by inch. Until now, she'd been willing to go along with whatever he said, because she was playing for time. He hadn't shot her immediately. Obviously he was saving her for something. She didn't want to think about what that something might be—using her to trap Lazlo, or worse. But now, as the lid closed above her, she realized that Roberto might just mean to kill her slowly. Maybe he was out of bullets.

She should have thought of that before. He might have been bluffing with the gun. Or maybe not. He'd gotten the knife away from her. If he wanted to kill her, he could have used that, too. She was too scared to think straight, to come up with an idea to trick him somehow, to figure out how to escape.

"Please don't," she begged, the most she was capable of at the moment. "Please. I'll do anything you want me to do. Don't lock me in here." The idea was more than she could bear.

He merely grunted with effort as he worked.

Suddenly, the branch snapped, sending him staggering back. He swore. She looked up through the gap, at the clear blue sky. He might not have sealed the box, but the lid was on far enough so there was no way for her to squeeze out.

He swore again, whacking the lid with the broken end of the branch. She ducked instinctively.

"What happens now?" she asked after he quieted—not really expecting an answer, but unable to stop herself from asking, her heart racing so fast she felt as if she was on the verge of a heart attack.

"You wait for me."

Like she had another choice.

She was alive. She tried to focus on that. It worked for about thirty seconds. Then she thought of something that chilled her to the bone.

What if Lazlo succeeded in killing Roberto, and Roberto never came back for her?

ROBERTO HEADED BACK toward his tent, as satisfied with himself as a man could be. He had a feeling that, when the prince had headed out that morning with a gun, the man was going after him. They were evenly matched now. Each had a weapon. That was why he'd decided to get some leverage.

Now the woman was his, and she was locked up. If things went well and he didn't need her, he could leave her where she was. She wouldn't get in his way again. And he would teach her a lesson, too, for hitting him over the head. He rubbed the bump and winced.

Yes, all in all, she had to die. But if things went badly, first he would use her as a hostage.

José and Marco were dead. Not that their deaths were a complete disadvantage. He might be able to better blend in without them once he reached the mainland. The authorities were looking for three men. Now he'd be alone.

And he had an idea how to reach the mainland. To
hell with the raft that could fall apart as easily as the
first had. He'd gotten this far. He didn't plan on drowning now.

Eventually, probably soon, someone would come
to pick up the prince and the others. There had been
four of them on the island. Which meant that probably
only one boat would come, two at the most. With only
a handful of escorts, if he was lucky.

He could pick them off one by one, as soon as they
reached the beach, before they knew what hit them.
And then the boat, and freedom, would be his.

WHERE THE HELL was the bastard? Lazlo went through
the campsite where he'd been tortured not long ago. A
fresh pile of dirt showed him where José was buried.
He checked the tent. No weapons. No radio. But he did
find the food and water the three men had stolen from
his guards. He didn't take anything. If he succeeded in
taking out Roberto and getting the radio back, he could
call for help and they'd be rescued before the day was
out. If he failed...

He wouldn't.

He couldn't let anything happen to Milda. She was
the one for him. He didn't stop to examine that thought.
He would think about that later. Right now, he needed
to focus on doing whatever it took to keep her safe.

As the sun moved higher on the horizon, he headed
for the top of the hill to give himself a better view of the
island. Waiting at camp would have probably worked,

Roberto would most likely come back to eat. But when? The man could be out there, wandering around the island all day. And Lazlo didn't want to wait. Milda was no longer as deathly sick as she'd been during the night, but he was worried about the poison she'd most likely ingested. He wasn't sure what the long-term effects would be. She needed medical help as fast as he could get it to her.

The sun above was merciless, although dark clouds were gathering on the bottom of the horizon—a storm that might hit before noon, or miss them entirely. Sweat rolled down his face. Low, prickly bushes scratched his legs. He kept going.

The heat was even more unbearable at the top. The faint breeze that moved meant little without any shade. He spotted a couple of fishing boats in the distance, all of them too far away to see him waving. Shooting his gun wasn't an option. Roberto could be close. Lazlo was reluctant to give away his location and have the man sneak up on him. Nor did he want to waste any of his few remaining bullets.

He surveyed the section of the island he could see from where he stood. The beaches and the rocky hillside were clear. Of course, Roberto could be in any of the wild groves. Or on the other side of the island. Taking a look at that required another short climb around the impressive rocks that blocked his way.

He made it over, handhold by handhold, was almost clear when he slipped and banged his bad knee. Sharp stones scraped his skin as he slid. He would definitely be adding new scars to the old ones on this trip. The least of his problems.

He went even slower, and paid closer attention to every foothold. Then he made it to flat ground at last and took a moment to take stock, using his shirt to stanch the bleeding. He didn't mind the pain—he was used to getting banged up on the racecourse—but he wanted to make sure that he was in good fighting shape when he met Roberto, and that meant he had to minimize blood loss as much as possible.

When his wounds were taken care of, he did take a more careful look around. Again, the beach in the distance was deserted. This side of the hill looked over a valley facing another hill that was somewhat lower. Etruscan ruins dotted the landscape here and there. From his childhood visit, he knew there were more among the trees as the elevation got higher. The Etruscans loved building their cities on the top of hills.

No movement anywhere.

He waited at least half an hour, scrutinizing every spot that he could see from his position. Then, when he was nearly ready to give up and try something else, he spotted Roberto, as the man hustled across one of the clearings near the beach.

Lazlo took careful note of the direction in which the man was headed, then took off after him. He aimed to cut him off, but when he reached the spot where he thought Roberto would be by then, he found it empty. Had the man turned? If he hadn't continued in this direction, that meant he'd either turned right, toward the beach, or left, toward his campsite.

Since food and water would be waiting only in the tent, Lazlo headed that way. He moved as fast as he could and as quietly as possible. He meant to end this deadly game of hide-and-seek today. After half an hour or so, he was rewarded by a slight noise up ahead.

He immediately stilled.

The noise was repeated. Someone moved in the woods about a hundred meters ahead, walking away from him.

He followed carefully, lengthening his steps to close the distance. He went around in a half circle, and this time managed to get in front of the man, which gave him the advantage of picking the ground where they would meet. He chose an ancient olive tree for cover. And stepped out in front of Roberto just as the man was plodding through a sparser area in the woods, with nothing to hide behind.

"Put your hands in the air." Lazlo kept his gun on the man.

Roberto didn't even have a chance to draw his weapon. He looked startled, but not particularly rattled. He even allowed a small sneer.

"I want the radio and your weapon."

"And if I don't give them, you shoot me?" The man foolishly mocked him.

"I'd prefer to secure you for now, then give you over to law enforcement later. You don't have to die on this island." He had to give the bastard something to make him cooperate.

But he didn't seem all that excited by the offer. "Better here than in prison." The man spat, his face reddening with anger.

"Toss your weapon and the radio."

Roberto hesitated then shrugged, as if he didn't care, as if he knew the gig was up.

But Lazlo didn't let down his guard. "The weapon first."

As if to spite him, Roberto reached for the radio on his belt instead, unclipped it, tossed it in a high arch. Lazlo could barely see it, having to look toward the sun. He had to move his hands for the catch. He couldn't afford to let the thing drop and smash on the rocks at his feet.

But as he stopped aiming the gun at Roberto, the man went for his own weapon. By the time Lazlo had the radio and the gun trained back on the man, he was facing down the barrel of Roberto's gun.

"There's no need for this. We can both walk off this island," Lazlo said, trying to reason.

"Me walking in chains?" The man shook his head.

"What do you want?" Lazlo pretended that he was willing to negotiate.

"You give back the radio and toss me the gun. And I'll let your girlfriend live."

Lazlo's blood ran cold. Then reason gained the upper hand. Roberto had to be bluffing. The overhang at Painted Rocks protected their shelter. Finding it was nearly impossible unless someone knew exactly where it was.

"She looked pretty sick. You better hurry." The man sneered.

And Lazlo knew that he spoke the truth. He wouldn't know that Milda was sick unless he'd seen her. And if he'd seen her...

The gun jerked in Lazlo's hand before he steadied it. "What have you done to her?"

"LAZLO!" MILDA SCREAMED again, her face pushed up into the gap above her. It wasn't big enough for her to stick her head out and see, but she figured her voice carried better if she shouted straight through the hole. Still, there was no response. She'd been shouting for so long that her voice was hoarse; but she couldn't stop, couldn't give up, even knowing that the surrounding trees trapped the sound, and that he would only hear her if, for some reason, he accidentally came this way.

And they never came to this part of the island. The valley was locked between two hills, without a view of the beach. It was too far from their shelter at Painted Rocks, too far from the creek.

She lay down on the bottom to catch her breath. Her fingertips were bleeding, her arms sore from the effort she'd been putting into moving the stone lid, to no avail.

She was buried alive, in a two-thousand-year-old coffin. And it was definitely some kind of sarcophagus. Enough sunlight filtered through for her to see the images carved along the walls. These were not as eroded by the weather as the ones outside. Faces of ancient gods and funeral processions decorated every inch.

Thank God, the grave robbers who'd long ago stolen anything that might have been valuable had also taken the body. At least she wasn't lying on someone's dry bones. But being locked in still freaked her out in every possible way.

The lid seemed immovable. Even Roberto could only shift it by using a branch for leverage. She had no tool to help her. However, she'd had some time to rest now. And her stomach was no longer as sick as the day before. She felt some of her strength returning.

She certainly had plenty of time to think. What could she use to help herself? There was absolutely nothing in there, save some dry leaves. She was looking straight up through the gap as she racked her brain. She saw storm clouds above and wished it would rain. Then she could push her face in the gap and drink.

Then another thought occurred to her. If they had one of those Mediterranean downpours, could water fill up the sarcophagus? She didn't fancy drowning.

Like she didn't have enough to worry about already.

Adrenaline shot through her, jump-starting her thinking. Maybe she could use her legs. Her leg muscles were much stronger than the ones in her arms. According to a Pilates teacher client of hers, the thigh muscles were one of the strongest in the human body. Milda bent her knees and set the bottom of her feet against the lid, then thought better of it and took off her sandals, thinking that she might be able to get better traction barefoot.

She pushed. Grunted. Nothing. She doubled her efforts until her thigh muscles burned and she felt like her bones were going to snap under the strain. When she thought she couldn't possibly keep up the effort any longer, she pushed harder yet. And then the stone lid moved, even if it was a small fraction of an inch.

Unfortunately, that small movement tilted the corner at the top into the sarcophagus. She caught her breath, desperately trying to support the weight, knowing she didn't stand a chance. But an inch or so below the top, the edge of a carving inside caught the slab.

Not that she could afford a sigh of relief.

That miniscule ledge wasn't going to hold a slab that weighed a ton. Not for long. In fact, she could already see the stone cracking.

And when that chunk broke, the lid would slide lower, tipping in. Sweat rolled down her face, her throat going dry, her heart racing as she realized that all that weight could come down on her at any moment.

"Lazlo!" she screamed, hoping more than ever that he'd be in time to save her.

Chapter Eleven

"Take me to her." Lazlo pointed his gun straight at Roberto's heart.

The thought of Milda being tied up somewhere in the woods, hurting and scared, was unbearable. As many times as he had tried to cajole, threaten or bribe her into going back home in the past five months, now he had a hard time picturing his life without her. Along the way, she had become a constant in his life. He might have even enjoyed their game of trying to outplay each other, their verbal sparring, her wry humor, the way she never gave up, not for a second.

"You will take me to her immediately."

"And if I don't?" Roberto sneered. "You'll never find her without me." Then he repeated his own demands. "Put down your gun and step away from it. *Por favor, señor,*" he mocked.

And after a long moment, Lazlo nodded. He lowered the gun, but then brought it back up again immediately, shooting for Roberto's right wrist. Except that Roberto must have expected some move on Lazlo's part, because the man dove to the side, squeezing off a shot of his own.

But he dove exactly the wrong way.

Lazlo lunged toward the falling body, swept the gun out of Roberto's limp hand. Blood ran out of the man's chest, from the bullet hole that went straight through his heart.

Time stopped as he watched that bright blood running down the man's clothes.

"Where is she?" Lazlo demanded as dark fear rose inside him, fear the likes of which he hadn't known existed. He'd always prided himself on being the cavalier, easygoing prince. Professional racing had been taken from him, so he'd been determined to enjoy what the rest of life could offer. He wasn't the type to get worked up over every little thing. Except Milda had gone from being a minor annoyance in his life to something else. She was important to him. The most important thing he ever stood to lose. The realization was staggering.

So they'd fought in the past. Fought a lot. That didn't mean she wasn't his match in every way. "Where is she?"

Roberto only looked at him with hate in his eyes. He understood that he was dying. He understood it and knew what that meant for Milda. A taunting smile came to his lips.

Lazlo pressed the heel of his hand against the hole in the man's chest. "Don't you dare die, you bloody bastard. You hear me?"

But as Roberto's eyes rolled back and his breathing

ceased with a violent shudder, he knew the man on the ground would never again hear anything. He stepped away from the body, staring for a moment, trying to wrap his mind around what had just happened. Then he sprung into action.

He wiped the blood off his hand, caring little about the smears on his pants leg, grabbed the extra gun and shoved it into his belt along with his own. He put away the knife, too, then took the radio from Roberto and turned the dial as he ran toward the Painted Rocks. When he found the security channel he knew was monitored 24/7, he immediately sent a message.

"This is Phoenix," he said, using his security code name. Each member of the royal family had one. "I need assistance. I repeat. I need assistance immediately. Over." No need to give his location. Royal Security would already have that. He couldn't put it by the Freedom Council that they, too, had somehow found a way to monitor radio transmissions. He didn't want them to know that he was in trouble and arrive before help did.

Barely a second passed before the response came. "Roger that. Assistance is on the way. Hang in there, Phoenix. Over."

"I need search-and-rescue helicopters. Over." He ran down the hillside at full speed, small rocks rolling beneath his feet. He took care not to lose his balance, but no longer needed to worry about making too much noise.

"You got it. Over."

"A full medical team. Over."

"Sending it immediately. Anything else? Over."

"Hurry. Over and out." He clipped the handheld unit onto his belt and kept running, a million things crossing his mind. A million ways she could have been hurt. A million fears that he could be too late.

"Milda!" he shouted every hundred meters or so. But no response came.

He kept himself in good shape, but even so, he was breathing hard by the time he reached their shelter. He'd put everything he had into the mad dash to reach her. But the crevice under the overhang was empty. No sign of struggle, no blood. He looked around carefully. No bullet holes in the rocks. That gave him hope. There was a fair chance that Milda was still alive. But where was she?

He thought of Roberto coming from the valley, and after drinking from their water supplies and grabbing a bottle for Milda, he began running that way. She could be tied to a rock in the punishing heat, for all he knew. He had no idea what kind of shape he was going to find her in.

He kept calling her name, but didn't slow until he reached the valley. Here he made a more careful inspection, called her name more often, waited in silence for long minutes, so that he could hear her answer even if her voice was weak.

Since he hadn't seen her from his vantage point on the top of the hill when he'd spotted Roberto, he guessed that she might be hidden in the woods, so he searched the thick of the forest first.

Nothing.

The thought occurred to him that she might be gagged, which sent a chill down his spine. If she couldn't respond, it might take days to find her on the island, even with a rescue team. And in this heat without a drop of water...

He made radio contact again. "This is Phoenix. I want canine rescue, thermal goggles and night-vision goggles. Over."

"On the rescue chopper already. Over."

"I appreciate it. Over and out." He kept moving, searching the woods. "Milda!" he called out, over and over again.

But no response came and he didn't see any obvious tracks on the ground. Except—

He bent and picked up a reddish bead he'd thought to be a small pebble at first. Then he looked at it more carefully. And up ahead, on the path made by wild animals, he soon found another. A green one. His heart sped. *Milda's love beads.*

Having to look for them slowed him considerably— they were nearly invisible amid the gravel and fallen leaves, but at least he knew he was going in the right direction, bless her brave heart and her always working brain. The fact that the beads were small and hard to see had worked in her favor. Roberto had never noticed her leaving a trail.

He followed the beads for over a mile before he could find no more. Was she here?

"Milda!"

No response came.

He searched every nook and cranny within a few hundred feet. Nothing, nothing, nothing. Could be she simply ran out of beads. The more he thought about it, the more likely that seemed. Her bracelet couldn't last forever.

Still, she could be here somewhere in the valley. Or Roberto had simply brought her this way, toward some other destination. There were a million hiding places on the island. The caves—not that he knew where they were—those Etruscan wells, the scattered ruins.

He'd seen ruins near where he'd spotted Roberto coming out of the valley. But where were those ruins now? The trees around him limited his field of vision considerably. He strode as fast as he could to reach higher ground, so he could figure out where, exactly, that he was in relation to those ruins in the valley.

Twenty minutes passed by the time he reached a high enough spot that wasn't covered by trees, allowing him to see farther than a few hundred meters. Man-made boulders dotted the landscape up ahead, to the east. That was all he needed to know. He was on his way.

The sound of several choppers came from the air before he reached his destination. He didn't even pause. He kept pushing forward. He could see one chopper disappear over the hill, probably touching down on the beach.

He grabbed the radio. "This is Phoenix. Send one rescue team to the valley, to the old ruins. The rest of them should comb the island and keep an eye out for a woman, possibly injured. Over."

"Roger that. Over."

"Thank you. Over and out."

He was at the ruins at last—and realized that he'd made a mistake. The boulders stood in solemn solitude. Nobody was tied to anything here. Any old buildings that might have stood in this place at one point had long ago fallen to the ground, the ruins too demolished by time and weather to hide anyone.

Anger coursed through him for messing up, for wasting precious time. On the heels of that anger came worry all over again. His gut said he was running out of time. She'd been sick to start with, and dehydrated since she couldn't keep anything down. She'd been out here for at least three hours now, in this heat. The climate was much different from mainland Valtria, where it was tempered by the presence of the Alps. Here, in the middle of summer and without any protection, a heat stroke was a serious risk.

He turned to leave, but something slowed him for a second. He saw no hope. "Milda!" he shouted anyway.

The hillside echoed his voice, nearly drowning out the weak response. "I'm here."

Then another frenetic moment came when he couldn't pinpoint where her voice was coming from.

"Where are you?"

"In a sarcophagus." The words came from behind a boulder.

He walked in the direction of her voice and spotted a stone chest. That's when he saw her slim fingers sliding through the crack at the top, and his heart about stopped from the sudden rush of relief. And then he was touching those fingers.

"I'll get you out of there. Don't worry."

Milda yelled, "Wait!" at the exact moment he realized the precarious position of the stone top.

Sweat beaded on his upper lip. From the gouge in the inside carvings, it was obvious that the lid had tipped in at one point and was slowly sliding toward Milda. If he'd gotten here any later, she would have been crushed to death. And that could still happen if he made the wrong move.

"Okay, I see it." He needed to lift that corner before he could do anything else.

"Get a strong branch," she suggested. "For leverage."

One lay by his feet, but it was too short.

"I'll be back." He darted across the uneven ground to the edge of the woods and immediately found a branch that was the right length, but too old and worm-eaten. It easily broke into pieces as he tested it.

"Hurry," came her voice from behind him, too weak for his liking.

"I'm working on it." He grabbed a sapling and heaved, straining his muscles to the tearing point. But he did pull the thing up, roots and all.

He wedged it under the top as soon as he got back to the stone coffin, leaned on the free end with all his weight. The top barely moved a millimeter. The sapling was too young, bending easily.

"I'll help," Milda grunted as scraping sounds came from below.

"Don't hurt yourself." He applied as much power as he could, feeling the veins in his temples bulging.

At last, the top came up a full centimeter. Twenty more and they would be in the clear. "Push again," he instructed.

And Milda did.

A helicopter hovered above, dropping a line some distance away from them. He would have radioed to tell them to bring the line closer so he could tie the stone slab to it, but he couldn't let up pressure now, or the slab would definitely fall on Milda. He kept all his focus on her, fighting for every precious centimeter, barely paying any attention to the men who slid toward the ground from the hovering chopper.

Then the slab was up and supported over the side. He collapsed against the stone coffin, his lungs heaving for air. Milda was panting below. He could only see part of her face. Although the lid was up now, she was still trapped inside.

"Need a hand with that?" Istvan said as he came running. "How the hell did she get in there? What happened here?"

"Careful." He didn't want his brothers rushing in to rescue her, with that wild thirst of adventure that ran deep in the blood of each. And they didn't understand the precarious position Milda was in. "I'll explain later."

"Take it easy." Benedek, his twin, came to stand next to them. "This is a very unstable situation." Assessing that fact only took a glance. He wasn't the best architect in the country for nothing. "Nobody touch anything until I have a look and figure something out."

Janos and Arpad came last. The brothers exchanged glances. For the first time in a long time, the Brotherhood of the Crown, a secret society of some historical significance, was together again.

And Lazlo relaxed a small degree.

One order after another came from Benedek, until he had everyone aligned to his liking. "When I say push, try to push and lift at the same time." He looked at the slab again, running his fingers over it. "I don't think the stone is going to crack, as long as we do this right."

Lazlo drew his lungs full. "We better work this right, then," he added.

Benedek took his place. "Push."

At first nothing happened. Then the stone wobbled. Milda let out a startled yelp. But eventually, between the six of them, the stone lid slid aside at last.

Then he was pushing his brothers out of the way and scooping her out of there. She was sweaty and dirty, her hair wild, her eyes squinting against the harsh morning light. She was the only woman he wanted, the only one he would ever need.

"Are you okay?"

She nodded and buried her face in the crook of his neck. It was a small gesture of trust, but that she would seek comfort from him made his heart soar. This was what he wanted—to hold her and protect her forever.

Istvan brought over the stretcher the chopper had lowered. She looked up, cringed. And Lazlo shook his head. "I'll carry her to the beach." He didn't want to let her out of his arms for a second.

Arpad had a bottle of water for her, and let her drink slowly as Lazlo held her.

Miklos was waving the chopper away, then strode closer. "I'll take her," he offered. "No offense, but you look a mite the worse for wear, brother."

But Lazlo moved forward. Only when she grew even more listless in his arms did he realize his brothers were stronger and could walk faster with her. He agreed to let them take turns.

"The guards?" Janos asked. "Where in hell were they when all of this was happening? Where are they now, for that matter? We tried to reach them over the radio as soon as the report about the boat came in, but they didn't respond."

"We managed to run into a couple of murderous castaways. If you put together a recovery team, I'll lead them to the bodies in a minute."

"What do you mean castaways?" Benedek drew up an eyebrow, as if Lazlo were making all this up.

"From the Sagro Prison break?" Istvan, too, had that look of incredulity in his eyes.

"Sagro Prison?" It was Lazlo's turn for questions.

"Three inmates broke out of Sagro Prison a couple of days ago. There's a massive manhunt going on for them on the mainland," Istvan explained.

Lazlo thought for a few seconds. "Could be them." The circumstances and timing certainly matched.

"How on earth did they get here? Sagro is miles away. They didn't even have a boat from what the news reports are saying."

"They found a way." Then a thought struck him. "How did you get here so fast?" Lazlo asked Arpad, the oldest of his siblings, the crown prince.

"Your boat was found off the Italian coast. A fisherman reported a sunk boat in about twenty feet of water. The Italian authorities contacted us about an hour ago. As soon as they said the name of the boat we got going."

He looked at Milda, but she didn't seem to have heard Arpad's words. Good. She didn't need that burden right now on top of everything else. "I've acted—" He looked down at his feet. "I'm to blame and nobody else."

Arpad opened his mouth, but Istvan lifted a hand to cut off his protest.

Nobody spoke until they reached the beach, except for monosyllabic instructions when they passed Milda over among them, trying to work out what would be optimum for speed. Then they walked out of the last olive grove, and the medical teams descended on the castaways.

Lazlo told them about the possible poisoning so they

knew what to look for, ordering them to give her their full attention, and not allowing anyone to touch him. But Arpad ordered one medic to stay, and there was no arguing with that. He never pulled rank with his brothers as a rule. But now that he had, the medic had to obey. Arpad was the crown prince. He outranked everyone here.

"What happened? You were supposed to come here on a fantasy date." Istvan spoke once Milda was carried out of hearing distance.

Lazlo glared at his brothers, who surrounded him in a ring while the medic worked on him.

"You set me up. Don't think I'm forgiving you for that. What happened to the code of loyalty? What happened to the Brotherhood of the Crown?" Irritation came swiftly. He didn't want them fussing over him like the old ladies of the court, for heaven's sake. He needed to go after Milda and see how she was faring.

Janos drew up an eyebrow. "The plan was for you to spend two weeks on a Mediterranean island with three of the most beautiful women in the country. We didn't think you'd complain."

Lazlo kept up the glare, but glanced toward Milda. Another medic was putting an IV into her arm. "They weren't more beautiful than Milda," he murmured under his breath, without thinking. Then wished he hadn't when he caught his brothers exchanging glances.

"So you noticed her at last?" Miklos bumped him in the shoulder. "Sorry," he said to the medic, who missed with Lazlo's IV.

"No problem, Your Highness. Almost done."

Lazlo kicked some sand toward his brother, the movement making the medic miss again. Not that he would tell them to stay still. The privileges of being a prince. "For your information, I noticed her from the beginning," Lazlo told his brothers, and stilled long enough for the man to get the needle into his arm. He seemed relieved.

"More like took off running every time you noticed her coming," Benedek, his twin, teased.

"I'm sorry I left you two stranded here. I had no idea you wouldn't be safe." Istvan at least had the sense to look pained. He was the most introverted among the brothers. For him, being stuck on the island with a bunch of women would truly have been torture. He loved the ruins, though. He'd conducted several digs here at the beginning of his career. "If I knew you and Milda were in danger… I just thought it would be, you know, romantic." He flashed a remorseful look.

Lazlo shook his head. "Only you would think that a deserted island with a bunch of old ruins is romantic." Then his brain backpedaled. "What do you mean, Milda and I? As far as you knew, I was supposed to be stuck here with the ladies."

"I had some second thoughts about the setup. I called to warn you."

The others scoffed. Miklos said, "Good to know that you could be trusted with a secret."

"I never got a call," Lazlo told him.

"Lady Szilvia answered your phone. She told me

what happened on the island and that they were on the boat, heading back to the mainland," Istvan clarified.

"And the reason why you didn't come to rescue us immediately was what?" Lazlo snapped at him, anger gathering deep inside, when he thought the nightmare of the past couple of days could have been completely avoided.

Istvan's forehead furrowed. "For one, I knew the island was secured. Miklos took care of that. I believed that you were safe. And I was glad for Milda," he added sheepishly.

"What are you talking about?" Lazlo looked around. All five of his brothers looked guilty.

"She would be perfect for you," Benedek put in. "Rayne said so."

Miklos cleared his throat. "Judi keeps telling me the same thing."

"Absolutely not," he snapped, more so because the realization that he was falling for her was still too new to him. He hadn't even shared it with her. He didn't want to share it with his brothers—not yet anyway. He couldn't stand it that his feelings were so transparent. He used to be better at keeping secrets. He'd always pitied men who wore their feelings on their sleeves.

She was smiling at him from a few meters away, as the paramedics poked and prodded her, her amazing eyes shining out of her grimy face. And he felt his heart turn over in his chest and his brain go all mushy. His body went all slack.

"Another one bites the dust," Benedek said next to him with a grin.

"Any guess as to what happened to the boat?" he asked.

"They found a hole in the hull," Arpad said, his voice grim.

Lazlo's limbs grew cold despite the heat.

"Explosives," Miklos added.

He saw red, his hands tightening into fists. "The damn Freedom Council." He got to his feet, despite the protesting medic who was running behind him with the IV bag as he paced. "They poisoned some of the food we brought," he said, then told them that story.

And it was his brothers' turn to look grim. "When you said poison, I thought she ate some poisonous fruit," Janos put in, his face etched in anger.

"So we do have one of their men in the palace. I knew I recognized that voice in the catacombs," Benedek said, looking pensive.

"But now we know it's someone with access to the kitchen. That narrows it down considerably." Miklos scratched his chin. "God help the bastard when I catch him."

The same sentiment sat on all his brothers' faces, and Lazlo suspected on his own as well. His only thought was how to get to the bastard first.

"If we'd known—" Arpad began to say, his tone turning to apologetic.

But Lazlo shook his head. "Never mind that now. It's over. Milda's recovery is the most important thing." But the Freedom Council was going to get its comeuppance. Too many good men and women had died because of them already.

"The gloves are off," Miklos murmured under his breath, then he said as he turned to them, "The second we reach home, I'm beginning a palace-wide investigation. I'll personally interrogate every member of the staff if I have to. The traitor *will* be found."

"I'll be right there to help," Lazlo said, and the murderous looks on his brothers' faces told him they stood ready to do their share to once and for all take care of the rebels.

His attention returned to the women he'd last seen driving off in his boat. "You suppose there's hope for the ladies?"

"Not after this much time. Even if they didn't get hurt in the explosion, there was a storm that night, with strong currents. They would have been washed out to sea." Arpad's voice was as somber as his face. "I'll make sure to personally notify the families. Each was being considered as a possible royal bride."

Lazlo winced.

Arpad clapped him on the shoulder.

Lazlo didn't say anything. The ladies had left the island in a huff because of him. He glanced at Milda, hoping she hadn't heard this last bit of news. She, too, would feel guilty, which was the last thing she needed at the moment. But judging from the tears rolling down her face, she had heard everything.

He took the IV bag from the medic and walked over to her. "Hey, it's not your fault."

Tears filled her dusky blue eyes as she whispered, "Isn't it?"

"Don't think about it now." He gathered her into his arms as much as the medics would allow. "Just rest and heal."

She burrowed against his chest, and it was the most wonderful feeling in the world. Until she said, "You were right. I shouldn't be doing this. I'm going home. I quit."

It was the one thing he'd been asking of her nonstop for the past five months, the words he'd thought would make him deliriously happy. Except, he felt as if his heart was being ripped out. He didn't care a whit about his brothers' knowing glances as he tightened his arms around her.

Chapter Twelve

Milda looked out at the majestic mountains in the distance, feeling small in the endless landscape. She grabbed the carved stone railing and held on tight. So many things overwhelmed her—the mountains; the remote hunting castle where Lazlo had brought her to recover; Lazlo's presence; her guilt over what had happened on the island; the thought that she would be leaving soon and probably never see Lazlo again.

Soft, veil-like clouds gathered above. One looked like a castle. The other... With that curve on the bottom, the other looked very much like her grandmother's face. What would she say if she could see Milda now?

She let go of the stone, blinked hard and turned back toward the double French doors that connected the balcony with her opulent suite. She had to get herself together. She needed to make some decisions. Or rather, she had to follow through on the decisions she'd made during the past two weeks since they'd been rescued off the island, during all those dark nights she couldn't sleep.

Unbidden, her gaze drifted to the right, to Lazlo's suite. And she caught him watching her through his window with that unfathomable look she'd been seeing on his face a lot lately.

He strode outside once he realized that she'd seen him. He was sliding a cell phone into the inner pocket of his jacket. "Miklos sends his regards."

"Any news at the palace?"

"They found traces of explosives around the hole in the boat. Different manufacturers have different markers in their material so it can be traced if those explosives are used in any criminal activity. The charge used to sabotage the boat was made of a faulty batch. If it weren't, it would have exploded much sooner, when I was on the boat. Anyway, only a few hundred kilos were sold before the company realized the mistake and recalled it. Miklos is working on getting the client list."

Which meant that they were likely to find a link to the Freedom Council at last, a link they could follow. Miklos was working the kitchen angle as well, investigating the poisoning. That would be another link. She could tell that Lazlo was excited.

She was happy for him. She could just never be happy *with* him. Too many things stood between them.

"I'm leaving." She was completely recovered from the poisoning—thank God they'd been rationing their food so she hadn't eaten a full portion. Her six-month assignment would be up in another week or so. She had no intention of making any further effort to match the prince, and hadn't once brought up the issue since they'd returned from the island.

A happy client had called her a puzzle master once, someone who had an uncanny ability to recognize pieces that fit together. But Lazlo was a piece that constantly kept changing shape just to spite her.

He was unpredictable, too passionate by half, too easygoing, too focused on the pleasures of life instead of duty—all things that she'd thought she didn't like about him, all things that she'd thought he should change. Except, at some point she'd come to understand that these qualities made him the man he was. The man she'd fallen in love with.

Stupid, stupid, stupid.

"Stay. I'll marry." He vaulted over the railing that separated their balconies. He landed a few short feet from her.

Her heart about stopped.

"Which one?" The three ladies had been found. The Lady Adel had broken both legs in the explosion, but the other two had dragged her to shore. They were all smart enough to wear their life vests, which had saved their lives. The ladies had been recuperating in a small Italian town.

With both of her legs in a cast, the Lady Adel couldn't travel, and the other two decided to stay there with her, out of solidarity. Lazlo had visited them the day before.

She tried not to be jealous. She wasn't succeeding.

He didn't answer her question.

The knife in her heart twisted.

Because the reason for no longer matching the prince wasn't simply her regret over what happened on the island and what happened with the ladies. She couldn't match him because she was in love with him. She'd broken the number-one rule of matchmaking. "I'm leaving," she repeated. "Tonight, if there's a flight."

She hadn't planned on going until tomorrow, but with a royal engagement coming, she felt she couldn't get out of there fast enough. She felt like she couldn't breathe.

"You'd quit on me?" He stepped closer, his stance and face rigid all of a sudden.

"I quit the business. You were right." She drew a slow breath. "When I thought that the ladies were dead, I had plenty of time to think about how I ended up where I was. Truth is, going into the family business was the easiest option I had. I already knew how to do it. My following in her footsteps made my grandmother happy, and I wanted to make her happy. And after she died..." She blinked back a tear.

Lazlo took another step toward her and took her hand.

"After she died, I had no other family. The business became my family. I thought it was who I was born to be." She lifted her gaze to his. "But maybe I'm not. Except that, if I'm not, then who am I?" She'd been struggling with that thought all morning.

"You're who you choose to be," he told her.

She scoffed. "Easy for you to say. You're a prince."

"And you're a vibrant, energetic, honest, intelligent woman."

He was making everything worse. How was she supposed to not fall in love with him even more when he told her things like that?

She stepped back from him. "So you're getting married." She needed to remind herself of that before she threw herself at him and begged for one last kiss.

"Hopefully. There hasn't been a proposal yet."

"The Queen will be happy."

"I'm not doing it for the Queen." He stepped after her. "Stay."

She looked away from him, out at the mountains, not wanting him to see the pain that sat in her eyes. "I can't." She was determined to save herself that torture. She couldn't watch him with someone else. "I'm going home to figure out who I am. Seems like something I should have done ten years ago, but it's never too late. I'm going to have fun trying new things." She could almost smile, as though she believed that.

"You could try being a princess. You never know, maybe it would fit."

A cruel joke to make. She was about to admonish him, but he was going down on half-knee, pulling a velvet box from his pocket that looked shiny with age.

"The thing is," he said, "I already know who you

are. You're the woman I love. And that's all I need to know." He opened the lid, revealing the most amazing pink diamond she'd ever seen, in an ornamental setting that took her breath away. "You don't know what I had to do to get this out of the treasury," he said when he caught her wide-eyed look. "Let me be by your side while you figure out what to do next. Then let's do it together."

Her head was reeling. "This is—I can't. You're a client." He couldn't be serious about this.

"Are we back to that again? Couldn't an exception be made for a prince? I'm used to having exceptions made for me," he added with a sexy grin.

"Why?"

"Because I love you."

Her heart turned over in her chest. She wanted this so badly, she had trouble believing that it was happening.

"The Queen wants a noblewoman for you."

"It's not going to be my mother's wedding, is it?" He brushed that concern aside with ease.

"But what will she think of me? She hired me to—"

"She'll think you accomplished the impossible and she'll be grateful for it. Believe me. Forget the Queen. What do *you* want?" he asked then, turning serious suddenly.

You, she wanted to say, but didn't. Everything seemed so surreal. "It would never work."

"Explain to me why."

"I'm not who you need. You're not who I need."

"Let me decide who I need," he said. "Who do you need?"

She used to be clear on that—she'd filled out the same questionnaire for herself that she had all her clients fill out.

"Let me guess," he said. "You'd like a Lithuanian American, someone who'd help you carry on family traditions. Someone who lives in New York. Someone who respects your business and supports you in it."

"Exactly. The fact that you don't meet any of those criteria can't possibly escape your notice."

"You want the right man."

"What's wrong with that?"

"What about a man who would make your heart sing?"

She couldn't argue with that. Those were her own words, almost exactly. Was he right? Had she been a fool all this time, making the same mistake most of her clients made?

"What about your precious freedom?" she asked. He'd always said that was the most important thing to him.

"If I'm free to love you, that's all the freedom I need."

"And I need an answer that's not quite that glib."

"I realized that loving someone is not a prison. Having your support and companionship wouldn't close any doors on me. It would open up a world of possibilities. I've never talked to anyone like we talked on the island. You made me see things in a different light. You made me understand a lot of things about myself. The truth is, I need you."

All she could do was stare at him.

He searched her gaze. "You don't love me. You still think I'm a no-good rake, is that it? I swear I changed. Let me prove it to you."

"No, it's not that." She knew he had changed. The island had changed both of them. "I do love you. I've been in love with you—but—"

He was on his feet the next second, crushing her to him. "Say it again," he ordered.

She looked up in exasperation and caught sight of that cloud again, the one that looked like her grandmother. She seemed to be smiling.

Her gaze drifted back to the prince. "I love you, but it doesn't mean—"

"Oh, yes, it does." And then he kissed her.

It was different from all the times he'd kissed her on the island. He kissed her like a man kisses a woman he wants to marry. His kiss held endless tenderness and love, desire, promises.

And she believed all of it.

So much so that she got completely lost in him, and the next thing she knew, she was in his arms and he was lowering her to the bed, onto the crumpled sheets she'd not long ago vacated.

"Are we rushing this?" she asked him.

He smiled. "How the tables have turned. If I recall correctly, a few weeks ago you were only too happy to rush me into marriage."

"That was hardly the same."

"I want to make love to you, only you, every day for the rest of my life," he told her.

"It's good to aim high," she teased, dazed by the passion that enveloped them.

He kissed her again, hard, on the lips. "I aim to please."

She had no doubt of that whatsoever. He was peeling her out of her clothes already. Then his hands were on her bare skin, heat and desire swirling through her, making her dizzy.

In another second, he was on the bed next to her, naked.

Wow. Whatever little brainpower she'd still had functioning shut down then—lights out, blinds drawn. She could only feel.

"I love you," he said again as he explored her body with his hands and lips.

"I love you, too," she admitted for the first time without prodding.

And that seemed to be the only permission he needed for thoroughly ravishing her.

"WILL YOU MARRY ME?" he asked much later, with her still sprawled on top of him after their amazing lovemaking, both of them still breathing hard, her body still tingling from the inside out.

"I don't think I should. I should figure out who I am and what I want to do with my life first."

"You mean a new career choice?" He kissed the heart-shaped mole on her neck.

She nodded.

He flipped her so she ended up under him. "Why can't you do that with me?"

"My life is in an upheaval at the moment. It wouldn't be fair to you. You already have everything figured out."

"Hardly," he said. "Except for the part about loving you."

And her heart softened.

"You know," he said as he nibbled her bottom lip, "people quit and start new careers all the time. It doesn't have anything to do with who they're with. We're in love with each other, let's firm that up and get married. Having that sure point will make figuring out the rest of life that much easier."

He was a smooth talker for sure. The more he kissed her, the fewer objections she could come up with.

"It's too sudden," she said in one last-ditch effort, studiously avoiding looking at the ring on the nightstand.

"We've known each other for six months and spent a considerable amount of time together each day," he said.

"Only when you couldn't figure out how to run away from me," she reminded him.

"More fool I. From now on, I'll only run toward you. I promise."

And she could see it all of a sudden, them coming out of some cathedral, rice being thrown and white doves being released. She could hear the wedding bells.

"And if I say no?" she asked, just to be contrary. He'd given her hell when she'd been trying to get him to marry. He couldn't very well expect her to make this easy for him.

"You can't. You make my heart sing."

"If you call me 'wild thing' next, this conversation is over," she joked, referring to the popular song.

"I'm not going to pressure you in any way," he said, apparently missing the joke. There definitely was a cultural gap. But it didn't matter. "I know too well what that's like," he went on. "Believe it or not, some people tried to drag me to the altar, not caring a whit how much I was kicking or how loud I was screaming." He looked at her pointedly. Then dipped his head to her nipple.

Pleasure shot through her. "I refuse to feel guilty for doing my job."

"I never said you should." He attended the other nipple, then moved lower. "All I'm saying is that I'm not going to push you, but I will keep making love to you until you agree to marry me." His tongue outlined her navel.

Heat and need gathered between her legs all

over again. "You can't be serious. We've just— It's impossible."

"People don't say that to royalty." He murmured the words against her lower abdomen. "When a prince wants something, a way is usually found to accomplish it." His hand was caressing her inner thigh, in circular motions, going higher and higher.

She melted into her pillow as she gave herself over to his ministrations. "Oh. Okay. Fine. I'll marry you, for love's sake. Eventually. But I'm not going to rush into anything."

"Why not? Speed is great." He kissed her silly and made love to her all over again.

She felt content. Complete. This was it, this was what she wanted. Everything else would work itself out. She'd found love, true love. For the moment, nothing else mattered. He was right—whatever else she needed to figure out, they would face it together.

Then he asked, "Are you sure you want to quit matchmaking?"

"What? Now you don't want me to?" The man was driving her crazy. "You were the one who got me started thinking about quitting in the first place. You made me question what I want. And I needed that, by the way. So what's this now?"

He kissed her. "Okay. First, I'm who you want, I'm what you need. But beyond that…" He kissed her again. "It couldn't have escaped your notice that I have three brothers who are all confirmed bachelors in their own way," he said with a mischievous grin. "Maybe you could help them?"

She watched him through narrowed eyes. "You want revenge, don't you? For them setting you up on the island."

"I just want them to know the joy of true love. What? What are you laughing at? Honestly!"

And then they sealed the future with a kiss.

* * * * *

Dana Marton's
DEFENDING THE CROWN *miniseries*
continues next month with
ROYAL CAPTIVE.
Pick up a copy wherever
Harlequin Intrigue books are sold!

Harlequin offers a romance for every mood!
See below for a sneak peek from our
suspense romance line
Silhouette® Romantic Suspense.
Introducing HER HERO IN HIDING by
New York Times *bestselling author Rachel Lee.*

Kay Young returned to woozy consciousness to find that she was lying on a soft sofa beneath a heap of quilts near a cheerfully burning fire. When she tried to move, however, everything hurt, and she groaned.

At once she heard a sound, then a stranger with a hard, harsh face was squatting beside her. "Shh," he said softly. "You're safe here. I promise."

"I have to go," she said weakly, struggling against pain. "He'll find me. He can't find me."

"Easy, lady," he said quietly. "You're hurt. No one's going to find you here."

"He will," she said desperately, terror clutching at her insides. "He always finds me!"

"Easy," he said again. "There's a blizzard outside. No one's getting here tonight, not even the doctor. I know, because I tried."

"Doctor? I don't need a doctor! I've got to get away."

"There's nowhere to go tonight," he said levelly. "And if I thought you could stand, I'd take you to a window and show you."

But even as she tried once more to pull away the quilts, she remembered something else: this man had been gentle when he'd found her beside the road, even when she had kicked and clawed. He hadn't hurt her.

Terror receded just a bit. She looked at him and detected signs of true concern there.

The terror eased another notch and she let her head sag on the pillow. "He always finds me," she whispered.

"Not here. Not tonight. That much I can guarantee."

Will Kay's mysterious rescuer protect her
from her worst fears?
Find out in HER HERO IN HIDING *by*
New York Times *bestselling author Rachel Lee.*
Available June 2010,
only from Silhouette® Romantic Suspense.

ROMANTIC
SUSPENSE

Sparked by Danger, Fueled by Passion.

NEW YORK TIMES AND USA TODAY
BESTSELLING AUTHOR

RACHEL LEE

BRINGS YOU AN ALL-NEW
CONARD COUNTY: THE NEXT GENERATION SAGA!

After finding the injured Kay Young on a deserted country road Clint Ardmore learns that she is not only being hunted by a serial killer, but is also three months pregnant. He is determined to protect them—even if it means forgoing the solitude that he has come to appreciate. But will Clint grow fond of having an attractive woman occupy his otherwise empty ranch?

Find out in

Her Hero in Hiding

Available June 2010 wherever books are sold.

Visit Silhouette Books at www.eHarlequin.com

SRS27681

Silhouette *Desire*

From *USA TODAY* bestselling author

LEANNE BANKS

CEO'S EXPECTANT SECRETARY

Elle Linton is hiding more than just her affair
with her boss Brock Maddox. And she's
terrifed that if their secret turns public her
mother's life may be put at risk. When she
unexpectedly becomes pregnant she's forced
to make a decision. Will she be able to save
her relationship and her mother's life?

Available June
wherever books are sold.

Always Powerful, Passionate and Provocative.

HARLEQUIN® *Romance*®

GIRLS'
Weekend in
VEGAS

Four friends, four dream weddings!

On a girly weekend in Las Vegas, best friends Alex, Molly,
Serena and Jayne are supposed to just have fun and forget
men, but they end up meeting their perfect matches!
Will the love they find in Vegas stay in Vegas?

Find out in this sassy, fun and wildly romantic miniseries
all about love and friendship!

Saving Cinderella! by MYRNA MACKENZIE
Available June

Vegas Pregnancy Surprise by SHIRLEY JUMP
Available July

Inconveniently Wed! by JACKIE BRAUN
Available August

Wedding Date with the Best Man
by MELISSA MCCLONE
Available September

www.eHarlequin.com

HR17663

Love Inspired

Bestselling author

JILLIAN HART

brings you another heartwarming story
from

the GRANGER FAMILY RANCH

Rancher Justin Granger hasn't seen his high school sweetheart
since she rode out of town with his heart. Now she's back, with
sadness in her eyes, seeking a job as his cook and housekeeper.
He agrees but is determined to avoid her...until he discovers
that her big dream has always been him!

The Rancher's Promise

*Available June
wherever books are sold.*

Steeple
Hill®

LI87601

LARGER-PRINT BOOKS!

GET 2 FREE LARGER-PRINT NOVELS

PLUS 2 FREE GIFTS!

HARLEQUIN®

INTRIGUE®

Breathtaking Romantic Suspense

YES! Please send me 2 FREE LARGER-PRINT Harlequin Intrigue® novels and my 2 FREE gifts (gifts are worth about $10). After receiving them, if I don't wish to receive any more books, I can return the shipping statement marked "cancel." If I don't cancel, I will receive 6 brand-new novels every month and be billed just $4.99 per book in the U.S. or $5.74 per book in Canada. That's a saving of at least 13% off the cover price! It's quite a bargain! Shipping and handling is just 50¢ per book.* I understand that accepting the 2 free books and gifts places me under no obligation to buy anything. I can always return a shipment and cancel at any time. Even if I never buy another book from Harlequin, the two free books and gifts are mine to keep forever.

199/399 HDN E5MS

Name	(PLEASE PRINT)	
Address		Apt. #
City	State/Prov.	Zip/Postal Code

Signature (if under 18, a parent or guardian must sign)

Mail to the **Harlequin Reader Service:**
IN U.S.A.: P.O. Box 1867, Buffalo, NY 14240-1867
IN CANADA: P.O. Box 609, Fort Erie, Ontario L2A 5X3

Not valid for current subscribers to Harlequin Intrigue Larger-Print books.

Are you a subscriber to Harlequin Intrigue books and want to receive the larger-print edition? Call 1-800-873-8635 today!

* Terms and prices subject to change without notice. Prices do not include applicable taxes. N.Y. residents add applicable sales tax. Canadian residents will be charged applicable provincial taxes and GST. Offer not valid in Quebec. This offer is limited to one order per household. All orders subject to approval. Credit or debit balances in a customer's account(s) may be offset by any other outstanding balance owed by or to the customer. Please allow 4 to 6 weeks for delivery. Offer available while quantities last.

Your Privacy: Harlequin Books is committed to protecting your privacy. Our Privacy Policy is available online at www.eHarlequin.com or upon request from the Reader Service. From time to time we make our lists of customers available to reputable third parties who may have a product or service of interest to you. If you would prefer we not share your name and address, please check here. ☐

Help us get it right—We strive for accurate, respectful and relevant communications. To clarify or modify your communication preferences, visit us at www.ReaderService.com/consumerschoice.

HILP10R

HARLEQUIN®

Showcase

On sale May 11, 2010

Reader favorites from the most talented voices in romance

Save $1.00 on the purchase of 1 or more Harlequin® Showcase books.

SAVE $1.00 on the purchase of 1 or more Harlequin® Showcase books.

Coupon expires Oct 31, 2010. Redeemable at participating retail outlets.
Limit one coupon per purchase. Valid in the U.S.A. and Canada only.

Canadian Retailers: Harlequin Enterprises Limited will pay the face value of this coupon plus 10.25¢ if submitted by customer for this product only. Any other use constitutes fraud. Coupon is nonassignable. Void if taxed, prohibited or restricted by law. Consumer must pay any government taxes. Void if copied. Nielsen Clearing House ("NCH") customers submit coupons and proof of sales to Harlequin Enterprises Limited, P.O. Box 3000, Saint John, NB E2L 4L3, Canada. Non-NCH retailer—for reimbursement submit coupons and proof of sales directly to Harlequin Enterprises Limited, Retail Marketing Department, 225 Duncan Mill Rd., Don Mills, ON M3B 3K9, Canada.

U.S. Retailers: Harlequin Enterprises Limited will pay the face value of this coupon plus 8¢ if submitted by customer for this product only. Any other use constitutes fraud. Coupon is nonassignable. Void if taxed, prohibited or restricted by law. Consumer must pay any government taxes. Void if copied. For reimbursement submit coupons and proof of sales directly to Harlequin Enterprises Limited, P.O. Box 880478, El Paso, TX 88588-0478, U.S.A. Cash value 1/100 cents.

HARLEQUIN®

INTRIGUE

COMING NEXT MONTH

Available June 8, 2010

#1209 THE BABY'S BODYGUARD
Bodyguard of the Month
Alice Sharpe

#1210 TWELVE-GAUGE GUARDIAN
Whitehorse, Montana: Winchester Ranch
B.J. Daniels

#1211 DADDY DEVASTATING
Texas Maternity: Hostages
Delores Fossen

#1212 ROYAL CAPTIVE
Defending the Crown
Dana Marton

#1213 MYSTERY LOVER
Shivers
Lisa Childs

#1214 NIGHT MOVES
Thriller
HelenKay Dimon